D0914921

Time and the Hour

Books by Howard Spring

Novels
SHABBY TIGER
RACHEL ROSING
MY SON, MY SON!
FAME IS THE SPUR
HARD FACTS
DUNKERLEY'S
THERE IS NO ARMOUR
THE HOUSES IN BETWEEN
A SUNSET TOUCH
THESE LOVERS FLED AWAY
TIME AND THE HOUR

For Children
DARKIE & CO.
SAMPSON'S CIRCUS
TUMBLEDOWN DICK

Autobiography
HEAVEN LIES ABOUT US
IN THE MEANTIME
AND ANOTHER THING . . .

Plays
THREE PLAYS
(*Jinny Morgan, The Gentle Assassin, St. George at the Dragon*)

Criticism
BOOK PARADE

Time
and the Hour

by HOWARD SPRING

Harper & Brothers
PUBLISHERS NEW YORK

TIME AND THE HOUR

Copyright © 1957 by Howard Spring

Printed in the United States of America

All rights in this book are reserved.
No part of the book may be used or reproduced
in any manner whatsoever without written permission except in the case of brief quotations
embodied in critical articles and reviews. For
information address Harper & Brothers
49 East 33rd Street, New York 16, N. Y.

B-H

Library of Congress catalog card number: 58–5426

S7688ti

Time and the Hour

160490

Time and the hour runs through the roughest day.

SHAKESPEARE
MACBETH

β β β β β β

1

A bove all things, young Chris Hudson would have liked to be on better terms with Anthony Bromwich. He thought at times that he would be ready to slave and sweat for him if that were necessary, but he would prefer not to do it, because he didn't want to slave and sweat for anybody. But if there *had* to be an exception, it would be for Anthony, who was all that he himself was not: good-looking, strong, and quick in the uptake with lessons. There wasn't a boy in the school who called Chris his friend, who wanted to walk home with him and share his life outside class-room hours. There were plenty, though, who were ready enough to make his life miserable. A week ago, in a corner of the playground, a group of tormentors had caged him. No one had touched him: the fun was in seeing him cry at the very idea that some harm might befall. And he did cry. Then Anthony Bromwich came along, smiling. Still smiling, without any sort of passion, he gave one of the boys a kick in the backside and another a sounding slap in the chops. "Leave the kid alone, can't you?" he said, and walked away whistling, his hands in his pockets. Chris was glad and furious: glad to be delivered, furious because his deliverer had taken not the slightest notice of him. He felt that he disliked Anthony Bromwich almost as much as the boys who now broke away and left him to himself.

2

That was on a Friday in March of 1912, when Chris was twelve years old. The next day Mrs. Wyke was in a ferment of what she called fettling. She yellow-stoned the doorstep. She polished the linoleum in the passage. She black-leaded grates, cleaned windows, and "turned out" Dick Hudson's bedroom. Dick Hudson was Chris's father. He was not often at home, but this week he was playing in Leeds. He would come here to his home in Bradford by an early train to-morrow, Sunday. He wouldn't have needed a home and the expense of keeping Mrs. Wyke had it not been for Chris. He would have been happy enough in theatrical digs. Even now he wouldn't want anything very stylish. Certainly not the sort of hotel where some of his fellow-players stayed, blueing their money and so laying up a future which, at best, would mean running a pub or sweating out their guts on some other such job. He could not yet believe his luck: after so many years of effort to be earning a hundred pounds a week! "The Great Hudson." Top of the bill.

He arrived early the next morning, before Chris was out of bed. The boy came down to find his father in the kitchen, eating his breakfast. He was a man of six feet, well made and handsome, with black hair that would have rioted into curls if it had not been close-cropped. Wigs played a large part in the life of the Great Hudson, and so his native furnishing was subdued. He was wearing a suit of brown tweeds that increased his bulk and this deepened the sense of something formidable with which Chris, a wizened shrimp, always regarded his father.

Dick got up and kissed the boy, and looked at him with the mingling of disappointment and compassion that he always felt for him. They met so rarely, and there was the never extinguished hope that Chris some day would spring a surprise, appear miraculously rosy-cheeked, confident and debonair. Well, here he was, home again, and the boy the same as ever. A transient look of pain shadowed Dick's features, and he did not know that the boy was subtle enough to be at once aware of it, to resent it as an unspoken and unfavourable comment.

There were kippers for breakfast, and tea and toast and marmalade. Dick ate as heartily as a hungry pike, while the boy nibbled like a minnow. Mrs. Wyke was out of the room.

"Shall we go on living here now?" Chris asked.

"What do you mean—*now?*" But he knew well enough that Mrs. Wyke had been talking and would probably expect another pound a week.

"I mean now that you're rich. And could I go to another school?"

"This is a nice little house, Chris. We're out on the edge of the town, and you can be up on Baildon Moor in no time. The air would do you good. Do you often get up there?"

"No. I don't like walking."

"You ought to try it, you know. We'll go up there this morning. I don't think it would be a good idea to give up this house. I expect Mrs. Wyke has been telling you that I earn a lot of money nowadays."

Chris nodded, nibbling a bit of toast.

"Well, that has only just begun, you know. It's no reason for lashing money about. You see, there's the future, Chris. I'm all right. I could get along somehow, however little I earned. But I don't want *you* to get along somehow. I want you to get along like a house on fire. The thing to do with money is not to dribble it away on every little thing that takes your fancy, but to save it till there's a big thing. That's the time to let fly. And you're the big thing, Chris. I don't amount to much. But you do, and you're going to amount to something more. Don't forget that."

He did not often let himself go, but now he had said it, and he hoped the boy understood it. "Why do you want to go to another school?"

"I haven't got any friends."

"Why, Chris, that's not a matter of a new school, you know. Still, it's something to be considered. And I have considered it. Between you and me, there wasn't much schooling in my life, and I've been thinking about putting it right in yours. You leave it to me. And now let's get up on to Baildon Moor and have a breath of fresh air."

They walked to Shipley, the out-sized man and the under-sized boy, and climbed up through the glen on to the moor. It was a place Dick Hudson loved. To-day it wasn't at its best, though a few sky-larks were trying to weave strains of joy into the glum air. But it was a reminiscent place. There were other days than this to think of. There were the days when he was a gangling lad working in a wool-merchant's warehouse, amusing his mates in the dinner-hour by tak-ing-off the boss and the manager and his mates themselves. "You ought to be on the stage, Dick," they used to say. "Come on. Do the boss again." And with no props, with nothing but the lift of an eye-brow, the twist of a lip, a trick with the hands, Dick would do the boss again. And one day, unknown to any of them, the boss, who was thought to be safely out at lunch, observed the performance through his window, and opened it, and said: "You—yon lanky chap—come here."

It wasn't the sack, as Dick had feared it might be. Sir William was a card, a character, in days when such things still existed, a bit of a humourist himself.

"What's your name?"

"Hudson, sir."

"Well, Hudson, you take me off very well. Do you want to earn a guinea?"

"I could do with it, sir." Twice his weekly pay!

There was a banquet that night at the Great Northern Hotel, and banquets were banquets then—eight or nine courses, and wines galore, and cigars, to say nothing of speeches that were only endurable because singers and comedians interspersed them with nonsense and sentiment. Sir William was to be the chief speaker, and the pleasant thought had come suddenly to him that if young Dick Hudson followed him, guying his famous and calculated mannerisms, that would put him even more emphatically on the map. He was thinking of himself, not of Dick, as a public figure loves to be the butt of a cartoonist.

It was an unforgettable night for Dick Hudson. For the first time he heard the sweet music of applause, and ate a grand dinner in the artists' room, and met Molly who sang sloppy songs in a voice of treacle. It had all gone on so swiftly from there. His services were sought for other banquets. He used to come up here to Baildon Moor and think out his repertory and speak his cracks, and sometimes Molly would be with him and would sing to him, and he didn't need the larks on those days. And up here he proposed to her, and one day told her the news: that he had been signed on as a music-hall performer. He was bottom of the bill on a third-rate circuit, but all the same it was the most wonderful news in the world. They married, and he left her in the little house from which he and Chris had walked that morning. He came back there between tours, but he was far away—in Middlesborough—when he learned that his son was born and that his wife was dead. There was nothing for it then but work, and there were times when he didn't give a damn whether he succeeded or not. But such times became fewer and fewer: Molly was not the sort of woman whose ghost would have durable qualities: and now, at thirty-two, to change from Dick Hudson into The Great Hudson gave him feelings of more than financial satisfaction. Not that he was unduly set up. He had never considered his sort of work to be of much importance; but, after all, it *was* his work, and to have got to the top of it was something. He took the "Great" with a pinch of salt; but it looked well on a bill. A sound chap, Dick Hudson. He would never want the Riviera. Baildon Moor suited him well enough.

That afternoon Chris trotted along Manningham Lane at the side of his father, a man he scarcely knew, and his cheeks would have been burning with shame had there been enough blood in them to warm a blush. Oh, God, he prayed, let none of the boys see him now! "We'll stroll down to town this afternoon, Chris," his father had said. "Be ready about four o'clock."

The day had become duller. A gleam or two had brightened the air at noon while they were up on the moor, but now the overhead grey was flat and still, and the coldness had a hint of snow. It was the sort of day Chris liked when he and Mrs. Wyke had the house to themselves. After supper Mrs. Wyke would make up the fire and sometimes say: "Now, you be cosy, Chris. Sit you down and have a good read. Lucky, that's what you are. Pity them that have to go out on a night like this."

She would be putting on her bonnet and cloak, and Chris would say: "Do you *have* to go out, Mrs. Wyke?"

"Ay, that I have, my lamb." (It made him writhe to be called my lamb, especially as he knew she didn't mean it.) "There's them as is coddled in this old world, and there's them that have to be out come wind, come weather. But don't waste your sympathy on me, my lamb. What is, is; and that's a fact."

He knew where she was off to, but it was part of the game that he should pretend he didn't. "Don't wait up for me. Put yourself to bed at ten. I've got my key."

Longing for her to be gone, he would urge her to stay; and when at last the front door banged he would hug his solitude. Now the house was his and he could be what he liked: not Mrs. Wyke's lamb, nor his father's "My boy," nor the hunted fugitive of the school playground. He had a great gift of identification, and a store of books—novels mostly—dealing with the lives with which he identified himself. Biographies were not so good. In them, men had ups and downs, and Chris had no use for downs. So he more and more sought out the tales of heroes before whom men cringed as they rode swift horses, or outwitted crafty Indian chiefs, or pleaded successfully in the courts, or stepped at a critical moment into a deadly breach. "Here's Mandeville. Leave it to Mandeville. He'll see us through," the book would say. And Chris would read: "Leave it to Hudson." The fire purred; the cat dozed on his lap; but around him stretched an arctic waste through which he lashed a team of huskies, hastening to the reserve depot for the food that would save

5

the other members of the expedition. Frostbitten and grey-faced, the leader had taken his hand. "You alone can do it, Hudson. Our lives are in your keeping."

One night, he did not put himself to bed at ten. He was up when Mrs. Wyke returned, opened the sitting-room door, and swayed on her feet, smiling at him amiably. "Oh, my lamb," she said, "you still up!"

He shut his book, shifted the cat from his lap, and stood up, not saying a word. "Oh, my lamb," Mrs. Wyke said weakly, "I got took."

He went straight to bed without answering her.

Mrs. Wyke's urgent affairs didn't call her out into the night for some time after this. Chris was sorry. He liked his dream-life of action and mastery. But there came a night when Mrs. Wyke's business could no longer be postponed. That night Chris was in bed by ten, and next day there was sixpence by his plate on the breakfast table. He left it there. "You can't bribe Hudson. No siree," the Sheriff said. The sixpence appeared every morning for a week, and then no more. He was glad to have this evidence that she knew that he knew; gladder still that she had tried to bribe him. For the first time in his life he enjoyed the feeling of power.

But this was not to be one of his favourite nights. Mrs. Wyke would not go out while his father was at home, and here was his father suggesting a walk. Dutifully at four o'clock he presented himself in the sitting-room, and he was never to forget the sight that met his eyes.

4

This was Dick Hudson's first tour as The Great Hudson. No more potty little music-halls in potty little towns—no more for ever, he hoped. Leeds last week, Bradford this week, and a fine big town in every week that followed. The Palladium in London. And wherever he went the Star's dressing-room. All because he could take people off, which meant, of course, put people on, represent them as living beings. He had begun humbly as Dick Hudson, Impersonator, imitating the stars, the radiant and as he thought unapproachable ones of his own profession. Then he lit out along his own lines: the cabman, the hot-chestnut man, the masher, the johnny. One day he wrote a little story with only two characters in it—a toff and a navvy. By quick work behind a screen which concealed changes of clothing he could play both characters. He was a patient chap was Dick Hudson. He practised that small act for a year in theatrical digs up and down the country before he was satisfied with it, and then it went on without a hitch. It was a success, and it showed him his line. In another story he managed three characters on his own; but when it came to four he had to employ a dresser, Harry Pordage, who lurked behind the screen, ready to fling the clothes on to him. Now that he was The Great Hudson, his simple screen had become an elaborate façade to meet the needs of the story: the front of an inn, or a fine house, or a public building, with several doors, so that he could disappear through one as a highwayman and appear through another as a buck or dandy. He could manage six people now, and his stories were romantic. The Great Hudson dwelt chiefly in a Regency world of pugilists and horse-flesh, heavy bets and heavier drinking, and pistol-shots behind the screen announcing that the plucked pigeon had taken the way out. He loved to challenge his own talents with the variety of his simple creations. Because of his fine build and handsome features he had no difficulty with the popular conception of Milord, and that is why he liked to do also little shrinking villainous ugly men. A critic once wrote of The Great Hudson's ability to *shrivel* himself, and Dick thought that a far-seeing compliment.

Before the tour started, Joe Kettle, his agent, said: "Well, I've pulled it off for you, Dick, as I said I would. Top of the bill and a hundred pounds a week."

"What am I going to do with all that money?"

"Money? You don't call a hundred a week money, do you?"

And so it was. A hundred a week was not for long "money" to Dick.

"Now I like my men and women to have a signature, if you see what I mean," Joe Kettle said, "and I've thought of one for you, Dick. Wherever you go, there's got to be something that'll make people stare in the street and say: 'There goes The Great Hudson!' See?"

"Well——"

"Yes. Well—now what you want to do, Dick, is walk through the public streets, at least once in every town you visit, wearing clothes that'll open people's eyes. What about the clothes you wear as Sir Frank Fotheringay?"

"Eh, lad," Dick said, becoming native Yorkshire in a flash, "Ah couldn't do that. Ah'd feel fair naked."

Which, oddly enough is just the effect it had on him, anonymity being the perfect disguise.

"You'll do it," Joe Kettle said.

And Dick did it. What made young Chris shake with shame was to be walking through the Bradford streets with Sir Frank Fotheringay. Upon Sir Frank's head was a hard hat of old-fashioned shape, slightly conical. A dark blue cape, lined with lighter blue, hung majestically from his shoulders. He carried a tasselled cane that he knew how to flourish. There was a froth of cambric at wrists and throat.

The March day was bleak as they set out from Frizinghall and strolled leisurely along Manningham Lane to the centre of the town. Night was closing in. A melancholy flake of snow fell now and then. There was hardly a soul in the streets, and Dick knew well enough that, as publicity, this was farcical. For all his fine air, he was as miserable as young Chris. But he had promised Joe Kettle to do this, and so he was doing it. Till now, he had always chosen the uninhabited prairies of provincial Sunday afternoons for his performance. He would get over this. In time, he would brazenly use the middle of the week's busiest day, thread his way with a buck's nonchalance through the crowds and eat his luncheon in the town's most popular grill-room. But that day he and Chris walked into the town, drank a cup of tea in one of the few tea-shops open, and walked back again. What added to Chris's woe was that Anthony Bromwich was one of the few people they met. Anthony stopped and stared open-mouthed. Then he took off his cap, and Dick returned the salute, raising his hat with a flourish and saying: "Good day to you, young sir."

Chris did not so much as let his eyes rest on Anthony after the first frightened recognition. His whole spirit shrank in the certainty that Anthony's gesture was ribald and derisive. But he was wrong. It was simply good manners towards a person, albeit a surprising one, seen in the company of a boy Anthony knew.

CHAPTER 2

❻ ❻ ❻ ❻ ❻ ❻

1

*A*nthony Bromwich had been
into the town because the only shop where Woodcock's Wonder
Weed could be bought was there, near the Midland station. Anthony's Uncle Horace smoked the weed which was said to be good for
asthma, one of his many mystical ailments. So far as ailments went,
Uncle Horace was like an insatiable gardener confronted by a seedsman's catalogue. He had only to get news of an untried specimen to
have a go at it. Anthony remembered the night when the asthma began. Till then, Uncle Horace had suffered only from rheumatism,
lumbago, and a heart that made it necessary to avoid such heavy work
as giving a hand with the washing up. He was delighted to add asthma
to his afflictions. He had come home from work on just such a night
as this, and after high tea had settled himself in his armchair by the
fire with Quain's Medical Dictionary, which was his favourite reading.
He gave a little wheezing cough. Aunt Jessie, who had many unguarded moments, said in one of them: "That sounds to me like a
touch of asthma."

"Do you think so?" Uncle Horace asked hopefully.

"Well——"

But it was too late now to temporise or turn back. The cough
came again, and he allowed himself to be shaken by a spasm. "I'm
afraid you're right, as usual," he admitted handsomely.

Aunt Jessie hedged. "Perhaps it's just a bit of a chill. If it's that,
we can do something about it. If it's asthma, there's nothing to do
but endure it."

"I've endured plenty in my time," Uncle Horace said, like a man
ready to brace himself to meet any number of new-come disasters.

9

Aunt Jessie sighed. "Well, you'd better get your feet into hot water and have some gin and arrowroot."

It was her specific for most winter ills, and soon Uncle Horace was enjoying himself no end. A shawl was hung round his shoulders, his long woollen pants were rolled up, his feet were put into the water, and gin and arrowroot rested in a bowl on his knees. For good measure, after an hour of this, Friar's Balsam was poured upon boiling water, and Uncle Horace disappeared into a tent of towelling to inhale the fumes, like an Eastern addict wallowing in hashish. Enough light filtered through the fabric to allow him to go on reading what Quain had to say about asthma.

Having thus, to his complete satisfaction, disrupted the household, he said that if Aunt Jessie would put a hot-water bottle into his bed and warm his bed-socks, formidable woollen tubes that reached above his knees where rheumatism lurked, he would retire early. He did so, and was well enough—as no one had doubted he would be, he least of all—to go to work in the morning. He set forth wearing a tartan shawl under his overcoat, an extra pair of socks inside his shoes, and galoshes outside them. In the passage he gave an experimental cough or two and said: "I'm afraid we haven't got to the root of it." Nor ever did. Asthma was a favourite plant in Uncle Horace's crowded garden from that moment, and Woodcock's Wonder Weed was the fragrance thereof.

2

Anthony's glimpse of the strangely-dressed man walking along prosaic Manningham Lane with Chris Hudson enchanted him. How on earth, he wondered, had that dreary shrimp got to know so splendid a fellow? He began to run, for one thing because of his excitement, and for another because the occasional flake that had been drifting down through the afternoon had now changed to a steady fall of snow.

Manningham Park made a pleasant break in the grey stretch of the road. He turned left at the great entrance gates and then left again into Megson Street. Any boy living in Megson Street seemed to him privileged, and he was the only boy who lived there. It was a *cul-de-sac* with six houses on one side and on the other a builder's yard. No traffic could pass through Megson Street, and between the stone setts of the road grass sprouted and in the summer dandelions bloomed. This gave the place a rustic air that pleased Anthony and his Aunt Jessie, but was a cause of friction between them and their neighbour Mrs. Wayland, who didn't hold with dandelions growing in the road. "After all," she said, truly enough, "this isn't a gipsy encampment." She would go out with a pen-knife and niggle away at the roots. She told Anthony that the very presence of the dandelions was enough to make him wet his bed. "The French," she said, and she was an encyclopædia on the ways of the French, "call them *pissenlits*." Aunt Jessie, told of this encounter, laughed and said she was ready to chance it, and on country walks she would gather the silver pom-poms of dandelion seed and at dead of night insert them between the setts. On the whole, she won that battle, and Megson Street was rarely without the bravery of dandelion gold in summer, but the poor things led a harassed life.

However, on that Sunday afternoon of March, summer gold seemed a long way off. It was five o'clock, and it was so quiet in the little tucked-in oasis of a street that you could hear the snow sighing as it fell. The linen blind of the Waylands' house, next door to Aunt Jessie's, was luminous, and *In the Shadows* was being tinkled on the piano. That was Lottie Wayland. She never played anything else, and to Anthony it sounded pleasant enough.

It was the general opinion in Megson Street that the widow Wayland gave herself airs. Her front window was the only one that was customarily lit up in the winter and shaded by a sun-blind in the summer. "I can't have the chintz in the parlour bleached," Mrs. Wayland said. A charwoman was in there once a week, and if Mrs. Wayland ever entertained a neighbour to tea it was always on the day when the woman was present. This, Aunt Jessie said, was so that she might have a chance of saying: "Serve tea in the drawing-room, Barraclough. We'll have the Sèvres."

"She and her drawing-room and her Sevvers and her Lottie!" Aunt Jessie would snort. "To say nothing of her Marlborough House!" This was a fling at the name on the gate. All the other houses had numbers, but Mrs. Wayland lived in—or, as she would say, was in residence at—Marlborough House. She used printed notepaper which ignored dear little Megson Street altogether. "Marlborough House, Manningham, Bradford."

If the front window of Aunt Jessie's house was not lit, the front door was. And a pleasing religious light it made, Anthony thought: all those splinters of red and blue, green, yellow and pink glass stuffed higgledy-piggledy between the threads of a leaden cobweb. It had warmth and welcome. He went straight in and walked into the back room. "It's snowing," he said.

"Then come and get something hot into your guts," said Aunt Jessie.

"What's to eat?"

"Cabbage and point, and not even that till you've washed yourself. Get upstairs, and don't keep your uncle waiting."

Anthony knew that his aunt's brusque manner need not be taken too seriously. He stayed where he was, warming his frozen fingers at the fire, happy in the comfortable jumble of the room.

What a clutter it was!—the walls especially. Hardly an inch of wallpaper could be seen for the photographs hanging there. Florrie Finch was not hanging. She stood alone, framed in silver, on the mantelpiece, and there she had been ever since Anthony could remember anything: a saucy-looking piece if ever there was one. With her shapely legs planted apart, she was wearing tights and a jerkin belted to a tiny waist. A hat adorned with a cock's feather was on her head, and over her shoulder was a bundle that wouldn't have held a dog's dinner, attached to a stick sturdy enough to knock down a raging bull. There was a milestone, with a cat sitting before it. You could almost hear Bow Bells. A dashing hand had splashed across the photograph: "For dear old Jess. God bless her. Flo."

Aunt Jessie would sometimes look long at this picture, and break away with a reminiscent sigh. "Gawd! She was a one!" For many years she had been dresser to Miss Finch. Then she had married Horace Pickersgill, twenty years her elder. There had been no children of the marriage, and Jessie's sister, Mrs. Bromwich, having died soon after giving birth to Anthony, they had taken the boy on the understanding that George Bromwich would reclaim his property when it was of an age that would not embarrass a widower. But George Bromwich had so lacked parental feeling as to vanish, no one knew whither. During all of his twelve years, Anthony had known no home save this, no relatives save Aunt Jessie and her husband.

Standing there with the warmth tingling back into his fingers as though they were being stung by innumerable bees, Anthony looked, as he had so often done, at all those girls and men pictured on the walls: dandies and conjurers and clowns, coquettes and dreamy-looking queens: and noted that they had in common a hearty slap-dash writing and an extrovert fervour of greeting. All except one.

12

From Florrie on the mantelpiece, to the sitting-room walls, to the staircase, to the landing, these players seemed to diminish in their interest and importance to Aunt Jessie. And in a corner of the landing, pinned above so utilitarian an object as the laundry-basket, was a youth whom you hardly saw in the daylight, for the landing was dark, but who, now that the gas was lit, suddenly caught Anthony's eye as he paused outside the bathroom door. He knew by heart all the inscriptions on those pictures, and suddenly he remembered what was written in a small careful hand on this one: "To Miss Jessie Wilsher, with grateful thanks. Richard Hudson."

When he was a tot, proud of being able to read, Anthony would decipher these inscriptions aloud; and he remembered that once, reading this record of Richard Hudson's gratitude, he asked his aunt what he was grateful for. She looked up from her work at the laundry-basket and considered Mr. Richard Hudson's picture for a long moment. Then she began to laugh with as hearty and knowing a look as Dame Quickly ever wore, and said: "A bit of the best, lad. But you wouldn't know about that."

Looking at the picture now, with the pricking in his fingers draining slowly away, Anthony found this name Hudson making him see again the opulent and exotic figure pacing along Manningham Lane, holding young Chris Hudson by the hand. He peered closely at the photograph. How different! And yet beyond doubt the same! Raw and awkward-looking, dressed in a lounge suit with a stiff stand-up collar, this was the chrysalis that had bloomed into the Regency butterfly. Forgetting to wash, Anthony ran downstairs and announced excitedly: "Aunt Jessie, I saw Richard Hudson this afternoon in Manningham Lane!"

"Oh, you did, did you!" said Aunt Jessie. "Well, go back and wash. I didn't hear the water gurgling out of the drain."

Uncle Horace looked up reluctantly from an article that gave him a faint hope that he was suffering from fibrositis, and asked: "Who is Richard Hudson?"

"No one you ever knew," she answered rather shortly.

When Anthony came down again they ate their high tea: a meal too plebeian for Mrs. Wayland. In the Wayland house dinner was served.

Anthony might never have met Dick Hudson, or at any rate the meeting would have been postponed, if the symptoms of fibrositis had not increasingly suggested themselves to Uncle Horace's imagination as he chewed his way remorselessly through cold beef and ham, stewed pears and pineapple chunks, bread and butter, cake, jam and parkin, which is a thick brown treacly slice. One thing Uncle Horace wisely avoided was an illness that would come between him and his fodder. As soon as the meal was finished he announced that he thought he had better go to bed. He didn't say why, but crept away, clutching his hot-water bottle and warmed bed-socks, like a man with some pretty startling news that he intends to keep to himself for the moment. When he was at the foot of the stairs Aunt Jessie said abruptly: "I don't suppose anyone will call, but if they do, don't bother to answer the bell. I shall be out."

Anthony heard these words with a sense of crisis, and so, it seemed, did Uncle Horace. His hunched and humbled figure went suddenly erect. "Out?"

"Ay. Now get up before those bed-socks are cold."

"Supposing I get worse?"

She didn't answer.

"Supposing I die?" he moaned ruthlessly, hunched again.

"I'll draw the insurance money. Now off with you."

She spoke with resolution, and after a moment's pause, as if summoning forces that refused to come, he creaked painfully upstairs. To Anthony, the prospect of a lonely evening was depressing. "Will you be away long?" he asked.

"Put on your coat and hat. You're coming with me. Galoshes, too. The snow's heavier."

That she should desert Uncle Horace in a moment of crisis seemed odd to the boy. That it should happen on such a night seemed to him odder still. He pulled on his overcoat with a growing sense of excitement.

3

The snow was falling now good and proper. The stone setts of Megson Street were dumb, and the dandelions were having a cold sleep below them. The Waylands' front window was bright, and the piano was sounding gaily. That couldn't be Lottie. "Looks as though Her Ladyship's entertaining," Aunt Jessie said with a laugh.

But she hadn't much time for Mrs. Wayland that night. "Fancy you meeting Dick Hudson like that!" she said. "He'd have been tickled pink if he'd known who you were."

"How could he know me?"

"Well, he'll know *me* all right. We're going to see him."

Anthony was strangely excited. He had been thrown too suddenly into an enchanted world. This white street with the snow whirling through the quiet and emptiness of Sunday evening, pricked here and there with the flowering street lamps; the odd sense of exaltation that flowed from Aunt Jessie; the prospect of seeing and perhaps speaking to the tall romantic man—it was all something outside his prosaic life till now: a life that had contained little save Uncle Horace reading *Quain* and Aunt Jessie reading *The Era*, wherein theatrical doings were recorded, and himself rushing through his homework in order to get early to bed, where he would light the forbidden candle and steal an hour with Henty or Manville Fenn.

"Did you know Mr. Hudson?" he asked.

"Well, he wouldn't have written that bit to me on the photo if I hadn't, would he?"

She beat at her clothes, shaking off the snow. "It was a night like this when I first met him," she said. "Years ago. In Newcastle. I was dressing Florrie Finch. I suppose Dick was about twenty. He hadn't been on the halls long, and he was first turn. That's what they give to the dogs'-bodies—you know, just a bit of work to fill in while the audience is coming along. Well, he got the bird."

Anthony didn't know what getting the bird was, and said so. "It's something I wouldn't wish my worst enemy. I'd heard of it, but I'd never seen it before and wouldn't want to see it again. There was an hour to go before Florrie's turn, and she hadn't shown up. I had everything ready in her dressing-room and was hanging round in the wings to watch this new chap. I was a bit of a Nosey Parker, and liked to know the ins and outs of everyone on the bill. Well, Dick Hudson was standing there by me, waiting for his bit of music, and he was trembling like a leaf. He was Yorkshire like me, so I gave him a smack on the behind and said: 'Go to it, lad. There's nowt to fear.' But by gum, wasn't there! They were stony-quiet for a bit, then someone in the gallery let out a whistle, and it was like a signal. Everyone started whistling and laughing, the wrong sort of laughing, if you know what I mean. Then the chap in the gallery gave a cat-call, and the people round him took it up, and other people started stamping. Oh, I could have killed 'em!" said Aunt Jessie. "It was plain bloody murder."

She shook her clothes vehemently, as if she were rattling together the silly heads of that far-off audience.

"He couldn't take it," she said. "He dried up, and stood there for a bit as if he'd been pole-axed. Then he ran off, right to where I was standing. And, d'you know, he was crying his eyes out. Oh, it can be a cruel thing, an audience, when it wants to."

"What did you do, Aunt Jessie?"

"Do? Why, I cuddled the lad," she said practically, "and let him cry a bit while the second turn went on. Then I said 'Well, I can't stand here all night mothering you, lad,' and we walked away together. He was sharing a mingy little dressing-room at the end of a corridor, and we were just passing Florrie's room when up she comes, smothered in furs and smelling of the cold night outside. A sort of sparkling smell. D'you know? She always had that smell—all alive and kicking."

Florrie looked at Dick Hudson and asked: "What's the matter with him?"

She was twenty-five—five years older than Dick, and old enough in experience to be his grandmother. Relaxed in her dressing-room, she loved to have her hands and feet massaged by Jessie Wilsher. Her hands and feet were long and fine. They didn't seem to belong to the slum she had come from. She would close her eyes and almost purr like a stroked cat. That was because the hands had been red and cracked from soda in the wash-tub, and the feet like leaden weights as she trudged upstairs with buckets of water to scrub the oilcloth in attics. A skivvy in one lodging-house after another. "You'd better dress, Miss Finch. You'll have the call-boy here any minute." "Go on, Jess. Another rub. Let 'em wait." But she never did. She was always on time. The sun-basking cat could in a second become the lithe and agile creature, with the long foot tapping the signature tune in the wings. She never let them wait. They would be there to send a wave of applause to meet her. She owed them so much. She never forgot that. But she didn't forget, either, as she looked at Dick Hudson with tears smudging his grease-paint, a lot of things she had known in her time, for she hadn't knocked 'em out with the first blow. Not by a long chalk.

The manager came along the corridor. "Good evening, Miss Finch. Hudson, could we have a word?"

Dick was visibly trembling. "Yes, sir."

Florrie said: "There's no need for any words from you. I can give him all the words he needs."

"Well, I'm not sure, Miss Finch. You see . . ."

"*I'm* sure. And don't you start rattling me. You know very well that I can't work unless I'm in a peaceful state of mind. Arguments upset me. So run along like a good boy."

It was as clear in Jessie's mind as though it had happened yesterday. But all she said to Anthony as they trudged through the snow was: "She put a bit of guts into him. They were about together all through that week. You know, there are people like that. They blow

16

the cobwebs out of you, and they blow the fresh air into you. She was a one, was Florrie. What she could do to an audience she could do to a man, if she put her mind to it. And she certainly put her mind into Dick Hudson. It was after that week that he gave me the photograph that's pinned up on the landing."

Across the road, a nest of snow that had built itself on the branch of a tree slipped and fell and, under the light of a lamp, burst in a noiseless feathery explosion. An electric tram, empty of everything but golden light, swung by like a galleon in an arctic sea. Oh, this is a grand night to be out in, Anthony thought, taking Aunt Jessie's arm and squeezing it with delight. "Did you go on knowing Mr. Hudson?"

"Well, yes and no. You see, a music-hall chap's on the go all the time, here to-day and gone to-morrow. Sometimes he and Miss Finch would be on the same circuit, playing in the same house week after week, and I'd see a lot of him. Other times I wouldn't. Then I chucked it all up to get married, and soon after that Florrie got married, too. I knew that Dick kept a house here for his kid, and I knew from the ads when he was playing in Bradford and would be at home, but I didn't worry him much. Just looked in on him now and then. Well, he's worked, has Dick Hudson, and I'm glad to see him top of the bill at last. And here we are. This is the street."

Like all the streets running off Manningham Lane, this one fell sharply away to the valley bottom. Down there was Frizinghall station, the hill on the other side of the valley rising above it, but invisible in the snowy darkness. A train had drawn in, and stood like a glowing dragon, a snort of steam blowing up out of its nostrils. Then it grunted and coughed and wormed slowly away towards Bradford.

Going downhill, they moved with care. "Do you think," Anthony asked, "that Chris Hudson will come tobogganing with me to-morrow?" Not that he wanted Chris. He wanted the son of The Great Hudson.

"You can ask him," Aunt Jessie laughed, "but why you should want to beats me. Gormless bit of nowt. He'll never forgive you if he gets his toes cold." She turned in at a little iron gate and rapped heartily with the knocker.

Anthony did not at first recognize the man who came to the door. He was wearing a tweed suit and smoking a pipe. The gaslight in the hall fell on Aunt Jessie's face and he knew her and said: "Well, God bless us, Jess! Shake off the snow and come on in for five minutes."

"Five minutes!" Aunt Jessie cried. "That's a fine welcome when

I haven't seen you for a year and have dragged this boy through the snow especially to meet you!"

"Well, come in anyway. The devil of it is, I'm due to be away in five minutes to take a cold collation, whatever that may be, and I don't know where I'm going."

They shook off the snow and hung their coats in the passage and followed Dick into the front room. Aunt Jessie introduced Anthony, who now realised that this was the dazzling apparition of the afternoon cut down to human size.

"Well, warm your behind, boy," Dick invited, and that seemed mundane to Anthony after the "A very good day to you, young sir," that the lips of the apparition had earlier pronounced.

Aunt Jessie sat in a chair at the fireside, her hands to the blaze. "Where's your lad?" she asked.

"Upstairs, getting into his best suit. He's coming to eat this cold collation with me. I don't fancy anything cold to-night, and what in hell is a collation? And, come to that, where's Marlborough House?"

Aunt Jessie began to laugh without restraint.

"'Ere, what's to laugh at?" Dick demanded. He knocked out his pipe on the fire-bars and took a letter from his pocket. "Now, listen 'ere, lass. This is about young Chris. I'm in the money now, as I expect you know. Well, I want to do something for the lad. Something about his schooling. I never had any myself, but he's going to have some. He's going to a public school—see? Well, he's got to be prepared for that, and he's not being prepared now because he's not happy where he is, and that's why he's learning nowt. He's sensitive, and he wants particular care, and that's what he's going to have. So I put an ad in the *Argus*, asking for someone who would be tutor to a young lad—see?—and give him individual attention. Well, I only got one answer, and this is it." He waved the letter. "You read it, lass."

Aunt Jessie read the letter aloud.

> "*Marlborough House,*
> *Manningham, Bradford*
> *March 6, 1912*

"Dear Sir,—In response to your advertisement in the Bradford *Argus*, I beg to offer my services in the proposed post. I am a widow with one child. For some years my husband held a commercial post in France, which gave me the opportunity to acquire a knowledge of the French language which I could impart to the proposed

18

pupil, not with the barbarous accent that no educated French person would comprehend, but as it is spoken in the best circles in that country. I am versed in the elements of mathematics, and need hardly say that I comprehend the refined usage of my native tongue. As you are no doubt aware, Bradford is not the best place for the acquisition of that accent which is desirable for a young gentleman destined for one of our public schools, but I may truly say that this house is a small centre of cosmopolitan culture which a pupil would imbibe as the air he breathes. I write a copperplate hand, as this letter testifies, and could impart this to my pupil. I invite you to take a cold collation here on Sunday night at 8 p.m., when we might discuss the wider question of whether the proposed pupil might not, with advantage, live here *en famille*, rather than come to and fro daily. There is a dainty bedroom that could be at his disposal. I think this, altogether, would be most advantageous.

Yours very truly,

EDNA WAYLAND

"PS.—I could impart the elements of the pianoforte to the proposed pupil."

As Aunt Jessie finished reading, the proposed pupil came into the room, with his hair plastered into a decorous parting and an Eton suit hung upon his skinny figure. The Great Hudson whose speech as a Regency rake would have been considered by Mrs. Wayland very *haut ton* wore the Yorkshire Doric with his tweeds and carpet slippers. "Well, lad," he said to his son, "hasta nowt to say to visitors?"

Chris had nothing to say, and Aunt Jessie did not help him. Dick looked at him in perplexity, and said: "See what I mean? Summat's got to be done. Now listen, Jess. A taxi chap that I ordered'll be 'ere any minute. Where's this Marlborough House?"

A bang at the knocker announced the taxi. "I'll take you there, lad," Aunt Jessie said. "It's on my way. If you're starving after the cold collation, just look in next door. That's where I live. Buckingham Palace is my place. But don't be nervous. I'll tell the sentries to let you by."

The taxi slithered through the snow. It was a short journey, cold and miserable, but it gave Anthony time to think what a dreary little tick Chris Hudson was; he hadn't a word to say to anybody. But, come to that, neither had Anthony himself. He was too perplexed by the contrast he had stumbled on: Dick in his carpet slippers and The Great Hudson.

Anthony would have been even more perplexed had he known what contrasts and contradictions inhabited Mrs. Wayland. He knew only the rather foolish exterior of that iron woman; Aunt Jessie's taunts and innuendoes helped to build a screen that hid the widow next door. Mrs. Wayland may have pretended, always, to be more than she was; but she did really and passionately *desire* to be more than she was. She was born in Nottingham, where her mother kept a fly-blown corner shop, and when she was sixteen years old she was working in a factory: hard, dirty work, rough on the fingers. It was slave labour, and she knew she was a slave, but she wouldn't accept all the conditions. She insisted on taking time off from slavery. When she was out of the factory she was not the girl who worked in the factory. Out of doors, her hands were always hidden in gloves. Indoors, they were busy making her own clothes, which she wore on Sundays to the Wesleyan chapel. There were plenty of Wesleyan chapels to choose from. Edna chose the one that the richest people attended. The gallery was free, but she didn't sit in the gallery. She rented a pew downstairs—that was what all the toffs did—and she found the money somehow. She didn't get on well with her mother, who called her a stuck-up little bitch: sometimes they came to blows. But Edna held to her way. She liked to be early in her pew, for both morning and evening service, and to listen to the organ playing its preliminary music, and to watch the toffs coming in. Almost all the men wore silk hats and kid gloves. The women, in large flowing hats and rustling skirts, smelled of exciting scents.

Edna didn't rent a whole pew. There were four or five seats in a pew, and she had the one on the gangway. She had chosen that one with a general's eye to the needs of battle. If you were first in your seat, then those who came later couldn't help noticing you as you rose to let them pass, and they would say good evening to you and might even smile at you. Mr. and Mrs. Wayland and Tom Wayland occupied the seats inside hers, and Tom Wayland, as he passed in, could not help now and then brushing her knees. He would blush and say "Pardon" before kneeling in prayer on his hassock. She liked this so much that occasionally she would forget her hymn-book, and Tom Wayland would share his with her. Hymn-singing was what she liked best. She had a clear soprano voice, as good, she was sure, as that of anybody in the choir, including Lottie Wayland, Tom's sister. She sang lustily because she was madly anxious to be invited to join the choir. The young people in it were all from the best families of the congregation. There was a *cachet* to it, and, for another thing, she would save the money she was paying for her pew.

Fine Sunday evenings in the summer were her especial delight. When the service was over, the sun would still be shining, and she would join the parade up and down the paths of a public garden near the chapel. She was eighteen now, and could lift a silken skirt with one hand and sport a parasol with the other as well as anybody. She had bought the wreck of a parasol for sixpence and beautifully re-covered it. She had learned to walk with a fine negligence, and, if she was no beauty, she was not bad to look at.

One autumn evening, she knew that the four Waylands were trailing behind her. She dropped her furled parasol, and in an instant Tom Wayland had picked it up and presented it to her, raising his hat. Lottie Wayland said good evening, and Mr. Wayland, too, raised his hat. Mrs. Wayland merely looked at her in the way in which a camel looks at most things. Then she found herself walking with the two youngsters behind the elders. She kept her head, but that night she walked home on clouds. She knew that Tom Wayland was taken with her. He talked to his sister about her voice, and said they should make room for her in the choir, and he invited her to come to the opening meeting of the Wesley Guild next week. He was to read a paper on the missionary work of David Livingstone.

Edna's mother, wearing the sack-cloth apron that was her favourite *négligé*, was sitting in the kitchen. "Well, your Royal Highness," she said. "Pick anybody up?" It was the sort of remark that was intended to lead to a quarrel, but that night Edna did not want to quarrel. She went straight to bed.

Thinking it over, she learned how easy it was not to quarrel, and how satisfyingly victorious one might feel over a person who was trying to quarrel all day long and whom one would not engage: victorious and virtuous. She needed the strength this gave her when she married Tom Wayland.

She didn't know what a fool he was, and tried to make herself worthy of him. It would have surprised her to know that he wasn't fit to lick her boots. They were never engaged to be married, but they began to go about together, and the first of Tom's attempts to quarrel with her came when she didn't want to go about so much. She was attending evening classes, and found to her surprise that she enjoyed learning. "You're good enough for me as you are," Tom said. She wouldn't fight about it, but neither would she give up her classes. For one thing, she knew that Tom's parents didn't approve of all this, and she wanted to do something that would make her seem better in their eyes. This was hopeless, for there is no class division so sharp as that between those who have a little and those who have nothing. In the pew Mr. Wayland, not Tom, now sat next to Edna, and he never offered to share his hymn-book; and presently the Waylands changed their pew for one nearer the pulpit: a clear enough hint. After all, you owe it to the mercy seat to approach it in reasonably respectable company.

It was a dreary and unsatisfactory time for Edna. She changed from the factory to serving in a milliner's shop, which was better for her hands. She went on with her classes in the winter and was about a good deal with Tom Wayland in the summer. On the whole, she was happier in the winter than in the summer, but she never reflected on what that might mean. She knew now that the Waylands would not accept her if they could help it, and a dull determination to make them accept her anyway obsessed her mind. But she would not have won her disastrous victory if Mr. Wayland had not himself handed it to her.

He was an accountant, and the treasurer of several funds. Odd thoughts must now and then have been turning in his mind as he knelt on his hassock and bowed his head. Could a thousand pounds from Fund A be transferred to Fund B in time for the annual audit; and, if so, what were the chances of covering that up with a thousand from C to B? That is simplifying it. There were complications more profound, and they had gone on for so long that even Mr. Wayland's accounting brain saw that soon there would be no accounting for them. A footpath went over the railway line at a level crossing; and perhaps this, too, entered into his thoughts as he moved softly from pew to pew passing the plate that was lined with felt lest the chink of lucre should defile the holy places. "The offertory will now be taken. The stewards will wait upon you." Oh, never, never, could a steward furtively abstract a solid and tangible half-crown, so different from figures in a book, little inky marks that could be taught to do such agreeable and profitable tricks. But only for a time, and then there was the foggy night when a man, going over the level crossing, might be held, by a stretch of the imagination, not to have heard the on-coming train. "The jury," said the newspaper, "returned a verdict of accidental death, and the coroner expressed his sympathy with the widow and her children."

And then another accountant looked into the little inky marks and it all came out. A lot of money had gone down the drain and no one knew whither. Perhaps the strange woman who turned up at the funeral could have said something. At all events, plenty was said about *her*. There was hardly a penny left for the Waylands, and Tom was now certainly no cop. But Edna had made up her mind to marry him, and she did so because she liked doing what she had made up her mind to do. She felt a grim pleasure in Mrs. Wayland's collapse, in seeing Lottie Wayland working, as she had done, in a milliner's shop, in saying nothing to her own mother. When the time came, she simply walked out with her things in a cheap suitcase and went to France with Tom Wayland. They were married at the British Consulate in Paris.

Not many people were kind to the Waylands in those days, but one of Mr. Wayland's old friends, a hosiery manufacturer, offered Tom a job in his Paris office, for it was a big firm with an international trade. Tom jumped at it. "You will be able to help your mother," his benefactor said. But Tom had no intention of helping his mother who had twitted him on his "low tastes" for years past. He hadn't a word of French, and one reason why he now clung to Edna was that she would see him over that hurdle. In her evening classes, French was her love. Her teacher for the last two years had been a Frenchman whose method was little more than conversation. Edna could now prattle tolerably, and though she had long ceased to think of making herself worthy of Tom, she was glad that this would be of use to him. She knew how he was longing to get out of a town where all his acquaintances knew the Wayland story, and where many of them thought they knew more than, in fact, had ever happened.

She was twenty-one.

The idea of living in Paris was exciting to Tom Wayland. Brought up in a stupid home, he had stupid ideas about most things, Paris among them. It wasn't what he had expected. His work was hard and uninteresting; his wages were contemptible; and he hadn't the resolution to take himself in hand as his wife had done. His temper was not improved by his knowledge of her contempt, never expressed in words. They lived in a meagre apartment, and Edna learned to extract value from every sou. She went to the markets and could soon chaffer over a ha'penny with the best. She read the French newspapers and French books and tried to bring Tom on by talking to him in French. He told her to stop that monkey-chatter. He was an Englishman, wasn't he?—and a Nottingham man at that, he added, as though that clinched it—and he didn't want any bloody foreign lingo.

"But, Tom, we're living in France."

"Let France learn English, then."

"Fortunately, some Frenchmen do."

That touched him on the raw, for they would have been near starvation on his wages, and Edna had begun to take in pupils. She taught by the simple method of talking to them and reading to them from books, and she was good at it. She soon had as many pupils as she could deal with; and there would be times when some would be in the apartment when Tom returned from the office. He could hardly wait for the door to be shut behind them before demanding if the place had to be littered with frogs. He hated them because he knew that his own inefficiency made them necessary.

She was twenty-three when Lottie was born. Lessons were abandoned during her pregnancy and for six months afterwards. That was a hard time. Tom quarrelled with her for giving him a child, and she replied that the child would be all right: it would be her responsibility not his. He said: "Some frog's responsibility, I shouldn't wonder," and all that had arisen from the titillation of knees brushing in the Wesleyan pew ended with those words. Edna did not answer them; she did not even look daggers, as they say; but if Tom wanted a woman after that he had to go elsewhere. She never knew, and never cared, whether he did or not.

Henri Hamel was among her pupils when she began again to teach. They had been youngsters till now, but Henri was twenty-one. He was from Provence, he had a small allowance from his father and a small apartment, and he was studying painting at Julian's. It did not take Edna long to perceive that she was a greater attraction than her lessons. It was difficult to make Henri talk English. He babbled away in French about painting, about books, about music. He wanted her to visit galleries with him, to go to concerts, to dine with him, and to visit his apartment. She put him off by asking what they could do with Lottie.

"Why," he cried, "we would carry her in turns. I have carried babies for many girls, and," he said, smiling hardily, "many girls have carried babies for me."

She liked him. He was impudent and amusing, and he knew what he was talking about. He brought books of reproductions and talked to her about pictures, and he was for ever sketching her and the baby. Soon all pretence that he came for lessons was over. She would make coffee, and Henri would produce a hip-flask and pour in cognac.

One afternoon he said: "Now there is one thing where this so terribly obstructive baby can be a help, not a hindrance."

A check cloth of red and black was on the table. He left the coffee things on it, took a baton of bread from the sideboard, broke it in two, and put that there, also. "A simple meal," he said, "coffee and bread, for this woman is poor. You remember, Edna, the picture I show you by Chardin? Well, this will be better."

He had brought a canvas and paints, and he now produced a handful of dandelion flowers and stuck them into a gay mug from Quimper. "You see, this woman is so poor she has used the leaves for salad, but she loves flowers and cannot afford to buy any, so she uses the simple *pissenlits*. Till now we have sketched. Now we paint."

He arranged and rearranged the things on the table; then finally put a kitchen chair where he wanted her to sit. He said: "The woman has finished eating. She is now feeding her child."

Edna said: "Oh, no, Henri. No."

He propped the canvas against the back of a chair, put another ready for work in front of it, squeezed a few colours on to the palette. "An art student sees many women, but he does not know them. I shall not know you. I shall be seeing only the poor woman with her child."

She bared her breasts, took up the child, and sat down. He came and took hold of her naked shoulders, and turned her about the way he wanted her. Then he arranged the stuff of her clothes, and as he did that his hands brushed her breasts. She trembled to the marrow.

He painted for an hour, chattering to keep her relaxed. Then he said: "To-morrow, at the same hour—yes?"

"Yes."

The picture was finished, and a month later Henri asked her to go with him to an exhibition where it was being shown. This time he did not wait for her to object that Lottie would be in the way. "There is the woman who cooks my dinner. She has nine children, and the youngest is now twenty years old. Between them, they weigh many tons. They are whales. She will make nothing of this sardine. She expects us at half past two."

It was a beautiful day of early spring. Henri carried the child. The flower-woman's baskets were piled with daffodils and mimosa. Edna had never been so happy in her life. She felt like a convict who has slipped his chains and got out on to the moor. They left Lottie with a huge complacent woman who asked when the child would be called for. Henri said: "*A dix heures—même onze.*" That seemed all right to the woman, and Edna laughed. "*Plutôt à cinq heures, madame,*" she said. The woman smiled broadly at Henri, whom she seemed to comprehend, and said: "*Nous verrons. En tout cas, restez tranquille.*"

But that was the last thing Edna could do. She felt as *tranquille* as champagne effervescing in crystal. Of her own accord, when they were in the street, she tucked her arm through Henri's. He patted her hand and said simply: "*Ça va mieux.*" He was in no hurry to get to the gallery. He trotted her along the quays and the boulevards. It was all new to her: she had never had time for this sort of thing. The barges on the water, the fishermen, the mist of opening leaves trembling against the blue sky, the jewels and dresses in the shops: she was so happy that she possessed it all while wanting none of it. "*Tu es contente?*" He had not given her a *tu* before. She nodded, too exalted to answer.

It was five o'clock when they came to the gallery: not much of a gallery, but a gallery flaming with glory, for Henri's painting was marked "Sold." They did not stay long. They hardly stayed at all, but she would always remember the picture she never saw again: the child's mouth at her breast, her own recognizable face, the dandelions shining in brave gold over the poverty of the broken loaf. She had hardly taken this in when Henri seized her arm and abruptly whisked her outside. She saw that he was crying, and said nothing.

But he was soon recovered: he was shot up, indeed, to an exaltation that matched her own. He laughed and chattered, but he did not speak about the picture. They drank a glass of wine at a table on the pavement, and then they walked again till the dusk came down: a purple dusk in which lights began to bloom and the pulse of the day merged slowly into the pulse of the night. They ate dinner in a restaurant noisy with youngsters whom Edna took to be students. Some of them passed the time of day with Henri, and one of them came up and slapped him on the shoulder and investigated Edna with frank eyes. She didn't know how she was looking, but she felt beautiful. The youngster said: "*Alors, Henri. Vous faites du progrès. Félicitations!*"

They went to a music-hall where the jokes were broad and the girls bare, and then they took another glass of wine. It was eleven o'clock when Edna reclaimed Lottie. The woman looked at them as though her eyes could divine and judge their day's doings. "*Ça marche?*" she asked with a smile, and Edna said simply: "*A ravir, madame.*"

"*Bon, alors!*"

Henri found a cab, and they drove to Edna's apartment with the sleeping baby cradled in his arm. On the doorstep he handed her to Edna, and then, as she stood there clutching that bundle, they had for a long moment nothing to say. The cabby whom Henri had told to wait shouted impatiently, and Henri said: "*Demain? À la même heure?*" She said: "*Oui. Et pour toujours si tu veux.*"

He kissed her rather hastily and said: "*Si tu savais comme je suis heureux!*" and hurried off.

She stood watching till the cab disappeared round a corner, then opened the door and climbed the stairs, almost unable to use her limbs for joy. Tom was in the small shabby sitting-room, which suddenly looked intolerable. "This is a nice thing," he cried—"out till nearly midnight, and with the child, too! Where have you been?"

She said: "In heaven," and wearily carried Lottie through to the bedroom.

She wondered, next day, what she should do about her pupils. Between three and six, she had appointments with four of them, and Henri would arrive *à la même heure*, which could be anything between two and half past. It was another day of magical weather, and she didn't want to spend it indoors. They would go wherever Henri wanted to go, and they would do whatever Henri wanted to do. She wrote a notice and pinned it to the outside of her door. "Madame Wayland regrets that she has had to leave town on urgent business." She fed Lottie, but she was too excited to eat anything herself. She put on the few bits of finery she had, and sat down to wait. But she could not sit for long. She was restlessly up and down, aware that soon many things would have to be considered, but unable to think, for Henri would be here at any moment.

He did not come—not on that day or any day. She left the notice on the door, and lay on her bed, overwhelmed, and heard callers come, and pause, and go. It was late in the afternoon when the thought struck her that perhaps Henri had been one of the callers, that he had read the notice, taken it for dismissal, and gone away. She went out then and tore down the notice, but she could not believe that he had come. He would not have stood there dumbly. Not Henri. He would have shouted and banged and rattled the handle; and anyway, she said to herself with sad insight, even if he had done none of these things, I should have known if Henri was there.

When Tom was due to return, she roused herself and cooked his meal. But Tom did not come, either. At breakfast that morning he had been morose and silent. She did not know that on the day which she had chosen for her joyous and revealing escapade with Henri, Tom had been given notice that in a week's time his employers would do their best to keep their affairs going without his assistance. He had come home in a mood of self-pity, and, more creditably, with a realisation for the first time of his own shortcomings. He was ready to go on his knees, to ask for pardon, and to promise an unlikely amendment. He had found an empty flat and a wife who, when at last she returned, was oddly lit up and too aloof even to give him contempt. So, to hell with her, he thought the next night: he would find his consolations elsewhere. He came home stinking of drink at eleven o'clock and fell on to his bed without undressing. It was not until the following Monday, when his notice was up, and he dawdled intolerably over his breakfast, that he told her. She still persisted in trying to make him speak French, and said: "*Dépêches-toi, Tom. Tu seras en retard au bureau.*" He grinned. "No more bureau for Tom. The bureau's given Tom a nice long holiday. Little Edna's the breadwinner now." At ten o'clock he took his hat and said: "They say that springtime is the best for seeing Paris. I'm going to check on that."

"Will you be in to lunch?"

"We'll see. On the whole, old girl, it may be best if I don't pry into your amours."

He never worked again, and became a fearful liability. Till Lottie was ten Edna worked like a horse. The pupils began to arrive now at nine in the morning, and sometimes the last of them left at nine at night. She was in a state of mental and physical and spiritual exhaustion when Tom died of the tuberculosis that his erratic life engendered. She looked without pity on the man in the coffin—the man she had once striven to be worthy of. She had kept a home of a sort for him to come back to as long as he needed it; and she had done so at tremendous cost. In all those years she had hardly stirred out of her apartment. She knew little of Paris save her immediate neighbourhood and when she thought of her day out with Henri she might have been thinking of a day in paradise accorded, as a refinement of torture, to one of the damned. She never solved the mystery of Henri's disappearance and never tried to. She would rather think that death had suddenly overtaken him than know that he was happily living, with her forgotten after a moment's aberration regretted. She remembered how, that day, whatever she may have looked, she felt beautiful. When she looked into the mirror now she saw that the woman in her early thirties was gaunt, greying, and a little odd.

This was the woman who for the past two years had lived next door to Auntie Jessie in Megson Street, and who couldn't bear the sight of dandelions. She left Paris as soon as she had put Tom, and so much else, underground. She came back to England with little more than a bi-lingual daughter ten years old and a not very good Sèvres tea-set. She didn't want Nottingham again. For aught she knew, her mother was still alive. But she wanted the sort of town she had known, and Bradford was as good as any. She wanted pupils, too, or she could not live; but now she would have to teach English people French instead of French people English. But no more pupils in the house, she promised herself. During the last two years, she had established herself, in her indomitable fashion, as a "correspondence school." It meant a lot of hard work, but she was making ends meet by that snowy March night when Dick Hudson rapped on her door, concerned about the future of his son Chris.

CHAPTER 3

9 9 9 9 9 9

1

*T*he houses in Megson Street were all joined together. Only a low iron railing separated the front doors of Aunt Jessie's house and Mrs. Wayland's. Aunt Jessie fumbled with her key long enough to give Mrs. Wayland time to come to the door and to hear her say: "Mr. Hudson, I presume?"

"Ay. That's me, and this is Chris," Dick said; and then they were inside; there was no more to be heard; and Aunt Jessie opened her own door.

"Well, it fair beats the band," she said in the passage; and then, sniffing, "He's up."

The aroma of Woodcock's Wonder Weed proclaimed that Uncle Horace was indeed up. He was in the sitting-room, with a fire blazing, his small pink face with its white moustache looking infantile and cherubic.

"I got better," he explained with simplicity.

"You're an old fox if ever there was one," said Aunt Jessie with affectionate asperity. "Couldn't trust me—that's the long and the short of it. Gnawing at you—that's what it's been—gnawing at you —the idea that I was having a night out. Well, we've been along to see Dick Hudson."

"Who's he?"

"You heard Anthony say he'd met him in Manningham Lane."

"Ay, but that don't tell me who he is."

Uncle Horace, who had never set foot in a theatre or music-hall, pretended, and indeed felt, a profound disinterest in Jessie's life before their marriage. A lot of poppycock and flapdoodle—people dressing up and making out that they were this and that when they were plain Toms, Dicks and Harrys like other folk. He was privately convinced that Jessie blessed the day when he rescued her from a life which he was sure only harsh necessity would make anyone accept. And a rum do that was, he sometimes thought with a chuckle, to find a wife when he'd gone to bury his brother. He supposed it was because the job had put him in a jovial mood. Who wouldn't be glad to bury a chap like Bert? He'd bailed him out of gaol more than once, and paid his debts in one thing, and advanced him money to set up in another, for almost as long as he could remember. And the devil of it was that Bert was younger than he was, so that it looked as though this would go on all his life. He couldn't afford Bert and a wife, and he was beginning to feel it was time he had a wife—someone who would sympathise with his delicate constitution as his landlady never did. And then for once Bert goes and does him a good turn—gets knocked down by a cab-horse on a foggy night in Leeds, and that's the end of him. Horace went over to Leeds for the funeral with a buoyant heart, and on the evening before it he was prowling about under the lights in the market, enjoying himself immensely. It was near Christmas, and the place was full of poultry and sides of beef and dazzling flower-stalls and hearty men shouting about good things to eat. He had come to buy a wreath for Bert, and the prices were a bit steep. It set him back half a guinea. That made him feel glum, and he must have looked glum when he entered a little alcove in the market where you could get a bite and a sup. There was only one other person in the place when Horace sat down and propped the wreath against his chair—a woman who looked what he would have called "booxum-laike." She considered him for a time with a sympathetic eye, and then said: "Was you bereaved, luv?"

"Nay, lass," he said, "not bereaved—relieved."

The only joke he had ever made in his life seemed to him so good that he began to shake with laughter, and that made him cough, and she said: "You want to watch that cough, lad. Have one of these."

She gave him a peppermint, and said: "You ought to be wearing a muffler on a night like this. And mittens wouldn't hurt you, either."

Such words fell as manna on the parched desert of Horace's spirit. This was a woman if you like! He said: "Well, it's something to have got a laugh out of Bert in the end."

Their tea and muffins arrived, and the alcove was warm and cosy, and he began to tell her about Bert and the funeral on the morrow. He hadn't enjoyed a talk so much for a long time.

When the tea and muffins were gone she said: "On a night like this you want summat solid in you. No wonder you get coughs."

So they ordered more tea and steak and chipped potatoes, with plum duff to follow.

"Now," she said, "that'll set you up for t'funeral. But mind you make a good breakfast, too."

"It'd set me up more if you'd come with me to t'cemetery," he said.

"All right, luv. Ah've nowt better to do."

That was how it began.

2

Mrs. Wayland was all solicitude when she went to the door and found Dick Hudson standing there. She apologised for the snow as though she had been personally responsible for allowing it to fall, and took Dick and Chris into the back room, which was the dining-room. By Dick's standards, there wasn't much in it: a table lit by four candles which made all the light there was, the chairs, a sideboard, and some low book-shelves filled with yellow-covered books. The walls were the colour of faded parchment, and there was only one picture, from which he hastily turned his eyes. It was over the mantelpiece: a reproduction of Manet's *Déjeuner sur l'Herbe*. Accustomed as he was to the stuffy and shabby fullness of theatrical digs, it seemed to Dick rather bleak, but the fire was bright on the hearth, and a small girl who had been standing before it came forward and made him a curtsey. "Lottie," Mrs. Wayland said, "this is Mr. Richard Hudson, and this is his son Christopher."

The child said: "Good evening, sir," to Dick, and gave Chris one of her attractive curtseys.

Dick said: "You're a bonny lass," and Lottie smiled at him and drew out a chair for him. With Dick, it was love at first sight. She was a child, but her manners were grown-up and without embarrassment. He found the combination irresistible. He looked at Chris, and his heart ached. The boy was as dumb as a stone, and as unforthcoming.

"Shake hands with Mrs. Wayland, Chris," he said, and Chris did so cumbrously, without a word.

The cold collation was already on the table. There were lamb cutlets with frills of pink paper on them, and a gay dish of salad. There was a salad cream that Mrs. Wayland had made, and Dick thought it better than the stuff he had been accustomed to pour lavishly from bottles. There was wine for him and Mrs. Wayland and water for Chris and Lottie, and the wine and water alike were in crystal. After this there was cheese of a sort Dick had never known. It was, in fact, Brie. And then there was coffee, served from a percolator on the table. The meal couldn't have been simpler, and Dick enjoyed it, but at the same time he was embarrassed by it, and he was annoyed that this should be so. Chris had not liked the cheese and was now saying ungraciously that he didn't want coffee. Well, that was all right. If you didn't like a thing you were entitled to say so, and if you didn't want a thing you could say that, too; but there were ways of doing it, and Chris hadn't got them. Lottie wasn't drinking coffee, either. Mrs. Wayland had asked: "*Du café, Lottie?*" and the child had said "*Merci, maman,*" whatever all that might mean; but obviously the child didn't want coffee and had said so politely.

Mrs. Wayland said: "Lottie, will you entertain Master Chris in the parlour for a moment?"

Chris gave his father a look of agonised enquiry. Dick replied with a brief stern nod. When the strains of *In the Shadows* came from the next room, Mrs. Wayland said: "Now, Mr. Hudson."

She was an intelligent woman. Like a statesman who, if he knows his business, goes to a conference with his conditions decided beforehand, she kept to the point and kept Dick to it. For a *fait accompli* to work from, she soon had Dick's consent that Chris should remain in the house that very night. They inspected Chris's bedroom, and Dick agreed that it would do. They discussed the charges for tuition and board and lodging. Dick agreed to these, too. Mrs. Wayland had them all written down, and they put their signatures to the bond.

"The lad's a bit nesh," Dick said. "Don't work him too hard."

"He'll be working from the time he gets up till the time he goes to bed," Mrs. Wayland answered. "But he won't know it. I shall bring him up as I have brought up my own child."

Dick recalled the pleasing image of Lottie, and hoped that Mrs. Wayland was speaking the truth.

When these main points were settled, Mrs. Wayland said: "May I enquire what your profession is, Mr. Hudson?"

Dick told her, and said: "A job like that means that I'm not in Bradford more than once in a blue moon. I'm thinking it'll be a bit daft to keep my house going here now that Chris is living with you. In other towns I make do well enough with digs."

Mrs. Wayland looked at him thoughtfully. "I shouldn't like Marlborough House ever to be called digs," she said. "But if you would care to come into residence here when your work brings you to Bradford, don't you think that would be a useful arrangement? Of course," she said, throwing away all her cards with generous diplomacy, "now that you are at the head of your profession, both you and Chris can live where you please. It might be to his advantage to go out of the provinces altogether and grow up in the capital, as Lottie did. You could find some pedagogue in Town who would gladly take charge of him, and a man in your position may well consider London rather than Bradford to be his headquarters."

Dick hastily brushed all this aside. "Oh, no," he said. "I were brought up in Bradford and feel at home here, and so does Chris. Coming to you will be a big enough change for him to begin with. Don't let's over-do things."

"I think you're wise to take that view, Mr. Hudson. But I felt obliged to put the option before you. If you still feel you want to give up your house, you can come here. You and Chris could have the parlour to yourselves. We have three bedrooms. Lottie and I share one, and that leaves one each for you and the boy. Think it over, and let me know some time how you feel about it."

"Nay," said Dick, "there's no need for shilly-shally. Let's call it a do."

"Very well. Now I think the children should go to bed. I believe in early hours for the young. Have you brought Christopher's pyjamas?"

"He sleeps in a night-shirt, and I haven't brought that. He can keep on the shirt he's wearing for once. It won't hurt him. When I were a lad I slept in nowt else. I'll bring his stuff in t'morning."

"Come then," said Mrs. Wayland, rather regally, and Dick found himself holding the door open for her. "Ay," he thought. "These are the little tricks t'lad'll have to learn."

The piano-playing had stopped some time before, and Lottie was trying to interest Chris in the first steps in draughts, not, it seemed, with much success.

"*Quelle heure est-il, maman?*" the child asked.

"*Dix heures juste. Faut se coucher. Dis la bonne nuit à Monsieur Hudson.*"

She came up to Dick, smiled at him out of her dark eyes, and gave him one of her curtseys. "*Bonne nuit, Monsieur Hudson,*" she said. "*Enchantée de faire votre connaissance.*" She turned to Chris. "*Bonne nuit, Christophe. Dormez bien.*"

Chris gave her a deadly scowl. She blew him a kiss, and went.

Mrs. Wayland said: "Will you take Christopher up, Mr. Hudson?

Christopher, we talk a lot of French. You will quickly learn what it means. To-night I shall wish you good night. To-morrow I shall wish you *bonne nuit*. It is easy, is it not? Good night."

Dick saw the boy into bed. "Now, Chris," he said, "you're going to have a chance in a million, lad. You'll be better off here than with Mrs. Wyke, and I think learning with Mrs. Wayland and that nice little lass will be better than a school class. There's a lot of rough corners on your Dad, Chris, because he never had much chance to rub 'em off, but things are going to be different for you. That's the only reason why I care tuppence about all this money I'm earning now, because it'll make things different for you. See? So learn all you can from Mrs. Wayland, and in a few years' time you'll be off to one of these public schools. And then you'll have to think about what you want to do with yourself, and I'll be there to help you. Always remember that, won't you, Chris? I don't want anything from you at all, except to let me help you. That's not much to ask of a lad, is it now? Well, no more jaw from the old man to-night. See you in the morning."

The snow had stopped, but it was a cold and slushy walk home. He felt very lonely somehow, not a bit like a dashing and devil-may-care Regency buck. He hoped he was doing the right thing, but it was hard for a chap like him to know.

CHAPTER 4

9 9 9 9 9 9

1

*W*hen Anthony Bromwich awoke the next morning it was to the silence of a snow-sheeted world. His room was full of pallid light that offered no invitation to be up and doing. He snuggled down into his warm bed like a rabbit into its burrow. His aunt bustled into the room. "Come on, lad." You could be very fond of Aunt Jessie, and yet suffer from the feeling of being perpetually at the mercy of a call-boy.

The sound of a shovel rasping upon the pavement broke the quiet and took Aunt Jessie across the room to the window. "Well!" she exclaimed. "That beats the band! It's young Chris Hudson clearing the snow." After a moment's cogitation she added: "See what that means? He must have slept there last night. She's got him!"

Then there floated up the light clear voice of Lottie Wayland. "*Bonjour, Christophe. Vous avez bien dormi?*"

The shovelling ceased, and Aunt Jessie reported: "He's looking at her like a stuck pig. Well, well! Dick Hudson's started something now." She came back from the window, and said as she went out: "Up you get. Don't keep your uncle waiting."

But when she was gone Anthony lay there for some time, listening to the scrape of the shovel that began again, and to the clear ring of Lottie's voice that was like a note struck from the sharp crystal of the morning air. He heard Chris Hudson's voice: "That'll have to do. I'm cold. Why don't you say something I can understand?" and Lottie's reply, in English this time, "My word, you are a grumpy one. Let's go in and have breakfast."

Anthony leapt out of bed and into his clothes. There would just

36

be time, before going to school, to make sure that the toboggan was in order. He would have fun with it in Ackroyd Park to-night.

On the whole, Anthony was obedient to his Aunt Jessie, but he could not give way in the matter of Ackroyd Park. "You keep out of Ackroyd Park," she used to say, and there was menace in her voice. But he was going to Ackroyd Park to-night, let her say what she would. Ackroyd Park was not a park. It was a street, running from Manningham Lane down to the valley bottom, the best toboggan-run, in Anthony's opinion, that you could find anywhere in Bradford. There were not many houses in the Park, and they were—or seemed to the boy—palatial. At all events, they were large, and each stood in a bit of ground, with a carriage-path through bushes to the front door. During an excursion into this forbidden region on a winter's night Anthony had seen one of those front doors open and a man-servant appear. That was the sort of place you meant when you said Ackroyd Park.

At half past six on that March evening Anthony's home-made toboggan stood side by side with a taxi-cab outside Mrs. Wayland's front door. Inside the house, Anthony, who had been complimented at school on his French composition, and who was trying to impress Lottie Wayland, was bogged down in the middle of a sentence.

"*Madame*," he said, "*je viens vous demander permission pour Christophe m'accompagner à . . .*" and then he stopped, feeling red all over, as well he might.

Lottie interpreted: "He wants to take Christopher tobogganing, Mummy"; and Chris said: "I hate tobogganing. I don't want to go."

The Great Hudson, who had ordered the taxi to be at the door to take him to the theatre, looked with anything but satisfaction at his son. "You go, Chris," he said. "It will do you all the good in the world. I don't mean the tobogganing, though that won't hurt you, but being out with other lads."

Chris said without enthusiasm: "All right. I'll go." And then, ungracious though this acceptance was, he made it worse. "Anthony Bromwich wouldn't have asked me if he hadn't wanted someone to pull the toboggan up the hill."

He had so much wanted to know Anthony Bromwich, who had never before spoken to him, and now, when Anthony approached him, this is how he must go on! Plunging even deeper into gaucherie, he said: "Anyway, wc'll be able to talk English." No one was pleased with him, and he was aware of it, and he enjoyed it.

Dick said: "Well, have a good time, lad. I must be off. I mustn't keep that taxi waiting."

Mrs. Wayland handed him a box, neatly tied. "Don't forget your supper," she said.

"Ay—I suppose it's a good idea," Dick said doubtfully.

Mrs. Wayland had shown a ladylike curiosity about Dick's work. She was ignorant of the ways of music-hall performers, and when Dick said that there was a long stretch of time between his first and second performance and that he'd go to a hotel to get "summat t'eat," all the scraping and saving years of her life in France rose in revolt. "You had a good meal at midday," she said, and Dick had to admit that it had been better than he ever got from Mrs. Wyke, who had a fixation on cold meat and pickled cabbage, "and what you want at night is something light but excellent. You don't need to squander your money in hotels. It's high time," she added, "that you, as well as Chris, had someone to look after you."

"Well, Ah don't know about that," Dick said with caution, "but thanks all the same. Mercy, madam." This damn thing is catching, he thought.

The boys watched the taxi-cab churn the snow and at last get a grip and move away. Anthony took up the rope of the toboggan, and Aunt Jessie, who was watching from the front door, shouted: "Mind you keep out of Ackroyd Park."

They were soon in Manningham Lane, where the day's traffic had flattened the snow. "Where are we going to?" Chris asked.

"Ackroyd Park. And not a word out of you to my aunt or to Mrs. Wayland."

Chris was not the boy to accept his blessings without question, even those he had longed for. "Why did you ask me to come?"

"To pull the toboggan up the hill. That is, if we survive going down."

"Why? Is it dangerous?"

"Well," said Anthony comfortably, "I've known chaps break their arms or legs. If you swerve into a wall, I suppose you might even break your neck. But you wouldn't know about that, so it wouldn't matter."

"If you did, and woke up in heaven, would you still have a broken neck?"

Anthony considered this. "I don't think so," he said. "If everybody in heaven is as he was when he kicked the bucket, it'd be a funny place, wouldn't it? Look at soldiers, and people in railway accidents, and people who get drowned or burned to death. There have been millions of 'em, one time and another. So I suppose there must be something about heaven that puts all those things right. It must be like sawing a woman in two."

"You can't saw a woman in two."

"Oh, yes you can. My Aunt Jessie told me about it. They do it in the music-hall. You put the woman into a long box like a coffin, and then you saw right through the box, woman and all. And then, when the box falls into two bits, the woman jumps out without a spot of blood on her. Well, that's how it will be in heaven. Even if you've been sawn in two, you jump up as right as rain and start singing with all the rest."

Having settled this point at least as satisfactorily as a medieval theologian could have done, the boys trudged on through the knifey air, beneath a wide glitter of stars. The snow under their feet was caked and rutted, but when they reached Ackroyd Park, which had been little disturbed by traffic throughout the day, they found the surface that Anthony had expected, smooth and reasonably soft, but already so many young sportsmen were upon it that it promised soon to be neither. With gay scarfs flying out like pennons behind them, boys and girls on hissing runners were hurtling down the roadway: from the great iron gates that aristocratically shut Ackroyd Park off from the main thoroughfare down to the valley bottom. In their excitement they were singing, shouting and screaming; and most residents in the Park were longing for softer weather, for rain that would clear the snow and put an end to this popular riot. It was not at all the sort of thing they liked to see staged within their exclusive enclosure.

3

Emily Freilinghausen did not share this view. She was enchanted by what was happening. She had a happy capacity for enchanting and being enchanted. "You are a child," her husband would say. "You ought to read nothing but Hans Andersen." She was in her middle thirties, but he was right: there were times when she looked a child. He would pull her on to his knees and loosen her hair so that it fell about her pert little face and caped her shoulders. Her greenish-grey eyes would peep at him through the auburn mesh like a winsome young animal's. "You are completely useless to me," he would say. "You are a dreadful spendthrift. You can't sew on a button. You're a wasteful housekeeper. You are for ever taking my mind off my work. And God help me if you ever left me."

The very earnestness with which he would say such things made her laugh. He never seized her with a lover's rapture, never groaned with unspeakable words. He would try to say everything clearly and logically. But she loved him, and he knew it. His strong surgeon's hands had with her an extraordinary gentleness. She tried never to think of his work. It could make her shudder to picture Ferdinand cutting his way through the intricacies of a human body as clearly and logically as he would carve the joint or the game at dinner.

His grandfather, Hans Freilinghausen, had come penniless to England, and died rich, one of the founders of the great wool firm of Freilinghausen and Zwemmer whose enormous warehouses were in the maze of small streets between the Midland and Great Northern stations. His father, Gustav Freilinghausen, tall, thin and bearded, now presided in those gloomy forts, driving in daily behind a pair of horses from a mansion at Cottingley. The ceremonial Christmas dinner there, which happened also to celebrate Gustav's birthday, daunted even Emily's young gaiety. Old Gustav and his wife Emma, looking every inch the matriarch of a tribe; Ferdinand's brothers Jacob and Joseph, with their wives, who had both come from Hamburg, and their plentiful children; Ferdinand's two unmarried sisters: all these, sitting round a vast candle-lighted table, with a portrait of Hans, the founder, peering through the encircling gloom, gave Emily a feeling of tribal solidarity with which she could never establish a link. No one there failed to give her the courtesy due to the wife of Ferdinand, the only son who had broken away from the family trade. They were all proud of Ferdinand, who had once been called into a consultation of doctors at Buckingham Palace, proud, too, that he never surrendered to metropolitan enticements but remained in Bradford doing much of his work for nothing among the poor. Even his taking of English nationality had not been frowned on. Indeed, Jacob and Joseph had followed this example. But as Emily sat at the table and listened to the incomprehensible German conversation and to the solemn singing of *Stille Nacht*, she felt a thousand miles away and longed for the moment when clicked heels and stiff bows would announce the end of the occasion and she and Ferdinand would be snug in her father-in-law's carriage driving back along the midnight road to Ackroyd Park. His large, warm, gentle hand would seek hers beneath the rug, his head would go down on to her shoulder, and she would know that he, like her, felt released from bondage into the only company that was the final and irreplaceable necessity.

4

Emily put on a fur coat and a fur hat and fur boots. She walked to her front gate—a big gate through which a carriage could come. But they didn't use a carriage: Ferdinand had bought a motor-car. Everybody was doing that now, except old stagers like Gustav who stuck to their carriages and pairs. Everything was changing, and Ferdinand, whose wisdom she never doubted, said that the changes seen now were nothing to those that would soon come. "If there is a war, everything will be speeded up enormously."

"A war!" she cried with horror. "What should there be a war about?"

"Oh, anything. A war comes when it is wanted. What excuse is made is a small point."

"But who wants war?"

He smiled at her; he did not like the harsh world he knew to touch her. "How would you like to change your name?" he asked with apparent irrelevance.

She would hate to change her name. It had taken some getting used it. Signing it had been a struggle at first, but now she had tamed it and was proud of it.

"You see, I am a captain—a medical officer of the British Army. I know we Territorials are laughed at—Saturday afternoon soldiers. I don't like being a British officer with quite such a German name."

"But, darling, Bradford is full of people with German names, and they're as English as I am."

He looked at her with speculation. "I wonder. But I, at all events, am English. My family for three generations, and I myself, owe everything to this country. I have been thinking of having my name changed to Fieldhouse."

He left it at that, and it didn't make much impression on Emily's mind. Ferdinand was an old sobersides who tended to worry about the oddest things. For herself, some immediate exhilaration could outweigh any amount of troubled thought, and it was exhilarating to-night to hear these joyous shouts in the road, to feel the sharp tingle of the frost, and to see the children shooting down the grey glissade under the shine of the stars. She watched them, leaning over her gate, and thinking: "For two pins I'd join them. But I'm afraid that would be a bit too much even for Ferdinand."

5

Anthony sat in front of the toboggan and Chris behind him. "To begin with, we'll go down like this, feet first," Anthony explained. "It's the way kids always start. But it's not much fun. Lying on the sledge, belly-down, and shooting along head first—that's the real fun."

They sat at the top of the run. Chris clutched Anthony firmly round the waist. "Don't do that. Remember, I've got to do the steering, and I don't want you pulling me about. Grab the sides."

"Let's play that we're in Siberia. Ponies are pulling us, and wolves are after us."

"You can play anything you like, but don't mess me about. I've got to keep my mind on what I'm doing."

They shot to the bottom of the hill. It wasn't much of a run. They were down well inside a minute. Then they pulled the sledge to the top and did it again. They did it four times.

"How are you liking it?" Anthony asked.

"I think it's dull—just running down a street and walking up again."

It's more than that, Anthony thought. It's the cold air brushing your face, and the shouts of the boys and girls, and the lighted windows reeling by, and the stars above you, and your breath like smoke. What's wrong with that? Why pretend it's something else?

"All right," he said obligingly. "We'll have the wolves this time. And, what's more, we're going down head first. You'll be at the back, so you can howl like a wolf. I'll be in front, so I'll neigh like a horse. But it won't be very good. I'm not much at neighing."

Anthony never remembered whether he neighed or not, or, whether Chris howled. What he remembered was the snowball thrown by a boy at the side of the road. It was a hard snowball that didn't explode in white dust but gave his eye a stinging and unexpected blow. The toboggan slewed beam-on to the run, and another, following it, crashed it amidships. He and Chris were lying in the gutter. The other toboggan, having heaved them aside, had recovered from its check and gone on. No one was going to allow a little thing like that to spoil a night's enjoyment. Chris Hudson was blubbering. Anthony said: "Oh, shut up. Let's get going again," and he got to his feet in order to do so. Then a howl was wrenched out of him. Someone was screwing a red-hot gimlet through his knee. He went down into the snow again with a crash. "Something's gone bust," he admitted.

Chris was on his feet, none the worse, and a woman who had been leaning in the gate nearby asked: "Are you all right there? Are you hurt?"

She came through the gate and looked down at Anthony lying in a heap in the dirty snow that was lit by a street lamp. "Are you all right?" she repeated.

Chris said: "He shouldn't have come into Ackroyd Park."

The woman laughed and asked: "Why on earth not?"

"Because his auntie told him not to."

"Well," she said, "I'm not sure that boys should always do what their aunties tell them."

This encouraging view of life and the agreeable scent that was coming from the lady led Anthony to ask: "Do you live here?"

"Yes."

"May I come in and sit down for a moment, please? I think my leg needs resting."

"Certainly you may come in," she said, "and certainly, if one may judge from the howl you let out, your leg needs more than resting. Go and ring at the front door," she commanded Chris, "and say I'd like Mr. Freilinghausen to come out here for a moment. And you," she told Anthony, "lie where you are. Don't try to stand on that leg. What's your name?"

"Anthony Bromwich, ma'am."

Lying there at her feet, he was not aware of the shock that passed over her face, or of the slight delay before she asked: "Why doesn't your aunt like you to come into Ackroyd Park?"

"I don't know, ma'am. But she's dead nuts against it."

Then there was a short black-out following a spasm of pain; and the next thing Anthony knew was that he was indoors. He was lying on a couch in a small warm room. A rather stout man was bending over him, and someone had removed his trousers and stockings and shoes. The man was aware now of being observed, and said: "I am Mr. Freilinghausen. You are lucky, young man, to have had your accident outside my gate. Now let me have a look at you."

He warmed his chubby hands at the fire, rubbing them briskly. "Now," he said, "you look to me the sort of boy who will not howl, though I expect you'll want to. Howl if you must."

The warm hands came very gently down on to Anthony's left knee, feeling softly, and then not so softly, while the face was turned away, concentrated, as though registering through touch, and without sight, what lay beneath the skin and within the bone. Anthony writhed, and everything within him called on him to howl, but he would not. He bit his lip, clenched his teeth, and held on, looking up at the dark concentrated face. Then suddenly he saw the face contract into swift resolution, and he felt the hands, which till now had merely explored, seize his knee like the two jaws of a vice; and now he could hold back the howl no longer, and it came out full-throated. And then the man was standing up, that stern concentration all gone, and he was smiling. "Well," he said. "Well, well. You were a good boy. I should have screamed the house down."

Anthony lay back. The sudden brief agony had drained him. But it was fading, and presently he smiled. The man said: "Well, now we must celebrate," and he touched a bell.

Then the lady was in the room, and Chris Hudson, and a maid carrying a tray.

The lady asked: "Is he all right?" and Mr. Freilinghausen laughed. "As right as rain. Nothing broken. Everything displaced. Now we have clicked it all back. See." He took hold of Anthony's leg, raised it, and gently flexed the knee. "It works," he said, "but he must not play football to-morrow."

"Will he be able to walk to-morrow?"

"Oh, yes. He could walk now, but he had better not. He had better sleep where he is, on that couch, to-night. To-morrow he can go home. You, young man," he said to Chris, "will perhaps explain to his people."

There were two bowls of soup on the tray that the maid had brought in, and Mr. and Mrs. Freilinghausen sat and watched the boys eat. The lady, Anthony thought, was very beautiful. He could not keep his eyes off her. Whenever she looked at him it was briefly: a glance, and she turned her face quickly away. And when Chris Hudson was gone and Anthony was tucked up on the couch for the night, his mind kept asking: "Where have I seen her before?" But he decided that he had not seen her before, that the night's unusual happenings were creating an illusion; and, with his pain ebbing away, he felt very tired and was soon asleep.

6

The window of the room faced east, and Anthony was awakened by pale sunlight looking in out of a pale blue sky. The surprise of finding himself there soon passed. He remembered. He gently stretched his left leg down to its full length, then raised the knee. There was no pain. Now he began to enjoy what had happened to him; it had been a great and wonderful adventure. The lady who had told him that a boy need not always obey his aunt came back to his mind, tantalising it. He knew her, and he was sure he was wrong in supposing that he knew her. In any case, she was something pleasant to think of: furry as a rabbit—hat, coat, boots, gloves—and smelling like violets. It had been like smelling violets in a snowdrift. He hoped he would see her again. Perhaps she would bring in his breakfast. Or perhaps he should dress and go and find out whether he was to have breakfast or just clear out now that he was all right?

The question was answered by the opening of the door and the coming of a maid carrying a tray. Coffee, eggs, bacon, toast, marmalade. Anthony began to feel very well indeed. This was not the young dimpled maid who had brought in the soup. She was older, tall and thin, and she didn't look as though she approved of bringing breakfast-in-bed to a boy who was well enough to be out and about. She thumped the tray on his knees and said: "When that lot's inside you, you can dress and go."

Anthony asked timidly: "Should I thank Mr. and Mrs. Frei—Frei——" He couldn't get the name.

She said: "Mr. Freilinghausen is out and Mrs. Freilinghausen isn't up yet. It's well to be some people."

"Should I send them a note of thanks?"

"Please yourself. But if anybody gets a note of thanks it ought to be me. Breakfast in bed!"

"Only one," Anthony said reasonably.

"I said two. I told you *she's* having hers up there."

Anthony was argumentative. A drink of coffee had fortified him. "Surely it's usual for Mrs. Freilinghausen to have breakfast in bed? So that's only one extra." It seemed to him natural to expect that such a lady, living in such a place as Ackroyd Park, where men-servants opened doors, should have breakfast in bed every day of her life.

"Don't you believe it," the grim one said. "Up with the lark she is, normal. Taking her exercises. Skipping, bending—you never saw the likes of it. As if she was ten years old. I'd exercise her! Well, I'm not standing here arguing with you."

"That's just what you are doing," Anthony said with a grin.

"That'll do. Cheek won't get you anywhere in this world. Not that I expect you'll get anywhere, with it or without it. Breakfast in bed! That's a nice start in life!"

Anthony thought it a very nice start for a day, anyhow, but he did not share this thought with her. She had gone, shutting the door noisily behind her.

Anthony finished his breakfast and dressed. He found sixpence in his pocket and left it on the tray for the grim one. It seemed to him a lot of money, a noble largesse, and he shyly made his way to the front door. A young man-servant, wearing a green baize apron, was polishing the brass. He winked at Anthony. "I heard," he said.

"Heard what?"

"Fish-faced Annie telling you off."

"I've done nothing to upset her."

"Oh, yes, you have." He coughed on the brass and rubbed. "You've upset the missus."

"How do you know?"

"Know?" He inspected his image in the door-knob, making faces at himself. "I know all right. Everyone knows when the missus is upset. That's what's the matter with old Fish-face, see? Worships the missus, she do, and when the missus is upset she flies off the handle at everybody, the missus included."

"I left her sixpence on my tray," Anthony said rather grandly. "That ought to cheer her up."

The youth looked at him, awestruck. "Sixpence!"

"Yes."

"Blimey—that's torn it!"

Incredulously, Anthony asked: "Isn't it enough?"

Green Baize slowly returned tins of polish, brushes and dusters to a vast pock on his apron. "Sixpence," he said sadly, as though so unfortunate a coin were about to unloose untold terrors on the household. "Sixpence for Fish-face!"

Where there had been satisfaction at having done the right thing, shame and humiliation flowed in. "Had I better go and get it back?"

"I don't recommend it. You better clear out. Tell you what. I'll shift it myself."

"Would you? Oh, thanks so much."

"Don't mention it. Now bunk."

Relieved to find such generosity in the world, Anthony went through the short garden, up the steep climb of Ackroyd Park, now a welter of thawed slush, and into Manningham Lane. Here was something to tell Aunt Jessie! he thought exultantly.

7

The thawed snow was running in rivulets down the gutters and dripping a cold rain from every shrub and tree. And—miracle!—where it lay on a lawn, thinned by the sun to nothing but a grey misty coverlet, a host of crocuses stood up like yellow trumpets, sounding the victory of spring. After all, it was March. There wouldn't be much more snow—perhaps not any. The lilacs and cherries would soon be out in the park and the dandelions between the stone setts in Megson Street.

And thinking of Megson Street reminded him that Chris Hudson was living there now, and he asked himself what sort of rigmarole Chris had carried to Aunt Jessie last night. Whatever it had been, it couldn't beat the reality for wonder: wonderful doctor, wonderful house, wonderful lady. He wanted to run, but his knee still felt a bit odd. However, his mind was running most vehemently when he turned into Megson Street.

And Aunt Jessie was a wet blanket! She met him with a dark face. He knew as soon as he saw her that something was wrong. She was dressed for fettling. When things were going well, Aunt Jessie took housekeeping easily: a flick and a rub and an occasional scrubbing-brush did all she needed. But when the world was against her she took it out of No. 6 Megson Street. She put on her uniform: a sackcloth apron, a duster round her hair, a pair of formidable boots; and she assembled her weapons: buckets and soft-soap, hard brushes and soft brushes, carpet-sweepers, carpet-beaters, and, on the kitchen range, every pan in the house boiling away, offering its steamy incense to her mania for duty. What she did seemed not to matter. She had been known to take down every curtain in the house and give them all a glorious communal boiling in the copper, lace curtains and velvet curtains and chintz curtains pell-mell, so that they all came out marvellously inter-married and with a care-free sharing of racial traits and colours. She had been known to shift every stick of furniture from the back bedroom to the front bedroom and from the front bedroom to the back bedroom; to take up all the carpets and drench the floors beneath them with water that took weeks to evaporate; and even to reduce the mangle to a collection of cogs and wheels and rollers and miscellaneous pieces of ironmongery that littered the scullery till a mechanic was called in to put it together again.

"Oh, so *you're* back!" she greeted Anthony, when he entered the sitting-room on that March morning. "Is your leg better?" Full panoplied, she was standing on a step-ladder, and glared down at him.

"Yes, Auntie, thank you." And, diplomatically: "I'm sorry I disobeyed you and went to Ackroyd Park, but Mrs. Freilinghausen——"

"I'm not asking you about Ackroyd Park," she said. "I'm asking you about your leg. If it's all right, that's all I care. And as for Mrs. Fry-whatever-it-is, I don't want to hear about her or any other foreigners. There's too many of 'em in Bradford, and so far as I'm concerned they can all go back where they came from."

"But I don't think Mrs. Freilinghausen is——"

"Will you shut up about that woman? I've got plenty to do to-day without listening to a lot of gab. Now, you take these pictures when I hand them down."

This was the shape of the battle to-day. Every one of these photographs that Anthony had so intimately known all through his life were swept away like the litter of a beach before a furious tide. When the living-room walls were cleared they started on the stairs and moved up to the landing, and by the time they were finished all were gone, from Florrie Finch in her silver frame on the mantelpiece to Dick Hudson tacked on the wall in his dark niche outside the bathroom door.

As they sat down to a snack at one o'clock, Aunt Jessie said: "Thank you, lad. That's the end of all that muck cluttering t'place up." She looked round at the walls, oddly nude and cold and blotched all over with dark squares and oblongs where the pictures had been. "Now to-morrow," she promised, "it'll be a *real* do. I'll get in some distemper and run t'place over. Then we'll get some proper pictures. I've got a few that I saved from *Pear's Annual*. There's a very nice sad-looking dog on his master's grave in the snow. I think that'll do a fair treat."

She seemed in a less aggressive mood, and Anthony wondered whether to venture again on the theme of Ackroyd Park. He decided that it would be unwise. "Must I go to school this afternoon?" he asked.

"Nay, take a rest, lad. And this evening we're going to see Dick Hudson do his stuff."

8

Uncle Horace did not go with them. Whenever his work was referred to he was called vaguely a foreman warehouseman, and

Anthony had no idea what he did with himself between his setting out at half past eight in the morning and his return at half past five in the afternoon. That day, he said he was far from well. The onset of the cold weather had shaken him up, and if you had hoped that the coming of the thaw would therefore settle him down again you would have been mistaken. He had, he said, been getting used to the cold, and this sudden change in the weather had shaken him up again, as though he were a medicine bottle full of something nasty to be taken twice daily. Making a long shot ahead, he referred to the flowering crocuses that Anthony had seen, and said that once those things were open the summer was on you before you knew where you were, and that was all very well for some, he added, looking darkly at Anthony, as though his robust health were an offence against the human condition, but was no joke for those who knew the horrors of hay-fever. Moreover, stripping the walls down to bare bones had made the house cold. Goodness knows, said Uncle Horace, who was very low indeed, he had never liked the look of all those stupid nincompoops with their gushing loves and good wishes to dear old Jess, but there was reason in everything, wasn't there, and couldn't they have taken down a few at a time and put up something else in their place?

Aunt Jessie refused to be rattled. She had now worked off whatever it was that had raised her spleen, and she assured him that she had a picture of a nice sad dog that was to be framed and hung over the mantelpiece. She went so far as to produce it, and it was indeed a nice sad dog, with a strong family resemblance to Uncle Horace. She cheered him by fixing it to the wall with drawing pins. Uncle Horace and the sad dog stared at one another for a few moments. "It looks like someone I know," he said autobiographically, and went upstairs to wash.

Although the cold caused by the taking away of the pictures was countered by the drawing of the curtains, the buzzing of the gas-jets and the roaring of a coal fire piled half-way up the chimney, Uncle Horace returned from his wash with a knitted Balaclava helmet on his head and a rug on his arm. He draped the rug over his shoulders as he sat down to a bowl of onion soup, feeding the stuff through the helmet with a fascinating dexterity. "I think," he said suddenly, his small eyes gleaming through their woolly environs, "that come summer I'll keep bees. They'll have all Manningham Park to feed on, as well as the dandelions."

"Well, a hobby'll be summat new for you, lad," said Aunt Jessie. "P'raps it'll keep your mind off your ailments."

"What I've got to do," Uncle Horace retorted, "is keep my mind *on* my ailments. I've just heard that bees' stings are good for rheumatism."

"A by-product like," said Aunt Jessie. "Well, I've heard that manure is good for the garden, but I'm not going to keep a Clydesdale stallion. Now you be reasonable and eat up your soup."

"There's a considerable difference," Uncle Horace said incontestably, "between the size of a bee and the size of a Clydesdale stallion."

"Well, anyway," Aunt Jessie persisted, "Clydesdale stallions don't swarm and fly about in great bunches. When your bees do that, you'll have to do your own chasing. There's more in keeping bees than getting stung for rheumatism."

This thought seemed to sober Uncle Horace, who finished his meal in melancholy silence, looking like someone who urgently needed the ministrations of Florence Nightingale. He took it ill when Auntie Jess said that she and Anthony would be attending the second house of the music-hall. "I don't think I should be left alone in a perishing cavern," he said, throwing another half hundredweight or so of coal on to the fire. "When I'm gone I suppose I'll be appreciated."

"Well," Aunt Jess said reasonably, "I'll be gone myself for a couple of hours. You can spend the time appreciating me."

9

Anthony had never before been to a music-hall, and as he sat there in the orchestra stalls (free tickets for Aunt Jessie, though he didn't know that), with the orchestra playing, and the lights shining through the blue fug of tobacco smoke left by the first-house patrons, he had no idea what Dick Hudson was to hand him. He had seen two Dick Hudsons: the elegant caped buck swaggering along Manningham Lane, and the rather dull chap who had brought Chris in a taxi-cab to Mrs. Wayland's. But when the curtain went up on Dick's act, neither of these appeared. Indeed, he could not believe that this was Dick Hudson at all. It was a shrunken little man standing outside an inn which a signboard declared to be the White Hart. He was polishing boots and singing a song about horses and hounds and foxes and tally-ho, meanwhile getting as much blacking on to his face as on to the boots and generally, Anthony thought, being a perfect example of the English rustic, who is notoriously inept, fumbling, and liable to get blacking in the wrong places. Then, taking up the boots, he disappeared round the side of the inn, and, almost at once, the front door was flung open by a corpulent and angry landlord, shouting: "Jorkins! Jorkins! Where is that fool? His lordship requires his boots."

Anthony found it hard to believe that this, too, was Dick Hudson, but the programme had assured him that "The Great Hudson, without the help of confederates, will ring the changes on six characters." This second character, despairing of finding the absent Jorkins, disappeared through the main door, and might almost be said to have jostled his lordship, so quickly did that personage appear, complete with all the swagger habiliments that had dazzled Anthony in the Sunday evening solitude of Manningham Lane. But now he was a more sinister lordship. It needed only a glance at his face to see that he was harbouring designs unbefitting an English gentleman. He looked up the road and down the road, like a hovering hawk inspecting a hedgerow for insuspicious mice. He took a pack of cards from his pocket and let them float with nonchalance from hand to hand. "So you are late, Mr. Middleton," he ruminated devilishly. "But late or early, I'll have the plucking of you yet, my pretty pigeon." And then, as the coconut shells clattered backstage: "Ha! He arrives at the back! He would remain unseen!" And, eager for prey, he launched himself through the front door.

He missed Mr. Middleton, who had a perambulatory habit and came round the side of the house, he, also, to look up and down the road, but with a sad and pensive air. Anthony's heart bled for him: a stripling who so clearly was about to be stripped. A nice lad, too, in a fawn overcoat with brown velvet lapels, and hair as fair as his lordship's was dark. "Perhaps," he pondered, "I look my last on these English fields," and he drew an ugly-looking shooter from his pocket. "But now, 'tis all or nothing. 'Tis fortune, and the right, Alice, to state my case, or, losing, to lose you and life together."

A cry of "Ho, there, Middleton!" caused the forlorn youth to run back the way he had come, while through the front door burst a jolly chap quaffing a tankard. "Gone!" he cried, on what seemed insufficient evidence. "Well, Frank, my boy, I'd have saved you from that beast of prey had it been in my power. My sister Alice is yours for the asking. She'll fly to you like a bird to a bough, be it rich with fruit or bare with winter poverty. Well, I'll to the pretty thing. She may need my comfort this night." And, banging the tankard down on a rustic table, he strolled away and disappeared into the wings, whistling so merrily that one might wonder whether his affection for his sister was all he cracked it up to be.

160490

Well, thought Anthony, counting on his fingers, there goes number five; and number six was not long in appearing. A shot rang out from the White Hart, suggesting close of play and ruin achieved in what must have been a record time even for so accomplished a pigeon-plucker as his lordship. But, to the pleasant surprise of the audience, his lordship had under-estimated his man. It was his valet who now came running through the front door, shouting: "My lord has met his match! Young Middleton has stripped him to the bone. He has sought the way out, but maybe he still breathes. Bring me his coach! His lordship's coach there, I say!" And as the coconuts clattered again Anthony, highly pleased with all that he had seen, would not have been surprised had a four-in-hand trundled round the side of the White Hart with Dick disguised as the leader. But, instead, the curtain swung down, and the applause broke out, and Aunt Jessie was lugging him out of his seat, and presently he found himself in the prosaic off-stage purlieus of the theatre, cold passages and stone steps and wire-caged gaslights, and finally in a little room where Harry Pordage, Dick's dresser, was hanging clothes on hooks, and wigs on stands, and Dick himself, sitting before a mirror, was wiping off his grease. With one side of his face wearing still the valet's haggard and hang-dog look, and the other clean and pink from scrubbing, he turned to Jessie with a grin. "Well, lass, d'you think Ah've come on a bit?" he asked.

"That'll do," she assured him.

"Remember the night I wept on thi breast?"

"Tha's nowt to weep about now."

Anthony said: "I'll bet Chris is proud of you, Mr. Hudson."

"He's never seen me, lad—not on the stage."

"I'll bet he'd like to, and to hear all those people cheering as they did."

"Ah'm not sure of that, lad. You see, all this has nothing to do with Chris, except that it's *for* Chris. Isn't that so, Harry?" he appealed to Mr. Pordage.

Mr. Pordage, a sallow little whippet of a man, went on with his work. "As you say, Mr. Hudson," he said without turning his head.

❦ ❦ ❦ ❦ ❦ ❦

CHAPTER 5

1

*P*ordage—not Harry but his brother Septimus—had a three-storeyed mind. Schoolboys knew this well. *Pordage's First French Course, Pordage's Second Course,* and *Pordage's Third French Course* brooded over them immutably; and if they went in for Latin, Spanish or Italian, Pordage was there, too, to drive them through the subject with his three-in-hand.

Harry and Septimus were an odd pair to come out of one family. Their father was a prosperous grocer in Halifax, and his ambition was of the simplest: Harry and Septimus should be prosperous grocers, too. He would set each up in a neighbouring town, and perhaps each would have sons whom *they* could set up, so that in time, over the best grocers' shop in every town of the West Riding the name of Pordage would glow with commercial rectitude. But things didn't turn out a bit like that, and the name of Pordage now glowed on nothing but a marble slab, mottled like a slice of Mr. Pordage's finest gorgonzola cheese, in Halifax churchyard, which did nobody any good, and on a gratifyingly large number of school text-books, which did Mr. Septimus Pordage all the good in the world. Harry was the first of the two to go, fired with ambition after paying a visit to the local theatre. He would never forget the morning after that visit, when a young lady, whom he had seen the night before driven by the schemes of a villain almost, but not quite, to make the supreme sacrifice, came into the shop and asked, as cool as you like, for a pound of sultanas. If she had asked for a pound of pearls or a league of lilies he would not have been surprised, and even sultanas, for a long time thereafter, hardly seemed to him mortal fruit.

Harry's present status as dresser to Dick Hudson is all that need be called in evidence concerning the murder of his dreams by the villainous years.

Septimus was a clever boy at his books, and Mr. Pordage grieved to see that even in his earliest teens Cæsar's Commentaries were more to him than the price of butter. There was nothing to be done about Septimus. You simply could not stop him from winning scholarships. He won them to the local grammar school. He won them to Oxford. He had a bee's ability to rifle every flower that took his fancy. He might have written a three-decker work on some one-decker person like Cheke or Lodge or Skelton and so established himself as a don of parts and repute. But that was not what he wanted. He put in a year or two as a master in a public school, and the squeaky voice issuing from his robust frame, his loathing for any sort of exercise, and his inability to come to terms with the young barbarians in his charge, conspired to make those years hellish. His refuge was in compiling *Pordage's First French Course*. Septimus could put on paper what he could not put in any other way. And now, in the middle age of Pordage, custom and ancientry had given his books prestige. In a thousand schools masters swore by him and boys swore at him and his portly self took its ease in Arcadia.

2

There was a lot to be said for Arcadia in April, Anthony Bromwich thought. His arrival there was sudden and unexpected. He had been granted no peep behind the scenes, nor, for that matter, had Uncle Horace. All that either of them knew was that on the Wednesday morning of Dick Hudson's week in Bradford Aunt Jessie said casually at breakfast: "I'll be out this afternoon. If I'm a bit late back, don't worry." She knew that Uncle Horace wouldn't worry, because his birthday was at hand and he would assume that she was going to find a present for him in town, as she had done before. It was a good alibi; but Wednesday is matinée day in the music-halls, and when Dick Hudson came off he found her in his dressing-room waiting to talk to Harry Pordage.

She and Dick, the day before this, had met in Megson Street and had taken a turn in the park together. "That's a glum lad—yon Pordage," she had chanced to say; and thereupon Dick had unfolded Mr. Pordage's story so far as he knew it, which was pretty well, for he had known Harry for a long time. He had watched the poor chap slipping down and down the music-hall bill, finally falling right through the bottom, all the time that he had been climbing up and up. He knew all about Harry's clever brother—the sort of man he wanted Chris to be, with letters after his name and all that, and he said: "Harry went to see him last Sunday. He lives out in Darton-in-Craven—you know, a little place not far from Smurthwaite. Grand country that is. I used to walk all round there when I was a lad."

It seemed that Mr. Septimus Pordage, in his middle age, was beginning to feel lonely, and had told Harry, a bachelor like himself, that he had been thinking of offering a home to a pupil if he could find the right sort of boy. "Not that he wants the money—he wants company like. It's a quiet place is Darton."

And this is what Aunt Jessie wanted to talk about to Harry Pordage; with the consequence that she and Anthony found themselves a month later in the train bound for Smurthwaite.

Anthony was far from happy. The house in Megson Street was the only home he had known, and it seemed hard to be leaving it now when the first dandelions were opening among the stone setts in a day of April blue. Auntie Jess and Uncle Horace were all he had known as relatives, and here he was now in the train, rolling out into the open country beyond Keighley, with Aunt Jessie talking rather breathlessly about a father of whom he had never heard, though he supposed he must have had one. "When all is said and done," said Aunt Jessie, "he *is* your father, though your uncle and I have brought you up, and little thanks to him except for a bit of money now and then. Always on the trot he's been, never satisfied with his own country, though I should have thought it was as good as most." And now this rolling stone, it seemed, had bumped to a standstill in South America, "and a better job than I ever thought he'd land"; and in his new-found affluence he was beginning to think of his son whom he hoped to meet some day. "So there it is," said Auntie Jess, helping herself to a sandwich, for she never took the shortest railway journey save in the expectation of starving before the end of it, "and if he says you must go to a tutor, that's that. He's your father, and he's finding the money."

It was all too sudden, unexpected and complicated for Anthony at twelve years old. He tried to understand, but gave it up. There were streams, and sunlight on white limestone, and a blue sky, and lambs in the fields. These things were immediate and uncomplicated, and he settled down to divide his attention between them and an enormous beef sandwich that was almost enough in itself to relieve the straits of a beleaguered garrison.

Mr. Septimus Pordage was waiting for them at Smurthwaite station. He was wearing a tweed suit and a wideawake hat, which he took off with a flourish to Aunt Jessie. He was a surprising creature to be the brother of Harry. They might have stood, side by side, as contrasting pictures of famine and plenty. Septimus's head was crowned with shining white hair, and his neat moustache was white, too. His cheeks were two little chubby pink hams, squeezing in upon two little blue eyes, and between the rounded chin and the white moustache two little lips pouted prettily.

Aunt Jessie shook his hand, which was a warm little pink cushion, and said simply: "Well, Mr. Pordage, this is the lad."

The lad stood beside his brown-enamelled tin trunk and looked non-committally at Mr. Pordage. He was acquainted with *Pordage's First French Course*, and said, in deference to its author: "*Voilà ma malle, monsieur.*"

Aunt Jessie regarded him proudly. "You'll find, Mr. Pordage, that he chatters the French lingo like a monkey."

Mr. Pordage spoke for the first time, ingratiatingly as a small mouse thankful for cheese. "I trust not, madam. If he does, our first necessity will be a set of remedial exercises." He struck the *malle* a smart blow with his ash stick whose end was as hairy as his tweeds. "To the transport wagon," he commanded, as though an army were about to march. Anthony took the handle at one end and Mr. Pordage hooked his stick through the handle at the other end, and they walked through the booking-office of the sleepy station to where, outside, the transport wagon was waiting. It won Anthony's heart at once, for it was a cosy little contraption, its upper-works all plaited yellow cane and red cushions, and in its shafts stood a fat white pony, sound asleep on his legs. He, rather than Harry, might have been Mr. Pordage's brother. Mr. Pordage chucked him familiarly under the chin and said: "Awake, Valpy, awake!"

Valpy awoke, and looked as soundly asleep as ever. His skin rippled at the intrusion of a few untimely flies. But for that, his head might have been on a pillow. "Why do you call him Valpy, sir?" Anthony asked.

Mr. Pordage dropped his end of the trunk on to the cobblestones and looked about him at this blue and white April morning across whose sky a few swifts were skating. He seemed in no hurry to put the trunk aboard, and he seemed in no hurry to answer Anthony's question. In fact, he and Valpy seemed in no hurry at all. "Valpy," he said at last. "Why do I call him Valpy? Why, boy, in pure derision."

He contemplated the morning once more, and then said: "Well, now, Darton-in-Craven. We must get to Darton-in-Craven. But not immediately. We can wait for Darton, and I am sure Darton will wait for us. Compose yourself to slumber for yet awhile, O Valpy."

Valpy had already done so.

"Coffee," said Mr. Pordage, and they set off, leaving the trunk on the cobbles. They entered the main street of Smurthwaite, with its grey shops, its grey-stoned roofs, its plane-trees opening their leaves in new green. "Will my trunk be all right, sir?" Anthony asked.

Mr. Pordage considered this as he rolled along without haste. "It is impossible to say yes or no, my dear boy. It is an experimental matter. If, when we return, we find your trunk safe and sound, we shall have demonstrated that our faith in Smurthwaite's honesty was not misplaced. If it is gone, we shall have learned a lesson, and next time we shall post sentries to the north, south, east and west of your *malle*. The chances are that we shall never find this necessary. Smurthwaite is not Babylon."

"Then you think the trunk is safe, sir?"

"I have said so as simply as possible."

"Thank you, sir."

"Well, here we are. There are fine sugar-coated buns to be had with our coffee in this place. We must take a few back for Valpy."

"Why do you call him Valpy in derision?" Anthony asked when Mr. Pordage had consumed four sugar-coated buns and two cups of coffee.

"Because," said Mr. Pordage, accepting Aunt Jessie's suggestion that she should order more buns, "Valpy was a grammarian who composed a *Gradus ad Parnassum* or, shall we optimistically say, a Stairway to the Stars. My Valpy, alas, will never make the grade, as you will discover for yourself. Give him a gradient of one in a hundred, and he'll expect you to get out and walk, and, what is more, carry your *malle*."

"Why do you call a trunk a *malle*?" Aunt Jessie demanded. "I carted that thing about for years on end and never called it anything but my old tin trunk."

"Now, Mrs. Pickersgill, you have embarked us on deep water that will wash us back to the Tower of Babel. It was there, I believe, that a beneficent providence conceived the idea of earning a living for the likes of me: a dispensation that I shall be the last to quarrel with. I beg you never to mention to me the word Esperanto. There are few ditches that a grammarian would shed his blood in; but my last

57

drop would ooze in any ditch embattled against the hosts of Esperanto. However, that is for the future. Let us take some buns to Valpy."

The trunk was where they had left it. Valpy was asleep in the shafts. A sheepdog that had been dozing in a patch of sunshine was still dozing in the patch of sunshine. Aunt Jessie said: "Things seem quiet like round here."

"Yes, Mrs. Pickersgill. It is a virtue of Smurthwaite that it does not harass its carcase. The passage of the year is recorded by the flowers in the station beds. You will notice that they are now daffodils. In course of time they will become chrysanthemums and dahlias. In between, this and that. Out at Darton, I often forget what month I am living in. I then ring up the station and ask what flowers are in bloom. It is as simple as that."

Valpy whinnied, and the sheepdog woke up. Observing these signs of activity, Mr. Pordage said: "Civilisation has struck its tents and is once more on the march. Heave the *malle* aboard, my boy."

Anthony did so. Aunt Jessie and Mr. Pordage went aboard, too, and Septimus said: "A walk will do you good, boy, but don't leave us too far in the lurch." The cavalcade set out for Darton-in-Craven.

It was not difficult for Anthony to keep up, and he was glad to be on his legs, for it was a wonderful day. Impossible to imagine that about a month ago he had been shooting down the snowy slope of Ackroyd Park, with the cold tweaking his ears and numbing his nose. Lambs everywhere, tottering about the fields and absurdly frisking. Green stuff frothing up in all the hedges and ditches as the yeast of the year began to make its ferment felt.

"This dog is following us, sir," Anthony said.

"And why should not the dog follow us, seeing that he is my dog? His name is Cerberus."

"Do you call him Cerberus, sir, in derision because he has only one head?"

"This is a bright boy," Septimus said to Aunt Jessie. "He begins to understand the Minoan Labyrinth of my mind. Well, boy, that is one reason. Another is that those who wanted to go to hell could get in by offering Cerberus a cake. That would still work; though it is my observation that those who want to go to hell can do it easily enough, without bothering about cake."

Cerberus was not a haystack sheepdog of the old English breed. He was a Welsh sheepdog with a short grey coat, one wall-eye, and one eye of dazzling blue. He knew that he was being talked about, and gave a self-conscious cough. Anthony, who shared Aunt Jessie's fear that famine might overtake one at any moment, and had prepared accordingly, took a sugar bun from his pocket and held it out to the dog, who consumed it with amused insouciance. "Yes, sir, it works," he said; and Septimus said: "Yes. But don't forget, boy, that if Hesiod is right Cerberus had fifty heads, and you would have your work cut out handling fifty sugar buns."

"I think," said Aunt Jessie, "that fifty mouths to be fed would make hard work for a dog with only one stomach," and Septimus conceded: "Yes, Mrs. Pickersgill; it is one advantage of a classical education that it can lead to fascinating by-ways of speculation."

Bemusing the way with such enchanting conversation, they covered the few miles between Smurthwaite and Darton, and came at last to a water-splash, a stream flowing from one field to another and crossing the road on its way. It was a gay, impetuous stream, not more than six feet wide, but full of life and sparkle. Had it been Euphrates or Mississippi in flood, it could not more dramatically have pulled Valpy to a stop. Cerberus had leapt into the middle, rolled luxuriously, and now, on the other side, was shaking an iridescent halo, a shining spectral extension of his own outline, into the bright air. But water was something Valpy did not take so lightly. "And now what?" Aunt Jessie demanded.

Septimus took up a wooden ball from the floor of his chariot. One end of a thin rope passed through it. The other end was attached to Valpy's collar. "This predicament," he said, "is not a new one. Science has dealt with it, as you shall see."

He threw the ball across the stream, descended from the trap, and crossed on the stepping stones at the side of the road. Then he took up the rope and gently heaved upon it. Valpy immediately crossed the water which hardly wetted his hoofs. But if he had induced a herd of wild stallions to cross a torrent Septimus could not have been more complacently self-conscious of mastery. He walked the rest of the way home, which wasn't much to do, for the stream was one boundary mark of his little property. "The stream here belongs to me," he explained as proudly as though he owned a mile or two of the Volga, complete with basso profundo boatmen. "And that's my house."

It was a good-sized cottage, long, low, white, with a stone-tiled roof and all the paintwork green. A lawn lay between it and the road, and on one side of the lawn the stream chuckled over its golden pebbles. On the other grew an untrimmed hawthorn hedge which would soon be in bloom. As lawns go, this was something that no horticulturalist would write home about. It was untended and full of weeds, but it was also full of daffodils. They grew in clumps all over the place and marched in a procession of swaying, singing gold along the margin of the stream. Anthony thought it the most enchanting lawn he had ever seen.

Away to the left of the cottage was a big stone barn. Telling Aunt Jessie to sit down on the bench in front of the house, Mr. Pordage led Valpy towards it. Anthony went along to help the unharnessing. The trap was left in the barn, but Valpy was shoo'd out into a paddock behind the cottage. The paddock, the cottage, the barn, the lawn, with the stream and the hawthorn hedge, composed Mr. Pordage's property—not more than a couple of acres, but encompassed by infinity.

Septimus and Anthony had rejoined Aunt Jessie on the lawn when the sound of a horn was heard and a pony came spanking down the road, drawing a trap in which the horn-blower was sitting. Mr. Pordage signalled with his hand, and went indoors as the trap pulled up. He returned carrying a letter which he handed to Anthony. "That is the postman," he said, "take him this." Anthony took the letter and read the address: "Septimus Pordage, Esq., D.Litt., M.A., Easter How, Darton-in-Craven, W. Yorks."

"You have made a mistake, sir," he said. "This letter is for you."

Septimus waved a chubby fist. "Do not keep His Majesty's mails waiting," he commanded.

Anthony took the letter to the postman, who gave him one in return, tootled on his horn, and drove away. The hand-writing was identical with that on the letter Mr. Pordage had brought from the house: "Septimus Pordage, Esq., D.Litt., M.A., Easter How, Darton-in-Craven, W. Yorkshire." Mr. Pordage put it in his pocket. "I shall read this later," he said. "It's only a letter. The real fun is when I send myself a parcel for my birthday or Christmas. Last Christmas I did me remarkably well: a box of excellent cigars and a dozen pocket handkerchiefs. I think I shall write a novel about me some day. It would make the oddest reading." He consulted his watch. "I sent me this for my birthday three years ago. An excellent present, I thought. One o'clock. Well, let's go in now and see what Mrs. Toplis has managed to do for us."

Mrs. Toplis had done saddle of mutton and the trimmings appropriate thereto, with apple-pie to follow; and after that there was cheese and coffee. "The lad won't starve," said Aunt Jessie.

"Not so long as I am his stable companion," Septimus agreed. "Valpy, Cerberus and I are among the best-fed beasts in the West Riding. Your nephew has come to a good manger."

Aunt Jessie said she would give Mrs. Toplis a hand with the wash-ing-up, and Septimus encouraged her in this, saying that the virtues of any civilisation could be gauged by the willingness of women to oil the domestic wheels, so that their smooth running was imperceptible to the creative half of the race. "Meanwhile," he said, "Anthony and I will inspect the scene of his own creative labours and deposit there the contents of his *malle*."

"Why, sir," said Anthony, "shall I not live in the house?" and Mr. Pordage replied: "God forbid. You will be abundantly educated by the mere superflux and waste product of my ego, a matter of con-tagion in such times as we are together. We shall be like two stars whose orbits occasionally bring them near enough for salutation. They exchange a celestial wink and set out on a few more million years of travel through inter-stellar space. If this proposition does not please you, say so, and let's have done with it."

Anthony said it sounded all right to him. His experience of school-masters suggested the ample joys of mere nodding acquaintance.

"Very well," said Septimus. "Let us beat the bounds."

They walked gravely round the property, keeping along the stream so far as it was Mr. Pordage's frontier, then turning left along the hedge of the paddock, and so coming at last to a big stone barn in which the trap had been housed. Septimus went in, exclaiming: "*Cherchons la malle*."

They brought it out, each taking a handle, and carried it round to a flight of stone steps. "Is there a room up there?" Anthony asked.

"Well," said Septimus, "I do not perceive that these steps vanish, like Jacob's ladder, into an infinity of aggressive angels. So we may safely assume some material destination."

To Anthony, the destination, though material, was enchanting. The oaken door was hung on strong wrought-iron hinges, and into the lock was inserted a big iron key. Mr. Pordage took it out and handed it to him. "This," he said, "is the key to your place. Remem-ber that no one—not even I—may come in without your consent. Always, my boy, whatever life may do to you, keep a private place. It is not for nothing that at our older universities a man may sport his oak, which is a phrase whose meaning you may learn in time."

They stood there, Anthony holding the massive key in his hand. After a moment, Septimus said: "I hesitate even to suggest that you should ask me in."

Anthony came to. "I beg your pardon, sir," he said. "Please come in."

He unlocked the door, and Mr. Pordage bowed, took up his end of the trunk, and they entered together. "Forgive me," Septimus said, "for banishing you to this place. I was brought up at Halifax, in the family sitting-room. How I longed for such banishment as this!"

Anthony cried with enthusiasm: "But it's lovely, sir! Thank you."

"You mustn't thank me. You must thank the previous owner of the property who had the sense to turn this loft into what you see. I will leave you to your exploration."

Anthony watched him toddle down the steps, then turned back into his lovely room. This floor of foot-wide oaken planks must have been put in centuries after the barn was built, but whoever did that had had the sense not to put in also a ceiling. And so springing up and interlacing above Anthony's head was a wonder of woodwork, and round him was the grey stone of the walls that had never been plastered. A semi-circular arch of stone was the fireplace, where a fire was laid, and on either side of the arch was a generous pile of billets ready for burning. The room was oblong, and in each of the longer walls was a tall round-headed window. The boy stood at one, and then at the other, and from each the view was much the same: white roads and pastures and the little stream and the rhythmic line of fells and sheep abundantly concerned with maternity and placid cattle browsing on the green spring grass. Brought up as he had been, it seemed incredible to Anthony that he could look so far and see nowhere the smoking chimneys of a mill. Blue sky, unsullied, arched over the full reach of vision.

He turned back into the room. A bed was near the fireplace, and a comfortable wicker chair. There was a table to write at, and there was a stored book-case. He looked at the titles. All of Pordage's three-in-hands were there, as well as what seemed to him, who had been brought up almost bookless, an immense array of reading matter. A washstand with a large basin upon it stood in a corner at the end of the room away from the fireplace, and there was a bucket on the floor. A letter addressed to Anthony Bromwich, Esquire, was propped against the wash-basin. Anthony Bromwich, Esquire, filled with pride at his grand appellation, took the letter to a window-seat, sat down and opened it. The paper of both envelope and letter was of a richness to impress: it soothed the fingers like vellum:

The Sunday next before Easter,
1912

DEAR MR. BROMWICH,

The utilitarian object to which this is attached is a wash-basin, satisfactory to the needs of countless generations of our ancestors. But in such places as Halifax, where I was brought up, and Bradford, where you were brought up, civilisation has richly advanced, befouling earth, air and water, and making necessary a recurring de-grimation of the human face and figure. To achieve this end, baths, washbasins in bedrooms, and all sorts of sanitary knick-knackery have been invented *ad majoram gloriam plumborum*. If you expect anything of this sort here, you are going to have the shock of your life. Cast down your eyes, and you will see a silly bucket on your deck. Take it in your hand, walk to my stream, and fill it. That should supply your casual ablutionary needs. For the morning bath, betake you to my Parson's Pleasure, which is where, on either bank of the stream, alders afford a privacy. Clothe yourself in a bathing suit if you like. For all I care, clothe yourself in a morning suit, violet suède gloves and top hat, or, cap-à-pie, in medieval armour. But it is better to wallow as Adam did in the river that flowed through Eden. That is what I do. Take no soap to the stream. Advertising to the civilised cities that heard our earliest pipes, I am aware that they have learned to put rivers to their proper use as receptacles of industrial and human filth and sludge, summarised enchantingly as effluents. In these more backward parts, we think that in our streams elvers are better than effluents and cresses than creosote. You must bear with these old-fashioned notions and foul not our fountains.

As for our studies . . . A-ha! There is no time like the present for deferring painful considerations.

Written with a goose-quill, and given under the hand of

SEPTIMUS PORDAGE, pedagogue.

Anthony had been taught by Aunt Jessie that letters should be answered. Not that he often received letters, and not that those which he did receive called for much to be said. But it was good manners, Aunt Jessie told him, to send some sort of answer. Perhaps, Anthony thought, Mr. Pordage shared Aunt Jessie's views, and how to answer this letter was a puzzler. Happily the solving of the puzzle was deferred. Sounds coming up through the floor suggested that Valpy had been led into the barn and was being harnessed to the trap. He went down to give a hand, but Mr. Pordage waved him away. "It is not my business," he said, "to invite Mrs. Pickersgill to invade your private quarters. Perhaps it will occur to you that it is yours. There is not much time if we are to catch the train, for I have no doubt that Valpy will be in a resentful mood. He dislikes doing two jobs in one day."

So Anthony took Aunt Jessie up to his room, and she looked about her, disturbed by its almost unfurnished space, which made it look different from anything she had understood as a room to be lived in. "Well," she said, "it's a bit bleak like, but you can't have everything in this world." She kissed the boy, and said: "Be a good lad now, and do what Mr. Pordage tells you. Mrs. Toplis says he's all right when you get used to his little ways. Still, that goes for men everywhere. You'd better not come to the station. Best to make a clean break."

Anthony felt he ought to send messages to someone, so he said: "Remember me to Chris Hudson and Lottie."

"If I see 'em. What about your uncle?"

"Oh, yes. Remember me to Uncle. I hope he keeps well."

"When he does, Ah'll begin to think there's summat the matter with him," Aunt Jessie said, establishing her cheerful grin. And off she went, for through the window they could see Mr. Pordage coaxing Valpy over the stream with the heaving-line. Anthony watched Aunt Jessie cross on the stepping-stones, climb in beside Mr. Pordage, and disappear round a bend in the road.

That night, as he was falling asleep, he did not feel that his room was bleak. After sunset the day had gone cold. He had put a match to his log fire, and the fireplace was still glowing, filling the room with pulsations of warm light. There were no curtains to his windows. He could see the stars, and on his feet he could feel the weight of Cerberus, who knew a good thing when he found it.

4

Unless you are used to it, an April morning is not the best time for plunging into cold flowing water. Anthony, sitting on the edge of his bed, with a hand absently fondling the ears of Cerberus, was wondering whether, in his answer to Mr. Pordage's letter, he should point out that, though a morning bath was referred to as something customary, his habit was to bathe in warm water once a week, on Saturday nights. However, he didn't want to start his life at Easter How with disobedience, so he pulled off his warm nightshirt, put on a mackintosh that made him shiver, and ran out to the head of the steps. He called to Cerberus, who opened one eye, gave him a knowing wink, and got his head down again between his paws.

The stone stairway was wet with dew, and cold. Anthony's naked toes curled and he stepped gingerly. But the sun was shining upon the daffodils, and the blackbirds and thrushes were full-throated in the hawthorn hedge. It was half past seven. The bleat of lambs came from the surrounding fields, and, too high to be seen, larks were in the sky from which the sun had not yet burned the last mists of the night.

Anthony stood still, listening, and he could hear the clear voice of the water, a silvery constant thread on which all the other sounds of the day were hanging. Suddenly, he was hearing nothing in particular, but everything was one thing, himself a part of it: the strengthening sunlight, and the flowers, and the birdsong, and the deep troubled voices of the ewes answering the quavering lambs, and the ripple of the stream, and Valpy snorting in the barn: and he ran down the stairs and across the lawn and along the edge of the water, his toes rejoicing now in the clear diamond wetness of the grass and his eyes in the golden blobs of water-buttercups—cups indeed, full to the brim with dew. And here were the alders enclosing what Mr. Pordage called his Parson's Pleasure, where the stream deepened to a pool, and hazels were among the alders, dropping from their boughs gold-dusted catkins, drying in the sunlight like the tails of new-dropped lambs.

He threw off his mackintosh and dived, and his fingers were at once among the pebbly nuggets that made the stream-bed an eldorado. He came up with a handful, gasping, for the water was as cold as though it were the sweat of a glacier, and he stood, dripping and shivering, while Cerberus, who had at last decided to follow, stood by, his red tongue protruding, laughing in derision, as if he realised, what only now occurred to Anthony, that he had come without a towel. Well, that was something to remember next time, the boy thought, wringing water from his hair, and this first time was something to remember, too. He put on his mackintosh, went back to his room, and towelled himself till he glowed. Never, he thought, have I till now started a day like this; and the memory came to him of the rush downstairs in Megson Street, and the rush through breakfast, with Uncle Horace coughing from some imagined catarrh, or writhing from some imagined lumbago; and then the rush to school, and the school-bell ringing, and the calling of the register. "Bromwich." "Here, sir." He felt as though he were in a dream: a dream, if one might so put it, full of absent things: blackboards, exercise books, chalk and little inkwells fitted into holes in desks.

He was awakened from the dream by the sound of a bugle: a sound appropriate to the morning, a sound that no boy on any morning could resist. He was dressed, and he ran downstairs, and he watched the soldiers tramping along the white road, packs on their backs, rifles in their hands, singing as they marched. As any other boy would do, he marched with them, crossed the steppingstones with them as they broke ranks at the water-splash, and turned with them into a meadow where field-kitchens were smoking and whence it was that the bugle had sounded, telling the arriving troops that breakfast was ready.

The men got rid of their loads, and with billycans and tin mugs filed past the kitchens, receiving their rations of food and tea. They sat upon the grass in the sunlight which now had warmth, and Anthony was beginning to be reminded of his own need of breakfast when a hand fell on his shoulder and a voice asked: "Well, how's that knee behaving?"

He swung round in surprise, and did not at once recognise the officer smiling down at him. Uniform made a difference: a shining Sam Browne belt, three stars on the shoulder, riding boots. Then he remembered Ackroyd Park. "Oh, Mr. Freilinghausen! It doesn't trouble me at all now, thank you."

Cerberus had arrived, looking as though, were his heads Hesiod's fifty, he could do with food for all his mouths. And the troops seemed to think so, too. Bits of bacon were being forked up and handed to him all along the squatting ranks.

Captain Freilinghausen shouted: "Stop that! That food is provided for you, not for dogs. Call him away," he commanded Anthony.

Easier said than done, but Anthony at last got the dog by the collar and hauled him out into the road. Captain Freilinghausen followed. "You see," he said, "we are a Territorial battalion on exercise. Part of the exercise is a night march. Those men have been on their legs for hours. They need food, and it is their business to eat it. As a medical officer I must see that they do. Well, that explains me. How do we explain you? I thought you lived in Bradford."

Anthony told of his changed life, and the captain said: "That is good. Take advantage of it. That is how a boy should be brought up."

Anthony wondered whether he should inquire after Mrs. Freilinghausen, but the chance did not come. An orderly approached and saluted. "The colonel is asking for you, sir." The captain abruptly left him.

By mid-morning the soldiers had marched away.

5

Anthony remained with Mr. Pordage for three years, and he was glad, when Septimus became famous, that he had kept all the letters he received from him during that time. Septimus became famous as a one-book author. He wrote nothing after *Me, About I*, by Ambrose Feend. It was published in 1919, and was at once shouted up as a masterpiece by the cleverest of the *recherché* critics. They were deeply mortified—indeed, they incredibly began to doubt their own judgment—when the *canaille* fell upon the book in avid thousands, rejoicing in its outrageous oddity, though perhaps unaware of what Septimus was talking about. It began: "On Quinquagesima Sunday in 1910, as I was walking down the main street of a quaint old Cornish town, I came face to face with Me, emerging from the Angel. 'Ho there, old Whorson Ape!' I cried happily, and Me stopped dead in his tracks, regarding I with deep remorse." For three hundred pages, I and Me had a remarkable day out, ending up by exchanging clothes, I entering the Angel, and Me going off down the street.

This opening paragraph—an average day's work for Septimus—was written on the morning in 1912 when Anthony saw Captain Freilinghausen for the second and last time. Its excogitation within the labyrinth of its author's mind could well account for his silence at breakfast. At nine o'clock Anthony went into the dining-room and found him already engaged with a large plate of fried lamb's liver, toast and coffee. A napkin as big as a hand-towel was tucked under his chubby chin. He was clearly in no communicative mood, and after wishing him good morning—a greeting acknowledged by no more than an inclination of the head—the boy applied himself to his own breakfast. Mr. Pordage was so far advanced through his meal that presently he stood up, exclaimed loudly *Benedicamus Domino*, and removed his napkin. The action showed that his general pinkness had been emphasized by a woollen tie shining with the new-cut-ham fervour of the Leander Rowing Club. He bowed to Anthony and hurried from the room.

The boy was at a loss. He had been told that his mysterious father, so long missing and so little missed, now in the money in South America, had charged Aunt Jessie with the task of finding an educator to prepare his son for a public school. Anthony's ideas about education having no basis beyond the practice in the board school he had attended in Bradford, he was prepared for serious and boring sessions; and to see his master walk calmly from the room, leaving him in the lurch, created a situation that puzzled him. He had, till now, taken his puzzlements to Aunt Jessie in the kitchen; so, piling the breakfast crockery on to a tray, he did the next best thing and carried the tray to Mrs. Toplis.

Mrs. Toplis was eating her breakfast. She wouldn't have put it that way herself. She would have said that she was snatching a bit o' summat, for she lived under the delusion that life chivvied her from pillar to post, and that all her sustenance was snatched, like a soldier's iron rations, in the heat of battle. In fact, when Anthony came in, she was doing herself proud, having just the sort of breakfast that Mr. Pordage had eaten, but rather more of it. But she had not spread a cloth upon her table, though there was no reason why she should not have done so, except the harassed prompting of her obsession. To have spread a cloth and laid her cutlery would have suggested a leisure she was determined to repudiate, so there she sat at an angle to a corner of the bare table, reaching for a knife from a drawer, a cup from the dresser, the sugar from a cupboard—anything to suggest the impromptu and movable nature of her feast.

Her hearty eating—for she was always snatching a bit o' summat at odd moments between canonical repasts—had failed to make a hearty woman. Mr. Pordage at all events showed the mettle of his pasture in the gloss of his coat; but Mrs. Toplis seemed to be string, bone and parchment. "Put it down there," she said to Anthony, with no thanks to him for bringing the tray, and she indicated the table at which she sat.

"Hadn't I better take it to the scullery? I could wash it up while you finish your breakfast."

"Put it down there," Mrs. Toplis repeated, not to be baulked of adding to the disorderly look of camping out that surrounded her. "As to finishing my breakfast, I don't begin and I don't finish. I just snatches. And as to washing up, I don't want no young ruffians in my kitchen creating messes for me to clean up that have plenty to be going on with anyhow." And to emphasise the way life pressed upon her she got up and wound the clock on the mantelpiece, took a swipe with a duster along a shelf, carried her plate for refilling from the frying-pan, and sat down again. "Maybe I'll have time to finish some time," she said, "but I don't see it in sight just yet. Well, go and wash up if you want to," she generously ended.

Anthony was a slow washer-up, but when he was through Mrs. Toplis was still snatching. She was kneeling before the fire with bread on a toasting-fork. "Finish this for me," she said in desperation, "or I won't have time for so much as a bite." She handed him the toasting-fork, resumed work on her plate, and when he took the toast to the table, said: "You'd better do another. I suppose this is the only bit of food I'll snatch this mortal day."

She was liberal with the butter, generous with the marmalade, and took a bite. "If ever the time comes," she said, "when I can sit down to a meal like other Christian women—and Christian I am though compelled to live like a heathen—then I'll feel I'm in Heaven, singing with the angels."

It was a pretty picture, Anthony thought: the immaculate choir in full cry, and Mrs. Toplis, seated at last before a reposeful spread, bringing in a word here and there through her chumbling chops. She would, he supposed, contribute a snatch.

"Mrs. Toplis," he said nervously, "what am I expected to do?"

"For one thing, you're expected to keep out of my kitchen."

"When will Mr. Pordage be starting my lessons?"

"When pigs fly, I should say," said Mrs. Toplis helpfully, wiping up with a piece of toast a rich deposit of butter and marmalade from her plate. "From what I know of that joker, I shouldn't expect him to start anything in a hurry, not if it means putting himself out. Anyway, don't you worry. For a boy to start worrying about lessons—well, that isn't in accordance with the laws of God or man. Lessons enough will come to you in the course of this mortal life," she moralised heavily. "There's no call to go out seeking them. Now where's that cushion? Well, if it isn't under my old b.t.m. all the time! That's how it is when you're rushed off your feet. You lose sight of everything."

She pounded the cushion and threw it on to two others that padded a wicker chair by the fire. From beneath them she drew out a copy of *Peg's Paper* and relaxed her bony frame into the chair's embrace. From a pocket she took a pair of pince-nez and snipped them on to her sharp nose. "We all have our rights," she said, "and we all have our wrongs, and if we don't look out we'll have so many wrongs that our rights will look like a row of pins given for a farthing's change. So if I'm not to have my poor feet worn down to my shinbones, if not farther, I got to have my little rest and my little read at this time of day." Anthony had begun to stack her breakfast things. "Leave that little lot," she said. "I'll snatch a minute to do 'em by and by. But I got to see what happened to Bernice. She was only a brick-layer's daughter, or thought she was; but if old Lord Tottering wasn't her father I'll eat my feather boa. Lessons! If you want lessons, you should read, like me."

So, while upstairs the pink and chubby Septimus was struggling with Me's confrontation of I, and down below the haggard Mrs. Toplis, as soon as Anthony was out of sight, was snatching forty winks, well deserved after the exhausting rigours of her breakfast, Anthony himself was strolling disconsolately about the paddock. But what boy could be disconsolate for long on such a day? Or, after he had tasted the joys of stretching his legs on the springtime roads and fells of the West Riding, on the days that followed? It was a week of glory, and at the end of it the postman tootled his horn, and the boy ran out with Mr. Pordage's daily letter to I, received Me's reply, and, to his surprise, received also two letters addressed to himself. One, for Mr. A. Bromwich, was in an unknown hand. The other, for Anthony Bromwich, Esquire, was in a hand now known well enough. He put them into his pocket to heighten the joy of the moment when he mounted his stone stairs in the dusk and lit his fire and his hanging paraffin lamp, and watched Cerberus stretch out, tired from the day's adventures he had shared with the boy, before the ripening warmth. Then he took out his letters and read them.

Dear Anthony Bromwich,—It was kind of you to ask your Aunt Jessie to give me your greetings, and I hope you are settling down and feeling very happy in Mr. Pordage's house. Your Aunt Jessie told me that your Mr. Pordage is a brother of Mr. Pordage who helps Mr. Dick Hudson in the music-hall. I told Chris Hudson this and he said the less he hears about any Mr. Pordage the better he will be pleased. And I said I sometimes think from what you say, Chris, that you'd rather I didn't talk about your Father much less any Mr. Pordage as if you were ashamed of him. And he said well come to that why shouldn't I be and wouldn't you be if he was your Father. So I said No I'd be proud of a man whose name was printed so big on the music-hall bills. Then Chris Hudson said well, that's a fat lot to be proud of I must say making an exhibition of himself like that and dressing up and walking along Manningham Lane on a Sunday and making me walk with him. There are times he said when I wouldn't care if I never saw him again. Who'd pay my mother then I asked, and he said that's right, rub it in. So I didn't say anything else because my Mother needs the money and the least said soonest mended. But I don't get on very well with Chris Hudson, and his French is awful. Well, that's all the news and I hope you have a very happy time. Yours faithfully, Lottie Wayland.

*The Friday in the Week next
before Easter: 1912*

To our well-beloved Anthony, greeting! What a sluggish toad you are. All about you the springtime world is full of creative energy. Birds are building nests in the hawthorn hedge; ewes are dropping their jolly little lambs in the fields; the fish, for all I know, are doing

70

whatever fish do to perpetuate their species in my Abana; Mrs. Toplis is snatching away like mad at her daily avocations; and I am deeply engaged on a work which could well cause the Blessed Damosel herself to lean so far out over the gold bar of Heaven, in order to have a peep, that one extra exertion could have her down among us, to our infinite confusion and dismay. And what are *you* doing? So far as I can make out, nothing but exercise a dog well able to give his own legs that limbering up which I had expected you would, long before this, have been applying to your mind.

We, Septimus Pordage, have no doubt at all that this letter will be read before your evening fire, for it appears that you do nothing unless wrapped in circumstances of indolence and sloth. Put down the letter, then, and walk to the book-cases which our foreseeing mind provided. Cast your eye along the shelves and make the effort to perceive that here is no haphazard collection of printed pages but a Royal Road. Go to the ant, thou sluggard, consider her ways and be wise; but stop short of entering my Presence imbrued with formic acid.

You came here to acquire certain Rudiments; and in my innocence I assumed that you would understand books to be footholds. But Oh dear, no! It seems that wisdom is to be acquired by gallivanting through the daisies with a dog-headed pal.

Quousque tandem abutere, O my Antonio, *patientia nostra?* I suppose you don't know what this means; but then what *do* you know, and what steps are you taking to make yourself know anything?

Pursue the primrose path, dear Mr. Bromwich, if it so please you. Dally in the dales, linger on the leas, frolic on the fells, revel in the river. What cares Septimus, who has his own fish to fry? But if some day it should occur to you that the great teachers, from Plato to Pordage, imparted their wisdom in answer to questions, then you will find me ready.

Written with the quill of a peregrine falcon, and given under the hand of

> Septimus Pordage, D.Litt., M.A., B.D., D.C.L.,
> and all that sort of thing, *ad nauseam.*

It was eight o'clock. Anthony sat with the letter in his hand, aware of its being a reproach, but not of much else. Presently he got up and walked down to the house. He found Septimus in the sitting-room, slippered by the fireside and happy with the pages of Fergus Hume's *Mystery of a Hansom Cab*, thus setting a taste in reading matter that was to be followed by dons and academics for generations to come.

"Sir," said Anthony, "I have just read your letter. I think I see what you mean."

"Astarte," said Mr. Pordage to his tortoiseshell cat, "here we have a rare phenomenon: a thinking boy." Astarte turned upon Anthony a look that combined disinterest and disbelief. She yawned at the fire, turned round three times, and went to sleep.

"Sir," Anthony continued, "I think I ought to have invited you to my room long ago. Would you care to come now?"

"I would, I could, and I shall," said Septimus.

"Why do you call your cat Astarte?"

"Because, like all cats of feminine gender, Astarte is a queen. Her temple, Milton reminds us, was built

> By that uxorious King, whose heart, though large,
> Beguiled by fair idolatresses, fell
> To idols foul.

Where Astarte is concerned, I am uxorious, and though I refuse to call her foul, she is an idol I have fallen for. I have sometimes thought of keeping a Jersey cow. They have such lovely eyes. I should call her Hera, for Hera, who also was known as Juno, was called ox-eyed. She must have been a remarkable woman.

> He, in delight,
> Smiled with superior love, as Jupiter
> On Juno smiles, when he impregns the clouds
> That shed May flowers.

However, there would be the question of milking. Would you care to milk a cow?"

"No, sir."

"Then that is that," said Mr. Pordage, "for nothing on earth would induce me to sit on a three-legged stool behind a four-legged beast, saying 'Get over, Hera.'"

Mrs. Toplis came in with a tray on which were two silver pots, one containing hot milk and the other hot coffee. "If you will bring another cup and saucer, Mrs. Toplis," Septimus said, "we will carry the tray up to Master Bromwich's eyrie, where the eaglet is anxious, I understand, to peep over the brink into the giddy abyss of knowledge." And when Mrs. Toplis was gone, he said to Anthony: "We shall also, this being a red letter day, stand ourself one of the cigars I sent Me at Christmas. They are rather outsize and lethal-looking. Indeed, Me thought I was rather ostentatious. Still——

72

> On such an occasion as this,
>   All time and nonsense scorning,
> Nothing shall come amiss,
>   And we won't go home till morning."

He went home long before morning, for ten o'clock was his bed-time, and if the last trump had sounded at that hour he would, all the same, have put on his nightshirt, got into bed, and there awaited the outcome. But it was an eye-opening visit for Anthony, who didn't need to wonder thereafter what to do with his books and his time.

CHAPTER 6

❻ ❻ ❻ ❻ ❻ ❻

1

*O*nce the ice had been broken between them, Septimus and Anthony met often, inviting one another, as though they were contemporaries, now to the downy old bird's nest, now to the eaglet's eyrie. For a year, Anthony did not return to Megson Street. Septimus, who had never had a lone pupil before, and who believed that he could create something special by the method that he called conversation and contagion, did not want his influence to be dissipated in long holidays; and as for Anthony, working when he liked, and playing when he liked, and seeing his educator when he liked: this seemed to him so agreeable a way of carrying on that he was content to stay where he was. His memory of school as a pupil, like Septimus's memory of school as a master, was strong and repulsive. Each thought that here was something better.

Letters from Septimus became fewer now that the working method was established; but special occasions still called them forth, and on an April day in 1913 Anthony read this:

*The Feast of the Anniversary of our well-beloved
Anthony's arrival at Easter How, 1913*

Salutatio Septimo Pordago! The contagion of the world's slow stain is about to seep into our Eden. Pordage has received a letter from his brother Harry, henchman and fiddle-de-dee in general to one Richard Hudson, known, like Alexander, as the Great. Greatness in this world—especially greatness self-announced like this—takes ostentation for its ally, and so Hudson is to shatter our serenity with what is known as a motor-car and smells like the bowels of that underworld whence its means of propulsion are obtained. The fiery steeds of Phoebus would perhaps affright Valpy, and the pards of Bacchus

74

have Cerberus on the run; but better they than what we are promised. Prepare, then, to meet thy God, for if petrol be not the God of the age now sadly dawning, the prescient eye of Pordage misreads the signs. The eye observes that Pluto's bowels spew forth petrol in desert places. The earth's desert places are wide and occupied by beggarly tribes, and beggarly tribes are not long left in possession of this world's riches. So petrol comes, like Cowper's "herald of a noisy world," with "news of all nations lumb'ring at his back."

Pordage's mind is cast down and bleak, but it must put on hospitality's smiling face, as you will do, he trusts, to the infantile companions of the main offenders: a Christopher Hudson and a Lottie Wayland. *Miserere nostri, Domine, miserere nostri.*

Under the hand of Septimus Pordage, deeply wailing.

2

The road with the water-splash that ran past the front gate of Easter How could not be dignified even by the name of secondary. It was an immemorial track that men had followed: it had come into existence by the mere fact of wheels and feet and hoofs going along it. Anthony had never seen a motor-car pass that way. The postman's trap, announced by the gaiety of a horn, was its most dashing vehicle. Occasionally a farmer trundled by, and every day at 10:45 a.m. precisely, there was the victoria. Anthony had noticed the victoria often enough before he could be said to have met it. Always it had the same occupants: a coachman with a cockaded top-hat, a severe-looking lady, and a girl whom he took to be a little older than himself. Nothing changed where this victoria was concerned: it appeared at the same moment, slowed down on the brief and easy descent of the water-splash, went over it with the horse going gingerly, climbed the rise on the other side at a walk, and then moved off on the flat road to Smurthwaite at a steady lope. In the winter the hood was up and the ladies' hats were small. In the summer the hood was down and the ladies' faces were shaded by large flowery hats and parasols. That was the only variety. Septimus said the lady was Mrs. Halliwell, and the girl her daughter Joanna.

It was on a day of midsummer, a few months after he had come to live with Mr. Pordage, that Anthony exchanged his first words with Joanna Halliwell. He was dawdling along the dusty road to Smurthwaite, accompanied as usual by Cerberus. In the hedges roses had taken the place of hawthorn, and honeysuckle was droning with bees.

It was a drowsy day, without cloud, and Anthony sat on the wayside grass among the dog-daisies and campion. Cerberus, however, was in no restful mood. He rushed at the boy, stopping suddenly, braked by splayed feet, barking, and doing all he could to say: "Come on, you lazy toad. This is no day for loafing in hedges."

Anthony was not responsive, and Cerberus trotted away to find fun elsewhere. The approaching victoria, drawn by this placidly-loping brown horse, looked promising, and he ran back to meet it. He greeted it with joy, running alongside and filling the scent-drowsed morning with a furious clamour of barking. The brown horse took no notice. He came steadily on; a fly on his flank would have been more discommoding. Anthony stood up and began to call, but Cerberus maintained his cheerful uproar. It accompanied the carriage for a few hundred yards to where Anthony stood. Then the lady said: "Stop," and the coachman pulled the horse to a standstill. The lady did not look at Anthony. She spoke into the air in front of her parasol. "Is not this Mr. Pordage's dog?"

"Yes, ma'am."

"I take it you are the boy who has come to stay with him?"

"Yes, ma'am."

"We had heard of you. Will you please take that dog by the collar."

Anthony did so.

"We are entitled, I should hope, to use the public roads without annoyance. Go!"

The last word was to the coachman, and the horse went. Cerberus struggled to follow, but Anthony held tight. Ten minutes later he went on towards Smurthwaite, pondering the brief encounter. A pair of stuck-up pieces if you like, he thought. The woman speaking into the air in front of her nose, the girl looking into the air in front of her nose. Neither of them—nor the coachman, come to that—had given him a glance.

Three-quarters of an hour later he was in Smurthwaite, and he remembered the place where, on the day of his arrival with Aunt Jessie, Septimus had taken them to eat sticky buns and drink coffee. Under the noble sycamores in their dark-green summer dress he walked to the coffee-house. On the glass door a notice uncompromisingly said: "Dogs not admitted." He looked down at Cerberus with a sigh. Cerberus looked up at him with a tongue-lolling grin of anticipation. He was about to turn away when the glass door opened and the girl of the victoria came out. "Are you wondering about the dog?" she asked.

"Yes."

"Bring him in," she said, smiling. "I'm sure they won't mind for once. They know me well."

She went back to the table at which she had been sitting, and Anthony followed. She said to Cerberus: "Lie down there!" and the dog miraculously obeyed. "You should be firm with dogs," she said.

There could be no sticky buns to-day. Anthony's pocket-money was small and ran only to a twopenny cup of coffee.

The girl said: "My name is Joanna Halliwell."

"I am Anthony Bromwich, and this dog is Cerberus."

"What are you doing at Mr. Pordage's place?"

"What has that to do with you?" He had not forgotten her bleak stare ahead on the road, and thought her now over-inquisitive.

She was not put out by his rudeness. "Nothing," she said. "However, I see hardly a soul from week's-end to week's-end, and so, when someone turns up, I ask these impertinent questions. Besides, I like to do what Mother says I mustn't do. You'd be surprised how many things I mustn't do. I mustn't even look at strangers, much less talk to them."

She was a fair girl, with pale shining hair and blue eyes. The blue eyes smiled at Anthony and he could not help smiling, too.

"I'm with Mr. Pordage to be prepared for a public school," he said, and added proudly: "I am learning French and Latin, English history, English literature and mathematics, though Mr. Pordage dodges the mathematics whenever possible. My father sent me to Mr. Pordage, but I have never seen my father."

"My father is dead," she said. "He died five years ago, when I was ten. He owned a woollen mill here in Smurthwaite. Now it is Mother's. She drives in every day to talk to the manager. I have my morning coffee here and then wait till she comes for me; then we drive back. It's a dull life. Perhaps it will be better in Switzerland."

"Are you going to Switzerland?"

"Yes—next week. I shall have a holiday till the school term begins there in the autumn."

There seemed nothing more to say to one another. They drank their coffee in silence till Joanna said: "Mother is never very long at the mill. I don't think there's any reason why she should go there at all. The manager looks after everything. She'd better not find me talking to you. So will you please take your dog to another table?"

However, it was too late for the move. Mrs. Halliwell came through the door. She was a determined-looking woman. She had been a mill-girl and her husband a mill-hand who had prospered. Joanna was wrong in thinking her mother's visit to the mill was unnecessary. There was not much that Mrs. Halliwell didn't know about a woollen mill, and she had just come from a stormy ten minutes with her manager. Anthony expected to be barked at, but Mrs. Halliwell said: "Joanna, what are you doing sitting there with that *strange dog?* Come at once, child!"

Joanna's back was turned towards her mother. She got up, and, as Anthony rose too, her blue eye gave him a wink. Wandering back to Easter How, he felt sorry that she was going to Switzerland so soon.

3

It was in the April of the following year that Anthony was walking towards Smurthwaite in the hope of meeting the motor-car bringing Harry Pordage and Dick Hudson, with Chris and Lottie, on their visit. It was a backward day. On Septimus's lawn the daffodils were out, but they had a look of not liking what they had found on emerging from the underworld. A cold wind, eddying, bowed them all now in this direction, now in that, so that they were like a Greek chorus, lamenting in turn to the left and the right. The birds were singing, more to keep up their peckers than from joy, and the clouds were inflated bags of grey, trundling with ungainly menace not very high overhead. A robin stood on a gate with an air of finding comfort in his red flannel waistcoat.

Anthony had almost reached Smurthwaite when he saw Joanna Halliwell coming towards him. She was not, as he had always seen her till now, over-dressed. She waved a gloved hand and said: "Hallo! Where's the dog? I've not seen you without him before."

"And I've not seen you without your mother. I haven't brought Cerberus because I'm expecting to meet some people in a motor-car, and he's not used to motor-cars."

Joanna said she was home for the Easter holiday. "A mistress brings us as far as London, and there all the girls who live in the country are met by their mothers." She added, with obvious pride in the fine word: "I am emancipated now, if you know what that means."

"Oh yes," said Anthony, not to be sat on, "it's from the Latin verb *emancipare*, to set free."

"We don't learn Latin—only French. We talk nothing else and all our lessons are in French."

78

"Who emancipated you?"

"I did. After all, I'm sixteen now. Do you know, till I went away I had never in my life gone a yard without Mother or my governess? And in Switzerland we don't, either. We walk about in crocodiles. So when I got back, I said to Mother: 'Mother, I must have my freedom.' She said: 'What you're going to do is learn to look after the mill when I'm too old to do it myself. In future you can come along with me each morning instead of sitting in a shop eating buns like a baby. It's not too soon to start, and it'll be something to do in the holidays.' "

"That's a funny idea of a holiday."

"I should think so. And what do I want with a mill? When Mother's dead, I shall sell it. I expect," she added complacently, "I shall marry on the proceeds."

"It would be far better," Anthony said wisely, "to give the mill to your husband, and let him do the work."

"Perhaps you're right. We shall see. Mother may live some years yet. Anyway, in the meantime, I'm allowed to be by myself now and then. I drove in with Mother this morning, and now I'm walking home."

She got down from the gate and set off along the way Anthony had come. He fell in alongside her. "Perhaps the motor-car will overtake us," he said.

"I want Mother to sell the carriage and buy a motor-car. Everybody's buying a car now. Jogging along behind that old horse is terribly old-fashioned, but I'm afraid I sha'n't shake Mother on that point. Old people are so obstinate. They make one feel madly helpless, and some of them live to be quite sixty."

"Mr. Pordage doesn't hold with motor-cars. He's very upset because this one is coming."

"Well, he'll have to be upset, that's all. There'll be plenty of them coming, whether he likes them or not. I expect, before we know where we are, we'll see these hedges down and a good road made into Smurthwaite. We'll be able to buzz in there from our place inside half an hour. Oh, much less than that, because motor-cars will be getting better, too. Better and faster. Don't you love the idea of going fast?"

Anthony wasn't sure that he wanted this young woman to subvert all that Septimus had taught him, but he soon found himself overruled, for the hooting of an old rubber-bulbed horn caused them to stop, to turn, and to see the car coming towards them in a cloud of dust. Anthony waved, and the car came to a standstill. The canvas hood was down. Harry Pordage, looking worried at the wheel, and Dick Hudson, who sat alongside him, were disguised with goggles. Lottie Wayland, wearing what looked like a piece of old net curtain on her hair, shared the back seat with Chris Hudson. She shouted excitedly: *"Bonjour, Antoine. Ça va bien?"*

"See here, Lottie lass," Dick Hudson said with massive patience, "this is Yorksheer. That thing comin' down t'road"—Anthony looked and saw Cerberus making a grinning approach—"is a dog, not what you call a chiang. You and Chris can parley fransay as much as you like when I'm not about, but a holiday's a holiday, so let's have a bit of God's good English. What say, Anthony? And how are you, lad?"

But Anthony had no time to answer. *"Mais, Monsieur Hudson,"* Lottie cried, *"c'est pour apprendre le français que Christophe se trouve chez nous. Il faut le parler toujours et partout."*

"Have it your own way, whatever you're talking about," Dick said with resignation. "Who's this lass, Anthony?"

Anthony made the introductions, and Joanna asked if she might have a lift as far as Mr. Pordage's house. They packed in somehow, Anthony jammed between Lottie and Chris Hudson, Joanna perilous on Lottie's knees, and, on Anthony's knees, Cerberus, who made an uninvited leap and looked round with great interest on this unaccustomed accession to his usual company. Harry Pordage, looking like a surgeon about to perform his first operation and hoping that God will be kind, fiddled with knobs and levers. Soon an intense shuddering shook the car and Cerberus began to bark with riotous joy. The car suddenly leapt forward like a steeplechaser who has decided to try the jump after all, checked, and threw everybody into a heap. It trembled violently, roused itself, and went sedately forward. "Good lad, Harry," Dick said. "Tha's gettin' on fine."

Joanna said: *"Moi aussi, j'aime parler en français,"* and that set them off: Chris, Joanna and Lottie. They chattered like magpies. Anthony could not believe his ears. French, as imparted by Septimus, expert grammarian but unskilled in conversation, had nothing to do with what he was hearing now. He didn't understand one word in six, and he was dismayed to find that Chris Hudson was as easy and voluble as the others. He was so downcast that he did not even try to join in. And so they came to the end of the journey: those three clacking away at the tops of their voices, Cerberus barking madly, Harry Pordage bent over the wheel as intently as Laacoon wrestling with serpents: to find Septimus standing at the watersplash holding out a red silk handkerchief nailed to a stick, and looking as though he wished it were a firebrand that would burn up everything that this shivering and already old-fashioned Humber represented.

4

This was a Saturday. The visit was not a long one as Dick Hudson had to be in Bradford for a matinée on the Monday, and, trusting Harry Pordage little enough as a driver, he told the party that they must be ready to leave on that day immediately after an early breakfast.

Luncheon was a miserable meal for both Anthony and Septimus. Neither of them could get a word in edgeways. Chris Hudson and Lottie Wayland, merely by talking in colloquial and idiomatic French, had everyone else silent. Septimus would have been capable of reciting passages in French from Ronsard to Rostand, but this was no occasion for scholastic virtuosity; this was something other. He was at sea, and he lapsed into an offended silence, growing pinker and pinker. Harry Pordage and Dick Hudson were content to give their attention to the food, accompanied by excellent wine, on which it had been Septimus's intention to say a few good words. He sulkily refrained, and merely pushed the bottle along from time to time. When the others were drinking their coffee he asked to be excused and went to his room, pausing at the door to say: "I speak passable English, Harry, and if either of these two young people would care for an elementary lesson I could spare a moment."

As he closed the door, Lottie said *"Touché"* and Chris Hudson laughed.

Anthony was furious for all sorts of reasons: because those two had shown him up, because Septimus had been caught out, and because Septimus had been so foolish as to give himself away by a feeble protest. He said: "You're overdoing it, Chris. Don't you think it sounds rather swank? Any guttersnipe in France could yammer away as you're doing, but knowing something about France and the French language and French literature—well, that's another matter, and that's where Mr. Pordage would make you feel a very silly little boy." He added: "And you're one without much in the way of manners."

Chris began: *"Mais, Antoine . . ."* and Anthony cut him short. "Oh, chuck it, you swank-pot. Anthony to you, if you want to speak to me at all."

He was glad to see Chris Hudson shrivel—almost cower, as he used to do in the school-yard. He had been surprised at the change a year had made in Chris. He had a self-confidence that made him seem a new person; but Anthony was wise enough to see that this defended him only when he was doing something better than it could be done by those around him. A sharp word, and it was gone.

Anthony apologised to Dick Hudson and Harry Pordage, and walked out of the room. Dick said: "You got what you were asking for, Chris. You shouldn't encourage him, Lottie lass. We all know by now that he can parley fransay with the best—and all thanks to you and your mother for that. But there's times and seasons like, and there was no call to be rude to Mr. Pordage, which is what you were."

Harry said lugubriously: "He's a queer fish, is Sep. Looks as well padded as a feather-bed, but if you tweak his nerves you can hear him screaming inside. So lay off it, Chris boy. As that young chap said, it sounded a bit too much like swank."

Chris was not one to take a reproof and ask whether he had earned it. He said: "The sooner we're back in Megson Street the better. I didn't ask to come."

"Ah, well, that's English, anyway," Harry said. "Come on, Dick. Let's give old Skinny Liz a hand with the washing-up."

"Shan't I do that?" Lottie asked.

"Nay, lass," Dick said. "Go and find yon Anthony. I expect he's been looking forward to seeing you after all these months. He'll want news of his auntie."

5

She found him in the paddock. She said: "I'm sorry about that, Anthony."

He had a stick in his hand, and swished at the grass with it, not looking at her. "So I should think," he said.

"Let's have a walk."

"It's not the day for it. It may rain any minute."

"Oh, no. It's cleared up a lot since the morning. Look at the sky coming through."

It was, and the wind had dropped. The daffodils down one side of the paddock were a golden file, standing at ease.

Anthony had been looking forward to her visit, and so he was the more annoyed that she had had her part in making it unhappy for Septimus. Now he didn't want to walk. But a maniac Cerberus came along, running round in tempestuous rings, a vital invitation to the dance.

"That dog wants exercise," Lottie said.

"Very well. Come along."

He chose to be glum for a mile or two, and Lottie wisely let him have his sulk out. She walked at his side, occasionally whistling to the dog, occasionally whistling a tune; and now the sunshine became warm and all the air rang with springtime music.

"You see," she said, "Chris can't help it. He *thinks* in French."

"That's more than he ever did in English."

There had been no letter since the one in which, almost a year ago now, she had told him how much she disliked Chris Hudson. "I'm surprised you didn't ask him to come with us, since you admire him so much," he said. "It would have been delightful to learn from him that these things leaping around are *agneaux*, and that the *soleil* is in good form."

She laughed. "Really, you are a fool. If you go on like this, I'll think you're as big a fool as Chris."

"You don't think he's a fool. You think he's a wonderful person who can think—in French at that."

She stopped, and stamped her foot in the dust. "I don't think he's wonderful, and I don't think you're wonderful. I think you're a pair of odious beasts. I have tried to be good-mannered with you, but you're not"—she puckered up her little face and got the word—"you're not reciprocating. Do you want me to go back?"

Anthony said gruffly: "Don't be daft. Come on."

"Very well, then. Listen to this. My mother told me when Chris came that I was never to speak a word to him except in French—never, not one single word about one single thing. And neither would she. Well, you can see what it's done for him, and we're both proud of it. He hated it for a long time, and then he began to tumble to it, and now he loves it. There's nothing wrong in that, is there? As for thinking him a wonderful person, that's a different matter. And I'm not going to say another word about him. I think it's time you said a word to me. How do you get on with Mr. Pordage?"

She looked fierce. She was laying down the law. And as Anthony's sharp word to Chris had taken the bounce out of him, so these words warned Anthony to watch his step.

"Let's just walk," he said. "Never mind Chris Hudson or Mr. Pordage. But he's a funny customer, I can tell you."

And, despite his "never mind," he began to tell her about Septimus's letters, and the big room in the barn, and the days on end when he would not so much as see Mr. Pordage except at meals, and other days when they would talk about everything on earth, sometimes in the barn-room, sometimes in Septimus's study, sometimes walking the roads and taking lunch in a pub or tea in a cottage.

"And that reminds me," said Anthony, "we could have tea out to-day. There's a cottage we're coming to . . ."

"No. It would be rude to Mr. Pordage. We ought to go back."

"Oh, he won't mind. 'You are not a felon in gaol, my dear boy, or a wretched beast in a zoo. Come in if you want to, and if you want to stay out, stay out. Sleep out, if that would please you. I often did when I was young.' That's what he said once, when I apologised for missing a meal."

"Did you ever sleep out?"

"Once. Cerberus found me, though, and kept on licking my face till I had to get up and go in."

"You couldn't sleep out in Bradford. Perhaps it would be all right in Manningham Park."

"The police would arrest you."

"Yes, and Mother would give me a terrific talking to. I think you're lucky. You have the best of it."

"I don't do so badly. Look, here's the place for tea. Have you any money? I've got sixpence."

"So have I. Will a shilling be enough?"

"I should think so."

"It seems a lot of money to spend. Mother says take care of the shillings and the pounds will take care of themselves."

"Then she would disapprove of Septimus. He said to me once: 'Despise the pounds, and the shillings will despise themselves.'"

"He seems a funny schoolmaster."

"He's funny whatever way you look at him, if by that you mean not like most people."

They had climbed a hill, and on the top of it was a cottage with roses, innocent yet of bud, climbing the walls, and with aubrietia and snow-on-the-mountain carpeting the small front garden. A notice nailed to a post said: "Stop here for a Reight Yorksheer Blow-out." Cerberus, who had looked with interest at the notice, had apparently interpreted it aright, and was thumping the door with his tail.

The woman who brought their tea to a table in the garden looked a Reight Yorksheer Blow-out herself: round as a barrel, blowsy as a bumble-bee. To be on the safe side, Anthony said: "We've got a shilling between us. Will that be all right?"

"What abaht t'tyke?" she asked. "Is he included?"

She looked at the immense earthenware teapot, the plates of ham, the bread-and-butter, scones and jam. "That lot'll be ninepence to a courtin' couple," she said. "Ah'll make up the bob wi' a bone for t'tyke."

She went in, and returned with what might have been the thighbone of an aurochs. "There, lad," she said to Cerberus, "get thy molars into that, an' tha'll not hurt."

"Thank you very much, madame," Lottie said with Parisian politeness and self-possession.

The woman grinned and said: "On second thoughts, tha'd better have that lot on the house. It'll bring me luck laike for t'season."

She disappeared into the cottage, which seemed a close fit for her, but which miraculously contained her double. The two faces appeared at the window, contemplating the children with the amused interest of archæologists who have unearthed a toy that a baby played with ten thousand years ago.

But Anthony and Lottie were not aware of that.

6

Soon after breakfast the next morning, which was Sunday, Joanna Halliwell appeared, riding a bicycle. Chris Hudson, Lottie and Anthony were standing near the water-splash, discussing the programme for the day. Harry Pordage and Dick had gone off in the car, proposing to be away till evening. Harry, as well he might, felt that the visit was not being a success. Lottie Wayland was the only one of the visitors in whom Septimus seemed to take any interest. Sensing his annoyance, she had set out to charm him, as she could, with her bows and curtseys and monsieurs. He had invited her to his study after supper and given her a lecture on calligraphy. Ranged on the long refectory table at which he wrote were bundles of quills. He showed her how they should be cut and used. He told her that he was writing a book, and said that it would be in three moods: stately and elegiac, for which he would use the quills of swans; soaring and romantic, for which he would use the quills of golden eagles; and harsh and discordant, for which he would use the quills of crows. He explained that during a holiday in the Highlands he had met a gamekeeper who, for a small consideration, supplied the eagles' quills, and the swans' quills came from a fisherman in Cornwall. "Crows' quills I can find a-plenty," he said. "I sometimes wish that fish were feathered. Their quills would be incomparable for passages of rippling liquid music."

He showed her with pride his parchment manuscript paper and the sepia ink that he made for himself. He displayed the writing produced with various quills, and she said it was the most beautiful writing she had ever seen, which was true; though—but she did not say this—she could see no difference between his elegiac and romantic hands. "You would have been very happy, sir," she said, "in a monastery, writing their beautiful books," and Septimus said rather wistfully that he thought he would; "but perhaps the cold would have been too much for me. I am not a very good man, my dear, not good enough to be able to endure discomfort. Still, it would have been pleasant to look out of a slit window and see that a gentle knight was pricking on the plaine rather than a motor-car a-sticking by my water-splash."

"I hope we have not disturbed you too much, sir."

"I shall survive. I shall survive. Now off to bed with you. Mrs. Toplis has built a nest somewhere, and she will expect you to snatch a little sleep. Do not disappoint her. Snatch."

This encounter put him into a better mood for the morning, but Harry thought it wise that he and Dick should be out of the way.

Joanna had come to invite Lottie Wayland to visit her house. "I had a job with Mother," she said. "But then I always have a job with Mother. You'd better bring your birth certificate and family tree."

"I don't want to go where I'm not wanted," Lottie said; and Joanna laughed. "Oh, come on. Don't be stuffy. I want you. If Mother's awkward, we'll just have to put up with it. After all, she won't last much longer. She's fifty if she's a day."

Cerberus, interested in the bicycle, bit through a tyre and inner tube and looked up with a smile, asking for approval, as the machine settled down on to the wheel-rim. Anthony thought that he alone had noticed this. He patted Cerberus. "Good dog," he said. He did not approve of a girl who thus casually took Lottie away and left him with Chris Hudson. The girls started to walk, Joanna pushing the bicycle. She was at once aware of the flat tyre. "Look what's happened now," she said. "Oh, damn!"

Chris said: "It was the dog did that. Anthony's dog. He bit through the tyre. I saw him."

The girls came to a standstill and looked back. Anthony said with menace: "D'you want a bath? You didn't have one this morning."

"I should think not." He addressed the girls. "Do you know

what Anthony does? He goes to the stream and jumps in with no clothes on. Disgusting conduct! He wanted me to go with him, but I wouldn't."

Joanna began to laugh. "You'd look a pretty sight if you did," she said.

Chris was no Adonis and no infant Hercules. This direct contemptuous comment on his physique stung him to blind anger. His fists clenched, and he said: "Oh, you—you——" He made to advance upon the laughing Joanna, but Anthony put a hand on his chest and shoved. Chris landed on his back in the middle of the water-splash.

Anthony did not wait to see the outcome. He crossed the splash on the stepping-stones, whistled the dog to his side, and walked away in the direction of Smurthwaite. Let 'em all go hang, he thought. Let Chris Hudson wallow, and let the girls go off, if they wanted to. He could do without any of them.

He did not get back till lunch-time, and he lunched alone with Septimus, who was in beaming good humour. He said: "Peace is upon this house. *Gaudeamus igitur.*"

"Where is Chris Hudson?" Anthony asked.

"He is embarked upon what he would call the *chemin de fer*— the iron road to Bradford, via Keighley."

"Was he very wet?"

"When first I saw him, he was very wet indeed. He looked remarkably like a newt that had clothed itself before emerging from the natal stream. 'Whence, O Christopher, this metamorphosis?' I asked; but chattering teeth were incapable of rational reply. He stood among the daffodils, gibbering with angry incomprehensibility."

"I threw him into the stream."

Septimus spread red-currant jelly upon a forkful of tender lamb. "Out of the incoherence," he said, "the name of Anthony Bromwich emerged, coupled with oaths and threats of lifelong feud. I was able to reach my own conclusions."

"He asked for it," said Anthony tersely.

"He said that he must leave this house, that he would not stay to be insulted. What could I do but bow? No thoughtful host could stand in the way of a guest's wishes so clearly expressed. Back to Bradford, he cried, back to Bradford without a moment's delay. I assured him that a moment's delay was imperative if he wished to escape rheums and agues, fevers tertiary and quarternary. In short, O Christopher, I said, you'll have to change your bags."

"I'd have let him go as he was."

"All nature cried out against it. He was a disgusting sight."

Christopher, having brought no change of clothes, was ordered to go to the barn-room and dress in something of Anthony's, and while Septimus walked among the daffodils filled with pleasurable meditations, a victoria drawn by a brown horse stopped at the gate, and a coachman wearing a cockaded hat approached and handed him a letter. With Mrs. Halliwell's compliments he was informed that Miss Wayland would be staying to lunch, and hoping that this short notice does not involve any domestic inconvenience, I am, yours faithfully.

"Inconvenience—oh no! My heart sang. To know that the widow Halliwell was mine—and faithful to boot—and to know that here was the *deus ex machina* for the conveyance of my dry parcel of boy to Smurthwaite station! A few sesterces pressed into that honest palm did the trick and permitted Valpy, whom I should have hated to disturb, to enjoy his sabbatic peace. And so you see, my dear Anthony, when others, by brutal violence, create a painful situation, Pordage's diplomatic service may be relied on to handle it with tact and discretion."

"He asked for it," said Anthony again; and Septimus said: "We all of us, my dear boy, ask for it in one way or another. Human history is little but the tale of frenzied men asking for it, sometimes getting it in the neck, and, with a frequency for which God be thanked, sometimes being allowed to escape the consequences of their own folly."

Mrs. Toplis came in with an apple-pie. "Quite like old times," she said. "Just the three of us. I must snatch a moment to warm that boy's trousers."

"O that some power had put it into a human heart to warm them with frequency and precision in the past," said Septimus.

CHAPTER 7

9 9 9 9 9 9

1

*P*ordage is not a widespread name, and Mrs. Halliwell, who was about the same age as Septimus, remembered the grocer's shop which she used to pass during her childhood in Halifax. She passed it because she could not afford to enter. Pordage's was a high-class shop—indeed, it advertised itself as "the Superior Grocer's"—and Mrs. Halliwell's traffic had been with two-pennorths from corner-shops. Even now, she thought of Septimus as superior—and how right she was! She had wanted to call on him and ask whether he was a Halifax Pordage, related to the illustrious alderman, church-warden, and public-talker-on-all-possible-occasions whom she remembered with an awe that her present easy circumstances had somewhat diminished. But she had not done so, fearing a rebuff, a jolt to the pride that sustained her uncertain social balance.

She needn't have worried. She was a formidable woman, well able to look after herself. She had been a half-timer in a mill, and then a full-timer, and so had Alf Halliwell, a thread of a chap with a pale fanatical face who had no intention of remaining the underdog that he had been born. His handicap was wretched health, and that was why, when he became under-manager of a small mill in Halifax, he took the first opportunity of going as manager to the mill in Smurthwaite, where the air was kinder to his hard-pressed lungs.

He married his Ada, and they looked around for a house in the country. A few miles farther out than Easter How, which Septimus had not then bought, they found a labourer's cottage. A rise of the fells threw a protecting arm in a half-circle round it. The little place looked south, downhill, and Alf Halliwell bought it with a few acres and made it habitable. He and Amy liked everything about it except the name, which was Horrocks's Bit. They changed this to Throstle's Nest. Alf rode in to Smurthwaite every day on his bicycle. It was still Throstle's Nest now that the cottage was gone, and the few acres had become ten, and a large red-brick ugly house stood where comely grey stone was to be had for the picking up. But to Alf and Ada this flaring eyesore was a symbol. The painfully formal gardens, the horse and victoria that took the place of the bicycle, the coach-man's cockade, Joanna's governess, the gardener and the cook: all were symbols that young Alf Halliwell, who had once been told in Sunday school not to come again unless his mother could sew an arse to his pants, was as good as some and better than most. For Alf not only owned the small mill in Smurthwaite, where he stayed because of the vital air, but, being a quick, not to say tricky, hand with finance, he had many desirable investments in the woollen industry. All of which did not prevent him from coughing his lungs up one day on the office floor and being taken home to die.

2

Perhaps Septimus would never have met Mrs. Halliwell had he not decided to answer the note she had sent about Lottie's staying to lunch. But when, on the Monday morning, the visitors were gone, and he had devoted a few hours to fifty words or so of the adventures of Ambrose Feend, he was overcome with excitement at the thought of addressing a letter to a vast carbuncular excrescence and calling it, on the envelope, Throstle's Nest. It would be, he pondered, like calling the Devil a mischievous little imp, or thinking of the Almighty as a good-natured chap. So he wrote:

"Mrs. Halliwell, my dear and beneficent neighbour—Our fledgling Lottie, returned from your Nest, reports a hospitality far in excess of what might be expected within the precincts of a few twigs glued together with mire and upholstered with a little moss. Indeed, she overflowed with praise, her young beak distended in adulation, both of you and your daughter Joanna. For which my ageing heart hereby sends its throb of gratitude.

Written with a goose-quill on this Monday of the first week after Easter, 1914. Septimus Pordage."

It was of no use for Joanna to speak the simplest French words to her mother, who would not have understood even *bonjour, maman*, but the poor soul was desperately anxious to hear her daughter prattle this lingo which she was paying good brass for her to acquire. She had often said, since Joanna's holiday began: "Come now, lass, let's have a few words in French," but the idea seemed so silly to the child that she blushed. "Really, Mother! I should feel the most awful fool on earth."

"Come on, now. There's only us two."

But Joanna would not open her mouth; and that was why Mrs. Halliwell, who sometimes doubted whether Joanna could indeed speak French, was overjoyed on that Sunday morning. Opening out of the dining-room at Throstle's Nest was a small room called the office. Alf Halliwell had spent much time in the office, and his wife, too, had taken care to acquaint herself with its secrets. Since his death she had used that room more than any other in the house, and if she said to Joanna or to some member of the staff: "I'll see you in the office," it was understood that, for good or ill, the matter was important. In a frame over the fireplace was a letter, the paper embossed with a Whitehall address. Mrs. Halliwell remembered how, on the day when Alf was brought home with a few hours to live, the postman handed in this letter at the very moment when the all-but-corpse was being carried over the doorstep. She did not open it till days later, and then she found that it informed "Dear Mr. Alfred Halliwell" that all was now in train for a representation to be made "from the appropriate quarter" to his Majesty that the honour of knighthood be conferred "for political services."

This sheet of paper was to Mrs. Halliwell more truly Alf's memorial than the rather fulsome words on his tombstone. Had his leaky bellows managed to puff for another few days she would have been Lady Halliwell, and sometimes she thought of herself as Lady Halliwell when she sat in the office on lonely winter nights. She knew that Alf's "political services" were to be reckoned in nothing but hard cash. He had never addressed a meeting or served on a political committee, but he voted Liberal and lavishly footed Liberal bills, and it was only right, she was sure, that a man should have what he had bought and paid for. She made another discovery in the office when Alf's frail presence was gone away from it for ever. In a stationery drawer was a mass of note-paper with this embossed at the head: "From Sir Alfred Halliwell, Throstle's Nest, Egremont-in-Craven, West Yorks." Alf had known what was in the wind, and had made ready for the great day. He hadn't said a word to her; it was all to be a surprise. She didn't burn the paper; it was still there in its boxes. She sometimes wondered what would have been the first letter Alf wrote on that paper. She thought she knew. It would have been something like this: "Dear Ada.—This means nowt much to me. It's for you, lass. Love, Alf." He wasn't wordy, except with a cheque-book. "Well, there it is, Mr. Halliwell." "Ay. All reight. Wheer's my cheque-book?" Even to her, he said most things with his cheque-book; and, after all, she wisely thought, that wasn't a bad test of whether he meant them.

Sitting there in the office that Sunday morning, she was considering a letter from her stock-broker about selling A and buying B, when she heard Joanna's voice in the paved terrace to which her window opened. She wasn't too pleased with Joanna. The child had taken to rushing about the countryside on a bicycle, and, now that there was no longer a governess, goodness knows what she would be up to. This morning Mrs. Halliwell had said: "Wouldn't it be nicer, my dear, to go for a drive in the carriage?" and Joanna had said: "Oh dear, Mother, what about my legs?"

"Your legs?"

"Yes. I want them to be beautiful."

Well, whoever heard the like of that?

"Your legs look all right to me."

"There's nothing wrong with them, but they need exercise. I think I'll go out on my bike. I should feel an absolute stupid idol sitting alone behind that old horse."

When Alf gave up riding his bicycle there was a pony and trap, and at last there was the horse. With the horse came the victoria, the coachman, the cockade. The pinnacles of gentility.

"And if one doesn't use one's legs," said Joanna—I wish she wouldn't keep on about legs—"what's wrong with a motor-car? Think of all the nonsense you could do without."

"Nonsense?"

"Well, you wouldn't have to dress up. You wouldn't need a horse or a coachman."

"I should need a chauffeur."

"Oh, no; you could learn to drive."

"At my time of life?"

"Oh, why not, Mother? You've got a few years yet."

"I hope so."

"You wouldn't have to worry about keeping the horse waiting, and harnessing, and unharnessing."

"Why should I worry? Roberts is well paid to do the worrying about those things. He wouldn't thank you if he found himself without a job."

"Oh, well. May I go on my bike?"

"Yes. But mind you're back in good time for lunch."

And here she was, back well before lunch, and chattering away in some unknown tongue that surely must be French. Ah, if only Alf had lived, thought Mrs. Halliwell, to hear his daughter now, talking French as easily as one might order a pound of cheese.

It was odd to feel so near to one's daughter through the very means—this uncomprehended language—that separated one from her. But that was how it seemed to Mrs. Halliwell. She wanted to speak through the window to Joanna, to let her know that she was listening with pride, but she understood that one word from her would dam the flow. So she sat listening, sad that Alf was not there to share her feelings, till the girls went out of earshot. It would have surprised Joanna to know how humble, how unworthy of her, her mother felt: this mother whom everybody at Throstle's Nest and at the Smurthwaite mill looked on with awe. But this was an important day for Mrs. Halliwell; and, when Lottie's visit was ended, the old lady marked its importance by returning her to Easter How in the victoria.

3

It had been an important day, too, for the girls. Mrs. Wayland, who thought her daughter safely in the company of Dick Hudson and Harry Pordage under Mr. Septimus Pordage's roof, would have been none too pleased to see her haring off with a stranger, leaving Chris Hudson forlorn in a water-splash. But both Lottie and Joanna had had a surfeit of chaperonage, and they flew together as naturally as though the way of the world till then had been designed to keep twin souls apart. Taking turns to push the punctured bicycle, they walked in silence till Joanna said: "You speak French much better than I do. Where did you learn?"

That set them off. Lottie had clear memories of her first ten years in Paris, and she chattered of that and of the odd household in Megson Street; and it seemed to Joanna that, compared with herself, Lottie was a woman of the world. Before going to Lausanne, she had known nothing but Throstle's Nest, with a governess, and three weeks' holiday at Scarborough—always at Scarborough, always in the same rented house year after year—with a governess. And here was a girl who had lived in Paris, not as one lived at Lausanne positively haunted by supervisors, but as one lived anywhere, walking about the streets, shopping, talking to people one met, if one wanted to; a girl who now lived in a house where there was a boy—and how

93

the Demoiselles Kempfer, those worthy Alsaciennes who had charge of her, swept the young ladies up from the threat of boys!—a house where occasionally a famous music-hall performer was to be found: oh, this was a sort of life very different from nid-nodding behind the same old horse on the same old road to Smurthwaite, and going to the same old house in Scarborough, where she wasn't allowed even to paddle with boys and girls she didn't know, which was a bit hard because she didn't know any of them; different, too, from the suave conducted walks on the shores of the Lake of Geneva. How could Joanna be expected to know that Mrs. Wayland's supervision had been of a gorgonian severity to match her mother's? A *jeune fille bien elevée* was Mrs. Wayland's ideal woman, and that woman was not produced by running helter-skelter about the streets, whether of Paris or Bradford.

As for Lottie, she with difficulty restrained her amazement and admiration. Throstle's Nest was beautiful. The careful unadventurous garden, the meek horse looking over the half-door of the stable, the servants, the decorous luncheon: all these things, which Joanna introduced with well-chosen slighting remarks, Lottie knew to represent her own mother's notion of how the good life was lived, and they didn't seem bad to her, either. And so, liking one another, each coveting much that the other possessed and thought little of, the two girls made a year's advance in friendship; and Mrs. Halliwell was enchanted to receive Lottie's accomplished curtsey and to be called Madame. She felt it was making a good impression on the servants. She even, when the visit was over, ordered Roberts to bring round the victoria and take "Maddermersel" back to Easter How.

But she was not prepared for what happened after dinner that night. Joanna, who had been rather quiet during the meal, said suddenly: "Mother, may I see you in the office?"

Well, this was a reversal of order! Never before had the invitation to the office issued from any lips but her own. "What is it, child? Can't you speak to me here?"

"It's a business matter, Mother."

Mrs. Halliwell smiled. "Very well," she said, and got up and moved towards the door to the office. Joanna was there before her, opened the door, and curtseyed. "*Entrez, maman,*" she said.

Mrs. Halliwell's smile deepened, but she was an expert in keeping smiles out of sight. "This is an act," she thought. "Something's coming." She sat in the swivel-chair at her desk and swung round to face Joanna. The girl stood uneasily before the fire, which was lit, for the spring evening was nippy. "Sit down, Joanna."

"*Merci, maman.*"

H'm!

"Now what's on your mind?"

"How much money shall I have when I'm twenty-one?"

"Who said you'll have any?"

"Oh, I know I shall. It was in father's will."

"What do you want to know for? I don't remember what it is," Mrs. Halliwell lied. "But it'll be a fair whack if you behave yourself."

"I thought I got it anyway?"

"Oh, no. Your father was pretty open-handed with his brass, but he was cautious for once. What he said in his will was that the money would be yours 'at the discretion of my dear wife Ada.' So you see it's for me to decide whether you get a brass farthing. And that's why I say if you behave yourself."

"If I tried to do good, would that be behaving myself?"

"It depends on what you call good. Plenty of people think they're doing good when they're laying up trouble for themselves or someone else. Throwing brass about is never a very good idea, if that's what you've got in mind. It was a weakness of your Father's, and"—with a glance at the framed letter from Whitehall—"it don't always bring home the bacon."

"But should it?"

"Now, child, don't ask daft questions. Let's have what's on your mind."

Joanna sat down. "It's about Lottie Wayland. She's as poor as a church mouse."

"So was I, and so was your father. There's ways of curing that."

Joanna had heard all of Lottie's story. "You mightn't have done it without Father," she said hardily. "It's not easy for a woman left all on her own like Mrs. Wayland. She has to sweat her guts out to make ends meet."

"That's not the sort of language I'm paying for you to learn."

"Well, I can't say she has to perspire her intestines."

"Joanna, that's the sort of silly remark I will not have you making. It's more offensive than what you said at first. All you need say is that this woman has to work hard. And what's wrong with that? So do most people, and it does them no harm that I can see. Keeps 'em out of mischief."

"Sometimes. There are some people who get into mischief that way, and some that get into the workhouse."

"And who pays to keep them there? Rich people have their place in the world."

"Would *you* pay to keep people in the workhouse if you didn't *have* to?"

Mrs. Halliwell admired the question, direct and personal. It was a punch below the belt, but it showed her that Joanna was no fool. It showed that Joanna knew something about men and women, and Mrs. Halliwell prized that beyond book-learning. She was well enough aware that the answer was No. "Yes," she lied, without batting an eyelid. "Of course I would. I have some sense of my Christian duty, I hope."

"Good," said Joanna. "I wasn't thinking of my Christian duty? I was being selfish, because I do like Lottie Wayland. Could I have some of my money now, to pay for her to come back to school with me?"

Mrs. Halliwell was staggered. Her first instinct was to bark: "No. I never heard such nonsense in my life," but the long look she directed at Joanna stopped the words. Joanna was trying to look cool and composed, one adult putting a reasonable proposal to another. She was sitting in an armchair, one hand on each arm. Her mother saw the brown, warm little fingers slightly trembling. Then she looked at the fair face, the blue eyes striving to be hardy, the hair so palely gold that it made her think of down on a day-old chick. She felt an impulse to go to the child and embrace her and comfort her. Instead, forgetting that she was all but Lady Halliwell, she said: "Well, it's nowt to be rushed at. But us'll see. Perhaps summat could be done."

And then the fingers relaxed, and Joanna rushed across the room and kissed her, and said: "Oh, Mother, thank you. I hope you'll live to be a hundred!"

Mrs. Halliwell grinned. "Well, Ah don't know about that. Ninety's my target. Ah reckon it becomes a bit wearisome after that. Now get to bed, lass."

And when Joanna was gone she pulled her hard swivel-chair up to the fire and leaned towards the flame, warming her hands and thinking of her husband. "You mightn't have done it without Father." She was a shrewd one was Joanna. She knew where a punch got home. It was true. She would have been nowt without Alf. And she remembered how Alf had sat here one night on the other side of this fireplace and they had fallen into reminiscence of their life together. She had urged him to accept an invitation that had just come: that he should stand as a Liberal candidate. "Nay, lass," he said. "There's two reasons against that. One is the old bellows, and t'other is that I never had no education. Plenty of chaps don't let that stand in the way, but I'm a bit sensitive like about it. I can't be like them. They pretend they're as good as the next and how a man speaks don't matter. But it do, tha knows. I'd have liked to have everything, but things worked out so as I couldn't. I'd have liked to be an educated man, but I'm not, and that's that, and so I'll stick in my own place, which isn't a bad place at that, and it's a useful place, too. But I've been thinking, lass, that one of these days I'd like to do summat for a promising lad here and there. An educational endowment or summat like that."

The old bellows had puffed their last before he got round to that. It was a long time ago, but, without knowing it, Joanna had enlisted a powerful ally.

4

Septimus pampered himself so shamelessly that in self-defence he pretended now and then to be roughing it. When he was younger he would put his things into a rucksack and say that he was off for a few weeks on the roads. "I shall sleep under a haystack or in a barn—whatever comes along—and live on an onion a day, with bread and salt and water. They make a Lucullan repast." And he would do this for a day. Then he would feed and sleep at cottages and country pubs, and if one of them had a *specialité de la maison* that pleased him, such as lobster salad in some inshore fishing village, he would stay there till his holiday was ended, roughing it with a book on a sunny sandy beach. He would go back not brown, for the sun was powerless against his sanguine skin, but a more enchantingly Leander pink, as though the lobsters had suffused their essence into his veins and tissue, and he would call on his fellow schoolmasters to witness the virtue of vigour and enterprise as he tossed down in the common-room the rucksack from which an onion or two and a hard crust would roll on to the threadbare carpet.

Mrs. Halliwell's Nest was a good three miles from Easter How, and he decided to rough it by ambling there on his own stout legs. He said at the breakfast table: "I shall not be in to luncheon to-day, Mrs. Toplis. Indeed, it is an open question when Ithaca will see me again. The Siren Halliwell awaits me and will enchant me with her throstle's song, and so, vulgarly speaking, you may expect me when you see me."

Mrs. Toplis said practically: "You'll want a bit of summat to snatch on t'road."

"The bleakest sustenance," Septimus said. "I shall travel rough." He reached beneath his chair and pulled out the battered rucksack of earlier journeys. "If I remember aright, I sent me last Christmas some tins of *pâté de foie gras* from Mr. Fortnum's and Mrs. Mason's expeditionary department. You never know when a soldier may have to recoil upon his iron rations. I think a dozen small sandwiches—reasonably small—you need not interpret the word too stringently—with some fruit and a bottle of hock—wrap it carefully, please, in a napkin—should see us over the first leg of the voyage. When we have made our landfall at Throstle's Nest, we shall perhaps be able to live on the country. We have been bidden to tea."

He was in a happy mood because his brother and Dick Hudson and Lottie Wayland were gone. Such glad release called for something in the way of a roughing expedition on the open road, and the widow Halliwell's surprising invitation to tea suggested an objective. "To discuss an educational matter," she said puzzlingly, and added: "The carriage will pick you up at 3.30 p.m." To which he replied: "My old friend Shanks's Mare, though no Pegasus, will bear me to your dwelling by 4 p.m., the hour at which the English are accustomed to indulge in *le five o'clock*. Trusting this will meet your convenience, I am, Yours sincerely, Septimus Pordage, D.Litt., ambulator."

It was a pleasant day. The spring-time had settled down, and it occurred to Septimus that Valpy, being dumb, would make an agreeable companion. So he went into the paddock, took down the washing-line that Mrs. Toplis had hung between two trees, and looped it round Valpy's neck. Anthony, watching them go from the window of his room, thought they looked like a pair of chubby twins. He would have been surprised had he known how separate they were and what parts they would fill before their trudge was ended. For, as Septimus plodded on beneath lark-song and young clouds at play, he was now this, now that, and Valpy had to change to meet his mood. He was an Arab with his steed, a knight limping home from a tourney, and, more surprisingly, a princess leading her white palfrey to a romantic encounter. Then he addressed himself aloud:

> To what strange altar, O mysterious priest,
> Lead'st thou that heifer lowing at the skies,
> And all her silken flanks with garlands drest?

This pleased him so much that he decided something must be done about Valpy's flanks. He tied him to a gate, and browsed along the hedge, seeking material for a garland or two and not having much luck. It was not yet the time for dog-daisies and campion and meadow-sweet. Even the hawthorn was tight-fisted, its pearls still under lock and key. The garland had to be of lush hedge-parsley, and, thinking things over, he did not see how he could hang this, or anything else, on Valpy's well-rounded flanks. So, with bits of string that he found in his pocket, he tied it into a large clumsy wreath to go round Valpy's neck; but as he approached, Valpy misunderstood his intention, snatched it with yellow teeth, and happily chumbled it. Septimus was not greatly put out by this. Valpy's greed made him think of his *pâté de foie gras*. He pushed open the gate to which the pony was tied and led him in towards a haystack in a corner of the field. Priding himself on being above all things a practical man, he found a pointed stick, drove it into the ground with his heel, and tied Valpy's rope to it. Now he was one of a cavalry troop halted on the march. He had fastened his charger in the picket-lines, and could take a moment's rest.

He moved to the sunny side of the haystack and eased himself down against its warm support. In this pasture the eager grass was richly green, and rising beyond it, a mile away, the fells were darker, the green of sage, with limestone blobs of light burning on their sides. Over that, the sky was blue, with here and there a small cherubic cloud, its shadow on the hills lightly but inseparably its fellow. It made Septimus think, as so many things did, of the mystery of his indissoluble I and Me; but he put the thought from him, murmured "How wonderful are thy tabernacles," and greedily turned to his rucksack.

What a surprising woman Mrs. Toplis was! How sensitively she interpreted the needs of roughing it! He had been wondering how he should drink his hock. The elemental circumstances of such a day demanded that he should knock off the neck of the bottle against a stone. But she had drawn the cork and lightly replaced it; and wrapped in tissue paper was his little silver cup. Dalliance was excellent sauce, and so, having unwrapped the cup and admired its shape, he did not drink at once but closed his eyes and recalled his one moment of athletic glory.

How he had loathed those playing-fields on which it had once been his duty to supervise the young barbarians all at play: a muddy, sweaty, panting phalanx, kicking clods into his eye with their leather-studded boots! His spirit shrank, his tongue cried: "Oh, well done, Thompson," and I called Me a hypocritical humbug. He knew they had him weighed up, that as he ran along the touchline, wearing the odious school muffler of grey and green, shouting, exhorting, they were all aware that his soul was longing for the fireside muffins and the comforting cup.

And yet I was longing all the time to show Me that I could do these stupid unnecessary things as well as the next man. There came the day of the frightful annual fiasco, when Old Boys played the school at rugby. Stockbrokers and accountants, advertising agents, men who were in tea or tin, put on their little blue knickers and woolly stockings and grey-and-green shirts, and panted about the field like bears and bulls pursued and worried by small loathsome dogs. If there was one thing that Septimus detested more than the average sensual schoolboy, it was the average sensual father thereof, boisterously in search of the childhood he should long have been proud to disown. But there they were, and there was Septimus, wearing football kit, running along the touchline as usual, shivering in the wind of a day darkening over the elms that edged the field. The streaky sunset sky was no bloodier than the thoughts in his heart. And as the game drew to its close with the school leading by three points, a hulking baldhead, who was in treacle or caramels—Septimus could never remember which—achieved a try at the dire price of a well deserved kick in the crotch from his younger son. He was carried groaning from the field, and Septimus, with a fine sense of timing— for the game had but two minutes to go—ran up to the headmaster and said: "May I deputise for the injured man, sir?"

The headmaster nodded dubiously, and Septimus pranced on to the field. The ball was placed for the attempt to convert the try, and the captain of the Old Boys—who was in truffles or Turkish delight— said with what little breath was left to him: "Have a go at it, Mr. Pordage." Septimus shut his eyes and had a go, and did not open them till the referee's final whistle shrilled in his ears, and Mincing Lane and Throgmorton Street closed upon him, slapped his back till he was black and blue, and carried him off the field like a slain bullock being manhandled into Smithfield. The Old Boys had won for the only time on record, and they subscribed to give Septimus this silver cup on which all their names were engraved.

Mrs. Toplis had not forgotten to include a fat slice of Dundee cake in the iron rations. Septimus spread a napkin on the grass and laid out the sandwiches, the cake, and a bag containing an enchanting *bonne bouche* of crystallised ginger. He took up the silver goblet and leaned back against the comfortable hay, re-living his moment. The Old Boys had taken him in tow that night and hauled him off, who was neither a boy nor an Old Boy but an increasingly odd betwixt-and-betweener, and had fêted him at the Mother's Arms in the neighbouring town. They were days when men did themselves well, and the Old Boys did themselves very well indeed. Gorged on half a dozen courses and swimming in the fumes of wines, Septimus, feeling like an owl that has had a night out among trustful field-mice, heard his health proposed by a man who was in aluminium or artichokes, and who, as a tribute to the house of learning from which he had just come, called him *Victor ludorum*. Septimus heard himself saying that yes, he had done a few things in his time, and instancing his stroking of the Oxford boat to victory and rescuing a Metropolitan policeman from drowning in the Thames by jumping off Waterloo bridge into a turbulent tide on a winter's night.

Then a report was brought from upstairs that the Old Boy who had received the Oedipean kick was still in great pain. They all stood in silent tribute for a moment; and the chairman called on them, "while still upstanding," to render thanks to their guest, and they sang He's a Jolly Good Fellow, Septimus still necessarily downsitting.

There were times when Septimus wished that all he had said that night was true, that there was an oar on his wall, and a row of silver cups on his mantelpiece, and a stuffed pike in the dining-room, a bear in the hall, a few miscellaneous horned heads grinning from the stairway walls, and a policeman's helmet, handed to him with the Chief Commissioner's thanks, hanging somewhere on a hook. In short, he was often tired of knowing himself to be an oddity and longed to be excessively something else. With the warm midday sun pouring down upon him, he put the silver cup on to the napkin, recalled the exploits which it was becoming increasingly easy to believe in, and presently was gently snoring. He was dreaming of his books: *Pordage's First Game-Fishing Course, Pordage's Second On-Safari Course, Pordage's Third High-Diving Course.*

He was awakened by Valpy's rubber lips investigating his back hair, and, coming suddenly to a world of facts, realised his deficiencies. The cavalry-man had driven in a most inefficient picket-peg. Valpy was dragging it at the end of Mrs. Toplis's washing-line, and from Valpy's mouth protruded a shred of tissue-paper. This tell-tale clue drew Septimus's eyes down to the napkin at his side. Gone! The *pâté de foie gras*, the Dundee cake, the apples and the crystallised ginger! All gone. The silver cup had been tried and found wanting. Valpy's yellow teeth had crunched it to a bit of tin-foil fit for a hospital collection. There was left a bottle of hock and nothing to drink it from. Septimus drew the cork, put back his head, and up-ended the bottle. It had been lying in the full sun, and the wine was not what it should be. "Valpy," he said sorrowfully, "with the whole of this green field to browse upon, with last year's harvest assembled in this haystack to which you have but to put your lips, you choose to rob me of my fragment of hardy fare. The sandwiches I could pardon, the Dundee cake I could understand, the apples were perhaps irresistible. But the crystallised ginger, Valpy! Would not even you agree that that was going too far?"

Forth they went again, and now there was nothing for it save to be a holy eremite, fasting, a creature of mere skin and bone, crossing the Pyrenees on his journey from Paris to Compostella to defend a thesis that was rocking the universities of the West. Joanna Halliwell met them at ten past four. "Go and look for Mr. Pordage," her mother had commanded. "Happen he's missed his way." Joanna lost no time in bringing Septimus down to earth. "My word, Mr. Pordage," she said, "you're late! Mother's waiting for you in the office."

In Septimus's ears it sounded like: "Pordage, the headmaster wants a word with you in his study." His poses fell away, and handing the clothes-line to Joanna, he hurried as fast as his stout legs would take him, and not without apprehension, to meet the formidable woman he had so often seen passing by in her victoria.

5

Mrs. Halliwell had decided that Joanna had better be out of the way. A fire was burning in the office grate and a comfortable chair was on one side of a low table, her utilitarian swivel-chair on the other. Septimus's eye swept the table and flashed a reassuring message to his brain: ham and tongue, toast, jam, cake. He looked at Mrs. Halliwell with respect. She was pouring tea from a silver pot, and the fireshine made valleys of darkness and ridges of light from the folds of her dark blue satin dress. He had never known his mother. Odd, he thought, that this should cross his mind as he looked at Mrs. Halliwell. Her hair was without a grey streak: black and vigorous. Her hands were thin but strong. She wore two rings: a wedding ring and one embellished with a chip of not very good diamond. Alf had been able to afford nothing better when they became engaged. He had given her rings in plenty since then, but she would wear none but this.

Septimus ate with a hearty appetite, but not heartier than Mrs. Halliwell's, who, presumably, had eaten a good luncheon, too. He apologised for his destructive attack upon the food; and she said practically: "It's there to be got rid of." He explained what had happened to his midday snack, and she was not amused. When he was glutted she said: "I understand you're an educated man, Mr. Pordage?"

"Madam," he said, "I could have delighted you by appearing in a number of gowns and hoods and doctor's caps, clutching in my hand an assortment of diplomas, certificates——"

She cut him short. "I've never seen a doctor in a cap," she said. "All the good doctors I've known have worn silk hats. And not only doctors. I used to see your father about Halifax, Mr. Pordage, and he always wore a silk hat on Sundays and a bowler on week-days, with a straw hat for summer. Only working chaps wore caps."

Her face gave no sign of it, but Septimus had a feeling that he had better watch his step, that she was deliberately misunderstanding him in order to prick his bubble. This might be Throstle's Nest, but winged nonsense did not flutter therein. Down to earth was to be the rule. Through the window he looked across the terrace towards flower-beds of such formality that they might have been a problem in geometry—not like the gay confusion that prinked his lawn. They seemed symptomatic.

"I wasn't aware that you knew my father," he said.

"I didn't say I knew him. I saw him about. The chaps I knew were them that wore caps. I married one of 'em."

Septimus thought of the chaps that wore caps when he was young in Halifax. Most of them wore clogs, too, and the behind of a chubby little boy attracted many an iron kick as he went through dark streets on winter nights from school to home. They had helped to give him his fear of boys in mass.

"Well," said his hostess, "we needn't start on Halifax. I wanted to talk about a scheme of my husband's. He wasn't an educated man—not in the way you are; and that was something he regretted for himself more than I regretted it for him. He was all right as far as I was concerned. But he had this idea of founding an educational endowment. He never got round to it, and there's no obligation on me to do it, but I want to do it all the same. For one thing, there's a girl who can benefit under it. That girl Lottie Wayland that's been staying with you. She got to know my Joanna, and Joanna's full of the idea of taking her to school in Switzerland."

"The child already speaks perfect French."

"There's more in being educated," said Mrs. Halliwell, "than speaking perfect French or perfect anything else. Otherwise, I wouldn't be wasting my money on sending Joanna abroad. There's manners. There's a way of speaking and looking and walking, and, if you like, a way of just *being* something. I know, because those are the things I never had and never will have. Not that that worries me. But they're a useful extra like."

Septimus saw how much the doubts were there in her, whether

103

they worried her or not, and admired her spirit. He saw that she knew, as deeply as he did himself, that these things were not "extra like," but of the essence.

"How can I help you, Mrs. Halliwell?" he asked.

"Well, you know educational people, as I don't. I know bankers and lawyers; and if you could have a talk with people on your side, and get some sort of scheme fixed up—say to help three girls to the tune of three hundred and fifty a year each—then I'll do all that's necessary on my side."

Septimus said impulsively: "You're a splendid woman."

She didn't warm to the compliment. She was still thinking that a thousand guineas a year was a lot of money, when all's said and done. She rose. "Well, thank you for coming, Mr. Pordage. I feel happier now that I've made myself take the first step."

He noted the word "made" and admired her the more.

She looked at the clock. "I ordered the carriage for half past five," she said. "It'll be here any moment. I didn't know you would be bringing your pony. I'll see that he's stabled for the night, and Joanna will bring him back to-morrow afternoon. By then, I expect you'll be kind enough to send a note by the child to let me know what you've done."

This was a disturbing notion to Septimus, who would have liked at least a week to get into his stride. The clock struck the half-hour, and as if in mechanical response, the carriage went by the window towards the front door. Septimus said: "I shall certainly do that, Mrs. Halliwell."

"Thank you, Mr. Pordage. I knew I could count on you."

"Say good night to Valpy for me—my pony."

"Very well."

She said it firmly, without a smile, and Septimus, sitting back a few moments later with a rug comfortably round him, could almost see her moving to her desk and writing in a business-like hand: "7 p.m. Valpy. Wish good night."

6

Before coming to stay with Septimus, Anthony had gone for his summer holiday, in every year that he could remember, to Blackpool with Auntie Jess and Uncle Horace. He had memories of the pair of them paddling in the sea, Aunt Jessie holding her skirts above her knees, her legs showing stout and white, and Uncle Horace with his trousers rolled up, showing legs that were thin and hairy. Even to the boy's indulgent eye, they looked a queer couple, walking solemnly up and down, with never a splash or a cry of joy; going through the ritual not for fun but as the pouring of a libation to Hygiaea. It was supposed to be good for Uncle Horace's rheumatism. "It is well known," he would explain, "that marine salts penetrate the epidermis, are absorbed into the blood-stream, and carried to every part of the body. Not," he would add, with a cautious eye on the coming winter, "that their effect is lasting. But they may see me through to Christmas."

During the two years Anthony had spent at Easter How there had been no holidays; but in the July of 1914 Septimus said at breakfast one morning: "Mrs. Toplis, from Monday next, Anthony and I will have to deprive you of the pleasure of our company. We shall sally forth *en vacances* to the North-east coast."

The news deeply excited the boy. He had come to love this life of freedom in which he had been taught to make his own bonds. But now he was ready for a change. He knew every road and lane for ten miles in any direction. He had bathed in every stream, climbed the fells in summer shine and winter snow. He had seen the seasons come and go, savouring them as one never could in a town. Behind him was a long count of evenings when, by the light of a fire or in summer's dusk, in his barn or in Septimus's study, he had brought out his problems and listened to the oddly-shaped but well founded wisdom that could always illuminate and sometimes solve them. He had been prepared for the steps ahead of him—"always barring those occasions, my dear boy, when we are presented not with steps but with chasms"—and he was becoming anxious to get his feet upon new rungs. Chris Hudson, he knew, would be going to a public school in the autumn; Lottie and Joanna were in Switzerland; he was beginning to have a feeling of being left behind.

Lottie had written to him from the Pension Kempfer:

"Dear Anthony,—It is such a relief to write to you in English. We are supposed to write, speak and think either in German or French. Even if our parents know nothing of these languages, we must use them when we write home. In theory, all our letters are read by one of the Miss Kempfers, either the one who neighs, looks like a horse and is mainly responsible for French, or the one who bleats, looks like a sheep and is mainly responsible for German. How profoundly either the one or the other would be shocked if she knew that I was sending this letter to a boy! The only boys we ever see are horrid little creatures who are brought in here for the dancing lessons and then seen carefully off the premises. The boot-boy doesn't count. He is a slave whom no *jeune fille bien élevée* would deign to look at, much less speak to. Fortunately, he lives out and is badly paid, and is thus always willing to earn a dishonest penny. A franc a letter is his fee, and I imagine he does fairly well, for, of course, we all write to anybody we please. There's not much to tell you, except that this is a lovely place which I should, all the same, hate if Joanna were not here. We are to stay here when this term ends, instead of coming home for the holiday. The Kempfers have arranged a perambulating holiday so that those who wish may see the famed Swiss beauties. Joanna and I are among the doomed six whose parents have consigned them to this horror. So I sha'n't see you and Mr. Pordage for a long time. Give him my love, and say I remember the evening I spent in his study, when he showed me his quills and how to use them. I promised to send him eagle quills, but eagles are not so plentiful here as he and I supposed. I haven't seen one, and, if I did, I should have no idea how to persuade it to part with a quill or two. What the Misses K. would do if they saw me engaged with an eagle I cannot imagine. We have nothing more adventurous than hens, kept in a remote part of the garden, and we are not supposed to know that they lay eggs. Yours till some unimaginable future, Lottie Wayland."

There was also a letter from Septimus.

Easter How

My dear Anthony Bromwich,—You will have heard at the breaking of our fast on the day when this reaches you that the anchor will soon be aweigh and the breeze abeam of us, insofar as a railway train can provide such amenities. For myself, I am prepared to forego these fabled delights. I distrust Yo ho ho, bottles of rum, the canvas running free, and all the rest of it. Those who think that "the hollow oak our palace is" may remain in that opinion so far as I am concerned, but I should have thought it one worthier of some downy old owl than of a human being in his right mind. I speak with no more experience than may be gained in a punt on the Isis, but *ex pede* . . .

The unvarnished truth is—and when truth is varnished keep a watchful eye on it—that we shall take the railway train to a Yorkshire village named Sleights, which lies upon the river Esk, a few miles inland from Whitby. There we shall dally for a week or two, with the moors about us, the sea at hand, and a reminiscence or two of the Venerable Bede in the atmosphere. Not that we need allow that to bother us. Then we shall return to Easter How and continue our studies, in the hope that, a year hence, you will be ready to enter a

106

public school. That, I am told, is the wish of him who pays this piper and calls the tune. A vehicle from Smurthwaite will be at the door at 9.30 a.m. on Tuesday. Be prepared. Septimus Pordage, bear-leader.

7

It was a small country house become a hotel. Anthony unpacked his few things and stood at the window, looking down into the garden. There was not much to be seen. The place was ringed with summer-bosomed trees. Within them was a lawn, a grey sun-dial, and many roses. No birds sang in the trees, but insects wailed through the hot hushed air of late summer.

He was tired from the long journey, glad to be in that cool room, with the quiet pool of the garden spread beneath him. So quiet that it seemed enchanted. The sunlight burned on one edge of it, but long soothing fingers of shade reached out from the other. In the shade was a white seat with a trellis behind it, covered with roses, and he watched the petals falling red and white and butter-yellow as a little wind lifted the branches of the trees. Then the immobility of the scene was broken. A waiter crossed the lawn and laid a tea-tray on the small iron table that stood by the white seat. A moment after-wards, a lady followed, sat down, and began to pour out tea. The waiter made to sweep the rose petals from the table with his napkin. "No," she said in a voice that clearly reached the boy's ears. "Leave them. I like them." She removed a hat that had been hiding her face and laid it on the seat beside her. Anthony saw that it was Mrs. Freilinghausen.

Septimus was in his room across the passage. The long journey had tired him and he had said that he would sleep till dinner-time. "If you wish for tea, my dear boy, ring for it. It's all on the house: that universally-providing paternal house of yours that lives in Rio or Antofagasta. This is our first spree. We shall not stint ourselves."

Anthony went down to the hall and found a french window there, open on to the garden. Seeing that this was a hotel, it was surprisingly quiet. Not a sound came from the kitchen quarters. He opened a door leading to a sitting-room. No one was in it. It was this that he always remembered of the moment: a quality almost of trance, as though in the summer heat the world stood still. A grandfather clock, standing where the stair made a turn, ticked solemnly, gave a rusty rattle, and struck four mellow notes.

Mrs. Freilinghausen looked up as he walked across the grass

towards her, but did not appear to remember him. However, she smiled. "Good afternoon, madam," he said. "I am Anthony Bromwich."

"Bromwich?"

"I expect you've forgotten me. It's a long time ago now since I had an accident with my toboggan outside your house in Ackroyd Park."

"Oh, you're *that* boy!" She took his hand, and held it for a moment, looking at him earnestly. When last he had seen her, she was all furs in the frosty weather. Now she was in a cloud of chiffons, aerial and fragile. She was looking very beautiful, he thought.

"You must have some tea with me," she said. "Go and tell the waiter to bring it out here."

He went back into the hall, found a bell marked "Waiter," and gave his order. When he returned, she moved along the seat and said: "Sit down here by me." And then: "No. Bring that chair and sit facing me, so that I can see you."

He brought the folding canvas chair and sat down. She looked at him, smiling, and said nothing till the waiter had brought the tea and gone. Then she said: "I heard of you from my husband—oh, it must be a couple of years ago. You were living in the country near Smurthwaite, and your dog wanted to eat the soldiers' food."

Anthony remembered the occasion. "Captain Freilinghausen was very stern about it."

"Yes. It's the sort of thing he would be stern about. He's a major now—Major Fieldhouse. You mustn't call me Mrs. Freilinghausen any more."

She poured tea for him. "I didn't know," he said, "that you could have one name to-day and another to-morrow."

"Oh, yes. I don't know how you do it, but it can be done. I'm Mrs. Fieldhouse now."

He finished what the waiter had brought for him. She had eaten nothing, had only sipped tea. "Finish these up," she said, giving him her plate of cakes.

He was hungry, and didn't need to be invited twice. She sat there, watching him eat, and he became aware of the silence pressing upon the garden, broken by an occasional sigh from the trees, and of the rose petals falling. She picked up one of the white flakes and held it on her open palm. It looked like snow that her warmth would make to vanish.

"It was in May that my husband changed his name," she said. "Only just in time."

He didn't know what she meant, and looked at her perplexed.

"You see," she said, "Freilinghausen is a German name, and he thought it wasn't good for an English officer to have a German name. And now, when we shall be at war with Germany—it is only just in time."

She looked at the petal curling in her palm, allowed it to fall to the grass.

"But shall we be at war?" Anthony asked, surprised.

"My husband thinks so. That is why he is not here with me."

The boy looked at her aghast. War! It was no more than a word to him, as to all of his generation: a word without content as yet. That would come. But a word sufficiently powerful to send a surge of excitement through him. "I didn't know," he said.

"How do you live?"

"Well, there's only Mr. Pordage and I. He's here with me. He's asleep now upstairs. I live with him at Darton-in-Craven so that he may teach me. But he's not like other men, not any men I know, anyway. For one thing, we never see the newspapers. Of course, there's Mrs. Toplis. She takes the *Daily Mail*, and she's been telling me how we'll have to give the Germans a lesson once and for all. But I've no idea what it's all about. Will Mr. Freil—Major Field-house—have to fight?"

"He thinks that he will soon have to be with the men who do the fighting. How old are you, Anthony?"

"Fifteen."

"And how long will you be staying with Mr. Pordage?"

"I am to go to a public school in a year's time."

"Are you happy with Mr. Pordage?"

"Yes, madam, very."

"Do you think you are learning the things you should know?"

"Mr. Pordage doesn't say much and he never has exams. But I think he's fairly pleased with me."

She smiled, shedding her sadness. "Well," she said. "I think he has good reason to be. Thank you for sharing my lonely tea. Now bring me a red rose."

Anthony chose one carefully, one not mature enough for there to be a danger of its petals falling. He smelled its musky sweetness, nipped off the thorns, and handed it to her.

A few people came into the garden, talking and laughing, shattering the silence. Mrs. Fieldhouse got up. "I must go in. I hope we shall see something of one another and that you'll allow me to meet Mr. Pordage."

Anthony rose and bowed as she passed him. He soon followed her. The newcomers were hurling a cricket ball about. "Well caught, sir!" The garden didn't seem the same place.

8

There were only about a dozen people staying in the hotel. The women had put on evening frocks, but none of the men had changed save Septimus. And he hadn't changed into a dinner-jacket as one would do to-day: his white hair and pink face shone above a starched shirt, white tie, and tails. It was eight o'clock when the dinner gong sounded not with metallic clamour, but like a roll of muted drums. Anthony, who had been in khaki shorts all day, was wearing a grey flannel suit with long trousers, the first he had owned, and felt grown up. Now that the sun was gone, the embrace of the trees made the room dark, and on each table an electric lamp glowed through a shade of golden silk. It was impressive to the boy, who had not before seen such a sight. It seemed to him to belong somehow to the presence of Mrs. Fieldhouse, who was sitting alone at a table, not lit but irradiated by her golden lamp. She was all in shimmering white except for the red rose at her breast.

As he passed her table with Mr. Pordage, Anthony bowed and she smiled at him. He had not yet said anything to Septimus about her, and Septimus, though he had noticed the bow and the smile, was not the one to ask intrusive questions. He took his seat, the lamplight turning his shirt-front to a burnished breastplate, shook out his napkin, and allowed his protuberant blue eyes to wander, with no hint of approval, around the company: the blazers, the tweed jackets, the tieless open-necked shirts of cotton or flannel. He looked with satisfaction at Anthony's grey shirt and dark blue tie.

As the meal was drawing to a close, Anthony told him of his meeting long ago with Mrs. Freilinghausen and of his surprised encounter this afternoon with Mrs. Fieldhouse. "She says she would like to meet you, sir."

Everyone else was gone. Those three had lingered in the room. "Then take me to her," Septimus said.

They went to her, and Anthony said: "Madam, may I present Mr. Septimus Pordage to you? I mentioned him this afternoon. Sir, this is Mrs. Fieldhouse."

Septimus's pink paw enveloped her slender white hand. "I'm glad," she said, "that you have looked after this young friend of mine so well."

110

Septimus said: "Thank you, madam. I've done my best."

She said: "Though it gets dark rather early now, it keeps warm in the evenings. What a summer it's been! We could have coffee in the garden. But I think I'd better put on a cloak."

She went, and presently rejoined them, holding a cloud of dark blue chiffon about her. "Will you be warm enough?" she asked Mr. Pordage. "Do you think you should put something on?"

"Perhaps Anthony will be kind enough to bring my light overcoat."

Anthony went upstairs, found Mr. Pordage's coat, and crossed the passage to his own room. He looked down into the garden. It was nine o'clock, and daylight saving had not been heard of. It was dark. On the seat where he had taken tea with Mrs. Fieldhouse he could see the glimmer of Septimus's shirt front, the fiery point of a cigar that he had just lighted. Alongside him, Mrs. Fieldhouse was almost invisible, but he could see a long streak of whiteness where her cloak was not drawn about her, and on her breast the dark stain of the red rose. On the eastward side of the garden, the trees were a pattern of lace against the luminosity of the sky. A full moon was rising.

He stood there for a long time, not wanting to break a moment that had a breathless perfection, and that seemed to him to have, too, a significance, a content, that he could not fathom. He felt intensely happy, and at the same time deeply troubled; but he could linger no more. He took up the coat and went down to join them.

9

Anthony remembered it as the holiday he had spent not with Septimus, but with Mrs. Fieldhouse. At breakfast, Septimus said: "I shall walk to-day to Goathland. There is an inn there where I can get a meal. I shall not be back till dinner-time, or perhaps in time to take a brief sleep therebefore. Mrs. Fieldhouse seems to be having a lonely holiday. See if you can amuse her."

To amuse, to entertain, so fine a lady seemed formidable to the boy. The least he could do, he thought, when he had watched Septimus sturdily depart, was to dress with decorum. So he took off his shorts and khaki shirt and dressed in his grey suit, with a stylish shirt and tie. He went down into the garden and found her reading the morning paper that had come through from Whitby. She was looking grave, but smiled when she saw him, and asked him if he was off to a wedding.

"No, madam," he said. "But Mr. Pordage has gone walking for the day, and I wondered if I might have the pleasure of your company? That is," he added gravely, "unless you are otherwise engaged."

To his surprise, she impulsively drew his head down and kissed him. "You are a dear boy," she said.

Anthony blushed. He did not remember to have ever been kissed—kissing was not in Aunt Jessie's line—and, even if he had been used to it, he had reached the time when he would prefer not to be: the awkward midway time between the kiss of mother and the kiss that he had not yet begun to imagine. He stood there fidgeting.

Mrs. Fieldhouse looked at him almost with apprehension. She said hastily: "It's very kind of you to offer to look after me. There's a pleasant river here. Let's go in a boat. Can you row?"

"Oh, yes. There's a park with a lake near where I lived in Bradford. I often rowed there. And I used to skate there in the winter."

"When you were not falling out of toboggans in Ackroyd Park."

The banter helped to re-establish their relationship. "You know," she said, "you shouldn't dress up to go out with me. Not at this time of day anyhow—and when you're on holiday. I noticed that you were not dressed up at breakfast. Would you like to change now? I think you'd be more comfortable in the boat."

So Anthony changed all over again, rather regretting the loss of adult status that he felt long trousers gave him, and hoping that shorts wouldn't make him seem such a little boy that she would want to kiss him again. But he was safe: it was the realisation that he was ceasing to be a little boy that had moved her heart. When he got down, she said: "We needn't hurry. I've asked them to put up some luncheon for us. We can make a day of it."

It was a day Anthony long remembered: so lovely a day perched on the edge of so appalling a chasm. She made him realise this. Dawdling on the little stream, with the sun blazing down, and the russet harvests being gathered in, and the deep autumnal peace smiling with its treacherous promise of permanence, she sat with a sunshade over her shoulder and the tiller ropes in one hand, and watched the boy lazily dipping his oars, just keeping steerage way on the boat; and she questioned him about his life, and his hopes, and Mr. Pordage; and she was happy that he was what she would have wanted a boy to be, except that she was saddened by the ignorance of what was happening in the world, for which not he, but Septimus, was responsible. She gently enlightened him, for her husband was a man who saw the road ahead more clearly than most, and had taken care that she should see it, too.

They had no objective. They were content simply to be on the sun-flashed stream. They got out and drank their morning coffee at a cottage on the bank, and they got out again to eat their luncheon among the stubble of a reaped wheatfield. After luncheon she said that she would like to sleep for a while, and he brought the rugs that she had asked him to carry down to the boat, and spread one upon the ground and another over her when she had stretched herself out. "Now go," she said. "Get back on the river, or have a walk. Don't think about me. I shall be all right. That music will send me to sleep."

The music was the noise of a reaper in the next field. Anthony climbed upon a stile and looked into it. Two horses were pulling the machine, their ears pricked up through holes in the straw hats they were wearing, and the sun was burning down on the white-gold of the wheat, and on the scarlet opened hearts of the poppies. He sat on the stile for a moment, looking at the immemorial scene, listening to the larks invisible in a sky whose blue was pale with heat, and he was troubled again with a pang of perfection, the more unendurable because of the grave matters that Mrs. Fieldhouse had revealed to him. When he turned back to her, her eyes were closed, and he stood for a moment looking down at the blue lids. Then the lids drew back, and a darker liquid blue opened to his sight. He thought again how beautiful she was. She smiled and asked: "Do you know any girls, Anthony?"

"Only two, madam."

"What are their names?"

"Lottie and Joanna. They are both at school in Switzerland."

"Joanna is a lovely name," she said, and shut her eyes again. He took it for dismissal, and went back to the boat, and idly paddled for an hour, noting the things he must tell her: the small blue thunderbolt of a kingfisher that buried itself in a rotten stump at the water's edge; the field where a kestrel ranged the hedges; the bank where the voles leapt out to paddle in a pool, for no other purpose that he could see than that they loved to do it.

When he returned, she was sitting up, and she at once asked: "Did you say those girls you know are in Switzerland?"

"Yes."

"If their parents are wise, they will bring them home at once or let them stay there till the war's over."

"They intend to stay there, anyway. I had a letter from Lottie Wayland, and she said it was arranged that they should spend their holiday in Switzerland."

"Then it will be a long time before you see either of them again."

Anthony folded the rugs, and they returned in silence to the boat.

There were only three more days of Mrs. Fieldhouse's company, and on each of them, to Anthony's surprise, Mr. Pordage found a good reason for going off on his own concerns. The three of them ate dinner together at night and breakfast together in the morning; but, for the rest, Anthony and Mrs. Fieldhouse shared one another's company. The boy had an odd sense that she was snatching at every moment. She spent a lot of money. She hired a car and a chauffeur, and she took him about the county. They visited the watering-places on the coast, and York Minster, and Jervaulx and Rievaulx, and they ate sumptuously in grand hotels. At least, Anthony did. She seemed content to watch him and to anticipate any of his thoughts of pleasure. On the third night, to his surprise, the hired car came to the door of the hotel after dinner. She said: "Let us go up on to the moors and see the moon rise." Septimus said that he had letters to write and asked to be excused.

They went up beyond Goathland and found a great rock rising from the heather, and there, on the stone still warm with the days of that incredible summer, they sat down, facing east, and the chauffeur went, with orders to be back in an hour. They looked out towards the North Sea or German Ocean, and the moon, dusky and immense, came up, and slowly shrank to a silent yellow ball. It was a silence that oppressed Anthony. He was restive, too young and inexperienced to guess what such a moment, with her eyes in such a direction, could mean to the woman. Wrapped in her cloak, and wrapped away from him in he knew not what thoughts, she seemed content simply to have him there; and it was not till they saw the lights of the car returning that she took his hand and held it. She said: "I shall be going home to-morrow. I must see my husband again."

He said tritely: "I'm sorry. I shall miss you."

Then, for the second time since he had met her, she put her arms about him and kissed him on the mouth. She could feel his lack of response, his all but resistance, and she got up and said with a trembling little laugh: "No one need worry about that. Even your Lottie or your Joanna."

She was gone in the morning before he and Septimus were up.

CHAPTER 8

𝕯 𝕯 𝕯 𝕯 𝕯 𝕯

1

"*My dear boy*," Septimus had written soon after the return from Sleights to Easter How, "I have tried to prepare you for the steps ahead of you, 'always excepting,' as I once said, 'the moments which are not steps but chasms.' I trust that in time to come you will look back with no regret on the years spent in my tabernacle in the sane wilderness. But now a chasm is suddenly at our feet. Our country is at war, and decisions must be made for you and me. I shall join the Army, or, if the Army will not have me, the Navy. I could be seasick in a washing-up bowl crossing a kitchen sink, but what of that? *Nihil obstat*. Nelson, I believe, could not keep his dinner down to his dying day, and in these scientific times we have the advantage of Mothersill's tablets. I have arranged with our roughly-diamonded neighbour, Mrs. Halliwell, to take charge of Valpy and Cerberus, and Mrs. Toplis will remain here, a rustic unwed Penelope, pending my return from the stricken field or flowing main. But she cannot be charged with continuing your education. I have, therefore, written to the headmaster of the school to which, but for the chasm, you would have been making your way in the autumn of 1915. He will receive you after the coming Christmas holidays. He is an old friend of mine, and will show you the less mercy on that account. There has been a falling off in the school numbers: so many of the older boys are already in arms. Such are the days we live in. I have made all this known to your aunt, Mrs. Pickersgill, to whom you will now betake yourself to await your going to school. I trust you to be not unworthy of Pordage, or of yourself, as forth you go *inter silvas Academi quaerere verum*."

It is no unusual thing to notice a few white hairs dropping the first snows of age upon a dark head; but never had Anthony seen this process in reverse till he came down from the barn on the morning after he received Mr. Pordage's letter. Septimus walked in to breakfast looking like one of those freak blackbirds that sport a sprinkling of white feathers. His eyebrows were a jetty black; his hair was an incredible piebald. Mrs. Toplis, coming in with the morning bacon, stopped open-mouthed at the door. "Well! What have you been up to now?" she demanded when she had slightly recovered. "You look as though you'd had your head up the chimley and then fallen into a bucket of whitewash."

For answer, Septimus took his spectacles from his pocket and handed them to her. "Take these, Mrs. Toplis," he said, "and destroy them. Grind them to powder beneath your heel. We must obliterate all traces of age and infirmity. I ran short of Indian ink. If you will go into Smurthwaite to-day, Anthony, and bring me all you can lay hands on, I shall be obliged. I would go myself, but, as Mrs. Toplis makes clear, I might induce wonder. I think," he added hopefully, "that when the job's done I may be taken for a robust thirty."

The job was done, and it was an unbelievable Septimus who climbed the steps to Anthony's room in the barn a few days later. Moustache and hair and eyebrows mourned in the lustreless black of a widow's crêpe, and the shine of the pink face, the glint of the blue eyes, achieved therefrom a startling luminosity.

To the end, he had observed the pact: he did not enter uninvited. Anthony had asked him to come up, with the hope of staging a neat ceremony of farewell. He had even committed a few words to memory, but when Septimus stood there translated in a beam of morning sun, there seemed to the boy to be something at once so grotesque and so moving in the sight that he could only stare, tongue-locked.

Septimus asked heartily: "Are ghosts about, demons, and grave-yard creatures?"

"I'm sorry, sir. It was only that you look so . . ."

"I know. It is my fate, and now I have made it apparent. So half-and-half. And the odd thing is that half and half do not always add up to one. If they did, life would be simpler. Well, up with the *malle*. V*alpy nous attend*."

So nothing was said between them; and it was not till he was half-way to Bradford that Anthony felt in his pocket the small edition of

Palgrave's *Golden Treasury* that he had intended to hand to Septimus with a few "well-chosen words." He decided to send it by post, and, speeding through the fading colours of the autmun, he pictured Septimus reading it by a camp-fire or among roaring seas. But Septimus's wary Third Man had no intention that I should permit Me to suffer either of these indignities.

3

In Bradford, Aunt Jessie met him at the Midland station. For once, she kissed him, and the kiss did not disturb him as Mrs. Fieldhouse's kiss had done. But all the same, it reminded him of Mrs. Fieldhouse, and as the taxi took them past the end of Ackroyd Park he said:

"That's where I dislocated my knee. Remember?"

"That was your own fault," she said sharply. "I warned you often enough to keep out of Ackroyd Park."

"Oh, but if I hadn't gone there I should never have met Mrs. Freilinghausen. Did I tell you that I'd met her again? She calls herself Mrs. Fieldhouse now."

But this was a matter about which, clearly, Aunt Jessie did not want to talk. She said dismissively: "She can call herself Mrs. Fieldmouse for all I care."

Anthony laughed. He suddenly recalled Mrs. Fieldhouse as he had first seen her: all fur and bright eyes in a glittering night. Fieldmouse! Very good. He wanted to tell Aunt Jessie about the encounter at Sleights, but she so obviously was not interested that he asked: "How is Uncle Horace?"

"Got a bit of a cough," she said. "He's been playing the last week." And from this it must not be assumed that Uncle Horace was out on the football field or anything of that sort. In Yorkshire, playing means not going to work.

This was unusual. For all his love of keeping a fine list of ills, and choosing one to wear now and then as a man might choose a coat from the wardrobe, Uncle Horace had never till now allowed an illness to prevent his setting out promptly at half past eight to his daily work. It was even more unusual, when the taxi stopped before the house in Megson Street, to find the door opened by Mrs. Wayland.

"How is he?" Aunt Jessie asked.

Mrs. Wayland said: "I've given him his soup, and he's just gone to sleep."

Aunt Jessie went straight up to look at the sleeping Horace. It was

117

Mrs. Wayland who helped Anthony to carry his trunk upstairs. They dumped it in the familiar bedroom, which looked unfamiliar now to the boy, a shrunken den after the wide spaces of his room at Easter How. He followed Mrs. Wayland downstairs. "Your uncle's very ill," she said, looking at him severely, as though he were responsible for the misfortune. "I'm superintending his diet. I'm afraid your Aunt is no exception to the English belief that boiled beef and carrots are God's plan for the human stomach. If your uncle survives, she'll have French cooking to thank for it. But I don't think he will."

"What's the matter with him?" Anthony asked.

"Nobody knows—the doctor least of all. But I haven't liked the look of him for a long time. Well, I must go and put my own house in order. Tell your Aunt that I'll be in again this evening. *Au revoir*."

"*Au revoir, madame*," Anthony said miserably.

He crept upstairs, and heard sniffling from the room Aunt Jessie shared with her husband. He opened the door quietly and looked in. She was sitting on a bedside chair, with one hand wiping her inflamed nose on a handkerchief, with the other holding the hand of Horace. Horace looked very small. In the enormous brass-bound Victorian bed he was a mouse in a palanquin. There had never been anything to him: an insignificant little man who trotted off punctually every day to do a job that any other insignificant little man could have done equally well, and who, in between times, was querulously concerned to give himself significance by being a perpetual nuisance. Now, with the pouting mouth half-open, his eyes shut, his once-round face peaked and pallid, he had significance at last: death is death, whether of sparrow or eagle. The darkening room seemed to be full of it, waiting.

It conditioned all the time between Anthony's coming home and going to school. He had been looking forward to Megson Street, but everything in it was shrunken and unsatisfactory. All day long there was Mrs. Wayland who seemed consciously efficient, with spoonfuls of broth, and trifles of steamed fish, and sips of champagne, and there was a morose Aunt Jessie who would have liked to do these things herself for Horace, but could not, and resented their being done by Mrs. Wayland. And there was a young doctor who seemed to think the radiation of his own abounding health and vitality was all that the case called for. Anthony listened to his confident footsteps going up to the bedroom, his cheerful tones coming down from it. "Well, and how are we to-day?" It was a voice that seemed to be for ever rubbing its hands. Mrs. Wayland, who was always there when he came, would say scornfully: "How are we to-day! That's what *he* should be telling us," but she was mollified by his daily prescription: "Well, keep on with the diet. It's not a case for medicine. Kitchen physic, Mrs. Wayland, kitchen physic." And at night there was the sense of Uncle Horace on the other side of the thin wall, and of Aunt Jessie, whose nose and eyes grew redder as the days went by.

It was a relief even to receive, unexpectedly, a letter from Chris Hudson.

"Dear Anthony Bromwich.—I hear from my father, who has heard, I suppose, from Mrs. Wayland, that you are back in Bradford. I shall be there myself soon, worse luck. My father tells me that your uncle is very ill and that Mrs. Wayland has taken the case into her own hands. She would! A boss if ever there was one—what she would call a *maîtresse-femme*. She drilled the lingo into my block all right, but was I glad to escape from her clutches! I expect Lottie was, too. I'm told that that extraordinary old chump Pordage that you were sent to had something to do with her going to Switzerland. I should not have thought him capable of so intelligent an action, and when we meet I sha'n't be surprised to find you half-way barmy yourself. A few years in that *ménage* would turn Plato into a village idiot. Still, I shall always remember that he helped to pack Lottie off to Switzerland where she is likely to remain till all this war stuff has blown over. They've got it on the brain here. All the small twerps worship the O.T.C. louts as gods, a worship which, I need not say, the O.T.C. accepts with smug complacency. Our house-master, I suspect, has just discovered Shakespeare. He rants all the appropriate bits at us till I'm sick of hearing him. 'Now all the youth of England is on fire, and silken dalliance in the wardrobe lies.' Well, this youth is not on fire, for one. The whole business leaves me stone-cold. However, enough of that. No doubt you see plenty of it, even in Bradford, which ought to do well out of making shoddy and dyeing it khaki. It's an ill wind. . . . I expect that woman Halliwell, whose daughter we met, will come out of this lot richer than ever.

"By the way, the last time I saw that girl I was lying in a stream, and she was laughing her head off. You may remember that you threw me in. I recall this so that you won't feel any embarrassment when we meet. You can forget it, as I have done. Let's meet as intelligent people, who have grown out of childish rowdyism. Perhaps I shall be able to give you a few tips on how to behave yourself at school, to which, I learn, you are going sooner than was intended. Ever yours faithfully, Christopher Hudson."

Anthony remembered how Chris Hudson used to be punched around the board-school playground, and began to understand why.

As he folded the letter and put it in his pocket Mrs. Wayland came into the kitchen, carrying a tray from the bedroom. "I've just had a letter from Chris Hudson," he said; and Mrs. Wayland, passing through to the scullery sink, said: "Well, that's more than I ever do, or his father, either." She seemed so disinclined to say anything more about Chris Hudson that Anthony let the matter lie.

He looked through the scullery door, and saw Mrs. Wayland's back bent over the kitchen sink, and smelled the disinfectant that she insisted on using when she washed the sick man's crockery; and it suddenly came over him that she need be doing nothing of all this, and that in those days Aunt Jessie was doing little but weep and moan about the house. He knew next to nothing about Mrs. Wayland: certainly nothing about the bad mother in Nottingham and the atrocious husband in Paris. He knew little save that she had always been Aunt Jessie's butt, and that he liked her daughter Lottie. He saw suddenly that her face was strained and tired. She had done with Horace's things and was beginning on what he and Auntie Jessie had used at breakfast. He went in and said: "Mrs. Wayland, let me do these."

She looked at him as though surprised. "Well . . ." she said, and he took the dishcloth from her hand.

"You mustn't do this any more," Anthony said firmly. "It's very good of you to do the cooking for my uncle, but you must leave the washing-up to me."

To his surprise, he saw that the face of the *maîtresse-femme* was far from tranquil. "It's Lottie," she said, as though in explanation. "Or rather, it's because there isn't Lottie. I can't stand the thought that she'll be away for years."

"Oh," he said comfortingly, "the war won't last as long as that."

"It will," she assured him, "and I get lonely, and so I come butting in here like this where I'm not wanted. . . ."

She looked utterly forlorn. "And I get behind with my own work," she added.

"What work?"

"Well, all my French papers. I teach by post."

That was something Anthony hadn't known.

"Even with Lottie at home there was plenty to do. She used to help me. She is a remarkable child for her age," she added with satisfaction.

"You should have kept her at home."

"Oh, no! She was so anxious to go, and it would have been wrong to stand in her light."

"You'll soon have Chris to keep you company."

She looked at him oddly for a moment, then said: "I loathe that boy."

It was so frank, and spoken with such venom, that Anthony was surprised.

"I shock you," she said. "Well, let me tell you this. There was a night when I was up to the eyes with work. But I scamped nothing. I could have given them a crust, but I cooked them a dinner, as I know how to cook. And I served it as it should be served. Then I said: 'Now, it will help me if you two children will do the washing up.' Lottie went off to the scullery, but Chris Hudson just sat there. I said: 'Now, Chris. Go and give Lottie a hand.' He scowled at me and said: 'My father pays you good money to wash up for me. *Moi, je ne suis pas laveur de vaisselle.*'"

There was not much that Anthony could say to this. Mrs. Wayland said: "Lottie told me that you threw him into a stream."

"I did."

"A pity you didn't drown him while you were at it," she said. "It might have saved a lot of trouble later."

4

Like a soldier on leave, whose first thought is to throw off his uniform—especially if he is a private, with no fine feathers to display—a schoolboy likes to shed school-kit when holidays begin. Chris Hudson was not a normal schoolboy. Unannounced, he turned up in Megson street, and throughout the holiday was to be found in the clothes he wore when he arrived: a short black coat, grey trousers, black shoes and socks, and a white collar with a dark blue tie. He wore no hat, and, cold though the weather was turning, no overcoat. If it was raining, he opened the umbrella which he always carried. It was never rolled. That, mystically, was one of the school things. Any small cad who, in his earliest days, didn't know this and went about with a rolled umbrella, was liable, by unwritten law, to be hailed before a prefect and beaten with the offending umbrella until the notion of the sacredness of conformity had entered his soul through the weals on his bottom.

Chris Hudson, who was observant and, from the beginning, on the look-out for the things that would belong unto his peace, had escaped this chastisement, which, he explained to Anthony, was an excellent thing. "It keeps the little sods in their place," he said. "You can't have them breaking out into all sorts of fancy notions. When you go to school, my child, keep your eye open for these little things. They have no meaning, none whatever, but the more important a chap becomes at school the more they *seem* to him to have meaning. By the time he's head boy—well, if some jackass in the seventeenth century had decided that, for the last course at dinner, you must go on your knees and lap it out of a plate like a cat, he would see the world crumbling if you didn't do just that. Which is precisely why you must do it."

"I wouldn't," Anthony said stoutly.

"Then you would be a fool. Suppose you lived in a religious community where everybody believed in heaven and hell and so forth, and suppose you believed none of it—well, you could get along much more comfortably in your disbelief if you went to church with the rest and said all the right words."

"I call that cheating."

"Call it what you like. It's what most people do, anyway. The only alternative, in days when people really did believe something, was martyrdom, and martyrs are such a nuisance. They bring out the worst in everybody, including themselves. I cheer with the rest when the silly-looking sods in the O.T.C. march by."

It was a fine clear day, but cold. The boys were walking along the road that crosses Baildon Moor towards Hawksworth. The flame of the heather was dimmer; the bracken was in golden ruin. As always up there, summer or winter, the skylarks were singing overhead. Anthony was puzzled by his companion. He had always thought of Chris Hudson as a wee timorous cowering little beastie whom one tolerated if not patronised, as he remembered tolerating him that night when they took the toboggan down the slope of Ackroyd Park. But Chris not only talked big: he had grown big physically. School had put a bit of meat on to him: he over-topped Anthony by a few inches, and a sense that it was he who was being tolerated now made Anthony uncomfortable. Still, he no longer felt that he wanted to throw Chris into a river. He even found himself hoping that he might like him, but the thought of the letter Chris had sent from school and Mrs. Wayland's frank dislike was at the back of his mind, so that his varying emotions could not be reconciled.

They came to the high road and walked along it in silence for a while. Then Chris said: "I'll tell you what we'll do. We'll stay out to lunch. We can walk over the moor to Ilkley. There's a pub there that does you well. Then we can get back by train."

"I've got no money," Anthony said.

Chris put his hand into his trousers pocket and produced a cheerful sound of rattling silver. "I'll stand you a meal and a railway ticket," he said. "The old man sends me plenty."

Anthony asked: "Do they allow that at your school? I'm told that where I'm going they're pretty stingy about pocket money. Not that I could expect to have much, anyway."

"There are always ways and means, my child, of getting round regulations. I suggested to the old man that a postal order in an unregistered letter was the safest thing. If you spend the money on yourself, no one knows you've got it."

Anthony hesitated. "I said I'd be back to lunch, and I ought to be, with my uncle ill and my aunt worried as she is. And Mrs. Wayland will be expecting you."

"La Wayland's expectations are no concern of mine," Chris said airily. "She's paid for what she's doing, and damned well paid, too. There are those rooms going begging all the time I'm at school. The old man doesn't use them once in a blue moon, and the rent's paid all the time. Mrs. Wayland knows a good thing when she sees it."

"Well, you've got to have some place to go to for holiday-times."

"I wish it was any other place. Once I'm through school I hope the old man will have the sense to pack it up. Even earning the money he is, there's no point in squandering it. It's a fantastic situation."

Anthony felt there was something wrong with the argument, and he felt, too, that he should go back to Megson Street. But he allowed himself to be persuaded, and the pair turned into the rough path that climbs up to the heathy wilderness of Ilkley Moor.

5

Insofar as Uncle Horace had symptoms, they were negative, and consisted in his having no symptoms of being alive. He lay from morning to night in a stupor. Aunt Jessie said he was fading away like a flower, and at all events he was fading away. But on the afternoon of the day when Anthony did not come home for lunch he had a moment's brightness. He suddenly heaved himself up in the bed and asked, "Where's Anthony?"

Aunt Jessie said soothingly that Anthony was around somewhere and that he'd appear at any moment. "I want some Wonder Weed," Uncle Horace said. "I want to smoke out this asthma."

"I'll go down and send him off for it right away," Jess said; and when she came back from this bogus mission Horace was on his back again, the old lifeless-looking log.

When Mrs. Wayland came in, Aunt Jessie told her of this odd flicker, and was sentimentally distressed because Anthony was not there when asked for. She began to make quite a case of it, heavily elaborating the ingratitude of the young for years spent on their bringing up. Mrs. Wayland cut her short. "Nonsense," she said. "It isn't a cheerful house at the moment. It's natural that a healthy boy should want to be out of it. And what has Mr. Pickersgill ever done for Anthony that he should be bursting with gratitude? Nothing that I can see."

Aunt Jessie was outraged. "How you can stand there," she said, "and speak like that of a dying man . . ."

Mrs. Wayland had done a heavy morning's work. She was tired and tactless. "Talking nonsense won't keep him alive," she said.

"Well," said Aunt Jessie, "that's the end of it. That's the end of it between you and me. I suppose you think it's your fancy messes that's keeping him alive? Let me tell you there's more to nursing the sick than fiddling about with French saucepans. There's love. . . ."

Mrs. Wayland, who had known more about love than Jessie ever guessed, looked at her for a moment with extraordinary bitterness. "Love!" she said. "You don't know what you're talking about."

She had come in to wash up the pots after the midday meal, but now she turned and walked back into her own house. Aunt Jessie sat down and wept. She didn't know that next door Mrs. Wayland had sat down and was weeping, too.

Anthony learned nothing of this encounter. He had enjoyed his day out, and came back feeling the better for having spent some hours away from the gloom that shrouded the house. He was aware that he was not in Aunt Jessie's favour, for when he asked how his uncle was she answered sharply: "None the better for your being away all day," and when, later, he commented on Mrs. Wayland's absence she said: "That doesn't surprise me if it does you. She's a proper flash in the pan, the sort that soon gets tired of giving a helping hand."

6

Anthony's enduring memory of that time was of gloom and taut nerves that he had to be careful not to touch, and of one more day out with Chris Hudson. Chris's father, Dick Hudson, was not at that time touring the music-halls. He was appearing as a buck in a

Regency play that was having a success in London. He wrote to Chris, and Chris showed the letter to Anthony.

"Dear Chris.—With me in this play I didn't think we'd have a chance of meeting for a long time, except that, if the thing is still running when you have a holiday in the spring, it might be an idea if you didn't go to Bradford but came and stayed with me because, not being on tour, I have taken a little flat. But if this thing pegs out and I go on tour again—well, we'll have to stick to Mrs. Wayland's for you to go home to. But there's a chance of a meeting cropped up because I'm going to be in Leeds for one day. You know all sorts of things are being arranged for the troops and they deserve that we should do all we can for them, and so there's this great show in Leeds where all sorts of leading lights of the profession are going to appear without charging anyone a brass farthing, and I'm going to be one of them, though a shocking rush it will be, leaving me no time to nip over and see you in Bradford. I'll have to travel to Leeds on a morning train, and then nip back to London first thing next morning, because that happens to be a day when we have a matinée here. So I thought we might manage to have a bit of lunch somewhere in Leeds—say in the restaurant of the station hotel that I can come to straight off the train, and then a bit of a walk. You better not bother about seeing the show because that would make you too late home to Bradford. Bring Mrs. Wayland with you. A day out won't hurt her. Well, how are you? Your loving Father, Dick Hudson."

Anthony handed the letter back to Chris, who smiled. "Well," he said, "pretty illiterate, don't you think? Still, I suppose I'd better oblige."

"I should have thought you'd be glad to go."

"Why should I be?"

"Well, I'd be, anyway—especially if I had a famous father. Aren't you proud of him?"

A look of frank astonishment came upon Chris's face. "Proud? What the hell is there to be proud of? Do you remember the first time you saw him?"

Anthony did indeed remember that Sunday night in Manningham Lane when the buck swept by with the great cloak about him, and under that wing a wizened Chris shrank from recognition.

"Do you think I was proud that night?" Chris asked. "If you do, you're mistaken. I was ashamed to look you in the face, and whenever I go to meet him now I'm terrified that he'll be playing the same silly bloody nonsense."

Chris seemed pleased with his new uninhibited vocabulary of

125

swear words, but Anthony did not like it. He remembered his own fall from grace. There was a boy he came across from time to time in Smurthwaite who could have given Chris a mile start at this game and beaten him in a two-mile race. Anthony was fascinated, and one day, when Valpy was being more than usually obstreperous at the water-splash, he told Septimus that he didn't know why he put up with the fat little sod's bloody nonsense. "Too many blasted oats. That's what's wrong with him."

The next morning, when he came in to breakfast Septimus was already at the table. He put down a book he was reading and roared at the top of his voice: "Damn and bugger it all, Mrs. Toplis! Are we to wait all day for you to bring in the bloody bacon? This poor little sod is damn near starving."

A well-rehearsed Mrs. Toplis, greatly enjoying herself, kicked open the door and stood there, arms akimbo. "What the hell d'you take me for?" she shrieked. "A bloody slave to jump about the moment you open your damned fat mouth?"

Anthony looked at them aghast. Septimus turned to him, eyes blazing. "What is one to do with such a feckless bloody jackass?" he demanded. He got up and stormed out of the room, roaring: "Bugger the breakfast! I must get on with my bloody work."

Anthony, deeply upset, himself did without breakfast that morning and the next day a letter came for him.

> *Easter How,*
> *St. Andrew's Day, 1913.*

Dear Anthony.—From the bottom of my heart I offer you apologies for the disgusting behaviour with which I ruined the breaking of our fast this morning. I behaved like an unmannerly pig, or like one who had forgotten the beautiful perfection of his native tongue. Forgive me, if you can, as I, in similar circumstances, would forgive a thoughtless child, and believe me to be, contritely, foul-mouthed Pordage.

7

Chris Hudson was in a very making-up mood, and invited Anthony to join him in the visit to Leeds. "I'll shell up," he said. "The old man enclosed a useful postal order, and there'll only be the train fare. He'll stand us a meal."

"Will you be paying Mrs. Wayland's fare?" Anthony asked. "I don't suppose she's too well off."

"La Wayland is not coming," Chris said. "I wouldn't be seen dead with the bossy old bitch."

"But your father asked you to bring her. Won't he be disappointed?"

"That's his look-out. I'll tell him she was too *affairée* to come. She is, too. Up to the eyes in this postal French course. She had the damned nerve to ask me to give her a hand with it. Some idea of a holiday! Not that it's much, anyway, in this hole. However, you can trust me to make the old man see reason sooner or later. I want a flat in London."

The boys were walking through the Cartwright Art Gallery in Manningham Park. Chris called a halt in front of a nude by Arthur Hacker. He studied it intently. "What d'you think of that?" he asked.

"I don't know anything about pictures."

Chris grinned. "I'm not talking about pictures," he said, and added with ill-founded optimism: "I should say that's pretty well the real thing. However, come on, my innocent child." And, switching the conversation in a way he had: "How much longer is this ancient uncle of yours going to hang on? From what my *maîtresse-femme* tells me, he's pretty well done for."

Anthony didn't know what to say. He hated Chris's casual and heartless question. At the same time he knew that Uncle Horace's illness seemed to him nothing but a bore. It was upsetting the house, but for the man himself he felt nothing, and never had felt anything. He disliked being made to recognize this fact.

Chris gave him a sly sidelong look that amounted almost to a chuckle at his discomfiture. "Old people can be a damned nuisance," he said.

They came to The Browning Readers—those demure Rothenstein girls sitting by the fire in a quiet library. "Now that's the sort of picture I like," Anthony said to break the moment.

Chris laughed. "Ah, well. A *chacun son goût.*"

8

Chris ordered a taxi-cab to be at Marlborough House, and as he and Anthony travelled to the station he said: "You know, Anthony, the Wayland woman has at least the beginnings of an intelligence. Marlborough House is certainly better than 4 Megson Street. It must impress her far-flung correspondents. I wish, though, that the name was embossed instead of being rather shabbily printed. I used her paper when I wrote to Courtice. He will join us at lunch. Damned decent of him."

Anthony asked who Courtice was, and learned that he was head boy of Chris's house at school. "An upholder of law," Chris explained. "He is one of the world's great conformists. What he is told to do he does; and through him others are told to do the same thing in the hope that, in time, they will tell yet others. And so on to the crack of doom. He'll probably become a first-rate administrator among coloured people. I loathe the sight of him. Well, here we are. We'll travel first-class in case Courtice is on the platform."

They had a compartment to themselves, and Anthony innocently asked: "If you dislike Courtice, why ask him to join us at lunch? Won't your father be annoyed? He has asked you and Mrs. Wayland, and you turn up with me and Courtice."

"You have no parents," Chris said, "and so I won't waste time in instructing you about keeping them in their place. As for Courtice, I don't dislike him. I loathe his bloody guts."

"Well, then . . ."

"Anthony, you really are the most dense-witted little sod. I am *using* Courtice. Don't you see that? I am putting him under an obligation: a very small one, it is true, but an obligation all the same. For one thing, he admires my father. He calls the music-hall a traditional form of English entertainment, and anything that's traditional is right with Courtice. He has condescended to tell me that he has seen my father's show and thinks it good. My father should be proud to be passed for publication by Courtice. You see the whole situation is not without advantages, especially as the old man will pay for lunch. Dick Hudson will bask in adulation. Courtice will be able to pay homage to tradition. I shall have the hope of Courtice's approval at school, and the whole damn' thing won't cost me a penny."

Courtice, at all events, was not traditional enough to be wearing his school clothes during the holiday. He was a tall, fair, undernourished looking youth with pimples on his chin and spectacles on his nose. He was wearing a tweed jacket and flannel trousers. He shook hands with Chris and said: "Well, Hudson, this is awfully decent of you."

"Not at all, Courtice," Chris answered. "It's awfully decent of you. I've brought this youngster along—Anthony Bromwich. You don't mind?"

"Not at all. Not at all." Courtice did not shake hands with Anthony; he looked at him with a kind but wan smile, as though Chris had produced one of his pet mice, and he himself did not care for mice. "I'm enormously looking forward to meeting your father, Hudson," he said. "A terrific honour—positively terrific. I think parental relationships are extraordinarily interesting and terrifically complicated. You have a famous father, and you hardly ever see him. My father is unknown—an estate agent—and I see him all the time. I call that enormously odd."

He looked at Chris with owlish earnestness, and Chris shook his head gravely to and fro, expressing assent to the profundities Courtice had uttered. He sloped his unrolled umbrella across his shoulder, and said: "The great point is, Courtice, that you *see* these things. Many a man is surrounded by equally difficult circumstances and they merely baffle him. You see to the heart of them."

Courtice said: "Thanks, Hudson. You help me to understand myself. It's awfully decent of you to put it that way. Please don't think that anything I have said is intended to be disrespectful to my father."

"No, no," Chris said. "I'm sure your father's an awfully decent man."

"Yes. So far as my respect goes, he has that, terrifically."

"And you'll soon be back at school."

"Yes." Courtice's eyes brightened at the prospect.

"You are valued at your true worth there."

"Without presumption, Hudson, I think I am. But thank you for saying it, all the same. I find it tremendously sustaining."

Courtice took off his spectacles to wipe them, and during this operation Chris flashed a wink at Anthony. Anthony reflected that Chris had not sworn once in Courtice's presence, and had not called his father the old man.

The train bringing Dick Hudson from London was due in about ten minutes. The three boys sat on a bench, awaiting it, and two second-lieutenants strolled by, themselves looking like schoolboys, fair and chubby, for all their new Sam Browne belts and solitary shining stars, well-rolled puttees and swagger-sticks. A pretty girl was with each of them, and Courtice looked at the quartette hungrily.

"I don't know why it is, Hudson," he said, "but no girl would ever look at me. Not that I meet many. But I've been to a dance or two this holidays, and I don't get on with them, though I have a tremendous desire to please." He fingered his pimply chin. "You know," he said, "one has to face up to the problems of puberty with a terrifically clean outlook."

"Definitely," Chris assented.

"And yet, I don't know. It must be tremendously difficult to make omelettes without breaking eggs."

He pondered this dilemma for a while, then said: "Well, I'll soon be through the O.T.C., and then I suppose I'll be in uniform like those two. Perhaps that will make things clearer."

"I should think it very likely."

"You don't mind my raising the problem? I know it's stupendously delicate."

"We must all face it sooner or later."

"Thank you, Hudson. That's well put."

Chris bought platform tickets, and they went to await the London train. When it came, and the passengers burst out of its seams all over the platform, Anthony thought that, during the few years since he had last seen them, Dick Hudson had swollen and Harry Pordage had shrunk. It was difficult to believe that this thin and apprehensive thread was the brother of the pinkly-blooming Septimus. "Take my stuff to the theatre, Harry," Dick said. "I'll see you there to-night. And take Dulcie's stuff while you are about it."

Harry Pordage disappeared obediently towards the luggage van, and Dick took Chris by the shoulders. Though Anthony and Courtice were standing by, and a dazzling young woman who was presumably Dulcie was worthy of attention, he seemed to see nobody but Chris. "Well, lad, well," he said. "Blow me if you're not putting on a bit of flesh at last." He seemed to find gratification in this, as though the more there was of Chris the better it would be for mankind in general.

"You're looking well yourself, sir," Chris said; and indeed, Anthony thought, the years had done Dick Hudson no harm. He was well dressed: a rather swagger full-skirted overcoat, wash-leather gloves, a malacca cane with a silver tiger head to finish it off. But it was not the clothes: a certain air of authority lay on him like the bloom of success. He continued to look approvingly at Chris, and Chris was looking approvingly at Dulcie. So, for that matter was Courtice, who was feeling deeply concerned about the pimples on his chin.

"You know young Anthony Bromwich," Chris said. "I brought him along as Mrs. Wayland couldn't come. She sends you her apologies, sir, and asks me to say she's terribly busy. And then I ran into Courtice here. Courtice is head of my house at school."

This seemed to impress Dick as deeply as though Chris had brought along the Prime Minister. He took Courtice's hand. "I'm very pleased to meet you," he said. "I hope you keep an eye on Chris."

At that moment, Courtice had an eye for no one but the young woman with the blue eyes and the silver-grey furs. He said absently: "Hudson needs very little looking after, sir. He's a tremendously decent type and gives no anxiety."

"That's fine then," Dick said, as pleased as though Chris had been mortally ill and a doctor had now declared the crisis to be passed. "Dulcie, what d'you think of these three? This is Chris. You've heard about Chris." Dulcie looked as though she had indeed heard about Chris and was a little surprised to find that he was not wearing a junior angel's gown. "This is young Anthony Bromwich, and this," Dick said reverently, "is the head of Chris's house at school." To the boys he explained: "This is Miss Dearmer, who's appearing in the show to-night. We travelled up together."

Miss Dearmer distributed a few smiles, like a commercial traveller handing round samples. "Dulcie Dearmer: smiling through" was her caption on a programme. She played an accordion encrusted with mother-of-pearl and flashing with what she hoped would be taken for diamonds, and she sang songs about streams and dreams and all such languorous things, in a slow, husky, dragging and drugging voice; and though most of her songs seemed to call for tears she smiled indomitably. It was one smile, prodigiously sustained for fifteen minutes. Anyway, she often thought, it's better than being Alice Box, daughter of a rural dean in Wiltshire, which is what, in fact, she was.

They all five lunched together, and after lunch Miss Dearmer said: "Dick, do you think someone could call a cab for me?"

Courtice, who had been a mere dumb worshipper, occasionally passing her the salt cellar as though it were a chalice, leapt to his feet, and said: "Give me that privilege, Miss Dearmer."

She shook hands with the other two boys and followed him out. Dick went after them, seeming to doubt whether a man of Courtice's eminence should be allowed to do so menial a job. Anthony said to Chris: "Well, Courtice didn't spare much time for your father, after all."

"No, but he'll never forget that it was through me he met Miss Dearmer. So things should be even better than I hoped. What a twerp she must think him! But what about the old man, eh?

Fancy travelling from Town with a bit of stuff like that! Makes you think. Did you notice that Pordage was travelling third, and those two first?"

Anthony had not noticed this. Chris said: "You know, it seems to me more and more important that we should give La Wayland the sack and find a London flat. Think of the people I'd meet in the holidays! And that reminds me, young Anthony. D'you awfully mind if you don't come on this jaunt with me and the old man this afternoon. I don't think he's too pleased with the idea of company, and then there are one or two delicate matters that I want to discuss. There's this question of London, to say nothing of life's financial aspect. He's looking damned prosperous, don't you think?"

So Anthony travelled back to Bradford with a first-class compartment all to himself, feeling very grand and rather lonely, and hoping that when he went to school next month he would not have a head boy like Courtice.

9

It was not a large school. It housed no more than a hundred boys, but to Anthony, after the years spent with Septimus, they seemed a multitude. He remembered his first day and how, after chapel, the headmaster came down from the pulpit and the head boy climbed into it and said: "Let us hold everlastingly in memory these names— boys of this school who, going hence, did not count the cost, but laid down their lives for us and their country."

It was January, 1915, and he read two names of boys Anthony had not known; and then, in the sad light of the winter day, the school sang "For all Thy saints who from their labours rest."

And he remembered how, on every day after that, this same thing happened, and there were three names, and ten, and twelve, and at last some of the names were of boys who had bathed with him in the river that ran through the school grounds, and walked with him about the hills, and laboured with him in class room and study. And the time came when he was head boy and said the words and read the names, and one of the names was that of the boy who had climbed into the pulpit on his first day there and read two names. On his last day in the school Anthony read seventy-seven; and that was in the autumn of 1918. On that same day he had received a letter from Chris Hudson, bearing a London address, and containing the words: "I shall be going up to Oxford—Merton—in October. Do you remember that chap Courtice you once met? He's been killed somewhere or other. Ah, well, he asked for it. Thank God *la gloire* and *la patrie* never stirred my bowels."

Uncle Horace was dead, too; and so was Major Fieldhouse. Every week Aunt Jessie posted to Anthony the *Yorkshire Observer Budget*, and in July of 1916 he took a copy with him down to the bathing-place in the river. He was with Joe Morrison, who came to the school on the same day as himself and cried when the first two names were read, for one was of his elder brother. Anthony cried, too, because of the strangeness and solemnity and loneliness. He felt lonelier than he had ever done when alone; and when they came out of chapel he and Joe Morrison, saying nothing to one another, walked together till their tears dried, and then they looked at one another, and the small red-headed Joe managed to smile. His face was freckled and his eyes were blue, and all of Anthony's friendless years seemed to rush out and put an end to themselves in Joe's smile. There was no schoolboy pact: nothing was spoken; they ran together like two insignificant streams that find the same channel through the shift of a pebble.

On that day of high summer in 1916 they skirted the cricket field where boys were at play, and the swallows were flying overhead, and in the river cows were knee-deep under the green nets of the willows. Across the Channel new names were being reaped for the list to which they would listen in chapel, but for the moment the cup was theirs, and they drank in happy oblivion. They swam like otters at play, and when they came out and lay upon the grassy bank with the sun pouring upon them Anthony reached out a hand and took the newspaper that had come from Auntie Jess.

It was thus that he learned of Major Fieldhouse's death when a shell had fallen upon an advanced dressing-station. There was a photograph and a brief biographical notice which ended with the words: "Major Fieldhouse is survived by a widow, who was once a popular music-hall favourite under the name of Florrie Finch."

It couldn't be! He was back in the homely warmth of the kitchen in Megson Street, with the piled winter fire, and the reek of Wood-cock's Wonder Weed, and the walls spattered with the men and women Auntie Jess had known. Over the fireplace was Florrie Finch, tights on her slender legs, a bundle on her shoulder, a saucy feather in her Whittington hat. And, as clearly as he saw that, he saw, too, the summer dusk at Sleights, and the tall lady talking so gravely to Septimus, a lady as far removed as anyone he could conceive from the rumbustious life of which Aunt Jessie was so apt to talk.

133

He lay there on his back, gazing into the blue sky, saying nothing to Joe, deeply perplexed, and feeling on the edge of mystery. A third picture came up. He was lying in bed at the house in Ackroyd Park, that oddly forbidden territory, with the pain of his injury ebbing away, and through the thick folds of coming sleep, Mrs. Freilinghausen's face was swimming into his consciousness. Where had he seen it before? Had he seen it before? He couldn't have done, he thought, as sleep overcame him; and the next day he had gone back to Megson Street to find Aunt Jessie sweeping every picture from the walls in one of her mad campaigns of cleaning. He sat suddenly upright. Why had she done that?

Joe Morrison stirred out of pleasant sleep, opened his eyes, and asked: "What's up? Seen a ghost?"

10

It wasn't a ghost: it was simply this enormous Why? He couldn't ask Aunt Jessie, and certainly, when he met Mrs. Fieldhouse again, he couldn't ask her. He was young, and, war or no war, there were pleasant things to do, and the question, unanswered, troubled him less and less. There was no one, he felt, to whom he could possibly open it save Septimus Pordage, and he was in France.

There had been no stricken field or roaring main for Septimus. A letter from him occasionally reached Anthony, and the last had been headed "G.H.Q., B.E.F., France, Candlemas, 1916." It was signed by Septimus Pordage, Major; and that had been something to think about!

"My dear Anthony.—Your revered headmaster, whom I have little difficulty in recalling as Puddingface Wilson, colleague of old and best-forgotten days, assures me that my pedagogic method has produced that *lusus naturae* a reasonable boy—'unbrilliant' says Puddingface, 'but balanced and dependable.' He is confusing you, I think, with the 'presentation timepiece' which we gave him when he left us to make the first step on his journey to headmasterly grandeur. I hope to check his diagnosis one of these days, for he has invited me to visit him during a leave. In the meantime, here Pordage is, far from shot and shell, insinuated into the intricacies of G.H.Q. like a nautilus within the convolutions of its pearly mansion. I have no doubt that I shall tell Me, when the war is over, that I have enjoyed Waterloos and Sedans galore, with an Agincourt or two for sidelines; but, till then, be assured that the hide of your venerable friend is inviolate, and likely to remain so.

"Mrs. Halliwell, my most faithful correspondent, sends me excellent news of Valpy and Cerberus; and Mrs. Toplis has taken to the keeping of runner ducks."

11

Septimus appeared in the autumn. It was a bleak day for September, and Anthony came running with Joe Morrison from the football field to stand arrested by the sight that met his eyes. Major Septimus Pordage was pacing the gravel in front of the old house around which the school had arisen. His hair and moustache had outgrown their baptism of Indian ink. They were silver, and his flesh was pink, and to this extent he was the old Septimus. But it had been impossible for Anthony ever to imagine this old Septimus in uniform. And what a uniform! Soldiers enough had come to the school, but none so unmarked by any suggestion of ordeal or catastrophe. Never had Septimus looked so rosy, round, and super-charged with corporeal well-being. All the leather-work about him shone like a chestnut fresh from its burr. All the brass of buttons, buckles and crown of rank twinkled like the knobs on Aunt Jessie's bits of fireside ironmongery. The puttees exquisitely rolled upon his chubby legs were of light fawn colour. So was his tie, and his coat collar was emblazoned with the red tabs of the staff officer. There were even, above the left pocket of his tunic, one or two dabs of coloured ribbon. His swagger-stick shone like the pointer of a celestial lecturer. He was strutting, a pouter-pigeon on a roof. It would not have been surprising had be begun to coo.

The headmaster was with him. They were walking on the gravel arm-in-arm. It chanced that at that moment an old boy—so old! eighteen if he was a day—who had left school the term before and was already in a private's uniform and had proudly arrived on his first leave from a training camp not far away: it chanced that this boy came up to speak to the headmaster and brought himself to a stand with a clang of one boot heel against the other and a brisk salute to Septimus. Septimus negligently lifted his cane in the general direction of his cap and turned aside to leave those two together. Thus he came face to face with Anthony. Joe Morrison had scuttled away.

Septimus did not speak, but presently he held out his hand and

135

the boy took it, with the odd feeling that he, and not the older man, was giving comfort, as indeed he was, though he did not know with what difficulty Septimus wore the disguise in which alone he could weather those dangerous years. There were moments when he could persuade himself that he was at last the man of action he sometimes wished to be; but the moments did not endure, and he knew his masquerade for the insubstantial pageant that it was, and longed for its end. Meantime, he passed his days and weeks making translations into exquisite English of rough-and-ready documents captured from the Germans. His dyed hair had given him a reputation for valour that he knew had never been seriously intended, and had landed him in a funk-hole that he found none the less loathsome for being gorgeous. He was very unhappy, and at this moment was feeling ashamed at having received a soldier's salute.

And so they stood and looked at one another with nothing spoken till the headmaster bustled up and said: "Bromwich, you have permission to be out of school to-night. Major Pordage is leaving first thing in the morning, and has asked permission for you to spend the evening with him. We haven't been able to put him up here. He is staying at Ickes's farm, which I expect you know. He tells me they can give you a bed for the night. Report back to me by nine to-morrow morning. Well, Pordage, *au revoir*. It's been good to see you again. Look after yourself."

"I'll do my best," Septimus promised.

Anthony ran in to change from his football togs and to put together his night things.

12

The dusk was thickening as they set off for Ickes's farm. There was even a nip of frost in the air, and Septimus had put on a British warm—a bum-length khaki overcoat—that sported a collar of grey fur. It was a two-mile walk, and they arrived in darkness to find an oil-lamp lit in the farm's stone-floored sitting-room and a fire of logs on the hearth. Septimus asked to be excused for a moment and Anthony, alone, studied a vast engraving by Doré, framed in rosewood: a Roman arena in which many Christian maidens lay mangled amid snarling lions, while the upper air was as thick with angels anxious to extend a helpful wing as an evening sky is with homing rooks. The click of the door-latch caused him to turn, and with an odd pang of relief he beheld no more a stranger but his familiar friend dressed in tweeds and at ease in carpet slippers. His smile of welcome—as though he had not seen Septimus till now—was so revealing that the old man beamed too, and said: "Off with the motley" as he sank heavily into one of the fireside chairs.

But he did not sit there long, for Mrs. Ickes, who had already set the table for their meal, came in with a tray, little smaller than a table itself. War or no war, there was no dearth in the English countryside. She apologised none the less for being unable to feed them as she would have done in peacetime while she laid down a charger wallowing in an overplus of lamb chops and uncovered dishes piled with potatoes and cabbage. There was a home-baked loaf to help out these things, and to follow them an apple-pie supported by a jug of cream. "There's cheese under that dish," Mrs. Ickes explained; and she carried from a sideboard plates that were gay with red apples and russet pears and a jar of red-currant jelly. She looked as though she herself had been weaned on such food as this and would expect it as invalid diet when preparing to go hence. Then she announced that she was "off to mash the tea," but had the happy afterthought "Unless you'd rather try my elderberry wine?" Septimus said that indeed he would, and a black dusty bottle was carried in. "Go easy on it," Mrs. Ickes warned him, drawing the cork. "I've known that stuff alter the history of this parish." With these enigmatic words, she threw more wood on to the fire and left them to it.

They overfed themselves by eating less than half of what had been provided, and the potent home-made wine dispelled the melancholy which darkened Septimus's life because of his sense of being a fraud and a sham, the simulacrum of a valour that he could never attain. When Mrs. Ickes had cleared the table they sat on either side of the fire, and after some time of companionable silence Anthony said: "Do you remember Mrs. Fieldhouse, sir—the lady we met at Sleights? Her husband has been killed. I thought I should write her a note, but I kept putting it off. I should find it hard to say the right thing."

"It is always hard to say the right thing," Septimus said. "A man who could do it whenever he opened his mouth or used his pen would be one of the world's marvels." He had taken the bottle to the fireside, and sipped from his glass. "I want to say the right thing to you now, but I find it difficult. I didn't come up here, you know, to see Puddingface Wilson. I came to see Mrs. Fieldhouse, and she has asked me to see you. I wish she hadn't. I wish she had done this job herself. When she made her first call on me at Easter How, I didn't bargain for what was going to come of it."

But there it was. She had made the call, and it was all his own fault. He would have liked to put the blame on to his brother Harry. If Harry hadn't messed up his life and got involved with that music-hall performer, Harry would never have met Mrs. Pickersgill, and consequently Septimus would never have met Mrs. Fieldhouse. But Harry had called on him at a bad moment. He was feeling low and lonely; and, to mitigate his boredom, he had dramatised himself as usual, had seen himself a Fénélon taking on the formation of a young mind. He hadn't put it like that to Harry: he had said only that he sometimes felt like housing a pupil, not expecting anything to come of it, and what had come of it was all this! What had come of it was that astonishing conversation on a day of late winter a few years ago when I was writing a long cosy letter to Me, and Mrs. Toplis had knocked at the door and said: "There's a person. Would you see her? She seems all right."

He had learned to trust Mrs. Toplis's intuition about the rightness or wrongness of callers, and said: "Show her up."

Certainly she seemed all right: a slender pretty woman. She had driven over in an open carriage hired at Smurthwaite, and her face was glowing from the cold. They shook hands, and she explained her business at once. "I've been told that you could board a boy here and look after his education?"

Septimus, who had already forgotten what he had said to Harry, now recalled it with dismay. "Oh, dear, madam, must we be held to all our thoughtless words and deeds?"

Her eyes, which he thought lovely, darkened, and he knew sorrow when he saw it. "Our deeds—yes," she said. "As for your words, you must please yourself. I wouldn't have bothered you if I hadn't thought my information reliable." She got up as if to go, and he saw that if she went it would be with much unhappiness, and he said: "Please sit down. Would you care to tell me something about this boy?"

Mrs. Freilinghausen, who sometimes found it hard to believe that she had been Florrie Finch, looked at him, and she had been accustomed to look at many men and to reach conclusions that were not often wrong. She saw in Septimus everything that no woman would want in a lover, and everything that many a woman would want in a father-confessor. She said: "The boy goes under the name of Anthony Bromwich. He is my son. He is illegitimate."

His own tortuous mind had given Septimus an admiration for the forthright word. He was not startled by her confession: nothing in human conduct startled him: he would have made an admirable priest till it came to imposing penance. He guessed that she was in her thirties. He was but in his mid-forties; yet, bearing premature banners of age, he looked and felt as though she might be his daughter. He was aware that she was under a strain through carrying a secret that the world would consider shameful. He said: "You do me a great honour in thinking me fit to receive such a confidence."

Mrs. Freilinghausen said: "I feel that you have decided to take the boy"—he nodded—"and now that that's settled, I should like you to know everything about him. I'm afraid," she added with a pale smile, "that that means about me, too."

It often pleased and amused Septimus afterwards to recall that it had gone like that: that when the question of the boy's coming was settled, they had not at once turned to ways and means and money. Such things had been settled, haphazard, much later.

"I should think," she said, "that you don't know much about music-halls."

"On the contrary, madam," Septimus said proudly, "when I was up at Oxford I once attended the Tivoli. It was on boat-race night, and," he added, embellishing as he had done when long ago he attended the old boys' dinner at the Mother's Arms, "I spent the night in the cells at Vine Street. I was fined and reprimanded as the ringleader of most disorderly conduct. I still have a button that I tore from a policeman's tunic."

"I don't remember," she said, "ever playing in the Tivoli on a boat-race night."

"Why should you?"

"Well, that was how I earned my living. I was a music-hall performer. I called myself Florrie Finch. Of course, that wasn't my name. I was Mabel Sanders. My father was a farm labourer in Somerset. I've had so many names in my time, I sometimes wonder who and what I really am. Does that seem strange to you?"

"Indeed it doesn't," Septimus assured her. "That is something I *can* understand."

"Well," she said practically. "I mustn't waste your time. We must talk about this boy. I was a very good music-hall performer, but I wasn't a very intelligent woman. I was always overfond of men. That's why my father threw me out when I was sixteen. He was a Methodist local preacher in Crewkerne."

There was no need for such precise detail: the name she first had borne, her father's status, and now "in Crewkerne." What did it matter whether it had been in Crewkerne or in Constantinople? She was, here and now, a beautiful woman, something emphatic and convincing in her own right, and he wanted to say: "There is no need for any of this. Send the boy along." But he guessed that he was listening to something that no one had heard before, something that it was necessary for her to have out and done with.

He said: "I once passed through Crewkerne during a tremendous walk I took when I was a young schoolmaster. I was rather noted as a walker. I thought it a pleasant little town."

"Yes," she said, "it is." And he was glad he had not interrupted the retrospective glimpse. "I was happy there."

She told him everything. She told him of a night in London. "I used to make an entrance then down a little flight of stairs. It was rather gay and saucy. The point was that there was a wind-machine under the stairs, and as I came down, it blew up my skirts and showed rather a lot of petticoat and what-not. Well, that night as I stood at the top of the stairs waiting for the curtain to go up, I suddenly felt like death. Those few steps looked a precipice, and the idea of tripping gaily down them terrified me. But I had to do it, and when the moment came I plunged at them blindly and fell from top to bottom."

As she lay there, not moving, the curtain swung down, and she was carried to her dressing-room. A few moments later the manager parted the curtains and asked: "Is there a doctor in the house?"

Dr. Freilinghausen had been up to London for an operation that he alone could perform. It had been an anxious day that had drained him. He must see his patient again that night, and in the meantime the nonsense of a music-hall would take the edge off his anxieties. But he wasn't much attracted by the thought of attending this impudent-looking little puss who had tumbled downstairs in a wind-blown froth of clothing. He hesitated. There wasn't time. He had his other, and very important, patient to think of. He waited for someone else to answer the call. No one did. Then he walked to the front of the house, and the manager led him to Florrie Finch's dressing-room. He considered her with a professional eye. Her bones looked like a sparrow's. No wonder they snapped. He touched her thigh bone. She winced and shuddered.

"He terrified me," she said to Septimus. "He looked at me as if I were not a woman but a collection of bones—a mere skeleton hanging in a medical lecture room. It was something new to have a man handling my legs and looking as cold as an iceberg."

He went to the manager's office and telephoned to a hospital.

140

He himself lifted her on to the stretcher, and she was aware of his tenderness. He gave orders as she was carried to the ambulance and put into it. Someone else could see to the rest of the job: a simple fracture of the thigh. He called a cab and went to see his patient. The man was dead.

It was the deepest shock of Freilinghausen's professional life. The operation called for great skill and delicacy. He had performed it thrice, successfully. He looked at the dead man, and he knew that, had the operation not been performed, he would not have lived a week. The thought did not comfort him, for if the operation had succeeded there was a chance that the man would have lived for years. That night he walked up and down the Embankment going over in his mind every moment of the long ninety minutes during which the man had been delivered to him, to save or lose. He could find no flaw. It was the old ironic story: the operation had been classically perfect, but the patient had died. He was overcome as never before by a sense of fallibility.

"By the next morning," Mrs. Freilinghausen said to Septimus, "I had forgotten him. I was surprised when he turned up at the hospital. Long after that, he told me about the man who had died, and said he had come to see me simply to have something to do, something to take his mind off that failure. He seemed to like me a bit better."

She looked beautiful and helpless. It was difficult to reconcile her with the saucily-dressed little piece he had handled the night before with some distaste. He realised with surprise later in the day that he had been thinking of her a lot, and of the man who had died less and less. He took flowers and fruit to the hospital next day, and then he returned to Bradford. A twinge of alarm sent him back to his job.

However, he could not forget her. He wrote to her once or twice. "They were almost business letters," she told Septimus, with a laugh—and when she was out of hospital and getting about a bit in the autumn weather he found an excuse for another visit to London—a visit that prolonged itself to a week, and he asked her to marry him.

"I had learned so much about him in that week," she said to Septimus, "that I couldn't understand why he should give me a second glance. I don't mean about his work. I can't say that I ever understood much about that. I mean about him. He was so good," she summed up simply.

But she knew now that she had not misunderstood the nausea that had made her fall downstairs.

"Should I have told him that I was going to have a child?"

Septimus pondered a point rather outside his range. "It would depend largely on the sort of child," he said, "and it was a bit early for you to know."

"I had heard a lot about his people," she said. "I didn't doubt that I was not the sort of wife they would want for him. They might just put up with *me*—but not with me and my sins. Even if he had known, and said 'It doesn't matter,' it would have let him in for a lot of unhappiness. Those things do matter, after all."

Septimus said nothing, but he was glad she had learned that much. Everything matters.

"How do you feel about things long after they are done?" she said. "That's the test. You may have thought them good things, and yet come to look on them with horror. Or you may do what seems a bad thing, as I did when I deceived him, and never regret it."

She left him in no doubt that she loved him, and she raised every objection that she could think of to the marriage: his family's feelings, their different backgrounds and upbringings, her all but illiteracy in face of his erudition. "My love," she said, "you mustn't blunder into something you would regret. In any case, I have arranged to be away for a year. I'm going to South Africa, where I have a sister."

That was true enough, but she had not heard from her sister for years and, when she got to South Africa, never went near her.

"Then marry me, and go away for a year, and come back," he said; and the temptation was great to leap at such a perfect solution of her dilemma. "But that," she told Septimus, "was something I could not do to him."

She said to him: "I shall come back, never fear; and I shall come back loving you. Be sure," she said, "that you still love me, when you've had so long to think it over, and then we shall know that nothing can go wrong with us."

She had made up her mind suddenly. It meant breaking contracts, and she left her agent to deal with that. She said that she was on the verge of a breakdown and had been ordered a long rest, and off she went to Capetown where the child was born. "There was only one person who knew what it was all about," she said, "and that was Jessie, my dresser. There was nothing you could hide from Jessie. She guessed the truth that night I fell down the stairs. There was only one thing wrong with her guess. Just before this I had met Dick Hudson, the man your brother dresses. I liked Dick Hudson. He was new to the game and in a dreadful funk about having started with a flop. I took him about all that week and cheered him up and almost kicked a bit of self-confidence into him. Still, this boy who's coming to you isn't Dick Hudson's, though I believe that to this day Jessie Pickersgill thinks he is."

She said after a moment: "I was all sorts of a casual fool in those days, and Anthony was the result of one of these foolish casual moments. Who the man was doesn't concern anybody but me, and he's dead now, anyway. He knew no more about the consequences of our nonsense than anyone else."

She looked at Septimus's pink benevolent face shining under the silver hair. His chubby hands were linked on his stomach. She felt happy. She said: "Thank you, Mr. Pordage, for letting me tell you all this. I shall feel at ease when Anthony is with you."

Septimus said: "All that you have told me is in a sense unnecessary, but I feel proud that you have shown me such confidence. I needn't tell you that it isn't misplaced. But the thing I *must* know is what the boy believes about himself."

"He believes that he is Jessie's nephew. She and I met when I brought the child home. She herself had just married Horace Pickersgill, and it was her idea to invent a sister who had died, leaving a child whose father could not look after it. That is what Anthony has been brought up to believe. He may talk to you about his father, who is supposed to be now in South America, earning enough to make the boy's coming to you possible."

"Why have you suddenly decided to take the boy away from Mrs. Pickersgill?"

"I always intended to do it when the moment came, and the moment was rather thrust on us."

She told him of the toboggan accident. "We were afraid he might tumble to something, for Jessie always kept my photograph stuck up in her house."

"Had you ever thought, once you were solidly settled down with your husband, of telling him the truth?"

"Yes, often and often. But I decided against it. What do we mean when we talk about telling people the truth? It's often wise to do nothing of the sort. And I don't mean clever; I mean really wise. I loved my husband. I still love him. But I have learned a lot of things about him since I married him. He can be very brusque and intolerant, almost cruel. He never is with me, but I've noticed it again and again in his dealings with other people. But that is not the truth about him. It's just a part of his make-up. The truth about him is made up of all sorts of things, and so I don't feel called on to tell him about his

143

shortcomings. That's all telling the truth amounts to with most people: just letting off a bit of spleen."

She thought for a moment, and then said: "I know that having had this child was an important thing. I hate to feel that I'm trying to justify what was wrong, but the wrong was not in having the child. It was in the sort of life that made it possible. And that was ended. I felt that as I accepted him, and loved him, with all his faults, so he should accept me."

"You must forgive me," Septimus said gently, "but your argument is unsound. He allowed you to know all his faults. You concealed yours from him."

At that, she began to cry, and he made no attempt to comfort her. "I know," she said at last. "I see the difference as well as you do, but I always try to hide it from myself."

He said: "I don't suppose you do that without a reason."

"No. My husband does not like children."

Septimus smiled at her. "Now we know where we are. You have been trying to be a sophist, but I see you are a very ordinary woman who has the commonsense to act in accordance with her human feelings. Let's leave Truth with a capital T out of it. That's rather a big subject for you. Even," he said, with a grin, "for me."

"Very well, then. I wanted so much to tell him about Anthony that I am sure I should have done so sooner or later if I hadn't found myself about to have another child. He was tremendously distressed, and he persuaded me to have the child done away with. The odd thing is that, though that shocked me at the time, it didn't in the long run change my feelings for him. But I learned two things: that I was a household pet—a pet who meant a lot to him and on whom he depended in his black moods, and that any thought of mentioning Anthony must be put out of my head for ever."

13

With an occasional sip from Mrs. Ickes's elderberry wine, Septimus stepped as delicately as he knew how through the business of making his revelation. "I did not see much of your mother," he said, and Anthony, who had never supposed himself to have a mother, was deeply disturbed by the word; "but we found opportunities to meet now and then, and, of course, when you and I took that holiday at Sleights her being there was not accidental. She occasionally saw you when you were in Bradford, but you didn't know that. Do you remember a coffee-shop there called Bonnet's?"

Anthony did, and recalled how, when Aunt Jessie took him there, she was apt to be fussy about his clothes and his manners; but he did not know that the occasions were arranged so that other eyes than Aunt Jessie's might look him over.

"That was where your mother saw you now and then," Septimus said; "but after you had come to Easter How she did not see you at all until we went to Sleights. I, rather than you, was on trial. I had to produce the more or less finished article, and I think I gave reasonable satisfaction. Your mother is still living in Ackroyd Park, but you need no longer keep out of it. Indeed, that is where you will go to for your Christmas holiday this year."

He was not finding it easy. He tried to make it all sound as natural and factual as possible, as though this were the sort of thing that any boy might sooner or later have to face. But Anthony felt all at sixes and sevens. He had had a father and no mother, and now he had a mother and no father. Uncle Horace had never been his uncle, and now Auntie Jess wasn't his aunt. He felt forlorn, and tried to say so.

Septimus swigged the last of the wine. "At all events you have Me," he said. "Let us take a turn in the air."

They put on their coats and left the overheated room, and went out into the nip of the night. The fields lay quiet under the light of the autumn moon. The farmyard pond was a plaque of silver, and the air had a pungent smell from a pile of grain that had been dumped from a malt house. This smell, and the cold smell of moonlight, always made up for Anthony that moment when his life split in two. They walked through the sleeping village without a word: there had been words enough, Septimus thought.

CHAPTER *9*

❻ ❻ ❻ ❻ ❻ ❻

1

*A*nthony wrote: "Yours very sincerely, Anthony Fieldhouse."

It was the first time he had ended a letter with that name, and he looked at the words lying on the page as though they belonged to a stranger. It was January of 1919, and here he was, in Ackroyd Park, which he had so often been told to keep out of. Here, as at Easter How, he had a place of his own. It hadn't the spaciousness of his room in the barn, or that room's view of loveliness. But it wasn't, either, like his bedroom in Megson Street whence he could see nothing but the builder's yard opposite. From here he could look across the steamy, smoky, industrialised valley of the Aire to the hills of Idle, and, though they were becoming thickly built upon, they had not lost all their trees, and at night they were starry with street lamps.

The room in Megson Street had been small and ugly, the room at Easter How spacious and austere. This room was of middling size and luxurious. He walked upon thick carpets. At the fireside was a chair that he seemed to sink in when he sat. His writing-table and the chair from which he now got up, his letter finished, were Chippendale. White bookshelves ran along one wall, but there were not yet many books in them. The walls were of ivory colour. Not much showed against them: one Chinese vase of blue and white, of which Dr. Fieldhouse had been a collector, and over the mantelpiece two water-colours, one by Cotman and one by David Cox. They, too, had belonged to the doctor. Anthony had not got over the feeling that neither the room nor anything in it belonged to him. It was as alien as the hotel room he had occupied at Sleights; and he knew that when, presently, he went down to lunch, he would see Mrs. Field-

146

house, whom he could not think of as his mother, with the same admiration—but with nothing more—that he had given to her there.

He sat in his easy chair and read what he had written:

Dear Joanna Halliwell.—Perhaps you won't receive this letter at all, seeing that you and Lottie Wayland will be on the move for England any day now. I wonder whether you will remember your native tongue after so long in a foreign land, and I wonder whether you will remember your native country? There's one thing to be thankful for—when you went away you were too young to know many boys, and so you won't have the shock of finding how many of them are dead. For most of the war I was away at school in Derbyshire, and when I was head boy it was my job every evening in chapel to read out the names of the boys who had been killed. It was sickening, and I suppose that sort of thing has been going on all over the country, to say nothing of thousands whose names nobody bothered to remember. Well, there it is, and now here we are at peace again, and your mother, I'm sure, looking forward to seeing you, and Mrs. Wayland to seeing Lottie.

You will find plenty of changes, and why I'm writing, really, is to tell you of a great change in my own life, so that it won't be a surprise to you. I expect Lottie will remember the night when I injured my leg while tobogganing with Chris Hudson in Ackroyd Park. I was taken to the house of a doctor who soon put me right. That was just before I went to stay with Mr. Pordage and met you. Well, this doctor was killed on the Western Front. When I read about his death in a newspaper I learned that his wife had been a music-hall performer under the name of Florrie Finch. It now appears that I am this Florrie Finch's son, born before she was married, and that Aunt Jessie brought me up for her. Now that her husband is dead, I am living with her and have taken her name, so that the signature need not surprise you. It all sounds rather odd, put in this bleak way, but please forgive me, for I am not yet used to the situation myself and *feel* rather odd. Now that all this has come out, the relatives of my mother's husband cut her dead, but she doesn't seem to mind, and I understand he left her plenty of money.

Now for news of people. My Uncle Horace died, and my Aunt Jessie is living here with us as a sort of companion to my mother, and I must say that makes things a bit easier. Tell Lottie that I have called in to see her mother, who is getting along fairly well, but is anxious to have her daughter home again. Septimus Pordage joined the Army and became a Lieutenant-Colonel at G.H.Q. He wangled his way out quicker than most and is back at Easter How, where Mrs.

Toplis survives. My mother and I went over to see him last week, and he met us at Smurthwaite station with his pony Valpy, looking just as he did when he met me and Aunt Jessie years ago. He was wearing the same suit, I think. Poor Old Cerberus, his dog, was at Easter How, but not up to larks any more. Do you remember how he stopped your carriage once and caused your mother to speak severely to me, and how you afterwards encouraged me to bring him in to the coffee shop where dogs, in theory, were not allowed? That was the first time I spoke to you. I found poor Cerberus very grey and morose. He didn't know me and snapped at my leg. There were ducks all over the place, and when I got home I received a letter signed "Septimus Pordage, duckherd."

Chris Hudson is up at Oxford, and has persuaded his father to give up the rooms at Mrs. Wayland's. They have a flat in London. Mr. Pordage's brother Harry is dead. Yours very sincerely, Anthony Fieldhouse.

2

It was not to be expected that there would be a telephone in the Megson Street house; and Septimus said the contagion of the world's slow stain could reach him easily enough without his laying it on like gas or water. So there had been no telephone at Easter How. A month after writing his letter to Joanna Halliwell, Anthony, sitting by the fire in his room, heard the telephone ringing downstairs and felt amazed that the sound excited and rather disturbed him. It had happened yesterday, too. He had been sitting here reading the newspaper when the bell rang, and he found that his ears had cocked and he was listening intently, and then he crept out of the room to the head of the stairs so that he might hear what it was about. It was apparently the butcher, ringing up about a joint.

He went back into his room and saw the Journal lying on his writing-table. His mother had thought of everything. She had taken out a library subscription; the most reputable newspapers and weekly journals were delivered to his room; and there was this Journal, a folio of admirable paper bound in green leather. Nothing had been said about it, but there it was, and clearly it was thought that he would like to confide in it.

Very well, then. He looked out at the frosty day sparkling over Idle, put some coal on to his fire, and sat down.

"February 10, 1919. Just now the telephone bell rang, and I almost jumped. Why was that? A telephone is a commonplace thing to most people, but it is not commonplace to me. I cannot hear it without expecting that it will bring some great or tragic or disturbing message. This is absurd. I am nineteen, and shouldn't act like a child. Why do I? I suppose my years with Septimus Pordage had something to do with it. Now that I have been away from him as long as I was with him, I can think of him more clearly. I haven't met many people, but enough to make me certain that Septimus is an unusual man, perhaps a great one. I am sure that he has given me something valuable, but it is on the reflective side of life, and I sha'n't know how strong it is till I am in the life in which men work and act. Then, after Septimus, school; and that, too, is something that shut me up out of the active world, so that I jump on hearing a telephone ring!

And this isn't all. Just before Septimus came to see me at school, to tell me about my mother, I had a long talk with Joe Morrison. I am very fond of Joe. He is just what I am not, full of fixed plans for his future, and full of energy that will enable him to carry them out. He's my own age, more or less. Our talk was about the future, and he did stir up in me a sense of the importance of having a goal and persistence in going towards it. I was foggy about what the goal should be, but, now that my Uncle Horace—as I thought him—was dead, I was at least aware of the importance of doing *something* towards looking after my Aunt Jessie.

Then Septimus came, and the bottom was knocked out of all that. I was to look after nobody. On the contrary, somebody would be looking after me. And here I am, all wrapped up in every sort of care and attention, while Joe is already helping his father, who owns and edits a small newspaper in Staffordshire.

If I had been told, when I first went to Easter How, that I was Mrs. Fieldhouse's son, I might have spent the years there, and the years at school, becoming accustomed to the idea; but I see that, so long as Dr. Fieldhouse was alive, this was impossible. However, to have the news broken to me during my last year at school, when I was on the verge of nineteen, to find a mother when many men are thinking of finding a wife, has created all this unsettlement that I now feel; especially as my mother is in as difficult a situation as I am myself. She has kept an eye on me from afar, but now to have a son in her home has overwhelmed her. It is at times almost as though I were a child, not a man. She can't resist showing what she feels about me, and though I know that this affection is something precious that I should value, I am embarrassed when, for example, she kisses me, and she knows this.

Well, this is a nice beginning to my Journal, I must say, but I wish life would treat me at any rate roughly enough for me to hear the telephone ring without jumping!"

3

But the next day, when the telephone rang again, he still jumped. However, he constrained himself to sit still. His mother came into the room. "It's a girl, darling—Joanna Halliwell. I remember you mentioned her when we were at Sleights."

He went downstairs and took the telephone. "Hallo, Joanna!"

"Well, Anthony! How are you?"

"Very well, thank you. How are you?"

"Very well, thank you, Anthony. How is your mother?"

"Very well, Joanna. How is yours?"

"Very well." Then a burst of laughter. "How long do we go on like this?"

"As long as you like. I think it's grand just to hear you. How is your mother's horse?"

"Very well, thank you."

"How is Septimus Pordage?"

"I don't know. I haven't seen him. But I wish they'd put that water-splash of his into a culvert. It's an awful nuisance when I motor that way."

"Oh, you've got a car, have you?"

"Yes. Mother bought one to be waiting for me. And she hired a man to teach me to drive. Guess who's here with me?"

"Lottie?"

"Yes."

"How is Lottie?"

"Very well, thank you. Her mother's here too."

"How is her mother?"

"Anthony, if you go on like that, I'll kill you."

"You can't. You can't reach me."

"Can you reach us? That's what I rang up about. Could you come over for a few days? We'd all love to see you and there's so much to talk about."

"I'd love to, but I'm not sure that I can. For one thing, a chap I knew at school is arriving here in a day or two."

"Well, that's easy. Bring your chap. There's masses of room in this barracks."

"That's very kind of you, but I don't know how my mother'd feel about it. I'm rather new to her."

"When you've had a mother as long as I have you'll know how to wheedle them."

"Well, I'll try. And I'll ring you up, shall I? And you're sure you won't mind Joe Morrison?"

"We'll see what he's like. After all, if he doesn't fit, we can lock him in a room with a good book."

"Have you got one, or shall I bring one with me?"

"We could go over to Easter How and borrow Pordage's Thirty-fourth Coptic Course."

"Well, good-bye. My love to Lottie."

He went upstairs feeling extraordinarily lighthearted, better than he had felt for a long time. Still, it wouldn't be easy to break the news to his mother.

There was no manservant in this house now. He remembered the first time he had entered it, and how, after breakfast the next day, he had found a youth polishing the brass—a youth who had purloined the sixpence he had left on the tray for old sourpuss, the maid. It was odd to think that so unimpressive a young man—his mother had told him of this—had won the V.C. and died in doing it. When he heard of such things he felt useless, a do-nothing. His hesitation to tell his mother that he wanted to go away for a few days made him wonder what she would say if he found some work to do and cleared out altogether.

The youth was gone, and sourpuss was gone. There were two maids who did this and that, and there was Aunt Jessie who was Mrs. Fieldhouse's companion, touchy if one of the girls entered Mrs. Fieldhouse's bedroom which she considered her sacred province. On the way to his room, Anthony heard her in there now, humming to herself as she made the bed. He put his head round the door, and said: "Auntie Jess, come into my room for a moment. I want to talk to you."

"Now, Mr. Anthony," she said, "I'm not supposed to do any such thing. You know that as well as I do."

"I know nothing of the sort," he said. "Come along."

One thing he would not have was nonsense from Aunt Jessie. No one had told her to keep out of his room. No one had told her to call him Mr. Anthony. But she felt that she "knew her place" and laid down all sorts of laws for her conduct that infuriated Anthony. She was the familiar cushion that prevented him from coming down with too hurtful a bump in these new surroundings, and he wasn't going to have her stuffing the cushion with stones.

She came in reluctantly, saying: "And what's more, Mr. Anthony, it's time you stopped calling me Auntie Jess. I'm no more your aunt than the man in the moon is my grandfather."

He put her into the easy chair by the fire and said: "Sit down and stop talking nonsense. I want to ask you about something."

She addressed her stoutening body to the chair with the reluctance that Mrs. Toplis showed in addressing herself to a square meal. Anthony took a cushion from his own chair, shoved it behind her, and gently pushed her back. "No soft soap," she said. "I can't stay here long. I've got my work to do."

He filled a pipe that he had recently taken to smoking, and said: "I wish I had. What would Mrs. Fieldhouse say, do you think, if I cleared out and looked for something to do?"

"Don't you go on calling her Mrs. Fieldhouse. She's your mother, and so she likes you to call her."

"Yes, I know. I try to remember, but now and then the other slips out. What if I were expected to call you Mrs. Pickersgill? Don't you think Aunt Jess would pop up now and then?"

"That's a different thing. She *is* your mother. I'm not your aunt."

"Things are what they *make* themselves," he said, trying to clear his own mind, "not what we call them. When I met her here, and when I met her years afterwards at Sleights, I liked her and admired her. I felt tremendously proud to be about with her that holiday-time, but even then it was a friendly stranger I was admiring. You see how different this is? You tie up with my life—with all sorts of nonsense— Woodcock's Wonder Weed, and that snowy night when we went to see Dick Hudson, and the dandelions in Megson Street. She doesn't."

"You got no right to talk to me like this, Mr. Anthony. I just took charge of you. You're hers. You count your blessings."

"That's what I was doing. And, anyway, you haven't answered my question. What if I cleared out?"

"You'll clear out in God's good time," she said with unaccustomed piety. "Men do. But let it come along. Don't go out after it. The day will come when your mother will be as anxious to see you flying as she is now to keep you in the nest. She's just making up for lost years, and that's only natural."

The gong sounded for luncheon, and Mrs. Fieldhouse appeared, as always, just as Anthony reached the dining-room door. This was so that he might open the door for her. She loved small attentions, and created occasions for them. He drew out her chair, thinking: if only I hadn't to do these little tricks, or could do them less self-consciously. If only I could say something rude to her and she could answer sharply. I'm sure we'd both feel the better for it in the long run, less like the ambassadors of two different countries, all stiff with politeness and protocol.

There were only two of them.

"Well, darling, have you had a good morning?" she asked.

"Yes, thank you, Mother," he said, knowing that she was longing to ask about the telephone call, but would not. Perhaps, he thought, Septimus, who had drilled into him the importance of respecting privacy, had had a word with her, too. He was still able to speculate about her as about a stranger. He knew almost nothing of her life. What did she do with herself all day long? She hardly ever went out, and, so far as he knew, she had no friends.

"We shall have Joe to share our meal to-morrow," he said.

"Yes. I'm very glad you asked him. I'm afraid you must find this rather dull at times."

He was on the point of asking: "Oh, Mother! How can you say such a thing?" but was impelled to honesty. "Well," he said, "I wonder now and then why we live such an isolated life. Do you think that odd of me?"

"It would be odd if you didn't," she said; "but you know, so far as I'm concerned, it all goes back a long way. I hope Mr. Pordage did his job well and told you all about me?"

Anthony crackled some toast into his soup and kept his head down. Try as he would, he could not bring himself to think dispassionately about what Septimus had told him. Septimus had been calm enough. All very well for him, Anthony thought. He was not involved as I am. There was something that disturbed him unbearably when he allowed his mind to dwell on the matter. But that was not often. For the most part, he shied away from it. He knew that if a stranger named Mrs. Fieldhouse, of whom his memories were all charming, had adopted him—unusual though it would have been for anyone to adopt a young man of nineteen—he would have felt happier than he did now when his charming memories had been confused by an episode that hurt him. It shouldn't. I know it shouldn't, he told himself. But it did, all the same, and there was nothing he could do about it. He looked up at her. "Yes," he said. "I think Mr. Pordage made it all clear."

"You see," she said, "when I first came here as Mrs. Freilinghausen,

I was terribly anxious to do nothing to hurt my husband. I wasn't used to the sort of people he knew, though that needn't have worried me, for I saw little enough of them. He was a very busy man, and when he had time for it he liked nothing better than to be alone with me. And I was the same way. I didn't gad about. I was afraid of myself, afraid of my accent, afraid of my manners. Manners are such odd things. The smallest point gives you away. My husband used to laugh at me, and indeed I needn't have worried. But, anyway, it all led to a life that was very lonely once he was gone."

No, thought Anthony, she needn't have worried. What she had been then he had no means of knowing. But the woman he had met here on a winter night, and at Sleights through those autumn days, need not have worried. That was the woman who could still charm his imagination, and he wished there had never been this other woman mixed up with her and blurring both images. He was terribly confused.

As usual, he thrust the confusion from him, and said with the cruel directness of youth: "Joanna Halliwell is just back after being in Switzerland all through the war. She wants me to go over there on a visit. I think it would be a good idea, don't you?"

She didn't think it at all a good idea. "Yes," she said. "It will be an excellent thing for you to get to know some young people. I suppose you'll be off as soon as Joe Morrison goes home?"

"Well, I suggested to her that Joe might come with me, and she says that would be all right. There's another girl there—a Lottie Wayland, whose mother lived next door to Auntie Jess in Megson Street. Lottie was in Switzerland, too. I believe Joanna's mother paid the bills. She's rather rich. She has a woollen mill in Smurthwaite. When I was there with Mr. Pordage I thought her rather a terror. I remember the day I first met Joanna. Mr. Pordage had a dog named Cerberus, and I was walking with him towards Smurthwaite. . . ."

He prattled on, and she encouraged him with a word here and there. By the time he had finished his coffee he realised with a little shock that he had been talking to her easily and without restraint for the first time since coming to Ackroyd Park. It was the way he had always wanted to talk to the beautiful lady at Sleights, but had been unable to do so because of the memory of her kiss. As for Mrs. Fieldhouse, she was thinking: Well, that was better. It could be a start. And then, with grief which she strove to hide, she thought: And this is the moment when he wants to be off!

He rang up Throstle's Nest, and a servant said that Miss Halliwell was out.

"Is Miss Wayland in?"

"No, sir. Would you wish to speak to Mrs. Halliwell?"

The last thing he wanted to do was speak to Mrs. Halliwell, but at that moment Mrs. Halliwell took the telephone from the servant's hand and Anthony heard her voice. "Who is that? This is Mrs. Halliwell."

"Oh, good afternoon, Mrs. Halliwell. This is Anthony Bromwich. Well, Anthony Fieldhouse, actually."

"What are you talking about?" The formidable figure sitting erect in the victoria swam into his view. "Who are you?"

"Well, I expect you remember Anthony Bromwich who used to be with Mr. Pordage? That's me—or rather I. But now my mother's turned up, and her name's Fieldhouse. I'll be able to explain better when we meet."

"What do you mean—when we meet?"

"Oh, perhaps Joanna forgot to tell you. She's invited me over and I'm bringing a chap named Morrison. He was at school with me."

"Thank you for letting me know," Mrs. Halliwell said ominously and the telephone went dead. But this wasn't as definitive as Anthony supposed. The next day he received a brief note from Joanna: "Really, Mother is the limit! We shall be calling for you and your Joe Morrison the day after to-morrow. J." Scribbled after the J was "and Lottie."

4

Joe Morrison had often spoken to Anthony about his father, who was a widower with no child save Joe now that his elder son had been killed in the war. "He's a proper card," Joe used to say, and it was evident that he held this card in deep affection. He always came back from holidays mightily refreshed. He once told the story of how his father handed him a pound note and said: "Joe, there's an illiterate fool somewhere who always translates the French communiqués wrongly. And the joke is that no English newspaper, so far as I can see, knows that they're wrong." He showed Joe a line in a newspaper that read: "The French are actually holding the positions gained yesterday." "Now, my boy, I'll bet you twenty to one in pounds that you can't see what's wrong there."

Joe studied the phrase and said: "Well, sir, I imagine that in the French the word used was *actuellement*, which doesn't mean *actually* but *now, at this moment.*"

"Out of the mouths of babes and sucklings, Joe!" He handed over twenty pounds.

"Now, Joe, I'll bet you twenty to one in pounds that you can't tell me what that word *actually* means, assuming that the sentence was not translated, but a piece of straight English."

"Well, sir, it means—well, actually is just actually, isn't it?"

"Hand over."

Joe handed over twenty pounds.

"It means nothing whatever, Joe. It's dead wood. I defy you to produce any sentence containing the word *actually* from which it could not be cut out, leaving the sense what it was before. Any sub-editor on my paper who didn't cut it out would be in danger of the sack."

"The cream of the joke," Joe said to Anthony, "is that I was actually a quid better off."

When Anthony met Joe at the station the next day, he was surprised to find him companioned by the card, who, it seemed to him, was Joe grown up. Leonard Morrison had his son's close-cropped red hair, blue eyes and ruddy freckled face. His red eyebrows bristled like prawns; that was the only difference, but no doubt Joe's would bristle, too, in time.

Mr. Morrison crushed Anthony's hand and said: "I'll just dump this bag in the hotel. I'm staying there to-night. Then we'll go on and have lunch at your place."

He put his broad shoulder to the swing door of the station hotel and left the boys standing there. "Your father takes his welcome for granted, Joe," Anthony said. "My mother's not expecting him."

Joe said: "He always takes his welcome for granted, and it always works."

Mr. Morrison soon joined them and said: "How far is this place of yours, Anthony? Can we walk it, or do we take a taxi?"

"We can walk it inside twenty minutes."

"Come on then. Let's walk while they let us. Take my word, inside twenty years walking will be a dangerous occupation."

He set a brisk pace up the hill of Darley Street, and they came on to the flat by the Theatre Royal in Manningham Lane. "Let's buy four stalls," he said. "We'll take your mother out to-night."

Anthony wasn't sure whether this was a good thing to do. "My mother may have something else in mind for to-night, Mr. Morrison."

"Ah, well. I'll turn the ticket in at the box office, and we three can go. Does your mother go out much?"

"Well, no, she doesn't."

"There you are, you see. We'll give her a night out. Do you take her out much?"

"I'm afraid not."

"You ought to. Joe's been telling me about her. I expect she'd enjoy it no end if you took her about a bit."

It was a new point of view to Anthony. It had never occurred to him to play the squire.

"I'll tell you one thing about women, young Anthony: mothers, wives, sisters, daughters, granddaughters and grandmothers, if you like: pay 'em little attentions, give 'em little treats. Don't use 'em like furniture. My mother died when I was one. I never had a sister or a granddaughter and I never knew my grandmother. But a wise man is entitled to generalise from small particulars. And so if a man comes grizzling to me about trouble at home I ask him: When did you last buy her a necklace? When did you last take her out to dinner or lay a rose on the breakfast plate on your wedding anniversary? So this is Ackroyd Park? Come on. Let's meet your mother."

He breezed along the path between the unlovely rhododendrons as though the place belonged to him, and Joe and Anthony tagged along behind, Joe with a rucksack on his back containing the things for his visit. A maid opened the door and Mrs. Fieldhouse was in the hall, which was a comfortable room with a fire on the hearth. She came forward to meet them, and it was Leonard Morrison who was first over the doorstep and striding towards her with extended hand. "Well," he said, "I never thought I'd meet *you!*"

She took his hand and looked at him, surprised. "Why," she asked, "have we met before?"

"Ay," he said, with a grin, "I'm a ghost out of your past."

She was not disconcerted, but she was perplexed, and her brow took on a small frown in her effort at memory.

He said: "My boy Joe here—Joe, shake hands with Mrs. Fieldhouse—Joe's been telling me what Anthony's been telling *him*, and that's how I know that you were once Florrie Finch."

"Oh, I see."

"I'll bet you don't," he said, standing comfortably with his back to the fire. "I was a young reporter then, and I used to do the music-halls among other things. I thought you were marvellous and I gave you marvellous write-ups. Why," he said, the impudent grin coming back, "you probably owe your career to me!"

She looked at him with a smile, and said: "Thank you for being a wonderful audience."

"Ay," he said, "and that's how I come to invite myself to what I

157

hope will be a wonderful lunch. Can you make room for me?"

"Yes," she said, "yes, I'm sure we can. If you'll excuse me, I'll go and have the table rearranged."

"Never mind the table. I don't want to eat the table. It's the joint I'm worrying about. How big is it?"

"Big enough," she said, and went out laughing.

It was a long time since Anthony had enjoyed a meal so much or felt so free of constraint in his mother's presence. There were so many things he wanted to ask her about the years hidden in a mist that, it seemed to him, she would prefer not to have dispersed; and Leonard Morrison had no inhibitions about ripping the veil. With a plate of roast beef and Yorkshire pudding before him, and, at his elbow, a bottle of Pommard from which nobody but he drank, he was a figure to loosen the tautest nerves and resolve the most tangled complications. Anthony recalled a night when Auntie Jess had said: "D'you remember that time in Birmingham—I believe Jack Pleasants was on the bill. . . ." And his mother had given her a grand lady look and a look that said *Pas devant les enfants*, and Anthony, who had pricked up his ears, hoping for a ray in the darkness, felt the curtain close down as if upon something unmentionable.

Everything was mentionable to Leonard Morrison, obviously a true lover of the old English music-hall, and he talked of Ella Shields and Fred Karno and Little Tich, and the Ten Loonies and Wilkie Bard, and Robey and Vesta Tillie, Harry Weldon and Clarice Mayne with her That. And he talked of all these things and people as though, naturally, they would interest one who had been among them and a part of them; and he was not daunted by his sense of her resistance, by her clinging, as if to a life line, to what lay between her and all that. "Now if I were ever to write a book about that old music-hall," he said, "and I've sometimes thought of doing it before all this revue stuff and boiled-shirt performers kill it stone dead, I'd still want to write about Florrie Finch as enthusiastically as I did when I was a youngster lording it in a free press seat in the stalls."

"For me," she said, "it's all dead."

"Don't you believe it, Mrs. Fieldhouse. Nothing's dead till the person who is the sum total of it is dead. And you don't look very dead to me. Don't you agree, Joe?"

"Dad, you know I've been brought up to agree with every word you say or else——"

"Ay," Leonard said, looking at him with affection, "he looks a whipped cur, don't you think, Mrs. Fieldhouse?" And without giving

158

her time to answer, he went on: "The trouble with you is that you're bottling up the most real thing in you. You've been worried to death that you wouldn't be able to play the grand lady, as though playing the grand lady mattered a twopenny damn to anyone. All this," he said, waving his hand in a comprehensive gesture that embraced the Pommard, the dining-room and the whole of Ackroyd Park, not to mention Bradford and the West Riding of Yorkshire, "all this shouldn't matter the twiddle of a lamb's tail against being able to say. 'I was Florrie Finch.' That's something real and important that you still are in your own right."

He finished his cheese, swigged what was left in his glass, and asked: "Would you call me a reticent sort of chap?"

She said: "Well, I wouldn't say you had ever learned to temper your hilarity with a modicum of reserve."

They both burst into laughter that surprised Anthony and Joe, who had never heard the old Robey gag.

"That's better," Leonard said, recognising a lowering of defences. "Now look. I came over with Joe because there's a chap here who may want to work on my paper. I'm going along to see him this afternoon, and then we'll all get out to the theatre to-night. Come and eat with me at my hotel first. How would you like that?"

To Anthony's surprise, she accepted with apparent pleasure, and said: "Anthony tells me your paper is a weekly. Do you have to make special visits to find talent for that sort of thing? I thought they just came out anyhow, full of local weddings, and obituaries of the dustman and chapel-keeper, and what the mayor said at the annual dinner of the football team."

Leonard settled back in his chair and lit a cigar. "You can go, Joe, if you like," he said, "and take Anthony with you. You've heard all this before."

Anthony said: "I'd like to hear it," for obviously Leonard had a lot on his chest.

"Well, then," he said, spreading his broad hands on the table before him, "in me you see an apostle." He looked a challenge, but no one denied it. "I know as well as the next man that weekly papers live on the insane desire of Tom, Dick and Harry to see their names in print. When Jinny Jones gets married—'a well-liked and popular assistant whose ready smile was known at Messrs. Marks and Spencer's local emporium'—we must be told everything she wore, pretty well from her drawers up to the 'going-away ensemble' that will grace some bed-and-breakfast establishment in Bognor Regis for the next week or so. And not only hers, but her mother's and her mother-in-law's, and we shall learn all about pages and bridesmaids and 'bride's attendants' and what *they* wore and what flowers they carried, and, above all, we shall learn their names, so that not one of them will fail to buy the paper and look popeyed at their names IN PRINT. When Bill Smith dies—'for forty years the respected groundsman of Totterington Athletic'—we must know the names of everyone who crawled behind his coffin and everyone who sent a wreath; and when the local amateurs put on *The Dover Road* you will discover not only how wonderful they were but the name of every man Jack and woman Jill down to the chap who sweeps up the shavings after the stage carpenter. The nearer you can make your paper to a list of names the nearer you are to a nice steady and profitable circulation. Well, then, *Damn the Circulation* is the motto of the *Longford Weekly Sentinel*. Here," he said, taking a sheet of paper from his wallet, "is something I have had printed and hung in the reporters' room, under the heading: A *Quick Way To Be Sacked. Write something like this.*" He read:

"An inspiring address on Peace in our Time was delivered on Wednesday to members of the Milnrow Methodist Guild by Mr. Tom Long, who was thanked by Mr. Dick Short, seconded by Mr. Harry Average. 'Oh, for the Wings of a Dove' was then acceptably rendered by Miss Olive Rook. An agreeable evening was terminated with tea, generously provided by the Mesdames Finch, Sparrow and Titt. The Mesdames Longbottom and Higginbottom poured, and the washing-up was expertly effected by the Mesdames Black, White and Green. The floral decorations gracing the festive board came from the Mesdames Trowell, Rake and Spade. A vote of thanks to all the ladies concerned was fittingly moved by Mr. George Smart, seconded amusingly by Mr. Henry Wagg."

He paused for breath or comment. There was no comment, so he drew breath and went on: "Still, we make ends meet. We don't make a fortune, but we exist. If you stop thinking about what people want, and give 'em what you think they ought to want, you're often surprised to find that they agree with you. So the Mayor can go round crowning beauty queens and opening the anglers' week and doing any daft thing he likes, and the *Sentinel* takes no notice of him because it doesn't think that that sort of thing belongs to the dignity of the first citzen. If he does anything sensible, it takes a lot of notice. It reports the Borough Council as thoroughly as *The Times* reports Parliament, and if there's a concert or a play it's dealt with by someone who knows what he's talking about and knows that he has full licence to tell the truth and to the dickens with the names. If people like to get married or buried, that's their affair, not the *Sentinel's*, unless they're people who've managed to do something a bit more important than run the local fish-and-chip shop. That's how everybody I employ is trained to look at things. And what's more, he's trained to write the King's English, as if he were writing for the *Manchester Guardian*. Well, if you want to know any more, Joe can tell you. He's learning. I must be off to see this chap. I like what he's been writing in the *Yorkshire Observer*, and I'm going to try and lure him."

When he was gone, Joe said: "He was on the *Manchester Guardian* for a year or two, and that's a disease that can never be worked out of the system."

5

Joanna turned up at eleven o'clock the next morning. It was bitter cold. She arrived, wrapped up in furs, in an open car, and she seemed to carry the nip of the hale weather indoors with her. The furs could not conceal her lithe tallness. She was taller than either Joe or Anthony. Anthony knew that she was a little older than he was. She must be twenty-one. He remembered her white-honey hair. It had been bobbed, and it curled round the edges of her fur cap. They had been flippant to one another on the telephone. Now they were both shy. She pulled off her gloves and they shook hands, and she said: "It seems æons, not years." "Yes," he said, "doesn't it? This is Joe Morrison."

She shook hands with Joe, and then they stood looking at one another not very helpfully.

Mrs. Fieldhouse came in, and she at least knew how to walk on to a stage. "So you're Joanna?" she said, and embraced the girl, and kissed her cheek. "Now take off that heavy coat or you'll miss it when you go out, and sit by the fire. Boys are barbarians, don't you think?"

The barbarians sprang to life. One helped her off with her coat. The other patted the cushions of a chair. Auntie Jess, doing a job that wasn't hers, but eaten up by curiosity, carried in the coffee tray.

Mrs. Fieldhouse poured out the coffee. "I'd thought there'd be two of you," she said. "Anthony has told me about a Lottie—Lottie Wayland."

"I dropped her at her mother's," Joanna explained. "We'll pick her up later."

"It's very kind of your mother to allow the boys to come. I should have thought that after so long an absence she'd want every minute of your time."

"I suppose she does," Joanna said, "but she's being very unselfish about it. Mrs. Wayland, too. Of course, they're both busy women. Even if they wanted to, they couldn't spare much time for us. My mother still goes into Smurthwaite every day. But the horse is gone. I drive her."

"Anthony has told me about those daily drives, and how he first met you when exercising Mr. Pordage's dog. Or should one now say Colonel Pordage?"

"Yes, Colonel, I think. He likes to be called colonel, and if you write to him, he likes you to address the letters to Colonel Septimus Pordage, D.S.O. I was once indiscreet enough to ask him how he won the D.S.O."

"And how did he?"

"He says that in the senior officers' mess one night he noticed his general eyeing the medal ribbons above his pocket. The general said: 'Pordage, why haven't you got your D.S.O. up?' Colonel Pordage said: 'I've never won it, sir.' 'Won it? At G.H.Q. the D.S.O. is *awarded*, not won. I must see to it at once. We can't have you here improperly dressed. What will the mess waiters think?' So that's how it was. At any rate, that's what he says."

"Life with Septimus," Anthony said, "would always be simpler if one could distinguish between what he says a thing was and what it was in fact. The trouble is that often enough he himself doesn't know."

And, indeed, Septimus at this moment was in a very complicated state, for now that he was back at his old trick of writing to himself, he addressed a letter on one day to Colonel Septimus Pordage, D.S.O., and on alternate days the answers came addressed to Septimus Pordage, Esq., D.Litt. His I and Me were dreadfully at odds, one in khaki and the other in cap and gown. However, he was finding some consolation by fighting it out in *Me, About I*, by Ambrose Feend, now nearing its end.

Mrs. Fieldhouse said: "Will you be staying to lunch?"

"If you'll forgive us, no," Joanna said. "I promised to be back. I think we should pick up Lottie and be away. Thank you very much for letting Anthony come."

"He's not a child to be allowed or prevented, and I know he wants to come. But don't keep him too long."

Anthony's suitcase and Joe's rucksack were ready, and they put

162

them into the car. The three young people climbed in, and Mrs. Fieldhouse leaned over the door and kissed Anthony on the mouth. He found it embarrassing, and even more so was the conduct of Aunt Jessie. She made an absurd pretence in order to see him off. She came running out with a fistful of handkerchiefs and thrust them into the car. "Here," she said, "I don't expect you've got enough of these." And then she, too, leaned in the car and kissed his cheek.

There was just room for the car to turn on the gravel sweep. Soon they had climbed the hill and were moving along Manningham Lane. Anthony had not looked back, and didn't know that his mother and Auntie Jess had stood there till the car was out of sight, waving as though in eternal farewell.

"Well, Joe," he said, "you should be thankful you have no women-folk to see you off when you go away for a day or two."

"I often wish I had," Joe answered. "It's something I shall have to see to one of these days."

They turned into Megson Street to pick up Lottie. Nothing was changed here: the same stone setts on which the war of the dande-lions had been waged, the half-dozen houses, the blank wall at the end. It seemed to Anthony incredibly small, and strange to see some-one he didn't know polishing the knocker of the house in and out of which he had so often run.

Lottie must have been on the look out, for the front door opened as soon as the car stopped and she ran out to greet them. And the odd thing to Anthony was that, like everything else in Megson Street, she hadn't changed at all. He had felt shy when he met Joanna, but Lottie left him nothing to be shy about. As soon as he was on the pavement she took his hand and held it and looked into his face, her own shining with pleasure. Ah, well, he thought, she's back in Eng-land after a long absence, and while she was here she knew few people and I was one of them. I join her up to what she was used to. There's no more in it than that.

She said frankly: "Why, you've grown into something quite hand-some!"

He thought it a left-handed tribute to what he had been, and noticed that she, too, had grown, if not into something handsome, at all events into something it was easy and somehow comforting to look at. Her face was round and merry. She was not tall.

"This is Joe Morrison," he said. "I expect Joanna told you I was bringing him?"

"Yes," she said, shaking Joe's hand. "Mother's waiting to see you all. She's got coffee ready. Come in. It's bitter out here."

Anthony said: "We've had coffee."

"I dare say. What you call coffee. I don't know what Mother'd call it."

They all traipsed into the little dining-room that had surprised Dick Hudson long ago. Nothing was altered in it, but something had been added: a print of a Chardin painting that made Mrs. Wayland think of a painting she knew when she lived in Paris: a painting of a woman holding a child to her breast by a table spread with a humble meal. Mrs. Wayland was percolating coffee, and everybody kept discreetly silent about having had coffee already. Anthony congratulated Mrs. Wayland on the excellence of the drink.

"You wouldn't think, would you," Lottie said, "that a little thing like coffee would change the course of our lives? Well, coffee and what goes with it. Has Joanna told you?"

Joanna had not told them. It was a week ago, and Mrs. Halliwell had invited Mrs. Wayland to come to Throstle's Nest and spend a day and a night there. Lottie was anxious to see Septimus Pordage, remembering the evening she had spent in his study listening as he expounded the art and mystery of calligraphy. Joanna drove Lottie and her mother to Easter How. Septimus came to the door wearing a solar topee, which he had bought on the chance that his war service would take him to India, and what looked like a nightgown.

"Will you stay to lunch?" he asked hospitably. "I am preparing it in the kitchen. Forgive my uniform."

He had, in imagination, for the last hour been Escoffier preparing a Lord Mayor's banquet.

"Mrs. Toplis," he explained, "is up aloft, groaning lamentably." He led them in and asked courteously: "Would you like to hear the groans?"

They could hear them. "The war," he said, "never took me so near to human anguish. Ever since this morning I have felt a seasoned warrior."

Mrs. Wayland said: "I'd better go and see what's the matter with her."

She went upstairs, and Septimus took Lottie into the kitchen. Mrs. Beeton's *Household Management* was propped open on the table. "I wished," he said, "to show Mrs. Toplis that I am not entirely dependent. Indeed, I promised myself to surprise her with a choice bit of invalid cookery. However, this entrancing book, which has passed through an enviable number of editions, held me from work. I have been studying the duties of a butler and how to stuff a wood-cock with truffles stewed in brandy, in case a marquis should look in.

164

But as you see, I have at last got down to something practical. I have obeyed orders and taken a dozen eggs. I am not told what eggs, so duck eggs have had to serve."

Lottie looked at a dozen eggs broken into an earthenware dish. "But here," said Septimus, "the fiendish woman has me foxed. 'Separate the whites.' That is the problem I was pondering when you arrived. How does one separate the whites? I have tried trimming one off with scissors, but was not notably successful. I went up and asked Mrs. Toplis, but she could only assure me that she was dying, an extraordinarily unhelpful remark in the circumstances."

Mrs. Wayland came down and said: "If I'm not mistaken that woman has appendicitis."

"Appendicitis," said Septimus, "once postponed a coronation. Is there any reason why it should postpone the banquet I am preparing?"

"You'd better get her into hospital right away," Mrs. Wayland told him. "You have a horse and a cart, haven't you?"

"They could be so called."

"Don't stand chattering. Get off those things and harness up. Lottie'll go with you. I'll get Mrs. Toplis ready."

With a reluctant look at his dishful of eggs, Septimus pulled a string and his white garment flowed down to his feet, as though a Lord Mayor had unveiled him. Standing there in his solar topee, he might have been an empire-builder, newly presented to alien eyes in some public park at Singapore or Rangoon. He stepped clear, and went off to the barn.

"Come up with me," Mrs. Wayland said to Lottie, and they went to the bedroom and with the help of blankets transformed Mrs. Toplis into a well-wrapped mummy. From her small leathery face, with the nose almost touching the chin, her beady eyes looked out with a glint of apprehension.

"Who are you?" she demanded. "Where are you taking me? You let me snatch a bit of sleep and I'll be all right."

Mrs. Wayland was a strong woman, and Mrs. Toplis had hardly more flesh than a mouse. The bundle was carried downstairs. "Now don't you wriggle," Mrs. Wayland admonished it. "Keep those blankets well round you, feet and all, and you won't hurt. Remember, it's a cold day."

"I'm not going to no hospital," said Mrs. Toplis. "I know what hospitals are for. They're for cutting you up. I'm not going to let no one cut me up."

Septimus was at the door with the pony and trap. "In with her,

Mrs. Wayland," he cried. "We'll carry her like the good news from Ghent to Aix."

Lottie got in first, and Mrs. Wayland handed her the mummy, which she nursed like a doll. Then Septimus got in and flicked his whip. Valpy looked round with annoyance at the unnecessary gesture and started off at a gentle lope.

When they were out of sight, Mrs. Wayland went into the kitchen, put Mrs. Beeton firmly on the shelf, clicked disapprovingly at the extravagance of eggs, and proceeded to prepare the luncheon. She had plenty of time. It was two hours before Septimus and Lottie were back with the report that the surgeons at Smurthwaite intended to cut Mrs. Toplis up that very day.

It is an illusion that all French people are good cooks. Some are and some are not, and that is true of English people, too. Mrs. Wayland was one of the good ones, and her years in France had taught her the best of both worlds. And so Septimus was surprised when he sat down to a late lunch that day. Mrs. Wayland had even rooted out a bottle of Beaujolais and had seen that it was properly *chambré*. "Forgive the liberty," she said. "I thought you might be cold."

When the meal was over, she and Lottie washed up, and Septimus loitered disconsolately near the scullery door. At last he said: "Mrs. Wayland, in my lusty youth I could live like an Arab on a handful of dates, or like an Irish peasant on bread and onions. And I often did so. Now, alas! I am no longer young, my Toplis has been snatched away, and I doubt if there is a date or onion in the house. Mrs. Toplis, I am told, will be fortunate if she looks upon my countenance again a month from now. Is it kind of you to choose such a moment for the display of your incomparable art?"

Mrs. Wayland said: "You can eat the cold meat for your supper to-night and have a cup of tea and biscuits for your breakfast. I'll come along and cook your lunch. And that's all I can do. I must return to Bradford in the afternoon."

She did so, and a few days later received a letter from Septimus.

Easter How,
Ash Wednesday, 1919,
A Day of Peculiar Desolation.

My dear Mrs. Wayland.—This is the first day of Lent. It should rejoice me to enter upon it with the flesh holding by a few meagre tatters to my bones. But I am not a spiritual man, and I do not rejoice. I have just returned from the intended assassination of a duck. Mrs. Beeton has much to say about ducks. She is now my favourite author. I permit her to haunt and taunt me, as anchorites of old were haunted and taunted in their caverns by apparitions of carnal felicity. So, last night, sleepless from famine, was I haunted by the combinations, permutations and transmogrifications of which the duck is capable in fulfilling its destiny upon the dining-room table. When at last dreams came, they out-soared the provocations of Tantalus. Ducks upon ducks upon ducks appeared before me, each differently prepared by Mrs. Beeton's ingenious hand, and each preparation excelling the last. Mrs. Beeton herself was there, wearing my solar topee and nightshirt, urging me to eat her ducks, and eat them I did, to such effect that where other men belch I quacked. It was Mrs. Beeton's elfin laughter at this strange accomplishment, whose discovery pleased me so much that I quacked and quacked, which brought me awake, only to discover that the sounds which had delighted me in sleep were, waking, no such matter. They were the hollow rumbling of all that within me—those endless convolutions by which nature mysteriously arranges that duck shall become Pordage—which now was crying out for meat.

Hence my assignation this morning with the ducks. Having breakfasted upon slices of raw turnip stolen from a farmer's field, I went forth with a heart black as Lady Macbeth's, but with the embarrassment that I must do the dirty deed myself. I took some corn, as I had often seen the stricken Toplis do, and I went to the paddock uttering traitorous cries of 'Ducky, Ducky, come to Uncle Septimus.' The ducks came and I threw the corn and they gobbled it up, and their little eyes twinkled appreciation of their benefactor. I said to Me: 'Now is the moment. One reaching down of the hand, one twist of the neck, and the deed is done.' But there was a little sunlight. It fell on the ducks' necks and had the colours of oil on water, and I thought of John Keats's lines:

> Vermilion-spotted, golden, green and blue,
> Striped like a zebra, freckled like a pard,
> Eyed like a peacock, and all crimson-barr'd;
> And full of silver moons that, as she breathed,
> Dissolved or brighter shone.

So I gave the birds some more corn, and here I am, defeated in the struggle for existence, writing to you; and, this letter done, I shall betake me to Smurthwaite, and there, at the Dragon, see the new Lent in with sinful plenitude.

But this cannot go on, and I write to lay before you two suggestions, cognate and conjoined. My publishers, who are Messrs. Periwinkle, Pulse and Parsley, or some such name, have written to me, seeking to impose a monstrous task. During the war the publication of school books languished and now is to be taken up again. To my dismay, it is suggested that all my works shall reappear in new editions—"brought up to date," say Messrs. P. P. and P.—and as some twenty books are concerned, Pordage foresees years of effort which can be undertaken only on two conditions: his body must be fed and he must have the help of a secretary. Did ever Providence, in laying a burden upon the back, more beautifully suggest the means to bear it when it whispered into my ear: Mrs. Wayland and her daughter?

So there it is. I cannot believe that you will deny me. I see Pordage facing years of fruitful labour, an admirable cook-housekeeper fortifying his physical integument, and, in the loft above the stables, the cheerful chatter of the typewriter proclaiming the mechanisation of his industry. As for Mrs. Toplis, she has told me often enough that her duty lies with her lately-widowed brother, and that she would be willing to come in to 'do the rough.'

Now I betake myself to Smurthwaite, rejoicing in the thought that within a day or two your letter will arrive, dispelling like sunshine the lamentable clouds now pressing down upon the head of your humble servitor, Septimus Pordage, D.S.O., Defeated by a Duck.

Lottie answered for her mother. "Dear Mr. Pordage.—My mother and I have had several long talks about your letter, and I hope that you are still alive to read this answer, which comes later than you expected. Though from the tone of your letter I shouldn't be surprised if this finds you a spectre. It wasn't an easy thing to decide. My mother, as perhaps you know, conducted a fairly successful correspondence school in French. The war caused her to lose many pupils, indeed most of them, and she had a harder time than I imagined while I was selfishly taking my ease in Switzerland. I found her anxious to set about re-establishing her school, and her idea was that we should add German to the curriculum, that part of it to be my job. However, that wasn't what I wanted, either for her or for myself. For her I wanted a complete change after all her years of slogging. Young girls are not often aware of the tribulations of their elders, and I was no exception. But I am now old enough to realise that she kept a roof over my head by labours that were positively damnable. I don't want her to go on with them, and I certainly don't intend to share them. I don't want to live in Bradford or in any town like it. For me, either London or the country—and I mean the country, complete and unspoiled as you have it at Darton-in-Craven.

Well, London is out of the question for the moment because I don't feel qualified to take the sort of secretarial job which is what

I'd like to have there. So you see what an opportunist I am. I shall love to come and work for you, so that I may learn to stand on my own feet and give you the push sooner or later.

I have at last persuaded Mother that it will be an excellent thing to have a change and leave all this scribing for ever. We shall come over to-morrow—that is the day you receive this—to discuss terms. I hope you will be able to give us good news of Mrs. Toplis."

The terms were soon settled, and by the time Anthony and Joe Morrison were learning of all this, Anthony's old quarters in the loft over the barn had become the office, living-room and bedroom of Lottie and her mother. It was big enough to absorb all their activities and still be spacious. Septimus had offered to divide it into rooms, but they both loved the austere stone walls and the tall windows and the view down the wide-planked floor from the door to the fireplace. Lottie's typewriter, filing-cabinets and long work-table were just inside the door; beyond that were two beds, foot to foot with plenty of gangway between; and at the fireside were a couch and two easy-chairs. For all the self-confidence of her letter to Septimus, Lottie felt almost sinful at being paid for living in a fashion after her own heart. She and her mother stood at the window when all had been arranged and looked out over the countryside on which, from that same window, Anthony had looked so often. It was a winter land-scape, but on its face there lay, for those who could see it, the faintest smile of spring.

"Well, Mother," Lottie said, taking Mrs. Wayland's arm in hers, "are you glad I persuaded you?"

"It'll do," Mrs. Wayland said.

6

Anthony crossed the corridor, knocked at the door of Joe's bed-room, and looked in. Joe said: "*Entrez, monsieur*. How d'you think I'm looking?"

He seemed to need reassurance. "I expect your personality will carry it off," Anthony comforted him.

"There are times," Joe said, "when I'd be prepared to print the Longford street directory *verbatim* in the *Sentinel*, if that would increase the old man's income. We live too near the line."

He took up the clothes brush and had a go at his shabby evening-suit, which was not improved by having travelled in a rucksack. "I asked the old man how long he'd had this, and he said ever since dinner-jackets came in. I suppose, for a posh dance like this, I ought to be wearing tails, anyhow."

Anthony was wearing tails and a white tie.

"This tie," Joe said, fingering his black one, "is made up. It can't come awash; that's one comfort. I hope there's no social function in Longford while I'm away, though the old man's capable of strolling into a coronation in his tweeds, and getting away with it."

Admiration of the old man and regret at having to share a dinner-jacket with him fought for mastery. He was already stout, but not quite so stout as Leonard.

Having now done all he could with limited resources, he sat down. Anthony stood about, feeling elegant. He had never worn tails before, or even a dinner-jacket.

Filling a pipe with a gesture absurdly like Leonard's—somehow the sagging clothes suggested to Anthony the man who should have been inside them—Joe said: "The old man goes too far. Hard up though he is, he pays more than the wages that are usual on our sort of weekly rag. He says it helps him to get the men he wants. Well, I suppose it does. But then they just learn all he's got to teach them—and that's plenty—and push off to something better. Which is what I intend to do myself."

"You don't want to settle in Longford?"

"Not on your life. But, of course, I don't breathe a word of that to the old man. How's your dancing?"

"Pretty ghastly."

"Mine's non-existent."

"It sounds as though the girls are going to have a good time."

"We'll just have to take hold of them and leave the rest to the moment's inspiration. Well, we'd better go down."

Lottie had not yet begun to work for Septimus Pordage. She was spending a few days at Throstle's Nest while her mother was clearing up her affairs in Bradford. Joe and Anthony found her and Joanna sitting in the office with Mrs. Halliwell. The war years had enriched Mrs. Halliwell and aged her. She was greyer and heavier, and she was worried about her daughter. It had been a bad thing, she thought, that circumstances had caused Joanna to be for so long away from her influence. She had never been clear just what she wanted to do with the girl, but she thought vaguely that if Joanna had been accessible something would have happened to show her the way. Now the girl had come back headstrong and full of ideas with which Mrs. Halliwell had no sympathy.

"But, Mother, you do see that after all those years of being sat on and treated like a child, one naturally wants to be a woman. And nowadays women don't sit down and twiddle their fingers. They go out and work at something."

"I see no call for you to work at anything."

"Why not? You were working when you were a mere child."

If there was one thing more than another that Mrs. Halliwell disliked it was to have her half-timer days recalled. Alf had wiped all that out for ever.

"There's no reason to throw that in my teeth," she said harshly.

"Really, Mother!" Joanna protested. "That's a shameful thing to say. It suggests that I despise you. Well, I don't. I admire you, and I sometimes wish I had grown up in the same way."

"You couldn't have done. Half-timers weren't allowed by the time you came along."

But Joanna felt acutely the way in which life had cut her off from immense tracts of experience. She remembered walking with one of the Misses Kempfer in the school garden as a winter afternoon was closing down, but no lights were appearing on the other side of the lake. Right opposite them was Evian-les-Bains, and that was in France. Miss Kempfer said: "It must be very sad to be over there. Just imagine standing on their edge of the lake, with darkness all around, and looking across at the lights shining over here. Yes, that must be very sad."

Joanna looked across the dark water at the invisible land, and from her safety pondered the dangerous unknown life that men and women lived there, where light was forbidden.

"At least," she said, "they are not in the war zone. Life may be difficult there, but it can hardly be dangerous."

"You do not know how dangerous," said Miss Kempfer, who had her own means of knowing at any rate something of what was happening in the sedate little spa across the dark water. "It is a repatriation town. It is full of French and English officers and men from the Sûreté Générale. Strange and dangerous things can happen there. As in the novels of Mr. Oppenheim," she added, for she kept up with the English classics.

She went in, and Joanna stayed on the clean raked gravel of the terrace overlooking the lake, and the lights behind her and about her glittered in shining rows and clusters, which, over there, must be seen as one steady peaceful glow from a country not at war. And safety suddenly seemed to her unbearable, and her mind was filled with speculation about what life could be for people loose in the world of chance and violence.

And so it was that while she talked to her mother in the ease of Throstle's Nest she more and more saw Mrs. Halliwell in the days when the nest for her was not especially downy, when she was, so to speak, one of those who lived in the dark town beyond the dark water and knew the secrets that life so watchfully veiled from Joanna's eyes. She no more understood what she wanted to do with herself than Mrs. Halliwell understood what she wanted to do with her, and so there were ragged edges where their lives touched, and a feeling that after the long separation they had not come together like mortise and tenon.

7

One thing Mrs. Halliwell could not understand was that Joanna admired her for the very things that she herself didn't wish to be remembered, whether for admiration or disdain. And this was because she still feared the disdain. She was not strong enough, as her husband had always been, to live in the present sum of attainment, not bothering about the integers that had added up to it, or, for that matter, about the missing integers that would have made it even more impressive. For example, he wasn't a speaker. Very well, then; he wasn't a speaker; and that was that. But Mrs. Halliwell, the more so now that Alf was dead, pondered on the things that Sir Alfred Halliwell might have been; and Joanna had not the imaginative experience to understand how, deprived of her company all through the war, her mother would spend lonely evenings in the office with the past, as much as the present or the future, for her companion. Out of her broodings came the conviction that she should do, for her husband's sake, the public things he had shunned. For one thing they were a refuge from loneliness, and for another they were the things that befitted Alfred's widow. So she was now a magistrate, a member of the West Riding County Council and of the Smurthwaite Borough Council, and she took a hand in many other of the borough's small affairs, as befitted one of its leading employers of labour. She never forgot, or, at any rate, never failed to tell herself, that this was all for Alf's sake rather than the natural expression of a *maîtresse-femme*; and it was to honour Alf's name that the ball was being held to which the four young people were going. The ballroom in Smurthwaite's charming Georgian Assembly Rooms had fallen into sad decay. The ceilings peeled; plaster fell from the walls; dreary streaks of damp proclaimed a leaking roof; and the taste of past members of the Borough Council, who owned the property, had bestowed upon the walls a colour-scheme derived, apparently, from diluting farmyard manure with water. Moreover, the floor was riddled with dry rot.

All this, Mrs. Halliwell decided, must be put right on one condition. The dance-room should henceforth be known as the Alfred Halliwell Memorial Hall.

Mrs. Halliwell was wise enough to know her own limitations and the limitations of Smurthwaite decorators. She went up to London and sought advice and found a young enthusiastic architect who had been invalided out of the army and who had never dreamed that at so unpropitious a moment a job like this would come his way. If he had small creative talent, John Shrubb had at least a deep reverence for Georgian architecture; and Mrs. Halliwell was as surprised as anyone else in Smurthwaite would have been to discover that the town contained a gem. John Shrubb knew all about it, and on the journey back to Yorkshire told her how Beau Nash had come from Bath to the opening, when the hall was built and handed over to the town by some eighteenth-century Newte, and had remained as Master of Ceremonies during a week of festivities. "It is generally agreed, Mrs. Halliwell," John Shrubb said, "that it was then as fine an example of an assembly room as anything to be found in the provinces. I am looking forward tremendously to seeing it."

When he saw it he wept, and also he doubted whether Mrs. Halliwell had any idea what the job would cost her. Sitting with her in the office that night, he didn't express the doubt, but he said: "Of course these are difficult times. Material, labour—you realise, Mrs. Halliwell, that we'll have to move heaven and earth, and even then perhaps come up against a stone wall."

Throstle's Nest had not reassured him. He looked in perplexity at its owner. She said complacently: "All that's got nothing to do with you. The money's there, and, as for the rest of it, I'll have the Borough Council behind me. I know nothing about your side of it, but you've been recommended to me by someone who knows what he's talking about."

John Shrubb contributed nothing to that room beyond a fanatic resolve to make it again what once it had been. The pale green walls, with their panels picked out in gold leaf, the four majestic chandeliers, which formerly, indeed, had contained candles but now blazed with electric light: these two things in themselves at once re-established the beauty of the room's proportions, and it smiled as it had smiled to welcome Beau Nash. There was one thing at which perhaps Nash would have raised his eyebrows. In one of the panels was a vast oil portrait of Alf Halliwell, with a brass plate beneath it telling the world that the renovation of the room was a widow's tribute to the memory of the sitter. Not that Alf had sat. But Mrs. Halliwell had entrusted a photograph to an artist with instructions to "copy it," and this the artist faithfully did. So there Alf was, with strip-lighting revealing his ravaged features, his air of faint surprise, as though, weighing up the situation in which he found himself, he was saying: "Eh! This is a rum do!" It was the second thing that caused Mr. Shrubb to weep, but there was nothing he could do about it. After all, that splendid room had been dedicated by the Borough Council to the storage of old chairs and tea-urns and crockery. He had been permitted to wave his wand and recreate the beauty, and a pimple on the nose was a small concession to make.

8

It was Mrs. Halliwell herself who introduced Joanna to Sir William Scroop. She watched the four young people go, with Joanna driving, and then went upstairs and changed into regal purple. The dress suited her. It emphasised the firmness and solidity of her character. She had not told them that she would attend this first public ceremony to be held in the Alfred Halliwell Memorial Hall, and indeed had been in two minds about going. But she found herself unable to resist seeing the young life aswirl in the room that she had awakened from the dead. She had ordered a taxi to be at Throstle's Nest at nine o'clock, and thought that this, at all events, was something that Joanna would approve: not so much her being at the dance as arriving there in a vehicle driven by petrol. Looking at herself in the glass of the big bedroom, where she still used the double bed she had shared with Alf, she surprised in herself a nervousness, a desire that Joanna should approve of her. She put on a necklace of rubies, and the colour of the dress killed it. She had never been to a dance in her life, and certainly she would not dance to-night. She had no doubt that this was the sort of thing that Mr. Arthur Geldersome, the Town Clerk, would not miss. She pictured him approaching her with a deep bow and asking for the pleasure of leading her on to the floor. She allowed herself a grim smile at the thought.

No. What she was going for, she now admitted, facing her own motive squarely, was to keep an eye on Joanna. It was very odd that, with all the desirable young men there still were in the country, even after this ghastly war had had its fill, the girl should have invited the two who were with her now. She had kept an eye on them and, saying little, had learned a lot. A chap whose father owned a tin-pot weekly paper that was probably losing money hand over fist, and this boy who used to be Bromwich and was now calling himself Fieldhouse. A proper mess up there. That sort of thing had never happened in her family, hard up though they'd been. She wasn't too pleased with either of them, though their manners were all right.

She decided against the rubies. They called attention to the skin of her neck, which was taking on an ageing woman's roughness. She rustled downstairs in her silk and opened the front door as the hall clock struck nine. The taxi driver was walking up the steps. Had he been but a minute late, she would have told him so, and ordered him home, and thrown up the whole thing. But he knew Mrs. Halliwell, and he was dead on time.

9

The Committee had sent an invitation for two to Mr. John Shrubb, who would have liked to take a pretty girl; but pretty girls were not much attracted by an ex-lieutenant who limped badly and was desperately in need of work. It was true that at the moment he had a few of Mrs. Halliwell's pound notes to rustle; but they wouldn't last long, and a nicely done job in remote Smurthwaite was hardly likely to improve his prospects unless it could be written about. It seemed to him that at the moment Sir William Scroop was better value than a pretty girl.

Shrubb had two small rooms in a street off the King's Road in Chelsea. He had been brought up in a well-to-do home; but, his father dying when he was still a schoolboy, his mother had married again, and the stepfather had proved a genius at dissipating money to which he had never been accustomed. Shrubb's life was lonely, his chief companion during holidays being the housekeeper, for his stepfather and his mother were forever gallivanting on the Continent. He had ended his course under Reilly at the School of Architecture in Liverpool and had spent a couple of years in a London architect's office, when two things happened on the same day in 1914. War was declared, and his mother and stepfather were both killed in a motor crash on the Corniche. Leaving lawyers to sort things out, Shrubb joined the army. And now here he was, with nothing saved out of the financial wreck, living on his disability pension and what few coppers he could pick up in the difficult post-war world. But he had a happy disposition and counted himself blessed because the house he lived in was owned by the housekeeper who had been the companion of his childhood and youth. She still called him Mr. John and never pressed him when money was tight.

Shrubb liked to stroll round at night to the King's Mistress pub in King's Mistress Yard and drink his strictly rationed pint of beer, and it was there, not long before, that he had run into William Scroop. They were of an age, and they had served together as lieutenants, but they had not met since 1916 when Shrubb was wounded. Shrubb remembered Scroop as a youth who was accounted wild and reckless even in these times when there was plenty to feed such a disposition. He was Mr. Scroop then, and Shrubb knew nothing of his family save that his uncle was the ninth baronet.

In the King's Mistress that night he exceeded his pint. Scroop's dark agile face seemed matched by an excitability of the spirit that disturbed and attracted him. They had much to talk about. When the landlord addressed Scroop as Sir William, Shrubb said: "That's news to me. I didn't know you'd succeeded."

Scroop said: "Succeeded! That's a bloody good word to give it! Failed is a better one. My old man was a crock as long as I could remember him, and his elder brother, my uncle Hector, who was the Ninth Bart, was as strong as an ox. A rip-roaring old devil who did everything to bring himself to the grave—drank like a fish, fornicated with all and sundry, and broke every bone in his body in the hunting field. My father cherished himself. They were twins, you know. My father missed the title by precisely three minutes. He married—so as to have a woman to coddle him, I imagine. The Ninth Bart was a bachelor, but he laid waste the family money more effectively than if he'd expensively brought up a clan. And then he died. As fit a man as you ever saw and only three minutes older than his puling brother. And he dies first! Just came in, took up a glass of whisky as usual, downed it, and dropped dead on the carpet. Now that was a dirty trick, if you like. If he had survived my father, I would have stepped into the title with only one cut at the death duties. But no. His brother, the Reverend George, became the Tenth Bart, kept a grim hold on life for two years, then pops off, and I, the Eleventh Bart, see another cut made at the little old Hector had left. And here I am, bloody well broke."

He banged a tankard on the table. The landlord came and refilled it.

"Not for me," Shrubb said; but Scroop insisted. "Come on! Damn it. It's not every day of your life you drink with an ancestral ruin. I can feel ivy growing through my chinks!"

Shrubb was a shy man with a few friends, and Scroop was not in any real sense one of them. But the war's vicissitudes had thrown them together. They had common memories of danger and endurance and the swift taking off of men they had known, and Shrubb was glad to see him. He suggested diffidently that they should adjourn to his rooms which were a few minutes' walk away and which he was rather proud of, for they were the only thing about him that was not beggarly. All that he had salvaged from the wreck his stepfather had made of his life was there in the form of excellent furniture, but the place was marred by his having to combine sitting-room and work room. His drawing-table took up a lot of space.

Mrs. Medway had kept the fire going, and Shrubb was not displeased with the look of things when he switched on the light. Scroop threw his overcoat and hat on to a sofa, and stood, back to the fire, looking about him. To Shrubb's surprise, he then walked across the room and peered keenly at a photograph pinned to the wall. "That's the Smurthwaite Assembly Room, isn't it?" he asked.

"How on earth do you know that?" Shrubb asked.

"Why shouldn't I? D'you take me for a clot?"

Scroop looked at the picture for a long time, drawing his hand down his thin dark jaws as though trying to lengthen his chin. "A bloody shame," he said at last. "A lovely thing like that going to rack and ruin."

"Do you know the place?" Shrubb asked.

"Yes—what's left of it. The Ninth Bart was very thick with old Newte. You know, the Newtes have owned all that country for centuries. The old hell-hound was rather fond of me, and he took me along once when he went to stay with Sir Titus. It was pretty well done for then, and I suppose by now it's finished."

Shrubb pulled out a drawer and spread on the table a dozen photographs which he had had the sense to have taken. "Look at that lot," he said. "Before and after."

Scroop looked at them long and hard. "Well, glory be to God! I didn't know that sort of thing was happening in England's green and pleasant land. Who did it?"

Shrubb said modestly: "Well, it was a co-operation between me and a woman of those parts who has oodles of money."

He told the story, and Scroop said: "That's just the sort of thing *Vanguard* wants."

"What is? and what is *Vanguard*?"

Scroop grinned. "The answer to the first part is oodles of money. The answer to the second part is a monthly magazine which may or may not come to birth. What are you doing tomorrow?"

"Nothing."

"Come and lunch with me. I'll meet you at the Café Royal at one. Then we'll go on to my place."

My place was in Soho Square. During luncheon, which was lavish, Shrubb learned a lot about Scroop. "If only money wasn't so bloody tight," Scroop kept on saying as he spent it regardless—brandy, cigars; it's an occasion, Shrubb; we can't economise *now*. He said that Rockhill, the Scroops' "place" for centuries, was rotting like an old tooth—"as everything decent is in this damned country." He never went near it now—let it rot. It had been going downhill ever since a Bart of the eighteenth century cleaned up at the top of the South Sea market before the bubble burst.

"He was one of the few wise guys. Old Sarah Marlborough was another. Even he began to spend as soon as he had the money—pictures, furniture, buildings. We've been spending ever since. Even the Tenth Bart, my old man, a proper bloody skinflint, had to spend on death duties, and then there was so little left that he went on spending to keep his mean soul alive in his shrivelled body. He sold every picture and every decent bit of furniture in the place. I've got nothing left now except the house in Soho Square. Come and see it."

He gave the waiter a fifteen-shilling tip, which made Shrubb wince.

"How did you get on after I left the show on the Somme?" Shrubb asked as they made their way through the back streets of Soho.

Scroop laughed. "As well as can be expected, sir," he said, "considering the mortality. However, I assaulted a brass hat during the breezy little outing at Passchendaele. He came along one day, looking absolutely bloody marvellous. Straight out of the show-case. 'Well, you men, how are you?' he asked. 'Everything *comfortable*?' It was so bloody funny that I began to laugh. And once I started I couldn't stop. I went on laughing and laughing, and he said 'Stop that!' Then I let out at him. He shied away and fell off the duck-board. I looked at his diminished glory and went on laughing."

Shrubb said: "Good show!"

"Well, it was up to a point. I suppose for smacking a G.S.O.1 in the kisser I could have been shot at dawn. As it was, I spent a long time in a nice establishment—in fact, it was a refined sort of loony-bin. I finished the war there."

He began to pull at his chin, and Shrubb laid a hand on his arm as he was about to step off the pavement in front of a taxi-cab.

The house in Soho Square was built by the Scroop who cleared a packet out of the South Sea investors. Sir William Scroop led Shrubb to the first floor. "Everything over this and everything below it is let as offices," he explained. "The rents are what I live on, I suppose. I don't think there's much else. I'm not sure about it. There's still an agent who looks after things and gives me a bit of money now and then. And I run up bills. Well, come in."

Although this room, that had once been the drawing-room, was immensely bigger than his, Shrubb saw at a glance that, like his, it was an all-purposes room. Relics of grandeur were mixed with the litter of the working day. A superb settee stood in front of the fireplace, and the great desk of red lacquer and ormolu in the middle of the room was a clutter of books and papers with a type-writer riding above the flood. The curtains were of a brocade that Shrubb thought heavenly.

Scroop struck a bell on his desk and a small dark man came from a back room. "Drinks, Gwilym," Scroop said. "And please get the fire going."

Gwilym, who was wearing a shiny navy-blue suit that looked like one of Scroop's cast-offs, said: "You'll get no more drink out of me to-day, Sir William, and there's no coal in the house."

Scroop laughed. He said to Shrubb: "Meet my grey eminence, Gwilym Williams, who was with me when I was learning to ride a pony at Rockhill, who was with me when I smacked down the brass hat, and who haunts me still. Not even beer, Gwilym?"

"Not a damned sip, Sir William," Gwilym said, and went out.

10

They met often after that. They were, up to a point, in the same boat. If Scroop had known luxury—for he had had little to do with his father and had been his uncle's favourite—Shrubb had known a moderate comfort, undisturbed by financial worry. Each of them had seen security vanish. The difference between them was in their reactions. Shrubb, with an inherited middle-class prudence and hatred of debt, thought of little save the re-establishment of his position. Sir William, knowing that the position of the Scroops was beyond recall, was ready to make hay while the scraps lasted. He was serious about *Vanguard*. What he had in mind was a journal devoted to the emergence of what he called elegance. He was a cast-back to the eighteenth century, which would have permitted him to enjoy with an equal gusto a building by Adam, a cock-fight, bear-baiting, a landscape by Repton or Lancelot Brown, a public hanging, and a collection of pictures and statues picked up during a grand tour. He might have been a great patron. It was as a patron that he saw himself now; he was pathetically certain that the world was full of young writers and painters and musicians and architects whom his journal could introduce to the public. But he was not serious enough to be devoted. Patronage, when all is said and done, was the dispensing of superfluity, and Scroop was too unstable to permit ends to meet, much less overlap. Everything was ready for the launching of *Vanguard* except money. Shrubb had read some of the articles piled up on the desk in Soho Square and thought them good, including those that Scroop had written himself. Others had been commissioned. "We'll pay when we've launched the boat," he explained to Shrubb.

Shrubb had taken to looking in at Soho Square, for he had little to do. Sometimes he would find Scroop at work, sometimes reclining on the couch before the fire, wearing a magnificent dressing-gown that had belonged to the wicked Ninth Bart and smoking a cigar. He was thus engaged one morning when Shrubb called. Shrubb found it impossible to be offended by anything that Scroop said, and put up even with the name Peggy, which referred to his game leg. Now Scroop greeted him with: "Well, Peg o' my Heart, Gwilym is permitting us one tot of whisky at 11 o'clock, and, as you see, the coalman has been squared and has delivered my ration. I have been brooding on the subject of my agent."

Gwilym came in with a small tot on a large tray. "One for Mr. Shrubb," Scroop said; but Shrubb declined.

"Well, now," Scroop said, "I have received a proposition from my agent, and I have composed my answer. Read it, Peggy."

He handed over a sheet of paper on which he had written:

> Oh, *agent mine, clod with commercial soul,*
> *Quibbling about the price of wood and coal,*

How dare you show your devil's cloven hoof,
By schemes to sell my dear ancestral roof?
Scroops are unscrupulous, but agents, surely,
Should live their little lives, like geldings, purely.

"I think," he said, "that should make him thoroughly ashamed of himself."

Shrubb said: "Don't send it. I don't know what it's all about, but don't send it."

Scroop sipped his whisky, drew on his cigar. "I can tell you what it's about. You know that this house belongs to me, and that all except this floor is let. The leases are about to fall in, and my agent has been approached by a firm who want to buy the place. Some bloody pottery people from up there where that chap Arnold Bennett comes from. They want to pull the place down, make a show room on the ground floor, and have what my poop calls administrative offices over that. Can you imagine it? Can you see the façade? Lavatory tilings and plate glass."

"I don't know," Shrubb said reasonably. "Business men aren't all hooligans nowadays."

"Oh, so you're in the opposition too, are you? Well, let me tell you this. No one's going to display W.C. pans in my front window."

"I doubt if they would. Still, what did your agent say?"

Scroop put down his glass and began wrenching at his jaw. "He said Sell! He thinks it's a chance that may not come again. He mentions some fantastic figure and tells me about the securities it would be invested in. He says it would guarantee me a comfortable competence. Who the hell wants a comfortable competence?"

He was beginning to shout, and Gwilym came through the door. He pretended that he had come for the glass and tray, but Shrubb did not miss the warning look he passed to Scroop.

Scroop tore up the lines he had written and tossed them into the fire. "Very well," he said more quietly. "I won't send that. Thanks for your advice, Peggy. But I'll tell him there's nothing doing. What I want is for him to arrange my affairs so that I—I and not some commercial firm—can spread abroad in this house—in this house as it stands, as it was built by someone who knew what building was."

"But how can he do that?" Shrubb asked. "From what you've told me, your affairs are in a pretty dicky state."

"Why can't he sell that damned great white elephant Rockhill? That's what I want him to do—sell that, not this. I want to keep this—every stone and timber of it. Oh," he said, his voice trembling again on an edge. "I feel so—so—bloody *trapped*!"

When Shrubb mentioned the ball at Smurthwaite, and suggested that Scroop should go with him and have a look at the renovated assembly room, Sir William took to the idea at once. "I remember the place," he said. "There's a very good pub there called the Dragon. Leave it to me. I'll write and engage a couple of rooms."

"All right. So long as you let me go fifty-fifty on the bill."

"Oh, don't bloody well quibble," Scroop said. "You've got bills on the brain like a shopkeeper."

"Why shouldn't I have? After all, my grandfather *was* a shop-keeper, and it was a damned small shop."

On the night of the ball they lingered over their dinner at the Dragon. "You see," Shrubb said, "dancing is off for me. I used to like it, and I was pretty good at it, but this peg of mine puts paid to it. So I shan't be taking a girl in to supper, and I don't propose to struggle for a sandwich and a glass of claret-cup on my own account. So we'd better eat now."

Scroop was of the same mind. "I haven't come to dance, either," he said. "For one thing, I don't suppose we shall find much here that is dance-worthy, and for another, all I've come for is to see what you've made of this place. And the time to see it, of course, is when it's alive, in use. That's the time to see any building, Peggy. It's always sad-making to see people gawping round an empty cathedral. The ghastly House of Commons is meaningless unless some debate is on. Even picture galleries give me the willies. The place to see pictures is in used rooms. Anything else is like think-ing you are seeing a man when you look at him snoring on a couch. This Montrachet is good. What about another bottle?"

"No, thank you. I've had enough."

Scroop laughed. "All right, Gwilym. Do you allow me brandy with my coffee?"

"As you will. Not for me."

Being away from London had been good for Scroop, Shrubb was thinking. He seemed to have forgotten the frustrations, the hourly reminders of loss, that afflicted him there. His thin dark face had lost its rather disturbing excitability. He was wearing full-fig eve-ning clothes. Shrubb had to be content with a shabby dinner-jacket. He was amused at being addressed as Gwilym, and rather touched. There's something about him, he thought, that will always make people want to give him the protection he scorns. He looked at the

182

brittle fingers clasped round the balloon glass, and said: "Knock it back, Bill, and let's get moving."

11

Mrs. Halliwell was glad she had come. She had seen the room before, but then it was empty and silent. Scroop was right. This was the way to see a room, and she was enchanted. The shine of the chandeliers, the music, all these young people swirling and laughing, and colours of skirts and of flowers. This was something like a way to spend a bit of brass! She was sitting under the portrait of Alf, with a feeling of his approval.

"Mrs. Halliwell, I hope it all comes up to your expectations."

It was that poor young Mr. Shrubb, with the damaged leg. She looked up at him, and at the taller, thinner man with him. She said: "It's very beautiful, Mr. Shrubb. No one could have done it better."

Shrubb said: "May I present Sir William Scroop to you? He's very much interested in buildings, and came along to see what you and I had made of this between us. Sir William, this is Mrs. Halliwell, who had the wonderful idea of doing all this."

Scroop took her hand and bowed over it, and then looked into her shrewd powerful face. "It was, indeed, a wonderful idea," he said. "Mr. Shrubb has shown me pictures of it, but I hadn't thought of it as quite so lovely. I for one would like to thank you."

"Oh, you needn't thank me. My husband and Mr. Shrubb— those are the two to be thanked."

Scroop said: "Madam, if you will permit me to contradict a lady, I should say you are wrong. Never underestimate the importance of money. It can do wonderful things. George the Fourth said to one of my ancestors: 'Scroop, my father was a better man than I am, but he hadn't my genius for screwing money out of the country. The consequence is that he will be remembered as the man who lost the American colonies, and I shall be remembered as the man who built Regent Street and the Pavilion at Brighton.' And how right he was."

They stood for a moment, one on either side of her, and then Scroop said: "Shall we circulate, Shrubb? I should like to take a look from different points of view. Will you forgive us, madam? And may I, a little later, have the pleasure of taking you in to supper?"

Mrs. Halliwell assented with a nod, and as the young men strolled away she looked after them with a thought niggling at the back of her mind. When it came to the front she couldn't believe it. Yet there it was. Alf! It was Alf that the young man reminded her of. Of course, there was all the difference in the world between them: Alf, who never bothered to mend his accent, and this one with his easy talk of ancestors and kings: but she'd bet her boots, she said to herself, that he needed looking after. It was the thin dark face with sadness in it that each of them had. It was that as much as anything that had drawn her to Alf. He was someone who had to be cared for, and this was another of the same breed. For all his lordly manners, he looked as though he wasn't getting enough to eat and as though he had plenty on his mind.

12

Joanna asked flippantly: "Who's the Adonis?"

Joe, very conscious of the old man's dinner-jacket, which wasn't quite such a good fit as he had hoped it would be, was not too happy. Joanna's dress was of gold *lamé*, but he didn't know that. He only knew that he was dazzled by a general sense of her goldenness: gold dress, gold shoes, hair like white wheat. She danced beautifully, or would have done, he thought regretfully, if he had been able to give her any help. Her blue eyes looking into his seemed to him to be full of mockery. She must be thinking him a clod, and he felt a clod, but also he felt deliciously disturbed by her contact and reluctant to give up his struggle for mastery of those steps which other youths seemed to take as easily as a blackbird took to song. He was ruining the night for her. He ought to release her and be sensible like Anthony, who was sitting in the sidelines, talking to Lottie Wayland.

But Joanna's smile was not of mockery. She liked Joe. His pug-nosed freckled face and eyes as blue as her own had an innocence and a candour that went to her heart, and she didn't mind at all giving him dance after dance. She wanted to say: "Relax now, and don't struggle with it," but that would have hurt him, so she did her best to dominate his movements as he should have dominated hers. As for the admirable young marionettes whose ease made Joe envious, he would have been assuaged had he known her opinion of them.

Joe followed the direction of her look and saw William Scroop and John Shrubb standing at the side of the room, gazing up at the ceiling, apparently oblivious of the dancing and the dancers. "Adonis?" he asked. "Which one?"

"Now, now," she teased him. "You know very well which one."

"If you mean the taller of the two, I'd agree that he's well-dressed; but Adonis," he added, with his father's impudent grin, "didn't bother to dress at all. Anyhow, insofar as he was anything, wasn't he Greek?"

"I don't know anything about him," Joanna said. "If, as you say, he was a nudist, Miss Kempfer wouldn't have allowed me within miles of him."

"Well," said Joe, "I can tell you one thing about him: when he was dead Venus turned him into an anemone, which seems to me a darned funny thing to happen to anybody. Still, it's not likely to happen to yon chap. He's about as Greek as I am. Looks more like a half-starved Celt. Sort of chap you'd find going down a coal mine in the Rhondda Valley, except that he's a bit on the tall side for that breed."

They had danced, or rather shambled, as Joanna would have frankly admitted, round the room, and now came once more within sight of Scroop and Shrubb. "Say what you will," Joanna said, intent on teasing Joe, "he's the handsomest man in the room, and the most distinguished."

"Have it your own way," Joe said. "I'm not competing. The Morrisons have never claimed to be handsome or distinguished. They get by with an irresistible *bonhomie*. Well, thank God for that," he added, as the music stopped. "I'm properly ashamed, Joanna, of the exhibition I'm making of you. I see your mother's here. Let's go and talk to her."

They joined Mrs. Halliwell, who said: "Well, Joe, I can see you've never wasted time on the lighter side of life."

"No," Joe said. "But there's something about me. Do you see those two chaps over there, looking around as if they're trying to locate a damp spot? Well, as we danced past them the tall one said to the other: 'Look at that youth dancing with the girl in gold. Evidently unaccustomed to these trivial occasions, but what concentrated power and energy! That's a man who will go far.'"

Joanna said: "Joe, will you push a way for me towards the buffet? There's one thing about you. You look as though you'd by a handy man in a scrum."

"Will you come with us, Mrs. Halliwell?" Joe asked; and Mrs. Halliwell said: "No, thank you, Joe. I've already been invited. Oh! Here is my escort."

Scroop, leaving Shrubb to his hobbling about the room, came up and bowed. Mrs. Halliwell got up, and he offered an arm. She took it. "This is my daughter Joanna," she said. "And this is Joe Morrison. This is Sir William Scroop."

Scroop bowed to Joanna, and said: "I saw Miss Halliwell dancing. I hope I shall be allowed the pleasure of dancing with her after supper? And once again, madam, now that I've had a chance of looking round, may I thank you for the superb thing you've done here?"

After his remark to Joanna, he took no notice of her, but gave his attention to Mrs. Halliwell, who was pleased to hear that what she had done for Alf could be so deeply, and obviously sincerely, praised. Not that she knew she had done a superb thing. What she had wanted was to brighten a dull room, and she was still more than a little surprised at the cost of what she thought of as a bit of painting and decorating. She contented herself with saying: "Thank you, Sir William. I certainly think Mr. Scrubb did very well."

Joe, taking a hint from Sir William, offered Joanna his arm, and they followed Mrs. Halliwell and the Eleventh Bart across the room. There was no need for scrum technique. Mrs. Halliwell's purple bulk, and something "Out of the way there, please," in Sir William's advance, cleared a path, and Joe and Joanna followed in the opened lane. "What did I tell you?" Joanna whispered, and Joe said: "Ay, he knows his stuff. He'd take some turning into an anemone."

Anthony and Lottie Wayland had been among the first to make their way to the supper room, and there, to Anthony's surprise, they found Septimus Pordage dressed up to the nines, one of the few who had taken seriously the words on the invitation card: "Orders and Decorations will be worn." On the lapel of his evening-coat hung a row of small medals, and his Order gleamed upon the burnish of his shirt front. He was standing by a table and held an ebony gavel into which a silver plate had been inserted. Anthony and Lottie approached him, but he frowned them away, and stood holding the gavel with some obvious public intent. When Mrs. Halliwell came in on Sir William's arm, he struck the table and cried: "Order, order."

It was unexpected. Everyone stood still, and the chattering gave place to a hush. "Ladies and gentlemen," Septimus said, "I have a few words to say about Mrs. Halliwell."

Scroop, with a sense of what was coming, and knowing that he had no part in this, released Mrs. Halliwell's arm, bowed to her, and moved into the crowd. She stood isolated but composed, and Septimus went on: "Mrs. Halliwell being what she is, we did not let her in on our schemes. Her modesty would have said No, and she being an unshakable woman, in every sense of the words, that would have been that. We didn't even know whether she would grant us the pleasure of seeing her here to-night, but here she is, and the last thing we must do is affront her with an oration. On the silver plate sunk into this gavel is an expression of Smurthwaite's thanks to her for raising beauty from ashes, and my very simple, but to me deeply moving task, is to ask you to show your appreciation."

When the cheers had died away, Mrs. Halliwell, who took them with no emotion, said: "Thank you, Mr. Pordage, and thank you all, ladies and gentlemen. I just had the idea, but the thanks should go to my husband for deserving this memorial, and to Mr. Shrubb who has made such a nice job of it. And now let's have supper."

13

When the music began again Scroop approached Joanna and said: "You didn't promise that you would dance with me, Miss Halliwell, but may I have the pleasure?"

She said nothing, but they began to dance, and this now was dancing. While she was at home she had not been encouraged to do much dancing, and in Switzerland it had been a formal and decorous matter. She had not realised that she could dance so well or that dancing could be so satisfying. "It's an odd thing," she said, "but I'm seeing this room for the first time. I'm realising that it was made for dancing."

"So were you," Scroop said.

He didn't smile as he said it. His face was dark, grave and concentrated, but she felt herself flush. She saw Anthony dancing with Lottie, and Joe Morrison trundling along like a conscientious steam-roller that had its stint to do and would do it if the skies fell; and she thought: They're boys. They've done nothing and seen nothing.

She was dancing with a man.

She looked at Scroop, and saw that as he danced a small tic was twitching his cheek. He looked sad, while all around them were smiles and broad grins and the occasional snatch of a poor little joke. He seemed aware of none of this, as though he were existing in some world of his own. And yet out of that remoteness had come those three words: So were you.

She felt inadequate, a bit afraid of him, and to break the tension she said: "Do you feel that about the room, too?"

He said: "Don't talk. Dance."

There was a short corridor leading out of the ballroom to a cloak-room, and whether by accident or by his contriving, they were near it when the music ended. He drew her into it and said: "Hold your head up high."

She thought it an odd thing to do, but she did it. He bent and kissed her on the throat.

He asked: "Does that surprise you?"

She felt confused and pleased and frightened, and she said: "Well—I . . . No, somehow it doesn't."

"Shall I write to you when I get back to town?"

She nodded, unable to speak.

That was all—a few seconds—and he was leading her across the floor to her mother, her hand resting lightly on his arm. He said to Mrs. Halliwell: "I have come to say good night, madam. Poor Shrubb is unable to dance, so I must take him back to our hotel and entertain him. We were comrades, you know, in the late regrettable skirmish in France."

Joanna thought: "He's saying this to me. He's telling me at any rate something about himself."

He bowed to her mother and to her, and went away to find Shrubb, who was sitting at the other end of the room.

Joe Morrison, who had shed the girl in an unsuitable shade of electric blue, asked: "Would you risk it again with me, Joanna?"

She said: "No, thank you, Joe. I shan't dance any more to-night. I'm rather tired."

"You're jealous," Joe chaffed her, "just because I gave that girl in blue the pleasure of my company. I wonder what you'd say if I became jealous of Sir William Scroop?"

"I suppose I'd have to grin and bear it," she said with an odd sense of fatality.

14

This dance was the culmination of the boys' visit. The next morning Joanna drove them and Lottie to Smurthwaite station so that they might catch the Bradford train. Lottie would be returning in a day or two to begin work with Septimus. The motor run to the station was cut rather fine, and the train was on the point of leaving when Lottie and the boys jumped in. Joanna had a sense, which puzzled her, of gladness to see them go. Now she could be alone. As the train pulled out she felt as though it were taking away her childhood. Lottie, with a boy on either side of her, was leaning out of the window. They were all waving, and Joanna waved, too, and, though they were out of earshot, she shouted "Good-bye." And then, looking round the empty platform, she said it again to herself. Good-bye.

ð ð ð ð ð ð

1

*I*t was as pleasant a domestic scene as you could imagine. Dick wearing a dressing-gown with red dragons spouting fire and cavorting all over a background of vicious green. Chris was in a neat lounge suit. The coal ration didn't go far, but Dick had had the fire lit to celebrate his son's visit. The remains of breakfast were still on the table.

Chris lit a cigarette and walked to the window. A dark London morning pressed down on the garden, little more than a square of grass with a few ornamental cherry trees at the end. But there was a passable brick wall round this little bit of St. John's Wood, and Chris was thinking that something could be made of the place. The grass should go. The whole square should be paved. Something could be done with water falling from a dolphin's mouth in the wall into a long narrow pond. Just that, and a few little trees in tubs, and a stone seat and a leaden figure here and there. Chris was always thinking of ways of improving his father and his father's surroundings and habits. He no longer disliked him. He felt a rather contemptuous affection for him. You couldn't take such a man seriously, of course, but as a character there was something to be said for him.

He flicked the ash of his cigarette into an ash-tray that made him wince. It was embellished with a picture of the Blackpool Tower. "What about that dressing-gown?" he asked. "Is it quite right?"

Dick stroked his dragons. They seemed to rear up with responsive affection. "There's nowt wrong wi' this," he said. "Cost me a pretty penny, that did."

"There's nothing wrong with the red," Chris conceded. "That

190

shade of red is one of my favourites. But the green! Damn it, it puts one's teeth on edge like sour apples."

"It's Oriental," Dick said, as though that explained and excused everything.

"And I'm not over-fond of dragons," Chris continued. "Their colour—yes. But there's too much of it, and there should be no green at all. What I suggest is a gown of dark blue shantung, with a girdle of that passable red. That would be distinguished."

"Damn it, Chris, I don't want to be distinguished. I want to be comfortable. And I'm used to these dragons. They're like dogs that've been about the place for years."

The dragons leered modestly.

"All right," Chris said. "Have it your own way. I'm only trying to help you."

He lit another cigarette and said: "Well, I sha'n't go back to Oxford till this afternoon. I shall be gated, anyway."

"What d'you mean by that?"

"Confined to barracks. Forbidden to leave college. It's what happens to bad boys who aren't in bed by the proper time."

Dick didn't like reproving his son, but he said: "I've warned you often enough, Chris. Why didn't you go back last night?"

"I should have been too late, anyway. Of course there are walls that can be climbed, but I dislike acrobatics. Good practice for getting out of Dartmoor, but who would want to climb *in*?"

Dick plunged his hand into a nest of dragons, pulled out a pipe, and lit it. He refilled his coffee-cup. "Now look, Chris," he said with a diffidence that somehow gave him dignity, "I don't want to pry into your affairs. You're a man now, the sort of man I've had in mind ever since those old days when I sacked Mrs. Wyke and sent you to Mrs. Wayland in Megson Street. It was a kind of bargain between us. I had to supply the brass, and that's not something I want to crow about, because making brass comes easy to me and there's not much to spend it on except you. So what the hell, as one might say. Your part of the bargain—not that we ever put it like this—in fact we never put it in any way—but what I'm trying to say . . ."

Chris interrupted. "Now take it easy," he said. "I know what you're trying to say, and I'm going to say something, too. I'm going to say just this: I think you've been splendid."

Dick smiled, and the boy thought: How easy it is!

He went on: "You're worrying about me. You're asking yourself whether I'm taking advantage of what you have so generously done.

As sure as eggs, I'm going to be gated because I've been out of college a bit too much. Well, that doesn't disturb me. I'm on top of my work. I can do what's expected of me, and more than is expected of me. I happen to be ambitious."

And this was true. Chris *was* ambitious, and he had discovered in himself a capacity for continuous and concentrated work. He knew well enough that a few nights out wouldn't count against the drive he could apply when he wanted to.

Dick looked at him with affection. Chris didn't often hand a bouquet, and he accepted it gratefully. "That's all right then, lad. But don't overdo it. Don't lose sleep. A young body needs a lot of sleep. You were very late in last night."

"Ah, well, I'll soon be back at the grindstone. I just happened to meet a few chaps."

He had met one chap whom he had known up at Oxford and who had now come down. They had had a drink or two and had then turned in to a music-hall. On the bill was *Dulcie Dearmer, Smiling Through*. Chris remembered how Dulcie Dearmer had appeared with his father one day on the Leeds railway station platform. He had gone over from Bradford to meet the old man, taking that young tick Anthony Bromwich with him, and they had met that super-tick Courtice who had later gone off and got himself killed. Sitting in the stalls of the music-hall, with a few drinks warm inside him and smoking a cigar—an indulgence he allowed himself only now and then, in expansive moments—he watched Dulcie Dearmer's performance, and thought little of it, and recalled the awe with which he and the two ticks had looked at her as she stood on the platform at Leeds, all fox fur and blue eyes and static smiling mouth. Well, well, he thought, what callow children we were. There was nothing about Dulcie Dearmer to startle him now. For two pins, he'd send up a note and ask her to meet him. The chap had to leave before the performance ended in order to catch a train to Amersham; and Chris, alone, was more and more tempted to put Dulcie Dearmer to the test.

2

It was a pity that the Reverend Robert Box had ever heard of Florence Nightingale and Octavia Hill and Mary Kingsley and other women of that sort. Grant Allen had written *The Woman Who Did*, a novel Mr. Box didn't like. He was obsessed by Women Who Did

Good Things. He was a widower, devoted to his only child, Alice, who was to become Dulcie Dearmer. She was a gay, pretty creature, and she had no use at all for formidable and contriving women. She preferred women like her mother. She could remember her mother singing her to sleep with charming silly lullabies. "None of your women ever got married," she said; and Mr. Box replied triumphantly: "There you are wrong, my dear. What about Mrs. Pankhurst?"

The thought of Mrs. Pankhurst was oddly unconsoling to Alice.

They lived on a small income in a large gloomy rectory adjoining the church. Church and rectory might have been built of carbon. They were black with decades of smoke and sulphur. The prospect from the front windows was of a churchyard no longer used. It was railed round with thick iron bars, discouraging to any ghosts who might rise up to seek a little sweetness and light. The tombstones tottered in the grimy grass, and the habitations that had known the ghosts when living reached implacably about the rectory in league after stony league.

In these dismal conditions Alice was happy. She went daily to the girls' grammar school, and Mr. Box was distressed by the periodic reports that showed her to be making no progress in any subject. But Alice didn't mind, and her father's gentle lectures, his exhortations that she should fit herself for a place in the world of women doing things, slid off her with no effect. She liked going to church because of the music, but she detested her father's rounds among the poor. He always took her with him, so that she might become acquainted with the social evils to whose curing good women applied themselves.

Mr. Box, who shrivelled as Alice bloomed, took all parts of his work seriously, and his work among the people of the theatre more seriously than most, for it seemed to him that they must necessarily be far from grace and in need of all that he could do for them. He was rather proud when the local newspapers called him "the actors' parson."

When Alice was in her middle teens, he took her with him on this mission, too. She was entranced. She had little to say, for, truth to tell, she was dumb in every sense of the word, endowed with nothing but pleasing looks and light-heartedness. As her father gave his little talks and his handshakes and his invitations to church, she was in a world peopled by such creatures as she had never imagined, for her first visit was to a pantomime company, and the girls with blue-shaded eyes and eyelashes clotted with mascara and rouged cheeks and painted lips, some in extravagantly ample clothes, some in tights and little more, powerfully worked upon her imagination. A box had been reserved for her and her father, and though the rector asked to be excused, saying that he had much to do, he was prevailed on, and once he and Alice had slipped into the box half-way through the show, the girl so earnestly begged him to stay that they remained till it was over.

"I was as dumb as they come—a proper little greenhorn," Dulcie Dearmer would say to anyone who cared to listen to her memoirs. "Incredible, isn't it? But there it is. I thought the whole set-up marvellous."

Certainly, the Reverend Robert Box found himself faced with a problem. The girl would talk of nothing but the theatre, begging him to take her whenever he made his visits. He did so for a time, hoping that her call was to be a female Damien among theatrical lepers. But her mania increased, and in alarm, perceiving at last its true direction, he forbade her the theatre altogether. To save these people's souls was one thing. To be so madly moved by what they were doing was another. Nell Gwynne and Mrs. Jordan had no place in his list of women who did things worth doing.

Alice had now left school. He had hoped—though not lately—that she would win a scholarship to help her through the university. He had even considered compounding his life insurance in order to pay all the fees. But, facing the question in his dark little study, he had reluctantly to admit that he might as well pour the money down the drain.

It was his custom to give an annual entertainment and bunfeast to the poor children of his parish. Alice helped. She would sing a song or two and tinkle the piano as the youngsters bellowed *Annie Laurie* or *Ilkla Moor*. She told him this year that she was going to give them something good, and certainly she gave them something astonishing. For weeks before the entertainment she disappeared every afternoon. She went to a public park and there practiced on odd instruments. She had a Jew's harp, a small cheap xylophone, a mouth organ and a tin whistle. She worked like a maniac on this improbable assortment, and on the day of the concert she went early to the hall and rigged up what she called a dressing-room with curtains in a back corner of the stage. Hence, when her "number went up," as she put it to herself, she emerged to the surprise of everybody except the curate who had given a hand with the rigging. He was newly down from Oxford where he had done a bit of amateur acting, and he had helped to assemble her make-up table. But even he can hardly have expected the sensational-looking harlot who stepped out

194

of the tent and bowed. ("My dears, though I'm long past the blushing stage, I still go a little pink when I think of it. My poor father!")

It was the worse for her poor father because he was sitting with Miss Batty, whom he had asked that very day to be his wife, and who had consented. She was a woman who did things, and had been a plague among the poor of the parish for years, inspecting their teeth and tonsils and deploring the strange foods they ate. Mr. Box was sure that in her he had an ally who would help Alice to see life clearly and to see it whole.

When the curtains parted, he was aware that Miss Batty stiffened. She was, normally, not supple; now she was as yielding as an iron bollard. He himself melted as she went rigid: he felt as if he hadn't a bone in his body.

Alice was wearing a stage costume of her own making. It showed too much of her budding breasts. It was tight round the stomach and then flowed down in frills of red, white and blue to her feet, shod in high-heeled scarlet. She had helped herself liberally from the make-up table. She had indeed given herself the whole works, putting the stuff on as if she were eating jam from a spoon. Her eyes were ringed with incredible blue; her cheeks and her mouth flamed with colour, and on to her face was nailed the immovable wide smile that showed her splendid teeth and was to become her professional trademark.

She smacked straight away at the xylophone. "Two eyes of blue come smiling through at me." And they did. The children loved it. They clapped. They hammered the floor with their boots. They shouted and they whistled; and Miss Batty turned round and glared at them as if they were a nest of vipers. Alice picked up the mouthorgan and rollicked into "Pack up your troubles." She made a mess of the Jew's harp, but an unbashful young ruffian, stimulated by the unaccustomed tone of the proceedings, leapt upon the platform and said "Lemme!" He took the instrument from her hand and showed himself a maestro. He was encored, ran through a considerable repertory, and was with difficulty induced to leave the platform. The curate lifted him down, kicking.

Alice then did what she could with the tin whistle, which wasn't much, and retired to her tent, leaving the curate to oblige with "We'll come up from Zummerzet" and "Tis Devon, glorious Devon."

Alice remained in her tent during the interval when tea was spilled down frocks and shirt-fronts and buns were crumbled all over the floor. They were wholemeal buns, too, dietetically ordered by Miss Batty, who stood behind the tea-urn looking like a Borgia who would for two pins unrepentantly poison everyone in sight, including the curate. He seemed to be enjoying himself more robustly than she felt a curate should, and she suspected him of collusion in Alice's extraordinary behaviour. It was time, Miss Batty thought, that Robert had someone to set the affairs both of his home and his church in order. She resolved to begin right away by taking the rest of the programme in hand, and sent the curate to tell Alice that there would be no more profane singing and playing upon instruments, and that, when she was decently dressed, she could emerge to take her part in round games.

The curate peeped into the tent and blushed to find his rector's daughter in a considerable state of undress. She was about to put on the second of her remarkable costumes. He said: "You'd better get into your ordinary clothes, Miss Box. La Batty is on the warpath. Whoopee is definitely off."

She asked: "Was I good?"

"You were good in parts, like my traditional egg."

Confronted by a generous view of parts which seemed to him very good indeed, he dropped the curtain regretfully, but with a sense of what was due from one who, after all, might some day be a bishop.

The rest of the evening was a dead loss to Alice. She played the piano for musical chairs, and rejoiced when Miss Batty, dashing for a chair, missed by an inch or two and went down on her behind. She dutifully joined in games of blind man's buff and round the mulberry bush, but what she wanted was to be alone on a platform, with an audience in front of her thinking her wonderful. And there was no more of that. It was Miss Batty who got on to the platform, when she thought it was high time Robert was going home to his Ovaltine, and said: "Now, children, let's have three hearty cheers for Mr. Box, who has given you this wonderful entertainment. And then you can all go home and tell your fathers and mothers that Miss Batty is a lucky woman because she's going to be Mr. Box's very own wife."

The assembled barbarians, who knew everything that was worth knowing about nuptials, and a good deal that wasn't, let loose a storm of ribald cheers, catcalls and whistles. They thought Miss Batty's turn almost as good, in its way, as Miss Box's, but they had their private opinions about what she could do with her wholemeal buns.

3

The next few years of Alice Box's life were unhappy. She was a cheerful hare-brained creature and it took a lot to depress her. However, the task was not beyond the resources of the new Mrs. Box. Alice was packed off to a secretarial school where she learned to use a typewriter, scribble shorthand and do a bit of bookkeeping. Then she was commanded to find work, and she did so. The carbon rectory, which had not daunted her childhood, became odious in her blossoming years, and she, who had never known either love or hate, but had taken all humanity on easy-going terms, learned to hate her stepmother with a blackness of which she herself was sometimes frightened.

Mr. Box could hardly fail to suffer from the chill change in the atmosphere of his home. He was a devoted priest and had overworked himself for years in squalid conditions, but this had not daunted him. He took sacrifice for granted. But what he could not take for granted was the miasma of unhappiness creeping under his roof. His health worsened alarmingly, and his bishop, who liked him and valued him, suggested a change to a climate and to conditions that would not tell so heavily upon him. And that was how, reluctantly, he became a rural dean in Wiltshire.

There was a frightful week for Alice when her father had gone south in connection with this matter and she was left alone in the rectory with her stepmother. She had been accustomed to go home for lunch, but that week she took sandwiches every day to the office, and she prolonged her absence by dawdling about the streets till nine o'clock when "second house" began in the music-halls, which fascinated her. It would be half past eleven before she got home, and then she would go straight to her bedroom. Mrs. Box, who had to wait up, for Alice was not permitted the freedom of a latchkey, looked black for three nights, and on the fourth barred the girl's way at the foot of the stairs. "Where have you been?" she demanded.

Alice said: "Keeping out of your way."

"Why should you want to do that?"

Alice, who disliked even now anything so real as a crisis, hesitated. Then she asked: "Do you really want to know?"

"I shouldn't have asked if I didn't."

"Very well, then. Because the sight of you makes me sick. Now get out of my way. I'm tired, and I want to go to bed."

Mrs. Box remained blocking the way up. She said: "It's time someone spoke to you frankly, young woman. You shall go to bed when I've had my say."

Alice did not answer. She was boiling, and wanted to knock the woman down. She was a robust girl and could easily have done it, but she contented herself with putting out an arm and sweeping Mrs. Box aside. She went past her without a look or a word, climbed the stairs on dragging feet, and got into bed.

Mr. Box had been born in an industrial town, and save for his Cambridge years had spent all his life in one. He loved the country, but detested the thought of deserting, as he called it, his black urban sheep. He knew as well as the next man that to stay among them would shorten his life, and had he remained a widower he would have seen nothing against that. But Mrs. Box saw a good deal, and so he returned from his visit determined to be cheerful, to report happily on what he had found. There was even work for Alice, he said. On the outskirts of the village there was a factory—"Nothing like the factories we have here, my dear"—for the reduction of milk to a powdered product; and he had talked to the managing director, one of his new church-wardens, who assured him that the office could find plenty for Alice to do.

Alice said: "I shall not be coming with you, Father."

She had not spoken to her stepmother since the episode at the foot of the stairs; but she might have got over that, for her father's sake, if Mrs. Box, infuriated by this sullen passive resistance, had not looked round for means of retort. The night before her father's return, Alice came in late as usual, and was met by a smell of burning from the kitchen. She went through at once, and found the grate choked with rags and paper. Beneath it was a pile of ash, which showed that burning and raking had been going on for a long time. What was smouldering now was an old dress, absurdly crusted with hundreds upon hundreds of small green beads, that had belonged to the first Mrs. Box, and that Alice had kept in her own wardrobe. And on top of this, licked by sickly flames, was a photograph of Alice's mother that had stood on the bedroom mantelpiece.

Mrs. Box, who had followed the girl into the kitchen, looked uneasy and ashamed. "I've been having a clean-up," she said. "The house is full of stuff we can't possibly take with us, and that dress is so old-fashioned that even the Poor would laugh if we offered it to them."

Alice had no deep feeling about the mother she hardly remembered. The dress had been no more to her than an amusing curio, and she hardly ever looked at the photograph. But she was shrewd enough to know that her step-mother was not aware of this, that she believed she was striking at a deep affection. And more than that, she was sickened by the thought of the woman invading the privacy of her room, fumbling with her things. She was so nauseated that it would not have surprised her to see a slug's slime on the strip of carpet by the bed in that cold little cell. She maintained her silence, gave her step-mother a smile of complete and candid understanding, pitying and contemptuous, and went to bed.

"I don't think there would be any point in my going down into Wiltshire," she said to her father. "I think it would be a mistake to break up the good start I have made here. I can easily find myself a room. I have prospects," she lied. "And I don't want to be a nuisance to you and your wife."

"Your mother, my dear."

"Your wife, Father."

Mr. Box knew that nothing could change the unhappy situation that he had seen growing for years; so, before he left the rectory, he made it his business to find a bed-sitting-room of the utmost respectability for Alice. She was not in it for long. She got a job in a theatrical agent's office in London, borrowed her fare and a few pounds to keep her going from the curate, and set off on what she was calling to herself her career. That was in 1908, when she was twenty; and so the woman who received Chris Hudson's note, and who looked about eighteen under the limelight, was a reasonably brazen trooper in her early thirties.

4

Chris was delighted. He felt himself the man of the world he had long wanted to be. Life had never washed from his mind the memory of the boy whom no one seemed to like, the boy kicked round the board school playground, under the ignoble necessity of being rescued by ticks like Anthony Bromwich. He could smile now at his childish escapes into heroism—"Lieutenant-Colonel Hudson is due at any moment, sir, with the finest troops on the frontier. He'll raise the siege, never fear"—but his feelings as he stood outside the theatre with Dulcie Dearmer were not greatly different from those. "That's Hudson with that fine-looking actress. He knows his way about."

But he didn't. He didn't know anything about restaurants or clubs, and his little note to Dulcie had merely said that he was Dick Hudson's son and would like the honour of meeting her. Dulcie was not excited: she was hardly interested: scores of similar notes came her way, and she tore up most of them. But she liked Dick Hudson. Most people did. And so she said yes to his son. He wasn't a bad-looking kid, standing there in the back alley on to which the stage door opened. He shook hands with her formally and said he was delighted to meet her and that he'd bet she didn't remember meeting him before. She didn't, and when he recalled the brief encounter in Leeds she still didn't remember, but said "Oh, you're *that* boy!" and Chris said: "Well, I suppose I was a boy then."

After that he seemed stuck, and it was all to be up to her, and she said: "What shall we do? Do you dance?"

He did. Dancing was the rage of that post-war moment, and it had caught him up, and he wasn't bad at it.

"I should love that," he said.

"Well, let's go to the Silver Star. Do you think you could find a taxi?"

("In no time, Hudson, who knew the town's glittering resorts as few men did, had whisked her off to the Silver Star, the most splendid of them all.")

But it wasn't so splendid as that. It was in a dark Soho street, and there was nothing to identify it save a many-pointed star of blown white glass that hung over a doorway. Within the door a young man in shirtsleeves said: "Ullo, Miss Dearmer."

Miss Dearmer said: "Ullo, Bert. I'm introducing a friend." She wrote the friend's name in a book, and said to Chris: "You can hang your coat and hat there," pointing to some hooks on the passage wall. Chris, who had been rather disappointed by this landfall, noted hopefully that black felt hats and the sort of coats and scarfs that go with evening clothes were hanging there.

Miss Dearmer asked: "Anyone here yet, Bert?"

"No one much."

"Do you expect Charlie to-night?"

"No. Nor for a good many nights, if you know what that means."

Dulcie said: "Oh, Bert! He promised he'd be here to-night. I haven't got a pinch left."

Bert looked blank. "I don't know what you're talking about."

"Oh, yes, you do. And you know very well that I can't . . ."

"Shut up, you silly fool," Bert said with a look at Chris; and Dulcie, looking at Chris, too, changed her tone and said: "Let's go in."

This had been a private house, with sliding doors between two

200

living-rooms. The doors were open, but even so the place was not large. There were a score of tables along the walls, with a replica of the silver star outside shining in miniature on each. Three tired-looking men were playing dance music on a small platform, and a few couples were dancing. More couples were dancing on the walls. The mural artist had let himself go. Silver stars were twinkling in the sky, and among dusty trees beneath them the couples danced: satyrs and fauns, Europa and her bull, Leda and her swan, and, mingled with these, many mortal men and women, naked as the creatures of myth. Chris thought this was much better than the Arthur Hacker nude which he remembered grinning over one day when he was in the Cartwright Art Gallery at Bradford with young Anthony Bromwich.

He looked sideways at Dulcie, and here, where the light, though discreet, was more revealing than in the stage-door alley or in the taxi-cab, he saw that she was not what Tennyson had called a "queen-girl of the rosebud garden of girls," though she managed to appear so under the limelight. Her hair had a brassy brilliance and her eyebrows were carefully shaped into thin lines. Her eyes, which, when he recalled that meeting in Leeds, always came back to him as gentian blue, were now washed-out, with blue a mere hint, as in a garment too long drenched by the sun. Once or twice she closed her eyes, as though she would gladly have nodded off to sleep, and then the colour applied to her eyelids could not make them seem other than integuments, taut and tired. Taut and tired: the whole face seemed that to his candid stare; and the painted finger nails called attention to the occasional nervous twitching of the fingers. What most struck him was the hardness of the features now that the professional smile had been taken off. His imagination had been giving her ten years less than her age. Now he was inclined to add ten years to it.

Chris could bluff himself with imagined situations just so long as reality didn't break in. Mrs. Wyke's return to the house in Bradford had always been able to wake him up; and he was pretty wide awake now. He was a bit disappointed at romance turning so swiftly to a banal situation which had landed him with a woman ageing before her time, but he made the best of it. He found the murals, at any rate, amusing; and it was amusing, too, to recognise some of the people drooping about the floor. Their faces were well publicised in *The Tattler*. He was now in command of himself and of his disappointingly cheap situation. He said to Dulcie: "Isn't that chap dancing over there Sir William Scroop?"

Dulcie came sharply awake. "My God," she said. "Is *he* here?"

"Yes, if I am not mistaken."

A waiter came to the table, and Dulcie dismissed him quickly. "You know what I always have, George. We'll both have it."

But Chris now was not prepared to be the small boy in leading strings. "Half a minute," he said to the waiter. "What is it that Miss Dearmer always has, and that I'm to have, too?"

"A dozen oysters, sir, red pepper, brown bread and butter, and champagne."

"Very well," Chris said. "But so as not to be ordered about, I'll do without the red pepper and have thirteen oysters."

When the man returned with the food, Dulcie said: "Has Charlie left anything for me?" and the waiter said brusquely: "I don't know any Charlie."

"A figment of the imagination apparently, this Charlie," Chris said with a laugh. Dulcie didn't join in. She was looking at Sir William Scroop, and Chris was looking at the girl with him. Where on earth had he seen her before?

5

Mrs. Halliwell and Joanna were staying at Brown's Hotel. It was the sort of place Mrs. Halliwell liked: as comfortable as anyone could want, but free of all those bits of glittering swank that she couldn't abide. Scroop laughed about it to Joanna. "Oh, yes, I've been there. The wicked Bart, my uncle, always stayed there when he was in town. He loathed the house in Soho Square, and he chose Brown's rather than one of the more shiny caravanserais because it was better cover for his disreputable doings. It takes the overflow of bishops from the Athenæum and the county people with their young. I've stayed there with the Ninth Bart, and flirted with innumerable small girls from places like Melton Mowbray. I was always a bit surprised that they didn't clatter downstairs to breakfast on ponies, with their pigtails flying. There was one I got on with awfully well. The honourable Molly something. She said to me one day: 'Would you like to see a photograph of my horse?' Well, that ended a promising romance."

Joanna let him run on. She loved to hear him talk of things and places and people that she had only imagined, even though his talk, as now, was not serious.

"Labradors, too," he said. "Couldn't your mother hire a few Labradors for the duration of your visit? They give an enormous prestige at Brown's. They bring in the shires and the scent of the heather and the crack of the gun. My uncle loathed them, and used to devise all sorts of counter-measures. Once he had a three-in-hand of Belgian griffons. You know the things—about as big as squirrels? He kept them on a sort of trident-lead of scarlet leather and saw to it that they tangled themselves in dowagers' legs. Another time he hired three appalling-looking Scotsmen and dressed them as ghillies. They had to come every morning and report about the bur-r-ns and the heather-r. To keep him *au fait* with the state of sport, they'd bring damn great salmon that he'd bought at the fishmongers and stags' horns that he'd found in secondhand shops. They had very loud voices, and always reported in the lounge where eminent-looking men were reading that eminent-looking paper *The Times*."

"I don't believe half of it," Joanna said, delighted; and he said: "Well, so long as you believe the other half that's as much as any man can expect."

Joanna looked round the room: that crowded room in Soho Square where Scroop was still playing about with the idea of launching *Vanguard*, and still wondering whether he could induce his agent to advance the money for the first number. "After that it'll start paying for itself." The agent had heard of too many things that would pay for themselves, but, mysteriously, didn't.

"Mother'll love this room," Joanna said, "if only for its size. When you've been brought up as she was, one of a large family in a few poky rooms, you seem to develop a thing about spaciousness."

There had been no pretences between them. He knew all about Mrs. Halliwell's beginnings, just as Mrs. Halliwell knew—or accurately guessed—what had happened at the Smurthwaite ball. She had observed the momentary disappearance of Scroop and Joanna, and had pondered on the girl's lit-up appearance as they drove home. She was aware of the letters that passed between them, not often at first, but then almost daily. After a few weeks, she said to Joanna, as the girl drove her in to the mill: "I'd better ask that Sir William Scroop if he'd like to come up here and spend a few days. He might like to look me over, and I'd certainly like to look him over."

Joanna said ingenuously: "Oh, Mother, how do you know about that?" and Mrs. Halliwell said: "Well, I wasn't brought up in a sort of convent, like you."

She thought there was reason for giving Scroop a look over, because by now she knew a good deal about him. She had written to advisers in London and asked to be told what they could find out about the Scroop family, and now she knew it all by heart, from the uprush on the tide of such speculations as the South Sea Bubble to the wastage that had been more or less continuous ever since, including the wicked Ninth Bart's inroads upon the estate. There was a lot in the story that, being the woman she was, she disliked very much, and she didn't intend to give Joanna away with a pound of tea.

What she liked about Scroop, when he came, was his candour. He was ready to discuss his family and his situation, and nothing that he said differed from what she already knew and kept to herself. He even told her of the scheme to pull down the Soho house and sell the site at a handsome figure. "But I'm not going to have that," he said firmly, "not if I starve. Do *you* think I ought to sell?"

Mrs. Halliwell noted the hand nervously pulling at the face from brows to chin, and said to herself that this lad was a bit overwrought. She also thought that his agent was not so good as he considered himself. She knew something about the value of London property, and believed that a lot more could be screwed out of the wealthy firm that wanted to buy.

Scroop looked at her pondering face, and said: "I want to keep *something* out of the wreck. If the place stays as it is, mostly let out as offices, and I keep my one floor, then perhaps some day it can all be brought back to what it was. But once you've turned the ground floor into a showroom the building's finished, and I might as well pack up. And it's a good building, believe me."

Mrs. Halliwell said: "When you're married to Joanna . . ." and Scroop broke in: "But you haven't said I may marry Joanna, and how can I marry Joanna . . ." and now it was her turn to break in. "You'll marry Joanna all right, and I must say that I'd prefer to have the pair of you living in the country. But she seems set on London, and you seem set on this house, so when you marry Joanna she'll want a proper home, not one floor. You can go on letting the ground floor to people who won't spoil it, but you'll need the rest of the house if you're to have anything like what *I* call a home, and I'll get it put in order for you as a wedding present. You'd better let that nice young man Mr. Shrubb do the job. And I daresay Joanna's money will allow you to live in the place comfortably enough."

6

Over their heads they could hear the decorators brought in by that nice young man Mr. Shrubb, and Gwilym had been in with morning coffee, and they were waiting for Mrs. Halliwell. It was a pleasant winter day, nippy but bright, and the world to both of them seemed lovelier and safer than they had ever imagined it could be. Joanna had not been in London since her return from Switzerland, and her life before that seemed infinitely remote. Her visits to London then were few and brief, and now all the throb of the place was there for her to discover, new and miraculous because she was seeing it through two pairs of eyes. Scroop said: "You want to see the oddest things, darling. My father loathed London. I don't remember his ever setting foot in the place. I discovered it in company of Sir Hector, and he never wanted to see the guard changed at Buckingham Palace or the ducks in St. James's Park. You're so innocent."

It was the essence of her charm for him. He thought of the many girls he had known, as beautiful as she, some more beautiful, all sophisticated. They would have laughed their heads off to hear her say, when he asked: "What shall we do to-morrow——?" "Let's get up early and see those men who carry the fish-baskets on their heads at Billingsgate." But those were the sort of things she wanted to see and do. They climbed to the top of the Monument, and inspected the armour in the Tower, and threw biscuits to the gulls on the Embankment and in Trafalgar Square. It was there that he told her to look at the portico of the National Gallery, and said: "It's odd to think of one of our Barts going through those pillars to take a meal with the Prince Regent."

"But how could he?" she asked innocently. "The Prince Regent didn't live in the National Gallery."

"No, but when they pulled down Carlton House, which is where he did live, the entrance was preserved and put up here as the entrance to the National Gallery. Carlton House was just across there—more or less where the Athenæum is."

"Oh!" she cried. "We haven't seen the Athenæum! Let's see it now. And then we can go down the steps and walk right along the Mall."

"You walk so much," he said. "It's time you did some dancing. Don't you remember that I told you in Smurthwaite you were made for dancing?"

She would never forget it.

And that was another side of life in London—alluring, round the corner, untasted as yet, but she wanted to taste it: the life that went on after darkness had fallen and she was sitting demurely in Brown's with her mother.

"I should love to take you dancing to-night," he said. "Do you think your mother would allow it?"

It seemed odd to him to ask that question, odd that there were still girls in the world to whom it needed to be put.

Of course there are, tens of thousands of them, he told himself, but they haven't come my way of late.

His way of late didn't please him. There was too much of the Ninth Bart about it; but the Ninth Bart wasn't ruined. He could afford to carry on with an air: sinning in his Sunday suit, as he called it. "William, my boy, always remember that sinners in Sunday suits are the ones that get away with it. If you ever find yourself without a shirt to your back, cultivate the approved virtues."

Old Hector hadn't been through the Somme and Passchendaele and a refined loony-bin. He hadn't come out of all that to find himself with hardly a penny but with a compelling drive to kick up his heels. Scroop doubted whether the old villain, in his place, would have had much use for the approved virtues. There was a sniff of cocaine to be picked up here and there, and, when life seemed a particularly depressing farce, that put a silver lining to things for a while. And in the clubs that were springing up like toadstools there were plenty of girls one could ask to dance without mother's permission. He had paddled in the fringes of all this, telling himself that once *Vanguard* was launched he would have something to do with his days and nights, something that all he thought worthwhile could be directed into, and then Gwilym wouldn't have to spend his days looking like a hurt spaniel. "You see, Shrubbo," he said, "we *must* somehow get this damned thing going. It's beginning to obsess me, and if it doesn't get born something's going to strangle inside me. It stands for what *I* stand for: preventing the wreck of all sorts of lovely things that's going on wherever you look. You *do* see, don't you, what it all means?"

And Shrubb said that yes, he did see. If only a bit of money could be come by . . .

"Oh, money, money, bloody, bloody money!" All his frustrations would surge up in him, and Gwilym would put his head round the door, and he would realise that he had been shouting again.

Even to think of these things now, as he was walking with Joanna in the Mall, made him tremble. A sudden appalling thought had come into his head and turned everything black with a suddenness he knew only too well. It was always, when thinking these moments over afterwards, the suddenness that frightened him. One minute, all was happy. The next, he was in a horrid gulf. He had thought now: What if Shrubb and Gwilym think I'm after her money?

Joanna said: "Are you all right, darling?"

Well, there was that. Thank God. There was Joanna to ask whether he was all right. He'd never had anything like that before, and he found it comforting. He got hold of himself and said: "Right as rain, darling. A bit of a shiver, that's all. It *is* cold, don't you think?"

"You should wear your gloves," she said in a motherly way. He hated gloves. She took both his hands in hers, having drawn off her own gloves, and said: "Yes, you are cold," and then she went on holding his hands and looking at his face, and he could feel that it was she who was trembling now. She was aware of such a gulf between them. The circumstances of her life—that long pause in her development because the war had shut her up on the wrong side of the lake—this made her feel, what indeed she was, a child; and she could not get over it that she was loved by a man. It was her first experience. She was like a bird that had awakened for the first time to find the air vibrant with the dawn song. For the moment there is nothing but that, and those who hear it and are part of it cannot believe in its tragic brevity. The wings that are yearning then cannot conceive of anything save heavenly flights. But a bucket clanks in a byre, and the first car races along the road, and a bolt shoots noisily back to open a house door, and even a dawn-singer must face the rough facts of fear and necessity, of time and the hour, that fill the day.

Still holding his hands, she said to him: "Why shall I always remember this moment?"

He said: "Shall you, darling? What's special about it?"

"Oh, I don't know. It's just an average sort of winter day, isn't it? And here we are, walking down this broad road with the dirt under our feet and the trees on either side of us with not a leaf on them. Why do I feel as though the sun was shining, and the trees were full of leaves and singing birds, and the air was streaming with banners? You said you were cold, and I took hold of your hands. Why does it do that to me? Tell me."

He looked at her with great tenderness and said: "When you took hold of my hands you comforted me. I felt suddenly very happy. My happiness must have tingled into your fingers from mine, and it made you very glad because I sent a message: my darling is helping me. Would it be something like that?"

She let his hands go and they began to walk again. "*Me* helping *you?*" she said. It seemed nonsense to her.

"What shall we do now?" she asked after a moment; and then she laughed and said: "Why do I always put things like that—'What shall we do now?' Never What shall we do now, Bill, or William, or even Sir William? I've never found a name for you. And William is dreadfully formal. And Willy is worst of all."

"For the time being you can go on calling me darling. Perhaps we'll hit on something in time. We must do as one does with kittens. They always have a long list of experimental names before the right one comes out of the blue. My father was never without cats about the rectory. I remember one that began as You There, and ended up as Malinskaya. In time, we may hit on something equally magnificent for me."

"Oh, no, nothing magnificent," she said. "You'll never be magnificent. Do you mind my saying that?"

"Say anything you like, so long as it's not good-bye."

"It's simply that I don't care for magnificence. If you'd been Sir William Scroop, eleventh baronet, with all your blushing honours thick upon you, estates undiminished, and everything in the garden lovely, I should have had to think twice about you. I can never understand how a sensible girl like Elizabeth Bennet could want that dreadful cad-snob Darcy."

"You read Jane Austen?"

"It's about all I do read."

"Then that's my five hundredth reason for loving you."

"Tell me about the four hundred and ninety-nine others. No!" She began to laugh. "Really, darling, we've never talked such nonsense. What's in the air to-day? Let's be sensible. What shall we do?"

"We shall get into the first taxi-cab that comes along and hurry back to Soho Square. Don't forget, your mother's coming this morning."

"And you will ask her to allow you to take me dancing to-night?"

"Yes. Did you bring with you that golden dress you wore at Smurthwaite?"

"Yes."

"Then wear it to-night."

"I wanted to surprise you with something new. Mother's had a wonderful dress made for me since we arrived."

"You surprise me every time I look at you. 'Capitano,' I say to myself, 'that girl loves you.' And then you could knock me down with a wren's feather."

"Capitano!" she said. "I shall call you Capitano. A name just for you and me."

7

She was wearing the gold *lamé* when he found her waiting at Tom Brown's, as he insisted on calling it. He had booked a table in the Savoy restaurant and had put on some relics of old splendour: a cape and an opera hat. Mrs. Halliwell, who had never before seen him as a lily of the field, looked at the tall, dark, thin figure with the lines of too hard experience etched on cheeks and brow, and she said: "You look utterly unreliable, Sir William. I'm not sure that Joanna should be entrusted to you. My husband once took me to see a play by a man called George R. Sims. The villain was dark, and looked just like you."

Scroop said: "I'll bet he had one advantage over me, Mrs. Halliwell. He was being paid a salary for looking like that."

He smiled. He felt supremely happy. He could smile at anything to-night, even his poverty. Mrs. Halliwell remembered Alf, and how he used to take her out. There was no Savoy about it. They would walk the streets of Halifax and Alf would smile at her. She knew that smile when she saw it now on Scroop's face. She understood why Joanna loved him. "Well, there she is," she said. "Take her away, and don't keep her out too late. Remember, we're starting off for Throstle's Nest early to-morrow."

In the taxi-cab Scroop said: "I wish you weren't going back to-morrow, darling. I sha'n't feel safe without you."

She teased him: "You'll have to make do with Gwilym and what Mother calls that nice Mr. Shrubb. And you'll write to me *every* day—long, long letters."

"And you'll write to me."

"Every day. I'll send you all the news of the province: what the cows are doing in the fields and how the snow lies on the hills and how muddy the road is between Throstle's Nest and Smurthwaite. And I shall sign myself yours truly Joanna Halliwell."

"What could be better?—truly, and mine."

He took her hand, and she rested her head on his shoulder and sighed. "I am, you know," she said. "Yours—truly, truly yours."

They ate and they danced, and, for all the crowd about them, they were alone in their world of warm delight. And at half past ten Joanna said, her mind recurring to that realm of untasted experience that she vaguely thought of as London night life: "I do wish we'd had a chance to go to a night-club. Is that a very provincial idea, Capitano?"

They were sitting at their table. Scroop wanted to go on dancing, but he was remembering Mrs. Halliwell's words: "Don't keep her out too late," and he guessed that eleven o'clock was the sort of time that Mrs. Halliwell had in mind.

"You'd be frightfully disappointed, darling," he said. "There are night clubs and night clubs, of course, but I don't think you'd like any of them as much as this."

He had, in fact, thought of taking her to a night club to-night, but at once put the idea aside, for her own sake and for his. She was a child. He saw her becoming a more and more desirable woman, but now she was a child, and she didn't belong to what he thought of as "all that." And all that, which had of late been part of his own life, a part in which he had found escape when frustration became intolerable, was something he wanted to leave behind now that, as he assured himself, he had escaped finally into something supremely beyond the possibility of such places to supply.

She said: "You think I'm just a child, don't you, Capitano? You know, your hesitation makes me all the keener to go. I feel I'm missing something deliciously wicked. I shall pine for it all the time when I'm eating buns in that little bun-shop in Smurthwaite. You're denying me the chance to tell most thrilling stories to Lottie Wayland."

He hated to deny her anything. "I'm afraid, darling, you wouldn't find it wicked, but boring beyond endurance."

"Well, that's what I shall be able to tell Lottie. 'My dear, we went to one of those vaunted night clubs, and I found it boring beyond endurance.' Shall we 'look in' somewhere, as they say, just for half an hour?"

Scroop said reluctantly: "Very well. But no longer, mind you."

She saw his reluctance, and said: "No, no, darling. If you don't want it we'll leave it alone."

"*You* want it," he said. "Come along."

8

It was some time since Scroop had been in the Silver Star. There had been "improvements." The murals, for one thing, were new. He was shocked. He would as soon have handed Joanna a pack of dirty postcards. He had not felt happy since leaving the Savoy. His blackness was beginning to take possession. He told himself that he was betraying Joanna, he was betraying Mrs. Halliwell, who would certainly have disapproved of the adventure. And he was betraying

210

himself. He was being as weak as ditchwater. He should have said No and meant No, and Joanna would have thought none the worse of him.

His jaw was afflicted by a tic, and he was in the mood when a small thing could tip him over. And he did not think the murals a small thing. He loathed their snickering indency, and as he danced with Joanna the figures in them danced, too, revolving before his eyes like an unending Priapus procession.

They danced once, and he said: "Well, that's a night club, fairly typical. Do you like it?"

Joanna said: "No. Shall we go now?"

"I think I should have one drink for the benefit of the house. Then we'll go."

Chris Hudson and Dulcie were dancing, and Scroop, looking for a table, saw the one they had been sitting at. He led Joanna to it. When the waiter came he ordered whisky. "A very small one and a lot of soda."

The waiter asked: "And the lady?"

"The lady is nothing to do with you. Get my drink."

The waiter shrugged and said: "Very well, Sir William."

"You seem to be known here," Joanna said.

"Well, you see, the place is a club. One has to be a member."

The music the band was playing faded out in a foolish snivel, and the dancers began to drift off the floor. Scroop had not noticed Dulcie till she walked up with Chris. "You've pinched my table, Sir William," she said.

He scarcely looked at her. He said: "It will be a pleasure to find another one," and got up.

Joanna was alarmed, both at the cruel words and at the tone of his voice. She got up when Scroop did, and looked at this girl who appeared to know him. She was horrified to see the tired brazen face suddenly crumple.

Dulcie was very unhappy. Not one of them knew much about her—not Scroop, nor Chris, and least of all Joanna. They did not know of the man she was to have married and who had been killed in the last days of the war. They did not know of the curate who had helped her to make up on the night of her first public appearance, whom she had kept in touch with, and who was now a vicar in the East End: one of those devoted vicars who go about bareheaded in skirts, with ropes round their waists, and sandals, and whom the people call Father. Dulcie could not resist a grin when he called her "my daughter." But she liked him, and called on him often, because through him she sometimes had news of her father. She had only once seen her father since the parting in that northern town. That was when she was at last successful and could go to him with what she hoped was the happy news that her gifts, such as they were, were recognised and rewarded. She took care to dress soberly, but it was all too clear that to Mrs. Box she was the whore of Babylon. This was bitter, because she was nothing of the sort, and it had not been easy to be nothing of the sort. She had been what she called to herself a good girl, and she remained so, even after that sad visit had made her see that she now had no base camp to retire upon and must fight things out as best she could on her own. To Mrs. Box's face she put on a show of humility for her father's sake but to a parishioner she was unwise enough to speak of her father and his wife as the Incumbent and the Incumbrance. This got to Mrs. Box's ears, and the woman, envenomed by the girl's success—she would have been happy had Dulcie come crawling apologetically home in rags—wept to Mr. Box about the undermining of her prestige, for she saw with what justification such a phrase would "catch on," and the visit that was to have been brief enough ended more briefly.

And the war came, and all that dancing and all that drinking; and towards the end of it there was the lieutenant, so much younger than she. He was a very ordinary young man, the son of a Westmoreland squire, but even ordinary young men were seen then in the context of the times, of the columns upon columns of casualty lists in the newspapers. They moved gigantic through emotional mists. They took on a combined stature, the proportions of sacrifice, and were hardly seen as entities. Such as he was, he was the substance of Dulcie's dreams, and she believed that she could happily give up the life she knew for one shared with him and his horses and hounds among dales and hills and lake water lapping. Such a life would perhaps have left her desolate; but so did his death; and consequently what she had imagined remained an enchanting mirage. She would brood about it, and about him: and it was in those days that she found Charlie and his anodyne. Once or twice she met Sir William Scroop. Someone had introduced them, and they were both forlorn. They danced together, and each discovered the other's secret commerce with Charlie, and this was an odd bond, because each recognised in the other some excellence and some self-loathing. They pitied one another.

Each of them had avoided the Silver Star for some time. In Dulcie's case, this was because she wanted above all things not to be what her step-mother would like her to be. Her self-loathing was because she knew she had begun to slide down towards Mrs. Box's idea of what she was. Somehow, not to do this was even more important to her than maintaining her father's esteem. She didn't give tuppence for Mrs. Box's esteem, but she did want to make it impossible for the woman to gloat.

In the morning of that day when Chris Hudson intruded himself she had gone down to Whitechapel to see her parson. They sat in his little fireless cell of a room, where he ostentatiously denied his body any comfort for the greater comfort of his soul. Not that his body looked much the worse. His close-cropped hair was on a round Norman head, and his frame was burly and robust. But there wasn't a picture on the white-washed walls or a chair that one could loll in, and his writing was done at a scrubbed deal kitchen table. The floor was covered with cheap oilcloth. He grinned at her, with the mischievous grin that she remembered from that far-off day when Miss Batty fell on her behind. He knew Dulcie inside out, and he understood her needs. The grin, recalling an ancient conspiracy, was useful to put her at ease.

She said: "Father, I want your help."

She had not called him Father before. She had never seemed to want to do more than gossip. Especially after that boy had been killed. She had come during that crisis several times a week and chattered twenty to the dozen, and he had understood why and let her go on. But he hadn't seen her for some time.

She said: "How does one give up taking cocaine?"

"Have you been taking it?"

"Yes. I began after Henry was killed. How does one give it up?"

"I can't tell you, because I've never taken it. I can tell you how to give up tobacco because I've done that. I said 'No more tobacco.' "

"I've said that with cocaine. It doesn't work. I've been saying it now for a fortnight, and it was working at first. Now I feel I must have it or founder."

"Then why not founder?"

"That's useful advice, I must say."

He had foundered himself, more than once, and knew that there were adventures of the spirit possible only to those who cried out of the depths. But these were not things that he could say to Dulcie. He thought sadly how few things there were that one could say to anybody.

She said with a sort of desperate finality: "I'm all washed up."

The familiar clichés came to his mind. How easy it was to think that by dragging them out again one was being true to one's calling!

He could say: "My daughter, though your sins be as scarlet, they shall be as white as wool." But what was the use? And he had sad news for her that was not going to help.

He asked: "Have you heard lately from Mrs. Box?"

"I never hear from Mrs. Box. I don't know her hand-writing, and if I did, and a letter came, I should tear it up unread."

Mrs. Box had not written to him, either. Mr. Box was an obscure person whose name would not interest the newspapers, and it was in a roundabout way that he had heard of the old man's death a week ago.

"Your father died last week," he said.

She took the news with apparent calm, and said with a brutality that did not deceive him: "Well, we all have it coming to us some time or other. He'll find the angels a refreshing change, I hope."

"I took my holiday in Wiltshire in the summer," he said, "and I called on your father. He loved you very much, you know."

"Yes," she said. "I know that."

"But perhaps you don't know that he was proud of you."

"Proud?" She was astonished without pretence.

"Yes. You succeeded in what you set out to do. After all, that is something. Your father said he wished he could say as much of himself."

"I wish he had told me."

"So do I. But I didn't feel it was a thing I ought to suggest. We parsons have a bad enough reputation as it is for suggesting the wise things other people ought to do. I sha'n't say the good things, because the wise things and the good things are the same in the long run. I don't go in much for advice. When people come to me for advice, I say: 'You know as well as I what you ought to do. So use your common sense, and don't try to shuffle the responsibility on to me.'"

"And that goes for me?"

"That goes for the lot of us. Come and have some coffee."

They were an odd-looking pair as they walked through the Whitechapel street: Dulcie in expensive furs, and the parson held together by his rope like a badly-tied parcel; and they looked odder still as they sat side by side in a rough steamy room full of carters and porters and drank a fearsome brew from enamelled tin mugs.

The parson walked with her through the grey winter weather to the Underground station. She said: "So you have no advice to give me?"

He said: "People never want advice unless it falls in with their

214

own wishes. Jesus Christ Himself couldn't *make* people follow His advice. Do you remember the rich young man? He asked for advice and he got it, and went away sorrowing, because he knew he had no intention of taking it. Jesus spent His life giving the best possible advice about everything under the sun, and you know what they did with Him. Really, I'm constantly surprised at the people who yearn for a Second Coming when I look around and see what we've made of the First."

She permitted herself the only smile of the morning. "I'm afraid," she said, "you'll never be a bishop."

He said: "God forbid. I want to succeed, like you, in my calling."

9

Dulcie had a flat in a mews tucked away behind the Marble Arch end of Oxford Street. It was a tatty place, full of ribbons and dolls and cushions and copies of *Vogue* and budgerigars. On the mantelpiece were photographs of her father and of the young man from Westmoreland, and of the young man's father's house, with three dogs sitting on the porch. The room was restless, like the budgerigars, who twittered and hopped and kicked seed all over the carpet and played with celluloid baubles that had bells attached to them—bells that gave out a constant tinny note that scratched the nerves. If anything went wrong with Dulcie, she assuaged herself by buying something for the flat, and it was always something that screeched in sound or colour. The walls were bright yellow, and the cushions were magenta and electric blue and a hot disturbing red. The young man from Westmoreland was there once, and laughed at the marvellous knick-knackery. "But don't you see, darling—it's Me," Dulcie explained.

She ate her lunch in Oxford Street and walked back to the flat. She dropped her fur coat on to a chair and sat down, feeling very tired. The faces of the two men looked down at her, one serene and the other innocent, and the grave house in the picture, stony and rather harsh, seemed rooted in the soil it stood upon. The room was quiet: the roar of Oxford Street was there, but muted to such a sound as the sea might convey to a house inland. She surrendered to it, and fell asleep.

She awoke feeling sad and refreshed, and for once she didn't try to put the sadness from her. In such a mood, it was her custom to do something about it, as she would say: go out and see a film, or put a gay record on to the gramophone, or ring up an acquaintance and have a long inconsequential talk about nothing. Anything except be Alice Box, who called herself Dulcie Dearmer, and who felt discontented and meaningless. But that day it was sadness, not discontent, and sadness is not without meaning. She couldn't analyse her feelings, and didn't try to; but the sadness was part of the refreshment, and she knew that it had to do with two dead men and a quiet house and the visit to the parson who made no pretences about what he could do for her, but who now, at this short distance of time, comforted her with a feeling that his own obvious strength must have a source. In short, the day's conjunctions had brought together the best things she had known, and, acting together, they had created this mood that was both sad and somehow, she felt, to be cherished.

She went into her small kitchen and made some tea and carried it into the sitting-room. As she sipped it, she heard the postman drop a letter through the slot in her door, and she brought it in and opened it with a piece of her knick-knackery: a thing that pretended to be a miniature fencing-foil, the hilt encrusted with bits of coloured glass. She saw at once who had sent it, and remembered what she had said to the parson: "If a letter came from her, I'd tear it up, unread." But she read it. The envelope was addressed to Miss Dulcie Dearmer, but the letter began "Dear Alice Box.

"Your father died last week, after a long and agonising illness. I feel worn to a shadow by the unremitting attention I gave him, and which such a saint richly deserved. He deserved all sorts of things that he never received, including the love of his daughter and a way of life on her part that would not fill him incessantly with shame. It was a comfort to him that you chose to live under another name than his; but this could do nothing to lessen the sorrow of his own heart, which undoubtedly shortened his days.

"My dearest wish, as you know, has always been to heal the breach between you two, and from the day you chose to go your own road up till the time of his death I have not failed to pray that this might happen. But it was not to be. I listened for any word that might suggest that he forgave you, but I have no comfort to offer you on that score. Indeed, insofar as such a dear man could be said to hate, I should say he died hating you.

"Now I am left penniless to face the world alone, while you wallow in comfort. But I do not envy you. The rest of my days, few though they may be, will be hallowed by the thought of what I have been able to do, while yours will be cursed by the thought of what you could have done but did not do.

"We heard from Mr. Austin Sinclair, who used to be your father's curate in the North, that you had become engaged to be married and that the young man was killed. It would not be surprising if others are marked for tribulation on your account. This is all that I shall ever have to say to you, but you shall remain in my thoughts and prayers."

Dulcie read the letter twice before burning it. She knew it was a compilation of venomous lies. It lifted the grave sadness from her heart and replaced it by a chill misery. But that was something she knew how to deal with. She whistled to the budgerigars and put on a noisy record. She put the three photographs from the mantelpiece into a drawer, thinking: "They nearly drove me cuckoo. Better not think of what's dead and done with"; and when Chris Hudson's note came to her in the theatre she said to herself with a laugh: "I hope this one isn't marked for tribulation on my account."

10

When Dulcie saw Scroop dancing she felt better. She was finding Chris Hudson a dull little bore. She liked Scroop. She liked his manners, even his way of always keeping a distance between them. He was refreshing amid so many men who wished blatantly to diminish the distance to the width of a bed. After a few dances he would thank her courteously and bid her good-night. He puzzled and intrigued her. She felt no more for him than that, but he fitted in to what she thought of as "good things," and it gratified her to dance with a man who did not treat her as though there were only one base motive for men and women coming together. She had endured an odd variety of emotions that day, and the sight of him comforted her. And then this, as she told him that he was sitting at her table: "It will be a pleasure to find another one." Like a duke ticking off a parlour-maid. She might have felt hurt, but she didn't. She felt merely abased, filled with a sense of worthlessness, and she began to cry.

Scroop saw at once that Joanna was horrified, and the resentment that had been working up in him—against this place, against himself for having been fool enough to bring her here—collapsed and left him horrified, too. He had turned away from Dulcie's table, but now turned back and said: "I beg your pardon."

Dulcie said through her tears, her bad side coming up: "It's all right. Go away. You've found better company."

Chris Hudson, who had been eyeing Joanna and liking what he saw and who was still puzzled by the thought that he had seen her somewhere before, said: "Now don't be silly, Miss Dearmer. Let's sit down and all be friends."

Scroop was still on edge, ready to fly out. "You find friendship easy, young man," he said, and he looked at Chris as if at a mess he might ask Gwilym to clear up. But Chris was not now in the schoolyard, ready to be bullied and contemned. He said: "I invited you to sit down, despite your insulting behaviour. Whatever you think of it, I call that a friendly act. Please yourself, but don't try high-horse stuff with me."

They were all four standing. Dulcie was dabbing at her eyes, and Joanna had gone white. They were beginning to attract attention. Joanna said: "We'd better go. I don't like this place." Scroop said to Chris. "Thank you. We'll sit down." His head was beginning to throb.

Joanna said: "I don't want to sit down. I want to go. Are you coming?"

The others sat, but she remained standing, terribly unsure of herself, caught in a situation that caused her to burn with humiliation. Chris suddenly got his bearings. "Aren't you Joanna Halliwell?" he asked.

She didn't answer him. He said: "Of course you are." He was beginning to enjoy himself. "You must remember me—Chris Hudson. The last time you saw me, I was wallowing in a stream. I'd been pushed in by a poisonous little friend of yours."

Then she remembered, but still she said nothing.

"Well," Chris said, "we can't be held to blame for our poisonous little friends. We all have them. Let's forget them for a moment and have a dance. Miss Dearmer and I have been dancing a lot. I'm sure she'd like a change. You dance with Sir William, Miss Dearmer. I'll dance with my childhood's sweetheart." He had drunk more than his share of the champagne.

Dulcie said: "Sir William hasn't asked me to dance," and Scroop, who had always thought of Dulcie as a harmless and unfriended little nincompoop, condemned himself for the unthinking hurt he had inflicted on her. He said: "Would you care to dance? Just once. It's getting late and I must see Miss Halliwell home."

Dulcie said: "Don't try to make amends. It's not necessary. I've already forgotten what you said. See Miss Halliwell home now." She had noticed the ring on Joanna's finger and had sized up the girl's bewilderment. "See her home at once," she said.

But Chris Hudson stopped that. "Now don't let's be silly just when we're all getting to know one another. If you two don't want to dance, you can sit down and have a talk while we do. Perhaps Sir William can tell you where to find Charlie."

Chris himself couldn't have said why he used those words. He had heard Dulcie asking for Charlie, but he had no idea who Charlie was or what was his significance. He threw his bomb innocently. As he spoke, he was standing alongside Joanna, about to take hold of her for the dance, and Joanna was shrinking away from him like a touchy filly. There was a flash in Scroop's head: a flash in which two things combined: an almost insane anger at the thought of this oafish boy laying a hand on Joanna, and a fear that the boy knew and would talk about things that, in fact, were unknown to him. They were things that Scroop had never got into deeply and that he was sure he had done with for good. His security and his salvation were in Joanna, and he saw them tottering. He stood up suddenly, and felt as though he had stood up drunk. The walls of the room swayed. The silver stars in the murals began to dash about like comets, like exploding shells on a battlefield. He was on the wrong side of the fragile table, and as he lurched towards Chris, it went over.

The dancing stopped, and the music stopped. The three bandsmen who looked so slack and debilitated were, in fact, strong-arm boys trained to deal with this sort of thing. They put down their instruments carefully, and then crossed the room with the agility of outraged baboons.

Chris Hudson was terrified, but he kept his wits. He seized Joanna and began to rush her towards the door. She resisted, shuddering at the touch of his warm moist hands on her naked arms. She made his good intention difficult to carry out; so difficult that one of the baboons got hold of her and of Chris, using a hand to each of them, shoving them through the door, along the passage, and into the street. She almost fell in the gutter. She had left her cloak behind her, and it was a bitter night. Chris Hudson said good night, and walked away. She stood there, cold and distraught, waiting for Scroop, longing for him, longing to say: "Oh, my darling, forgive me." For had she not overpersuaded him? Was not the whole disgusting episode of her own making?

So there she stood, cloakless in the cold, wearing the gold *lamé* dress and the gold shoes, and he didn't come, and her disgust turned to fear. A couple of prowling men spoke to her, and, in a neighbourhood as foreign to her as Timbuctoo, she began to run blindly. She could feel the hands of the baboon on her, and trembled as she ran. A policeman stopped her and asked cheerfully: "All right, miss?"

She managed to stammer: "Brown's Hotel."

A taxi was passing. The policeman stopped it, opened the door for Joanna, saluted, and said: "Brown's Hotel. Pretty pronto, too, I'd say."

The baboons hustled Scroop and Dulcie down a dark passage and through a back door, and dumped them amid the dustbins in an alley. Then they went back grinning and began to play again and one of them crooned about seeing you soon under the moon.

Scroop got up from the pavement and leaned against the wall. Dulcie said: "Well, this has been quite a day for me, one way and another. How are you feeling?"

Scroop laughed and said: "All right, sergeant. My name wasn't on that one."

She said: "Be serious. Are you all right? Can you make your way home?" She thought that, even for baboons, they had been a bit rough with him. He was swaying against the wall, smiling at her in a half-witted way. It would be easy enough, she thought, to persuade a taxi-man to come round to the alley and take him home. Easy enough if she knew where his home was. She didn't.

She began to be anxious. "Look, Sir William," she said. "It's cold, and it's time I was in bed. If I find a taxi, can you make your way to your own bed?"

He said: "Thank you, Gwilym. Has Shrubbo called?"

Dulcie said under her breath: "Hell, he's gone cuckoo. Now I'm landed with something."

Then it occurred to her that the girl who had been with him was perhaps waiting for him at the front door.

She said: "Stay where you are now. Don't wander off. I'll be back in a minute."

Scroop saluted, and she ran round to the front, her back aching where a baboon's knee had been pressed into it. She found the street empty. Looking up and down it in the midnight desolation, she herself suddenly felt desolate as though at the far end of a cold uninhabited world. The purging sadness that she had known briefly in the afternoon came back and flooded her. She felt calm, somehow almost happy. She found a taxi-cab, and the man bundled Sir William in. Sir William's opera hat lay squashed flat on the pavement. The man sprang it open, and without comment put it on Scroop's head as he lolled in a corner.

Scroop said: "Thank you, Gwilym."

"Where to, Miss?"

Dulcie got him upstairs, and, somehow, into her own bed. She fell asleep, utterly exhausted, on the couch in the sitting-room.

11

Mrs. Halliwell, too, slept soundly. She had done what needed to be done, as was her way, and it seemed to her natural, then, to sleep. At half past six she was called, and she put on a dressing-gown and went to Joanna's room next door. It was still pitch dark outside. She was not surprised to find a shaded lamp lit by the girl's bed.

She asked conventionally, knowing the answer: "Did you sleep well?"

"I haven't closed my eyes." It was true. She was haggard with grief, and her mother's heart was rent. But there were other things to do, Mrs. Halliwell thought, than indulge in soft talk.

"Get up and have your bath," she said. "That will freshen you. Then come to my room. I've asked for breakfast to be served there at seven. A car will be here at eight to take you home."

"But, Mother! William is sure to come round. He will expect to find me."

She looked so lost that Mrs. Halliwell would have found it easy to give her all she wanted, but she was sure that easy things would be wrong things at this moment. She said: "He will find me here. I shall not be coming with you. You needn't be afraid. Sir William and I have always got on very well. You think he's all you've got. Well, you're all *I've* got and I happen to love you."

Love was a word Mrs. Halliwell so rarely used that Joanna was surprised and shaken. Mrs. Halliwell said: "This isn't something that can be washed up with a few kisses. Go and have your bath now."

Then she had her own bath and pondered on what she had done. It seemed to her that nothing had been omitted. She had been sitting in the lounge when Joanna came in last night looking half dead with shock. She said: "Where's your coat?" but the girl went straight up to her bedroom without answering, and she followed. There she listened to an hysterical story that didn't make sense to her—even now she had no idea of what in fact had happened—but she knew that, Joanna being the unsophisticated girl she was, it was something serious that would demand her staying in London to investigate it. But Joanna must go home at once, and not by train. She was in no condition to be turned loose. It happened that during her stay in London she had met a Bradford business man whom she had long known—a friend of Alf's—and who had told her that he was driving himself home the next day. Although it was now one o'clock in the morning, she rang up his hotel and had herself put through to his bedroom. He was not surprised at the unseasonable call: her ruthlessness had always amused him and he knew she had too much sense to do such a thing without good cause. He said he was starting early and would be at her hotel at eight, and that he would go out of his way to drop Joanna on her own doorstep.

Then Mrs. Halliwell decided on more nocturnal disturbance. She dragged her housekeeper out of bed at Throstle's Nest and told her as much as she ought to know, which was little enough; and her mill manager out of bed at Smurthwaite to say that she would not be back for a day or two. Then she ordered early breakfast to be served in her room, got into bed and slept like a top.

At eight o'clock she wrapped one of her own voluminous coats round Joanna, saw her into Bill Murgatroyd's big Daimler and watched the car slide away down Albemarle Street. A name had stuck in her mind out of Joanna's story: Dulcie Dearmer. She went in to see if the telephone book gave Dulcie Dearmer's address. It did.

12

Scroop woke up at seven that morning. The curtains had not been drawn, but the room was almost dark. Only a haggard light revealed the window-pane. He had no idea where he was and he felt ill. He found that he was half-dressed in a strange bed. He dressed himself, and walked out into a short passage, with doors to right and left. He opened one and peeped in. Dulcie was asleep on the couch.

Well, that told him where he was. He didn't wake her. The door at the end of the passage opened on to a stair. He went down into the courtyard of the mews, and thence into Oxford Street. He wandered about till he found a coffee-stall, and, having drunk, he felt better. Better, but confused. He tried to recall what had happened, and couldn't. There was dinner and dancing at the Savoy, and then there was the Silver Star where he and Joanna had danced again. Then Miss Dearmer. She had a boy with her, whom he thought offensive. Standing there in his full-fig evening clothes, his thin cold hands warming themselves round the coffee-cup, looking at people hurrying through the damp morning on their way to work, he tried to urge his mind over the next hurdle, but he couldn't get beyond the name of Charlie. He remembered that boy saying something about Charlie. What then? Nothing. Nothing whatever. And that was how it had been when he came out of what he called to Shrubb the refined loony-bin. He was as rational as he had ever been in his life, but he could not remember what he had been doing that had caused him to be taken there.

He thought of Joanna, and he had never known such fear. What had happened to her? Did she get safely home? He began at once to walk in the direction of Brown's Hotel, and then noticed a long tear in his cloak. He took off his hat and saw that it was filthy. He looked into a mirror in a shop window and his gaunt white face and un-shaven chin were disgusting. The idea of presenting himself thus to Joanna and her mother appalled him, and yet he knew that he should go at once. He decided to go first to Soho Square, have a bath and a shave and change into decent clothes. He called a taxi-cab and lost no time, brushing aside Gwilym's persuasion that he should go to bed. He was at Brown's soon after half past eight, and was told that Miss Halliwell had left, and that Mrs. Halliwell was out.

As soon as she had seen Joanna on her way and had found Dulcie's address, Mrs. Halliwell rang up Scroop's flat and was told that he was not at home. She deduced that a man who was not at home at eight in the morning had probably been out all night, and her apprehension deepened. "Who is speaking?" asked the sing-song voice that she recognized as Gwilym's. "It doesn't matter," she said. "It's quite unimportant."

But it was important to see this girl Dulcie, whoever she might be, at the earliest moment. That couldn't, in decency, she decided, be before nine o'clock; but she didn't feel like sitting down; and ten minutes before Scroop arrived at the hotel she set out to walk.

Dulcie felt like death. She had slept in her clothes, had awakened at half past eight to find her visitor gone, and had decided to have breakfast before she did anything else. Crumpled, un-made up, with her back still aching from the thrust of the baboon's knee, she looked, and felt, a wreck. She switched on her electric fire, took the cloths off the cages of the budgerigars, who began to fill the room with distracting cries, and sat down to her coffee and rusks. She had to think of her figure, but at the moment thinking was all she could do about it.

While she was wondering what on earth had happened to that

nice girl last night the doorbell rang. Feeling not fit to be seen, she opened the door a crack and put her nose through. A large woman with a scrubbed sensible face asked: "Are you Miss Dearmer?"

"Yes, and I'm just having my breakfast."

Mrs. Halliwell detected the note of hostility, and though she didn't much like what little she could see of Miss Dearmer, she called in aid all she had learned while sitting on touchy committees where she usually got her way by not being touchy.

"I smell coffee," she said. "I wonder if you could spare me a cup? I've had no breakfast," she lied. "I'm that worried about my daughter, Joanna Halliwell. I believe she was with you and Sir William Scroop last night."

Dulcie had lived in the North long enough to recognise the accent, and she was surprised that this old body was the mother of the young beauty she had seen last night. She had taken her to be some society girl that Sir William had hooked up with—the sort that likes to get about the night spots under male protection.

She said: "I hope your daughter got home safely?"

"Oh, yes," Mrs. Halliwell said, in the passage already, "but what happened to Sir William I have no idea. I gather you're an old friend of his, so naturally I turned to you—rather rudely, I'm afraid, at this unearthly hour. What pretty birds!"

She was in the sitting-room, making clicking noises to the budgerigars, and noticing the disorder, the smears of old make-up that made Dulcie hideous, the lack of solidity.

Dulcie poured her some coffee, and she asked: "May I sit down?"

"Good gracious, yes," and Dulcie put a maroon cushion on the chair and stuffed a magenta one behind Mrs. Halliwell's back.

Mrs. Halliwell said: "Joanna went out last night with Sir William to dance at the Savoy. I waited up for her and she came back very late without him. She was upset about something—so much upset that she couldn't talk very intelligently, so I sent her straight to bed. However, she did mention your name as someone she'd met in the course of the evening, so I looked you up in the telephone book. You don't mind? Perhaps I shouldn't have called till later in the day. But I was very anxious."

"I'm sure you were," Dulcie said. "I could see with half an eye that your daughter wasn't used to that sort of place. And then for that to happen!"

"What sort of place? She went to the Savoy."

"Well, I met her in the Silver Star. That's a night club. I'd gone round there after the show."

"You'd been to the theatre?"

"No. I mean after my show. I'm a performer in the music-hall."

Mrs. Halliwell didn't think much of music-halls. Her anxiety did not lessen. She said, looking round the room: "Ah, that explains it. I guessed you were some sort of artist."

"Well, I suppose you could call me that," said Dulcie, not displeased.

Mrs. Halliwell said: "Work like yours must be very interesting, but also very tiring. I can understand how you need relaxation, and a place like that must be a godsend to you. But Joanna and I are country people. We don't often get to London. I've never been in a night club, though I've often longed to see such places. But I'm a little bit afraid of what my neighbours would think if they found out."

Dulcie began to feel quite fond of the dear old soul. "Well," she said, "when you get to know them, night clubs can be dreary, but there's always the danger of a row breaking out, like the one last night. Then things can get rough enough to be pretty terrifying to a child like your daughter. I got a nasty kick in the back. It's aching still."

"I'm sorry to hear that," Mrs. Halliwell said, full of simple solicitude. "Are you sure you shouldn't be in bed? Should I go?"

"Oh, no. I'll get over it. But it was a bit of a shock even to me. I've never run into that sort of trouble before. But something made Sir William see red, and . . . ."

And then Mrs. Halliwell had nothing to do but sit back and listen. From her placid mask Dulcie could not learn how deeply she was disturbed. Not one thing about it pleased her. She couldn't understand Sir William taking Joanna to such a place and she couldn't understand Joanna's consenting to go. She went hot and cold as she thought of hired bullies laying hands on Joanna, throwing her out into the street, but she laughed and said: "I can see it was quite a night. But how did Joanna and Sir William get separated?"

"Well, she got thrown out through the front door and Sir William and I through the back. I went round to look for her, but she'd vanished."

"That was very kind of you," Mrs. Halliwell said: but she felt she still hadn't heard the whole story.

"Why did Sir William get so excited? He's always seemed to me a bit on edge, but hardly the man to act in that way. Was he drunk?" she asked frankly.

"Oh, no. Sober as a judge. He certainly drank nothing at the club, and I should say that before then he'd had no more than anyone might drink with dinner."

Mrs. Halliwell didn't understand it. She was a magistrate, and she felt that she was up against the real point of the case but that the witness was holding out. And that was true. It was the word Charlie that had made Scroop see red, and, for her own sake and his, that was a name Dulcie did not intend to mention. Mrs. Halliwell let it go. She asked: "What happened to Sir William? It seems that he didn't get home last night."

Dulcie refilled Mrs. Halliwell's coffee-cup. She felt that her visitor was not going to like this. "Actually," she said, "he spent the night here."

But even that didn't ruffle Mrs. Halliwell on the surface. Inwardly, she winced, more hurt than by anything else in this sorry affair.

"You seem to know Sir William very well."

"Not particularly. I've never met him except at the Silver Star. We used to dance a bit, and I liked him. He always treated me with great courtesy," poor Dulcie said, "and it went to my heart. I was used to that sort of thing once."

She looked meditative, as if on the brink of her life story, and Mrs. Halliwell didn't want to hear that. Not now, at all events. "I can understand that," she said. "I should have been surprised to hear that Sir William didn't treat women properly."

"Ah, well," said Dulcie, "plenty of them don't, believe me, Mrs. Halliwell. Anyway, I liked him well enough to look after him when he couldn't look after himself."

"But why couldn't he? And why couldn't he look after Joanna? You say he was sober."

"He was sober all right. But he was acting in the queerest way. He didn't seem to know where he was. You may not know it," she said, beginning to be ruffled by the very imperturbability of this clean healthy woman, "but some young men had a bit more than they could take in France."

Mrs. Halliwell paused, sensing that the witness was not only resisting but resenting the questions. After a moment she said: "That's very true, my dear. I know that Sir William, for one, had plenty to put up with."

Dulcie said with sad defiance: "My sweetheart had to put up with being killed, and I had to put up with having him killed. It's not wrong, is it, it's not wicked, if you think of those things and do your best to help a man?"

226

A tear began to steal down the side of her not very attractive nose. "Well, there it was," she said, using her handkerchief. "I brought him here and shoved him into my bed, and I slept on that couch. When I woke up he was gone. And that's enough questions about it. It's time I had a bath and put on a face."

Mrs. Halliwell took a taxi-cab to Fortnum and Mason's, and bought an immense box of crystallised fruits and an immense bunch of unseasonable spring flowers and had them sent to Dulcie's flat. Then she went on to the house in Soho Square. The faithful Gwilym said nothing of his master's absence overnight. He reported that Sir William had gone out early and had not returned. Mrs. Halliwell was glad to hear it. She did not want to see Sir William yet. She asked if Mr. Shrubb were there, and was taken to the top of the house where Shrubb was painstakingly worrying his head about Georgian stripes for window-curtains. He hobbled towards her, leaning heavily on a battered old ash stick, and she was suddenly overcome with compassion for young people everywhere in those days. This nice Mr. Shrubb and William and Joanna, and that poor young thing she had just been talking to in that horrid little flat: the war had knocked them all to pieces in one way or another. She and Alf had had plenty to put up with in their young days, but nothing that resolution could not face and overcome.

She said: "Where do you usually take your lunch, Mr. Shrubb?"

Shrubb pointed with his stick to a battered cardboard case. "It's in there," he said. "I take it here. One of these days I shall bring a dream true. When we had nothing better to do in France we sometimes talked about the high spots we'd hit after the war. I used to say: 'You'll see me taking a girl to lunch at the Ritz.'"

She asked: "How will I do for the girl?"

Shrubb blushed. She was going to be generous, she was going to take him out. But that wasn't the dream at all. In the dream he was doing the taking out, doing the paying from a comfortable income, and the girl. . . .

She sensed his discomfiture, and felt rather ashamed. The war, that had smitten so many, had enriched her. She said rather brusquely: "Well, anyhow, meet me in the Ritz lounge at one o'clock."

He thanked her, and she went back to Brown's, where there was no message from Sir William. It was eleven o'clock. She rang up the Ritz and went to bed till a quarter to one.

14

After lunch they sat in the lounge, and Shrubb was smoking an unaccustomed cigar. She asked: "How long have you known Sir William Scroop?"

"We had a year or so together as fellow-officers during the war. Then I got this." He slapped his knee. "It's quite useful in a way. A lot of chaps could do with a permanent disability pension. However. . . . Well, I didn't see Scroop again till just before my bringing him along to Smurthwaite. I ran into him unexpectedly in a pub. We got talking and discovered common interests. Architecture, you know. And there was that magazine he wants to bring out."

"You don't look the sort of man one would find in a pub, Mr. Shrubb. My husband *never* went into pubs."

Shrubb smiled. It was almost as though Victoria had said "My Albert"—or would it have been Our Albert?—both as example and reproof. "Oh, I don't know," he said. "Pubs are what you make them, like anything else. I find my local comforting. There are plenty of men like that at the moment, you know. They're rather at sea—looking round for something in place of lost comrades. Anyhow, I can't afford to go to the devil that way."

She felt as she had done with Dulcie: that the witness was answering back, telling her where she got off.

She asked: "Have you seen Sir William to-day?"

"No."

"Did Gwilym tell you that he didn't get home last night?"

"No."

He was all defensive—the man who wasn't going to give away a comrade. She thought none the less of him for that.

She said: "Mr. Shrubb, I need your help. I need it very badly. If you refuse to give it to me I shall have nothing to complain about. You've met my daughter. You know that she's engaged to be married to Sir William. Well, I have to decide whether I can allow the engagement to stand."

She looked at him appealingly. He fidgeted, very uncomfortable. At last he said: "I'm not very happy in this place, Mrs. Halliwell. Let's go and talk in my rooms in Chelsea."

"Very well," she said, "if that will make you happier. But I feel that I'm being unduly profitable to taxi-drivers to-day."

She herself felt happier in this room. It was more like her office at Throstle's Nest. Shrubb sat opposite to her in a wicker chair, with his game leg on a footstool. He lit a pipe and said: "That was just a dodge, you know, bringing you here. You put me in a difficult position, Mrs. Halliwell, and I wanted a quarter of an hour to think it over."

"If it will help your thinking, you can begin with this: what I'm looking for is not some reason for stopping this marriage, but some reason for letting it take place. And I'm not all that sure," she added, "that I could stop it if I wanted to. I can't lock Joanna up, or Sir William for that matter, and so long as they're loose there's no saying what they'll do."

Shrubb said: "Tell me what it is that has upset you."

She told him all she knew, and he was impressed by the fairness and clearness of the story, and by the firm way she had gone about what she had to do.

He said: "So Joanna told you that Scroop just blazed out when that boy mentioned the name Charlie?"

"Yes."

It didn't surprise him. He knew who Charlie was.

It was in the first days of their re-union, before the visit to Smurthwaite. They had spent an afternoon in this room of Shrubb's discussing *Vanguard*, and Scroop had been full of energy and enthusiasm. Then suddenly he had wilted, put his elbows on his knees and his head in his hands, and said at last: "You can't fool me, Shrubbo, and I can't fool you. We haven't a penny between us and it's all a bloody mirage."

"He's a pretty good draughtsman," Shrubb said, "and he'd been as happy as a kid with a box of crayons, drawing this and that to illustrate what he'd been talking about. He got up in a blazing temper, tore it all to bits, and threw it into the air."

Shrubb comforted him, and said: "Let's go and have one at my local."

Scroop replied: "The wolf's not at my door, Shrubbo. He's inside, chewing my blasted vitals. There's only one way to assuage the beast, and that's not with a pint at your local. Put on your beautiful garments, and let's blue our last penny."

Shrubb put on his unbeautiful dinner jacket, with a moth-hole eaten through the satin of the lapel, and dabbed ink where the white lining showed. They took a taxi to Soho Square. Scroop changed there, and demanded drinks from Gwilym, and at half past eight they arrived in the Café Royal and ate an expensive

229

dinner with expensive wines. Scroop said: "You see, my dear Shrubbo, a man need never despair. It's always possible to take on a new lease of death." He called a taxi-cab, and they went on to the Silver Star. It was before the murals had added to the gaiety of the place, and Shrubb thought it rather dreary. He sat at his table, and his leg ached, and he watched Scroop dance with a number of girls. The performance always ended with a polite bow and a return to the table where Shrubb patiently endured and thought of his bed.

It was late when Dulcie Dearmer turned up. Scroop introduced her to Shrubb and then invited her to dance. He brought her back to the table and gave her a drink and asked if she had seen anything of Charlie lately. She hadn't, but they had quite a conversation about Charlie, and Shrubb was in no doubt as to his status. He didn't think it was his business to pry into Scroop's habits, but he was glad when he saw him safely over the doorstep in Soho Square. By then, Scroop was depressed. "I was looking forward to a night's sleep," he said. "Now it'll be the old merry-go-round. Do you see merry-go-rounds when you can't sleep, Shrubbo?"

"Never. I sleep like a top."

Scroop slapped him on the shoulder. "Admirable Shrubb! Sound as a bell! Eupeptic bourgeois! I see the most marvellous merry-go-rounds: white unicorns and golden panthers, black swans and fiery flamingoes, all bright and beautiful. I want to get up among them, but the music never stops, and I'm a poor kid on the fair-ground, without a penny."

He told Mrs. Halliwell about this, and added: "I suppose it was saying things like that to the wrong people that got him put away."

That was the first she had heard of it. "Did you know him then?"

"No. Shall I get away from facts and tell you some of my private fancies?"

She nodded, and Shrubb said: "The first thing to remember about Scroop is that he's an artist who can't express himself in any art. There are people like that, you know, just as there are people who have a superficial knack of producing pictures, or music, or what not, while not having a spark in them. Some of 'em do very well for themselves, too. Scroop knows more about painting and writing and music than anyone I've come across. That's the deepest thing in him, but when he tries to draw or paint there's a blank between what he feels about it all and what comes out. I expect the psychologists have a good word for that, but that's what it is, and the consequence is an overpowering desire from time to time either to hit out or to say 'What the hell' and go on a binge. It was something like that that landed him in what he calls 'a polite sort of loony-bin.' That was before I met him. I imagine it was rather a strict nursing-home."

Shrubb's landlady came in with tea, and Shrubb put a match to the fire which he couldn't, as Mrs. Halliwell guessed, afford to keep going all day. It was odd, she thought, at her time of life and after all she had gone through, to find that she had forgotten the small sad economies of the poor.

Shrubb gave her tea and said: "Now this is where my views about Scroop become rather high falutin', and you can stop me if you like."

"No, no. Go on, Mr. Shrubb."

"Well, an artist like Scroop doesn't *have* to express himself in paint or notes. He can do it by living. And that's what he's been doing ever since he met Joanna. I liked him before he met her. Since he met her he's been wonderful. I'm no fool, and neither are you, and I'm sure we both understand how the ending of his financial worries has made him happier. That was one of his nightmares, and it vanished. But, believe me, that was a small part of it. You know, loving and being loved gives a man style."

He looked at her timidly in the darkening room, wondering if this was going beyond her. She said: "You know, Mr. Shrubb, I'm glad he met you."

"I once went to a show of caged birds," Shrubb went on, warming up. "There was a gorgeous thing there—I don't know what it was—blue and gold. I thought: 'My God! I'd like to see you flying with your mates along a wood in the sunshine. You'd have style!' That's what I mean."

She said nothing, and Shrubb went on: "There's *sense* in style. People think it's an extra, but it isn't. It's the *thing*. And ever since meeting Joanna, Scroop has been utterly sensible, complete, a joy to be with. So I ask myself: What happened last night to cause the break-down?"

"Yes, indeed. How did they come to be in that horrible place at all?"

"I can give you no more than a guess, and here it is. A girl like Joanna, who hasn't seen much of life, is quite naturally curious about things, anxious to get around. Scroop told me that she'd heard of night clubs and thought they must be wonderful places.

He assured her that they weren't, and he told me that he had no intention of taking her into one. Well, it's very likely that last night she over-persuaded him and they went."

"Supposing it was like that. I still don't see why Sir William started throwing the furniture about."

He thought hard before making his last revelation. "Mrs. Halliwell, did you know that Sir William used to take cocaine now and then?"

"No, indeed," she said; and he hurried on, seeing that this had surprised and hurt her.

"He hasn't touched it since I've known him, though once he tried to get it. Since he's known Joanna, nothing—I'm sure of this, Mrs. Halliwell—nothing would have induced him to take it. We've got to remember this: that the Scroop we've known since Joanna came along is Scroop."

"Then I'm baffled," she said. "I can't explain last night."

"I think I can," Shrubb answered. "I'm tiring you out, but please allow me to go on."

"Very well."

"Scroop's blazing out always came when he'd been on top of the world and something happened to throw him down. Well, what sort of thing could that have been last night? We can't have any doubt about the top of the world feeling while he was with Joanna, and then this boy you speak of mentioned the name Charlie. Charlie was the man who supplied cocaine. Everything to do with Charlie was done with, and then there the name was, and I can imagine Scroop's fear that Joanna would learn who Charlie was and what he meant. So he lashed out, and when that sort of thing happens in a night club anything can follow."

They were silent for a long time. Then Mrs. Halliwell said: "Your guesses make sense, Mr. Shrubb. I can well imagine that everything happened just like that. But I'm not satisfied. There have been these things in Sir William's life, and I think it would have been common decency for him to tell me about them and let me decide what I wanted to do. Honestly now, Mr. Shrubb, do you think it a good idea to hand a young girl over to a man who was once given to cocaine and who's been shut up in what you call a nursing home?"

Shrubb said: "You have no right to ask me such a question. The responsibility is yours."

"All the same, I repeat the question. I should be obliged if you would answer it."

232

Shrubb hesitated, but said at last: "I haven't known Scroop for long, but I think I know him pretty thoroughly. I've known Joanna for even less time. Still, I think they were made for one another. Does that sound old-fashioned?"

"I like old fashions."

"All right. Perhaps Scroop should have told you. Perhaps not. I certainly wouldn't spend much time pointing out my flaws to a prospective mother-in-law. In his case, it would be a good thing if he knew that you knew, and if he knew that you accepted him despite everything. After all, you've got no more right than the next woman to expect perfection."

"You are a frank young man."

"I expect that's because I've got nothing to lose by it. And I happen to like and admire Scroop. Since he's known Joanna, he's been a glorious chap. It's up to you to decide whether to throw him back."

She got up, and said with a grin: "The least we can do for you, Mr. Shrubb, is to ask you to be best man. Now, will you do one last thing for me? Call a taxi-cab, and come with me to this Silver Star."

Shrubb did so, and as they drew near to the wretched place his heart began to beat rather quickly. He didn't want to be involved in trouble. However, Mrs. Halliwell looked calm, and she talked pleasantly to the taxi-driver, who had a rich Yorkshire voice. He said that he came from Heckmondwike, which sounded to Shrubb an odd place to come from, but it seemed all right to Mrs. Halliwell. When the cab stopped outside the club, she looked at the young man, six feet of roast beef and Yorkshire pudding, and said: "I'd like you to come inside with me, if you don't mind."

He said he didn't mind, and she rang the bell. When the door opened, the stale smell of the place hit them. The man in shirt sleeves looked surprised as Mrs. Halliwell's plebeian bulk moved past him. "Are you members?" he asked.

She said: "Don't be daft. Do we look it?"

Her eye ran over the coat hooks in the passage-way. They were empty. "Lead me in," she said to Shrubb.

He did so. The man in the passage had pressed a hidden bell-push; and as the three came into the empty dance-room a couple of waiters and what might have been a manager slid in from the back quarters.

The manager asked: "Can I help you, madam?" and Mrs. Halliwell said: "Nay, lad, Ah've come to help myself."

She had seen Joanna's fur cloak hanging on a wall. She lifted it down, and handed the manager her card. "Keep that," she said, "in case you want to prosecute me for theft."

The young man from Heckmondwike was standing close to her, as if hoping things would not end as tamely as this. But they did.

Then Mrs. Halliwell became aware of the murals. She gave them a long appraising look, and said to the manager: "You ought to be ashamed of yourself. A big boy like you should know better. If you did this sort of thing in Smurthwaite you'd be had up."

Then she walked out. In the street she said: "Ah wasn't leaving that! Two hundred and fifty pounds that cost me."

She gave the taxi-man thirty shillings and said: "Now drive me back to Brown's Hotel, and then take Mr. Shrubb on to Chelsea."

15

When Scroop found that Joanna was gone back to Yorkshire and that Mrs. Halliwell was out, he walked away from the hotel in utter misery. He still did not know what had happened last night, and this made things worse. His imagination came into play and suggested enormities. The only thing clear to him was that he and Joanna had become separated, and he broke into a hot sweat as he thought of the probable and improbable things that could have befallen her. He had no doubt that he had seen the last of her. Her train had been due to leave in mid-morning, and her going away so much earlier suggested that Mrs. Halliwell had firmly removed her from the possibility of meeting him, and Mrs. Halliwell's absence from the hotel at a moment when she would not yet have had her breakfast said clearly enough that she, too, wished to avoid him. He didn't blame her, and he didn't intend to thrust himself upon her. He walked to his club in St. James's Street. He could not have afforded to belong there, but the wicked Bart had bought him a life membership. It was his funk-hole, the place he used when he wished no one to find him. Neither Shrubb nor Gwilym knew that he was a member.

He ate some breakfast and went into the writing-room. No one was there, and he began to feel more composed. What ought he to do? It was characteristic of him that his first thought was of Dulcie Dearmer. Whatever had happened last night, he had obviously involved her in it, and she had done what she could for him. Using

234

"second" sheets, with no address printed on them, he wrote to her, sending apologies and thanks.

That done, he felt better, able to tackle the more serious job of writing to Joanna. It took him all the morning. It was his Apologia. He told her everything: the nursing-home, the cocaine, his hopes and frustrations. "You should have known all this before, and you *would* have known all this before if I hadn't felt that it was meaningless, because done with. But in feeling that, I was mistaken, as I now see, and my mistake has involved you in a situation that I can only imagine." It was a calm, factual letter, and he didn't ask her, having read it, to try to understand and forgive. It was written on the assumption that, whether she understood or not, she would not forgive and that he had no right to expect forgiveness. It was a good-bye letter, and when he had posted it at noon and eaten some lunch, he went to the smoking-room and fell asleep, as exhausted as if he had performed some heavy physical task.

16

Bill Murgatroyd, who was entrusted with taking Joanna home, did not make his visits to London merely to discuss wool. Mrs. Halliwell, who knew most things about those she dealt with, knew this, and was pleased that Joanna would have such an escort. Bill was a ladies' man, and what he didn't know about keeping a woman in good humour wasn't worth knowing.

Bill was enchanted with his mission. He had heard of Mrs. Halliwell's daughter who was being brought up abroad, and indeed had seen her when she was a child, but the grown woman was better than he had expected. He looked forward to a pleasant journey, even though the girl was for some reason as glum as she was beautiful. The honey-gurgle of the Daimler's horn as he turned out of Albemarle Street was not fruitier than his own voice as he began a bit of friendly talk about having known her when she was so high and his pleasure at being able to do her a service.

She said: "It's very kind of you, Mr. Murgatroyd, but you're doing Mother a service, not me. I wanted to stay in London."

"Well, Ah'm not surprised at that. It's a good place, but I expect your mother knows best."

"I wonder," Joanna said, settled her head back, and closed her eyes. She had had no rest all night, and as the perfect car, perfectly

235

driven, slid along the road, she was lulled and was soon asleep.

Murgatroyd looked sideways at the lovely tired pale face and thought "Poor kid" and wished he was twenty years younger. But no. Twenty years ago there was no Daimler and all that went with it. He wondered what had happened, and guessed, and wasn't far wrong. Let her sleep, he thought; and she was still asleep when they reached Derby. Only one sound had come from her, and that was something between a sob and a cry that moved him deeply. She woke with a start when the car stopped outside the railway hotel, looked about her wildly, and remembered. She remembered that only yesterday she had been walking in the Mall with Scroop, and had asked him why the commonplace day was wonderful. Bill Murgatroyd had got out of the car and was coming round to open the door on her side. She asked: "Why have we stopped?"

Bill turned back the cuff of a pigskin glove and looked at his watch. "Ten to one," he said. "Lunch."

She said: "Can't we go straight on? I want to be at home."

He grinned. "Nay, lass," he said. "It's one of the disadvantages of having me for a gaoler that I must prolong the agony by eating. Ah'm like that—can't go on unless Ah'm stoked up."

She was contrite. "Oh, Mr. Murgatroyd," she said. "Have I done that—have I been treating you as if you were a gaoler? I really am most obliged to you."

"Well, then, come and show it by putting a bit of food into you. Ah can see, there's some trouble about, but Ah never met the trouble yet that wasn't helped by a bite and a sup."

She got out and relented far enough to give him a pale smile and to take his arm as they walked into the hotel. "I feel a little better," she said.

"Ay," he said simply. "One does. One gets over things."

He was proud that she had taken his arm, though with a chaste technique imparted by Miss Kempfer, who had not carried the instruction far enough to say that the gentleman might then squeeze the lady's arm. However, Bill chanced it, and got no response. Having been kissed by Scroop, she was aware of headier pressures.

She would have liked to gratify her escort by eating a hearty meal, but she didn't feel like it. However, ashamed of having slept all through the morning, she did her best to be a polite companion in the afternoon and succeeded only too well. Nothing, Bill thought, was so putting-off to an oncoming man as this ladylike yes and no and do you really think so, Mr. Murgatroyd? Presently she fell silent again, and as the northern winter afternoon wore on to darkness

Bill gave it up. He'd deliver his parcel, and then beat it hell for leather for his fireside in Bradford.

It was quite dark when he carried her suitcase up the steps at Throstle's Nest. She remembered her manners again and asked him if he'd care to come in for a drink. It went against his inclination to refuse such an invitation, especially from a pretty girl, but he said no, he had things to see to in Bradford. He had reversed the car almost before the door was open.

What he didn't know was how great a strain upon her emotions it had been for Joanna to talk to him at all, even in so perfunctory a fashion. As the door shut behind her and the housekeeper shot the bolt and pulled the chain across the lock she felt utterly drained, and heard the sounds of these customary nightly operations as though again hearing the sounds of imprisonment. The old and privileged servant, whom she had known all her life, embraced and kissed her, aware of trouble but not of its nature.

"I've got a lovely little dinner ready for you," she said, but Joanna, unable to speak because of this show of solicitous affection, shook her head and ran up to her bedroom. Here the affection pursued her in the shape of an unaccustomed fire. The room was all ready as though for an invalid: warm, curtained, welcoming. She impatiently pulled the curtains back, threw open the casement window, and looked out over the countryside where not a light showed anywhere except for an icy twinkle here and there in the inaccessible sky. The owls, which she had always loved to hear, began their tremulous calling, and all was so accustomed and familiar that the one thing lacking bore down on her with overwhelming power, and she flung herself upon the bed and began to cry without restraint.

In the morning she was haggard and red-eyed. What had happened to Scroop? Daylight brought no answer to the question that had been beating at her mind for so long that it was bruised and numb. She had never felt so cast off and abandoned. The moment when that boy Hudson had walked away and left her shuddering in the empty street was the most horrible she had ever known. She felt as though she were standing there still: the moment went on and on, like the dark and sordid street itself, which contained nothing but nameless evil.

The old housekeeper tapped at the door and came in with a tray. She who had expressed her love for the girl by leaving everything snug was met by a rush of wind, by the sight of the open window and the dead hearth. The tidy bed told her that Joanna had not slept, and Joanna was not sitting in the easy chair but on a hard chair at the bedside, determinedly crucifying herself. She put down the tray, shut the window, and said: "Now then, luv, this won't do. You'll make yourself ill."

She went round the bed, took hold of the girl, and persuaded her to sit upon it. She put pillows behind her and spread the quilt over her. "Be sensible now," she said, "and eat something. And then you'll find a nice fire in the drawing-room." She took the girl's cold hands and chafed them. "You're like death," she said.

She brought the tray and placed it on Joanna's knees. "Now be sensible," she repeated, and tip-toed out as though from a sickroom. Joanna looked listlessly at the tray and saw a letter propped against the tea-pot. She recognised Scroop's boyish handwriting, and the dull weight of misery changed on the instant into a wild excitement. Her heart had seemed a dead lump. Suddenly she felt it, and literally heard it, beating in her breast.

She gave herself the fearful pleasure, almost unendurable, of putting off the reading of the letter. She took it up and felt it and rejoiced at its thickness. She put it down and stared at it. She poured herself a cup of tea, and the tea wavered into the cup and into the saucer as if she were pouring it in a railway train jolting over points. She drank, and she ate some toast, and then she got out of bed and undressed, and locked the door. She got back into bed, pressed the letter against her naked nipples, and at last opened it.

It was Scroop's Apologia, written in the club, a letter from which he had deliberately strained all warmth and emotion. "My dear Joanna," it began. "You are of course wondering what happened to me last night. I wish I could tell you. But I can't. I don't know *what* happened, and this is to tell you *why* I don't know, and to tell you other things which I should have told you long ago."

It was the longest letter she had ever received from him: ten pages, covered on both sides. She felt as though she would die as she read: page and page and page, and not a loving word. "Well, that is William Scroop. He thought, after he had met you, that such things were done with, and that, therefore, nothing would be served by telling you about them. Whatever it was that happened last night, it has shown me that I was wrong in thinking this, for what happened then could happen again, and that would not do if I were married to you. I cannot face the thought that I am liable— God knows why, but I am—to place you in a position that might mean recurring humiliation."

For a time she was numb. It was a hard point for a young and inexperienced girl to consider. She blamed herself. It would never have happened if she had not almost insisted on his doing what he had not wanted to do. And then she felt a sober gladness. If they had not gone to the Silver Star she would have married him without knowing what she knew now. And she was glad she knew. Love for him flooded her, the greater for the dam that now went down and allowed her feelings to rush unhampered. She was arrogantly certain of her love's power to take in its stride such things as he had written about. The very thought of them suggested a need in him, and that was something new. It gave her feeling a great tenderness. At all events, there was now something that could be done after so many hours of helpless misery. She dressed and went downstairs and put through a telephone call to Soho Square. When it came, she took it on the extension in her mother's office. She recognised Gwilym's voice, and when she asked for Sir William he recognised hers. "He's not here, Miss Joanna. Went away he did in a hurry this morning."

Her heart sank. "But where to, Gwilym? Did he leave no address?"

"No, Miss Joanna. Packed a bag and just said to expect him when I saw him. That was not an hour ago."

She put down the receiver and wandered into the drawing-room where, as the housekeeper had told her, a bright fire was burning. But she was not aware of it, or of anything save the cheerless winter day that she gazed on through the window, and of the foreboding that once more made her heart feel like lead.

17

On the evening before this, when Mrs. Halliwell had seen Shrubb go off in the taxi, she rang up the lawyers to whom she had applied some time before for all the information they could give her about Scroop and his family. "There's one thing I'd like to know," she said. "Does he belong to any club?" They gave her the name of the club.

She had been surprised to find no message from Scroop, and came to the conclusion that, for whatever reason, he was hiding himself. And in what more likely place than his club, wherever that might be? She knew enough about clubs to be aware that men fled to them when they had had enough of women's company. Even Smurthwaite has its Constitutional Club, and she had no doubt that it served other purposes than upholding the constitution. She didn't ring up: that would have given Scroop a chance of escape. She had had enough of taxis for the moment, and she walked round to St. James's Street. The formidable maleness of the place would have daunted most women, but not her. A venerable being who could have been an archbishop turned butler looked a little shocked as she came into the hall, but allowed himself to unbend enough to ask her business.

"Is Sir William Scroop in the club?"

"I'll see, madam," he said, well accustomed to finding members who told him emphatically that no—they were not in the club. Anonymous and invisible, they resumed their sleep or billiards.

It could well have happened to Mrs. Halliwell, but at that moment Sir William walked down the stairs. She was shocked by his haggard look. She said, as if to a small son: "Get your hat and come with me."

He did so, and she walked him to Brown's. They didn't speak a word on the way, and they said little over their meal. Then she found a quiet corner of the lounge and said: "I don't want any explanations about what happened last night. I happened to run into that music-hall girl, and so perhaps I know more about it than you do. It's all been a bit of a shock to me."

She didn't look as though it had. Scroop said: "I can well believe it. It's been a shock to me. I thought I'd done with all that."

"What 'all that' amounts to you needn't tell me. I know about it. I had to *find out* about it. And that's what upsets me. I don't like having to find out things. It's not a nice occupation. You've made me spend my day like a third-rate detective, and I resent that. Why didn't you tell me and Joanna long ago?"

"Joanna'll know about it all right in the morning. I've written to her and told the story from A to Z. You're not likely to have Joanna worrying about *me* any more."

She said: "Well, that alters everything."

"Yes. I can see that. I intended that it should."

He looked so woebegone that she was deeply moved. "Oh, Bill," she said, "how little you understand Joanna, or me for that matter! Don't you see?—the change is all for the better. You've given us your confidence—a bit late, but you've done it. We can talk to one another now, can't we, with all the cards on the table. I'm a Yorkshire woman, and that's how I like to go about things, not creeping into people's homes to pry into this and that."

He saw that she had spoken truly: that she had been deeply shocked: that she had spent a day in a most dislikeable fashion. She was now near to tears. He laid a hand on hers, and said: "I've been feeling dreadful all day. I haven't given a thought to how you've been feeling. Forgive me. Being with you is making me feel happier."

"I love Joanna," she said simply, "and I'm proud of her, and I should have felt betrayed if she'd married you first and found out those things later. Thank you for telling her."

He said with a wintry smile: "Don't thank me for writing my death warrant. We Scroops have been a crumbling lot for some time, and there's nothing crumbling about Joanna. I thought she'd prop us up at last. Well. There it is. . . ."

He seemed unable to understand what she was telling him.

She said: "I'm worn out and I'm going to bed right away. I advise you to do the same. You know the time of the northern train to-morrow morning?"

"Yes. I've taken it once or twice."

"Very well. Meet me on the platform. You'd better have Joanna's answer in person. I've not much doubt what it will be."

She got up, and for the first time offered her cheek, almost shyly, to be kissed. Scroop went home in a daze and said to Gwilym: "I'm going away to-morrow. Expect me when you see me."

18

They arrived in the darkness. Mrs. Halliwell said to her house-keeper: "Where is Miss Joanna?"

"In her bedroom. She's eaten next to nothing all day."

"Tell her that I am back. Say nothing else."

She and Scroop stood side by side in the hall, and presently saw Joanna come to the top of the stairs and look down. She was wearing a dressing-gown. Her face was white and her hair untended. Mrs. Halliwell said: "Well, we're back."

Then she stepped into her office. Joanna hesitated for a moment, looking down as though awe-struck and unbelieving. Then she gave a little glad cry and ran like a child seeking safety, and Scroop folded her in his arms.

❦ ❦ ❦ ❦ ❦ ❦

CHAPTER 11

1

*O*ver the fascia of the premises in Baker Street you read *François: Gâteaux*. There is a shop on the ground floor, stuffed with delicious cakes and chocolates, and over that there is a refined tea-room. If you climb the next flight of stairs you find yourself—or did—facing a door painted olive green. On the door in 1921 you would have found an ivory oblong incised with the words *Mr. Anthony Fieldhouse*. Hanging outside this door was an electric light fitting in beautifully wrought bronze; and, looking at that and at the ivory plate, you would have said to yourself that Mr. Anthony Fieldhouse, whoever he might be, did himself well. If you had rung the bell and been admitted, you would have seen that you were right about that. Passing through a narrow hall that contained nothing more distinguished than Mr. Fieldhouse's hats, overcoat and mackintosh, you would have been in the main room of the flat. The window looked upon Baker Street, which is to say that anyone who found the view pleasing would have been easy to please. The buses and taxi-cabs grinding and hooting along did not look as though they contained romantic or nefarious or distinguished clients seeking audience of Mr. Sherlock Holmes or of Dr. Watson in one of his conveniently recurring abstentions from medical practice. Still, this being a brisk morning of early April, the sky above the roofs deserved attention, gay as it was with small white active clouds that seemed to be kicking up their heels like woolly creatures in a blue meadow. This touch of spring had come into the room and alighted on a mahogany table that shone before the window, carrying a vase of yellow tulips and the young opening leaves of copper beech. Standing at the back of the room and looking at the table and the flowers and, behind them, the long muslin curtains alive in the wind, for the window was open a little, Anthony thought the effect very pleasant.

The carpet was sage-green, and a fire was burning in the grate of the marble fireplace, which was fortunate for a couple of cupids who, in the way cupids have, did without clothes. They balanced the mantelpiece on their curly heads, and, though this was no mean feat, they smiled as uninterruptedly as Dulcie Dearmer, Smiling Through. There was a Georgian wing chair on either side of the fire, and there were bookcases against the stone-grey walls, and over a small writing-table in a corner was a newly-painted portrait of a lady we should know well enough, for she had been Florrie Finch and Mrs. Freiling-hausen and Mrs. Fieldhouse, though now she was Mrs. Morrison. Anthony, who was awaiting Joe Morrison's ring on the bell, stood before the picture. She looked happy, and he hoped she *was* happy, and that she would be happier now. The telegram had come that morning from her husband, Joe's father: "A whopping great son. All going well." A birthday present of a sort, for this was Anthony's birthday as well as the whopper's. He was twenty-one.

When Joe came they would go down to the floor below and drink coffee, and he expected to meet Joe again to-night at dinner in Sir William and Lady Scroop's place in Soho Square. Septimus Pordage would be there, too, with his secretary Lottie Wayland, and Mr. Shrubb. They were to celebrate the appearance of the first issue of the new monthly, *Vanguard*. All these people were doing some sort of job. All except himself. His life, he reflected with satisfaction, was unacceptable to any right-thinking person, and very pleasant. Shopping in the morning. Because there was nothing else to do he took a lot of time over this and chose things with care. The best meat, the choicest vegetables, delicate salads, unseasonable fruits. He made do with a snack for luncheon, but dinner was a serious matter. He cooked it himself. There were plenty of cookery books to consult, and he discovered an aptitude. His small kitchen became his workshop. He would put on a white apron and go to it gravely. He began to study wines and to match them with the food. The thing became an obsession, and for a meal that he had cooked himself and that he would eat alone he would write a neat menu card, dated, and place it on the table. He had a collection of these now and occasionally looked over them, as a writer might look over his books, and told himself where he had improved and where he still had a lot to learn. Once, when Mrs. Wayland had left Easter How to spend a few days with Lottie in town, he invited them to look in one evening, and surprised them with a dinner. Mrs. Wayland was impressed, and they spent a happy hour in the kitchen. She thought some of his methods wasteful and showed him how to economise, and she offered to look in each day during that visit and supervise his work. Anthony was surprised to find how happy this made him. They had the old days in Megson Street to talk about, and new sauces to invent, and the success of Septimus's odd book to discuss, and altogether he discovered that Mrs. Wayland was not the ineffective shadow she had seemed in his boyhood.

Well, this was all part of his pleasant life, and there were walks in the parks, and visits to art galleries and museums, and, above all, the sweet taste of being alive and young and unfettered.

The telephone bell rang. It was Joanna Scroop. "Oh, Anthony! Such sad news! All our arrangements for to-night are knocked endways. The woman who was coming in to cook the dinner has gone down with flu."

"Well, that can hardly seem a disaster to an efficient housewife like you."

"Oh, but I'm not anything of the sort! You wouldn't believe the odd things I learned *chez* Kempfer. I can do the national dances of several countries, but the national dinners of none."

"So what happens? I've been starving since yesterday in the hope of glutting myself."

"I don't know. William is out. I suppose he'll arrange something with a restaurant. I'm just trying to catch everybody now, in case they're elusive later on."

Anthony said: "Look. Here's a thought for you. Dinner at a restaurant wouldn't be the same thing at all, would it? It was to be an intimate occasion. Well, make it so still by telling everybody to come here. I'll cook the dinner."

She laughed. "Really, Anthony, you do say the maddest things. I wouldn't trust you to feed my goldfish."

He was nettled. "Haven't you heard of my cooking?"

"Should I have done? Is the news all over the town?"

"Look," he said. "I'm serious. When you get hold of Lottie, ask her whether I'm talking sense."

She realised that he was indeed serious. "I was rude," she said. "Forgive me. I didn't know that you'd so much as boiled a potato in all your life. I'll see what Lottie says, and ring you later."

2

The telephone bell rang. It was Joe, calling from the office of *The Banner*. "I can't come round, Anthony. I'm just about to hop into a taxi. Several interesting pieces of a woman have been found under a milliner's counter at Penge."

It may or may not have been true. It was the sort of thing with which Joe often cancelled an engagement. But at all events it meant that Joe was being packed off somewhere in a hurry by his paper.

"Are you all right for the dinner to-night?"

"So far as I know. Nothing is certain now that I'm one of the stars on the star-spangled *Banner*."

Joe was not a star. But the editorship of the *Banner* having recently fallen to a friend of his father, the boy was being given a chance.

"Well, if you can make it, come here—not to Sir William's. Have you heard the news about the whopping great son?"

"Yes. Each of us has a half-brother. Which half do you claim?"

"I hadn't thought about it. Let's toss when we meet."

"Right. Well, the taxi's panting. I must be off to Penge. Sounds a place where the darkest doings could break out. Au revoir."

It was a year ago, Anthony reflected, that he and Joe had been among the small company who stood on the steps of Throstle's Nest and waved good-bye to Sir William and Lady Scroop after the wedding. They went away in a motor-car, with Joanna driving. She looked superb, shining with an almost visible light of joy. No sooner had the car disappeared than a taxi-cab drew up, ordered to take Joe and Anthony to Smurthwaite. It was not till they were in the train for Bradford, where Joe was to spend the night at Ackroyd Park, that he broke a long silence. "I'll never forget that," he said "—the way she looked when Scroop got into the car alongside her. There was nobody else there: not her mother, nor you nor I nor Lottie. She looked like a young angel who has been privileged to conduct the Almighty on a tour of heavenly places."

Anthony was tired, and did not answer this hyperbole. Joe asked: "Have you ever been jealous?"

Anthony laughed. "Don't tell me, Joe, that you're jealous of Sir William Scroop!"

"Said like that, it puts me right in my place, doesn't it? Sir William Scroop, umpteenth Bart. Joe Morrison, general dog's-body on his old man's weekly paper. And yet I'm as jealous as hell. What do they mean when they talk about being in love with a girl? Perhaps I'm too young to know. But that night when the Assembly Rooms were opened I danced with her—if you can call it dancing—and with no one else. Later on that night, when she danced with Scroop, I was sitting on the sidelines, and again and again they swirled past me, and

I could see that this was something else for her. Just as it was an hour ago. She didn't see me. I felt as miserable as sin."

There wasn't much Anthony could say to this; and Joe went on after a moment, the blue eyes in his young ingenuous face scanning the growing dusk beyond the carriage window, as if seeing there all life's hope shredding into mist: "I'm a pretty realistic sort of chap,"— Anthony had to allow himself a private smile at this—"and I said to myself that this was the first girl I'd ever met and that a week or two would put me on my feet again. Well, I never saw Joanna after that night until to-day, but there's never been a day when I haven't thought about her. And at this moment I'm feeling just about as gay as a duck that's been shot but not killed and is floundering in the sedges."

Anthony remembered, sitting by his fire in Baker Street, how, when Joanna had come out of the house to go away, she had been so be-mused into a world not there to other eyes that she had forgotten to put on a coat. She stood holding the handle of the car door, waiting for Scroop, wearing a rather thin suit, and a cold wind was stirring. Mrs. Halliwell said to Joe: "Joe, go and get the coat that's lying on the chest in the hall," and Joe brought the coat and Mrs. Halliwell motioned to him to put it on the girl. But Joe was as if petrified at the thought of touching her, and Anthony himself took it, and held it for her to slip her arms into the sleeves, and she turned to him with a start, her eyes lit up, and then, this not being Scroop, the impulsiveness fell from her and she said evenly: "Oh, my coat! Thank you, Anthony." He helped her into it and felt none of the tremor that Joe feared would betray him. Then Scroop came almost at a bound down the steps, and they seemed to flash into the car. In a second, with no more than a perfunctory waving of hands, they were off, like a projectile set in motion by the sharp clang of the car's door, like something urgently fleeing from them all.

When Joe and Anthony reached Ackroyd Park that night, Aunt Jessie was alone in the house. Anthony said: "Would it be much of a bother for you to bring us some supper in my room, Auntie Jess?"

"All right, Mr. Anthony," she said. "I've got a fire lighted there for you. You go on up."

As they were on the stairs, she said: "Your father's here again, Mr. Joe. They're out at the theatre as usual."

Anthony disliked hearing Aunt Jess call him Mr. Anthony, but it had to be Mr. Joe, because Joe's father was finding one reason after another for visiting Bradford, and he was Mr. Morrison. The boys

246

exchanged glances at news of this latest visit, and when they were sitting by the fire Joe said: "You know, Anthony, something tells me that I am about to have a stepmother and that you are about to have a stepfather."

The idea had for some weeks been faintly stirring in Anthony's own mind, but to hear it plainly expressed was a shock. And, he admitted, not altogether an unpleasant one. It was useless to pretend that he and his mother had for one another the normal feelings of mother and son. On his side there had been a lack, on hers a superfluity. If she were not his mother at all, he thought, but someone who had adopted him as a child, that could have worked out well. Life would have woven threads to bind them securely enough. But now he was irked and uneasy with her, as though he had been adopted when a man, and he must be for ever, by duty and politeness, making amends for the absence of those deeper emotions which, he told himself, frankly, he did not feel. On her side, there had been long years through which she had covertly watched him and provided for him, and her feeling for him had banked up like water behind a dam, and now that the obstruction was removed her emotion was vivid and ebullient, washing here and there in an effort to establish in fact something she had too long dwelt on in imagination. Anthony was aware of all this, and at times suffered sharply from his inability to respond with more than a temperate affection to the demands of her love. Sitting there with Joe, the coffee-pot and chicken sandwiches before them, he was visited by a thought that made him blush. He had read of women, disappointed in love, taking up with another man "on the rebound," as it was called. Could that happen in the case of a mother who had failed to win the love of a son?

3

Anthony fitted the leaf into the Sheraton dining-table and put three candlesticks down the middle. Each of them held three candles. He decided not to use shades. Nine points of candle-flame reflected in the bare wood: that would be all right. He would use the Spode dinner-service that his mother had given him. There had been a lot to spare when she left Ackroyd Park for good, and much of it was here: wood, silver, porcelain, damask curtains. She had given him a comfortable but not extravagant income. He didn't know how well-off she was; she had simply told him, in one of her few business moments, that she had inherited not only Major Fieldhouse's capital but a block of shares that had belonged to him in the great family wool business of Freilinghausen.

He stood right back, leaning against the door, looking at the table, seeing it as it would be that night: as he would have *made* it that night, the artist in him said, though not consciously. He had not yet reached the realisation that to create such highly civilised scenes as his mind was now engaged with would give him the deepest satisfaction he was to know. Joanna, he supposed, would be wearing the golden dress he had first seen on her at the opening dance in the Smurthwaite Assembly Rooms. Scroop had a "thing" about it. Lottie? He couldn't see her. Perhaps, he thought, she was too familiar to be clearly seen. He had known her ever since the days when she sent *In the Shadows* tinkling out through the window of Marlborough House while her mother grubbed up the dandelions in Megson Street. However, she was a good-natured useful girl, and he decided that as a lot of shopping would have to be done he would ask her to give him a hand. It was going to be rather a lopsided dinner party: five men and two women. But Scroop wanted only those who had been in with *Vanguard* from the beginning. That meant Scroop and Shrubb; and Joanna because she was Scroop's wife; and Septimus Pordage because, in the full flush of fame that his book had brought him, he had written an article that would in itself, he said, sell out the first number; and Lottie because she was Septimus's secretary; and himself and Joe because—Well, we've nothing to do with the thing, he said, but I've known Joanna a long time now, ever since we shared a bun at Smurthwaite, and she insists on Joe simply because she likes him so much. Moreover, Scroop said you never knew when the press might be useful, and perhaps Joe would manage to smuggle a paragraph about the dinner into Inquisitor's column that everyone read in *The Banner*.

He put on his hat and overcoat and went out into the brisk morning. His first call was at a restaurant a few doors down, where he had a word with Georges, who was a waiter friend of his, and Georges said that yes, certainly he knew an excellent waiter who was free that night, his brother Henri. Anthony arranged that Henri should be at his flat an hour before dinner time, and then he crossed the road, turned into a side street and climbed the stairs of a house where Septimus Pordage had rented a top-floor flat.

"My dear boy," Septimus said, "I was hoping you would call. Every artist wishes to share the beauty he has created, and the probability is that I shall never do better than this."

He was wearing a morning coat and sponge-bag trousers, grey spats

248

and a dark blue cravat. A grey topper was in his hand. He put it on and tapped it to a rakish angle with the ivory knob of his malacca cane. "A man," he said, "owes it to himself to make the most of the parts life thrusts upon him. You have seen me red-tabbed and martial-looking as only a non-combatant staff officer can look. Now you behold Ambrose Feend about to enlarge the public conception of the well-dressed man. I have invited Me to take a walk. Unfortunately the wind demands an overcoat, but all need not be loss."

And indeed it wasn't, for the overcoat was a tight-waisted garment with three large dark-pearl buttons at the back, and flowing skirts. Anthony thought he looked like a buck of Dick Hudson's early days, run to fat.

Septimus put on lavender suède gloves and considered himself in a looking-glass. "Yes," he assured himself. "Yes. I shall toddle into Oxford Street, consider the pleasing pile of *Me, About I* in Messrs. Bumpus's bookshop window, saunter into Bond Street, and make my way to St. James's Park. I wish to see the mandarin ducks, with whom at the moment I feel a sharp affinity. I should like to invite you, Anthony, to come with me, but there are moments when a man must commune with his sweet and virtuous soul."

"I'm a pagan, sir," Anthony assured him, "concerned only with the stomach. I have to get out and order the things for Sir William Scroop's dinner to-night. I wondered if you could spare Lottie to come with me for an hour or so."

"The body and the soul, young Anthony," Septimus said, "are the homely cart and the precious cargo, the wine and the bottle. You may think of them as things apart, if you like, but, if you do, so much the worse. Rather think of them as things in harmony, or that should be so. I shall bring my soul along to-night. My body is in your hands. Do it proud, my boy. Some great songs have sprung from the cravings of the flesh. Read your Keats, or your Tennyson. *All Danaë to the stars.* Think that out. Well, I mustn't deprive the populace any longer. Au revoir. Remember, *je suis fine bouche.*"

They listened to him toddling downstairs, and then Anthony turned to Lottie and said: "He's given it to me."

"What has he given to you?"

Anthony hesitated, then said: "Oh, I expect you'll think I'm crazy, but—mind you, only in the vaguest way—I've sometimes wondered whether I could make a living out of running a restaurant. I'm sick of mooching about, living on my mother. I've never had any sort of training. There's that awful Chris Hudson reading for the Bar, and Joe starting in London journalism, and Scroop launching a magazine, and you earning your living with old Septimus. Well, I *can* cook."

"Yes. Mother says you have the makings."

"Well then, I can go on from the makings. While I was walking across here I was thinking—What if I had a restaurant? What should I call it? And Septimus has just handed it to me. *La Fine Bouche*."

Lottie said in her temperate way: "Yes. That's good. But it would take some living up to."

"So does everything worth doing. Look, let's talk about this dinner for to-night. And then, will you come and do the shopping with me?"

4

Lottie sat idly in the flat. There wasn't much to do as Septimus's secretary. He was having a high old time being the literary celebrity of the moment, but Lottie knew that this was only a pause, that they would soon be back at Easter How, with Septimus in his country tweeds again. They would take up once more the work of revising the long list of Pordage grammars, and Lottie didn't want that. Beneath her calm, she was as restless as Anthony, and her stay in London had done nothing to quiet her longings. Septimus had written his only book, and knew it, and said it. He was delighted to play his part so long as the fuss lasted. He accepted every invitation to literary lunches and cocktail parties, where he chattered as Ambrose Feend was expected to chatter. He had lectured on the Mystical Approach to the Obvious, and had laughed to Lottie at what he could get away with. "What do you make of it, my dear?" he asked when she handed him the typed copy, and she said frankly: "To me it's double Dutch." "So it will be to everybody," he said, "and that is the reason why they'll all find it wonderful. They're terribly afraid of not understanding the latest thing, which is why Scroop's *Vanguard* has a good chance of success. In the van. That's what they're all after, although a good many vans are like the vans on railway trains, bringing up the rear. It's not that they love painting or music or writing. It's simply that they must be in the *fashion* of these things at the moment. Old-fashioned. They'd do in their dearest friends rather than be called that. And yet, there are few fashions that matter, and they're all as old as the hills. So this," tapping the typescript, "will go down in a big way, and bring me a fat fee."

There was a standing invitation to visit Joanna—one of those "look in any time, darling," invitations that punctilious or sensitive persons find hard to accept. Especially at this moment, thought Lottie. Joanna had been married for a year, but she was still shut up in a world inhabited only by her and William. Lottie had been to Soho Square several times, and didn't like the feeling of warming her hands at someone else's fire of happiness. She liked Scroop as a man, but she didn't like him as unvaried conversational diet, and at times she felt apprehensive and wished that life would harden Joanna a bit and not keep her in this warm flux in which she now existed. She was sensitive, too, about Joanna's beauty, incredibly ripened, and about the splendour of Joanna's circumstances; Mrs. Halliwell's money translated into elegance. At Miss Kempfer's one hadn't thought of such things, and at Throstle's Nest Mrs. Halliwell's money was dowdy and commonplace and roughly comfortable; but in Soho Square it had been put to other use. The splendid drawing-room in which Scroop and Shrubb had untidily laboured had been cleared, and the affairs of *Vanguard* were conducted in a couple of hired rooms not far away. Under Shrubb's care, the drawing-room had been restored as beautifully as the Assembly Rooms at Smurthwaite. The painted ceiling was cleaned, the walls were done in green and gold, and every piece of furniture was in the best taste of the Georgian hey-day when the house came into being. Gwilym hardly dared to move, "and I wouldn't want the job of cleaning that chandelier," Lottie thought.

The joke of it was that Joanna didn't praise Mother from whom all blessings flow: she praised Scroop. She had plenty to praise him for. His love was undoubted and overpowering, and that was another thing that made Lottie uneasy in Soho Square. She was at times almost physically aware of the house as a big bedroom, and of herself as an intruder who should get out so that the important matters of life might be carried on.

The glances that sometimes passed—suddenly, at unlooked-for moments—between Scroop and Joanna: glances both reminiscent and full of immediate suggestion: were enough to make Lottie go hot all over. And that could happen even when there was company. There was a night when she and a couple whose names she could not remember were the last to go. Scroop and Joanna stood under the fanlight, seeing them off, his arm round her waist. When the door shut on the midnight street, Lottie went in one direction and the young couple in the other, and Lottie heard the man say: "Well, did you ever!" and the girl answered: "I'm not shocked, darling. I was brought up on a farm." Lottie hated them; but those were the kind of moments when she thought of the whitewashed room over the barn at

Easter How where she and her mother had truckle beds, and the windows opened on to a view of the fells, and the owls' cries trembled on the cold air, and from down below came the comfortable sound of Valpy shuffling in his straw.

And yet. . . . She knew that she did not want to go back there. Especially now, after this shopping expedition with Anthony, she did not want to go back. Standing at the window of Septimus's flat, a poor enough shabby place rented only for a moment of passage, she looked out at the unprepossessing picture: bricks, windows, chimney-pots. The briskness and young gaiety of the morning had passed as the day grew cold and sullen. She admitted to herself that she had long wanted Anthony to ask her to do something, if only to go shopping. How many years ago it was since he had asked her to do anything at all! Not since a day that had proved disastrous to poor Septimus: the day when she and Chris Hudson had arrived in a motor-car at Easter How with Chris's father. They had chattered colloquial French to Septimus's discomfiture, and she had tried to make it up to the old dear by listening to his lecture on quills and calligraphy. And—"Was it the next day?" she questioned Anthony, as she recalled this moment after they had set out—he asked her to go for a walk. They had quarrelled and made it up, and the day had turned bright, and with a few coppers in their pockets they had gone into a tea garden. She was amazed to find how sharply it was all cut into her memory: how the woman had smiled at them—"and we must have been an odd-looking pair, you'll admit, Anthony"—and there had been a large bone for poor Cerberus, now dead, and the garden had touches of brightness from spring's earliest flowers. But Anthony seemed not to remember much about it.

And then there was going away, and the war that kept her away for so long; and almost as soon as she was back there was that affair in the Smurthwaite Assembly Rooms. There she met this different Anthony, a young man, well-dressed and well-to-do, mysteriously transmogrified and seeming to her, who felt unchanged, stand-offish and aloof. She had learned to dance in Switzerland, and hoped he would ask her to dance, but they had done nothing but sit together and talk about things that didn't matter.

She had seen him a little since coming to London; she had been to his rooms with Septimus; but his air of a young man-about-town with nothing to do had not been encouraging. He had never once asked her to join him in the agreeable business of doing nothing. And now he had asked her to go shopping!

5

He was very polite, and nothing can be more devastatingly a barrier than that. He was apologetic for having asked her, and explained that he had dared to do so only because he so much valued her advice. He was careful to carry the heaviest things, and he was talkative enough. No one could complain that he was a dull companion, but it was all, she said to herself with a flick of annoyance, so damned "matey." At any moment, she felt, he might tell her that she was a good sport, and that would put the tin hat on it all. What seemed to interest him far more than she could do was this notion of running a restaurant. She said she thought it would be a dog's life unless the place were absolutely tip-top and successful, and he said calmly: "Oh, it would be that all right." At last they dumped all their packages into a taxi-cab, and he dropped her at her door and then went on to Baker Street.

Septimus was not back. She never knew what he would do. Apart from breakfast, which she prepared, they ate out of the flat. Sometimes he would come in from his morning toddle and take her out to lunch, and if he didn't she went out and ate alone. It was difficult to know why she was here at all. Septimus was merely marking time; he was doing nothing but warm himself in his passing gleam of glory, and when he was tired of that he would go back and live sensibly in Yorkshire. But it pleased him to have his secretary with him, though it would have been much cheaper, she reflected with her mother's practicality, to send his few bits of typing to some office that did that sort of thing. She felt unnecessary and unwanted, a rather plain girl with her living to earn and few friends.

There was Shrubb, of course: the strange and almost anonymous Shrubb. She didn't remember ever to have heard his Christian name. Joanna and Gwilym called him Mr. Shrubb, Scroop called him Shrubbo, Mrs. Halliwell spoke of that nice Mr. Shrubb. He was now officially a member of the staff of *Vanguard*, and sometimes he was cast for a rather important moment: he had been Scroop's best man at the wedding. But he gave, even there, the effect of being a little outside everything. With his shy diffident manner, his hesitant speech and his limp, he was like a footman in a farce who, to satisfy some trick of situation, is playing the part of a member of the family, but will soon be a footman again.

She remembered how, a week or two ago, she had called in the morning at the house in Soho Square. For some reason Scroop had not been to the office of *Vanguard* that day, and, as she was leaving, he said: "Lottie, there are some papers here that Shrubbo ought to have at once. Would you mind dropping them in as you go by?"

She had not been to the office before, but she knew where it was, in a street that had once been smartly residential. A plaque alongside the door, announcing that once a famous dramatist had lived there, did nothing but emphasise the sordid decline of the region. Inside the open door, a newly-painted strip of board told her that *Vanguard* lived on the first floor. She knocked and heard Shrubb trailing his leg across the floor inside. When the door opened, his rather sad face warmed to a smile. "Oh, come in, come in," he said. "I was just starting lunch. Watch your step. Festus is about somewhere."

"Festus?"

"Yes. There he is. Come here, boy." He knelt with great difficulty, and a large white rat scampered from a corner, leapt to his shoulder, and looked at Lottie with eyes as pink as spindleberries.

"Give us a hand," Shrubb said. "Getting up is not so easy as getting down. Put a hand here—under my elbow."

She did so, and slowly eased him up, her eyes in horrified proximity to Festus's scaly-looking tail.

"Don't you like him?" he asked. "I think he's a remarkably handsome chap. And highly intelligent."

She hadn't the heart to say that she didn't like him a bit, but he sensed this, and said: "Well, old boy, you'll have to go to beddybyes."

This was, or had been, a rather fine room. A door opened from it into a much smaller one, and into this Lottie followed Shrubb. "Excuse me," he said in his attractive nervous way. "I'm afraid you'll think this rather fancy. I made it myself."

"But it's lovely, Mr. Shrubb," she sincerely said.

It was Festus's home. There was a mahogany stand, and on this a small house in two storeys. In the right-hand corner of the ground floor was a perfect panelled door. For the rest, this floor was shut in with small-meshed wire. An inclined run led through a hole in the ceiling to the upper floor which had two neat windows with white-painted sashes. The roof was crowned with a chimney at each corner, and scales of grey-painted wood made the slates. Lottie thought Festus's house much more attractive than Festus, though she looked at him with a tolerant eye now that he had run to the upper floor and peered out through a window.

"I found him," Shrubb explained. "I was going home one night when there he was cowering behind a dustbin. Well, if he'd been a rough sort of chap he'd have been able to look after himself. But a rat like that has obviously been someone's pet. So I thought he might miss all the little attentions he'd been used to. I brought him back and put him in a drawer for the night, with a few biscuits. Sir William didn't take a good view the next day. He said: 'You can't infest us with rats, Shrubbo.' That's why I call him Festus," he said with a shy grin. "Scroop doesn't mind so much now that he has a home. I always let him out for a good run through the two rooms while Sir William's away at lunch. I think he's getting rather fond of me. I hope so."

The bigger room had two curtained windows looking on to the street. This inner room had one small uncurtained window looking upon a shabby chaos of back yards. The quarterdeck and the lower deck, Lottie thought, and felt resentful on Shrubb's behalf.

He washed his hands at a sink in the corner and said: "I was just about to have my lunch."

On the table was a bottle of beer, a glass, and a small package which, Lottie supposed, contained sandwiches. She thought of Sir William who would now be sitting down with Joanna to a swell meal: cut glass and silver and all the accessories. Steady now, she told herself. These things are, and I suppose Mr. Shrubb sees nothing wrong about that. But all the same, a small swell of resentment rose in her breast, and she said impulsively: "Can you leave the office? Can you come and have lunch with me for a change? Mr. Pordage is out to lunch with Lady Sybil Colefax."

"Well," he said, "that's uncommon civil of you, Miss Wayland. Really, I'd like that." He slipped the sandwiches into a drawer. "These'll see Festus over a day or two," he said.

Lottie had been thinking of giving herself a bun and a pot of tea in a Lyons tea-shop; but now she remembered a little Italian restaurant not far away, and she took Shrubb there and they ate a great dish of macaroni and tomato, laughing as they twirled it up on their forks into hanks of disordered knitting, and they drank a flask of rough Chianti which she wasn't at all used to. When she got back to the flat she lay down and had a sleep, remembering that she had promised Shrubb to call at his place in Chelsea on the following Saturday afternoon.

She made that visit. It was the first time she had been in Chelsea, of which she had heard much, and read much, and expected much. She was disappointed. It seemed to her a grimy unprepossessing place, living on the memory of a few great names, a place that would be intolerable without the river. The day didn't help. It was March, and no wind was awake. The trees were dark and sodden and the very air seemed afraid to move. Everything was suspended, and as Shrubb took her round repeating the familiar Chelsea litany: Carlyle, Whistler, Rossetti, Oscar Wilde: she felt as though she were in a graveyard and he was reading the names on the tombs. He took her to lunch in the King's Road, and then they crossed the river and walked for a while in Battersea Park. Here, beneath the leafless trees, he said: "Do you mind if I take your arm, Miss Wayland? It helps me. I've walked rather a lot to-day."

She was full of contrition and suggested that they should go back at once, but he wouldn't hear of that and pegged along, one hand on her arm and the other on his stick. Undoubtedly he was tired, but he was also, she knew, being a little disingenuous. He wanted to take her arm but had been too shy to do it without excuse. This reflection made her infinitely sad. It opened a window on Shrubb's life. His loneliness became part of this stagnant day; and she thought of the back room in the *Vanguard* office, with the old-fashioned sloppy sink in one corner and the gas-fire in another, and Festus's house, and the uncurtained outlook upon back yards full of dustbins and broken crates and rusting bedsteads and all the miscellaneous rubbish of human living. And she said to herself: "It's all in me and not in Battersea or Chelsea. If this were spring and the trees were budding and I loved Mr. Shrubb, then it would all be different. And if I loved Mr. Shrubb it would all be different anyhow."

She wondered if he felt any tenderness for her, and remembered the smile that had lighted his sad face when she arrived at the office with the papers from Sir William, and how eagerly he had entered into the fun of her little lunch in the Italian restaurant; and she thought that yes, he probably was at this moment, because of her, happy in his quiet way, and this seemed to her the saddest thought that had visited her all that day long.

And as she stood there in Septimus's flat and these memories engaged her, Septimus himself came in, buoyant and eupeptic. "My dear child," he said. "There is nothing more to wait for. I have now seen it all. Miss Edith Sitwell was upon my right hand. We shall attend this dinner of Sir William Scroop's to-night. To-morrow to Smurthwaite. To familiar woods and pastures that are none the worse for not being new."

6

When everyone else was gone, and there was no sound save the clatter Henri made as he washed up in the little kitchen, Joe Morrison said: "They proved to be old ham bones. How do these things happen? How does a respectable Penge milliner develop so strange an addiction—to keep ham bones under the counter? How does someone discover them and report the matter to the police? And how does so trivial a thing swell in the public mind to such proportions that news of it reaches every office in Fleet Street? The boys were frightfully disappointed. It looked like the makings of a lovely sexy and sadistic crime. All disappointed except me."

"Why—what did you make of it?" Anthony asked.

"I asked just the questions I've been asking you. I wrote a nice little piece on the birth of rumour. I had the pleasure of seeing it go on the spike. Still, it was exercise. But there's something more important than that."

Anthony was tired. He wanted to sit here thinking of the dinner, of the compliments he had received, of the ways in which it might have been better still. But Joe was indefatigable. He was one of those men who begin to wake up at 11 p.m.

"Well," Anthony said, "I suppose this is where I ask: What is more important than the birth of rumour?"

Joe stuffed tobacco into a foul pipe, and Anthony winced. One did not smoke a pipe after a dinner like that.

Joe said: "The suppression of rumour," and looked wise.

"Well?" Anthony obliged him.

"All over this country, all over Europe for that matter, there are things being hushed up. If I can make any sort of reputation in Fleet Street, the sort of reputation that will give me a chance more or less to choose my own work, I want to get about and do a lot of unhushing. Now take . . . ."

Happily, Henri came in from the kitchen. "I may go?" he asked.

"Yes, Henri. And thank you very much. You were a great help."

"I give my felicitations. We try again some time?"

"I hope so."

When Henri was gone, Joe said: "I suppose it *is* your night, not mine. So I'd better stop cackling. It really was a marvellous dinner, Anthony. And didn't Joanna look smashing?"

"It was a good dinner," Anthony agreed, "but I hope to do better. And Joanna looked very well indeed. Now I'm off to bed. I'm travelling north to-morrow. I think I ought to see my mother."

"And my father."

"And our half-brother."

"Yes, give him two kisses—one on your half, one on mine."

"I hope he hasn't got your red hair."

"You won't be able to tell yet. It'll just be a furry scribble on the scalp."

"I wouldn't know a thing like that. I've never seen a newborn baby."

"Neither have I. I'm guessing. I wonder whether Scroop has put Joanna in the family way yet?"

"Joe! Of all the things to say!"

"All right. You don't have to have my imagination if you don't want it. But the thought of those two haunts me. And thoughts sometimes take on a very personal tinge. Well, good night, Escoffier. My greetings to the old man."

7

While a schoolboy, Anthony had several times been to Longford with Joe during the holidays. They had not been very lively times because of the war, but he remembered them with pleasure. He liked Longford and he liked Joe's father. The town was small and Joe's father was big, and between them they achieved a medium sort of sanity. Enclosure, they say, was good for agriculture; and the "multiple" stores are an Enclosure of trading, squeezing out the small man and bringing in a lot of brass and brassiness *ad majoram gloriam investorum,* as Septimus might put it. But Longford was small enough to have escaped this kindly intention. There wasn't even a taxi-cab at the station, and, walking into the town with his bag, Anthony thought it was a pleasing place. It's architecture was half of brick, rosy with the centuries, and half of grey stone. The tall many-storeyed silk mill was of brick, and already lights were in its windows. It was a long straggle of a town, with hills throwing a protective half-circle round one side of it, while the other side wandered into a plain through which a small river ran, the river whose power had once worked the mill. There had been a little snow, and the hills were white, recalling to Anthony adventures that he and Joe had up there on disastrous home-made skis.

He wondered what his mother and Mr. Morrison had made of the Old Court, which was a picturesque note in the main street. It was a happy-go-lucky street which refused to recognise that business was one thing and private life another. The town hall, and shops, and dwelling houses, and the doctor's place, and the local solicitor's office, and a market-hall jostled companionably together, and half-way down one side was the Old Court, which once had housed the family who built the silk mill. But that family had disappeared, and the mill was owned by a limited liability company, and for years the Old Court had been empty. The façade was right on to the cobbled pavement. It was a three-storeyed brick building, warm and mellow, obviously the work of a local builder turned architect, unpretentious, well-proportioned and satisfying. There was no bow-window fantasy. The façade was flat, but whether by luck or insight, the builder had apportioned the windows and the doorway to the brickwork with a nicety that made the Old Court the finest thing in the street.

It was not to this house that Mr. and Mrs. Morrison had come on their marriage. They had lived for a time in the small stone house, close in under the hills, where Joe had been born. It was there that Anthony had visited them when they came back from their honeymoon. He recalled how, on an evening of late summer, he and his mother had climbed up the hill behind the house. They sat on a boulder and looked across the town to the plain which, in the almost-darkness, might have been stretching to the sea. Anthony recalled the day at Sleights, when he had not known that this was his mother, and they had sat waiting for the moon to rise on the North Sea, and he had been aware of an edge of tension in their relationship that had puzzled and disturbed him. She was holding his hand now, as she had done then, but no quiver of over-heightened emotion passed between them. What passed between them—and he was glad of it—was a warmth of understanding, on his side of gratitude to her and dissatisfaction with himself.

He pressed her hand and said: "What a disappointment I must have been to you, Mother, after all those years."

She said: "They're all wrong, you know, when they say you can't eat your cake and have it. When you've eaten it you have it—part of you for ever and ever and for better or worse. If you keep it—well, it soon ceases to be eatable cake, doesn't it?"

"Is Joe's father turning you into a philosopher, Mother?"

She said: "He's turning me into a very happy woman," and he knew that she had never looked happier, her blue eyes more lovely.

She said: "It's all a big If now, and nothing is so foolish as worrying about the Ifs. But if I had wanted a son I should have eaten my cake and damned the consequences. One of the consequences, I suppose, would have been that I wouldn't have married Mr. Freilinghausen. I'm quite sure that he wouldn't have stood for you. And that would have been a great loss to me. He was a very wonderful man. But I would have had a son."

259

Anthony said: "I'm sorry, Mother. I don't want you to talk about this. I don't want you to feel that I'm prying into your life."

She gave a little laugh. "My dear, your very existence pried into it from the beginning, believe me, and that wasn't your fault, was it? It was my fault if, when I could say 'This is my son,' he wasn't my son in the way I wanted. How could he have been?"

"I should like to have been, Mother."

She said: "I have been given far more than I had any right to expect—all of Mr. Freilinghausen, and a bit of you, and now this."

She waved a hand vaguely into the night in which a few stars were appearing, as though Joe's father had given her the world.

He did not see her on that day of his arrival at the Old Court. But the next day Auntie Jess took him to the bedroom, and a ray of wintry sunshine lit the white room and the bowls of daffodils and tulips that seemed to make it a bower, and there was his mother, looking absurdly younger than ever, with a small face in the crook of her arm. It seemed for a moment like nothing on earth, and then, as he shyly stroked a cheek with his finger, the eyes opened, blue, and a grin appeared on the face, and—yes!—the down was indubitably red! "Well, I'm damned!" he cried. "It's Joe! It's not a bit like me."

Mr. Morrison, whose radiance seemed to fill the room, said: "Well, that's a good start," and took him downstairs at once, and gave him sherry and biscuits.

He went back from that visit feeling closer to his mother than he had ever been. Now that she really had a son—and not, he said to himself, a great oaf who looks as though he might be her slightly younger brother—her love was all-embracing. He was included in it with a freedom he had not experienced before, and he was able to give back her love, because he felt unchained from her anxious wish that he should do so. Before going, he kissed her, and he had never been able to do that till now, though he had accepted her kisses. They smiled at one another, and there were happy tears in her eyes as she said: "I haven't deserved that it should all turn out like this."

CHAPTER 12

19 19 19 19 19 19

1

*D*ick Hudson had a reputation in his profession as a close customer. He had gone fairly early to the top and earned a lot of money and hadn't splashed it about. His own success never failed to astonish him. It had been so easy, he said, forgetting the hours he would spend on perfecting a glance or a gesture. If he was modest, he was also cautious. Plenty of his fellows parted cheerfully with their money to the book-makers, and some even went in for owning race-horses. But not Dick. He had seen too often what that led to, and there was Chris to think about. Once, long ago, he had been tricked over a money matter, and he had taken the business to Rudolph Schwann, a small swarthy solicitor, with offices in Serjeants Inn. Schwann had got him so neatly out of his difficulty that Dick asked him to handle his affairs. He had never had cause to regret it, and the years since this arrangement was made had been profitable both to him and to Schwann. Dick didn't want to totter to his grave across a music-hall stage. He wanted to retire while he still had a few years before him. "You allow me just what I need. Invest the rest, and when I can chuck up this caper you pass me the word."

It was early in 1923 that Schwann passed him the word. He bought the small house that till then he had rented in St. John's Wood, and in the autumn of that same year Chris came down from the university and began to read for the Bar in the chambers of Mr. Farrington Roberts in the Inner Temple. Nothing, Dick thought, could have been more satisfactory than this. His quarterly cheque came in from Schwann, and his real life was beginning in the life of his son. As for himself, he could now start on his own education. He dutifully read books that Chris recommended, and he spent a lot of time wandering

261

about in picture galleries and museums. He would say to Chris things like this: "Look, Chris. Now suppose I went to a first-class concert. They're half-way through playing something. I want to feel at home. I want to be able to say 'Beethoven' or 'Schumann' or whatever it may be. Now, what's the book for that?" Or pictures: "What's the book that'll let me say 'Constable' or 'Turner' at a glance?"

Chris would explain that he himself had never studied music and knew little about pictures. Dick couldn't understand it. "After taking that degree at Cambridge?"

"Just keep on with it, Dad. The light will dawn. To travel hopefully is better than to arrive."

"Who said that?"

"Stevenson."

"Where can I read about him?"

That was easier. Chris would produce the book and go off whistling to the chambers of Mr. Farrington Roberts. It was a good life, he thought. He could look back even on Mrs. Wayland with toleration. The *maîtresse-femme* had taught him to speak French as few Englishmen spoke it. Then the old man had given him a public school from which he hoped he had drawn something better than warts like Courtice could draw. He had enjoyed Oxford. So long as you kept away from what he dubbed all this bluism, left the rowing alone and dodged the hearty chaps who came in steaming from the rugger fields in winter dusks, there was something to be said for the place. You didn't have to get emotional about crumbling stone, and What is her secret? and all that sort of thing. The thing was to work. It was a good place for work, and he had found that few things gave him more satisfaction. Work was the way to power and influence. The law was alluring him, especially criminal law. "It's a difficult case. The fellow's got no more than a hundred to one chance. Better call in Hudson. Marshall Hall? Rather a back number, don't you think? An actor, not a lawyer. Hudson's got a brain packed in ice."

Of course, a man needn't be such a fool as to do nothing but work. But he should relax like a man, not a cat who found release in clambering about roofs and pinnacles. An occasional trip to town was the thing, and it wasn't always necessary to let the old man know about that. An odd type, the old man. One had always thought of music-hall people as raffish men and pretty hot-stuff women, and so they were, most of them, so far as he knew them. But the old man was an exception: a bit of a Puritan, and his present phase of going out after culture was rather pathetic. Still, it made it easy for one to jolly him along. "He can start morning prayers if he likes," Chris thought, swinging along happily through the spring morning, umbrella in one hand, brief-case in the other, a bowler hat on his head. He always walked to the office when the weather was fine. It gave him reasonable exercise, and exercise, like everything else, should be reasonable.

Yes, he thought, even morning prayers could be borne so long as this comfortable harbourage was maintained until he was ready to push off in his own boat. And it was very comfortable. A room on the first floor at the back of the house was his as a study-sitting-room, with a mere cubicle of a room opening off it for his bed and wardrobe. He could be sure of his privacy. The old man never disturbed him there. He would as soon have butted into the sanctum of the Lord Chancellor. There was a Mrs. Butterworth to look after their physical needs, and a little woman like a dusty rumpled sparrow came in "to do the rough." All very nice, Chris thought. Couldn't be better. He never failed, when a chance came, to thank Mrs. Butterworth and even the sparrow for looking after him so well. Nothing like it, he thought. Keeps 'em on their toes. All in all, he considered himself a wise youth, *mens sana in corpore* reasonably *sano*. The spectacles he had lately taken to wearing gave an owlish benevolence to a face that was chubby and promised to be fat. But anyone who thought Chris Hudson benevolent stood a good chance of waking up with a start.

2

Mr. Rudolph Schwann occasionally took a bit of business along to the chambers of Mr. Farrington Roberts, and Chris Hudson would covertly watch him. Schwann had a habit of sitting relaxed, however exciting the conversation, one of his hairy hands palm-downward on each of his knees. There the hands lay unmoving, like a couple of moles. Only his eyes moved, his quick and rather oily brown eyes, darting to right and left. Hair sprouted from his ears and nostrils, but so much of it had been used elsewhere that there hadn't been enough to cover his head. His tonsure was leathery brown, and so was the skin of his stout clean-shaven face. He dressed with care. The moles emerged from burrows of spotless cuff, each enhanced with a golden link. Chris watched him, fascinated. The quietness of the man's pose was in such contrast with the restless darting of his eyes that Chris thought of a snake sunning itself on a warm rock, but alert to disappear in a flash. "A tricky customer that," he summed up to himself, and felt a wish to be acquainted with Mr. Schwann more closely. He didn't know that Schwann was his father's man of affairs. Dick never discussed that sort of thing with his son, and Schwann, though he knew of the relationship, did not discuss his clients' affairs with anybody. But already there was the beginning of a link between the two, if only because of Schwann's dealings with Dick Hudson, which gave him a mild interest in the boy, and Chris's feeling of satisfaction at having a dubious customer to observe. There were few things he liked better.

"Mr. Christopher Hudson, K.C., cross-examined the accused. In his characteristic attitude, his hands clasped behind him under the tail of his gown, his eyes looking coldly above the head of the person addressed, he asked: 'Tell me, Mr. Schwann, can you add up two and two?' 'As well as the next man.' 'And do you always make it two-and-a-half or three, when four would more nearly represent the interests of your client?' The judge intervened to ask: 'What exactly are you suggesting, Mr. Hudson?' 'I thought, m'lud, it would be clear that I was suggesting a not unprofitable inexactitude in the prisoner's mathematical processes.' (Laughter.)"

He came to with a start. He was walking along Fleet Street and almost collided with Schwann. Indeed, Schwann laughingly fended him off with the ferrule of his ebony cane. "Steady, steady!" he said. "Do not allow your mind to run so deeply on torts and malfeasances that you can't see the world about you."

"Sorry, Mr. Schwann," Chris apologised, beaming through his spectacles at the prisoner so abruptly transferred from the lonely dock to the bustling pavement. "My mind was rather occupied."

"Come and occupy your stomach, or allow a dozen oysters to do so."

They were outside the Falstaff and went in together. Chris followed Schwann's example and ordered a dozen oysters, brown bread and butter and a pint of lager beer. They followed this with cheese and biscuits. "A snack is all one needs at this time of day," Schwann said. "At night one can really give attention to food."

"I'm afraid I have to give attention to masses of work. My father and I have a very simple meal, and then I get up to my den."

"Don't overdo it. You should give yourself a break at least once a week. I get out more often than that."

"Well, naturally I don't stay in every night," Chris said. "Perhaps we'll be able to get together some time."

"Make it to-night. Would you like that?"

Chris would like it very much, but he made a pretence of reluctance. "I think," he said, "it's just possible that. . . . Well, yes. I could put that off. Yes, to-night then?"

264

Schwann gave him a card. "Call for me there about half past seven."

3

The flat was the top floor of a house in Berkeley Square. A man-servant let Chris in, took his hat and coat, and showed him to the room where Schwann was waiting. A fire burned on the hearth. The curtains were drawn and a gentle light filled the room from some hidden source. Chris looked about him surprised. "My word," he said, as Schwann came forward and shook his hand, "you do yourself well!"

"Why not? I have no one to think of but myself. Never clutter yourself up, my dear Hudson. Wives, children, school-bills, measles, whooping-cough—dear me—no, no, no! What will you drink?"

He looked sleek in his dinner-jacket. Chris apologised for not having changed. "Don't give it a thought," Schwann said. "Just a habit. Coster puts the things out, I put them on, and honour is satisfied all round. If I didn't, he'd leave me. He was with a duke. Sit down."

Chris sat down. The fire purred. The soft light seemed apologetic for being light at all. Schwann moved soundlessly on the mossy carpet, bringing a dry Martini.

"That's a Rouault, isn't it?" Chris asked.

Schwann looked at him with admiration. "Yes," he said, "but most people who see it merely ask: 'What on earth do you call that?' Do you know his work well?"

Chris sipped his Martini and smiled. "Just a trick," he said. "Visual memory. I know nothing at all about painting, but I like wandering in galleries. When I've seen a few pictures by a man, I've got him. They all have their little tricks, haven't they?"

"Well," Schwann said, "I'd call it more than that."

"Maybe. But the trick's there—a sort of signature. And it gives one prestige to recognise it. Think how I could have imposed on you as a connoisseur to-night."

"Not for long you wouldn't," Schwann assured him. "Try it on some day, my boy. Bring me a Rouault with all the tricks, but that isn't a Rouault just the same, and have a go at selling it to me." He laughed and refilled Chris's glass.

Chris felt warm and happy and relaxed. This was his idea of civilised company, and he had never tasted it before. He thought of what he had known till now. An occasional invitation to tea with a housemaster and his wife in a shabby room decorated with photographs of Kandersteg or some such place where they had spent a

265

honeymoon or done a bit of winter sporting. Tea, muffins, an embarrassed housemaster's wife desperately trying to find something to talk about to one of the ticks she'd be glad to see the back of. "Do you shee, Mr. Hudson, or should one call it skee?" There hadn't been much at Oxford. The same thing, in fact, with a tutor's wife in place of a housemaster's. He'd made no friendships, and would have been bored to tears but for the work. One thing he'd looked forward to on coming down was what he thought of as man-of-the-world society. There was nothing that Dick Hudson could do to provide that. All that Chris sighed for was what Dick would give his ears to avoid. Hope dawned when Farrington Roberts invited Chris to eat dinner one Sunday night with him and his family. Now this was going to be the thing, Chris thought, for Roberts was a notable man in his profession. Chris put on his dinner jacket, and Dick handsomely stood him the cost of a private-hire Daimler to Hampstead and back. The boy leaned on cushions in happy dreams of the glittering company he was to meet, the sparkling conversation in which he hoped he would have a chance to play his part. He found a comfortable house enough, but there were no festive lights and the maid took him up to Mr. Farrington Roberts's study, a room no bigger than his own at St. John's wood. Roberts looked a little surprised at the dinner jacket—he was in an old velvet jacket and was smoking a pipe—but said nothing about it. "Sit down, Hudson. I was just getting through a bit of work while my wife's out. She doesn't altogether approve of work on Sundays, but it has to be done sometimes. She and Ada won't be long."

She and Ada soon returned from the evening service at a nearby Methodist church, and at once they went into the dining-room and sat down to roast mutton, while Mrs. Farrington Roberts gave them a terse précis of the sermon she had listened to. The girl Ada, who was about the same age as Chris, was bored and silent, as indeed she might well be at hearing for the second time a discourse that didn't sound outstandingly worthy of being listened to once. However, she brightened up towards the end of the meal, which was bread-and-butter pudding, and said: "We always have Dickens on Sunday nights, Mr. Hudson. I don't think Father altogether approves of him. He was so disrespectful to lawyers."

"And I hope, Mr. Hudson," said Mrs. Roberts, "that you won't think that I altogether approve of his being read on a Sunday. However, you know what modern girls are. I well remember my father thrashing my brother for reading *Tom Jones*, and not on a Sunday at that. But I suppose one must move with the times."

This happy permission being granted, they went into the drawing-room; and Miss Roberts became quite animated by the pleasure in prospect. There were three complete sets of the works of Dickens in a bookcase. "We read dramatically," she explained to Chris, "each taking a part. We're doing *Oliver Twist* now. Here you are, Father. You're Fagin and I'm Nancy. Mr. Hudson had better be Bill Sikes."

If Mr. Farrington Roberts in his velvet jacket looked an odd Fagin, that was nothing, Chris thought miserably, to what he must look as a Bill Sikes in spectacles and dinner suit. There seemed to him no reason why Miss Roberts should not speak Nancy in her own voice, but she led off in a high tremulous falsetto, and he growled his reply in such a voice as he imagined a burglar-murderer might be expected to use in addressing his doxy. Mr. Roberts, as Fagin, threw new light on the forensic conception of cringing villainy; and Chris could believe his hostess when she assured him that, little as she liked Sunday night fiction, still she must say she had never heard Dickens read like that before.

He was startled from his reverie by Schwann, who said: "Take a prowl, Hudson. There are one or two things worth looking at." He went silently out of the room, pressing a switch at the door which caused lights to spring out and illuminate some of the pictures. There was fairly recent French stuff: a Sisley, a Renoir, a Berthe Morisot, and lovely little Boudin. There were one or two English painters: a girl on a beach by Wilson Steer, a wishy-washy Conder, a brilliant little Augustus John, and a French peasant woman by his sister Gwen, a thing of tranquil sadness.

Schwann came back, wearing a light overcoat. "Have you looked in the book-case?" he asked.

Chris said that he hadn't. "Well, some other time," Schwann said. "There are a few things worth attention."

The shelves themselves were worth attention, Chris thought, black and shining. "Ebony?" he asked.

"Yes. I'm surprised it's not used more."

"Perhaps because it's a bit expensive."

"It is. That's what I mean when I say you mustn't clutter yourself. Have only what is essential. To me, luxury is essential. I could have a sizeable house like Farrington Roberts's, and everything in it shabby and third-rate. I prefer this small flat and everything with a touch of distinction. Well, come along. Coster tells me the taxi is at the door. So long as you live in town, Hudson, don't clutter yourself with a motor-car. Petrol, garage hire, licence, insurance—all clutter, and taxis at every corner."

He continued, as they went down in the lift: "Ever heard of a taxi in an accident?"

"I can't say I have."

"No. Always private cars. Taxi-men know their business. Leave it to them, and don't clutter yourself."

In the taxi, he said: "There's a place in Dean Street I want to have a look at. D'you know that Inquisitor column in *The Banner?*—man-about-town stuff?"

"I look at it now and then."

"Inquisitor keeps an eye on the restaurants. He's usually reliable, and he had a paragraph about this Dean Street place. *L'Esculent* they call it. It had better be, or they won't see me again. Well, this looks like it."

4

It was just a year since Anthony Fieldhouse had cooked the dinner that inaugurated the journal called *Vanguard*. An incredible year it seemed to him, chock-full. He had gone to Longford to see his mother and his step-father and his half-brother, and, being a young man of leisure, he changed his mind as he was walking with his suitcase down the long main street to the railway station. He had intended to go back to London. Now he decided to take a short holiday in Smurth-waite. He reached the town as dusk was falling, and it didn't seem to him so long ago since he had first arrived there with Auntie Jess and the *malle*, to find Septimus and Valpy and Cerberus waiting to welcome him. That was soon after his evening out with Chris Hudson on the toboggan, and in the meantime everybody seemed to have grown up except himself. His aimlessness troubled him. To be able like that to change his mind and come along here with no compulsion beyond a sudden whim! There was no sense in it, and his casual talk about settling down as a restaurateur seemed empty even to himself.

He walked up the main street of the little town, beneath the winter-bare trees that lined it, past the Assembly Rooms to the Dragon, where he booked a room and, having unpacked his few things, went down to the lounge. The log fire, the shining brass, the cosy leather chairs and a glass of sherry put him into a better mood. "What's wrong with this?" he asked himself with a grin. If Chris Hudson chose to swot in the dusty precincts of the law, and Joe Morrison to spend his time chasing after ham bones in Penge, and Lottie Way-land to drudge over Septimus Pordage's triple courses in this that and the other, and Joanna Halliwell to become Lady Scroop: well, so be it. But, for him, this was all right. He ordered another sherry, and was pleased to see the sparks fly up the chimney as the hall-porter threw more logs on to the fire.

To his surprise, Mrs. Halliwell came into the lounge. It was not a place where he would have expected to see her. As it happened she had been attending a meeting of the Smurthwaite Town Council, and there were one or two points she wished to discuss with a fellow councillor, a robust-looking farmer who was with her. He was not of her opinion, and she knew his partiality for a cosy drink and talk. It was not long before she had helped him to believe that perhaps he had not been right after all. Anthony, half aware of the comedy, noticed that she herself drank nothing, and was not surprised when her companion rose and said heartily: "Well, there's summat in what tha says, lass. Ah'll think on."

When he was gone, Mrs. Halliwell, who had given Anthony no more than a nod on entering, beckoned him to join her. As he did so, he had an odd feeling of being a culprit, caught out. This was Mrs. Halliwell's territory, and he should have announced his arrival in it. He declined her invitation to have a drink, and said that he was just about to go in to dinner. Would she care to join him? Rather to his surprise, she accepted, and sent a message to her chauffeur to let them know at Throstle's Nest that she would not be in, and to come back for her when she rang for him.

"So you use a car now?" he asked.

"Well, I have to get about a bit. It's useful."

"When I was a boy staying with Mr. Pordage I used to think you awfully grand, driving by in your carriage and stirring up the dust."

"I don't know that I was ever very grand," she said simply, "and we don't stir up any dust now. That road's been relaid, and the water-splash by Mr. Pordage's gate is in a culvert."

"Oh dear! That must have broken his heart!"

"Well, it gave us plenty of trouble in the County Council. He drew up a petition and got lots of people to sign it."

Anthony smiled. He could imagine Septimus's petition. "I hope you kept a copy of it," he said.

"No, I didn't. So far as I'm concerned, it was double-Dutch. There were great chunks of poetry in it about Dryads, whatever they may be. The County Council was properly baffled."

"I'll bet they were!" Anthony said. "Did you vote against him?"

"Ay. I thought a better road was a good idea." Her mind was as direct and uncomplicated as that.

"And what does Mr. Pordage do now? Does he still use his pony and trap?"

"Ay, unless he's in a hurry, and then he borrows my car and chauffeur," she said with a grim smile.

"I can't imagine him in a hurry."

"Neither can I. But sometimes he pretends to be, just to have a ride in the car. And as for his water-splash," she said, "except that it isn't a water-splash now, it's as good as ever. The water's still clean. What more does he want?"

They went in to dinner, and the Dragon, as usual, did them proud. It was an old and celebrated inn that had known the arrival of the solitary horseman and the family coach and the public stage-coach, the sound of the horn and the shouting of ostlers and grooms. It belonged to days when men ate and drank lustily, and the feet of generations had sagged its floors and grooved its stone. Mrs. Halliwell was a woman who enjoyed her food. She made no dainty pretences. She smacked her lips over her roast duck and apple sauce, and said: "Well, when you start this place in London, your customers will be lucky if they get anything as good as that."

Anthony put down his knife and fork and looked at her in surprise. "What do you know about a place in London?" he asked.

"No," she said to the waiter. "I don't want a sweet. I'll just have a bit of Wensleydale cheese," and, to Anthony: "Well, things get about, you know. After all, Lottie Wayland *has* been seeing a bit of you in London."

"She's been seeing a lot of things in London."

"Happen so, lad. But none of it seems to have stuck in her head like a morning out shopping with you. That was when you talked to her about starting a restaurant. She thinks it would be a good idea."

"Oh, she does, does she?"

"Ay, but perhaps that's just because it's *your* idea."

He thought her look was full of meaning, and felt deeply embarrassed. He dropped Lottie out of the conversation. "Well," he said, "it was just a thought. I can't say I was very serious about it."

"It's time you were serious about *something*," Mrs. Halliwell said bluntly. "I can't say running a restaurant in London is my idea of how to earn a living. I go out to a few of these places when I'm in Town, and it seems to me there's more bowing and scraping and fal de diddle in general than good food to eat. And you pay twice as much as you would for an honest bellyful in a place like this. Still, all that's as may be, and I daresay there are plenty who know no better and like that sort of thing. 'Everything satisfactory, Madame?' Just to see a chap rubbing his hands and asking that makes 'em believe everything *is* satisfactory when it's about as satisfactory as Sunday's mutton hashed up on Wednesday. But if you want to do it, do it. That's the point. Make up your mind, and when you've made up your mind,

270

work. George," she called to the waiter, "ring up Throstle's Nest and tell 'em to send the car at once. And Mr. Fieldhouse won't be staying here to-night. I'm taking him along with me."

"But Mrs. Halliwell," Anthony protested, "you can't upset their arrangements like that."

"Oh, yes I can," she said calmly. "I own most of the shares in this place. I'd like to catch 'em writing the menus in French!"

"But——"

"Now, Anthony," she said, "there's no but about it. Just run up and pack your things. You shouldn't come to Smurthwaite without letting me know."

And somehow, looking at her plain resolute face, he felt that he had committed a social sin, that he should indeed have let her know before intruding into her territory, and he went humbly up the sagging oak stairway and packed his things, as ordered.

There was a fire in Mrs. Halliwell's office. She put Anthony into the easy-chair, which was the only easy thing in the room, and herself sat very straight up in the wooden swivel chair behind her desk. How is Joanna? How is Sir William? How is that nice Mr. Shrubb? What do you think of this paper of Sir William's? Will he make a go of it? That was how it went. Joanna, and everything to do with Joanna, was all she wanted to know about. Anthony felt a mischievous wish to say: "I am very well, thank you. And my mother has never looked better. And my small brother is a peach. And my step-father is a caution. As for Joe Morrison, he's smelling out murders that don't exist, while biding his time to be one of those chaps who send signed despatches from abroad. Would you believe it, his latest is to have made friends with a French family and a German family, so as to learn to speak their languages well. I remember he was the best chap at languages that we had at school."

He was rather tired with the journey, and the warmth of the Dragon, and the warmth of this room, and these thoughts were floating about in the back of his mind as he answered Mrs. Halliwell's questions. Presently he was aware of her saying: "Well, if you ever do get down to anything serious about this restaurant, just let me know. You don't begin a thing like that on tuppence. I know a bit about London rents. You won't want to start shabby, either. You'll want the best. And all that means brass. I don't mind investing a bit in you, so long as I'm satisfied that you're serious and that the set-up is sensible. Well, you'd better get to bed now. You seem tired."

Anthony suppressed a yawn, apologised, and wished her good-night.

5

Anthony's stay with Mr. Pordage seemed to him now to have been so long ago that the memory of it had set into a pattern like the memory of childhood when we begin to get old. It seemed to him that all spring times then had been an uprush of glory, all summers fecund and autumns russet-ripe. But when he woke in his bedroom at Throstle's Nest he did not need to walk to the window, or even look at the window, to know that here was winter as winter seemed always to have been. It was in the quality of his first conscious breath. There must have been times when snow was a burden, and frost almost too bitter to be borne, and rain a cold continuous misery; but what he remembered was this: the air like chilled wine, astringent and energetic. Before he got out of bed, he knew what he would see; and there it was: the fields white with a frost that had sharpened in the night, the sky cloudless, the distant fells beginning to shine under a sun that had not yet got down to serious business. How often, in his loft over Valpy's stable, he had leapt from bed, heaving the drowsy Cerberus off his feet, and run to the window to see exactly this which he was once more seeing! And as this thought came to him he remembered who was tenant of the loft now. Perhaps at this moment Lottie Wayland, new risen from bed, was standing at the window, filling her lungs with this unforgettable West Riding ether.

A glance at the clock on the mantelpiece told him that this was improbable. He had overslept. It was nine o'clock, and Lottie Wayland was a working woman. So was Mrs. Halliwell. When he went downstairs half an hour later she was gone. But she had remembered him and ordered his breakfast, having her own ideas of what a still-growing man should eat. And in this atmosphere he felt like eating it, as he would not have done in Baker Street. He disposed heartily of his bowl of porridge, his kidneys and bacon and fried potatoes, his toast and marmalade and coffee. Then he opened the note that lay by his plate, addressed to him in Mrs. Halliwell's handwriting. "I wish Joanna could be here to enjoy a bit of this decent air, but seeing that she can't, mind that you do. I shall call at Mr. Pordage's on my way to Smurthwaite to ask him to give Lottie a day off as you're about, just as they do in schools when some big nob comes along. And not so big as all that sometimes. They even did it once when I went to hand out prizes. Well, have a good day, and of course you'll stay to-night?"

Ever since the thought of Lottie getting out of bed in his old room had crossed his mind he had been considering the idea of calling on her. He could pretend that he was calling on Mr. Pordage, who would certainly be annoyed if he didn't. He had quite made up his mind, and then Mrs. Halliwell's note made him wonder whether he should go after all. A bit thick, he thought. Taking a liberty, I call it. What right had Mrs. Halliwell or anyone else to go to a third party and announce his coming? And then he walked out on to the gravel and really began to taste the air, and his annoyance melted before that lively medicine. Third party! How absurd one could be! Lottie Wayland a third party! She had been there from the beginning, from the days of poor old Uncle Horace with his foot-baths, fumigations and Wonder Weed. It would be odd indeed if a man couldn't take a friendly walk with a girl he knew so well. He said to Mrs. Halliwell's housekeeper: "I shan't be in to lunch. I'm going to have a good long walk." And he left a note thanking Mrs. Halliwell and saying that he'd be delighted to stay that night.

6

He found Septimus walking in the garden, a picture of agitation: wild-haired, wild-eyed, and wild of words. He wrung Anthony's hand with the fervour one might expect of a general, with a starving garrison behind him, welcoming the raiser of the siege. "At last!" he cried. "I thought you would never come!"

"Why, sir, what is the matter?" Anthony asked, alarmed by his bearing.

"If I am any judge," said Septimus, "every bone in her leg broken. That's what's the matter. I would have harnessed Valpy and been on my way long before this, but the poor creature is beyond the effort. Amble, amble. Shamble, shamble: that's all I can get out of him now."

"What has happened? Whose leg? Whose bones?"

Lottie answered from the front window, which was open. "Good morning, Anthony. Don't let Mr. Pordage rattle you. There's nothing much wrong."

She was sitting on the window-seat, her legs stretched out in front of her. "Don't move!" Septimus shouted. "And don't talk. Conserve your strength."

Anthony walked to the window. "Good morning, Lottie," he said. "What's up? What can I do?"

"A pirouette!" said Septimus. "I saw the whole performance. A pirouette! You observe that the pathway from garden-gate to front door is made of stones set in the grass. You observe that even now a residue of frost makes the stones treacherous, and from that you may deduce that in the early morning hours they were filmed with ice. And on those icy stones she decides to treat us to an exhibition of pirouettage."

"Why?" Anthony asked.

Lottie said: "Mrs. Halliwell called to say you would be paying us a visit to-day. I walked as far as the gate with her, and when she was gone I danced back to the house because I felt happy. There was no pirouette about it. It was a hop, skip and jump."

"Pirouette, fandango or Highland fling," said Septimus, "you've probably broken every bone in your leg."

"Strained a muscle, more likely," said Lottie; and Mrs. Wayland, who now appeared at the window, said: "We'd better see what it is, anyway. You should have the telephone put in, Mr. Pordage. It would save a lot of trouble."

Septimus reddened under his white tousled hair. "Ha!" he cried. "How like a woman! They are capable of turning everything, even a disaster like this, to their own petty profit. Is she thinking of her daughter's agony, my boy? No! She is thinking how convenient it would be to ring up for a pound of rice or a scrag end of mutton. And to give her that satisfaction I am to have a tap in the house through which every intrusive bore can drip his inanities into my ear. Never! Not if this dancing mænad dies on my hands!"

"Well," Lottie said, "what it boils down to is that we want a doctor. So, if you wouldn't mind, Anthony—Whistle! Whistle!"

The cry surprised Anthony, but not, apparently, Mr. Pordage. He whipped out of his pocket a silver whistle attached to a blue ribbon that passed round his neck, and blew two shrill notes. "Don't bother, Anthony," he said. "Remain here in charge of the women. I'll see to this."

A motor-car was coming down the hill towards the front gate. Septimus ran out into the roadway and stood there blowing his whistle and waving a red silk handkerchief. The car had either to stop or run over him. It stopped; there was a flurry of conversation; and he was off towards Smurthwaite, waving his handkerchief gaily.

Anthony went into the house and pulled down the window. "That was an interesting performance," he said.

"Oh, we're used to it now," Lottie assured him. "He's a perfect old fraud. He loves riding in motor-cars, but he won't admit it, and

274

if there was a house with a telephone on the other side of the road he'd be there cadging the use of it every day. Mrs. Halliwell is so used to his tricks that her chauffeur has orders to slow down whenever he passes the house, in case Septimus wants to whistle a lift in to Smurthwaite. He puts it all down to Valpy's increasing age, of course. 'My dear, we must not overburden old friends who so generously gave us the strength of their youth.' Do you know what I noticed when I came a cropper?"

"No."

"I lay there face down, and right under my eyes were the buds of the daffodils, just showing through the leaves."

"I suppose they'll be in flower already in places like Cornwall," Anthony said, "and the London shops are full of them."

"I've been told," she said, "that in Cornwall they even have camellias blooming in the open air before Christmas."

"I don't know that I'd like that. I like winter to be winter and spring to be spring, and I think this time of year in Yorkshire, when we're right on the edge between the two, is glorious. A frosty night like last night, and then a sunny day like this. I came to ask Mr. Pordage to give you a day off, you poor wage-slave. D'you think he would have agreed?"

"Oh, yes. He's very kind. He would probably have said: 'My dear, Smith Minor can go on panting for another day for Pordage's revised edition of the First French Course. That won't hurt him. Indeed, if I know my Smith Minor, he would gladly and indefinitely postpone the pleasure of meeting me unless upon a bier, which he would cheerfully heap with bays.'"

Anthony laughed. "You are good at languages," he said. "You have quickly picked up Septimese."

She said: "When Mrs. Halliwell said you were coming, I *did* hope you were going to suggest a walk. We've known one another such a long time, but I can remember only two walks with you in all my life."

"I remember them, too. There was one when we were infants, and we took poor Cerberus with us."

"Yes, and you were as cross as two sticks. At the beginning, anyway."

"And there was the one the other day in London. Far more prosaic. Just a matter of stocking the larder."

"Oh, but I enjoyed it," she said. "I really did."

Then, shifting her position uneasily on the window-seat, she could not repress a little groan. Anthony, who hated pain and sickness, felt as though the shock had gone through his own body. "I'm so sorry, Lottie," he said. "Is it very bad?"

She managed to grin. "Well, I *did* give myself a wallop while I was about it. And just at this moment I feel rather like a violin that's being tuned. But go and talk to Mother. And Mrs. Toplis is somewhere about. You'd better snatch a moment to give her a word."

He found Mrs. Wayland in the kitchen, preparing the lunch. "Do you mind if I watch?" he asked half seriously. "I shall need all I can pick up if I'm to open that restaurant."

"I hope you're not going to be such a fool as to do your own cooking?" she said.

"I may, at the beginning," he assured her. "And whether I'm doing it myself or not, I shall want to know what the cook's up to."

"It sounds to me," she said, briskly whipping up eggs, "as though you'd better start a coffee-stall on the Embankment and have done with it."

"You impress me as not approving of my plans, Mrs. Wayland."

"It seemed to me you hadn't made any, that's all. I suppose, as well as doing the cooking you'll do the waiting and the washing-up?"

"I haven't thought about such things. Naturally, I haven't gone into details."

She laughed. "Oh, it's natural, is it, to want to do something and think that's the end of the matter! I should have thought it was natural to sit down and do a bit of thinking, and consider every possibility that might turn up. You talk about doing the cook's work. D'you think you could run a restaurant worth having on one cook? Good lord, child, you'll need a pastry-cook, and a cook for this, that and the other, and a man who knows about wine, and. . ."

"Here, half a minute! All that may come. But it won't be the Savoy Restaurant or Simpson's to begin with."

"What it'll be in the long run will depend on what it is to begin with, and if it's to be anything at all you'll have something more to do than hiding yourself in the kitchen. Get the best cook you can, and leave it to him—or her. To me, for example."

Anthony had been sitting, to Mrs. Wayland's annoyance, on the edge of the kitchen table. Her last words astonished him. He got down and looked at her. "Do you mean that?"

"It's common sense, isn't it?"

"I see. You've been talking this over with Lottie."

"No, I haven't," she said, going on unconcernedly with her work. "But I've been thinking it over *for* Lottie."

"And where does she come in?"

"She could look after the accounts. She's good at that sort of thing."

"And where does poor old Septimus come in when you've left him on his beam ends?"

"*Chacun pour soi*," she said calmly.

"Do you know what the insufferable Chris Hudson used to call you?"

"No. But if he ever turns up in your restaurant, pass word along to the kitchen. I'll put arsenic in his soup."

"He used to call you the *maîtresse-femme*."

"Well, he was right for once. Marriage does different things to different women, and that's what my marriage did to me. Listen! I think that's the doctor. Let me know what he says. I must get on here."

"You think you're impressing me by showing devotion to your art."

"I don't care whether I'm impressing you or not, but I must get the lunch ready. And I don't suppose there's anything wrong with Lottie that a cold-water compress and a day's rest won't put right."

It wasn't so easy as that, but neither was it so bad as Septimus had pretended to suppose. There was nothing broken, but it was a week before Lottie was able to put her foot to the ground without the help of a crutch, and throughout that week Anthony stayed at Throstle's Nest. It was a week that got better as it went on, and by the end of it no one could doubt that the turn of the year had come. There were lambs in the fields, small green flames licking the black of the hedgerows, and the birds were having moments of delirium.

"I suppose," Lottie said, "if we were living some thousands of years ago, we'd be up to the neck now in ceremonies to make the year a kind and fruitful one."

"But as it is," Anthony answered, "here I am up to the neck in schemes for prosaically earning a living."

It was the last day of the week. To-morrow he would be returning to London. He couldn't remember such a week since the one in Sleights long ago when Mrs. Fieldhouse, as she then was, had hired a motor-car and taken him about the county. Now it was Mrs. Halliwell's car. She had insisted on Lottie's having the use of car and chauffeur. She herself went to and from Smurthwaite in a taxi-cab. Each morning Anthony went to Easter How and collected Lottie and her crutches. Over night she would have studied the road maps and decided the course of their tour, and away they would go, leaving Septimus to gaze enviously after them. "I've never had a real *day out* in one of those abominable things," he said, and Anthony told him heartlessly: "You must try it some day, sir."

He didn't want Septimus or anyone else to share those journeys *tête à tête* with Lottie, sometimes quite literally *tête à tête* when a hairpin bend would throw her shoulder against his and her brown hair would brush his cheek. It was all unexpectedly and increasingly pleasurable: sitting on a hilltop, with the rolling county below them; helping her out of the car and adjusting the crutches under her arms so that she might hobble into a hotel for lunch; holding her hand warmly under the rug as they made their way home in the failing light. They didn't talk a lot. Their background had so much in common that large areas of experience could be taken for granted. On this last afternoon he said: "The other day when I called at Easter How—the day you had your fall—I was going to ask you to take that walk again. The walk we had when we were babes with about sixpence between us."

She laughed. "Going back to do a thing like that all over again doesn't usually work out. But at least we'd have found one thing unchanged, and that's my financial set-up. I haven't become a person of independent means, like you."

"Well, perhaps we'll do it later on in the summer—some day when you're able to walk again."

She said: "No. I'm glad we didn't go. Let's just leave that. Something to look back on, always with pleasure."

"Always?"

She said simply: "Yes, so far as I'm concerned, always."

Anthony didn't think he was in love with her. He had seen Joe Morrison go white when talking of his love for Joanna, and he knew of the incandescent feeling between Joanna and William Scroop. That was love, he thought, and it frightened rather than attracted him. He was sure he would never feel like that about any woman. Certainly, he didn't feel like it about Lottie. When he woke up in the mornings at Throstle's Nest, the first thought that swept into his mind was of the day's journey ahead, and of course Lottie was a part of that. It would be rather dull spending the day looking at a chauffeur's neck and without a companion.

They were nearing Easter How, and there would be no drive to-morrow, except to Smurthwaite station. This was the end of it. He was holding Lottie's hand beneath the rug, rather absently, but aware of its comfortable warmth, and now, with a little sigh, she began to withdraw it. He resisted this, held it closer, but she still tried to draw it away, and a small struggle developed, hand fighting hand in the darkness. It excited him, and he thought: "If I want to hold her hand, I'll hold her hand," and he closed his fingers upon hers quite cruelly. Then her hand stopped struggling and lay still in his, warm and living like a little creature that had surrendered because of the futility of struggle. He remembered a night in Megson Street when Aunt Jessie's cat had come in making triumphant noises through its clenched teeth and with a mouse dangling beneath its whiskers. He had managed to take the mouse, unhurt, from the cat, and Aunt Jessie cried: "Kill it, Anthony! Kill it! We mustn't have mice about the place."

But he didn't want to kill it, though he had no feeling for mice. He held it surrounded in the cage of his two hands and felt it struggling wildly and imagined its small heart battering at its ribs as its small body was battering at his fingers. And then it stopped struggling, as though aware of protection, and he opened his fingers cautiously, and the mouse did not run away. It sat in his hands, looking up at him with bright black eyes. It seemed to the child to be asking what he was going to do, while sure now that what was to be done would be good. It was a summer night, and, stroking the mouse with one finger, pleased with it because it had trusted him, he carried it to Manningham Park and set it down gently amid some bushes. He stayed out till the park closed, thinking of the mouse and feeling happy.

With Lottie's unresisting hand in his, he looked sideways at her, and saw that she, seeming very sad, was looking sideways at him. He leaned nearer to her and kissed her, rather experimentally. She returned his kiss warmly, and then they sat primly apart, and let go one another's hands, lest chauffeurs, like school-teachers, should have eyes in the backs of their heads.

7

When Mrs. Halliwell came in that night, she said: "I've asked Mrs. Wayland to look in after supper. There are one or two things that I think should be talked about."

It was an eye-opening talk to Anthony. He had been like an inexperienced subaltern who sees the enemy and says: "Well, we'd better have a smack at them." But that was not the way Mrs. Halliwell fought her battles. Her fighting-force was cash, and that was something which she didn't commit to an engagement unless the chances of winning were high. Anthony found that a company would have to be formed, and that meant shareholders and directors and annual meetings and all sorts of formal matters that had not entered his head. How much capital could he provide, Mrs. Halliwell asked? He said he didn't know and would have to consult his mother about it. She looked at him grimly, contrasting him unfavourably with what her Alf had been at the same age. "Anyhow," she said, "there'll be a year or so to go into all that, because you'll have to spend at least that time learning something about the job. Just being able to cook a bit of food doesn't mean that you can run a restaurant—not in London, anyway, where the competition is pretty hot."

Anthony protested that he didn't know anybody connected with London restaurants, and she explained patiently: "There aren't many things or many people that you can't get to know if you are ready to pay for the privilege."

"Well, may I leave that to you?" Anthony asked.

"Ay," she said with a grin. "I'm getting used to it. People seem to leave everything to me except money in their wills."

And that, Anthony had sense enough to realise, was what she liked. It catered to the feeling of power in which she was at home. She always knew somebody who knew somebody. It wasn't long before she had arranged for him to spend an apprenticeship in a small but elegant restaurant in the West End. When the place was mentioned to her, she went to it anonymously more than once before being satisfied that it was the right school. She was not a woman who took things on trust.

It never entered Anthony's head to wonder why she should bother with him at all. If it had, she would have found a simple answer. She believed she could make a profit, and Anthony was a friend of Joanna. Her love of money and her love of Joanna dictated most of the actions of her life.

It was Mrs. Halliwell who found the premises in Dean Street and engaged that nice Mr. Shrubb to oversee their decoration. She knew somebody in the Potteries who supplied the china, and she bought the glass, napery and cutlery of a restaurant that went bankrupt. Like many other people, Mr. and Mrs. Anthony Fieldhouse had a lot to thank her for. They were married a month before L'Esculent opened. When the company was formed, Mrs. Halliwell and Anthony's mother held most of the shares in it. Anthony was pretty heavily committed, considering his slender resources, and Mrs. Wayland had a token holding of a hundred pounds. So had Septimus

Pordage. "My dear Anthony," he said, "I can't refrain from invest-ing in a concern whose claims are so modest. Esculent, as I under-stand it, means no more than eatable, and you can hardly fail to live up to that. Though," he added, "my brief sojourn in the Metrop-olis showed me that, even in the most publicised establishments, this failure, though difficult, is not impossible. I warn you that you will find me a vigilant and captious shareholder at your annual gen-eral meetings. I shall take it out of you for stealing my secretary and my cook and throwing me back upon the snatchery of Mrs. Toplis."

Anthony was rather conscience-stricken. The old man might joke about it, but he was going to be very lonely. There would be no one in the room over the barn, and no friendly Valpy in the straw below. It was during a week-end of Anthony's apprenticeship, when he had gone up to Easter How to pursue his courtship of Lottie, that Valpy died. Lottie had learned to drive the pony, and she proposed on the Sunday morning that they should go for a jaunt in the trap. They went to the stable to harness up, and Valpy was lying on his side. If he had been dead, Anthony thought, it would not have been so bad, but there was just enough life left in him to turn his eyes upon them in the way doomed animals have, which suggests unconquerable faith in human beings. "Ah! Here they are! Now something will be done for me." And nothing can be done, and you stand and watch them die; and if it is the first death you have seen, as it was with Anthony, then, even though it is the death of a pampered pony, it is death and the sadness and the revolt that death brings.

When Lottie knelt in the straw by Valpy's grey head, and put her brown head down to his body, and listened, and at last stood up and said "He's dead," then he clutched her as he had never clutched her before, aware of transience and of the need of com-radeship. He was thinking of how Septimus and Aunt Jessie, with the *malle* aboard, had ridden behind Valpy, and he had followed with Cerberus, and life had seemed endless and changeless. He was ashamed of his tears but could not hold them back, and Lottie comforted him.

It was thus that Septimus found them. At a glance he compre-hended all. He did not seem surprised at their distress. He said simply: "Go for a walk now," and they went, and it was the saddest walk they had ever taken, and the one in which they understood one another the most deeply.

When they got back Septimus had already begun to dig a pit in the paddock. He never mentioned Valpy, who was buried in the

281

pit, and over his body the runner-ducks found the grass unusually green and succulent.

When Mrs. Fieldhouse, returning from a visit to London, reported to Aunt Jessie on the Baker Street *ménage,* Jess couldn't believe it, couldn't understand it. She was a static woman, devoid of the principles of growth, one of those who move, substantially unchanged, from the cradle to the grave. It surprised her to be told that someone who had once been thus was now quite other. Mrs. Wayland—"She and her Marlborough House and Sevvers china!"—had been a figure of fun, and it was necessary to Auntie Jess's well-being to deny that she could ever be anything else.

However, Mrs. Fieldhouse went home from her visit happy to know that Anthony and Lottie were in excellent hands. She had gone up to town because she was doubtful of Anthony's wisdom in inviting his mother-in-law to share his home. The experiment might not have been successful if Lottie, Anthony and Mrs. Wayland had not been united in a resolution to make *L'Esculent* a success. Mrs. Wayland was the buyer, Lottie was the bookkeeper, and Anthony was learning to keep an eye on everything as he walked about in black coat and striped trousers with a smile that was happily natural, a developing gift for remembering names and the tables that clients preferred, and a nice balance between friendliness and deference. He was discovering who preferred to be called "Sir" and who "Mr. Jones," and if Mr. Jones came in alone he would enquire about "madame's" health, and if Mr. Jones came in with a lady who wasn't madame, he wouldn't. It was all very subtle, he thought. You must know when to pick up a perfectly polished glass and with an air of annoyance tell a waiter to take it away and bring one that was polished. It gave a sense of unfailing vigilance, but it mustn't be done too often or with the wrong people lest it suggest slovenliness.

Mr. Shrubb had done well. You came from the street into a brightly-lit vestibule with stairways opening off it, leading to cloak-rooms above. In the vestibule were settees whereon diners might wait for their friends. The walls were white and a chandelier lit everything up splendidly. It had cost a pretty penny, that chandelier, and so had other things. Anthony sometimes shuddered to think what bills had been run up before the place began to make a penny. But Mrs. Halliwell had been firm. "No trumpery. This isn't a coffee-tavern in Smurthwaite. If you want the flies," she said with an unaccustomed dash into imagery, "your web must be attractive."

The restaurant itself was a long and rather narrow room. It was a surprise to enter it from the contrived radiance of the vestibule. The contrast was intended to strike you, and did. Out there, everything glittered. Here, everything smouldered. The walls were a matte ox-blood red, and along them on either hand ran sconces whose light came softly through old-gold vellum. It was rich, simple and impressive. The tables stood along each wall, banquettes in deep red upholstery behind them and chairs in front. Down the long alleyway the waiters' trolleys could be trundled. There was just room for them to pass one another. At the far end the coloured bottles of a bar looked cheerful, and on either side of the bar was the In and Out for waiters. Up and down the carpeted alleyway, with an occasional peep into the kitchens beyond, was Anthony's daily and nightly beat. Sometimes he would pause at the desk just inside the vestibule door where Lottie sat. Another pretty penny, he would think; for that nice Mr. Shrubb had decided that a commonplace and clerical-looking desk wouldn't do at all. So Lottie sat in a Regency chair behind a red-leather topped table whose cabriole legs sported a lot of brass work. Anthony would sometimes give her a covert wink, but she wasn't having any. She would not return it. In the flat it was all right, but here it was another matter. This table had to be paid for. And how right she is, Anthony would think. The first annual general meeting of L'Esculent Limited had come and gone, leaving a sense of tempered hope rather than rejoicing.

Anthony looked at a list in his hand and wondered who this Mr. Schwann could be who had rung up to order a table for two.

9

On the morning of this day when Rudolph Schwann and Chris Hudson visited L'Esculent there was unhappiness in the atmosphere of the Scroops' house in Soho Square. The night before, the Scroops had been to a dance. That, in itself, was something unusual. Each of them had wanted no one but the other. Occasionally they would ask a few friends in; but if in return the friends asked them out, there was, more often than not, a reason for not going. Just now and then an invitation would be accepted, and the acceptance was always regretted. It was a post-war moment of vulgarity and nonsense that often sank to something worse. For all her beauty that had increased since marriage, Joanna was a Yorkshire country girl. She was nauseated by the sight of young girls lying boozed across the knees of glassy-eyed young men, and Scroop, who had inherited a tradition of style, would meet her eyes, see their disgust, and take her home early, cursing himself for having exposed her to ignominy. So they more and more accepted their need of one another as the best thing they knew and earned a hermit reputation. Especially, Joanna put an absolute ban on invitations which would take the party on to a night-club. She remembered her only visit to such a place, and like a nightmare there sometimes came back to her mind the moment when a youth whom she vaguely remembered to have seen before had taken her into the dark street and there abandoned her. The recollection could still make her shudder, and the thought of the man who had so casually strolled away fill her with anger.

Last night she and William had been out to a most prosaic and proper affair. William's agent was in hopes at last of selling that white elephant of a country house that he had for so long wished to be rid of. William had met James Frinton, the prospective buyer, a rich industrialist, and had been invited to come with Joanna to a dance which the man and his wife were giving for their daughter in a London hotel. They accepted the invitation with smiles at their mercenary intentions. They were expecting no pleasure, but they thought they might advance the prospect of the sale.

Mr. and Mrs. James Frinton were in the news. He was a self-made man who liked to remind you of it. He had made a fortune before the war, and the war itself had done his fortune no harm. The couple had four daughters, two pairs of twins, with only a year between the pairs. Within the last twelve months three of the girls had been married off: one to a viscount, one to the heir of a baron, one to a baronet. The gossip columns in the papers hinted at an even more splendid marriage impending for the last of the batch. It was for this girl that the dance was being given. Joe Morrison, who liked to pick up a guinea now and then by contributing a paragraph to *The Banner* column called Inquisitor, was free that night. He put on his glad rags and took himself off to the Dorchester. He was late arriving, and he found Joanna Scroop sitting unattended on the edge of the dance-floor. With his heart beating insanely, he asked her to dance.

She was fond of Joe. She remembered that the first time she had met him was when he came to Throstle's Nest with Anthony for the Smurthwaite dance. She had almost had to drag him round the

284

room. He had improved, and she congratulated him with a smile. "How do you find time to learn?" she asked him. "I understand from Anthony that *The Banner* keeps you busy day and night."

He told her about *The Banner*. He told her about his own ambitions to be a foreign correspondent and about what he was doing to make them come true. She was aware for the first time of a fierce drive in him. His talk was different from the platitudes or sly innuendoes that she was accustomed to hearing from her partners when she infrequently went out. "Not a word to anyone," he said, "not even to Anthony, but there's a dog's chance that I may get a start. A vacancy's turning up in the Paris office, and I've been given a hint—no more, mind you—that I may get it. My French is pretty good, and I'm taking steps to make it better."

She looked at his eager face, with the deep blue eyes and the strong chin, and she realised that here was a young man who would always take steps. He wouldn't sit and wait for things to come to him. The dancing stopped, and while they stood in the middle of the floor in that absurd attitude of applauding their own performance, or the band's, or whatever it might be, he was still talking. "Of course, it's an enormous business to get the hang of—I mean the state of Europe. Everything disrupted, sprawling, all these little new countries cock-a-hoop, so many of the old ones bitter and angry."

The music began again, and Joanna said: "Joe, you make me feel like Wellington's partner at that dance in Brussels on the eve of Waterloo. If he danced. I don't know."

"Neither do I," Joe said. "But Waterloo'll be nothing to what might blow up out of the present state of things. Do we go again?"

"Yes, let's," she said.

Presently his face went solemn, and he asked with diffidence: "If there was anything worth writing about—assuming, that is, that I get this Paris job—would you think it all right if I wrote to you now and then? I mean, Sir William wouldn't mind, would he?"

Joanna's impulse was to laugh. The idea of William feeling jealous of Joe Morrison—for surely that was what was hinted?—seemed to her unthinkable. Then she was aware that Joe, who had been doing fairly well as a dancer, was missing his step, was hopelessly confused and agitated, and she saw that more would depend on her answer than she supposed.

"Let's sit down," she said. "I feel rather tired." And she led him off the floor. "Of course," she said, "William and I will be delighted to hear anything you have to tell us. We shall expect to hear that you're doing famously. Write to him, and he'll read me your letters."

She saw his disappointment. "Good," he said. "I'll do that." She guessed he never would. And he never did.

Scroop came up to them, looking profoundly unhappy. He said at once: "It's all off, darling."

"What is?" Joanna asked.

"The sale of my house. The miserable shack is quite unsuitable for a marchioness."

Joanna was more interested in the romance than in the failure of the sale. Why should William worry so much about getting rid of his damp and, she thought, dreary house? They had money enough.

"So she's landed him?" she asked.

Scroop said: "Yes. There they go."

The young woman danced by, starry-eyed, her hair nestling against the face of a youngster with a fair moustache.

"You know," Joe told them, "he hasn't got a bean."

Scroop said: "Mr. Frinton was very apologetic. He liked the place, but she didn't. It was intended for her, you know. I gather Frinton didn't think she'd land him. A younger son without a place of his own was what he thought it would come to. But now the money'll go into building up this chap's ruins."

"It really is definitely fixed?" Joe asked.

"Oh, yes. But I promised Frinton to say nothing. It's not to be announced for a day or two."

Joanna thought that not since their marriage had she seen him so gloomy. He was at his old trick of pulling his hand down his jaw, and that frightened her. It was associated with the awful moment before their cloud miraculously lifted. She said: "You look tired, darling. Shall we go now?"

"Yes," he said. "There's not much point in all this, is there?"

Joe wished them good night, and they sought out Mr. and Mrs. Frinton and thanked them, and then they found themselves in a taxi sliding along Park Lane. She took his hand, and he had nothing to say. He'll be all right when I get him home, she thought. She had great faith in the curative property of their lovely drawing-room, associated as it was with quiet contentment that could burst at a touch into ecstasy.

Gwilym, in his white jacket and black trousers, was surprised to see them back so soon. Joanna said: "Bring Sir William a whisky and soda, Gwilym, and then you can go to bed. I sha'n't want anything."

286

The lighting was subdued. The fire was burning in the big basket grate. It was difficult to imagine that they were in the heart of the vast town. Hardly a sound reached them. She sank in a rustle of silk on to the couch alongside him. Presently Gwilym came in and put the whisky on a table in front of the couch. Scroop said: "Thank you, Gwilym, but I shan't need that."

Gwilym said in his airy way: "That's all right, Sir William. I'll leave it in case you do."

Scroop, with his hands in his pockets and his eyes on the fire, said quietly: "Gwilym, I don't want to be told of your intentions. I merely want you to obey my orders."

Gwilym did not answer. He took up the tray and went.

Everything was quiet save for the purring of the fire and the soft click of the latch as the door closed behind Gwilym. But Joanna felt as though a bomb had exploded. Ever since her marriage to Scroop—and that, she realised, was a fair time ago now—she had known a sense of utter safety. His few quiet words to Gwilym, the tightening of his face as he spoke, and Gwilym's look of pain and bewilderment which she had glimpsed as he bent over the table, opened a crack—no more than a crack, but through it she saw Scroop as he had got up in the night club, a dangerous-looking man whose image had disappeared beneath the sometimes rapturous, sometimes placid, surface of their lives together and that she thought her in-fluence had destroyed for ever.

She looked at him, and saw that he was smiling. He said: "When you feel a failure, an absolute wash-out, it's comforting to find that you can give orders to someone and see them carried out."

She thought: "Oh, William, my darling, that is wrong, that is unworthy." She sat closer to him, and he took a hand from his pocket and put an arm round her, but casually, not with the warmth she wanted to stir in him. She said: "I'm listening, darling. I'll listen all night if you like. What's the matter?"

He gave a wry grin. "Weltschmertz. The Sorrows of Werther."

"Darling, that doesn't tell me much, does it? Don't let's generalise. I want to know about the sorrows of William, whatever they may be. Every one of them is my affair."

"I'm a failure."

"No, no. It went something like this, didn't it? You went to the dance to-night hoping to hear from Mr. Frinton that he'd bought your house. You dearly wanted that to happen because you've stuffed your silly old head with the notion that everything you have comes from me, and you wanted to say: 'Well, there's *my* contribution. There's fifteen or twenty thousand pounds.' That would have made you feel good, and quite naturally so. I should have loved it if you'd been able to say that, and I can understand that you feel disappointed. But what's that got to do with either failure or success?"

She waited, hoping to strike some spark of answer out of his apathy, but none came. She said: "Even if Mr. Frinton had bought the house, what would that do to make you a success? You would simply be getting money for something your ancestors created."

"It would be better," he said, "than getting it out of you."

"Oh, William! How horrible it is to be talking like this! Do realise that you're getting nothing out of me. Not money, anyway, though God knows I give you everything else, and to give you that is the only happiness I know. As for the money, it doesn't come from me, though it comes through me. It comes from Mother, and if taking it makes you a failure, then I'm a failure, too. But I don't look at it that way, and I never shall. If success is a matter of money . . . ! Well, I don't believe it. You have been enormously successful, darling. Do believe that. You have been, you are, the loveliest creature, making me miraculously happy. Isn't that how we should measure success? Think of the rich people we know, miserable, unfaithful, squalid. . . . Oh, they make me sick, and I won't have you measuring yourself against *that* sort of yardstick. Let me ring for Gwilym. Tell him you'd like that drink after all, and give him a look that will make him feel happy."

"Your solicitude for Gwilym is very beautiful, darling. It does you credit. But I don't want a drink."

She said: "Don't speak to me like that!" And in the silence that followed, for he answered with nothing but a shrug of the shoulders, she heard her own words going on and on, echoing in a cave of terror which suddenly she seemed to be inhabiting. For she realised that she had spoken sharply, in a raised voice. It was the first time she had spoken to him except in the accents of love or affection, and she was afraid, because she knew that now, more than ever, he needed her, gentle and compassionate.

He got up and stood with his back to the fire and looked down at her, his face working. "I beg your pardon," he said almost formally, and she thought in desperation: "Oh, God! Don't go by the book of rules. Come and kiss me."

He said: "You seem to think that not selling the house has got under my skin. Well, it has. But that's not the only thing. It's just the last straw. Everything I do seems fated to be a wash-out. Look at *Vanguard*."

She would have preferred not to look at Vanguard, because she knew that this was where he was being hurt most. All the first-rate things that he cared for were concerned. She was sensible enough to know that anything real and vital would persist with Vanguard or without it. It could never be more than a mirror of excellence that would still be there if unreflected. But she would dearly have loved William to be able to think that what he gave so much time and thought to was influential.

He said: "It started well enough. I suppose that was just curiosity about a new thing. And now it's sunk back, stuck at a point where every issue is a dead loss. It's not as though Shrubb and I didn't work like horses. And, as you know, I don't take a salary and Shrubb gets very little—hardly more than the typist."

"Come and sit down, darling," she begged him, patting the couch, but he stayed where he was, as though to inflict on her the sight of his unhappy face.

"There are things that can be done about it, you know," she said, trying to be practical. "You could make it a quarterly instead of a monthly, for one thing."

"That would be a retreat, and it's always the first step towards going out altogether."

"It needn't be. And at the worst it would mean that we were losing money only four times a year instead of twelve."

"We? There's no we about it. It's your money."

She looked at him despairingly. She had known times when he was even jocular over Vanguard's losses, and though she was too much of her mother's daughter to be altogether pleased about that, it was at least better than this.

"Well," she asked, "what do you propose?"

He yawned, and said: "Being very tired, I propose to go to bed. As for Vanguard, it can go to blazes."

She got up, feeling defeated. "You'll regret it," she said.

He pulled his white tie loose, and somehow that gave him a look of drunken desperation. "Well," he said, "what does one more regret matter?"

10

A night's sleep seemed to do Scroop good. He was reasonably cheerful at breakfast, and apologised to Gwilym for his rudeness of the night before. Gwilym said in his forthright way: "That's all right, Sir William. But you want to keep a hand on yourself. I thought that sort of thing was all over since her ladyship came."

"All right, Gwilym. I'll do my best. Has the *Banner* come?"

"It's there under your nose on the table," Gwilym said, pushing it across.

Five minutes later Scroop went into the bedroom where Joanna was breakfasting in bed. He was grasping *The Banner* like a serpent that he wished to strangle, and he looked furiously angry. "Well," he said, "you've got some pretty friends, I must say!"

She was still full of alarm over the events of last night. She had awakened with a headache, and Scroop's appearance did not soothe it. "Darling," she said, "I'm a bit under the weather. Is this something that could keep?"

He ignored her plea, and said: "That Morrison boy has betrayed my confidence. Look at that!"

She waved it away. "Is it about that Frinton girl's engagement?"

"Yes. I was told in confidence. I mentioned it to you in confidence in Morrison's hearing, and there it is as large as life. What on earth will Mr. Frinton think of me?"

She asked wearily: "Does it matter what he thinks? And how do you know the information came from Joe Morrison?"

She could see Joe's blue eyes and ingenuous face, and she felt a need to defend him, though she believed he was guilty. But she was wrong. The time was to come when Joe Morrison would be told far more important secrets than that of Miss Frinton's engagement. His reputation as a man who could keep his mouth shut till the right moment was valuable. The fact was that Mr. Frinton had not kept his own mouth shut. What he had told Scroop in confidence he had told in confidence to half a dozen people, and if Scroop had cared to look he would have found the news, such as it was, in every paper. He said an absurd thing: "Frinton will think I've done this because of resentment about his not buying the house."

Suddenly the whole thing seemed to Joanna so trivial, and Scroop's annoyance so disproportionate, that she could have wept with frustration. She had hoped that this day would be good, that she would soon get up feeling well, able to make headway against Scroop's despair. And this absurd outburst seemed at a stroke to hurl them back into last night. She said: "Nothing could interest me less than whether Miss Frinton's engagement is announced in the paper or who is responsible for its being announced. Will you please take away my tray, William?"

He took up the tray, moved half-way across the room, then stopped and said: "I don't understand your attitude. Can't you see that my word is involved?"

She said: "Please, William!" and as he went he saw her pull the bedclothes about her and curl up.

She woke at noon, and a maid told her that Sir William had rung up to say that he would not be in to lunch. That didn't worry her. Now and then William would take Shrubb out to lunch, and that could well happen to-day when the affairs of the paper were weighing on his mind. She bathed and dressed and felt more cheerful. Her headache was gone and the day looked good. Then Joe Morrison rang up, and his voice was so full of happiness and optimism that his mere "Good morning, Joanna," was a tonic. She said: "Good morning, Joe. Has your rich uncle died?"

"Something much better than that," Joe said. "Things were moving quickly without my knowing, and now the news has broken. I've got to pack and get off to Paris to-day."

She was genuinely pleased. She liked people to be happy. "I'm so glad, Joe. It's a tremendous step-up for you."

Joe laughed. "Well, if to be an office-boy is a step-up, it's a step-up. I'll be little more than that, you know, in the Paris office. But anyway, it's a step in the right direction. I'm just crazy about getting on the inside of doings on the Continent. There's only one regret."

There was a tone in his voice that expected her to say: "And what's that, Joe?" She said it.

"Well"—his words came more diffidently now—"it's been sprung on me in such a hurry. There's only time to pack and go. And I should have loved to ask you to a farewell lunch."

She didn't know what to say to that, so she said in a noncommittal way: "That would have been very kind of you."

What Joe wanted to hear was: "I should have loved to come." There was a moment's pause, and she could almost hear his sigh. He said: "There's one thing I want to explain. About that Frinton girl. I hope Sir William doesn't think that I was responsible for spreading the news. I would have done it like a shot if he hadn't asked me not to."

Joanna was glad it hadn't been Joe. She lied: "I was sure you wouldn't do a thing like that. As for William, nothing could interest him less."

"Good! I just wanted to get that off my chest."

"Well, now, I mustn't hold you up, Joe. All my very best wishes. Good-bye and good luck."

She felt as though she had dismissed him, and wondered whether she should have tried to sound more enthusiastic about the lunch. With William away it would have been possible. She was rather surprised that the possibility seemed to her a pleasant one. During the few visits that Joe had made here for a meal or a talk he had proved a companion who was both amusing and informative. Joanna remembered an occasion when she and Scroop at a party had casually met the second Baron Dunkerley, son of the man who had founded *The Banner*. She had had a few moments alone with Dunkerley, who was notoriously addicted to isolating attractive young women and talking to them in corners.

"Now, Lady Scroop," Lord Dunkerley said, "where have I heard your name before?"

Joanna modestly suggested that perhaps it was her husband's name he had heard of in connection with *Vanguard*.

Dunkerley laughed. "No, no, Lady Scroop. I'm afraid *Vanguard* isn't my line, though I can imagine that at one time my father might have played with it, and if he had, by God, he'd have made it pay! What's its circulation?"

Joanna, who knew all too well, said she didn't know.

"Never mind," Dunkerley said. "I'm sure I never heard of you through *Vanguard*. Ha! I have it! Joe Morrison!"

He told her that he believed in keeping an eye on his young men. "If a boy's promising, I have him to dinner. You know, over a *tête à tête* meal, you can learn everything about a man."

"And did you find Mr. Morrison promising?"

"Well, a bit of wire-pulling comes into these things—into most things, come to that. The editor of *The Banner* is a friend of young Morrison's father. That's how the boy came to us, and that, I suppose, is why our editor called my attention now and then to his work. So I thought I'd better have him to dinner. Yes, I thought him promising."

Joanna knew enough about the way of the world to be sure that to be thought promising by the head of the vast Dunkerley chain of publications was something most young journalists would give their ears for. All the same, she wondered how at the *tête à tête* dinner her name had cropped up. But Dunkerley seemed to have forgotten that small point; his conversation turned personally complimentary, which was a way it had with pretty girls, and Joanna found a means of escape.

And so, thinking now of Joe's hint at a lunch alone with her, she thought also of that conversation with his employer and wondered how or why her name had been mentioned. It piqued her not to know, and she found it nagging her mind disproportionately as she ate her solitary meal.

11

A letter had come for Sir William Scroop by the midday post. It was a fat bundle of stuff in an envelope that was registered and marked "Urgent." Joanna supposed that it was a contribution for *Vanguard*. Poor boys, she thought. They all saw what they wrote as urgent and deserving the protection of the registered post.

She decided to take a walk after lunch, and as she was about to leave she noticed the letter still lying on a tray in the hall. Perhaps it *was* urgent. She could go a little out of her way and drop it in at the *Vanguard* office. She had never been there before. It was a "thing" with William that she didn't belong to the office and that he didn't want to see her there.

She was repelled by the look of the place. The London County Council plaque announcing that it had once been a famous person's home somehow enhanced its present squalor. The stairway was shabby, even dirty, and on the doors, as she climbed, she read the names of small businesses on unpolished brass plates. When she came to the *Vanguard* floor, things were a bit better. The plate was polished, and the mahogany door was shining. She didn't know that the place displeased Shrubb as much as it did her and that he did these small jobs. The sight of Georgian panels neglected threw him into action as vigorously as a good groom would be thrown by the sight of a thoroughbred's neglected coat.

She rang, and Shrubb appeared and asked her in. The room she entered was not bad. It was Sir William's. The window was clean and had good curtains. There was a bit of carpet on the floor and attractive prints were on the walls. The desk and chairs had come from the house in Soho Square. Joanna was surprised not to find William there, and Shrubb was equally surprised that she expected to find him.

"He hasn't been here to-day," he said.

Joanna was disturbed by this, but did not allow it to appear. She put the letter on William's desk and said: "Well, now that I've made a visit at last, perhaps you'll show me the rest of the premises, Mr. Shrubb."

Shrubb said: "There's only one other room, you know. Just give me a moment. I'd better put Festus away before you come in."

"Festus?"

"It's a small pet of mine."

"But I love pets," Joanna said, and went close behind him into the other room.

Shrubb said apologetically: "We intend to put this room to rights as soon as we've got a bit of spare cash. I'm afraid it's not up to much."

Joanna thought this an understatement. The place seemed to her revolting. The only lovely thing in it, she thought, was Festus. She was one of the few women who do not dislike rats or mice, and Festus was certainly a rat in a million. His white coat shone; the gleam of his pink coral eyes and the fine spread of his whiskers spoke of abounding health. He was sitting on the table amid Shrubb's papers, eating a peanut. Shrubb took him up and put him into his house, which enchanted Joanna, and for a moment she forgot her apprehension at William's absence and the shabbiness of the room. Then she strolled to the window, looked on the deplorable prospect it offered, and turned back into the room with a sigh. The wash-basin in one corner, the gas-ring in another, offended her, especially as the gas-ring assailed the nose as well as the eye. She didn't think it could be very good for Festus to breathe day and night in such an atmosphere, and said so to Shrubb. "Oh, I think I've got on top of it now," he said easily. "There was a small leak, but I've dropped a blob of sealing-wax on it."

A plate, a cup and a saucer were in the wash-basin, and a tin kettle stood on the gas-ring. "You make your own meals?" she asked; and Shrubb answered: "Yes. They tend to be pretty vegetarian. Quite sustaining, really." And quite cheap, she thought sadly.

They went back into William's room, and, looking down from the window, she saw that the ground floor of a house opposite was a tea-shop. A man was coming out, carrying a tray, and she said: "Look, Mr. Shrubb, will you go down there and bring something up? We'll have a little meal together."

Shrubb started to hobble away, and she stopped him. She felt ashamed. She was always forgetting other people's troubles and disabilities. "No, stay here," she said. "I'll get it. You put a match to the fire and make this place a bit more human."

"But Lady Scroop. . . ."

She turned to him with a laugh. "Mr. Shrubb, not so many years ago I was a schoolgirl who delighted in smuggling forbidden things into a dormitory and having a feed with her friends. I don't feel all that much changed by becoming Lady Scroop."

What a lie! she thought as she went slowly down the stairs. I am changed utterly, and I've just had lunch, and I couldn't eat a mouthful. But she felt, as Lottie had once felt, a great sadness in Mr.

294

Shrubb, and for that matter in those two rooms where, it seemed to her, failure dwelt like a grey presence.

She came back with the tray: tea and muffins: and the fire was lit and the room seemed human. It was not a very heartening day, so she drew the curtains and switched on a light. "We'll sit on the floor," she said. "That's what we used to do at school." She took cushions from the chairs and put them on either side of the fire and laid the tray on the mat between them. She poured his tea and waited for him to get on with the muffins before sipping her own. There was a lot she wanted to know.

"Where does the typist work?" she asked.

"She used to share my room. But she's been gone for some time, you know. What typing there is I do. We had to cut our expenses. My pay has been dropped by a pound a week. Mind you, that was voluntary. I offered to do it."

"It's a good thing you don't belong to a trade union," she said with a laugh. "They'd soon stop that sort of altruism." But her heart wasn't laughing, and she was thinking: "Oh, William! Why don't you tell me these things? Why don't you let me share it?"

She said: "I don't like that room next door, Mr. Shrubb. I don't think it's good enough either for you or Festus."

"Well," he said, munching away, apparently quite reconciled to his poverty, "as for Festus, he's registered no complaint so far; and as for me, I'm rather indifferent, you know, to surroundings. I know what that little room *could* be. I could make it pretty good, and, oddly enough, what I live in is the room as I see it, not as it is. Does that sound crazy?"

She said a little bitterly: "The joys of the imagination are lovely to fall back on. I've no doubt when you were in the army bully beef went down all the better if you could think of a spread at the Savoy."

He said simply: "Now, Lady Scroop, you must have patience. Remember, *petit à petit l'oiseau fait son nid.*"

She answered, not at all with patience: "But my dear Mr. Shrubb, the nest *is* built *petit à petit*. The bits get added on. Here, you're lopping them off. The typist, for example."

He looked crestfallen, and pulled his pipe from his pocket. "Of course," he said, "put like that . . ."

"How else can one put it?" she asked, more impatiently than ever. "Oh, light it. Light it. No. I don't mind."

He lit his pipe and she refilled his cup. "Now look," she said. "So far as I can see, the prospects of *Vanguard* paying its way are as bright as my chance of becoming the Queen of Sheba. The loss isn't sensational, and, so far as I'm concerned, I don't mind meeting it. If we look at the thing like that, we can go happily on because we've accepted a fact, however disagreeable. But we can't go on with a bluff. Now, to begin with, for goodness' sake allow me to do something about that deplorable room of yours."

Shrubb said: "That's very kind of you, Lady Scroop. I'd like it, but Sir William wouldn't allow it."

"Why not?"

"We were talking about the paper the other day, and he had an outburst. When I first met him, he used to have 'em pretty often, but I don't recall one since he married you. Well, he said: 'Shrubb, do you remember how it was before the paper started? I used to think "Oh, money! Bloody, bloody money!" and kid myself that if we had the money to get started the thing would go. And now we've got the money and we've got the paper and it isn't going. It's got nothing to do with money, Shrubb. It's got everything to do with me. "The fault, dear Brutus, is not in our stars, but in ourselves, that we are underlings." ' And then he started calling himself all sorts of things I don't care to repeat. So, you see, he wouldn't look favorably on spending money here unless it was coming out of profits. Otherwise, it would only make him feel worse."

"And I suppose that was when you docked your salary?"

"Well, yes, it was," he said reluctantly. "I wouldn't mind working here for nothing. It's not as though I had to rely on my *Vanguard* pay for a living," he boasted, and Joanna thought with compassion of his small disability pension and the few guineas he earned by giving advice on interior decoration. "I could get along," he said. "But if I packed it in here I'd be rather lonely. I haven't many friends, you know, and I admire William. He deserves better luck."

Joanna was close to tears. What she had intended for a gay little party had gone flat. She looked at the litter of crumbs on the tray and felt like a bird-feeder in a bitter frost. Too, too many birds, and far too small a tray.

"I must be off," she said briskly.

Shrubb got with difficulty to his feet and hobbled to open the door. She said: "You keep these panels very nice. It's a lovely door."

He stroked the wood. "It's no more than it deserves," he said. "I'd like to have a go at this whole house."

She walked slowly down through the whole house with its exudation of poverty and making-do. She thought suddenly of red-haired, blue-eyed Joe Morrison, at this moment setting off, a "promising" young man, full of hope and enthusiasm. She was glad it hadn't been possible to have lunch with him. It would have seemed like treachery to William and Shrubb.

12

The Frinton enterprises were not housed in a couple of rooms in a back street of Soho. They were in Piccadilly, in a new building that symptomatically occupied the site from which a duke's London house had been swept away.

"Don't you see that my word is in question?" Scroop had said to Joanna, and watched her curl up under the bedclothes. This withdrawal, that was due to her feeling far from well, hurt him, touchy as he was about what he considered Joe Morrison's betrayal. He thought it a withdrawal from himself, as a creature one makes to stroke will withdraw as if scorning one's companionship. He was in a mood that had rolled back two centuries. He was ready to call Joe Morrison out. That the idea crossed his mind didn't seem to him absurd, and what was biting most deeply into him was the belief, mistaken as it happened, that a point of honour was something Joanna would not understand.

He walked about the town aimlessly till eleven o'clock and then made for Piccadilly. He sent his card up to Mr. James Frinton and fumed for twenty minutes before Mr. Frinton rang down to a commissionaire to say "Send him up." The fact was that Mr. Frinton was in no mood to see him. He had no idea what this visit portended, and didn't want to be badgered any more about buying that house, which he thought the most likely reason for a penniless baronet's call. Well, he said, I'll pretty soon shut him up if that's it, and he rang down.

"My dear Sir William," he said graciously. "How good of you to call. Come and see our view."

He was proud of our view. He took Scroop to the window, and our view was something to be proud of. Across the roar of Piccadilly's traffic the spaces of the Green Park extended to the lovely silhouettes of Whitehall lying upon the grey of the winter sky. They looked in silence for a moment at that familiar beauty, and then Scroop said: "You are very kind to me. I didn't think you would receive me, unless to tell me what you thought of me. I've come to give you my apology."

Frinton looked at him in surprise. "I don't get you, Sir William," he said. He looked at Scroop's pale face and said: "Sit down, my boy. You're not looking at all well."

Scroop sat down. The place was as comfortable as a boudoir, with its deep leather chairs, thick carpet and lively fire. Mr. Frinton opened a cabinet, produced a bottle of whisky, a soda syphon and two glasses. "Say when," he invited.

Scroop took his drink, and when Frinton was sitting opposite him he said: "It's about your daughter's wedding, sir. You gave me the news in confidence, and I see it's in this morning's *Banner*. I want to tell you, on my honour, that I didn't give it to the press."

To his surprise, Frinton laughed heartily. "Good God! You haven't given yourself the trouble of coming along here just to say this?"

"Yes, sir. I felt I had to clear myself."

Frinton could judge men. He looked at Scroop and saw that, for him, this was something that went deep. He got up and put a hand almost paternally on Scroop's shoulder. "Look, Sir William," he said, "I want you to know that I appreciate what you've done, and you can believe that never for a moment did it enter my head that you had betrayed my confidence. But, good lord, don't take things to heart like that. It doesn't do nowadays. Saying 'Keep it under your hat,' as I did—well, that's hardly more than a matter of form. Why, sometimes I say that when I want a thing to get about. It's a sure way, believe me."

"I must seem old-fashioned to you," Scroop said stiffly.

"Well, yes, you do."

"I'm sorry. I'm taking up your valuable time."

He made to get up, and Frinton gently pushed him back. "You haven't finished your drink," he said. "I can see the way your mind's been working over this. I noticed last night that that youngster Morrison from *The Banner* was with you. You probably let a word slip to him—in confidence, of course—and now you're worrying because you think that's how the news got round."

"In fact, sir, that's just how it was."

"Well, you can take one thing from me. If you told Joe Morrison anything in confidence, it was as safe as the Bank of England."

Scroop looked at him in surprise. "You know young Morrison?"

"Yes. A lot better than I know you. When this place was opened a couple of months ago *The Banner* sent him to do the story. It pleased me, and I take some pleasing. I asked young Morrison to call on me, and we had a long, interesting talk. He seemed to me to be the man I was looking for. I was after a publicity officer for Frinton

298

Enterprises. I wish I could have got him, but he's full of damn-fool notions about being a foreign correspondent. I offered him a thousand a year as a starting salary, and he's not getting that now by a long chalk. But nothing doing. As it happens, I was talking to his boss, Lord Dunkerley, a few days ago, and I told him frankly I was trying to steal Joe Morrison. He said if I did he'd put the whole of Frinton Enterprises on the paper's black-list. I'd like to see him try it! I'd put his papers on my advertising black list. That'd make him think!"

Scroop was in an alien world, lost and bewildered. Black list. Blackmail. They didn't seem too far apart. He said: "It sounds as though I owe young Morrison an apology."

Frinton said impatiently: "Sir William Scroop, get it into your head that nobody's so keen on receiving your apologies as you seem to be on imposing them. Now, good morning to you. Thank you for calling."

He pressed a bell, and that was that.

13

Scroop ate luncheon at his club and passed the afternoon there. He was very tired. The failure to sell the house and so to shake off some part of his irking sense of dependence; his consequent rudeness to Gwilym and the first breach in his perfect understanding with Joanna: all this, added to his not having slept and to Frinton's opinion that he was a back-number doodling with notions that no sane man any longer entertained, had exhausted him, and he fell asleep in the smoking-room.

Dusk was deepening when he woke, and for a moment he could not remember where he was. It was so long since he had used the club. He recalled the last time he had been there, and the recollection did him no good. It was after the night when he had blacked out and awakened in the flat of that music-hall girl whom he had met when he and Joanna were at the Silver Star. He had left the girl asleep and come here and written to Joanna. He remembered all this very clearly, and it crystallised round the fact that he had blacked out. Once that had entered his mind it stayed there, and it frightened him, because all through the happiness of his marriage he had not given that, and what it meant, so much as a thought. That the remembrance had now leapt out of some compartment of his mind that had seemed for ever securely built over was alarming. So alarming that he at once went out and took a taxi to Soho Square. It was no distance to walk, and he liked walking, but the idea came to him that he might black-out before getting home. He said to himself that he was taking no chances, and this made him feel cunning and competent. Scroop, he said, was not such a fool as jumped-up people like Frinton took him to be. He knew how to look after himself.

14

Joanna returned to the house in a heavy mood, suffering for both Scroop and Shrubb. She did not see that she could do anything about Shrubb. If William insisted on the paper's being self-supporting, then that was the end of Shrubb—so far as *Vanguard* went, at any rate—for the paper, she knew, would never pay its way. "What's the circulation?" Lord Dunkerley had asked; and, as the concern's financier, she knew that its peak—and not a paying peak—was reached some months ago, and that since then the sales had gone steadily down and the income from advertising had gone down too. She would gladly have been rid of the whole thing: she didn't like losing money: but she was aware that William's self-esteem was concerned. And yet, if it was his dependence on her money that undermined his self-esteem, it must be the more undermined by the drain the paper made. It was a wearisome dilemma in which money and certain moral considerations seemed to cancel one another out.

She put the thing out of her mind, rang up *L'Esculent*, and had a talk with Anthony Fieldhouse.

"Anthony, have you a spare table to-night? I'd like to bring William to dinner. We're both rather ashamed that we haven't been before this. I'm told it's very splendid and very successful."

"We've nothing to complain of, your ladyship."

Joanna laughed. "Ladyship, indeed! Hoity, toity! How's Lottie?"

"Well, Joanna for this once. But it's a rule here. When our friends are our clients, they are addressed as our clients, not as our friends. So to-night don't call Mrs. Fieldhouse Lottie. She certainly won't call you Joanna."

"Very well, Mr. Fieldhouse. At eight o'clock."

Well, well. More oddities of human behaviour. She went to bed. She hoped William would come home soon, and it was in bed that she wanted to receive him. She wasn't happy about his absence from lunch. In the past when he couldn't come he rang up to say so. This was the first time he had left her flat, and she had insight enough to connect it with his mood of the morning aroused by the announcement of the Frinton wedding. "Can't you see that my word is involved?"

When he came in and was told that her ladyship was in bed, he went straight up. He was in an almost gay mood, pleased with himself at having arrived thanks to his clever taxi plan. She was glad to see the smile on his face and was careful to say nothing about his midday absence. "Well, darling," she asked, "what have you been doing all day?"

"D'you know," he said, accepting the invitation of her open arms and kissing her, "Joe Morrison didn't let us down after all."

"I'm glad that's off your mind," she said; and, sitting on the edge of the bed, he gave her an account of his meeting with Frinton. "Not a bad chap I should think, though there are points we wouldn't see eye to eye on. I apologised, thinking I was responsible because I'd mentioned the thing to Joe, and Frinton seemed to think me over-fussy. He as good as laughed in my face."

She noted that much of the day was unaccounted for, but let that go. "You must be worn out," she said, "and we both need some relaxation. So I thought we'd go along to-night and see how that place of the Fieldhouses' is doing. I rang up Anthony and ordered a table for eight o'clock."

"Thank you. Just what I should like."

"Come to bed then. We sha'n't need to leave here till a quarter to eight."

15

Rudolph Schwann seemed to know everybody, by sight at all events, and Chris Hudson felt himself to be in the great world at last. To begin with, there was the fun of snubbing Lottie Wayland. You could have knocked him down with a feather when he saw her sitting at what he called the cash-desk. Good lord! The girl who helped her mother to make his boyhood miserable in Megson Street and whom he could remember standing by the stream at Easter How, laughing when Anthony threw him in! Reduced to this! Handling the change in a London restaurant! She was not the sort of person one would want to introduce to Rudolph Schwann. He merely nodded to her and said: "Well, Miss Wayland, fancy this!" and walked on with Schwann before she could reply.

And then there was Anthony Bromwich walking down the carpet and saying: "Good evening, Mr. Schwann," and Schwann shaking hands with him and saying: "Good evening, Mr. Fieldhouse. Thank you for finding room for us."

Chris thought that he had better shake hands, too, though his uninstructed mind wondered why a man of the world like Mr. Schwann should shake hands with a chap like Bromwich who seemed to have some job here comparable to a shop-walker's in a store. "Well, Anthony!" he said. "I see you've got Lottie Wayland in the cash desk! And why Fieldhouse?"

"Fieldhouse goes for her, too," Anthony said. "She's my wife." He pulled out the table for Schwann to slide in to the banquette, raised a finger for a waiter, and left them.

"You know Mr. Fieldhouse?" Schwann asked.

"Yes, very well. It's a surprise finding him here."

"An interesting young man." He looked round the restaurant with a connoisseur's appreciation. "If he goes on as he's begun we'll be lucky to get a table here soon."

"You don't mean to say that he *owns* the place?"

"Well, no doubt he's had to raise capital from here and there, and it looks as though whoever put money in is going to be lucky."

He studied the *menu*, and Chris studied the scene. He was a quick learner. The quiet opulence impressed him. He saw that he had made a mistake with Lottie, and resolved to put that right as soon as possible. He had nearly made as bad a mistake with Anthony. Men like Mr. Schwann didn't shake hands with shop-walkers. He must watch his step.

Schwann had ordered the meal without reference to Chris, and now he was in consultation with the wine-waiter. "The Clos Vougeot," he was saying; and the words fell on Chris's ears like music. This wasn't *Oliver Twist* at Hampstead on a Sunday night. This was the sort of thing he must learn to do as easily as Mr. Schwann was doing it. "The Clos Vougeot."

Schwann leaned back and looked about him and gave Chris a Who's Who. "That lean fellow with the pretty little red-head is Maurice Dekker. He's making that *Joseph in Egypt* film at Elstree. Going to drop thousands on it from what I hear. The girl is Susie Stirling. She's playing Potiphar's wife. I wonder what Dekker's wife thinks of her."

Oh, this was the stuff, Chris thought. The low-down. The worldly-wise. He was hardly aware of what he was eating, so fascinated he was by Schwann's conversation, but he was aware that it was supremely good. The Clos Vougeot gave the scene an exciting vivacity.

Schwann said: "That's Sir William Scroop just coming in," and looking up, Chris saw Anthony Fieldhouse pulling out the table and Joanna Halliwell settling herself straight across the room from him. "I take it," Schwann said, "that'll be the Yorkshire heiress Scroop was lucky enough to find."

Chris had drunk two Martinis at Schwann's flat and a sherry here in the entrance lounge. He was half-way through his second glass of Clos Vougeot, and this all added up to more than he was accustomed to drink. He was very far from drunk, but the fine edge was off his mind, and, looking at Joanna, he said: "Heiress my foot!"

Schwann was sitting with his hands, as usual, placid. The little moles were lying on the table-cloth. He said sharply, without looking at Chris: "Don't speak to me like that!"

Chris was shaken. The sudden change from gracious host to stern reprover nettled him. He told himself that he knew more about Joanna Halliwell than Schwann could possibly do. Hadn't he seen her with Lottie Wayland, pushing an old disreputable punctured bike uphill in Yorkshire? Some heiress if she went around with people like Lottie Wayland! He looked across the room. Certainly she looked something nowadays, even more attractive than she had been at their second time of meeting. He wondered if she remembered that and whether she felt as grateful to him as he thought she should? He didn't often recall that moment, but when he did it was with admiration for his own resource. This man whom Schwann called Sir William Scroop was with her then. What had caused him to go berserk that night Chris did not know; but he did know that he had saved Joanna Halliwell from a mauling. He had got her safely out into the street. If she had expected more than that, she had come to the wrong shop. He had met her only once before, and that was when she had shared Lottie Wayland's laughter at his humiliation in the water-splash. That being so, she should be thankful to him for saving her skin. She could hardly expect him to hang round and play the knight-errant in a *sauve qui peut* moment like that. And now the damned girl's presence had earned him a rebuke from Mr. Schwann, with whom he had been getting on so well.

He took a gulp of wine and thought: And that's another thing. Who does Schwann think he is? He said: "What do you mean, Mr. Schwann—don't speak to you like that?"

His voice was a little bellicose. Schwann said patiently: "I mean don't contradict me. Especially in the uncouth accents of a boor. When I tell you a thing, it is so."

"But Mr. Schwann, let me tell you. . ."

"Please!" The moles made a movement of deprecation, sitting up

303

on their sterns, then falling with a gentle plop to the table. "Ah! The *crêpes Suzette*. Here is something on which we can be agreed."

16

Anthony remembered throwing Chris Hudson into the water-splash, and that Joanna had seen him do it. So far as he knew, that was the only time the two had met. He wondered whether one would cross to the other's table, or wave a hand of recognition. Neither of these things happened, and it was none of his business to intervene. A couple who had dined early, at a table near the door on Schwann's side of the restaurant, got up to leave, and Anthony went to speak the customary courtesies. Then, as he was walking back down the restaurant, Joanna said: "Mr. Fieldhouse."

"Your ladyship?"

"Do you expect anyone else to-night at the table that's just being cleared?"

"No, your ladyship."

"I'm sorry to worry you, but could we change over?"

"Certainly."

He saw the change made, and was distressed. Obviously, Joanna couldn't stand the sight of Chris Hudson, looking her full in the face across the narrow room. He didn't know why. Had he known Chris was coming, he would have made different arrangements, but Schwann had ordered a table for two, not naming his companion.

Joanna laid a hand on Scroop's and said: "Forgive the fuss, darling. Somehow, I like this side better."

She had been alarmed, both for herself and for him. Was she ever likely, she wondered, to forget the man sitting there looking at her with an intent recognition? For long after that night at the Silver Star he had been in her dreams, dwindling down a vista in which there was nothing but him, smaller and smaller, and then not so much as a human dot, only herself, terrified, abandoned. It had faded at last as a continuing content of her dreams, but there were times when it came back to her mind, and in those moments Chris Hudson's figure in the lonely street was the incarnation of betrayal. Had they never met before it would had been bad; but he himself had reminded her that night of a previous meeting—something that gave her a claim, however tenuous, upon his fidelity. And he had gone, in her moment of direst need. No, she would not ever forget Chris Hudson.

And she was alarmed for William. What had lain behind it all she did not know or want to know, but she knew that the consequence of William's last encounter with Chris Hudson had been disastrous. A couple of hours ago William had awakened in her arms and she had said: "Darling, we've never been to Cornwall."

"No."

"I had a letter this morning from Julia—I've told you about her, haven't I? She was at school with me in Switzerland."

"Yes."

"She's married, and lives just outside Penzance. She tells me they have mimosa and camellias blooming in the garden, and millions of daffodils. Imagine that—at this time of year! It must be heaven."

"Yes."

He was so unresponsive she could have wept. "Why shouldn't we go down there? Right away. I think London's getting a bit stale on us. Let's go and have a good lazy month in the sunshine among all those flowers."

"But I'm used to London. I get nervous in strange places among strange people."

"Well, Yorkshire, then. If the weather's good, the air there is marvellous in winter. Mother'd love to have us."

"I'm not so sure of that. She's a very busy woman. That's one thing. And another is that she'd wonder what right I had to be loafing about doing nothing. She's spent money enough on me already."

She didn't know whether to feel outraged or despairing. "Darling! Do you think such an idea would enter Mother's head—or mine?"

"The trouble is it enters *my* head."

She sat up naked and looked about her. A luxurious room, no light save the fire-flicker, the man she loved lying in her bed. She had everything, and for the first time since she had married him she felt afraid. Never before at a moment like this, had he been other than tranquil, relaxed.

She said: "Darling, should you worry so much whether *Vanguard* is a success or not?"

She knew that everything had come suddenly to a dark knot in his mind: the failure to get rid of the house, Frinton's cold misunderstanding of the point of honour, *Vanguard*. She was aware that *Vanguard* had become to him a symbol, something against which he was measuring himself, and she mentioned it not without fear.

He didn't answer her question, and she said: "Don't let it become an obsession."

It was an unhappy word. He knew and he feared what it was to be *obsessed*. He remained silent, and Joanna said: "I should think Mr. Shrubb is very good at his job. Couldn't we let him see to the next issue? Then we could get away for a month—anywhere you like. After all, we could keep in touch with the office by telephone, and if Mr. Shrubb ran into difficulties you could put him straight."

He said simply: "I don't think it would be a good idea." He kissed her to show that he loved her and that he understood how she was thinking of his welfare, and then he got out of bed and went off to have a bath and dress for the evening.

17

When Joanna asked Anthony to put them at another table Scroop thought with a secret smile: "How clever of her! She knows that man is bad for me." But she was not the only clever one. He was pleased to observe that he was waking up himself to the badness of some things. The thought recurred to him that he had been clever in going home by taxi. Walking alone about London would have been definitely among the bad things. And this man, though he could not remember who he was, was a very bad thing indeed. When Joanna apologised for being fussy, and said: "I like this side better," he laughed and answered: "I'm not surprised. That's a bad man."

She was horrified. There had been a ghost of a chance that he would recognise Chris Hudson, but she had hoped not: after all, he had seen Chris only once, and only for a few moments. She asked: "Who, darling? What man are you talking about?"

The very question clarified his mind, and he answered pat: "The man we met in the Silver Star. He talked about Charlie."

His mind was desolated by his own answer. He felt himself swept by a dark wave against a rock on which he beat in vain, because recollection ended there. He could remember the man and the name Charlie, and he could remember waking on Dulcie Dearmer's bed. But what lay between those two moments he could not remember. He knew only that it was something terrible, something that was not Scroop but that could get hold of Scroop and inhabit him. He told himself that he had to be careful, to remember always to take taxis, and to give nothing away. So he said to Joanna: "But why should we worry our heads about a man like that? You order the dinner, darling." Having had the wit to circumvent the moment in that way, he felt victorious and relaxed. He was rather silent as they ate their dinner, and they didn't linger at table.

306

Joanna was not reassured. He was there at her side, but she knew that she was not there at his. If she spoke to him he answered, but from a distance. This had never hapened before. There had been moments enough when the continuing misfortunes of V*anguard* had made him moody and unhappy, but she had always been a sufficient medicine. She knew that this time she was not. There was more here than she could fathom. Her heart turned towards her mother who had never failed to solve her problems. As soon as William was out of the house in the morning she would ring her up. She would try and persuade her to come to London. Something must be done about Scroop and the wretched paper. For the first time she cursed V*anguard*. It had let her down. She had hoped that, win or lose, it would keep William occupied and happy. She thought of it now as a poison that she must somehow prevent him from taking. Perhaps Shrubb would have some ideas. She would find a way to see him alone tomorrow. However, when they got back to Soho Square Gwilym said that Shrubb's landlady had rung up to say that he was down with influenza and would have to keep to his bed for a few days. This news unduly depressed her, and she had been disturbed by William's odd behaviour on leaving L'*Esculent*. The commissionaire stopped a taxi, and as she was about to step in William said: "No. Tell him to drive on." They got into the next cab, and William said: "I didn't like the look of that first man, did you?"

She felt uneasy, but managed to laugh. "Really, darling, when I start choosing my taxi-drivers for their looks I shall expect you to fear the worst."

Scroop said sharply: "He didn't look a man one could trust."

18

Joanna slept deeply and was awakened by the sound of the breakfast tray chinking into the room in a maid's hands. The girl switched on a subdued light and said: "Good morning, my lady. It's proper foul. You can't see across the square for fog." She left the curtains drawn as usual and put the tray on a table by the bed. Joanna would not stir from beneath the bedclothes till she was gone. She was shy of revealing that she slept naked. Every evening her nightdress was laid along the bed. She would put it under her pillow, and in the morning throw it, crumpled, on to the eiderdown. Body to body: that was how she liked to sleep, as once everyone did.

"How is Sir William?" she asked.

"Fit as a flea, my lady. Which is surprising on such a day. Talk about fog! All thick and swirly-like. And not a trace when I came in last night."

"What time was that, Eva?"

"Later than it should have been, I don't mind admitting now that I'll be leaving you. It was just that extra half hour that did it. We fixed it up."

She switched on the electric fire and went out gaily, and Joanna sat up wondering whether it was the overflow of Eva's own happiness at having fixed it up that made the girl think William was cheerful. Or was he, really? She hoped so.

She thought of Lottie, working away to help Anthony, and she thought of this pert little Eva who doubtless would work away to help her boy, a Covent Garden porter. She looked about the room and felt dissatisfied with herself and with her life. This habit of breakfasting in bed. It was lazily typical of so much of her life, which, since her marriage, had been nothing but a prolonged honeymoon. She thought of her mother and of the father she could hardly remember, and her own life seemed shocking. She wondered for the first time whether she had been what William needed, whether her obsession with him had not drained him of some guts, slackened him in fibre? She was living in the hangover of last night's depression and was desperately unhappy.

When Scroop had eaten his breakfast, he stood at the window looking out into the square. It was nine o'clock, but might have been midnight. Indeed, at midnight those lights burning in windows on the opposite side would have been steadily visible. Now they came and went as blear blinks in the thick drift and eddy, sluggish yellow eyes whose lids were briefly raised. The thought pleased Scroop. It peopled the morning with unknown creatures. When, on his side of the square, a figure moved by, coat collar up, hat down, quickly seen, then gone, it had a furtive and conspiring air that caused him to watch it intently within the narrow moment of its apparition. If ever there was one, he thought, this was the moment for taking no chances. That was a dangerous world out there.

The same idea seemed to have visited Gwilym, who came in and asked: "You going to the office to-day?"

"Oh, yes, Gwilym. And as Mr. Shrubb won't be coming, perhaps you'll hack me a piece of cheese for Festus."

"You'd better not walk it. I'll ring you a taxi."

Scroop looked at him with sharp suspicion. What did Gwilym know? Why should he want to protect him?

"I shall walk," he said.

"All right," Gwilym said. "I don't recommend it, but you're the boss. Watch your step, that's all. Don't fall off the duckboards."

"Duckboards?"

"Ay. Don't tell me you've forgotten what duckboards are. I'm speaking figurative. I'll get the cheese."

Scroop put on his overcoat and, like all the other conspirators, turned up its collar and pulled down the brim of his hat. He put the cheese into his pocket and stepped out into the fog, thinking of duckboards.

Gwilym was right, he told himself. You couldn't be too careful about duckboards. A false step could put you up to the neck among the mules and men who had already been there too long to be comfortable companions. Of course, duckboards had their points. He remembered knocking an offensive fellow off one. Whoops! He was off one himself. It was only the edge of the pavement, but he hopped back with a sharp apprehension that shook him. Happily, he hadn't far to go to the office of *Vanguard*, and though this thought pleased him for a moment, it then confused him. What had duckboards to do with *Vanguard*?

Whoops again! He turned a corner and collided violently with a man. Gone as soon as seen, or rather felt. He hadn't been seen, and that was bad, because you wanted to know who was knocking around on a day like this.

Anyhow, that was one corner turned. There were three that had to be missed, then one to be turned. But had he missed three, or only two? Or perhaps four? He looked up, and saw a brown sluggish ceiling. He looked about him, and saw brown sluggish walls. Well, thank goodness for a landmark at last. Here was the shop where he was accustomed to buy his tobacco. He went in and cried gaily "Good morning, Bill," to the back that met his eyes. The man turned, and it wasn't Bill. Bill was in the room behind the shop, but Scroop didn't know that. He left the shop in a rush, and floundered off the duckboards again. A bad one that time.

On a clear morning he could have reached the office in ten minutes. To-day it took him three-quarters of an hour, and he was not sure how he had got there at all. Anyhow, what a place it was! He had never before noticed, as he climbed the stairs, how silent the doors were. What went on behind them? *Who* was behind them? He went up very slowly, oppressed by a feeling that once he had shut his own door behind him he would be cut off. Still, precautions could be taken. He turned the key in the lock. Anyone who wanted to get at him now would have to batter the door down.

Usually, he found the fire laid in his grate and had only to put a match to it. But to-day the grate was full of dead ashes. The fog was so thick that the charwoman from Battersea had stayed on her own side of the river. He switched on the ceiling light and saw that even here indoors the air was thinly webbed with mist.

There was a gas fire in Shrubb's room, and he decided to work in there. He went in to ask Shrubb's permission and was surprised to find the room bleak and empty. Then his hand met the packet of cheese in his pocket, and he remembered. He walked across to Festus's neat little Georgian house, and there Festus lay in the upper storey, looking none too well. His pink eyes were open and his whiskers twitched, but he remained lethargically outstretched when Scroop spoke to him. Scroop opened the door on the ground floor and put in the cheese. Then he sniffed, and remembered how often Shrubb had promised to have something done about the gas leak. He lifted up the Georgian house and carried it through to his own room, throwing up the window and happily watching Festus revive. It was half-an-hour before the rat decided that he was well enough to go downstairs and have his breakfast, and by that time the fog had oozed so thickly through the open window that the room seemed sub-aqueous. Scroop felt almost as though he were swimming as he went back towards Shrubb's room. His mind as well as his body seemed invested with a gentle air-treading quality. He had forgotten what caused him to carry Festus to the open window. He shut the door behind him and sat down at Shrubb's writing-table. Lying on the blotting-pad were a few quarto sheets inscribed in Shrubb's italic hand: "For Sir William. Some suggestions for reforming Vanguard."

Scroop laughed. Faithful, conscientious Shrubb, he thought. No, no. The time for reform was past. Shrubb didn't realise that all the world was in league against Vanguard and what it stood for. He pulled some sheets of paper towards him and dipped a pen in the ink. He must set out for Shrubb's benefit the iniquity of the forces opposed to them. He wrote: "Going on is out of the question. The time has come to end the whole thing."

He sat back to arrange in his mind the points he would have to make. It was not only what immediately concerned Vanguard. There were all those points of view that created a climate of opinion opposed to the success of good intentions and clean endeavours. There were men like James Frinton who laughed at a notion of honour. . . .

And having started on that tack, his mind swiftly recurred to what had happened to him since leaving Frinton's office: his fears in the streets, the strange re-appearing of that man whom he had met disastrously at the Silver Star; and on and on, and round and about,

310

and in and out his mind went, so bemused by phantasmagoria that he wrote nothing more, forgot where he was, and only came to with the realisation that his head was aching and that the room was very cold. He told himself that he must light the gas fire before putting his thoughts on to paper, and got up to do so. He was surprised at the haziness both of his legs and his head, but he managed to waver to the fire, kneel down, and turn on the tap. Then he felt in his pocket for matches, and no matches were there. They must, he thought, be in his overcoat pocket in the other room. He tried to get up, but found it difficult, and said it would be easier in a moment. Then it seemed pleasant enough just to lie there. He was very tired. He mustn't waste his strength, he thought. He would need it all, because, by God, old Shrubb was right, and the thing to do was not to give up.

The coroner had no doubts. It was touching, he said, that before taking his own life the deceased had been careful to put a rat in a place of safety and to provide it with food. That he had taken his life was beyond question when one considered the farewell words he had written.

CHAPTER *13*

௫ ௫ ௫ ௫ ௫ ௫

1

*F*rancis Scroop, 12th baronet, was born at Throstle's Nest in June of 1924. He was christened in the parish church of Smurthwaite, and Septimus Pordage was his godfather. It was six months since Sir William Scroop had died, and Joanna had not yet recovered from the shock of that affair. She had had to remain in London until the inquest was over, and then her mother had taken her back to Yorkshire. She felt numb in body and spirit, oppressed by a sense of failure. She had given Scroop all she had, and it had not been enough. There were desperate moments when she felt herself his killer. She told herself that she had been lazy, idle, self-indulgent, when the circumstances demanded a tonic companionship rather than an enervating perpetual love-affair. Living now alongside her mother, with an insight she had not had before, she marvelled at Mrs. Halliwell's industry and understanding, and she was ashamed of herself. She remembered how, in his last days, William had again and again spoken of his failure. Surely it was she who had failed him, and she had failed any potentiality of usefulness that may have been in herself. What she found worst to bear was the remembrance of having persuaded him, so long ago as it seemed, to take her to the Silver Star, when obviously all his will and wish had been against it. She saw the ruin that now lay around her as touched off on its course from that moment, for it was then that William had first met Chris Hudson, and that first meeting, she was sure, was linked with the second, and the second, in some way that she did not understand, had helped to precipitate the desperate end.

Mrs. Halliwell let her be. She was wise enough to know that this was a time for nothing but love, which could be something other than a love affair. She had been a passionate woman; she knew well enough

312

how things had been between Joanna and her husband, and she was pleased that it was so. But this was a moment for another aspect of love, and she quietly allowed its cloak to lie about Joanna, without fuss or ostentation. She encouraged Septimus, for whom she had discovered an odd amused affection, to visit Throstle's Nest; and, as the spring quickened towards its first lovely touch with summer, the old man and the sad beautiful girl walked together through the countryside, with many a pause by some young stream or on a warm seat of rock, and they would let the sun soak into them and not talk much; and in these companioned silences Joanna would find comfort and now and then begin to catch again some glimpse of meaning in her life.

There was an afternoon in late May, when it might already have been June, so lazily warm it was, so full of bee-drone and herb-scent, and so full-bosomed the trees were, heavy and opulent like Joanna herself, when she laid her hand on the old man's pink podgy paw and asked simply: "What is it all about, Mr. Pordage?"

"If I could tell you that, my dear," he said, "I should be God Himself, and I fear I still have some way to go before I qualify for that degree."

"You are at any rate a wise old man. Tell me: how does one get through life? How does one bear its sorrows?"

"How," he asked, "does one deserve its joys? Try not to think of life in terms of the moment. Life isn't joy and it isn't sorrow. It's something one gets through, and if you ask me how, I can only say that we have to, and that's the end of it. And what we can get through is surprising. You can say to yourself that you never, never, never will get over the loss of loved ones, but the odd thing is that you do. The bleeding stops, and the scar forms, and perhaps the scar will always be there, but it doesn't hurt any more, and often enough the scar itself goes."

"I wonder," she said, still holding his hand.

"The joke about life," Septimus said, "is that it isn't a bread-pudding. It isn't all one stuff, and whoever mixed the ingredients didn't forget the gall. But it's all there is to eat, and, anyhow, there's the final consolation that the meal ends at last."

"Would you call that a consolation?"

"Well," he said, smiling, "it's a booby prize for those who have no other. That it all ends is the only consolation Shakespeare could give us. 'Time and the hour runs through the roughest day.'"

She said: *"Tout passe, tout casse, tout lasse.* Is that all there is to it?"

313

"No," he said, and he put his arm round her warm young shoulder. "That is really a foolish little proverb. *Tout passe*, to be sure. But our life itself is the passing, and if some of it is pretty rum, a lot of it is not to be sneezed at."

The birds had not yet fallen upon their midsummer silence. The air was full of song, and a flight of gold-finches went by shining. "Look at that," Septimus said. "Have we any *right* to think only that the winter may kill them off? Of course it may. And we shall rightly feel the sorrow of it. But is it common sense to say: 'I have loved these birds so much that never again will bird-song give me joy'?"

"Parables from nature," she said, but not too maliciously. "I wonder whether reflections of this sort have ever really helped a person in distress?"

"Possibly not," he said frankly. "And never pretend that they do if they don't. When all is said and done, there's not much we can do for one another, is there? Except stand by, just in case."

They went slowly on towards Throstle's Nest, and he said cheerfully: "Well, that's a day's march nearer our *accouchement*."

At that, she really did laugh. "*Our!* Come, Mr. Pordage!"

"Well," he said, "Pordage will suffer with you in spirit, dear lady."

"It will be comforting to know," she answered, "that you are standing by. Just in case."

2

She got out of the train at King's Cross and walked into the street that was bitter cold with an east wind blowing. She pulled her furs about her and told the taxi-man to take her to *L'Esculent*. She was glad that she didn't have to say "In Dean Street." The taxi-men knew the name, and she was glad for Lottie's sake and Anthony's. It was nice to know that one's friends were succeeding by their own efforts. As for her, she was richer than ever, and there was irony in some of the riches having come through poor William. He was hardly in his grave when the white elephant house was sold as a school, and what she got out of that was nothing to what she got out of the house in Soho Square. She wished never to see it again, and William's agent used the chance to approach the firm of pottery manufacturers who had long wanted to pull it down and build on the site. The sum offered seemed to her immense; but Mrs. Halliwell intervened. Mrs. Halliwell didn't believe in selling an important piece of London ground, and Joanna remained the ground landlord. Already, she understood, the housebreakers were in, smashing the place where she had known her brief and vivid bliss. She had left that house when William's long absence disturbed her; and, because already a fatal premonition was in her, she had asked Gwilym to go with her, and they had found the door of the *Vanguard* office locked on the inside. She would never forget the sound of Gwilym's knock, tentative at first, then loud and louder, falling on her heart as well as on her ears, or the look of growing desperation in Gwilym's eyes. At last he stood back and smashed the flat of his boot into one of the panels that Mr. Shrubb had so lovingly cherished, and had reached his hand up through the hole and withdrawn the key. "Now you'd better go away for a moment," he said, and looked at her with an appeal that she should do so; but, choked beyond speech by the turmoil of her feelings, she had shaken her head and they had gone in together.

It was a year ago, almost to the day, and she could think of it now at any rate without terror. She had survived a shock which, at first, she had hoped would kill her. Septimus was right. A skin was forming over the wound, and she found herself thinking more and more of Francis's future than of her own past and William's. Francis was at Throstle's Nest. Joanna hoped that the nurse her mother had engaged, a rather startling young creature bristling with all the degrees and qualifications that seemed to be demanded nowadays of those who had to warm a drop of milk and wash a few napkins: Joanna hoped that this nurse would stand between the child and spoiling. Mrs. Halliwell might pretend to be brusque, but she was a bit too fond of speaking of Sir Francis; and what Mr. Pordage might do, given his head, was beyond her conjecture. She had come into the nursery and found him standing by the cradle, holding in his hand a short length of toy railway line.

"What is that for, Mr. Pordage?" she had asked.

"I have been explaining to our child," he said, "a scheme which we shall build up bit by bit. We shall lay down at Easter How a transport system. We shall bridge the stream, and tunnel under the hill, and roam about the prairie, of which my paddock will supply an adequate representation. Sidings, stations, signal boxes—why, bless my soul, you should see the catalogue I have secured from Messrs. Bassett Lowke! Believe me, my dear Lady Scroop, Sir Francis and I are in for a high old time. He is a little young, I admit, but it behooves me as the senior partner to launch the enterprise."

Joanna said dryly: "Yes. He is a little young."

She looked down at the child, who had nothing of Scroop and was all Joanna; and from the rounded pink cheek in the cradle she looked up at the rounded pink cheek and blue eyes of Septimus. "You're remarkably alike," she said. "A pair of Holy Innocents."

3

While she was eating her lunch she was my Lady to Anthony, and she was glad of the formality because she wanted this moment to be free of personal content. She wanted just to sit there undisturbed, to put her heart and nerves to the test. The place was full, and she spared a moment to rejoice in its prosperity for Lottie's and Anthony's sake. But what she had come for was to challenge the feeling that she must never see the place again, to test the strength of the skin that was forming over the wound. As the train was approaching London she had asked herself where she should lunch, and so much in her said "Not at *L'Esculent*" that she knew she must go there. She mustn't be hag-ridden. There was much that, even now, she didn't know about Scroop and would never know; but she knew that fears had been his companions, never deep below the surface, always up and about if given a chance. So here, where they had surged upon him for the last time, she sat and ate her lunch and found a normality in the moment and the scene, and was glad that Scroop's infection had not corroded her.

She forced herself to think of that night, and especially of Chris Hudson. That the boy had had, for William, some peculiar and sinister significance she knew; but now that William was gone it was as though Chris Hudson had been exorcised. She found that she could think of him calmly as nothing more than a young man whom she did not like. Even that dreadful night at the Silver Star took on proportions of sanity. And this again was because William was gone. She would never know what it was about Chris that had caused William's outburst and breakdown: neither, for that matter, would Chris: but it was nothing that could touch her; and as for Chris's abandonment of her in the gutter, she was able to see it as no more than shocking bad manners on the part of a person she was not likely to meet again. She herself, she said, had acted that night like an overwrought and emotional little fool.

She felt satisfyingly grown up and sophisticated, a woman who had had a hard knock and learned that emotion was best kept on a chain. When she got up to go, Anthony said: "If you've got a moment to spare, come and have a word in the office."

She was glad not to be her ladyship now, and in the small room that was the office Anthony kissed her. The warm gesture moved her deeply. She felt as though she had been received back among friends, liberated from too much love and too much sorrow. She sat down weakly and said: "Why did you do that?"

Anthony said: "Because you look such a child." She noticed that he himself was not looking a child. He was maturing. There was grey at his temples and he was pale. "Child indeed!" she said to slide over the moment. "You forget that I am the mother of a baronet eight months old."

"When you came in," he said, "my memory made an enormous leap. I was in Smurthwaite with Mr. Pordage's dog, and I looked through the door of a bun-shop that had a notice 'Dogs not Admitted.' You were inside and you ordered me to bring the dog in. You were high and mighty, a law unto yourself, an imperious child. And, what pleased me even more, you paid for my buns and coffee. So now *L'Esculent* is going to pay for your lunch. But don't regard it as a precedent."

"Thank you, Anthony. But I don't feel high and mighty at the moment. Do you know why I came in here to lunch to-day?"

She told him, and the telling eased her mind. She said: "When I was a girl I had a mania for coral island stories. You know the thing: just you and someone you love. Nothing but beauty about you. The world miles and miles beyond the horizon. Well, I had it. Just that. But I hadn't thought of tornadoes and lethal waves. Well, I came in here to see if there was a hope of crawling back to firm land."

"Bless you," he said. "You'll make out."

"Yes. I think I shall. How is Lottie? I see there's a strange girl at the receipt of custom."

"Lottie's expecting a baby. Any moment now I shall be the father not of a baronet but of a simple boy or girl."

"I must be the god-mother. May I?"

"You can't escape it. It's all been arranged. And Joe Morrison is to be the god-father, if he's in England."

"How is Joe?"

"Doing very well, so far as I can see. His name often appears over his stuff in *The Banner*."

"I'm so glad. He's a nice boy."

Anthony, who had seen Joe quivering with emotion at the very thought of Joanna, let the cool appraisal go without comment.

He said: "This infant of ours is going to make a difference to the set-up. We don't fancy bringing up a child in Baker Street. It is not as though we intended it to be a detective. We've bought a house out at Pinner. Lottie won't be coming back here. It was a tough business, you know, getting going, but we're round the corner, thank God, and can afford to pay a cashier."

"I should think so," she said, "considering your prices. Give my love to Lottie and Mrs. Wayland. I'll look in as soon as I'm allowed."

"Where shall I find you?"

"For the moment, at Brown's Hotel. I'm looking for a flat."

4

She took the flat in Baker Street and then she went out to Chelsea to find Mr. Shrubb. He had been much on her mind, and he was embraced within the plans she had made for the conduct of her life henceforth. The plans had not readily commended themselves to Mrs. Halliwell, who would have liked nothing better than to have Joanna at Throstle's Nest until she found another husband, which was something Mrs. Halliwell thought certain to happen before long to a rich and beautiful young woman. But another part of her approved what Joanna wanted to do. She knew that the girl was in revolt against the sort of life she had led since her marriage, that she wanted, as she put it, to justify her existence; and if London seemed to her the place for doing this, well, it might be the place for finding a husband, too. As for the work involved, Mrs. Halliwell told herself that work never hurt anybody and it might help to take Joanna's mind off her troubles. Secretly, she rejoiced at the thought of having more or less of a free hand in the bringing up of Francis.

Joanna was on her way to Shrubb's lodgings and divagated down to the Chelsea Embankment, and it was there that she ran into Shrubb. She saw him and recognised him when he was a long way off, leaning on the embankment wall and watching the swans who breasted the flowing tide, taking the scum of the fouled river upon their feathery prows. It was all grey and white: grey water, grey cloud, and a grey sneaking little wind and grey of granite; white of the birds: swans and gulls. Shrubb belonged to the greyness. He looked a bit of pathetic flotsam on the tide of the day. His face was thin, and so was his overcoat, and a grey woollen muffler wrapped his neck. She felt a sinking of the heart and was aware of the effort with which she summoned a smile to her face.

Shrubb turned with a start when she laid a furred hand on his shoulder. They smiled at one another: a tentative, almost evasive smile, as though they wondered what there was to smile about; and then she said absurdly: "Are you very busy?"

"Not overwhelmed," he said.

They took a taxi-cab to Baker Street, and there, in the tea-shop below the flat, she gave him a meal. He made no bones about being very hungry, and the muffins, dripping warm butter as plentifully as a ripe comb drips honey, vanished magically. He wiped his lips and turned to her with a shy smile. "I don't mind telling you," he said, "that that was necessary, and very welcome."

She was pleased with his tact. She had feared that she might have to tell him that she did not want to hear William's name; but he seemed to know this, and she guessed rightly that for his own sake as well as hers, that was a name better left unsaid.

She said to him: "You know Anthony Fieldhouse, of course? You did the restaurant for him."

"Yes."

"He lived here, you know. There's a flat over this place. He's moved out, and I shall soon be moving in. At the moment, I'm living at Brown's, but I don't want to be in a hotel any longer than I can help. Could you take on the job of getting the flat ready for me?"

Shrubb's face wonderfully brightened. "What do you want me to do?"

"Everything. Decoration, furnishing, lighting. I don't want to bother with any of it."

"Let's go and have a look at it."

"No. Here's the key. Go and look at it by yourself. Keep that key till the job's finished."

Shrubb hesitated. "Well, my lady," he said, "I haven't had many jobs of this sort, as you know; but for my own sake and my client's I like to have some idea where I stand. It wouldn't do to walk through a thousand pounds and then find that your client had been thinking of five hundred. I'd better see the job and work something out and give you an estimate in about a week's time."

"Do that," she said, "if you would prefer it. But you'll want some cash in hand."

She had already prepared the cheque for five hundred pounds, and handed it to him. He looked at it, speechless, and she found it an awkward moment. She said flippantly: "Of course an item on your bill will be 'expenses,' delightfully vague. Well, I shan't enquire too closely if a good dinner for yourself to-night is included."

She took up her hand-bag and walked out with dignity, but she felt like running.

5

Some time in the sixteenth century a farmer, working the good loam of Middlesex, built himself a small house of brick on the hill behind the church at Pinner. It stands there still, with four hundred years of weather in its brick, surrounded by a couple of acres of the old farm land, now a garden with lawns, shrubs and fruit trees. It didn't look its best on a winter day, especially such a day as this, for there had been a little snow in the night and the sky was still heavy and overcast, but Auntie Jess said to Mrs. Wayland: "Well, it looks better than Megson Street. Of course there's no Marlborough House to give it tone like, but you can't have everything."

They were walking up the gravel path towards the front door of iron-studded oak, and a curl of blue smoke rising from the chimney suggested the cheerful hearth within.

"The woman can't leave well alone," Mrs. Wayland thought. She knew as well as Aunt Jessie did that her life had had its foolishness; but she had grown out of a lot of it and didn't relish the reminder.

"I'll bet," Auntie Jess said, "Lottie'll have her work cut out here in the summer if she has a fancy for keeping down the dandelions."

You're a malicious old fool, Mrs. Wayland thought. You learn nothing and you forget nothing. Thank God you'll be gone in the morning.

The house was no distance from the church, and they had walked up together from the christening. Anthony and Lottie with the small mite Elizabeth and Mrs. Morrison, whose grandchild this was, though it was little younger than the child Mr. Morrison had given her, had already arrived in a taxi-cab; and tagging along a few hundred yards behind Jess and Mrs. Wayland were Joe Morrison and Joanna Scroop, who had just sworn, as god-parents, to do all sorts of things that they had already forgotten. Joe had flown over from Paris and would be flying back. He said so casually, but not without pride. Joanna was impressed. "It seems odd," she said, "that not so long ago I was driving every day into Smurthwaite with my mother behind an old brown horse. Now I've been married, and I've become a widow, and I have a son, and my friends say airily that they've flown in from Paris."

"Friends?"

"Well, a friend."

Joe looked at her. She was all grey fur, and her face was glowing from the cold. His mind was inflamed by romantic ideas. Watching her holding the child in the church, he had thought she looked like a madonna. She said prosaically: "This is a nice little house that Lottie and Anthony have found."

The nice little house was now only a few hundred yards away, and Joe wished that it were a few miles. Soon the company would snatch her from him. When Anthony had written to ask if he would be the child's god-father, he had not been anxious to make the considerable effort for the sake of what he thought a formality. Then the letter said: "Joanna Scroop, who has taken over my old flat, will be the god-mother," and Joe moved heaven and earth to get his brief leave. This ten minute walk alone with her was his reward, and it was nearly over.

He said: "I shall have to get a train back to town pretty soon. Lord Dunkerley, alas! has heard that I am in England, and I'm commanded to report to him. Happily, I don't have to dine with him. He has some public dinner to-night and will squeeze me in before going on to it."

"Why happily? I know that he thinks well of you. A dinner with him would do your career no harm."

"I say happily because it leaves my dinner-hour free."

He looked at her with a meaning she could not fail to understand. She respected him for not making it an invitation, for merely throwing it out like that for her to take or leave. He must have heard from Anthony of what she had been through, and she was pleased with his delicacy in not pressing himself upon her. She said: "I've promised Anthony and Lottie to stay for an evening meal. I shan't be getting back to town till late."

She was aware that he was bitterly disappointed, but here was the house now, with the front door open upon a welcome and Anthony standing there shouting: "Come on, you two. Elizabeth Augusta Victoria Fieldhouse—Liz to you—is already in bed and we're waiting to drink a toast."

She said quickly: "I'll walk down as far as the station with you, Joe, but then I must come back."

The living-room of the old house, ribbed with black oak, low-ceilinged and warmed with a fire of logs, seemed unreal to Joe Morrison, so taken to another world he was by that quickly-spoken sentence. He had expected nothing, so that to receive this seemed to him an immense boon. He was hardly aware of the champagne-glasses twinkling on the Jacobean gate-legged table or of Anthony thumbing the cork out of the bottle. It all seemed very odd to Aunt Jessie, too. Mrs. Wayland was the grandmother of her dear Anthony's child, and so was Florrie Finch Freilinghausen Fieldhouse Morrison. When Mrs. Wayland raised a glass and cried: "A *la santé de notre chère petite. Qu'elle soit heureuse, belle et sage!*" Auntie Jess belched at the onset of the bubbles and said: "Well, Ah don't know what all that means, but here's wishing little Liz all the best. She's a bit of a mixed grill, if you ask me, but I hope someone'll find her good eating one of these days."

6

It was nearly midnight when Joanna switched on the light in her sitting-room in Baker Street. Mr. Shrubb had done a good job, but she was not in a mood to take much notice of it. She put on her electric fire, sank into a chair before it, and was very worried about the five minutes that had just ended. When she walked to Pinner Station with Joe Morrison after the toast had been drunk, she wondered whether she had been wise to do so, whether it would give an unintended encouragement. It was almost dark and the frost was sharpening and Joe's tongue seemed as frozen as the night. He hadn't a word to say. If he had chattered of this or that—she wouldn't have cared what, the christening, or Paris, or anything in between—she would have felt more comfortable, but Joanna, as Scroop had taught her, was all woman, and she was aware of and upset by the emotion behind the silence. She could almost feel the tingling of Joe's nerves as he loyally forbade his arm to stretch out and take hers. They had cut it rather fine, and she thanked God that the train was almost due as they climbed the short ascent to the station. Behind the railings there, the shrubs wore snowy coats that were stiffening under the frost, though a touch of sunshine would rouse them to life and movement. Thinking this as Joe, in the train, leaned out of the window, she gave his hand a warmer grasp than she had intended and said: "Well, good-bye, and mind you write to me, Joe."

It was the touch of magic warmth, and his face lit up, and he said: "Oh, may I, Joanna?"

She couldn't go back on it now, and she said: "Yes, please do, Joe."

"Thank you, thank you," he said, and the train bore him away.

She went back then to the dinner party at Anthony's, and at last took a late train to town. The day had tired her, and she was aware that the heaviest contribution to her fatigue came from the few moments with Joe Morrison. Physically, it was difficult to tire her, but if anything disturbed her emotionally she was sunk. What disturbed her about Joe was that his infatuation was obvious, and she didn't know whether she wanted to encourage it or kill it. As the train drew into Baker Street station, she thought thankfully that a five minutes walk would land her in bed. When she came to the station barrier there was Joe Morrison waiting for her.

They had said good-bye. That he should now be there had an unmistakable import, and they both knew it. She said: "Well Joe!" and then nothing more was said for a time as they walked out into the almost empty midnight Baker Street. It stretched before them, long, dull, straight as a ruled line, and the unappealing perspective reminded Joanna of the frightening street in which she had found herself with Chris Hudson when they were thrown out of the Silver Star. But things were altered. She was not the inexperienced schoolgirl bemused by love that she was then. This empty street had no terrors for her. What was wrong with it was that it was *not* empty. She felt a mounting annoyance as they walked along wordless. She was determined not to be the first to speak, but Joe's silence almost dragged words to her lips. She fought them back. This was his situation. Let him handle it. And yet she thought of him pityingly. It was a bitter night. He had not known on which train she would return, and he must have watched the passengers come off train after train. She sighed so heavily that it was almost a groan. Hearing it, Joe said: "You must think I'm mad."

Still she wouldn't speak; and he went on: "Well, so I am. So I have been for years. Before you were married. When we danced together at Smurthwaite—that was the beginning of it."

Now he was launched, and not only what he had restrained that day but what had been dammed up in him ever since he had known her spilled over.

"We were children," he said, "just out of school the pair of us. It's not so long ago, but we've grown up. You've been put through the hoop in quick time—marriage, your husband's death, your child. And as for me, well, my sort of life encourages growing up too. What I mean is, if I were going to grow out of you I'd have done it by now. But it doesn't happen. I just grow more and more mad about you, and I can't bottle it up any longer. I intended to push off to-morrow and leave it all unsaid. But I couldn't do it. I was just going to bed in my hotel when I thought 'To hell with it. Tell her.' I was half undressed, and I put my things on again and got a taxi. I remembered how you shook my hand as I was leaving

Pinner station. You shook it warmly. You know you did, Joanna. What did that mean?"

They were standing outside the door of her place. A street-lamp spot-lighted them, and a passing policeman looked at them with professional curiosity, so tense and dramatic they seemed. She said: "Surely, Joe, a warm shake of the hands is not unusual among friends?"

He said with insight: "I don't know when you first began to be aware of what I feel about you. But you've certainly been aware of it all through to-day. You've been fighting me off. And you haven't been sure whether you wanted to or not. So I said to myself that if you'd really wanted to shake me off you'd have given me a frozen mitt, or nothing."

She had taken her latchkey from her handbag and was holding her coat closely round her against the cold. He said: "You're cold. Let's continue this discussion inside."

His face was pale under his red hair, and his blue eyes seemed alight. His look and his words destroyed the image of herself that he had himself created. Suddenly she was not the woman of the world with much experience crowded into a few years. She was a girl, frightened. She said: "No."

It sounded so definitive that he took it for the answer to all his argument, all his pleading. He didn't look stricken. She thought he looked as proud as Lucifer. He said: "Well, it's taken me a long time to make up my mind to talk to you like this. There were moments when I could hardly stop myself from doing it even when Scroop was alive. You appear to be the more resolute character. You can dispose of everything with a word."

She said, almost pleadingly: "You must write to me, Joe."

He laughed. "About economics and the state of Europe? No."

He took the key from her fumbling gloved hand, opened the door, and handed the key back to her. When she was inside, it was he who pulled the door to. Standing there, she heard his footsteps die away along the pavement. Sitting by her electric fire, feeling too exhausted to go to bed, she still heard the footsteps, and then she heard the whirring of propellers, and then she heard the footsteps again, sounding in a Paris street. And Paris seemed a long way off.

7

When she came to London she hadn't been sure what she wanted to do. She could speak, read and write in English, French and German. Septimus Pordage's suggestion that she should become a dragoman was romantic, but she pointed out that it would involve learning Turkish or Arabic, too. Hardly to her surprise, she found that he was serious. He said he knew a man who could teach her both, but she put him off. "After all, Mr. Pordage," she said, "I should be a dragowoman and somehow that doesn't sound quite respectable."

The immediate point was far less exciting. It was simply to see that Shrubb had enough to eat, and when she had arranged that in her own way she walked about the town with her eyes open, hoping that something would suggest itself. A shop window in Brook Street attracted her attention one morning. It contained a couple of gilt armchairs upholstered in moth-eaten velvet and a few trivial bits of pewter on a dresser made of heavy oak. This mingling of a broken-down Georgian boudoir and a Welsh farm kitchen was so incongruous that she was not surprised to see pasted across the window: "Sale: Reductions." Whoever ran that little shop had an unerring instinct for the road to ruin.

This was the shop which she now rented. Her first thought had been to consult her mother, but she didn't do this. She had come to London to make her own life, as she put it, to prove that she was not an idle, luxurious, over-loving wench. And so, instead of going to her mother she went to a solicitor. She knew nothing about solicitors, but she guessed that they would be congregated in the precincts of the Law Courts. She walked down there one morning and turned into Serjeants Inn. She did this simply because the small tucked-in court looked attractive, and she wondered if Mr. Serjeant Buzfuz had lived there. On a brass plate she saw the name of Mr. Rudolph Schwann. Mr. Schwann chanced to be in. He would not normally have been much interested in so small a transaction as this proved to be. He would at best have passed it on to one of his clerks; but the name of Lady Scroop stirred a memory. It was just about a year ago that Sir William Scroop had committed suicide—or so the coroner had found—and Schwann recalled that immediately before that he had seen Sir William and his lady at *L'Esculent*. He had thought her very beautiful and he had heard that she was rich.

Schwann's room looked into the courtyard of the inn. When Joanna was shown in there she was surprised, and her face showed it.

Even a less observant man than Schwann would have been aware of this, and Schwann missed nothing. He shook hands with her, glad that his recollection had not belied her beauty, and said: "I'm glad you like my room, Lady Scroop."

"Well," she said, "it's not a bit what I expected. I don't remember being in a solicitor's office before, but I've read of them, and in tales they're always dusty and dingy and cluttered with black japanned deed-boxes and bundles tied in red tape, and there are engravings of Lord Chancellors on the walls and drawings by Spy, with mould-spots on them."

"Any mould-spot that made its way in here," he said, "or for that matter any drawing by Spy, would be at once arrested for contempt. Sit down, Lady Scroop."

She sat facing him across his wide desk, which seemed the only utilitarian thing in the room, but was, all the same, lovely. He fascinated her as much as his room had done. "No," he said with a smile, reading her thought, "I never take snuff or smell of parchment or wear mulberry-coloured small-clothes."

She blushed, and he thought the blush became her. He was now in his Buddha pose, perfectly still, only his eyes moving, his moles peeping out from the immaculate cuffs on the desk before him. "Now," he said.

When she left the office it was eleven o'clock. She walked up Fleet Street towards St. Paul's and found a coffee-room and sat down to sort out her impressions. She thought with a smile that her mother would not approve of Mr. Rudolph Schwann. A solicitor who conducted his business at an uncluttered Georgian desk in a room with walls painted a charming pale matte green, with only one picture in view, and that, she'd dare swear, a Renoir—the bathing girls were rather blush-making; a solicitor whose carpet was Aubusson and whose mantelpiece above an Adam fireplace held nothing but a Chinese-looking horse: this solicitor would hardly be Mrs. Halliwell's cup of tea. But when all is said and done, she thought, Mother soon gets to know a man apart from his circumstances and idiosyncracies, so perhaps she would have approved of Mr. Schwann after all. For, once they had begun to talk of the business in hand, Mr. Schwann certainly smoothed things out as neatly as a flat-iron going over good linen. He shook hands with her on parting, and, sensing her complete inexperience in affairs, told her not to worry her head about the matter. She understood that it was all a trifle that could be quickly dealt with, that in due course she would be asked to put her name to a few papers, and that would be that. And so, indeed, it proved. On that night when Joe Morrison walked along Baker Street with her, Joanna had been running the shop for a month.

8

Schwann's father was a German Jew. Adolf Hitler was not the first person in Germany to dislike the Jews, and Heinrich Schwann came to England and worked as a chemist with his fellow-country-man Ludwig Mond. He married an English woman, but he never became an Englishman in law. He had two sons, Rudolph and Wilhelm. He was dead now, and so was his wife, and Wilhelm was living in Berlin. His heart had always pined for the land of his fathers. He was a German first, and a Jew a long way behind. With him as with Rudolph, Jew was a secular label. It had no religious significance for either. Wilhelm was twenty when he returned to Germany, and that was twenty-five years ago. He taught classics in a high school, was married, and had a son and a daughter. He had fought for Germany in the first world war and been severely wounded. Rudolph, who had become a naturalised Englishman, had fought for England. In the twenty years of their growing up together, a deeper than usual affection had bound them, and the tragedy that cast them on different sides in the war deepened this. Wilhelm had never returned to England, but, more often than not, Rudolph spent his summer holiday in Germany and had watched young Magda and Fritz grow up. He wrote to Wilhelm every week. It gave him a sense of family that he deeply valued, the more so because of his own unmarried condition. During the moral and financial chaos of Germany after the war, he had been more like a Dutch uncle to Wilhelm than a slightly younger brother. He had managed to tide the small family over the worst of those disasters, and this gave him a feeling of responsibility for them all that deepened as time went by.

In the evening of his meeting with Joanna he sat down in his Berkeley Square flat to write his weekly letter. He liked to hear from Wilhelm all the little things that made up his life as a schoolmaster, and in return he sent him news of his own daily doings in so far as discretion permitted. He had come to love England, and English law he looked on with reverence. When he was a boy his father had been summoned to a county court to answer some charge against him by the man from whom he had bought the small house the Schwanns lived in. During the hearing this man used the expression "a proper bit of Jew-boy dirty work." Rudolph would never forget the quiet but emphatic anger of the judge as he ordered the man to withdraw this remark. The man refused; the judge persisted; and the man became abusive. He was then committed for contempt of court. The boy's already calm logical mind was impressed by the inevitable sequence of events in support of justice. And now he had only to hear such a phrase as "slippery as a lawyer," or "a slick attorney" for that odd deep silence to come upon him which showed that he was simmering within. The sense that he, a foreigner (as he considered himself despite his naturalisation), was admitted to the fraternity of the English courts was precious to him, and the last ha'penny of a client's money could have been entrusted to him as safely as to the Bank of England. And a client's affairs, too. He was an oyster. Yet, loving England and English law as he did, his sentiment for Germany was deep. It had been suggested to him years ago that he should change his name by deed poll to Robert Swan; but he would not do this. There was a loyalty involved here, too. Who was he to abandon a name that his family had borne for centuries?

"My dear Wilhelm," he wrote. "I have had a very beautiful client this morning—a Lady Scroop, a young widow, very rich. No, Wilhelm, do not pull a long face. I do not intend to marry her. Fritz and Magda can still count on old Uncle Rudolph. But I was interested in this young woman because of the circumstances in which I last saw her. I had gone out to dinner with the son of a famous comedian. What an odd life you must think I lead! Rich young titled widows, and comedians and their sons, while you day after day see the same dull boys and try to drive some beauty into their heads! But there it is. Like a journalist or a doctor, a solicitor is always shuttling about among all sorts of people. For example, when I had discussed my three-penny-worth of business with my young client this morning, I had to go through all sorts of deeds and settlements and what not, with a vast fortune involved, consequent on the very sudden death of a millionaire peer. That is how my life is, Wilhelm. The comedian is one of my clients, too! That is how I came to take an interest in his son, who is studying law, and will soon be putting up his plate, as they say, as a barrister. But I have not come to like the young man. You always laugh, I know, when I tell you that I can read most people like a book. But I can, you know, and what I read about this young man is that he thinks I am a bit slippery, if not a downright rogue. What do you think of that, eh? Poor old Rudolph a very bad boy! Well, this makes me go about with the young man now and then for my amusement, and I discover that what he thinks of me he thinks of everybody, so I am consoled.

"Well, when I am taking dinner with this young man Lady Scroop comes into the restaurant with her husband. This morning I remembered her very well, but she did not seem to have noticed me so I said nothing. Poor lady! She had reason that night not to notice strangers, though why that was so is no business of yours.

"Now she is going to start a little shop here in London. That was what she came to see me about, though why she should do this, being so rich, I don't know. But I can guess. Her parents are what we call self-made. Sometimes that is bad for the children. They do nothing but live on their parents' money; but other times the impulse of the parents lives on in the children, and rich though they are they must all the same work. And that is good. That is what I like; and so I hope this Lady Scroop will make a go, as we English say, of her shop.

"Well, Wilhelm, I know you like to hear these little details of my life and work, which help you to see old Rudolph under steam. Tell me now of you. How go those promising boys you spoke of? Do they get their scholarships and go on to the University? All the little things, please, especially about ugly Fritz and beautiful Magda, whose Dutch uncle, neither one thing nor another, can impartially send them lots of love. And to you, old boy, from your loving Rudolph."

9

Over the shop now was the word Decorators. All that Joanna asked of it was that it should pay its own way, repay her, in time, what she had put into it, and give Shrubb a better living than he had had at any time since she had known him. Shrubb's loyalty to William caused her to look upon him as a trust that she must honour. But she told herself that she must have no nonsense with him. The *Vanguard* episode had done him no good. So long an association with foredoomed failure would do no man any good. That day when she saw him loitering on the embankment at Chelsea he had seemed to be wearing failure as a cloak, and almost to be taking some perverted satisfaction from it. "What we are trying to do is too good for this stupid world. Very well, let them do without it." No, no, Joanna thought, with Mrs. Halliwell uppermost, that won't do at all. We must find the best we can make people take, and sell it to them. She had paid Shrubb generously for the work he did on her flat, and when he turned up, in response to her invitation, at the shop in Brook Street she was annoyed with him. It was a bright May morning, and she was wearing bright May clothes and feeling full of enthusiasm for the adventure before her. The shop and the cubicle behind it were empty and smelling of carbolic soap. She had had the place scrubbed to within an inch of its life. Mr. Shrubb was a little late, and this in itself annoyed her, so hopping with energy she was and not so much as a chair to sit on. When he did come, Shrubb looked more deplorably uncared for than ever. He might, she thought, at least have bought himself a decent suit and a new pair of shoes with the money he had made out of her, and he might have tried, on such a morning, to look a bit less like Rachel sorrowing for her children. The fact was that Shrubb hadn't a penny. He had paid his landlady a lot of money that he had owed her, and had also, in gratitude for her tolerance, bought her an electric sewing machine. Deplorable of course, but Shrubb.

Mr. Shrubb showed no curiosity about the reason for his summons, and looked round the antiseptic smelling room without asking any questions. His attitude was so apathetic that Joanna didn't know how to open the question of her great enterprise. The sun streamed through the window, and she could do no more than stand there in its beam, slapping one hand with the lilac gloves that she held in the other.

At last she said in desperation: "Let's take a walk." She locked the door behind them and gave Shrubb the big iron key. "Keep that," she said. "It's yours. I'll explain presently."

They didn't go far. She had noticed along the street a shop selling things that looked fabulously expensive, among them a pair of velvet curtains that had once been green but had faded to a silvery grey, with yet a hint of mossy green remaining. They went into the shop, whose muted atmosphere seemed to invite reverence deeper than a cathedral would be entitled to. An acolyte, beautifully dressed, permitted them to handle the curtains, as some sacristan might have permitted the toe of a relic to be kissed. "Exquisite," he breathed. "From Brocklehurst."

Brocklehurst was yet another lordly house sold up, but Joanna was not impressed. She asked as bluntly as her mother might have done: "What do you want for them?"

The acolyte sighed. "I don't know that you can have them at all. Mrs. Lomax Mencken may be taking them back to Detroit."

"Then that's that," said Joanna, turning to go.

"There's just a possibility," the acolyte said. . . .

When she had bought the curtains, Joanna took Shrubb to drink coffee in Bond Street. She said: "I wanted those curtains. They'll do for the shop window. But I also wanted you to smell the atmosphere of a place like that." More diffidently she added: "I hope you noticed how that young man was dressed?"

Shrubb asked, naturally enough: "What's that got to do with me?"

She told him. She expounded the whole scheme: decoration principally, at which he was an expert—"and you'd better see that you always have good workmen on tap"—but lovely things to be in the shop as a reminder that homes could be not only decorated but, if necessary, furnished as well.

"You've got the key," she said. "I don't want to see the place again until this day fortnight. That's when we open. What's your bank?"

Shrubb seemed surprised at the question. He said he hadn't a bank and never had had one.

"Then you'd better open an account at once and let me know where, so that your salary can be paid into it weekly."

Shrubb went back alone to the shop, feeling that he had never known Joanna before, as indeed he hadn't. He sat on the bare boards and looked about him. A good cornice. Some nice moulding in the ceiling. Yes, something could be made of the place. He took out a notebook and began to make notes and drawings and to see colours. When he stood up he reached for his stick. His leg was giving him hell, and he thought sadly of the acolyte.

10

It was another May morning, a year later. Dick Hudson might have been going to Ascot or the Royal garden party at Buckingham Palace. All that he wore he had worn on the stage; and now he was wearing it in the public streets with none of the shrinking and the shame that he had felt when he wore a stage outfit for a walk down Manningham Lane with Chris so many years ago. He was thinking so intensely of Chris that he was unaware of the grey topper, the tailed coat, the silvery tie and the white carnation. The years had dealt well with him. He carried his six-foot odd with dignity, remembering not that he was The Great Hudson but that he was the father of a barrister.

That walk with Chris down Manningham Lane was very present in his mind as he walked through his leafy blossomed suburb under the blue sky. Then and now. It was then that he had made up his mind to do something about Chris, and now it was done. In the Inner Temple, at the foot of a stairway, among many small brass plates there was one which read Mr. Christopher Hudson. That was what he was going to see, and that was why he was dressed up for a holiday. He would look at that plate with more emotion than had filled him when he looked for the first time at a bill with his name at the top: The Great Hudson. This was the end of something to which he had set his hand so long ago; but for Chris of course it was only a beginning. His thoughts flew and sang like the birds in the flowering cherries: Mr. Christopher Hudson, K.C. Mr. Justice Hudson. Well, you never knew. If he could get to the top, starting from nowt, why shouldn't Chris, with every advantage that money could buy?

Mind you, his self-communing went, admitting reluctantly a doubtful note, Chris wasn't perfect. He would have liked the lad to be a bit more—well, friendly like. Still, there it was. You paid to make your children better than you were, and they became better, and if somehow they gave you a feeling that you weren't in their class, that was a bit of the rough that you had to take with the smooth. After all, Chris *was* better. No argument about that. Still, a chap like him, getting on in years, would have liked a bit of company now and then, but Chris had kept to himself, burrowed into the four corners of his own room, and when he went out never had a word to say about what he had been up to.

And now this flat. Breakfast-time a month ago. Chris sitting there reading *The Times*, which somehow seemed always a reproof to Dick for reading the *Daily Mail*. *The Times* carefully folded and put into the brief-case on the table at Chris's elbow.

"Father, I wonder if you know how much I appreciate all you've done for me?"

"Why, dammit, Chris, you've got nothing to thank me for. It's been a sort of self-indulgence like."

"It's very good of you to look at it in that way. But everybody wouldn't, you know. George Cording—that's a young barrister I know—tells me his father's kept most careful accounts of every penny spent on George's education—school, university, and while he's been eating his dinners. Now the bill has been handed to George."

Dick looked outraged. "Well, I call that a bit thick."

"I was sure you'd see it like that. Not that George intends to pay a penny. To begin with, there's the Statute of Limitations so far as the school money goes, and as for the rest, there's no contract. The

332

old man's done it all off his own bat and must stand the consequences."

"I don't like the sound of that, Chris—stand the consequences. It sounds like as if doing what you can for your boy is a mistake after all, and that you'll regret it because there was nothing in it for you."

"I know that's how *you* look at it, and sometimes I've felt I could kick myself for taking it all for granted. But I don't any more. I assure you that I understand the way you've sacrificed yourself. That's what makes me feel such a dead-weight in continuing to ask for your help."

Dick lit his pipe and said: "Well, lad, you won't be doing that much longer. Your plate's going up, and once you start to practise you'll go ahead like a house on fire, never fear. Meantime, you've got a good home here. As good as I can make it, anyway," he said humbly.

Chris got up and tucked his brief-case under his arm. "I was rather thinking," he said, "of setting up a little place of my own. As you say, I'll be paying for it myself before long, and of course I shan't bother with it at all if you find the financial side the least bit inconvenient."

Dick was surprised and hurt. For a moment, of which he felt ashamed, he wondered whether the conversation had led him up the garden path. He dismissed the thought and said: "Aren't you comfortable here, Chris?"

"If comfort were the only thing, I should thank God for it," Chris said, looking devoutly at his father through his thick lenses. "But there's work. I want the feeling of being on the spot. I've been offered a little place on a top floor in Chancery Lane. A cupboard and a bathroom is about all it comes to. But you see, I could nip to and from the Temple in no time. Convenient when there's work to take home. The rent's a flea-bite, but alas!" he added, allowing himself a heavy humour, "I've no fleas of my own."

The remark tricked the boy's father back into a laugh. "You should have been on tour with me in the old days," he said. "In Ackers Street in Manchester they weren't fleas. They were man-eating tigers. Well, we'll see what can be done, Chris. You're ready for launching, lad, and we won't spoil the ship for a ha'porth of tar. But I'll be lonely."

"That's the devil of it," Chris conceded, looking sorrowful. "I wish there was another way out."

But now that the point was gained he didn't delay. It was always like that, Dick thought, standing at the window and watching Chris go down the garden path: dark overcoat, striped trousers, black felt hat, dispatch-case, rolled umbrella. He would have liked Chris to say some week-end: "What about taking a train into the country, Dad, and having a good walk?" or, some night: "Let's go out to dinner." But no; that never happened; and, of course, he said to himself, it was a bit romantic-like to wish for things like that.

Chris had moved into his flat without delay. The man who had rented it before him was going abroad and wanted to sell the furniture. "Just a few worthless sticks," Chris explained. "I can have the lot for a hundred and fifty pounds. Another flea-bite. I wouldn't inflict it on you if it wasn't so ridiculously small. As for my professional expenses, I'm keeping them down to the bone. It's decent of Farrington Roberts to let me share his chambers and his clerk. Believe me, a good clerk is a jewel."

Dick had no idea what a barrister's clerk was or what he did, and it was characteristic of Chris that he did not enlighten him. There was so little that he knew about Chris. It would have surprised him, for one thing, if he had heard a conversation in the flat in Chancery Lane. The young man who was clearing out, and was not going abroad but getting married, wanted to make the best bargain he could for his furniture and diffidently asked a hundred pounds. Chris laughed. "What! For this collection of Tottenham Court Road rubbish? I'll give you fifty, and you can count yourself lucky."

"But, damn it, Hudson, it cost me the best part of a hundred and fifty."

"I daresay it did. I suppose that was when you were demobilised after Waterloo. Look at the stuff!"

The young man looked at the stuff, and looked at Chris, and loathed him. "Well, I *was* demobilised in 1919 anyway," he said, "and that's more than you were."

Chris laughed easily. "I took care," he said, "to be born when I was a bit young for the last war and will be a bit old for the next one."

He got the furniture for seventy-five pounds.

On the whole, Dick Hudson hadn't much to be gay about as he walked in his fancy dress to inspect Chris's new plate, but he didn't know this, or at any rate resolutely covered up any whisper from little devil doubt that might be stirring in his heart.

And there it was. He had never been in the Inns of Court before and took his time, sauntering among the old red brick, admiring the opening leaves of plane trees, listening to the splash of a fountain, looking at the lawns and the flowers and the sun-burnished pigeons, and feeling reverent towards the men in wigs and gowns who now and then passed him on their way to cross over Fleet Street to the Law Courts. He was consciously delaying his moment. Chris was part of all this. He had made Chris part of all this. The very names at the foot of the stairways moved him romantically. Some of them he recognised: names that you saw every day in the newspapers. And one of them, it happened, was in the list that included also "Mr. Christopher Hudson." There it was. He could hardly believe it. Chris every day would be climbing the same stairway as Sir Henry Belton! Sir Henry might say: "Good morning, Hudson."

"Good morning, Sir Henry."

He stood there, leaning on his cane, dreaming among the cooing pigeons, no doubt at all in his heart now, and Chris, coming towards his staircase with a companion, saw him there, made an excuse, and retraced his steps. My God! That was a lucky escape. He might have run into him. He might have had to introduce him. In that fancy dress—looking like some fatuous toff in a musical comedy. He broke out in a sweat, as he had done years ago on Manningham Lane when he saw Anthony Bromwich approaching and knew there was no escape. He peeped cautiously out of an alley-way after a few moments, and saw that his father was gone. Then he ran quickly across the open pavement and bounded up the stairs two at a time.

11

The Elizabethan farmer who built the small house at Pinner was called Fenton, and Fentons had lived there, usefully and notelessly, for so long that the place was still called simply Fentons. On that May morning when Dick walked to the Inns of Court Anthony Fieldhouse was up early, thinking himself lucky to have such a place. The lawn was dewy, the small birds were singing, and the big ones making their cheerful clamour. Wistaria was blooming on the porch, and the roses would soon be out. He brought his small car round from the garage, and stood by it, waiting for Mrs. Wayland. He had kissed Lottie and the young Elizabeth who would presently, when the dew had dried, be brought out here and put down naked on a blanket to kick in the sunshine. The small morning rituals gave him pleasure. He sometimes wondered why they should—especially why the thought, the feeling, of Lottie filled his life. They were both rather undemonstrative, and they had drifted together rather than passionately flown into one another's arms. They knew how it had been between Joanna and William Scroop, and Anthony knew of Joe Morrison's stormy feeling for Joanna. Nothing of that sort had ever visited them, and Anthony would tell himself with a smile that there was a lot to be said for being a couple of tradespeople with a job to do and no time for nonsense.

But now his heart was lifted up by a morning like this and by the thought that Elizabeth, in an hour or two, would be kicking on the grass!

Mrs. Wayland came out and got into the car. Anthony took her, as usual, to Covent Garden, left her there, and drove to *L'Esculent*. She enjoyed this morning job. It reminded her of Paris and the Halles, and if that should seem small reason for enjoyment, for her life then had been sad and grey, there was at any rate the enjoyment of contrast. All, then, was strife and insecurity. Now it was not. She liked, when she had done her bargaining, to go to a small eating-house where French confectionery could be bought, and coffee was served in a percolator in the French way, and she would let herself go in a bit of French gossip with Madame who ran the place. It carried her on to eleven o'clock; and then, when she came out into the morning, the May sunshine had taken hold, heartening but not embarrassing like a midsummer grill, and she was tempted to take a little walk. She went East, and presently found herself in Fleet Street, and the thought of the river allured her. It was not the Seine, but it was something. She turned into the Temple to make a short cut, and she saw Chris Hudson and his companion. It was a long time since she had set eyes on that young man. Her news of him came through Anthony, who had told her of his reading for the Bar. She kept him in view, and saw him hesitate and withdraw. Then she saw Dick Hudson in his glory, leaning on his cane. It didn't need a sharp wit to read the situation, and Mrs. Wayland's wit was enlivened by her old dislike for Chris, which surged up and almost choked her with rage. She watched Dick walk away and Chris return, and when the boy had bounded up the stairs she went across and read his name on the plate there. She was almost glad that he had run so true to her prognosis.

She followed Dick and came up with him as he was reaching the Embankment. "Good morning, Mr. Hudson," she cried. "You look rather jaunty."

He was feeling lonely, and was pleased to meet her. He raised his grey topper with an air and bowed over her hand as he took it.

"There's reason to be," he said. "A grand day like this, and a great day in my life."

They braved the motor-cars and tramcars and crossed over to the river side. They were an odd-looking pair: he so festive, she in the rustling black that she wore as her business costume. They looked down at the sparkling water, and at the busy traffic of the bridges, and at a string of lighters piled high with esparto grass.

"Tell me about the great day," she said. "You look as if it's a wedding at least." She felt almost a tenderness for him. They belonged to the same stock. They had both come from hard life in industrial towns.

"Well, it's Chris," he said. "You remember Chris?"

Did she not! "Yes, I do."

"The lad's done very well. And we've got you to thank for some of that, you know."

She let it go, and Dick expounded the virtues and achievements of his son. They were walking towards Westminster. "Well, there it is," Dick said. "That first night when I brought him to your place in Bradford I was a bit vague like. I just wanted the best for him, but I didn't see far ahead. However, once I'd got him on the road he was no worry at all. He just went forward on his own. He knew what he was after, and now—well, there he is."

"And here you are."

"Ay, here I am, and I don't mind telling you that when a job like that's done, a man feels a bit loose-ended, a bit lonely."

"And sometimes, I should think, a bit disappointed."

He looked at her sharply. "Well," he agreed, "perhaps. But that's a man's own fault. You get into the way of thinking that you're building something up for yourself. You know. You kid yourself. You forget that while the boy's becoming a young man, you're becoming a bit of an old man. And the moment comes when you realise that you've got to get out of the light. That's the thing at last that you've got to give to your children. And it's the hardest of all to give."

Dick was surprised to find himself so eloquent, to have analysed his own thought, and to have found it bleak. "The fact is," he said, "he's set up a flat on his own. I was hoping he'd stay with me till he got married, if he ever did. And how's that lass of yours that I met once or twice? She went abroad to school. I never saw her after that."

"Oh, she's married now and has a daughter. She married young Anthony Fieldhouse."

"Don't know him."

"Oh, but you do, Mr. Hudson. He was Anthony Bromwich. You remember?"

"Of course I remember Anthony Bromwich, but I never heard of his changing his name. What's he doing now?"

Mrs. Wayland was shocked. That boy had known all this. He had been in and out of *L'Esculent*. He knew of the marriage; he knew of Anthony's change of name. What on earth sort of life had Mr. Hudson been living with him? No small talk. No family gossip. They were at Westminster Bridge, and she looked at Dick with anxious speculation. All dressed up, and no place to go. "You'll be telling me next," she said, "that you don't know that that woman who called herself Anthony's Aunt Jessie wasn't his aunt at all."

"Then who the heck was she?"

"I'll tell you what, Mr. Hudson. You'd better invite me to tea. What you need is a good gossip."

"That'll suit me fine." He handed her one of his cards. "I'm not on the telephone, but I'll stay in every tea-time till you come."

"You can make it to-day," she said. "Four o'clock. But for Heaven's sake change your coat and trousers before I come."

Dick called a taxi, drove her to *L'Esculent*, and then went home feeling lighter-hearted than he had done for a long time. Her tea-time prolonged itself to a three-hour visit, and at the end of it he was lighter-hearted still. They had had what he badly needed: a wallow in commonplace gossip. He had always thought of Mrs. Wayland as a superior sort of woman. Her fluent French, her charming little daughter, her well-run house in Megson Street: all had made him think her a lady who had come down in the world. They became very confidential. He learned of the factory in Nottingham, and of the drunken husband in Paris, and the desperate work to make both ends meet. And now he liked her all the more as a lady who had come up in the world. He swopped his life-story for hers. He learned for the first time that Florrie Finch was Anthony's mother and that she was married to Joe Morrison's father. They sat looking out into his garden patch, gay with a few flowering shrubs, and he was amazed that while he had dallied alone with Chris in this pleasant backwater so much had been happening to the people he once had known.

"And you mean to tell me, Mrs. Wayland," he said, "that Chris knew about all this?"

"About most of it, anyway."

She got up to go. "Well, it's been good to see you," she said. "It's

338

time you stopped being a hermit. You must come out and see us all at Pinner."

"Ay, I'd like that. Ah were fond of that lass of yours. A mother, eh? That beats the band."

She said practically: "Well, it tends to happen when people marry."

He went with her to the front door, and said he would see her as far as a nearby taxi rank; but as they reached the gate a taxi drew up and Chris got out. He said good evening civilly to Mrs. Wayland, and she nodded to him distantly as she detained the taxi and asked to be driven to the Baker Street station. Chris and his father entered the house.

"You staying to supper, Chris?"

"Oh, no. I'm dining with a man in an hour or so. I looked in to pick up a few books. I must say the last thing I expected to find here was Mrs. Wayland. Quite like old times."

"Ay, it was," Dick said with satisfaction.

"How on earth did she find you out?"

"Just an accident. I was taking a bit of a stroll and ran into her. I'd no idea she was in London."

"Well, I expect the idea will dawn on you now in all its beauty. She'll take a bit of shaking off."

Dick had followed Chris upstairs, and stood behind him as he rummaged on his bookshelves.

"What have you got against her, Chris?" he asked quietly.

"Well, in general terms," Chris said without turning, "I loathe her. Need I go into details?"

Dick said rather sharply: "You're a bit flippant, lad. I'm no lawyer, but I know that when you make a charge against anyone, you *do* go into details. If you're not prepared to do that, you should keep your mouth shut."

The little back room was darkening. The sharp tone surprised Chris, who turned and saw that his tall father's face was stern. This was something altogether new. Instantly, school, university and Inns of Court dropped off him. He was a small boy in a board-school yard, with bigger boys looking unfriendly. He said: "Sorry, Father. You're quite right about that. I should have merely said that I have a vague dislike of Mrs. Wayland. I have, you know. I suppose boys get that feeling towards people put in authority over them, and somehow in her case the feeling has persisted."

Dick said: "Yes, boys feel like that; but when a boy becomes a man he should have the sense to know that authority is something you've got to put up with. It was I who gave her that authority, and so in a sense it was my authority that was being exercised. I think she did a good job."

"Well," Chris said. "Let's agree on that. I'm prepared to believe my feelings are all wrong."

Dick was still rattled. The great pleasure of his long talk with Mrs. Wayland was on him, and he disliked the thought that the mere presence of Chris had thrown cold water on it. He said: "A man shouldn't be prepared to believe that his feelings are all wrong merely because someone's annoyed when he expresses them. He should believe they're wrong when they're shown to be wrong, and not a minute before."

Chris took courage to laugh and say: "Good lord, Father! You argue like a lawyer. It's you should have read for the Bar." He put a strap round his books, glanced at his wrist-watch, and said: "D'you mind if I bolt? I'm rather pushed for time."

He went, and Dick did not go down to see him out. He stood in the dusky room, annoyed, yet somehow oddly pleased with himself. He had stood up to Chris! That was something he hadn't done before, and he hadn't come off badly, either. And if he hadn't met Mrs. Wayland he could never have done it. An extraordinary woman, that. He remained there pondering for a long time. Talk about guts! Fancy getting out of that factory life, and defying her old woman, and fighting like the devil for existence in Paris, and bringing up that little girl so well! When he went down to supper he was still thinking of Mrs. Wayland rather than of Chris.

12

There was no reason why Joanna should go to the shop in Brook Street. It was well looked after without her. Mr. Shrubb and Mollie St. Mellons did all that was needed. Mollie St. Mellons was a decorative name, and Mollie was a decorative girl. She hadn't much to do, but someone had to be in the shop when Mr. Shrubb was out of it, engaged in consultation about a job or supervising the doing of one. So far, these occasions for his absence were few, but they were becoming more frequent, and Joanna had a feeling that the graph of this business would go up as certainly as the graph of *Vanguard* had gone down.

But all the same, Joanna went to the shop daily and punctually. There was no reason, she told herself, why Mrs. Halliwell should go daily to her office in Smurthwaite, but she did, and Joanna was more and more seeing her mother as someone whose precept and practice should be followed. She remembered saying to her mother long ago: "Why do you have to go to Smurthwaite every day?" and Mrs. Halliwell's answer: "There's nothing like the boss's eye. Thou God seest me."

And so, on a June morning in 1929 Joanna set out for Brook Street, rejoicing in the lovely weather and looking forward to reading Mr. Pordage's weekly letter about Sir Francis. It had come on the morning post together with one having the Paris post-mark, which she knew was from Joe Morrison.

"Good morning, Mollie."

"Good morning, Joanna."

Mollie was sitting in a Regency chair, reading *Crome Yellow*. She had blue-black eyes and bobbed black hair. She was wearing a bright yellow djibbah and goatskin sandals. An uncut chunk of emerald hung from her neck on a silver chain. She was a doctor's daughter from Acton, a pin-money girl, not trained to do anything in particular, but vivacious and quick in the uptake. She liked to think of herself as something she called modern. She tried to be up-to-date in her reading, but hadn't got beyond Aldous Huxley. Kafka had floored her. "Oh, not literally," she would say, she hoped daringly. Joanna valued her as *décor*.

"Any millionaires this morning, Mollie?"

"Not yet. But any moment, I should think."

"You *will* rise from that chair, won't you, when you see them through the glass? And pick up *The Connoisseur* instead of *Crome Yellow*?"

She went into the cubby-hole behind the shop, read the morning mail, which consisted of one letter, and made up the accounts which didn't take her long. It was comforting that Mr. Shrubb was out interviewing a possible client: a nice job if he could pull it off.

It was rather dark in the cubby-hole, even on a midsummer day, but it was comfortable enough. The room was carpeted and contained a roll-top desk (because there was one in The Office at Throstle's Nest), a filing-cabinet, a desk chair, and an easy chair. She sat in the easy chair and read Septimus's letter first.

"My dear Joanna.—This from Pordage, on a deck-chair by his singing stream, unto you, benighted Babylonian. Your recent visit for the fifth birthday of Sir Francis Scroop, Bart., may seem to you to have been, for me, an occasion to display a monstrous incivility. Not once did I permit Me to stray within the mossy security of

Throstle's Nest. But this was because Me's heart was shaking with fear, yet valiant. Fearful lest you might, in maternal zeal, find yourself unable to resist a decision to take the minute Bartlet to London; valiant because, by lurking within my own tent, I refused to influence you. Once, you called upon me; but I saw you coming from afar and instructed my housekeeper to say, as you will remember, that I was gone on a mission to Afghanistan. You took the hint.

"Of course, the time will come when Mr. Bartlet must be separated from his Pordage, but you have held your hand for the moment and dealt me only the minor blow of leaving an Iceland pony for the boy's delight. He has decided to call it Pordage, for it is shaggy and it ambles, and, despite its youth, has an appearance of venerable age. For the moment, the pony has diverted the boy's mind from our far-flung railway network which now embraces all the paddock. It is a pity, because I had just imported two new hands for Clapham Junction Station: Bill Boffin, who is married, rather worried, and has seven children; and Bert Barnes, a younger fellow, living with his widowed mother in Islington, and rather rough on luggage. Only last week, he mislaid a seal which was on its way to a circus. Boffin found it at last, looking over the edge of a water-tank, near Platform No. 6. However, at the moment, Mr. Bartlet is Colonel Cody, riding roughshod over Pawnees and Crees and things of that sort. I feel that at any moment my housekeeper may exclaim with temperate surprise: 'Lawks, Mr. Pordage! Wherever is your scalp?' To which I shall reply, off-hand: 'Oh, is it gone? I suppose Cody has taken it to hang on his belt.'

"In between these exciting adventures, we find time for the alphabet. No slates and scratchy pencils. Not for Pordage! I am starting him off with a goose-quill, and he progresses. He can write Cat, but has progressed no farther into the production of literature. But could Keats write Cat at five years and one week? I doubt it. Still, I must not unduly fire your hopes. There is, after all, a bit of intervening territory between Cat and *Lamia*. Still, Pordage is at hand. The approach of Cody, glimpsed from the corner of an eye, compels him to inscribe himself ever, my dear and beautiful lady, your devoted Septimus."

Joanna smiled. She was sorry not to have seen the old man, not to have had the chance to thank him for the warm affection that gave security to Francis's days. There was a nurse, but she seemed to have nothing to do save walk with Francis to Easter How in the morning and leave him there. As often as not, he ate his midday meal with Septimus. Mrs. Toplis was now snatching her eternal rest.

Her successor was a colourless woman who had, in Septimus's eye, only one virtue: she could cook food that a child would eat. "I've had six, and he'll get what I gave them, baronet or no baronet. Seems to me a baronet's guts works much the same as other folks'."

Joanna tucked the letter into the Pordage dossier, and took up Joe Morrison's. She did not hurry to open it. Joe's letters were few. He had gone off, after that midnight walk along Baker Street, intending not to write at all, but this resolve was beyond the strength of keeping. He wrote about once a month, so formally that Joanna could almost hear him gritting his teeth to prevent words of affection from stealing in. It was a moment of glib disregard for old formalities. A man was calling you by your Christian name before he knew your surname, and a kiss on greeting was an empty gesture. And so Joanna was the more amused that all Joe's letters ended "Sincerely yours, Joseph Morrison." She hadn't known that his name was Joseph: for ought she knew, he had been christened Joe, and certainly his stuff in *The Banner* was signed "Joe Morrison," which seemed to give it a man-to-man touch. And Joe's first book, *France Now*, had Joe Morrison on the title-page. She had read the copy he sent her with disquiet, for France now, if Joe was right, was a glittering coach that would turn into a rotten pumpkin on the midnight stroke of doom. The book had caused a certain amount of excited comment, and most people said that Joe was talking through his hat. She always answered his letters, calling him "Dear Joe" and trying to find a middle way between his hurt *farouche* stand-offishness and a familiarity that might put the wrong idea into his impetuous red head—that head which never wore a hat, anyhow, for him to talk through or for any other purpose. She signed herself, "as ever, Joanna."

She opened the letter.

"Dear Lady Scroop.—*The Banner* has sent me my packing-up orders. I am to report back to London as soon as a substitute arrives here. The trouble is *France Now*. It has made me *persona non grata* in news-gathering quarters, and if some of the stuffed shirts on the Quai d'Orsay had their way my head would roll. Why in hell do people go on living in the past and guzzling on *clichés*? You still hear them quote that old ruffian Dr. Johnson: 'When a man is tired of London, he is tired of life.' I ask you! Even Johnson wouldn't believe it to-day, but people still trot it out. And Manchester is still someone or other's 'noble town,' and France is du Bellay's *'mère des arts, des armes et des lois.'* Well, we shall see.

"So far as my career with *The Banner* goes, this has done me no harm. Lord Dunkerley was passing through Paris recently, and made one of those unexpected descents on the office that set everybody dithering. However, he was all right with me. He took me out to dinner, congratulated me on my work for the paper, and said he thought *France Now* was sound in the main. 'In the main,' of course, was thrown in to make me believe that he knows more about the matter than I do (which he doesn't), and to prevent me from thinking that he wholly approves of me (which I hope he does, but his policy is never to say so). One senses rather than knows which way the Dunkerley wind is blowing, and I imagine it's favourable to me at the moment. After he had returned to London came the interesting news that our second man in the Berlin office has been made chief, and the chief has been recalled to London to take over the foreign editorship. That leaves a niche in Berlin, and if I read things aright I'm to be popped into it. That would suit me down to the ground, because what may happen in that country will decide the fate of Europe, and possibly of Asia, for a long time to come. But if you ask me what may happen, I can only say 'Anything, and I hope I'll be there to see it.' And that's all for the moment. Sincerely yours, Joseph Morrison."

She sat there with the letter in her hand and a sense of urgency in her heart. Joe somehow always conveyed this sense. She had been aware of it at the dance in Smurthwaite, but then it was latent. In his letters from Paris it was on the surface. One had the feeling of a petrel gazing down from a stormy sky into a stormy sea, aware, at that point of vantage, of disaster unseen from the comfortable shore. The very reticence of this letter, on the personal side, disturbed her. It was as though a dynamic force for a moment disregarded her because aware of being able, when the time came, to deal with her and her hesitations. She went to her desk and wrote at once: "Dear Joe.—I'm so glad that the almighty Dunkerley approves of you and that there is a chance of your being moved to a town where you want to be. I'm not posting this to Paris because you may have left before it gets there. It is just to say that I'm free for luncheon almost every day, being quite anti, or at any rate un, social now that I have a job to do. Ring me up, and let's eat together before you fly away again to the Continent. As ever, Joanna."

She addressed it to *The Banner* office, and marked it "To await arrival." She sent Mollie St. Mellons to post it at once. "I'll wait in for Mr. Shrubb," she said. "Go on to your lunch."

A matter of business had taken Rudolph Schwann into the West End, and, being there, he had been tempted by the fine day to linger. Suddenly he remembered the shop in Brook Street, and, having strolled by the window to make sure that Joanna was within, he went on to a florist's and bought a dozen deep red, almost black, carnations. He took these to the shop and presented them to Joanna with a bow.

Joanna was rather taken aback. She had not expected to see Mr. Schwann again, but his own lack of embarrassment put her at ease. Watching her arrange the flowers in a tall cut-glass vase, he said: "I hope these are much too late to be a good-luck offering. Surely already the luck is with you?"

She said: "Well, Mr. Schwann, we're working hard, and I think we shall make the place pay. I don't know whether luck comes into that?"

"Oh, yes," he said. "Plenty of people work very hard indeed, and all the same life does not smile at them. Luck is something else."

She thought of Scroop and *Vanguard*. Mr. Schwann was right. But what was she to do with him? What did he want? Evidently he had not come in as a client. Then a taxi-cab containing Mr. Shrubb stopped at the door. A neat Mr. Shrubb, wearing a grey lounge suit and a Guards' tie, got out, and seeing Joanna engaged, passed through to the small office at the back. As he went, he gave her a thumbs-up sign, which meant he had landed the job he had been angling for. It was the biggest job yet, and she felt enormously heartened and justified. She wanted to do something to celebrate it, and she said rather impetuously to Schwann: "Well, since you're on my territory and it's nearly one o'clock, may I offer you lunch?"

Mr. Schwann protested. A cab would have him back in Fleet Street in ten minutes. He didn't eat much at midday. He had only looked in, being in those parts, to wish her good-day.

"Rather expensively," she said, looking at the carnations and knowing what they cost in that part of London. "It was sweet of you, Mr. Schwann."

He didn't need much persuading. She had never talked to him before except on business matters, and they hadn't amounted to much. She found him a lively and intelligent companion, agreeably free of the flirtatious on-coming attitude that, as a handsome rich woman, she met too often and detested. He was soon telling her, with an affection that she liked, of his brother's family in Germany, and of his visits to them, and of his fears for them, because they were Jews.

She was surprised by this. "Surely, Mr. Schwann," she said, "that sort of nonsense doesn't still go on in the world?"

He looked at her, as if pitying her innocence. "Nonsense? It was not nonsense that drove my father out of Germany. And Germany now is a very unsettled country. Never since the war has there been stability. And you may see from history that in a time of instability the Jews do not do well. Things go wrong. What is the cause of that? The Jews. And so, if they are rich you rob them. If they are poor, you kick them. It is simple."

He sat with his quiet hands on the table. He said: "My brother's children are very diluted Jews. He himself is half English, his wife is half French, and the children are very fair, with blue eyes."

Then he apologised for having made his conversation so personal and so gloomy. "And on such a day! A day that must be joyous to you. I know, for I saw the light-heartedness of your young assistant, and his happy signals."

There is not much, she thought, that Mr. Schwann misses. "Please don't apologise," she said. "There is a cult of conversation about nothing, and I get very tired of it. As it happens, I received a letter from a friend this morning who takes as grave a view of things as you do yourself. I expect you know him—or know his name, anyway. He writes in *The Banner*. Joe Morrison."

Schwann said that he knew Joe Morrison's journalism and had read *France Now*, which he thought to be near to the truth.

"Joe thinks," Joanna told him, "that he may be going to Berlin soon. He'll welcome the change, for his name seems to be mud in Paris."

"Then some day, if he gets about a bit, he may meet my brother and his family. It will perhaps be fatal for him, for Magda is very beautiful and very good. She is eighteen."

He smiled at the playful thought, and Joanna said: "Possibly, but I'm afraid he has a fixation on an English girl."

"Then she should realise her good luck and marry him soon, for he is an exceptional person, if his work is anything to go by. And young men loose in foreign parts can't be counted on to maintain their homeland fixations."

He smiled again, then looked grave, and said: "Still, I shouldn't advise entanglements in Germany just now."

Joe rang up the next morning while she was having breakfast. "Look. I'll be occupied with Dunkerley all day. I can lunch with you to-morrow. Where do we eat?"

After the conversation with Schwann she had given that matter much thought. "Here," she said. "*Chez moi.*"

Joe said: "I thought I wasn't allowed over the doorstep? Wouldn't you feel safer if we set up a trestle table in Trafalgar Square? I'll provide a large umbrella to prevent any unpleasantness from the pigeons."

"Don't rankle, Joe. Don't be tiresome."

"And we could lay a sword along the trestle table between us. Between courses, I could read *Holy Living and Holy Dying*—d'you know it? Awfully good—and you could do some knitting. No danger of insidious conversation."

"Chuck it, Joe."

"And the buses are so handy there. After the meal you could hop on one going west, and I'd go east. And never the twain shall meet."

"You're drunk."

"How wide do you think the table should be? I'm thinking of knees. Most dangerous things, knees. Four feet, do you?"

She said firmly: "Here. To-morrow. One o'clock. All right?"

"O.K."

It was to be a cold luncheon, and so she didn't have to be fiddling in the kitchen. The weather remained beautiful, and she went into Baker Street to give herself the pleasure of seeing him come along. There was no mistaking him, even though to his hatless red head was now added a forked red beard. His step was quick and eager, and girls, she noticed with complacency, turned to look at him. He didn't see her, and she entered the front door behind him, and called when he was half-way up to her flat: "Good morning, Joe!"

At once he ceased to be so emphatically a gamecock. He could be saucy on the telephone, but now, face to face, he was not so assured. He greeted her and stood aside, and she went ahead of him and unlocked the door. When he came in, she shut the door and gave him a kiss. She had never done this before, and he looked so surprised that she started back and said: "Good lord! You're not Joe Morrison, are you?"

"I am."

"Oh, do forgive me. I thought you were someone who'd crashed the party. You know modern manners? One always kisses a stranger, but never someone one knows, lest it be misunderstood."

"I suppose the beard misled you."

"Yes. If you were a bit taller you'd be like Bernard Shaw in his offensive youth. Do sit down. I'm afraid this will be an unadventurous meal. I'm not a cook like Anthony. He can ponder over a sirloin as lesser men do over a sonnet."

There was cold chicken and salad and a bottle of hock. When they had sat down Joe said: "I don't want to talk about sirloins or sonnets. There are only two things that interest me at the moment: you and me. Which shall it be?"

It struck her that there was a third subject: you *and* me: but she didn't say so. She said: "Tell me about you, Joe. Are you going to Berlin?"

"No. My guess was wrong. I'm going to Rome."

"Are you disappointed?"

"Well, yes and no. I should have preferred Berlin, but if I went there it would be to play second fiddle. In Rome I shall be chief. And Berlin will come. It's a matter of waiting."

"You've had a lot of practice at waiting, Joe."

He looked at her keenly, wondering whether the words were a challenge, whether he should take it up. He let it go. He said: "I know in my bones that the real boil-over in Europe will come in Germany, and that if the boil-over is in the direction of France, France will be like a basket of rotten pears in front of a steamroller. That's why I want to be there. But there's plenty to be going on with in Italy. That fat frog Mussolini is blowing himself up so much that one of these days it'll be someone's moral duty to puncture him."

She removed the plates and put a cold fruit pie and cream on to the table. Meanwhile she watched Joe closely. His young face, aged a bit by the beard, was so set and fierce that she thought of some fanatical *conquistador* let loose in Mexico or Peru. Was he thinking about her at all?

"You take your moral duty very seriously, don't you, Joe?"

"You can put it that way if you like. When I was a schoolboy with Anthony, the war was on. Every day the names of the dead were read out. That went on and on for years. It seems to have done something to me."

"But that's all over and done with."

"Oh, my God!" he said, pushing his plate away with an impatient gesture, which made her notice his fine thin hands. "Don't you realise that *nothing* is *ever* over and done with? Every damn-fool

348

political party there ever was has its 'programme' for settling the world's problems. But they're never settled and never will be. Government, as I see it, should be immovable principle and unending fluid improvisation. And foresight. But, my God—foresight! You have only to direct their eyes a few yards ahead, and they bay at you like a pack of hounds."

She guessed that he resented some of the reviews of *France Now* and his cold shouldering—virtually his expulsion—by the Quai d'Orsay.

"Eat your pudding," she said soothingly.

"All right. I suppose that's the answer. Eat your pudding."

"A man who can make a parable of a simple remark like that is far gone," she said with a smile.

He looked at his watch. "Well, this man will literally be far gone in a few moments. I told a taxi-man to be here at 2.10 and it's now 2.5. He's bringing my bag along with him and taking me to King's Cross. I'm catching the 2.30. Dunkerley has given me a week, and I'm spending it with my father. Thanks for placing the sword."

"What on earth do you mean, Joe?"

"Setting me off on my hobby-horse. I'm told that was the only way Mrs. Patrick Campbell could keep Bernard Shaw from rolling in the hay. The sound of his own voice could make him forget even his passion."

She was aware of disappointment. As she had pictured the occasion, the lunch was to be the fixed principle, and what happened after that would need unending fluid improvisation. She said: "I did hope there'd be time for a bit of *private* talk, Joe."

"Well, then—how's young Francis?"

"Flourishing, thank you."

"How's your mother?"

"Never mind my mother. Give me a kiss."

He kissed her awkwardly. "I'll write to you when I get to Rome," he said, making for the door.

She followed him and said: "Yes, and for heaven's sake don't write about Mussolini. There are other topics."

They were on the pavement, and he climbed into the taxi. He put his head through the window and said: "Thank you for the kiss, Lady Scroop."

The taximan gave her a wink and a thumbs-up signal, and she turned back to the stairway blushing.

She hurried up the last few steps because her telephone bell was ringing. It was Mrs. Wayland.

"Are you desperately busy to-day, Joanna?"

"No. I'm finished with the shop. I go there only in the mornings."

"Could you give me a cup of tea this afternoon and listen to a long story?"

It wasn't so long as all that. "Do you know Chris Hudson?" Mrs. Wayland asked.

"Not well. I've met him once or twice, and I've heard a good deal about him from Anthony. Of course, you must know him very well indeed. He grew up in your house, didn't he?"

"Yes. But I'm only using him to introduce something else. Did you ever meet his father?"

"Once. Long ago. I was at home on holiday and Mr. Hudson motored from Bradford. He brought Chris with him, and Lottie was there, too. I can't for the life of me remember what it was all about. I didn't see much of any of them except Lottie."

"Mr. Hudson was working in the theatre then," Mrs. Wayland explained. "He was quite a celebrated man, you know, in his own way. He had a dresser named Pordage, who was a brother of Mr. Septimus Pordage. That's what it was about. It was just a meeting between the brothers."

She seemed ill at ease, and Joanna was surprised at this rambling circumlocution from a woman usually concise. Mrs. Wayland said: "I thought perhaps you knew Chris's father a bit better than that."

"No. That was the only time I ever saw him, and I can't even remember what he looked like."

"There's nothing wrong with his looks. I should call him a handsome man. And I don't altogether like the idea of sharing that house with Anthony and Lottie at Pinner. Especially now there's Elizabeth. Young people should have a place of their own."

Light began to break in Joanna's mind. She noticed that Mrs. Wayland, who usually affected an almost peasant simplicity of dress, was smarter than she had ever seen her. She looked at her hat, and that clinched it. She said mischievously: "I'll tell you what. Let's call together on Mr. Hudson. Then I can say whether I approve of him for you."

Mrs. Wayland was too hardened by life to be capable of a blush, but her face softened and she smiled at Joanna. "Do you think I'm an old fool? That's what I'm afraid of—that people will think me an old fool. Not that I know many people, and not that I should care much what they thought anyway. I'm only fifty," she said simply, "and I don't suppose Dick is much older."

She looked at the younger woman thoughtfully and tenderly. "You've been in love," she said, "and I expect you will be again. So have I, when I was in Paris and about as old as you are now. It never came to anything but sorrow. All the same, I know what it is. And I know that this isn't it."

"Oh," said Joanna, trying to make it sound gay, "there's all sorts of ways of being in love."

"There are not," Mrs. Wayland said, "and you know it as well as I do. Cauliflowers in Covent Garden look to me like cauliflowers, not like fleecy lambs each curled up and asleep in a bit of green meadow. That's how I've seen them in the Halles. No, this isn't it."

Joanna poured some more tea. She didn't know what to say, and indeed what could she say? But she was touched by Mrs. Wayland's confidences.

"But this could be something else, good enough in its way," Mrs. Wayland said. "I've known Dick for many a year. All the time Chris was with me, he used to stay in my house whenever he was in Bradford. I became very fond of him. Glad though I was when Master Christopher went, I was sorry to think I wouldn't see Dick any more. And then I ran across him by accident the other day. Since then, I've seen him quite a lot."

"And he's asked you to marry him?"

"No. But I intend to see that he does. He needs someone to look after him. We shall get along very well in our middle-aged way."

Joanna said, not without admiration: "You talk like my mother."

"Why, has she got her eye on anyone?"

"No, and I don't think she's likely to have; but if she did she'd have her way."

Mrs. Wayland said with a laugh: "I'd better warn Mr. Pordage."

"Poor Mr. Pordage! I'm half in love with him myself. But that's how he is. No woman could find the other half. It would be too much like abducting a shabby old angel."

"Don't get Mr. Pordage wrong. He knows how he wants to live, and he lives that way. In his fashion, he can look after himself. But Dick can't. I could screw the neck of that son of his and rejoice to hear the click."

"Anthony doesn't like him."

"Does anybody? He's sucking on to his father like a leech, and at the same time shamefully neglecting him. Living in his own flat! What d'you think of that? With that house there for him to use. And Dick paying the rent of the flat!" She looked grim. "Master Christopher will have some surprises yet."

Joanna said, alarmed into wisdom: "No! Don't marry the father to revenge yourself on the son."

"All the time he was with me he was an unmannerly and insulting little brat."

"He once did me a great wrong, too. But I don't think he intended to. Anthony tells me he's a barrister now. Perhaps some experience of life will help him to mend his ways."

Mrs. Wayland got up to go. "Thank you for listening to me, Joanna," she said. "I wanted to be sure you wouldn't call me an old fool."

"I shall probably call you whatever you prove yourself to be," Joanna said. "Don't make me an accessory before the fact."

᭡ ᭡ ᭡ ᭡ ᭡ ᭡

CHAPTER 14

1

*I*t *was* odd, Anthony thought, to have your brother, or at any rate your half-brother, calling you "Sir." It made him feel more than his thirty-three years. There had been a lot of anxiety in the last few months and Lottie had taken to twitting him about the distinction that grey hair gave to his looks. In the train coming down to Longford he thought there had been plenty to get grey about. On his advice, the company which owned *L'Esculent* had sold up and bought premises in Piccadilly where *La Fine Bouche* was founded. There was one thing about it: he had started the new venture not as the enthusiastic amateur who had opened *L'Esculent*, but as a deeply experienced restaurateur who saw the matter less romantically but far more shrewdly. And now his anxiety was passing. He had carried a lot of the old *clientèle* with him: it looked as if the place would go.

What with *L'Esculent* and *La Fine Bouche*, it was a long time since he had taken a holiday or even permitted himself a few days off. Even when Aunt Jessie died a couple of years ago he had not gone to the funeral. But the news from Longford now was very grave. Three days ago his mother had been sitting at dinner with her husband and their son, young Harry Morrison, who was home from school for the summer holiday. They were discussing where they should go that year, though they all three knew well enough. They would go to Sleights, for which Harry's mother had a liking the boy did not understand. His father would motor off to the nearest golf course, and his mother would say: "Let's spend the day on the river." And they would do so, lolling about in a boat, sometimes he pulling, and sometimes she; and they would get out and lie in the sun on the bank and open a luncheon hamper. While they were talking the matter over at dinner

Harry was sure that this year would be like any other, but it wasn't, for his mother, gay and excited by the prospect, as she always was, with no warning at all suddenly said "Oh dear!" and slipped from her chair on to the floor. That was three days ago. She had not left that room. A couch was made up there, and she had lain on it without speaking a word. Mr. Morrison had rung up Anthony at once, and now he was on the way. There was no hope.

It was August of 1933, and in the railway carriage the heat was intense. He sat with his coat thrown up on to the rack, his sleeves rolled up, unable to read, unable to think constructively, unable to do much save experience a sense of wonder that his mother's forthcoming death left him sad, as the thought of any death would do, but no more. He knew of those annual holidays at Sleights, and he realised their significance; and he sometimes wondered whether there had been a lack in young Harry's life through his playing on those and other occasions an understudy's part without ever knowing it. He had no doubt whatever that it was he who was with her then, and that, worshipfully though Joe's father had surrounded her life, she had never forgotten that her grand campaign for the completeness of a mother-son relationship had failed. He was old enough now to realise what plotting and scheming there had been, how near to the reefs of disaster she had sailed; old enough, too, to guess that if he knew who his father was he might have the key to the matter. She had allowed him to know many things, but never that. As for him, he had seen her in boyhood as a radiant and beautiful lady, and he had been shy and diffident with her. In young manhood, when he knew she was his mother and he lived with her, it was too late. He had no memories of being in revolt, of crying and kicking in opposition to her, and then of feeling the loneliness of the separation this brought, and then the happiness of giving in and lying on her breast and sleeping there with the broken world fitting its bits together again in wholeness and peace. He had known the lack, and she had known it, and she had found Joe's father and made what she could of that.

And so, approaching Longford, he wondered whether he was an exceptionally callous person; but he couldn't believe it. For the very sight—and now the very thought—of his six-year-old Elizabeth and of Lottie kissing her cut knee or comforting her if she woke up frightened in the dark could make his heart swell with tenderness. No, it wasn't that. It was simply that there couldn't be love at first sight between a mother and son. There must be the growing up, the tension and the struggle, the relapsing into peace, and all this going on and on. And there had been none of it. She had never slapped him, as he had once slapped Elizabeth because she had picked up a sickle that had carelessly been left lying about and had wantonly slashed with it at a rose bush. She had not cried. She had looked at him with a face of surprise and utter misery. It was he who had cried, hiding himself behind the toolshed. And there Elizabeth had come to him and given him shyly one of the damaged roses, and he had caught her up in his arms, and carried her about the garden, singing

Elizabeth is a sad slut, nor heeds what we have taught her;
I wonder any man alive will ever rear a daughter!

And so he felt only grey and sad, incompetent to deal with this young half-brother Harry, who was thirteen, and who met him at the station with the announcement: "Our mother died this morning, sir."

2

Harry was at the school where Anthony and Joe had spent their young years together on wretched wartime food and in the wretched wartime atmosphere. The boy was wearing the same sort of blazer that they had worn then, but nothing about him reminded Anthony of the young blue-eyed pugnacious Joe. Harry was slight, thin and dark, with rather long silky hair. His manners were formal: he had held out his hand at once to his mature half-brother.

"My father will be glad to see you," he said.

Our mother—my father. It must be difficult for him, Anthony thought. I must seem an odd hybrid. As they walked down the long main street he clutched at the school as a link, and he asked about the head-master and the form-masters he had known. They all seemed to be gone, and his questions only deepened his sense of young Harry as a creature of another world.

The boy said, with what seemed startling inconsequence: "We shall have our holiday after all. I thought this would put an end to it, but my father says we'd better get away."

Anthony said: "Well, that's not a bad idea, Harry. I should like to take a holiday myself, but I'm afraid it'll be impossible this year."

"I suppose that's because of your new restaurant. My father"—again that proud possessive pronoun—"my father's been telling me about that. Don't you find it rather an odd way to earn a living? I should get sick of watching people over-eat all the time."

"Oh, they don't necessarily *over*-eat. And I rather like the job. One sees a lot of famous men and beautiful women and all sorts of odd types. I'm never bored."

"But surely, sir, you would see all sorts of people if you were, say, a doctor? And you'd feel you were doing a job that was worth while."

Anthony was amused rather than annoyed by the grave young moralist. A bit of a prig? If so, where on earth did that come from? Certainly not from Florrie Finch or Joe's father. "What are *you* going to be when you grow up?" he asked.

Harry said: "It's surprising how many people ask a boy that. It seems just a conversational gambit."

"A thousand apologies."

"In this changing world it's almost impossible to answer such a question. What I'd *like* to be is another matter."

"And what's that, Harry?"

"Well, either a millionaire with masses of money, or a priest without a penny."

They walked on in silence for a while; then Anthony said: "Well, I hope you'll have a good holiday. Where are you going to?"

"The only thing decided so far is that it's not to be Sleights. I rather insisted on that. Apart from that, I don't much mind. When there's just the two of us, my father can't go off all day and leave me alone. It'll be a marvellous chance for us to get to know one another."

They reached the house where, Anthony saw at once, the blinds were down in the room where he knew his mother lay. On the doorstep Harry said: "Well, we part for the moment; but I hope the chance will come for us to get together and have a good long talk."

"I shall be delighted, Harry. You must try to buy me or preach me out of my evil way of life."

"Oh, no," Harry said. "Let's leave personalities out of it and talk about principles."

"Right. Let's do that. It sounds jolly."

3

In the hall, the boy turned abruptly into the sitting-room on the left, and Anthony went into the dining-room on the right. Mr. Morrison was sitting on a hard Sheraton chair by the bed, his head in his hands. Seeing Anthony come in, he got up, wrung his hand with a desperate agony and went out without a word.

The room was in a green twilight, for the lowered blind was green. What moved Anthony was that she was lying there, in the dining-room. In a bedroom the impression would not have been so deep, for in a bedroom one lies down daily to a little death. But here, where a grandfather clock was ticking loudly in a corner, and there was a wooden bowl of fruit on the sideboard, and the chairs and the table belonged to the daily festivity of eating, here amid the vivid paraphernalia of living it was shocking to see her lying dead.

He stood looking down at her face. The stroke had pulled it askew, leaving open one eye that looked at him—that *seemed* to look at him—with an intent regard. Something in that petrified look so betrayed his memory of her beauty that almost in desperation his mind searched backward for her as she had been; and at that moment the clock in the corner struck the hour of four. As the notes fell into the hot hush and the pale green light, his mind rushed back. He was the boy Septimus had taken to Sleights, and he was standing at his bedroom window and saw her cross the lawn and sit down to tea at a little table. He recognised her as Mrs. Freilinghausen, and he walked down to the quiet hall, full of tree-greenness and summer heat, and as he stood there the grandfather clock on the stairs struck four. Then he went out and introduced himself to her.

And now, as if time had come full circle, the four strokes that had rung for their meeting tolled for their good-bye.

His eyes were hot with tears that would not flow. He looked up from the face that one blow had turned from beauty to horror; and he saw red roses in a vase on the mantelpiece. He remembered the waiter who had wanted to sweep away the rose-petals that had fallen on to her table. "Leave them there," she said. "I like them." Later she said to him: "Now bring me a red rose," and that night she had worn it on the white dress which he remembered shimmering in the darkness of the garden.

So now he took a red rose from the vase. There were thorns on the stem, and he snicked them off with his finger as though they might hurt her. He placed the rose between her calm hands and knelt down with his head bowed over them. He said: "Forgive me. Forgive me." And he hated young Harry because he knew he had not loved her; and he hated himself and wished that he were at home where his love could freely flow. For even now, even now, he told himself, here it could not flow. His tears, yes. But not his love.

4

It was towards a midsummer sunset when he got out of the train at Pinner, glad that it was over, glad that he had escaped a discussion of principles with Harry, glad to be back. He liked walking up the main street of the village, even though the plate glass of multiple shops was ousting the old façades. A good deal was left. The church pleased him. He liked to remember that it was there when Yeoman Fenton built Fentons, and he liked to picture Master and Dame Fenton, in their Elizabethan rig, strolling down to morning service and joining the excited company in the churchyard, who were discussing whether the rumour could be true that the invincible Armada had been cut to pieces. And, more than this, he liked to think that in five minutes now he would be kissing Lottie and hurrying on tiptoe to peep into Elizabeth's room. But that night he didn't have to tiptoe or to peep. Elizabeth was in the garden, alone.

The sky was full of sunset, calm and windless. His few tall trees, elm and lime, hadn't a moving leaf, and the limes were in flower, pouring out a fragrance that mingled with the scent of roses. Elizabeth was crouching over a flower-bed, industriously opening the buds of poppies. The close-packed crinkled paper of the petals seemed to disappoint her. How did one enchant all this compressed material into the flourishing work of art that was a poppy?

He let the gate fall-to, and at the sound she was up at once, running towards him. She went straight into his arms, and he held her up, his hands under her armpits, and their faces smiled each into the other. And then he saw it for the first time as he was to see it again and again, coming and going in wayward flashes. Elizabeth's was the young image of the face he had seen in Ackroyd Park, and in the garden at Sleights, and in the strained days when they had made believe that after long vicissitudes they were happily at one. And how he loved Elizabeth! Warmth and comfort flowed into him at the thought. Perhaps this was how it was to be. Perhaps this was the way he was to give back her love.

He said: "You've been stealing the raspberries."

"No," she said.

"You lie, woman. Look at this."

A raspberry pip was sticking to her lip. He picked it off and showed it to her.

"It must have flewed there off the bush," she said. "How is my grandmother?"

She had been told only that he had gone to see her grandmother. "She has not been well," he said. "But I left her in a good sleep."

"Did you peep in at her and kiss her as you do me when I am having a good sleep?"

"I peeped in at her, but I did not kiss her."

"Were you afraid of waking her?"

"No. She was sleeping far too deeply for that. And why aren't you? It's long past your bedtime."

"Because I was a little madam and howled."

"Oh. Well, you'd better come in now and tell your mother you're sorry you were a nuisance, and ask her to put you to bed."

"I'll put her. You go in and see Lottie. Come along, darling."

Auntie Jo was *persona gratissima* and then some with Elizabeth. The child at once took her hand.

"Hallo, Joanna! What are you doing here?"

"Go in and see Lottie," she said.

But Lottie was coming out, and when Joanna and the child were gone, he kissed her, and they walked on the warm grass, his arm around her, and then they sat on the white seat under the lime tree. "What a nice person Joanna is," he said. "How well she contrived that."

"Yes. I'm very lucky in my only friend and my only husband. Well, how did it go, darling? Not too bad?"

"Not too bad as death goes. I'm glad she had those years with Mr. Morrison. I'm sure they were happy ones."

"And how is young Harry?"

"A holy horror. Tell me about Elizabeth. How has she been behaving?"

"So, so. She knew you'd be back to-night, and raised Cain when I tried to put her to bed."

"I find that gratifying. She's becoming a proper little liar," he said with satisfaction. "There was raspberry juice all over her mouth, and she said she hadn't picked any."

"That sort of lying is easily cured."

"Tell me, O Solon."

"Don't forbid her to pick the raspberries."

"Good. We must try that on burglars. D'you know what I noticed to-night? She's the image of my mother."

"I've noticed that, too. It comes and goes."

They went on and on, and the small familiar talk soothed him. The sky went green and a star or two appeared. He said: "Darling, I feel real. I no longer have an aunt who isn't my aunt. I no longer have a father who doesn't exist. I no longer have a mother who was for too long a fairy godmother, not a native of the common world. For the first time, I'm just Anthony, on his own, with his own life to live. I like the feeling."

"You're not on your own," she said. "You've got encumbrances."

"If anyone else called you that, I'd want to knock his block off.

But you are privileged. My encumbrances . . . . Lottie . . . . Elizabeth . . . ."

She said: "And A. N. Other. Sex unknown."

"No!"

"All right. I'm only giving you my opinion. But it's a subject on which I have all the necessary information."

Presently Joanna came out and said: "I stayed till she was asleep. She didn't need long. Let's go in and have supper."

Anthony said: "Oh, Joanna! Lottie's going to have another baby!"

"I could have told you that," Joanna said. "She's been keeping it very quiet, but I've noticed what she's been knitting the last few days."

5

The next morning Anthony drove Joanna to town. She said: "I haven't seen that *Fine Bouche* of yours. Will you keep a table for three to-day, for dinner? I shall be bringing a couple of friends. You know one of them, I think—Mr. Rudolph Schwann?"

"Oh, yes. He used to come often to *L'Esculent*. I haven't seen him in the *Fine Bouche*."

"You'll see him to-day, with his German niece, Magda."

"You seem to know him well."

"Fairly well."

"How do you come to be a lady of leisure, spending three days at Pinner? I thought you went to your shop every day?"

"Well, the place is more or less on its feet. I still go there whenever I'm in town, but I'm taking a bit more freedom. If I want a long week-end with my mother, I motor up there without any pangs of conscience. And in September Francis will be going to a school in Kent. It'll be a bad idea to badger him, but I'll be about in case I find the temptation irresistible."

"How has he got on with Septimus?"

"Splendidly. He passed his entrance exam without any trouble. What bothers me is how Septimus will get on without him."

"There are the long holidays."

"Yes. But I expect I shall be taking Francis abroad mostly. It'll be an excuse for me to go myself. I'm getting stale and insular."

He looked at her sideways and laughed. "Stale? Does anyone ever tell you nowadays what a beautiful woman you are?"

"Yes."

"I should think so. It's quite a thrill for me to be driving you into town."

"That'll do. I shall complain to Lottie."

"Anyhow," he said, "according to Joe, there won't be much fun soon in going abroad. Did you read that new book of his, *Italy Now?*"

"Yes. Pretty gruesome. I wonder whether he's wise?"

"In what way?"

"Well, there he is now, in Berlin. And Berlin doesn't sound a nice place, does it?"

"Anything but."

"I'm afraid he'll run into trouble. He goes there with the reputation of those two books behind him. It's the reputation of a man who opens his mouth pretty widely about dirty work wherever he finds it."

He thought of Joe's passion for her, and wondered how things were between them. He said: "When Joe was last here, preparing for Berlin, I was up to the eyes in my move to *La Fine Bouche*. I hadn't time to see much of him. Did you?"

"Not a lot. I see more of Mr. Schwann."

He gave a whistle so full of meaning that she was deeply annoyed. "Anthony, if it didn't involve the risk of an accident, I should act like a fishwife and slap your face."

He spared her a look, despite the traffic crossing, and saw that she meant it. He was horrified. He could think of nothing to say except: "Sorry, Joanna. I take that back."

They were in the thick of the town's traffic. She said: "It's a nuisance for you to take me to Baker Street. Drop me here and go straight on to Piccadilly. I'll pick up a taxi."

"Oh, nonsense. It won't cost me five minutes."

"Please Anthony!" It was imperious, and he drew in to the curb. He waited till she was in the taxi, then drove away. Joanna gave the taxi-driver Mr. Schwann's address in Berkeley Square. She had not intended to, but her annoyance with Anthony made her change her mind. She stopped on the way to buy roses for Magda. The poor child! She seemed lost. It would be a pleasant welcoming gesture, she told herself, seeking to excuse her too early call.

Mr. Schwann's man Coster said that his master and Miss Magda were already away. "They are spending the whole day on the river, my lady. A lovely day for it."

My lady got into another taxi-cab, and went on to Baker Street. Half an hour later she was at the shop, and, with the briefest greeting to Mollie St. Mellons, passed through to the office. "Deal with anything that comes along," she said. "I don't want to be disturbed."

Joe said to her, when he came home from Italy: "Don't let's eat in Anthony's place. I can't stand the sight of him. He looks so damned happy."

"Why shouldn't he?"

"Why should anybody? Believe me, my girl, this world is not a happy place, and the sooner some of you folks over here realise it the better."

She was aware of a deep change in him. They went to a little Greek restaurant where the food wasn't very good and the wine tasted of resin. She said: "Why did you bring me here, Joe? To mortify the flesh?"

He hesitated for a moment, then said: "Talking of mortifying the flesh, take a look at this."

He unbuttoned the cuff of his shirt sleeve, pulled the sleeve up, and held out his arm. A long red scar ran from the elbow half-way to the wrist. "Well, that's it," he said, quickly buttoning up again.

She was frightened. She knew he hadn't shown her that for fun. Her voice shook as she asked: "What happened?"

"Just five minutes," he said, "—no, hardly that, about two minutes—of European reality."

In Rome he had had a bedroom and a sitting-room. You turned into a narrow street and, off that, into one that was little more than a lane. Then you climbed two flights of stairs, and there you were. It was lovely in summer. You were on a hill. Mauve bunches of wistaria framed the window. The long view was of ancient mellowed roof-tiles; the near one of a courtyard with a cypress standing up alongside a carved well-head. But it wasn't lovely that night of last winter. The wind whizzed round corners like flights of frozen arrows. There was no one about. The streets were badly lighted, and the lane was not lighted at all. Neither was the staircase, but Joe carried a small torch. However, a torch doesn't help you to see round corners, and as soon as he reached the turn at the first landing a blow to the chin hurled him against the wall, and the torch fell from his hand. But he had had time to recognise his visitor—a villainous youth of the local Fascisti. They were locked in one another's arms for a minute, heaving and struggling with their breath coming hard. Then they broke free, and Joe felt the slash down his arm. He knew that it was not intended for his arm, and reached out, infuriated, trying to grasp his man. He found that he was clutching the wrist of the hand that held the knife. He managed to get his other hand on to the hilt and pulled it clear and threw it behind him. Now the fight was on even terms, and he was not afraid. This Jacopo whom he had recognised was as wiry as a bit of steel cable and as slippery as an oiled eel, but Joe was in better shape, not given, like Jacopo, to over-indulgence in wine and women. He managed to gather up his adversary's coat-front into a firm handful, and held him steady, though his arms were still flailing like the tentacles of an octopus. "Now, Jacopo," he said, "this one is for you." He crashed his right fist into the man's face. Then he picked him up from the floor, and said: "And this one is for the Duce." He planted his foot in the man's behind and heard him hurtling downstairs. He followed, and made his way to a discreet anti-Fascist doctor, who put ten stiches into his arm. When he returned Jacopo was still lying at the foot of the stairs. He stepped over him, and went up to bed. The next morning Jacopo was still lying at the foot of the stairs. His neck was broken. No one had bothered about him. It was better not to interfere in matters of that sort.

"That," Joe said, "*is* a bit of European reality."

Joanna looked at him aghast. "You killed him!"

"With no more pangs of conscience than I would have crushed a bug. Wouldn't you have done?"

She couldn't find an answer, and he said: "Anyway, it was suicide. I was the instrument he chose for his own destruction."

"You didn't mention it in your book."

"Why should I? It was too trivial. It's happening all the time. I didn't want it to be felt that I had a private axe to grind. That was just a personal matter between me and the Duce."

She said: "I'm glad you're going to Germany. I'll feel you're safer there."

He looked at her without a smile. She noticed that he didn't smile as much as he used to. "Well," he said, "that is on the knees of whatever gods may be. I wouldn't put much money on it."

He took up the wine bottle and made to refill her glass, but she put her hand over it. "Come," he said, "let us eat this remarkably sinewed goat, drink this vinegar-and-resin and be merry. For to-morrow we go to Germany."

"You always wanted to."

"I still do. Even Mussolini can't open the eyes of the people or the politicians in this country. Half of them think he's rather a good chap, curing the Italians of those care-free happy-go-lucky ways that are so repugnant to solid anglo-Saxon virtue and thrift. In fact, he's a blown-up megalomaniac butcher, who employs other people to do his knifing. I've tried to tell people so, and I haven't succeeded very well. Perhaps Hitler will do it where Mussolini failed. He's a bit nearer home."

At last he did achieve a smile. "Well, Joanna," he said, "this is all a long way from young Joe Morrison and young Miss Halliwell footing it on the floor of the Smurthwaite Assembly Rooms. I wonder what would have happened to us both if Sir William Scroop had not turned up there?"

He reached across the table and laid his hand on hers. She trembled a little, thinking of the scar that ran up above that hand and of the man he had killed. One of Mussolini's rats, but in the shape of a man. She noticed then that his hand was not trembling. His gesture was friendly—nothing more.

"And another thing," he said. "What a long way this seems from that night when young Joe Morrison and Lady Scroop stood on the cold pavement in Baker Street in front of an obstinately closed door. Poor old Joe!"

Was he telling her that he was finished with her, except in a temperate friendly way? And, if so, was she glad or sorry? She thought of William. How long was a ghost valid? She withdrew her hand and looked at Joe's face. It was not the face of a man awaiting the answer to a vital question. He was right. It was a long way from Smurthwaite, a long way from the closed door in Baker Street. She had never doubted his love for her—never till now; but, for herself, she still didn't know how her heart would make her respond if he tried to take her by force.

"You see, Joanna," he said, "when I die you'll find Joanna written on my heart—all over it, as many times as there's room for writing—like one of those hoardings where the kids write up Joe loves Joanna. But Joe's left it too late. He can't marry Joanna now—even if she would want him to, and he doesn't think she would, Joe can't marry Joanna in a world where Jacopos wait in the dark with knives and Jacopo's kindred souls are all over the place. God grant, Joanna, that the time may come when all that will be ended and men and women can smile at one another and speak to one another without each wondering whether the other is the devil in disguise. But then it will be very late indeed, and so it's a future that Joe refuses to budget for. Now, let's go."

She was trembling when they got outside. She said: "Joe, would you like to come back with me to Baker Street?" And in her bones, as she said it, she found her own answer. She knew that she didn't want him to.

He said: "No, no. That's not how I ever saw it."

He called a taxi and took her to her doorway and then drove off. She climbed her stairway with eyes misted by tears.

7

The next morning she received an invitation to a sherry party in Lord Dunkerley's flat. It came jointly from his lordship and Miss Hesba Lewison. She had met Hesba Lewison and knew something about her. She often acted as hostess for Dunkerley, and that gave the guests at the parties plenty to gossip about. Had she been his mistress? It was said that in his youth, when his powerful father—so different a man from him!—was building up the great house of Dunkerley, he had been deeply in love with Miss Lewison, but that she had married a brilliant and erratic youth named Alec Dillworth, who died soon afterwards. Miss Lewison, as she continued to be called, was then a writer of books for children, and it was this which caused Joanna to go to one of the joint parties, for the books were still in print and Francis adored them. Joanna wished to meet the woman who had given her son so much pleasure. It was then that she first heard the gossip about Dunkerley and this Jewish woman, who attracted her enormously. Miss Lewison was short and stout, with close-cropped grey hair and black observant eyes. She dressed rustily and smoked cheroots. She had never, Joanna decided, been beautiful, but she could well imagine that in young womanhood she had had a disturbing vitality. Whether, after her young husband's death, she had become Dunkerley's mistress no one would know. That they were now bound by affection and common memories was obvious. It was a long time since Miss Lewison had written one of her famous children's books. She wrote novels for grown-ups, and few of those. But when one did appear, it was received by the critics with a reverential awe that separated it from the packet of novels flipped over and briefly sent to the devil. It was reviewed by itself, under two-column headlines, by a pundit. And, indeed, Joanna thought, when you tried to read one of these novels you saw that it was right that this should be so, for they were appallingly cerebral. The grace and glory that would make the children's books live for ever were departed—perhaps with the youth who died untimely?—and intellectual ashes alone remained.

That first time of her going to a party where Miss Lewison was to be met she had felt enormously flattered. There was competition for Miss Lewison's attention and she did not expect to have more than a word with her, if that; but when Dunkerley led her up to where the old lady was sitting and said: "Hesba, this is Lady Scroop," Miss Lewison looked at her as though seeing a ghost, and said: "But, Laurie, it can't be! Surely you can see who it is as well as I can?"

Dunkerley looked puzzled, and Miss Lewison said: "My dear Dunderhead," which was usually her unflattering name for him, "surely you can see it's Grace back from the grave?"

Dunkerley considered Joanna for a moment, then said briefly: "I hadn't noticed it, but there is a likeness," and walked away.

Miss Lewison got up from her chair and, to Joanna's surprise took her arm. "Come with me, my dear," she said. And, adding to her reputation for eccentric rudeness, she led Joanna out of the room, leaving a knot of adorers to gaze gloomily after her. She said to a waiter: "Bring some food and drink in there," pointing to a door, and through this door Joanna followed her into a small room where for a moment they sipped their sherry and nibbled their almonds.

At last Joanna shyly spoke of Francis and his love of the books Miss Lewison had written so long ago, and added: "I hope you liked the person I seem to have recalled to you. I should hate to have brought back an unpleasant memory."

Miss Lewison blew strong-smelling blue smoke from her cheroot, and said: "You have given me a terrible shock. I attended her funeral last week. It was the funeral of a woman withered and wrinkled by years of pain, and now she has burst out of the grave as she was when we were young. She was the wife of the Bishop of Foxminster."

Joanna sat uncomfortably under the scrutiny of those bright black eyes. Some accidental flash of likeness, she thought, has turned the old girl's head.

Miss Lewison said: "I'm surprised Laurie didn't see it at once. She was his cousin, Grace Satterfield."

She got up and took off Joanna's hat, and her pudgy little hand felt Joanna's hair. "Everything," she said in wonder. "The hair, the eyes, the height. But your voice is different and your hands are not quite so long."

Miss Lewison went back to her chair, and Joanna noticed that she walked slowly on short legs that age had thickened. Her ankles bulged over her shoes. It's her own youth that I have startled back upon her, Joanna thought, as much as the budding-time of this woman who has died. She must have been a proper little dynamo. There's still fire in those eyes.

Miss Lewison began to talk. She talked of a Sussex house called Dickons, that Joanna knew to be Dunkerley's country seat, though he was rarely there; and of a summer morning long ago, when Dickons had just been built, and of herself and young Laurie—Dunderhead—and Grace Satterfield lazing in the sun on the terrace. "I thought it was all dead," she said. "What should we do to people who bring back things like that—bless 'em, or damn 'em?"

Dunkerley put his head round the door. "People are beginning to go, Hesba," he said.

She waved her cheroot at him impatiently, but got up and tottered out on her swollen legs. "All right," she said, "all right. Why do I bother with them, or with you?"

Dunkerley said: "Well, I thought you might have wanted to bother with Rudolph Schwann. However, he's gone. He only looked in for a moment."

8

When the invitation came on the morning after Joe had said he would love her for ever and wished her good-bye she thought of Hesba Lewison and she thought of Schwann. Either was worth meeting, and, if Schwann was in the habit of attending Dunkerley's parties, she might meet both. She didn't believe that when Schwann brought the carnations to her shop he did it because of some isolated impulse. She remembered that at lunch that day the name of Chris Hudson had cropped up. Schwann had said at last that he must get back to his office. "There's a young barrister I have to meet—a boy called Christopher Hudson. He's just put up his plate and has never had a job. There's a small thing I think I can entrust to him, just to see how he handles it." He laughed. "I am a most forgiving man," he said, "because I don't like Mr. Hudson. I know his father a little, and so I tried to know the son. I am like that. I experiment with men and women, and usually my experiment is a wash-out, as with young Hudson. There can be nothing between us. But he has chosen a hard life, and perhaps I can do a little to help."

She did not say that she knew Chris Hudson, but when she was back in her flat she thought of what Schwann had said: that he had "experimented" with him, and she wondered whether the carnations were the beginning of an experiment with her. They appeared to be, for the next week he invited her to dinner. She found him a fascinating companion. She guessed him to be in his middle forties, and though she herself was in her early thirties she didn't look it, and he seemed to her much older than the difference in age suggested. For

367

one thing, he was bald but for a fluffy halo round his tonsure, and he had a deep quiet gravity. Save for Septimus she had never before been in friendship with so old a man, but she was from the beginning aware of a liking for him. At dinner he proved to be both an amusing gossip and a practical man. As Chris Hudson had found, he appeared to know everybody, and in the restaurant had entertained her with diverting or scandalous stories about them. They were dining at *L'Esculent*, and she had heard the first rumours of Anthony's intention to move on to something bigger. She mentioned this to Schwann, and said that the amount of new capital that would be necessary for the sort of thing Anthony had in mind was terrifying. Schwann said: "I know Mr. Fieldhouse. Perhaps I might have a word with him about that. I often advise clients about investments." In the long run, it was he who smoothed out some problems that were worrying Anthony sick, and he became solicitor to the reconstructed company.

After dinner he said: "You have never seen my flat, Lady Scroop. Would you care to come along, or should I be boring you?"

Joanna was not in the habit of visiting bachelor flats, but she had no hesitation about going to Schwann's. The large sitting-room delighted her. He talked about his pictures. He showed her his rare editions. These were his two loves. It was a new world to her. After all, she reminded herself, she had never known a man who had ventured into it. Anthony was a business man. Joe cared for nothing of the past nor for the loveliness which the present could produce. He wanted only to be at the boiling-point of contemporary events. The house in Soho Square had been full of beautiful things, but they had all been collected by William's ancestors. William had loved them, but had added nothing to them and had stayed still among them. But now surrounding her was something that was Rudolph Schwann expressed in the terms of what he wanted as the setting for his daily living. He had told her nothing of his family, but she guessed it was as bourgeois and commonplace as her own. Ancestry could have contributed nothing to this taste. It was Schwann, and she found that it deeply satisfied her.

She said little, but Schwann was aware of her quiet pleasure. "You decorators!" he twitted her. "As soon as I go into a room I can tell you whether you have been at work or whether the room has grown out of the person who lives in it. Your Mr. Shrubb! Admirable fellow! I have found him all over the town, and I am glad he keeps the wolf from his door. But when I go to visit Jones, his room should make me say 'Ah, Jones!' not 'Ah, Shrubb!' I was in a house last week, and my hostess said to her husband: 'Alfred, those Chelsea figures are not as Mr. Shrubb arranged them. Have you been changing them about?' He said that he had, and his wife said: 'You shouldn't do it. Mr. Shrubb knows best.' "

Joanna smiled. "I don't believe it," she said.

"Well," he admitted, "perhaps it doesn't belong to the eternal verities, but it's not a bad parable."

They met once or twice after that, and then his attentions suddenly stopped. She hadn't seen him for a fortnight, and realised that she missed him. When the Dunkerley invitation came on the morning after Joe had left her in tears she remembered that, from what she had heard Lord Dunkerley say, Mr. Schwann was a friend of Miss Lewison. He might be at the party. She decided that she would go.

9

She arrived when the party was in full screech. Dunkerley's flat was the top floor of what had been a Park Lane mansion. A private lift led to it. She found, thankfully, the windows open on to the view of Hyde Park. It was a hot night, and the shrill talk and tobacco smoke created a little hell. Miss Lewison, with her swollen feet on a footstool, was sitting near a window, hemmed in, and, like a body-guard, Schwann and a lovely girl were standing one on either side of her. Now and then the two exchanged a look or a smile, and, when their eyes were not thus meeting, the girl's still remained on Schwann, and she had a look of loving dependence that Joanna found disturbing. She seemed about twenty. She was slender but not tall, blue-eyed and fair-haired. In that well-dressed and carefully made-up assembly she stood out if only because she was rather shabby-looking and innocent of paint and powder, a garden flower in an orchid-house.

Joanna turned away and found Dunkerley watching her with a smile. He lifted a drink off a passing waiter's tray and brought it to her. "Lovely, isn't she?" he said.

"Who?" Joanna dissembled.

"I don't know," he said. "Schwann sidestepped me and made straight for Hesba as usual, taking her with him." His practised eye considered the girl. "A Gretchen goose-girl," he said, "but capable of development. Well, have you seen anything of your friend Joe Morrison while he's been here?"

"I had one meal with him."

"He flew off this morning. He's been making my blood run cold

369

with his prognostications. The devil of it is that he usually knows what he's talking about."

"And what is he talking about now?"

"Well, he's met this chap Hitler. He's always had a thing about Germany, as perhaps you know. Last year, instead of spending his holiday as sane people do, he went over from Rome to Berlin to have a look about. And he wangled a long off-the-record talk with Adolf. He says the man's as mad as a hatter, that half the time he was talking he was literally frothing at the mouth, and that he really believes himself destined to rule Europe."

"He's not the first."

"No. But Joe says he's the most dangerous, and he almost went on his knees begging me to start a rearmament campaign. That wouldn't half queer my pitch. Why, the Labour chaps would start frothing like Hitler himself, and I can't see the Tories either rallying under that banner at the moment."

"And what did you tell Joe?"

"That we must wait and see."

"He must have been enchanted."

"Yes. He said: 'All right. You'll do the seeing before long.' And he went out and banged the door."

He drifted away and Joanna found Schwann at her side. "I have been neglecting you," he said. "I come to make my apologies and to give you my reason. There, that is my reason." He looked towards the beautiful girl still standing sentinel by Miss Lewison's chair. "My brother's child, Magda."

The girl was staring towards him, as though imploring him to come back. Joanna felt an almost physical pang of hurt as she looked at Magda's face. The beauty was a mask on utter desolation.

"Whatever has happened to her?" she asked impulsively.

"A very little thing," he said. He took her by the arm and led her to a corner of the room that was not too crowded. "As you see, she is but a schoolgirl. Well, just out of school—at the university, in her first year. She was attending a lecture, and she had with her a book on the subject—rather a costly book for a poor girl. A youth sitting next to her picked it up and put it in his satchel. Naturally, Magda protested, and the boy said: 'You Jews had better keep your mouths shut from now on.'"

He looked at Magda, and his face was infinitely compassionate. "Well," he said, "she had heard of this sort of thing, and now here it is. It is with her. But she was not dismayed. She turned to a girl on her other side—a girl who had been her great friend—and she said:

'Tell him he can't do that.' Her friend said: 'Can't he?' and turned her face away. Then Magda waited till the lecture was over and protested to a professor. He was honest—a good honest coward. He said: 'I'm afraid you'll see a lot of that. For me, I have a wife and children to keep.' That is all of the small happening. A mere trifle."

Joanna said: "She looks utterly German—almost ideally German."

"But she is a Jewess," Schwann said. "Her mother is Burgundian, and her father's mother was a Cheshire woman. But she is a Jewess."

Joanna thought of Joe, talking to the man frothing at the mouth.

Schwann said: "Magda did not go back to the university. She was now afraid. Her father asked me to take her for a while, and here she is. It is difficult. I am out all day, and she will not leave the flat alone. Would you be her very good friend, Lady Scroop? Would you take her about a little? Miss Lewison cannot. She is hampered, as you see, in moving."

"But, my dear Mr. Schwann," Joanna said, "of course I will. I shall be delighted. Why didn't you ask me before?" And to quiet his expressions of thanks, to change the whole sad subject, she asked: "How do you come to know Miss Lewison so well?"

"I am just what you call a fan," he said. "I have read all her novels, and I think she is a very good writer because she has known much sorrow."

"I have tried to read them, but I must say they beat me."

"Perhaps you are not yet old enough or wise enough," he said patiently, "to read between lines. However, I think I told you once that I like experimenting with people. Well, I decided to experiment with Miss Lewison. I had the impertinence to write her a long letter, and she answered very kindly, and at last we met, and—well, there it is. We took to one another. We are both Jewish. That is, in blood. But I think we have no fetishes. We are grown up."

Joanna saw much of Magda after that, and therefore, necessarily, much of Mr. Schwann. And that was why, when Anthony whistled as he drove her in to town, she was deeply annoyed. Suddenly, Anthony, her contemporary, seemed a boy for all his façade of a successful business man and family man. She suddenly felt old, and involved with life's sorrow and struggle, and she could, quite literally, have hit him in the face.

🙂 🙂 🙂 🙂 🙂 🙂

CHAPTER 15

1

*O*n the other side of the Park, in the Bayswater Road, Hesba Lewison had a flat that was not sumptuous like Dunkerley's. Indeed, she never called it a flat. She called it her lodgings. She had gone to live there when she was a girl just down from the university and making her way in a world that was dominated by Dunderhead's father, Dunkerley the Great. Her landlady now was the married daughter of the woman who had been her landlady then. She had grown into the rooms like a nautilus into its shell, and she couldn't imagine living anywhere else. So much had happened to her here. She remembered her dear friend Grace Satterfield, Dunderhead's cousin, walking away from the rooms with her handsome parson, Theodore Chrystal, who was now, most venerably, the widowed Bishop of Foxminster. She remembered young Laurie, who had grown into the worldly-wise second Lord Dunkerley, calling on her after the tragic death of her husband—a young Laurie still dominated by his forceful father, still dewy-eyed and hopeful that he could mend the bits of her shattered life. He was probably glad, she thought, that she had sent him away. She wasn't now much that a man like Dunderhead could have valued. And he had turned out a flitter, one decorative girl after another. However, out of all the strands that made up the stout cable of life he and she had many in common and they could not leave one another alone. She knew of the gossip that linked their names, and she smiled at the times she lived in. Poor young things, she would think, looking at the cackling, screeching mob that Dunderhead liked to assemble. They were so without the wisdom of roots, so proud of varnish and glitter, so up to the minute that they couldn't remember even the name of last night's lover. There was hardly one of them who didn't know how to make a better world; and there was not one of them who seemed to know, or to want to know, how to make a better life.

It was late autumn, and she sat at her window overlooking the Park, and called herself a black old Jewish spider in her web. A thin mist was creeping across the grass, hanging grey woolly stoles upon the arms of the trees, but the brave gold of the leaves shone through. She loved those trees. In good years and bad they gave her their beauty, of green, of gold, of dark indomitable resolution when ice encased the twigs which yet bore within them the spring again. Roots. It was all a matter of roots, she would tell herself.

She rang the bell, and said to her landlady: "Mr. Schwann and Lady Scroop will be here any minute. Bring in the muffins as soon as they come." She sat by her fire and chuckled. Muffins! "My God!" she said. "I've eaten so many muffins here that I must be made of muffins." But there it was. A fireside, tea and muffins. It was easy, and she couldn't be bothered to make changes. Besides, she liked the buttery grease.

2

Rudolph Schwann bent his bald head over her hand, holding it lightly in his hairy paw. She liked his devotion because she knew it sprang from understanding of what so few seemed to understand; but she allowed herself a half-malicious grin and said: "One of these days, Mr. Schwann, you'll call me *chère maîtresse*, and then the fat will be in the fire, for I shall have to decline the title. Joanna, will you please pour the tea? Once I settle into this chair my back and my old knees seize up, so that I hate leaning forward."

She watched Joanna pour out the tea and rejoiced in the young woman's likeness to Grace Satterfield. Perhaps she exaggerated it; but attending Grace's funeral had been a black winter moment, and seeing Joanna had been the miracle of the new leaves.

"Now tell me," she said to Schwann, "all about Magda."

"She is very well," he said, "and we have Lady Scroop to thank for that. All through the summer of last year they were not long apart. Magda's English became very good, and so, as you know, she was able to go to Bedford College in the Autumn. She has ceased to be frightened, except for her family. She even talks at times of going back. But my brother begs me not to allow that. I fear that all is not going well with my brother. He does not tell me, but I think he has lost his job. But that is my affair, and I must not trouble you with it. Then, all through the long holiday this year Magda has been with

Lady Scroop in Yorkshire. Now she is back, and her skin is toasted, and she will begin her second year at Bedford College. You see what we owe to Lady Scroop."

Joanna said: "It was self-indulgent of me. Magda took my son off my hands."

"That is a way of putting it," Miss Lewison agreed, "but not a very good way. You don't see much of your son, and I should think it unlikely that you wanted him off your hands."

Schwann looked at Joanna fondly. "That is true," he said. "When a mother is young, that is the time when her heart is storing up the things she will always remember. Her son will be off her hands soon enough."

What a wise pair they are! Joanna said to herself. She thought of Anthony and his mother, and of how few things their hearts had stored up to remember, and of the cold unpeopled land that seemed always to lie between them. "You are quite right," she said. "I should have liked Francis all to myself, but he didn't want me as he wanted the others."

"Who are the others?" Miss Lewison asked.

"Magda and an old gentleman named Septimus Pordage."

"Ah!" said Miss Lewison. "Now that is the strange man who called himself Ambrose Feend and wrote the wonderful book! Why does he not write anything more? I met him when he came to London."

Joanna explained: "He says he will never write anything more because most writers start quietly and climb to their top note, while he began on his top note and has no intention of spending his life in a decline."

"Well," Miss Lewison conceded. "There is wisdom in that, too. And how did he get on with Magda?"

"He gets on with everything that is young," Joanna said, "because he's just a great baby himself. The four of them had a splendid time."

"There are now four?"

"Yes. There is also an Iceland pony."

"Of course," Septimus had said, "we shall need panniers for the pony. He and I are ill-adapted for our parts, but he will have to be an overfed Rosinante and I a gross Don Quixote. I do not see Sir Francis as Sancho Panza, if it comes to that, but the genius of a producer lies in making the best use of the material available. Never fear, Lady Scroop, never fear. We shall make do; and, from what you tell me, this German girl at least will make an adorable Dulcinea del Toboso."

"And where do I come into this?" Joanna asked.

"You can be an innkeeper and put us all up for the night."

It was the week before she had brought Francis away from school. She had gone down to Throstle's Nest to make the arrangements with her mother and had found Septimus sitting on the grass verge of a roadside while the pony grazed lazily beside him. Francis had entrusted the pony to Porger, as he called him, and it was housed in the barn where Lottie and Anthony had watched poor Valpy die.

"Sit down," Septimus invited, patting the warm grass, "and share my frugal luncheon."

She lowered herself beside him, and he opened his rucksack and brought out a bottle of Chambertin, chicken and ham sandwiches, cheese, biscuits, fruit and a large box of chocolate tied in magenta ribbon that flourished into a bow.

"Who was it," he asked, "who wrote those lines about 'a scrip with herbs and fruit supplied, and water from the spring'?"

"I don't know."

"Neither do I, dear and beautiful lady. But he was in the rights of it. Now, if you will be content with one half of an anchorite's forbidding fodder . . . . ? I sometimes regret that we cannot, like the wise beasts, get down on all fours and simply browse on Nature's plenty. As it is, permit me to draw this cork."

He took out the sort of knife that schoolboys love, furnished with everything, it seemed, from a two-foot rule to a telescope, and from among its complexities unfurled a corkscrew.

"Now concerning the panniers," he said. "It is fortunate that I have been attending basket-making classes in the Smurthwaite Technical School. I made myself an easy-chair, but I have not yet ventured into it, because, trying it first on my cat, I saw a tendency to cant when she sprang upon it. Unlike a cat, Pordage has not nine lives, not consecutive lives anyway, though concurrently believe me, Lady Scroop, he has many more than that. But panniers are within my scope, and I have thought of trying to build up a connection with the Grimsby fish trade. My own domain provides the necessary willows, and incidentally disproves the popular notion that harps hang upon willows. I have never seen one doing so, and, as you know, I believe in hard facts and eye-witness. Well then, I shall make the panniers—ample ones that will hold tents in case we decide to sleep out. It looks to me as though the dales and fells of the West Riding are in for a high old time."

She motored down to the school and collected Francis, who was becoming too thin and tall for her liking, and whose first words were:

"Hallo, Mummy. How's Porger?" On the way up to London she outlined Porger's schemes, and found that they, despite her absence from them, were received with joy. They stayed at the Baker Street flat for the night, and in the morning went to Berkeley Square to pick up Magda. Joanna was ashamed to find herself almost hoping that Francis would dislike the girl. But though she was pale and tired from overwork in college, they got on well enough, and once Porger had taken them in hand they became deeply attached and well-looking and happy. The holiday went off very much as Mr. Pordage had planned. Once or twice they even used the tents and slept out. They lit fires, and grilled chops and kippers, and bathed in Septimus's Parson's Pleasure, and under the stars listened to Septimus reading poems or unfurling the story of Don Quixote.

It wasn't a very good time for Joanna, but Mrs. Halliwell said: "Leave them alone. The young ones like to be together."

"Does that go for Mr. Pordage?"

"Oh, yes, especially for him. You just stand by, Joanna, till you're wanted. There's not much else a mother can do, and the time usually comes."

And now Francis was back at school, quite happily, and Magda was working with young furious energy at Bedford College, and here was she taking tea and muffins with a woman old enough to be her mother and a man old enough to be at all events her much older brother. She felt oddly adrift between the generations. The young ones got on very well without her, and her touch with the old ones was fragmentary and uncertain.

She got up to go, and Schwann rose, too. They left the house together, and he said: "If you are not in a great hurry, shall we take a turn in the park? There is still light, and we shall not have many more evenings like this."

They walked in silence for a time, and silence was so unusual with Schwann that she began to feel uneasy. He never prattled, but he was rarely without something interesting or amusing or serious to say. At last, to break the constraint, she asked: "How is Christopher Hudson getting on? You told me you had passed some work on to him."

"I don't think," he said, "that he will come to much. Though let us be fair: he is young and it's a bit early to judge. I've put a few things in his way now, and he deals with them—well, adequately. He does a bit of work on the Oxford Circuit, and perhaps his acquaintance with the barristers' mess will humanise him in time, but I gather he's not tremendously popular there at the moment. He's appeared once as junior to a K.C. in the Law Courts here, but that was just devilling. Well, there is my report."

And, indeed, it sounded so much like a report, and a dull and dreary one at that, that Joanna laughed, and found herself compelled to change their customary roles and take charge of the conversation. She told him of the night in the Silver Star, though William did not come into it. She merely said: "Believe it or not, I'd never stayed in London before, and I had exalted ideas about the gaiety and glamour of night clubs. So I persuaded a friend to take me to one," and she went on from there.

"For years after that," she said, "I would dream about being abandoned in that long empty street, and I built poor Mr. Hudson up into a symbol of evil. It took me a long time to realise that he was just a not very resourceful young man, frightened out of his wits and saving his skin. Well," she added fairly, "he did save mine, too. At least he prevented me from being manhandled by those bullies."

Schwann listened gravely, and said: "Yes. I think he is like that. He will do half a thing."

Then he fell again into such brooding that she said: "What's on your mind to-night?"

"I should not worry you. What have my troubles to do with you?"

She sensed that this was something deep and important. "Tell me," she said, and put her arm through his. He pressed it to his side, and she felt that he was trembling, and knew that this had nothing to do with whatever news he had to impart.

"It is a letter from my brother's wife," he said, "Magda's mother. They came for my brother last week."

They! All over the world They were coming into their own, the anonymous They, the nobodies, the hoodlum scum with an itch for the power their own capacities could never give them. So They opened their meagre pipe lines to the boundless rivers of evil power, and this flowed through them, through millions of them, ennobling them with the sense that They were men of destiny.

So they called one night on Magda's father, and they tramped through the house and opened drawers and desks and threw things around. Revolvers were strapped about them, and when Magda's father asked them what was their warrant for coming there, one of them pulled his revolver from its holster and said simply: "This." They found nothing, but after an hour of wreckage they took Magda's father, Mr. Schwann's brother, away with them in a noisy car. He came back twenty-four hours later, pale and exhausted-looking, but unharmed. Unharmed but silent. He had nothing to say to Magda's mother. "And that is the terrible thing," she wrote to Mr. Schwann. "He is all in himself, as he never was before. He no longer plays upon his flute. Do not tell them that I have written. He has forbidden me to do so, and he will not write to you himself. And when you write, do not mention anything of this. Just begin your letter with the words 'I am busy to-day,' and that will tell me that this has reached you. I am entrusting it to safe hands."

All this Schwann told Joanna as they walked in the misty park through the evening of late autumn, and she kept her arm in his to comfort him. And so they came at last to the Marble Arch Gate, and within it were the speakers on their rostrums, and one of them was bawling: "And so I say 'To hell with Hitler.' I am a Jew. I'm not half a Jew or a quarter of a Jew. I'm a Jew with a Jewish father and a Jewish mother, two Jewish grandfathers and two Jewish grandmothers, and this doesn't prevent me from being a faithful citizen of this great empire on which the sun never sets. I'm Jewish and I'm British, and I say to hell with any man and any country that persecutes the Jews. Now let me tell you something of the contribution the Jews have made to the greatness of this old Empire. Take Disraeli. . . ."

Schwann and Joanna had stopped to listen with the apathetic crowd. Behind them was a group of young men in black shirts and riding breeches and leggings, listening with grins of derision on their faces.

"Take Disraeli," said the orator, "or, if you like, take that eminent Jew, Albert the Good, Consort of Victoria the Great. A Jew was good enough for Victoria, and I'm saying this to those scum of the British Fascists, the B.F.'s, that I can see there lurking in the crowd. The government of this great Empire should put them behind bars, preferably in the monkey house at the Zoo. Standing here in this hallowed temple of free speech, where that great patriot George Bernard Shaw so often upheld the banner of truth . . ."

A tomato broke upon his face and ran in red streaks down his sparse wagging beard. He was a foolish-looking little man, but good-humoured. He clawed the muck out of his beard and said: "The aims of the British Fascists are evidently excellent, but I can now testify that if they were achieved we should all have a rotten taste in the mouth."

This raised a titter, and annoyed the blackshirts. They didn't intend to let him get away with a crack like that, especially as it had swung the audience a little in his favour. As soon as he began to speak again they started a monotonous chant of "Blah—blah—blah." They pressed closer into the crowd. Joanna could feel them at her back. She said to Schwann "Let us go," but Schwann was fascinated. This was a small example—or perhaps only a parody—of what was happening in his brother's world. It held him, and he hesitated. Then a swift change overtook the moment. A robust-looking Cockney, who might have been a coalheaver or a stevedore, said: "Stop your bloody row and let the little bloke speak. He got a right, ain't he?"

Somehow, the words spoke right into Schwann's heart: they were the voice of England. "He got a right, ain't he?" He said almost involuntarily: "Hear, hear. Let the man speak."

One of the blackshirts said: "Shut your gab. You look like a Kike yourself." Then they went on chanting.

The heavyweight said ominously: "I've warned yer." And as they still took no notice, he grabbed one of them by the shirt front with his left hand and sent his right fist into the man's midriff with the force of a pile-driver. The man shot back into the midst of his companions and then fell groaning to the ground. The Cockney said with satisfaction: "That's the only way to get a bit of peace and quiet out of beggars like you. Armaments is the answer."

An athletic-looking youth, who was standing, oddly enough, under a banner inscribed "Prepare to meet thy God," now hoped to increase his audience, and shouted: "No, brother! On behalf of Jesus, the King of Peace, I declare unto you that armaments will settle nothing. Come to Jesus, brother, and learn the ways of peace."

The coalheaver said: "You go an' chew coke, brother. Jesus said 'I come to bring not peace but a sword.'"

Joanna felt she was living in a nightmare. All the sad and tragic things that had of late intruded into her life seemed to be summarised in this swift and tangled moment. There were They, the ominous ones, who had caused poor Magda to flee, who had broken into her father's house like burglars and carried him off and the peace of the family with him. There was Joe, knocking the life out of the furtive Jacopo, and there was Joe again telling Dunkerley that armaments were the answer. It was all here: all that she had heard of was being enacted as if in some fantastic pantomime.

She took Schwann's arm and tried to pull him away, but the blow that sent the blackshirt down had changed everything. The thin crowds that had been listening to this speaker and that coalesced into a sizeable mob, shouting and arguing and hemming in Joanna and Schwann. It was pretty clear that if the little Jewish orator had been a joke, his case had swiftly altered and he was now a victim of oppression. There were howls against the blackshirts, and they began to fight their way backwards towards the railings on the other side of the broad road. Willy-nilly, Joanna and Schwann were swept that way; and the youth who had called Schwann a Kike kept slashing out a fist decorated with knuckledusters. Joanna's hat was knocked off and trampled underfoot—even in the hot moment she could think ruefully "A new one!"—and then the Fascists were jammed against the railings and the fight was a standing one.

It soon broke up. The police were on the fringes of it by now, saying placidly enough: "Move on now. Move on. Push off," and they had, as always, without much fuss, their almost mystic dissolvent effect of hot water on sugar. The youth who had taken an especial dislike to Schwann was still slashing at him, and while there was yet crowd enough to cloak the action Rudolph stood back a pace and kicked him with all his force in the crotch. "That," he said in a quiet reasonable voice, "is for my brother, and for having the bad manners to knock this lady's hat off." Then he took Joanna's arm, and, trying like everyone else to look unconcerned in the moment, they sauntered slowly away.

3

They both now were exhausted, emotionally and physically. They said nothing, but felt as though they had lived through a long revealing time. In fact, not more than seven or ten minutes had passed since they had stood to listen to the Jew. Presently they turned left out of the park into Park Lane, and Schwann stopped a taxi. Without asking whether she wished to come, he gave the address of his flat. Magda would not be there, he was glad to remember. Thank God, in whatever world they lived, young people could find some joy. Magda would be going, after her college session, to a friend's home, to dine with her parents and go on to a theatre.

He did not take her hand or her arm as they sat in the taxi. She leaned back in her own corner, thinking of that kick. Odd that such a thing should entirely reconstruct her opinion of a man. What were the adjectives she might have used of him? Suave, urbane, civilised. A bit too much so, she had sometimes thought. Everything about him so neat, so polished: his clothes, his linen, his furniture, books, pictures. His flat was exclusive. Everything there was excluded except what could be covered by the three adjectives. The curtains shut out the world. One wanted to whisper. One's very feet whispered on the carpet. His man had a low soothing voice. And now, out of the heart of this hushed being, had come that swift effective act of brutal violence.

She hadn't known many men, and she thought of those she had known, most of them casually, and she could not think of one who would have done what she had seen Schwann do—not one, that is, except the man she had loved, and the man who wanted her to love him. She was quite sure that Scroop and Joe Morrison were capable of violence; indeed, she knew each to have been violently engaged, though William, she thought, might have refrained from this particular act through disdain. But William did not have a brother in Germany. William, Joe, Rudolph. A strange trio of musketeers. She even achieved a smile.

As for Schwann, he was sitting away from her because he was trembling, and a touch would reveal it to her. He did not want that. She was so innocent. She did not, he supposed, even know what a knuckleduster was, and certainly had not realised that those black-shirts were wearing them. In the stress of the moment, she had supposed, he was sure, that the hand which knocked off her hat was intended to do no more than that. She had been too excited to know that the knuckleduster had grazed her cheek, had drawn a little blood which was now lying in a dry smear upon her skin. He saw it as the ruffian struck at her, and it was then a living thing, a few red drops, Joanna's blood, oozing out of her. And that was what drove him to violence. That was why he kicked. He was amazed at the surge of his own feeling. What had happened to Magda, what had happened in his brother's house, had saddened and depressed him. But this had infuriated him. It was as though all the tragedy of Europe had written itself in that red hieroglyphic on her cheek. And yet he knew it was more than that. It was Joanna's cheek.

And so they sat apart, each profoundly aware that the other had been revealed.

The taxi-cab stopped in Berkeley Square. When it was gone, they stood for a moment on the pavement. How peaceful! The drone of Piccadilly traffic was remote, almost soothing, emphasising the quiet. The plane trees were as still as if petrified. Stars were shining, and the autumn air was crisp and tonic. You could believe that the world was suave, urbane, civilised, and that comfortable curtains could contain a private life within a warm corner of it. No clutter, and the essentials charming.

They stood caught in this mood, knowing it to be hollow, when a car shot suddenly at a great pace into the square and hurled past within a few feet of where they were standing. Another followed even quicker. The first stopped with a nerve-rending scream of brakes, half on the pavement. Two men leapt out and bolted down a side-street. They saw policeman jump from the second car and follow. Then the quiet was down again, but threaded with violence. All in a few seconds.

"What is it?" Joanna asked, alarmed.

"Smash and grab, I imagine. Just serving notice on Berkeley Square that an underworld exists."

They entered the house and climbed the stairs to the flat. In the small entrance-hall, little more than a cubby-hole, Joanna saw her face in a mirror. No hat. Her hair gone haywire, a streak of blood down one cheek. "Good God!" she said, "I look like a prefect after a dirty game of hockey! I've never been in such a state in my life!"

He said: "All the same, you look adorable," and kissed her.

For months she had guessed that this kiss would come, but the moment took her by surprise now that it was here. To gain time she said: "I could understand the games-mistress doing that to her filthy little heroine, but, for myself, I'd like a moment alone with some warm water, a face-cloth and a flapjack."

He said: "Forgive me," trembling uncontrollably. "You see now why I kicked that man. I saw him strike you."

They went in, and he showed her the bathroom. In there, behind a locked door, while repairing the ravages, she found her legs weak. She cleaned the blood from her face, did what she could with her hair, made up her lips, and looked despairingly at her trampled shoes. She lifted her skirt and saw what she feared—a run in a silk stocking. She was playing for time, and dallied, looking about the room. How like Mr. Schwann! And how unlike William! And, she imagined, how unlike Joe Morrison, too. In Soho Square the bathroom had been a stern utilitarian place with brown linoleum on the floor, varnished paper on the walls, and little to encourage dalliance. Here, the thick rubber flooring had the silence that was the note of all the flat. The bath was of pale-blue porcelain and the walls were tiled in matte turquoise, pleasantly rough to the touch. One wall was a mirror incised with fishes and water-plants, and she thought it would be amusing to take off her clothes and see herself pictured there, subaqueous among the swim and undulation. Warm pipes enervated the place, and thick luscious towels hung upon them, pink, daffodil-yellow and the pale green of Edinburgh Rock. The white bath-mat seemed about a foot thick. Everywhere were mirror-fronted cupboards. Chromium shone. A rubber tent could be drawn around you as you took a shower, and all the lighting fell, gently modulated, through a glass ceiling, which, like the mirror-wall, was incised with marine life: sea-horses, nautiluses, and, to crown all, a sailor in a dinghy. Joanna thought it would be a blushful affair to lie in the bath beneath the able-bodied seaman's regard. He couldn't help, she said to herself, peeping over the dinghy's edge.

There was so much to see in the bathroom, where even the taps were shaped like dolphins, that she long exceeded the time any reasonable woman would need to repair her appearance. However, she was glad of that, for she found the trembling of her legs diminished and felt she could meet Mr. Schwann more robustly.

He had repaired himself, too. He had changed into a dinner suit. He was standing with his back to the fire, and before him was a little table agreeably furnished.

"Sit down," he said. "You must be very tired. It has been a terrible afternoon for you. Listening to the sad story of my brother, and then those ruffians, and then your host forgetting his manners and kissing you. But I could not help it."

"Rudolph," she said, using that name for the first time, "you are the oddest man I've ever met. You kiss something that looked like a jumble-sale in the church hall, and now, when your marvellous bathroom has put me more or less to rights, you can find nothing better to do than apologise. Well, then, here you are." She got up and kissed him.

"Thank you, Joanna," he said. "Now what would you like to drink?"

She knew that this was a truce, an armistice, not the end of what was between them. She accepted it as such. She drank sherry, and he lit a cigarette for her, and said: "I have rung up the Berkeley. We shall have dinner there presently. I thought you would like that."

Joanna said: "I'm not fit to go out. Even your Babylonian bathroom didn't offer me a hat, and look at this."

He looked at the ladder in her stocking and said: "Yes. I noticed that as you got into the taxi. I have arranged about that, and about the hat. Of course, you could have found stockings in Magda's room, but she hasn't many. We shall buy them."

"At this time of night?"

"I have arranged it. I have rung up a young friend of mine. She has a hat shop here on the corner of the square, and she lives over it. She will let us in. She says she can do stockings as well as a hat."

Now what does a girl do about that? Joanna wondered. Does she accept stockings and a hat from someone she's not sure about—not sure of her own feelings? Her mind switched to her mother, and a laugh forced itself from her as she thought what Mrs. Halliwell would say about such a proposition. "Joanna, I'd like a word with you in the Office."

"Thank you, Rudolph," she said. "You're very, very kind."

"It was all my fault. You asked me to go from that meeting and I stayed, and even interfered. But now I am glad, because it gives me the opportunity to make you a little present."

She was ill at ease. She didn't want to hurt him, but she didn't know whether she wanted to encourage him. She didn't know. She said with a shot at light-heartedness: "It may not be such a little present as all that. I don't go in for cheap hats."

Schwann, too, was ill at ease. He had never bought a girl a hat or anything else. He had expected her to refuse, perhaps with indignation. And he couldn't get over his temerity in ringing up the girl in the hat shop. She was a young vivacious Jewess. He had met her through taking Magda there to buy some things, and had liked the girl and found time to give her a few pleasant words if he passed her in the square. When he rang her up, she said: "Oh, something for Miss Magda, is it?" and he said No, he was bringing a lady-friend around. The girl said: "Oh, I see," and he wondered what mistaken thing she saw, and felt foolish. It was natural, he admitted, the world being what it was, that she should jump to conclusions; and then he was overcome with an inner confusion as he imagined that Joanna, too, might be saying to herself: "Odd. How on earth does he know a little milliner well enough to ring her up after business hours?" Which was, in fact, one of several questions that Joanna was turning over in her mind. Living above a shop in Berkeley Square could be very convenient.

But when she was trying on hats a few minutes later, all such thoughts flew away: she was simply a rather choosey woman buying a hat. It was a cosy little *salon*, and the hats were good, and there were plenty of them, and when at last she was satisfied the milliner said: "But, of course, madame, it is Mr. Schwann also who must be pleased," and she led Joanna to the little hole of a waiting-room where Rudolph was sitting ill at ease.

"It is all right, Monsieur Schwann? It pleases you?"

He got up, looked briefly at the hat, and said: "Yes, thank you. It is very beautiful." He would have said the same if it had been a greengrocer's bowler. He had wanted to buy Joanna a hat, and he had done it. That was what mattered.

Then Joanna went back and put on a pair of stockings, and the girl said: "These we need not display. We shall expect Monsieur to take them for granted—yes?"

The remark, and the pert look that went with it, turned Joanna all Halliwell. "You will send the bill to me," she said. "Take my address."

She dictated it in all its ladyship, and the poor girl looked so conscious of having put her foot into it that Joanna's mood instantly changed, and she said with a laugh: "Never mind. Tear that up and send the bill to Mr. Schwann, or he'll be disappointed."

Then she joined him, and they strolled along to the Berkeley.

4

A few days before this Joanna had taken Magda out to dinner. It was difficult to make the girl give up an evening, but, if she was conscientious as a student, Joanna was equally conscientious in obeying Rudolph's suggestion that she should keep an eye on Magda. She didn't see why even an earnest German girl should turn into a mere learned goose. When she was Magda's age, living in the Swiss *pension*, she would have given anything to be taken out now and then; and, too, Magda was a decorative child to take about. Schwann was as generous to her as if she were a beloved daughter. She had plenty of clothes, and she didn't need make-up. With her fair hair cut like a mediæval page-boy's, her light blue eyes, and her skin which never reddened but kept still some of the biscuit-brown from the holiday in Yorkshire, she looked like a just opened flower. Joanna called for her at Rudolph's flat and found her wearing a white dress with a golden sash and golden shoes. Her cloak, lying across a chair, was of golden velvet, lined with white silk. Schwann's little dark eyes were swimming with happiness as he took up the cloak and laid it on her shoulders. She turned and kissed him, her long brown arms going round his neck. Across her head, he looked at Joanna, inviting her to join in the conspiracy to make this child happy. She smiled at him, loving his loving-kindness.

Magda said: "Why do you not come with us, Uncle Rudolph? It would make me happy."

"Does it not make you happy to go with Lady Scroop?"

"Oh, yes," she said hastily, fearing a *gaffe*, and loosing him to turn and smile at Joanna. "But with the three of us would it not be even more happy?"

"Perhaps we shall all go out together some night," he said.

"Though if I were going out with Lady Scroop I should not over-insist on a third party."

Magda said: "Perhaps you will love her, and then you will throw me out to earn my own living."

"Yes," Schwann said, "perhaps we shall do that. But now you had better go."

Yes, Joanna thought. We had indeed. "Come then, Magda," she said. "I'm keeping a taxi expensively ticking over; and that's something my mother would never approve of."

"Your mother is a firm woman," Magda said as they went downstairs. "Do I mean firm?"

"I think you mean stern—severe—something like that."

"Yes, stern. But to be relied on. Send her Magda's dear love when you write."

In the taxi she rested against Joanna like a child, and wriggled with the excitement of going out. It was her first big occasion. "You will spoil me, Lady Scroop," she said, "you and Uncle Rudolph between you. There is Latin that I should be doing. I shall never be a learned woman if you go on like this."

"Oh, well, there are other things. And please call me Joanna."

"That would not be rude?"

"Not now that I have asked you to do so. I should like it. Lady Scroop makes me feel terribly old."

Magda sat up and looked at her. "To be beautiful, that is the thing," she said. "You are beautiful. Uncle Rudolph thinks so."

"Did you see much of your Uncle Rudolph before you came to England?"

"Oh, yes. Every year he would come to Germany, and my father would say 'Not married yet?' and Uncle Rudolph would say: 'What, with you lot to keep?' And he would laugh and look at my father and mother and me and my brother, and say: 'Why clutter myself up with a family when I have one ready made?' And he would take us all out to dinner and to the theatre, and there would be a big box of chocolates to eat while we watched the play." She was suddenly silent; then added: "And now it is not any more like that."

Joanna was still considering this attractive portrait of Schwann when the taxi drew up under the canopy of the Savoy.

She had ordered a table near the dance floor. There was no one for Magda to dance with, but she thought the girl would enjoy the spectacle. She wondered whether she should give her wine, and asked: "Do you ever drink wine, Magda?"

"On my birthday, Joanna. I am allowed one small glass of hock."

"Very well, then. You shall have one small glass now."

"Yes. It shall be my baptism into the life of gaiety."

She was looking about her with wide eyes. Everything was new and strange and exciting. It was not to such restaurants that Uncle Rudolph took them in Germany, but to sedate places that suited their tender years. She said: "Oh, Joanna! I should be doing my Latin, but I am glad that I am not!"

"You must make up for it to-morrow."

"Who knows? Perhaps you are turning me into the paths of unrighteousness."

Joanna smiled. "You really are picking up some extraordinary English, Magda."

"Tell me—what is wrong? I wish to speak correctly."

"It isn't wrong. That's the joke of it. It is too, too correct."

"What should I say?"

"Well, I suppose an English girl would have said: 'Perhaps you're leading me astray.'"

"I shall remember. Leading me astray. Are you?"

"I hope not. Well, here is the hock. Your very good health."

"Your very good health. *Prosit*."

5

Chris Hudson had been dining with a man he wished to cultivate. He was not friendly with him, but he liked to be seen about with him. He was a handsome youth and his father was a judge and he was altogether the sort of person Chris thought it advantageous to know. So this night he had asked him out to dinner and had taken him to the Savoy. ("Only the best is good enough for Hudson, you know.") They had dined well, and at ten o'clock Chris's companion gave thanks for a good meal which was welcome but which he couldn't quite understand being invited to share, and asked to be excused. He must be off, he said.

This suited Chris. He had seen Joanna come in with a beautiful girl. For the last half hour he had been watching them, and when he was left alone he ordered more coffee and a brandy and lit a cigar and continued to watch them. He thought them a rewarding spectacle. Joanna Scroop was the last word in sophistication. Her severe black dress, the arrangement of her hair, the very way she sat or addressed a waiter, spoke of a woman at home in this *milieu*. But it was the girl who intrigued him. Her eager way of looking about at something obviously delightful because unaccustomed, her simple white dress with the touches of gold, the way she would stop eating to watch the dancers, her foot in the golden shoe tapping the measure, the friendly smiles she gave to waiters: it all added up to something that was worth waiting for. So Chris Hudson waited, smoking his cigar, sipping the brandy from the big balloon glass.

And now they had finished their meal, and Magda said: "Oh, Joanna, it has been so beautiful. Thank you." She took up Joanna's hand and put it to her lips, "If only I could now dance! I am in the mood to dance."

"Did you dance much in Germany?"

"Oh, yes. But not in lovely places like this. But I am good at it."

"You should be. You have a good figure. Next time you come to dinner with me I must try and bring a dancing partner for you."

"Shall it be often?"

"What about the Latin?"

"But now and then? And we shall bring Uncle Rudolph to dance with you."

"Does he dance?"

"Yes, indeed he does. He has danced with me many many times. But I can teach him nothing. He does not give. He is not elastic."

"Flexible."

"Not flexible. He remains all in one block."

Chris Hudson strolled across to their table. He bowed to Joanna. "Good evening, Lady Scroop."

What could you do? The young man who had left you flat when you were an inexperienced girl, little older than Magda was now. It was so long ago. There was all her life with William in between and all the growing-up of Francis. You couldn't harbour resentment for ever.

She said: "Good evening, Mr. Hudson. Are you alone?"

"I've been dining with a man, but he had to go early."

Joanna said: "Magda, this is Mr. Christopher Hudson. This is Magda Schwann. I think you know Mr. Rudolph Schwann? Magda is his niece."

And now he was shaking hands with that beautiful girl, and saw her eyes were chicory-blue and that her skin was a silk tan, and that she was living in wonderland. He was deeply moved.

He said: "Lady Scroop, it's a long long time ago since we last met. Do you remember?"

"Yes. Sit down, Mr. Hudson."

He sat, and went on: "I don't want to recall to you what happened that night. But again and again I've been deeply ashamed of it. I'm glad to have this chance to say so."

"Well . . ." She considered him across the table. Well dressed. Not bad looking, if only he would discard his thick-lensed spectacles. A bit heavy in the body. Probably, she told herself, just an average man. Certainly not one who at all appealed to her, but was it sensible to cling to that old feeling of aversion?

"You hesitate," he said. "And that doesn't surprise me."

She smiled at him, but didn't commit herself. "Let me order you a drink," she said.

"Thank you, Lady Scroop, but I shan't drink any more tonight. I'd rather dance with you, if you will allow me?"

She got up and they moved on to the floor, and he put an arm round her. She didn't like it. At his touch, the old aversion swept over her, but she concealed it, and she admitted to herself that he danced well. It was a waltz, and that was a test of a dancer. Anyone could make a show of shuffling over the floor in what they called dances nowadays. The demoiselles Kempfer had been obsessed with the waltz. In youth they had lived in Vienna. There wasn't much Joanna didn't know about the waltz, and not much it seemed, that Chris Hudson didn't know, either, despite his stocky build. As they walked off the floor, she thanked him and congratulated him. He beamed with pleasure. "If we meet again in—what is it?—ten, fifteen, years' time, you will have a happier memory of me, Lady Scroop."

She said: "Don't harp on it."

They let the next dance take care of itself. Chris Hudson addressed himself to Magda. "I know your uncle, Miss Schwann," he said. "He has been very helpful to me. I'm a barrister, and when a barrister isn't well known he's glad of a solicitor who puts work in his way now and then. Mr. Schwann has done that, and I'm beginning to get more or less on to my feet."

"Uncle Rudolph is helpful to everybody. Now, do we dance?"

Oh, dear, Joanna thought, I must be getting old. For she was shocked by the girl's ingenuous eagerness. Magda had half risen to her feet and was looking at Chris Hudson with starry-eyed invitation.

"Magda!" she said; and Magda dropped into her chair. "I do wrong? I am very sorry."

She looked utterly crestfallen, and again Chris Hudson was moved by her youth and inexperience. He said to himself "I love that girl," and he had never said that, never felt that, before. How wise, he had always thought, Rudolph Schwann was to keep clear of

389

clutter! When a man had made some headway, that was time enough to begin thinking of a wife. He said: "It would give me great pleasure to dance with Miss Schwann, if you will permit me, Lady Scroop."

What was that eager light in her eye? Joanna wondered. Was it this occasion, so strange to her, these rich surroundings, her new white dress and golden shoes, her sheer youth and well-being? She hoped so, and her heart was shaken by both joy and sadness. The child was so happy, and she was glad of that; but she had a beauty that seemed to invite calamity. Joanna said: "We mustn't be out too late. Have this one dance."

Watching them, she felt old and forlorn. She, Joanna Scroop, whose body was in its prime, whose emotions were urgent, however much she had learned to keep them under control, she sitting there a chaperone, a duenna! She could have laughed at the situation, but it was not, from any point of view, a laughing matter. Christopher Hudson was as old as she, and, for that matter, not so well preserved. His face was heavy, his body thick, but when they were dancing she had not noticed that. She looked at him now and suddenly remembered the night of the ball at Smurthwaite where so much had begun. She had danced for a long time with Joe Morrison, and she recalled how he had held her, distantly, timorously, as if fearing a contact that she might think disrespectful or presumptuous. And then, out of the blue, there was William, and his arms seemed to wrap her up, and she could feel her body responding to his, almost indecently eager, and all her emotions in a turmoil. And this, with two women now, not one, was being re-enacted. For while they were dancing, Chris Hudson, for all his mastery of the waltz, had shown an aloofness both of body and spirit that she had approved and reciprocated. But how differently he was dancing with Magda!

She watched them with anguish: bodies touching, Magda's head on his shoulder, her eyes almost closed as she gave herself to his direction.

She had not seen Magda dance before. The child floated like a windflower. Joanna longed for the dance to end, feeling an impulse to snatch Magda and run away with her; and when the dance did end, the pair remained there on the floor, clapping their hands, waiting for the music to begin again, and when they had done clapping they stood with their hands lightly held together. They were on the other side of the floor, near the band. There was nothing Joanna could do. She endured through the next dance, which was lively and even tempestuous, and which at last restored to her a

390

Magda laughing and out of breath. Chris led her to Joanna's table, with a hand on her arm, bowed, and said: "That was very lovely. Thank you, Miss Schwann. Thank you, Lady Scroop. Will you pardon me? I must go and burn the midnight oil."

Magda cried: "Oh, must you go so soon?" Disappointment spread ingenuously on her bright flushed face.

"Yes," Joanna said, "of course Mr. Hudson must go. He has told you. He has work to do."

Chris bowed again and went. Magda sat down and said: "Thank you, Joanna, for letting me dance. All my dances have been tied up in me for so long! They came out like a little puppy that has been shut up in the house and is at last let free to run about like mad. I must tell Uncle Rudolph all about Mr. Hudson."

"Yes," Joanna said. "Do that, darling." She was enormously relieved. She knew that Schwann had no high opinion of Chris Hudson, and she felt that she ought to let him know what had happened. If Magda chose to do it herself, so much the better. She didn't relish the part of dragon.

"Put on your cloak, darling. We must go. It's nearly midnight."

"Yes," Magda said, "all good things end. But perhaps I shall see Mr. Hudson again."

6

This was a few days before Joanna, wearing her new hat and her new stockings, dined with Rudolph at the Berkeley. It was a nervous dinner, for they were both aware that the kiss he had given her when they returned from the Hyde Park meeting that day had started something that was not yet ended. And so they talked defensively of commonplace things, and soon after ten went back to Schwann's flat. It was but a little way to walk, and he took her arm, not casually as a friend might do, not confidently like a lover, but in a way that made her feel he was apologising for touching her at all. It was the way Joe Morrison had held her at Smurthwaite, the way Chris Hudson had held her at the Savoy dance, and she thought of Scroop and the way he had swept her up, like quicksilver touching a drop of its own kind and becoming instantly one with it.

"Magda is gone to the theatre," Schwann said. "She should not be very long now. Would you like to wait and say good night to her?"

She wondered what Magda had told him about the Savoy dinner and the dancing with Chris Hudson, and so she went in and put the question to him directly. "I know you don't much like young Hudson," she said. "But there was nothing I could do about it. He was there, and that was that."

"You know him as well as I do," Schwann answered. "Indeed you have known him longer than I have. What do you feel about him?"

"What one feels about a person—can it be put in one word? Well, I'll try. I should call him unreliable."

Schwann was evidently perplexed. "You know," he said, "young Hudson did what they call the honourable thing. He rang me up and asked if he might call here to see me, and when he came he told me what Magda had already told me about the dance, and he asked my permission to see her now and then. It gave me an odd feeling—as though a burglar were asking permission to break into my flat."

"Do you dislike him as much as that?"

"Well, I share your feeling that he is unreliable. That is not in itself a fault. There are plenty of people who are unreliable because they move and develop. Look at Picasso now. I happen to be a great admirer of Picasso, but how unreliable he is! As soon as all the little men have caught up with him he is off again on something surprising. And how easy it would be to defeat a reliable general whose strategy was all of a piece! And so to be undependable may spring from an inventiveness of the spirit which is always after new forms of creation." He looked at her with a smile. "What a tiresome old pedant old Schwann is!"

"He is very unreliable," she admitted. "Now he is buying you a new hat and stockings, and before you know where you are he is philosophising about the creative spirit."

"Yes," he admitted, as though taking a good look at himself, "he is an odd old creature who pampers his carcase with luxury bathrooms and rich carpets, but whose spirit despises what his body cannot renounce."

"It must be fascinating," she said, "to lie in that bath of yours and think how much worthier one would be if lying on spikes like a fakir."

"You are right to laugh at me," he agreed. "But we have left Mr. Hudson in the lurch. My feeling about him is that he would be completely reliable where his self-interest was concerned, but one jolt to that would send him flying. Do you know his father?"

"I met him once, long ago when I was a girl at Smurthwaite. Recently he's married the mother of a dear friend of mine, Anthony Fieldhouse's wife."

"Another odd thing about old Schwann," he said, "is that he used to have a great passion for the music-halls. He hasn't now, because the halls have become starched and shiny. But they were wonderful. Toulouse-Lautrec loved them, and so did Rouault and Sickert. Well, young Hudson's father always delighted me, and when I first began to know young Christopher I said to him one day: 'Are you any relation of the Great Hudson?' I could see at once that he was shocked, that he despised that great artist, and he began to stammer silly things. When it dawned on him that I admired his father, he changed his tune on the instant. That is what old Schwann's roundabout rigmarole is getting at. That small thing taught him a lot about Christopher Hudson. The old man is as simple a soul as you could find, with no education and little intellect, but in his own line he was a great artist, and for his sake I used to take Christopher about, but I don't see much of him now."

"Well, what did you tell him when he came to you with his honourable proposal?"

"The days when you could show a suitor to the door are past. I told him that Magda was a child, that she had endured great sorrow in Germany, and that her release from it had disposed her to make a rather exaggerated response to ordinary kindness and courtesy. I told him that he should be careful, therefore, not to assume that her reactions at the moment were normal. I said, too, that she was a student whose evenings were occupied, and that the best thing would be for him to give her friendliness if they met, but not to do anything to blow the thing up into a significance that perhaps it didn't possess. I happen to know that Christopher Hudson is rather well in with these Mosley toughs, and so, to give him the full works, as they say, I said: 'You know, of course, that Magda is a Jewess?' "

"And what did Master Christopher say to that?"

"I blush to tell you. He said: 'Well, if it comes to that, Jesus Christ was a Jew.' How I hated it! You hear it again and again, and always like that—used to gain a point of self-interest. When he said that, I not only disliked him: I despised him. Jesus was born in the house of a Jew, but he is the daysman. In him is neither Jew nor Greek."

"I don't know that word—daysman."

"You will find it in the book of Job—'There is no daysman betwixt us, that might lay his hand upon us both.' There is, now, a daysman."

She looked at him, sitting quietly with his moles upon his knees, and she was moved and perplexed. "I must go," she said. "Magda is later than I expected. Say good night and kiss her for me."

He saw her downstairs, and she said she'd walk down to Piccadilly where she would be certain to find a taxi, but when he had shut the door she strolled round the quiet midnight square, thinking of Rudolph. No day since she had known him had shown her so much of him. The kick in the Park, the bathroom, the kiss, the hat-shop! What an odd perplexing creature he was! And the daysman! What a beautiful disturbing thought to be so casually produced, as though his being were a jumble from which he might at any moment fish up a jewel or a rag of frippery! It was peaceful under the stars in the still night. This peace seemed but a continuation of the peace she had felt as she sat listening to Schwann's quiet talk. And the prospect of being endlessly at peace, listening to quiet talk, appalled her, for increasingly she felt, her body was starving for rapture.

7

It was half an hour after midnight when she climbed the stairs to her flat in Baker Street. A letter was lying on the mat, and she saw that it was from Joe Morrison. She was tired, and her impulse was to put it aside until the morning. Then she saw that though the writing was Joe's the stamp was English, not German. Joe was in England or he had entrusted the letter to someone leaving Germany. In either case, she wanted to know at once all about it. She removed her hat and threw it on to the table. She looked at it in surprise. A strange hat. Then she remembered where it had come from. This brief but total gap in her memory of Schwann, whom she had seen so recently, startled her, no less than her eagerness to discover what Joe Morrison had to say. She switched on her bedroom fire, warmed some coffee and got into bed. With the drink on the bedside table, she opened the letter.

"My dear Joanna.—I don't know whether you trouble your lovely head with what I write in *The Banner* concerning things as they now are in Germany. If you do, you will know that I have no illusions about what we are heading for, and you will perhaps guess that life, which became rather difficult for me in Italy under bullfrog Benito, is no easier under the jackal-afflicted-with-rabies whose inspirations run the show here. And even if you do read *The Banner* you don't know much. Our good Dunkerley keeps an eye on me and sees to it that the blue pencil deals with what he thinks my wilder extravagances. Of course, he's not the only newspaper proprietor who has a sneaking feeling of admiration for both the bullfrog and the jackal and a wishful think that they somehow are a useful buffer between us and Russia, and, come to that, there are crawlers in the Government, too, to say nothing of some of the financial gentry.

"However, I mustn't complain. I am allowed to write *something* —just enough so that Dunkerley will be able to say 'We told you so' if I turn out to be right. But you know that I couldn't keep my mouth shut about France and Italy, and I've almost finished my new book about Germany. It's my biggest stinker yet, and, as always with me, every fact is authenticated. Whether it will do any good I shouldn't like to bet. The English capacity for shutting their eyes till they find someone poking them out is phenomenal.

"What surprises me is that I have become nervous, and that will surprise you, too, I think, seeing that you know the brash and over-confident Joe pretty well. I have seen so much indecency in this country, with no effective protest made from anywhere in Europe, that if anything happened to me I can imagine Dunkerley saying: 'Play it down. This is no moment to stir up trouble.' Anyway, I've been taking great care that the typescript of this new book shan't fall into the wrong hands. One of Goebbels's boys said to me the other day with an innocent smile: 'I suppose it won't be long now, Mr. Morrison, before you present us to the world in our true colours?' I laughed it off, but when I got to my rooms that night I found it was no laughing matter. They are very skilful, these searchers of rooms, when they want to be. Sometimes they don't, and delight in leaving a mess; but, unless I had known what to look for, I shouldn't have known that they'd been. Of course, my landlady said nothing. She's scared stiff; and it would have been foolish to ask her.

"I buy my matches from a chap who sells them in the gutter. He was once a professor, but he didn't bow down in the house of Rimmon. I type on wafer-thin paper. A good many sheets, folded up, will go into a match-box. I never speak to my old match-seller— not there in the street, anyway. I simply snatch my box of matches, drop my coin on his tray, and my box of typescript at the same time. It is easy enough for him to sell it later to an unimpeachable party member, and so it goes right out of harm's way, for this unim-peachable member is, in fact, one of my most valuable contacts and informants. He is occasionally sent to England, and when the type-script is finished he will see that it reaches my publisher, as he will see that this letter reaches you.

"Do you feel, my dear Joanna, that you have now been put in touch with a world of melodramatic madmen? Well, you have; and sometimes I think I am becoming one myself. The thought of Eng-land, with all its blindness, is extraordinarily alluring, and, thank

God, I shall be there soon. Next week, in fact. I am taking a fortnight's leave.

"What does this news do to your heart? It plays Old Harry with mine, on which, I once told you, the name Joanna was for ever inscribed. I said good-bye to you, didn't I?—good-bye for ever. Well, well. What fools we are, and how we over-estimate our powers of forgetfulness, or our powers to go on existing despite what can never be forgotten; and I shall tell you one of the small things. It was the day of your marriage, and you were going away with Scroop by car. You came out of the house looking like an angel walking on the floor of heaven. You had forgotten such earthly things as the cold wind. Your mother told me to go into the house and bring your coat, and when I brought it she told me to put it round your shoulders. I just couldn't, and Anthony did it for me, and you didn't know, I swear, that a coat had been put on you. You knew nothing except the feeling of Scroop's arm as he swept you into the car, and then you went and never looked back.

"When are you going to turn your head and see Joe Morrison waiting with a warm cloak?"

The letter ended without signature. She put it under her pillow, saw that she had drunk no coffee, switched out her bedside light, and sank into a warm impassioned sleep.

8

When she woke she remembered the letter at once, took it from under her pillow, and read it again. Suddenly she trembled. Last night the ending of the letter had excited her imagination. Now the long preamble filled her with foreboding. Joe confessed himself to be nervous, and if Joe Morrison was nervous, then ordinary mortals had cause to fear. Why should she worry, except as one would worry about a friend in a danger that might or might not spring a trap upon him? Her foreboding, she knew, went beyond that.

She carried her breakfast into the sitting-room, where also she took her meals, and she saw the foolish pleasing little hat lying where she had thrown it last night. As she ate she thought of Schwann, and thinking of Schwann took her ruminations on to his friend Hesba Lewison. "Another, and another, and another," she remembered Miss Lewison saying, dropping letters from hand to hand one day when she had called upon her.

"Another what?" Joanna asked.

"Another Jew asking for help. What can be done about it all? I have found work for a professor of literature as librarian in a duke's mansion, and for a girl who is a promising pianist as nurse-maid to a stockbroker's children, and for a novelist as an under-gardener. Happily he is a very good gardener. But where can it end? Do you know the pictures of Hieronymus Bosch?"

"No."

"Oh, they are hell on earth, a world peopled with distorted beasts. And that is what Germany is now. Nothing is safe there that is decent."

Firelight played on the old woman's black shining satin and dark face and grey mop of hair. She looked like something painted by Rembrandt—a face into which he had concentrated a lifetime's experience of sorrow.

Eating her breakfast, Joanna thought of that—of Joe Morrison in a world peopled by distorted beasts, and he full of a rash courage that would not pull a punch, whether at a Jacopo or a Hitler. "Joe Morrison waiting with a warm cloak." She managed to laugh. She knew there would be no warm cloak with Joe Morrison.

The sight of the frivolous hat annoyed her. She took it into her bedroom and put it out of sight on a shelf. Then the telephone bell rang, and there was Schwann himself.

"Good morning, Joanna. Did you sleep well?"

"Like a log."

"In the cold light of morning, do you still like the hat?"

"It's utterly adorable."

"Could we have lunch together somewhere to-day?"

There was the slightest hesitation, and then she lied: "Sorry, Rudolph. I'm already fixed up. And I may have to go out of town for a few days. Something to do with the shop. Mr. Shrubb, alas, is down with influenza." That at least was true. "Did Magda get home safely?"

"Oh, yes. She was very, very happy." But he didn't sound as though he wanted to talk about Magda, and she said hastily: "I'll let you know when I'm in circulation again. Good-bye," and hung up.

9

Schwann had heard a good deal about Margaret North, and was grateful to that young woman, whom he had never met, because she extended her friendship to Magda. She was at Bedford College, and it was to her house, Schwann understood, that Magda had gone to dinner and on from there to the theatre, returning, as he said to Joanna, very, very happy. The next day he himself was not very happy because he had caught that slight hesitation in Joanna's voice when she said she could not go out to lunch with him. He didn't blame her: he blamed himself, and chided himself for his impetuosity. Joanna had become to him something so radiant, so shining in the dullness of his life—though it had been a pleasing life enough till now—that her slight rebuff depressed him. And so he reacted more sharply than Magda had expected when she said at breakfast: "Margaret has asked me to go out to a dance to-night. Do you mind, Uncle Rudolph?"

"My dear child," he said, "do *you* mind? Do you mind neglecting your studies? Do you mind taking the risk of failing in your examinations? In these unhappy days I am responsible for you. I owe it to your father to give you good advice, and though of course I don't advise you to forget that you are a young girl who is entitled to some pleasure, still you were out last night. Would not one night's play in a week be a good idea?"

She looked more crestfallen than he had expected. Indeed, she looked, beyond all reason, crushed. How could he know it?—but this was because she loved him so much and hated to deceive him. But had not Chris warned her that it was necessary to deceive him? "I have called on him," Chris said, "and though I don't suppose he'd mind if we accidentally met, I'm dead sure he'd never allow us to meet by arrangement." This was last night, when she had deceived him with the story about dining at Margaret North's, and she and Chris had danced and danced. They had walked part of the way back to Berkeley Square, and Chris had drawn her into a dark corner and kissed her, and she had felt on fire and hung on to him, body to body, as though she could never have enough of his kissing. She said to him: "You know I'm a Jewess?" and his only answer was to kiss her again till her bones melted.

So much that was horrible had happened to her that she had ceased to believe in herself as a person. They were little things, but they went to the soul. There was the matter of her stolen book in the classroom. And there was the matter of the dance. She had been dancing with a boy whom she knew only slightly, and as they walked off the floor another boy came up and said to her partner: "You're asking for it, Otto. That's a Jewess." As though he had said: "That's a poisonous reptile." It had made her feel unclean, and she had run home, and her father had said gravely that she had

398

better stay away from public dances. So she felt she had to say to Chris: "You know I'm a Jewess?" and if he had started from her then in horror she would not have been surprised. His response re-established her, made her a woman, and she kissed him with a woman's passion.

He was surprised. He was a prudent young man and knew that he was in no position to marry. That was one point, he told himself, on which old Schwann was dead right. Life could be squalid without money, and he didn't want squalor. At the same time, it was pleasant to have a girl to take about. He had had little experience of girls. The few he had met had shown no enthusiasm for him. Only once had he overcome his nervousness and "tried it on," as he put it. It was just as it had been to-night with Magda. The girl had agreed to go with him to a dance, and afterwards he had pulled her into a dark corner and started to kiss her. She had slapped him in the face. His spectacles were knocked off, and while he was fumbling for them on the ground she walked away. Physically, the smacks didn't amount to much; but his pride was smarting. It was Magda's experience in reverse. It was as though he had been a slug brushed off a leaf. The experience made him careful with girls. Subconsciously he knew that there was not much to him: that was why he glorified himself in day-dreams of valour and distinction: he couldn't bear that what little there was should be humiliated.

When he saw Magda with Joanna at the Savoy he trembled. She was so lovely that the thought of speaking to her carried with it his fear that she would react in a way to humiliate him. He was careful, therefore, to ingratiate himself, to establish his credentials, by asking Joanna to dance first. And then he and Magda were on the floor, each uplifted—though neither guessed it of the other—by a sense of release. Magda remembered that Joanna had said "This is Mr. Rudolph Schwann's niece," and so he must know that she was a Jewess.

But did he, after all? she asked herself later. Schwann was not necessarily a Jewish name. The question troubled her for days. She had taken more hardly than any other member of her family the insults and ignominies of her position in Germany. It was because she was so clearly undermined physically and in spirit that her parents got her out of the country. She had taken to lurking in the house, like a doe in ambush, afraid of the dogs. The thought of her unresolved question now brought back all that tension of body and mind, and, Chris Hudson being associated with it, his image gained in her imagination an importance it might never, otherwise, have had.

She hated herself because she, who owed so much to Uncle Rudolph and who loved him, was going to deceive him. Chris's address was in the telephone-book. No one was more surprised than he to receive her letter. She said nothing about the ruse of the Norths' dinner-party and theatre. She said simply that to-morrow night she would call on him at 6.30, and could they go somewhere to dance? Don't answer. Tell me when I come.

It was so innocent and inexperienced a letter that Chris was oddly moved. He thought of going to Schwann's office, and, in however roundabout a fashion, making him acquainted with it and asking his advice. But he didn't see how he could do it without getting Magda into hot water; and so the thing fell out, and they ate and danced, and afterwards in the dark street he fell to kissing her, and she said "You know I'm a Jewess?"

Magda had had no premonition of what would happen. She had not expected to be kissed, and she had known no kisses but those of friendly affection. She was startled and bewildered and frightened; but, above all, she was stirred. The fright and the bewilderment faded into a rapturous invasion of her body that was new and ecstatic; and now she felt more than ever that everything depended on the answer to the question which she had pictured herself putting timidly, judicially. But she had to break from his arms to put it breathlessly; and then he was kissing her again. That was answer enough.

Later, Chris said to her: "When shall we meet again?" and she said without hesitation: "To-morrow night."

"But can we? Mr. Schwann——"

"He must not know. I shall arrange it. I shall call for you."

She had deceived him once; it seemed easier and not so painful this time.

10

And so on the morning after Schwann had bought Joanna a hat, and when he was feeling depressed because Joanna obviously did not wish to meet him that day, Magda brought out her story of the invitation to the dance. She had innocently supposed that Schwann would assent without question, for innocence goes hand in hand with the egotism of youth which cannot understand why its wishes should be thwarted. And this was more than a wish: it was a burning desire. She had hardly slept. The night had been a living over again of the dancing and the kissing and the awakening. Chris Hudson was no Perseus, heaven knows; but what people are does not matter. What matters is what they seem to be to other people; and to this young Andromeda, chained for so long to the rock of her humiliation, he was the liberator of her mind; and what made it worse was that he had been at the same time the awakener of her body.

When Schwann pointed out the importance of her studies she could only wonder at the denseness of grown-up people who esteemed such trivial things. What seemed to her important was that the unspoken gauges of last night should be re-affirmed.

They were at the breakfast-table, set near a window of the flat, but neither was aware of the urban beauty of the morning: the pale blue sky, the quiet light on the house fronts, the golden cloud on the trees, and the patines of bright gold on the rimed grass. A boy went by, clacking a stick along the railings, and inside the railings a lazy over-fed red cat dozed in a patch of sun that he knew would strengthen soon. They saw none of these things. She saw only his patient face that seemed to her obstinate. He saw only the look of undisguised frustration that puzzled him because of its disproportion. He was too experienced to allow his own feeling of frustration to appear; but it was in his heart and it enlightened his mind. Good God! he thought. We're both in love; and it seemed odd to him that this lovely opening child and himself—getting old and slothful—should be visited with identical torments. He remembered what Joanna had told him of the meeting with Chris Hudson at the Savoy, and he remembered Chris's call upon him. He didn't like any of it, and he didn't know what to do.

Magda was profoundly depressed by his brooding face, whose sorrow she took for condemnation that could harden into a stand against her; and she could feel a tide of rebellion stirring where hitherto nothing but love and gratitude had had a place. She would have liked to tell him everything, but Christopher had warned her not to, and her first duty was to that deliverer.

The thing to do, Schwann was thinking, was to write to his brother, tell him all the circumstances as he saw them, and let him decide. But it might be a week before an answer reached him; and here was Magda, risen from the table and speaking in a voice tight with emotion, a voice, he knew, that could not have anything to do with an invitation from Margaret North. "Well, I must gather up my books and go. What about it?"

He said: "I love you, Magda, and out of my love I advise you not to accept this invitation. But you must please yourself."

She bent down and kissed him swiftly and went as swiftly out of the room. She seemed to skim away from him like a bird released from a trap.

When she was in the street Magda knew that there would be no sense in going to Bedford College that day. The release from the tension of her brief struggle with Schwann left her with trembling legs and palpitating heart. And she couldn't drag her imagination away from that half-hour's dalliance in the dark street. It had been so unexpected and so heady; she could think of nothing but drinking again from that cup.

All the same, an undercurrent of sorrow dragged beneath the sparkling surface of her mind. She could not put Schwann's unhappy face away. She had wanted to tell him, because she was sure he would have rejoiced in her happiness. She still supposed that his worry was about neglect of her studies. She must tell someone, and she thought of Joanna. Christopher had laid down no embargo there.

Already when nine o'clock was hardly passed, she was at the shop, and Mollie St. Mellons was astonished by the young radiant apparition. She looked like a bride lit up by a honeymoon, and Mollie hoped she had come to feather an expensive nest. When she said she was a friend of Lady Scroop and had called on a personal matter, Mollie put her into the cubby-hole and thought that Joanna had all the luck, in friends as in everything else.

Joanna arrived soon afterwards and was taken aback by the unexpected visit. "Why, darling, you're going to be late for a lecture, aren't you?" she asked.

Magda said, clinging to her and kissing her: "Oh, Joanna, I've got so much to tell you." And she told her. It bubbled out of her with an innocent frankness that spared no detail and left Joanna astonished and dismayed. "The one dreadful thing about it is having to deceive Uncle Rudolph. I'm longing to tell him, and when I am allowed to do so he'll be so happy!"

Joanna paced the few yards of her cubicle feeling as miserable as a panther newly pushed into a cage. She thought of Schwann, so unhappy, she didn't doubt, and of Schwann's problem put now on to her plate. What on earth was she to do with it? She said suddenly: "Since you've got a whole day off, you ought to meet Chris's father."

Magda was delighted. "Oh, could I?" she cried.

"At any rate we can see. I'll ring up."

Mrs. Hudson answered the telephone. "Well, Joanna," she said, "what a long time since I heard your voice."

"Yes. I feel dreadful about it. Could I call on you to-day? I want to bring a small wedding-present for you and Mr. Hudson. I shall have a young girl friend with me. Would you think me terribly intrusive if I asked you to invite us to lunch?"

11

When Joanna had done the few things that needed to be done in the shop, she said: "We shan't have many more autumn days like this. Let's go and walk in the park."

They walked along the Mall, and the sun was taking strength, burning the last of the morning mist out of the air and intensifying the colours of the autumn leaves. Joanna remembered another day, when she had walked here with William in wintry weather, and, winter or not, her heart was alight and every common thing seemed to have caught a shine from paradise. How much more, she thought, must this day, richly glowing, be stirring now the heart of this child! What she was about to do made her feel an assassin. She looked at Magda, wearing the severe and unattractive clothes that served her for college, but so entranced that, had she been wearing wings, she would not more obviously have been afloat, off the earth. She had gone a little ahead, as though she had forgotten Joanna, but this small physical distance was nothing to the continents of separation that Joanna felt to lie between them. Magda was in the world that is tragically evanescent in the happiest outcome, and Joanna was chilled by the notion of cutting short even so brief a felicity.

She called softly: "Magda!" and the girl started, turned, and waited for Joanna to come up. "I'm sorry, darling. I was running ahead."

They went into the Park at Hyde Park Corner, and Magda said: "Tell me about Christopher's father. It will be lovely to meet him."

"Hasn't Christopher told you about him?"

"No. You see, I've only met Christopher twice. That night with you, and then again last night."

"How did you come to meet him last night?"

"I'd been thinking a lot about him, and so I wrote and suggested that we should meet."

Joanna was shocked. But how easy it is, she thought, to be shocked by what other people do. She knew that had there been no way of meeting William again after their first encounter save by writing to him, she would have written. Like her, Magda had been awakened at a touch. She looked at the girl with profound sympathy.

Why should she interfere? Well, Chris Hudson was not William Scroop. That was the long and the short of it. And it was no good saying: Who are you to be the judge of such a matter? There was common sense.

She said: "I don't know Mr. Hudson. I only know *about* him. I knew his wife better, but she is not Christopher's mother. She is Mr. Hudson's second wife."

"Oh, well. Let us not talk about him. I can wait. It's lovely to have things to wait for and to know that they will all be good. Being happy, I think, makes me wicked. I am very wicked to be talking about nothing but myself. I have not told you to-day how beautiful you are looking."

Joanna laughed. "For you to-day, my child," she said, "the witches on the blasted heath would be beautiful."

"I know the witches. They are in *Macbeth* which we read at school. I think they too are beautiful in a terrible way. But they were birds of ill omen."

"How do you know that I'm not a bird of ill omen?"

"You—my beautiful Joanna? Oh, no. How lovely the policemen look on their horses!"

"I was thinking how beautiful the horses looked under the policemen."

"Well, that also. All is beautiful."

So they dawdled through the morning, and at half past twelve they got into a taxi-cab and went to St. John's Wood.

12

You couldn't blame Chris Hudson for not having been at the registry office when his father and Mrs. Wayland were married, for it was Mrs. Wayland's own wish that the affair should be private. Not even Lottie had been invited or told the day. It was lovely summer weather, and she took Dick off to Paris, which she had not seen since she had lived out her miserable marriage there. She trotted him about the boulevards and took him to the *Folies Bergère* which shocked him, but less than it might have done, for he didn't understand a word that was spoken. They had a thoroughly good time. It was the first holiday Mrs. Hudson had had in her life, and when she told Dick this he said that he'd always managed to get in a week at Skegness, and that in future they could do that together. They were good friends, happy and contented in one another's company, expecting no more, pleased to have so much. "There's one thing," Dick said, "you won't have to worry about getting to know my family. It's a family of one—just Chris—and you know him like the back of your hand."

"Ay," she said non-committally. "I do."

When they were back and established in St. John's Wood, Dick rang Chris up and broke the news to him. "There's one thing, Chris," he said, "you won't have to worry about getting to know your stepmother. You know her well enough."

"Yes," Chris said. "I do."

"Well, lad, don't let's bother about formal invitations. You're always welcome here. Just blow in any time you feel like it."

"Good. I'll do that. Be happy."

So far, Chris had not blown in.

13

Magda was pleased with everything: with the meal, with Mr. and Mrs. Hudson, with the cosy little house and the garden at the back, where a wall was sheeted in flame by Virginia creeper. "It is so lovely," she said to Mrs. Hudson, "to be here with all these things that Christopher must know so well. Thank you for allowing me to come. You have made me very happy."

"Oh, so you know Master Christopher, do you?"

They had taken coffee into the drawing-room and were sitting at the open French window. The mild sunlight fell on the dahlias and the Michaelmas daisies and on a leaf detaching itself now and then from the wall of creeper and spinning down, its brief life ended. It seemed a paused moment, and yet it wasn't. Each leaf as it fell spoke of inexorable continuity, the secret scene-shifter preparing the winter set. To Joanna it was very beautiful till Mrs. Hudson spoke. Then, so sharply was her mind in sympathy with Magda's, the moment seemed to darken, and she would not have been surprised if all the leaves with one sigh had rustled down together, leaving them nothing to look at but bricks and mortar and rusting wire stretched upon rusting nails. And yet, she said to herself, why did you bring her here if not in expectation of this moment? You wanted to open her innocent eyes, but you shrank from doing it with your own words.

"So you know Master Christopher?"

It was said with an asperity that cut Magda like a knife, for in her exalted state she could not believe that Christopher was not the object of everybody's love and admiration. "Oh, yes," she said. "I know him very well. I love him."

Could innocence go farther? Joanna could have died of grief.

Even Mrs. Hudson was taken aback by the simplicity of that declaration, and Dick shifted uneasily in his chair. "Chris is a good lad," he said, "but at the moment he's up to the eyes. It stands to reason that with his way to make in a hard profession he's got little time for visiting. That's what worries Mrs. Hudson. He don't call on us as much as she'd like."

"He's not called once since we married," said Mrs. Hudson, "and that's quite as often as I'd like." She had never forgotten the sight of Chris dodging his father that morning when Dick had gone to the Temple, all dressed up, to gloat on Chris's new plate.

Dick said hopefully: "You must bring him here, lass. If he's fond of you—well, perhaps that'll make a new element in t'situation and he'll get on better with Mrs. Hudson. He's all right fundamentally is Chris."

Magda listened, bewildered and distressed. Fundamentally. The very word seemed full of doubt and reservation. And this was Christopher's father speaking! She watched another red leaf fall, and it was like a bit being torn out of her heart.

Mrs. Hudson was as distressed as the child. Her feeling for Chris was not a vague dislike. She detested him. He had grown up in her house, and she was convinced she knew him as his father did not. The more his father did for him, the more offensive he became; she was sure he regarded Dick's marriage as a disastrous alliance with a servant. Her policy was silence. She never mentioned Chris, and if Dick mentioned him she brushed the subject off as quickly as possible. Looking at this beautiful child, she was deeply wounded at having been jerked into saying the things she had. She wished Joanna had had the sense not to bring her. Above all, she feared that a discussion of Chris might open a breach between her and Dick. She hoped that nothing more need now be said.

But Magda decided otherwise. She repeated: "I love Christopher. And because I love him I want to know about him. I am not a child," she said pathetically. "I have already suffered much, as Lady Scroop could tell you, for I am a German and a Jewess. And I could suffer more. I could suffer hearing why you hate Christopher," she said, turning directly upon Mrs. Hudson, almost accusingly. "He is not your son. You cannot know him as his father does."

"Ay, that's true enough," Dick said.

"No," Mrs. Hudson said. "It is not true. I could tell you things—But no. No." She pulled herself up, appalled at what she was about to say.

Dick said reasonably: "If you know anything wrong about the lad, you should say so."

Mrs. Hudson's mind had gone back to a day of long ago when Dick had come to Leeds during the war and had written inviting Chris to go there to meet him. He had asked the boy to bring Mrs. Wayland, suggesting, in the kind way he had, that a break in her routine would do her good. Chris had said nothing whatever to her about it, but had gone to Leeds with his friend Anthony. Mrs. Wayland had found the letter dropped on the floor, and, picking it up and noticing her name, had read without compunction what had concerned her. She had thought Chris's action that day the meanest and most revealing of the many acts that she disapproved, and it was this that she had been on the point of saying.

"Dick," she said, "will you please allow me to say nothing more? I'm sorry for what I've said already."

It was with this doubt hanging in the air, with this hint of un-revealed perfidy in her mind, that Magda sat, white and silent, in the taxi-cab that Dick had called. Joanna held her hand, but was given no encouragement to speak. She could as easily have spoken to a priestess who had been told, but refused to believe, that her altar was lath and plaster, unsanctified.

14

At nine o'clock that night Joanna rang up Schwann. "I didn't go away after all. May I come round and see you?"

"Yes. I shall be very happy to see you, Joanna."

"I'll be with you in ten minutes."

"Try and make it nine."

Well, she thought in the taxi-cab, he is capable of a small joke. Perhaps he's not so bad as I have been fearing.

She had been thinking about him ever since Magda had wandered off home from Baker Street. She had wanted to take the girl straight to Berkeley Square, but Magda had said: "No. It must appear that I come from my lessons," thus being frank enough with Joanna to make it clear that she did not intend to be frank with Schwann. Of the matter that was eating her up she said nothing except: "I like Mr. Hudson. I do not like his wife."

Joanna, who knew Mrs. Hudson's opinion of Chris, would have liked to try and put her in a more favourable light, to say that, if Magda knew all, she would think Mrs. Hudson's conduct restrained. But what's the good? she asked herself. She was like a doctor who knew the symptoms of the disease all too well because he had been afflicted by it himself. However, what Schwann might wish to do was another matter. She knew how deeply he felt his responsibility towards the girl, and had no doubt that so percipient a mind would be aware that something was in the wind. Should she tell him just what it was? She decided that she should.

She found the customary scene that somehow always depressed her a little. It was not that the flat was over-furnished or badly furnished. But everything in it was so perfect and so inevitably always in the same place that it gave her a sense of unreality, of its being a stage set. The fire was burning; the table with drinks was before it; Schwann was wearing his dinner-jacket with the impeccable shirt-cuffs protruding an impeccable inch; and the Rouault clown over the fireplace, that had hung an inch askew when she last saw it, had been made to toe the line. Schwann's man Coster announced "Lady Scroop, sir," in his velvet voice, and she walked on to the stage, wearing the hat Schwann had bought.

"I know," he said, "that you like your sherry sweet. This Cream Oloroso for you then." He poured himself a Tio Pepe. "You have a good taste in hats," he said. "You must give me the name of your milliner."

She told herself firmly that she must not get on to the subject of hats. She had worn it hoping that it might help to cheer him up, but he didn't seem to need cheering. He was almost perky.

He said: "Would you call me a cruel man?"

"A runner-up to Caligula."

"I hope," he said, "I have been sufficiently cruel to stop what looked like being a bad business. I asked young Hudson out to lunch to-day."

"Why?"

"Oh, come, Joanna! Surely you don't suspect an *arrière pensée* every time I ask a man to eat with me?"

"Well, your preamble didn't suggest that you invited him out of sheer kindness of heart."

"And so you ask why. In a word, because I didn't want him to meet Magda to-night."

She looked so startled that he said: "Oh, it was only a guess,

408

a shot in the dark. Do you remember that when you were leaving last night you said 'Magda is rather late.'?"

"Yes."

"Perhaps it didn't occur to you that it was *very* late. It was midnight when you left. Magda had been out to dinner and on to the theatre with the Norths. Or so we understood. Well, theatres don't keep going until midnight, do they? The whole North family was at this festival, we understood. Now Mr. North, with a young inexperienced girl under his care, would surely have seen her home? I don't know whether he has a car, but surely either in that or a taxi-cab he would have had Magda on our doorstep by eleven at the latest?"

Joanna looked at him with respect. She wondered whether she had needed to intervene in Magda's affairs after all.

Schwann was standing with his back to the fire, watching the smoke from his cigar. "When Magda came in," he said, "I knew, apart from the time, that she had not been to the theatre." He considered how to put it. "She was blazing like a torch," he said. "I kissed her, and told her to get off to bed. This morning she was in a very odd frame of mind indeed. She told me that the Norths had invited her to go dancing to-night. It didn't sound likely. Naturally, I wondered who the man was. She has had so little opportunity to meet men, and she hasn't seemed to *want* to meet them either. I could think only of young Hudson, and I knew from his call on me here that he was taken with her. Well, there was poor old Schwann's problem. What was he to do?"

Joanna asked, because she wanted to hear his comment on what she had done herself: "Why should you do anything?"

He said: "Magda is nineteen. She has suffered terrible humiliations. She was almost convinced that there was indeed some taint, some shame, in her blood. She used to creep about the flat hardly daring to look even Coster in the face. If he spoke a kind word to her she would look at him with a sort of incredulous gratitude that hurt me. I know that she is an extreme case. She has no toughness. She is a shellfish without a shell. Most Jewesses even in Germany, I imagine, could put up a better fight. But there it is. We must take her as she is made. If I am right, she met young Hudson last night, and I can understand how all her repression would lead her to respond to his squiring. And I am pretty sure that her engagement to-night is to meet him again. Very well, then. You ask why I should do anything."

Joanna said: "I came round to-night to tell *you* things. But you don't seem to need much telling. However, before you go on, I can say that you are right so far. She did meet Christopher Hudson last night, but you can't blame him for that. It was her own suggestion. To-day she didn't go to college. She is infatuated, and she is meeting him to-night."

"I pretended," Schwann said, "to accept that she had been invited by the Norths, and tried to persuade her that her work was more important. That was no good. I thought of writing to my brother, but that would hold things up. I had to do something at once, and if you ask me why, I am not at liberty to tell you. I can tell you only that I dislike young Hudson and know that he would let her down in the long run. But that is not all. However, it was enough to make me see that he had better let her down in the short run. It will be hard for her, but that must be accepted."

15

A few days before this, Schwann had been to see Dick Hudson. He had always liked Dick for his simple and unpretentious ways; and his curiosity about human things took him out to St. John's Wood because he wanted to see Dick in his new part of married man. So he used the pretence of discussing his finances and suggesting some new investments. He was pleased with what he found, thought Mrs. Wayland a woman of good common-sense, and expressed the hope that Christopher was doing well, though this was a matter on which he knew he was better informed than Dick. However, the feeler gave him what he wanted. It touched Mrs. Hudson off at once. "We know nothing about Christopher, Mr. Schwann. His only connection with this establishment is to draw a weekly dole from his father. Fancy that—at his age!"

"Now, lass," Dick began; but Schwann wasn't going to let an argument develop. He apologised for an indiscretion, handed over the little wedding present he had brought, and took himself off.

As soon as he had got to the office on the morning of his unhappy clash with Magda he rang up Christopher and invited him to lunch. He was aware of the note of caution in the young man's voice, for Christopher, if not in love with Magda as she was with him, had found his adventure with her pleasant, and was looking forward to seeing her again. His thought was that Schwann had sniffed something, and so his reaction was towards refusing the invitation.

410

However, there was his career as well as this girl, and the good-will of a solicitor of Schwann's importance was not to be neglected. "Thank you very much, Mr. Schwann. I think I can manage it." Schwann smiled as he put down the receiver. He knew that the young man could manage to spare far more time than he would need.

When they were sitting at the meal Schwann used his call on Dick Hudson as the ostensible reason for the meeting. He spoke warmly of Mrs. Hudson and said how lucky Chris was to have so admirable a step-mother. It tickled him to note Chris's acquiescence. "Yes, indeed. I've known her for a very long time. I grew up with her. So she's not one of those step-mothers who bring something new and disturbing into a home. I never knew my mother. Mrs. Wayland, as she then was, took her place."

"That explains her affectionate interest in you," Schwann said. "My experience has been that step-mothers fear and dislike their husbands' children. They want a man all to themselves. They're sure they can give him a new start and that to clear out what they consider the old encumbrances is one way of going about it."

Chris looked a little startled by this turn of the conversation, but he could not go back on the step he had taken. He laughed and said: "This is the only step-mother I've ever had, so I'm not an expert in the matter. I'll take your word for the rest of them."

"Mind you," Schwann said, laying his paws on the table, "there's something in their point of view, especially when a child, as in your case, is a child no longer. Supposing him to be like you—started in a profession, set up by his own wish in his own establishment, but not yet able to stand on his feet and therefore drawing an allowance from his father. Well, his father's new wife might well cut up a bit rough about that. Women like to control the purse-strings, and a young man in those circumstances is very lucky indeed to have a step-mother who sees his point of view and realises that the one thing he wants above all others is to cease being an encumbrance."

Chris said airily: "Oh, that won't take me long."

"I'm sure it won't," Schwann said comfortably, tipping his moles over suddenly on to their backs and considering their pleasing pink bellies. "When the right sort of solicitors become aware of you, I've no doubt you'll go ahead."

He allowed it to sink in, and then said: "It's a pity a man can't just go ahead with his work and not get involved in domestic issues."

"I remember," Chris said, "that that was a point you made to me when you first took me to your flat. No clutter. Don't get involved."

"Yes, but it's not always easy to toe the line you mark for yourself. This hyena Hitler has upset my apple-cart. There is this niece of mine. I find myself practically in the position of a father to her. She must prepare herself to earn her own living, or, if she should marry, to be fit to marry something better than a nincompoop. In either case, she has a long time of study before her, and I have to be constantly on the look-out to ward off distractions. I shouldn't regard them too kindly. However, I mustn't worry you with my troubles. I know that a young barrister with his way to make has plenty of his own."

They walked to the cloak-room, and, as Chris was helping him on with his overcoat, Schwann said: "By the way, what are you doing to-night?"

"Nothing in particular."

With his overcoat on, Schwann turned to him with a smile. "Oh, happy carefree youth! Nothing in particular. Don't young men read Kipling nowadays and learn to fill the unforgiving minute with sixty seconds' worth of distance run? Try to-night to run a long way from the dangers of nothing in particular. Be wise."

The conversation gave Chris plenty to think about. He told himself that, taking one thing with another, he had better be wise. He wondered what that bitch of a Wayland had said about him to Schwann, and whether she was in a position to induce his father to stop his allowance, and whether Schwann would have the nerve to put her up to it. He decided that he had better leave Schwann's niece alone. He had discovered what could be done with girls, and there were other girls. Should he wait for her and tell her it was all up? He could imagine the scene and hadn't the nerve to face it. When Magda knocked and knocked at his door, and at last turned away bewildered, frightened and ashamed, he was buying his ticket at the Palladium.

16

When Schwann had given Joanna the outline of this story she was deeply alarmed. What had happened that afternoon at Dick Hudson's had shaken Magda, and it was easy to imagine with what expectations of comfort and reassurance she had hastened to meet

Christopher. If Schwann's plot had succeeded and Christopher had let her down, she would be utterly foundered. What would she do then? Joanna put the question to Schwann.

"Naturally," he said, "I could not leave Magda to her own resources. In my work I have something to do with those dubious types called private detectives. I briefed one of them this afternoon. He rang me up just before you arrived, reported that Christopher Hudson left his flat just before seven, that Magda arrived there at about a quarter past, that she walked up and down the Embankment for an hour, and that she is now in that Lyons tea shop that faces across to the House of Commons."

She looked at him with admiration. "Magda will suffer terribly over this," she said, "but she has a lot to thank you for. You are so dependable."

She was sitting on a couch running at a right angle from the fireplace. Schwann had remained standing, facing her. Now he threw his cigar into the fire and sat at her side. "I wish," he said "that *you* had something to thank me for, Joanna. But, alas! it is all the other way about."

She was startled and tried to ward him off with flippancy. "I have this hat." She took it off and threw it on to the couch.

To her surprise, he gave a deep groan. "I can look after Magda," he said, "but who is to scheme for me? Who is to advise me that it would be better never to see you again? I advise myself, but it is no good. When I rang you up this morning and asked you to lunch, I was ready to let Magda go to the devil. If you had said Yes, I should not have invited Chris Hudson. So you see what counts most with me. But you lied to me and said you were going out of town. I knew you were lying, but I didn't mind that. When you rang me up to-night and said you were coming round, I knew that this was about Magda, not me. But I was very happy. That's the sort of fool I am."

She turned to him and put a hand on his arm. She said: "Rudolph, please don't think of me like that. If I loved you, I would say so and be happy about it. I should have no doubts. I can imagine a woman saying Yes to a man, even though she had all sorts of doubts and knew that she was letting herself in for trouble. But if she loved him she wouldn't mind that. With you, I know that I could count on safety and loyalty and everything that is sound and solid. Thank you for offering me all that. But I don't love you, and I should be a fraud if I pretended to."

"You forgive me for kissing you?"

"Oh, for God's sake!" she said, deeply upset. "What do you take me for? It's a long time since a kiss here and there had anything to do with marriage."

She put her arms round his neck and kissed him, and said: "Now then. Do you forgive me for that?"

Schwann said: "I would rather you hadn't done that, Joanna, but I shall always remember it."

She could feel that he was torn between desire and a prompting to put her aside. And they were thus, her arms still round his neck, her cheek against his, when Magda quietly opened the door and walked in.

She stood for a moment like a pale, horrified and accusing ghost before they were aware of her. In the attitude they had taken, Joanna's skirt had ridden up above her knees. She had beautiful legs. To Magda, utterly distraught and wounded in both her love and her new self-esteem, the couple made a picture of lascivious abandonment. They got to their feet, and the girl, without speaking, surveyed them for a moment with hatred and disgust, and then walked out of the room.

ⱺ ⱺ ⱺ ⱺ ⱺ ⱺ

1

O_n the surface, life for Schwann and Magda went on as usual. She did not speak to him of that night, nor he to her. She became again the praiseworthy student, trotting off promptly to college, keeping to her books at home on most evenings. But she was frozen. When Schwann kissed her in the morning and again in the evening she seemed literally cold to his lips and to his fingers that stroked her face. There is a way of dealing with seeds. Leave them lying here and there for a long time in any casual conditions and they will deteriorate. Many of them will never produce a plant. But put them into a refrigerator for months, or even years, and then, when they are brought again into warmth, they will spurt into sparkling life. Schwann knew nothing about horticulture, but he was full of foreboding about this ice maiden who had known the frenzy of waking up in the sun and the bitterness of eclipse. He had not fully interpreted the look that Magda had turned on him and Joanna before silently leaving the room; but Joanna was in no doubt about the girl's false deduction. This made it difficult for her to take up again her position of guide and protector. She didn't feel called on to explain or excuse that moment, but, in order to see how Magda would react, she invited her a few days later to call at the flat in Baker Street after leaving college and to stay for a talk and supper.

Magda accepted, and when she came, looking dowdy and like a spiritless schoolgirl, she at once tossed on to the table a brooch. It was a small cluster of gold roses, each with a zircon at the heart.

"Oh, Magda, thank you!" Joanna exclaimed. "I've been very upset about losing that. The catch is defective and I've been intending to get it repaired."

Magda threw a satchel of books on to the couch, and said carelessly: "I thought it was yours, Joanna. I found it behind the cushions on the couch in my uncle's sitting-room."

That was all, and they went on at once to talk of other things; but Joanna felt that the throwing down of the brooch was a declaration of enmity.

It was an uneasy evening. They went down to the tea-shop below the flat and had tea, and then they went back and talked till it was time for Joanna to prepare supper. Then they talked again, but Joanna felt herself being fended off as if by a boathook that was blunt enough as a rule, but now and then had a sharp point.

In an effort to interest Magda, she told her of Joe Morrison's coming visit to London. "That's somebody you *must* meet," she said. "I expect he'll have plenty to tell you about how things are now in Germany."

Magda said: "I shall not need telling about that. I sometimes read the English papers, and if your Mr. Morrison is like most of the correspondents, he either knows nothing or is a liar. I find Englishmen not particularly reliable. They take fright and run away."

It was so sad and naïve that Joanna could have wept for the girl. Certainly, as she knew, Chris Hudson could easily take fright and run away; but O heavens! she thought, what a yardstick to measure other men by!

"I think," she said, "you won't find Joe Morrison like that."

She told Magda of Joe in Italy, of Jacopo, and of the book Joe was writing on conditions in Germany. "He's not good at running away," she said.

"Oh, Italy!" Magda replied. "Italy is not Mussolini. It is civilised. But Germany is Hitler."

She didn't seem much interested in Joe Morrison or in anything else, and Joanna was glad when at last the girl said: "Well, now, I must get back and spend an hour or two on my books. Thank you for asking me."

"I'll call a taxi and see you as far as Berkeley Square," Joanna said. "It will save you some time."

Magda looked at her with young painful cynicism. "Thank you very much," she said, "but have no fear. I promise to go straight home."

2

When Joanna got out of bed the next morning she saw that autumn, the golden link between summer and winter, had snapped.

People were hurrying along Baker Street from the Metropolitan station overcoated, brisk, lashed by a wind which she could not feel here in her warm room, but which blew out mufflers and fichus into pennons, and did its best with bus tickets and crumpled hand-bills, a poor substitute for the golden playthings it must now be finding in the parks and the countryside.

Wearing a dressing-gown of blue crackling Chinese silk that Septimus Pordage of all people had given her on her last birthday, she went into the sitting-room, switched on the electric fire so that the place should be warm for breakfast, and then, in the kitchen, made the toast and coffee that were all she would need. Then she went to the bathroom—not so stern as William Scroop's or so Byzantine as Schwann's. Dropping Septimus's dressing-gown on to a chair, and thinking of him and Schwann, a sad amusement filled her mind.—Septimus had said in a note that came with the dressing-gown: "If only I were a century or two younger, dear and beautiful lady, there would be some sense in the palpitations that afflict me as my mind contemplates you arrayed in this," and whenever she ran up to Yorkshire for a week-end he was fussily attentive. A dress-ing-gown from Septimus, who must be seventy; a hat from Rudolph who was—what? A man of indecipherable age, with the stolid sense of a wise centenarian. She said to herself that her love-life was hardly exciting or adventurous. She was thirty-seven, and the tombstones in many a church made it clear that, at that age, women once were accustomed to be buried, bowed off the scene with pious commen-dation of their fortitude in having borne a dozen children. She could picture the patient withered wrecks, gladly laying down the burden, all too glad for the monumental masons to move in. She didn't feel a bit like that. She surveyed herself briefly in the long mirror. No, she still had plenty to give. Her breasts didn't need a scaffolding or her stomach a rubber tube. Juno was about it.

Back in the bedroom, she saw the brooch of gold and zircon. It was full of memories. Scroop had given it to her, and she had first worn it on the night she persuaded him to take her to the Silver Star, the night of Chris Hudson's defection. Odd that it should return to significance at this moment when Chris was once more in the news. She had no doubt that it was significant—that Magda, finding it on the couch after her own desertion, saw in it a symbol of sin, pictured perhaps in her young fevered imagination Schwann's fingers undoing it in an exploration of her clothing.

Poor Magda! On one side of the dressing-table was an elementary make-up set that Joanna had bought to give the child some idea of

417

how to do something with herself, and on the other was a bowl of yellow roses, put there to make the room look festive in case Magda had gone in there last night to touch herself up. But she had not done so. She had been *farouche* and unreachable, her young beauty in eclipse, like a camellia that has miraculously shone through a day of winter sunshine, only to turn to a drab parody at a touch of frost. Like Schwann, Joanna thought she was in a dangerous state. She had leapt up like a Jack-in-the-box, but now the lid had shut her down, flattened and disfigured her. If at this moment another hand released the spring anything could happen.

Wearing nothing but the bright blue dressing-gown, tied with a broad sash of darker blue that was finished off in a fringe of crimson threads, she stood there sadly pondering her own state and Magda's when the door bell rang. It was a loud imperious ring, startling to her pensive condition. She dropped the brush with which, automatically as she mused, she had been burnishing the long honey-coloured hair that streamed over her shoulders. She walked on bare feet to her small entrance hall to see if letters had been dropped through the slot, though the ring was not the postman's gentle salutation, which she knew. There were no letters, and as she stood doubtfully there the imperative ring sounded again. Then the letter slot was pushed inwards and held there, and a voice said: "This is Joe Morrison. He can see light blue silk and dark blue silk, so don't pretend you're not at home, Joanna. That's not the charwoman's outfit."

Her heart began to beat excitedly. She said: "Go away, Joe. Or stay there if you like. But give me a moment to get some clothes on. It's lucky for you that there's no charwoman to-day. She's gone to a wedding in Limehouse."

He said: "Kneel down and peep through as I'm doing."

She did so, and they looked at one another's eyes, and she saw the red gleam of his hairy face.

"You look fine," he said. "A much more satisfying sight than those What the Butler Saw peep-shows on the pier. Now let me in."

"I'm not dressed."

"Good. Let me in."

An hour later she sat up in bed, languid and relaxed. She took up the bedside telephone and rang up the shop. "Oh, Mollie," she said. "I'm in bed."

"I'll say you are," Joe said, his pointed beard wagging with laughter.

She put a hand over his mouth, and he kissed it.

418

"Oh, no, nothing much," she said. "I'm not feeling very well, that's all."

She put back the receiver and Joe said: "Oh, you're not, aren't you? Well, I must see if I can do a little better."

At four o'clock she said: "I'm terribly hungry, Joe," and got up, dressed, and sang as she made the tea.

3

"What would you like to do, Joe?" she asked. "Shall we go out somewhere to dinner and to a theatre, or what?"

"I should much prefer to get some practice in domesticity. It's something I know nothing about, and I suppose I'll have to learn. So why not stay where we are? I'll be reading a good book, if you have one, and you can be knitting some socks. We'll occasionally look up at one another and grunt."

"Yes," she said. "Let's do that. It sounds enchanting. I've never had a husband who grunted."

The cold wind of the morning was still blowing, and now rain was falling as well. The afternoon darkened quickly. The sky over Baker Street was a scamper of dirty rags; the pavement was awash.

"Will you light the fire for me, Joe? This electric thing is all very well, but on special occasions I believe in atmospheric pollution."

He lit the fire, strolled to the window, and looked out. He stood there for so long, his hands in his pockets, his head sunk in to his chest, that she walked to his side, stood with her arm round him, and asked: "What is it? What are you seeing?"

He drew the curtains on the uncomfortable night, switched on a standard lamp that suffused the room in a gentle gold, and sat by the fire. "Isn't this lovely? All those poor devils paddling through the rain to Baker Street station under that sky of a witches' sabbath, and here are we, out of it all."

"That's the prologue," she said. "Tell me the tale."

He filled and lit his pipe. She sat by him, and he took her hand.

"It's no good!" he burst out. "How the devil can we wake people up? Not only England—all Europe, to say nothing of America, is full of us: men and women with the blinds drawn, refusing to see what's happening outside where it's dark and damned miserable and blowing up for something that I don't suppose you can even begin to imagine. But I can."

She put her head on to his shoulder and said: "I know how you feel about all these things, Joe. Why not leave it alone for to-night? What about our domesticity?"

He put her away from him and pointed to a chair near the fire with the stem of his pipe. "Go and sit there, Circe," he said, "and let me talk. Besides, if you like to hear such things, I get a better view of your legs. They're quite something."

He said: "I've been in England for three days now. I went up to see my father and that monstrous little half-brother that I share with Anthony. He informed me he was rather attracted to the ideals of Karl Marx. I told him that so far as I was concerned he could be attracted by the ideals of Karl and all the other Marx brothers rolled into one. Then I went over to Smurthwaite to see your mother."

"I heard from her this morning. She didn't tell me."

"I asked her not to. I wanted her permission to propose to you."

Joanna rocked with laughter. "Really, Joe, you are the most extraordinary person! How old do you think I am?"

"Perhaps I've got a fixation. Perhaps I always see you as the girl of the Smurthwaite ball. Anyway, I wanted the thing to be in order, and she consented."

Joanna said: "She would be fascinated if she knew how you interpreted her consent."

"That's as may be. Well, I was back in London yesterday, to hear glad tidings from Dunkerley."

"Good. And what were they?"

"That he's thinking of sacking me."

"No! Oh, no, Joe!"

"Oh, yes, Joanna. He's not going to do it at the moment. He merely indicated gently that it was on the cards if Joe Morrison didn't watch his step. He's got the wind up."

Joe got to his feet and knocked out his pipe on the fire bars. He stroked her silken leg as he passed by, and then sat down again.

"First of all," he said, "Champagne Charlie is not at all pleased with the way I'm carrying on."

"Who is he?"

"Alias Ribbentrop. I'm told he keeps a very good table at his Embassy, and Dunkerley, as you may know, is partial to good food and to girls who are not so good as their mothers would like them to be. Champagne Charlie can always provide a few Nordic types of beauty and a plentiful trough, at the same time whispering to my lord that that bloke Morrison is endangering those happy relations between England and the Reich that the God-inspired Fuehrer sets such store by."

"How on earth do you know that, Joe?"

"I know everything. It's my job to. Then there's Neville, the sisal-grower from Brummagem who, in God's mysterious Providence, became Prime Minister of Great Britain. He doesn't like poor little Joe, either."

He stuffed tobacco fiercely into his pipe. "The editor of *The Banner*," he said, "and sundry other assorted editors, have been summoned to Whitehall and had it impressed on them that the Fuehrer's tender feelings are hurt by the news their wicked representatives are sending from Germany. In the interests of world peace, these boys had better lay off concentration camps, and the incineration of Jews, and midnight visits, and beatings-up, and military preparations, and the death of the free press, and other trifles of that sort. Whitehall doesn't like these things getting about. It just isn't done to criticise what a sovereign state chooses to do within its own borders. These glad tidings Dunkerley communicated to me yesterday. So I am to watch my step in future. Our Prime Minister is on the side of Jacopo. He'd like to shut my mouth."

"Will he, Joe?"

"That doesn't rest with me. What I write is one thing. What Dunkerley chooses to publish is another."

He put some coal on to the fire, and they listened to the cry of the wind and the lashing of rain against the window.

"You see," Joe said, "the dangerous type you've got mixed up with. And I haven't told you all of it."

"Oh, darling. There can't be anything much worse than that."

"Well, you shall judge. You know I wrote to you about a chap in Goebbels's department who was double-crossing the Reich and being very useful to me?"

"Yes."

"Well, I'm afraid he's what you might call a double double-crosser. My book on Germany is nearly finished, and all the typescript so far is in his hands. He was due for one of his visits to England and was to deliver it to my publisher. I saw my publisher yesterday, and it hasn't reached him."

"Perhaps he didn't come after all."

"He did. I know that he has been in England for three days."

"Perhaps he hasn't found a chance yet."

"Oh, yes. There are plenty of perhapses. But my guess is that Joe Morrison's opinion of Germany is now being gloated over by Mr. Goebbels."

"Would that be serious?"

"It could make Germany even more unhealthy for me than it is now."

She loved him. She had no doubt of it now, and everything in her made her want to say: "Why go back? Why not let Germany stew in its own juice?" Everything except her respect for Joe. She said: "When will you be going back?"

"I don't know. Perhaps in a few days. At most in a week."

Even at that moment she could afford a laugh. She asked demurely: "Seeing that we have the consent of my son's grandmother, could we marry before you go?"

"We could, but we shan't. We've waited a long time, Joanna. I think now we'd better wait till the world's a bit more promising. Besides, think what we shall save on income-tax if we live in sin. It's the only private enterprise that the Chancellor looks on leniently."

She said: "Very well, Joe," but she said it so sadly that he went over and kissed her. "I'm acting wisely, my darling," he said. "I know more than you do of what is involved. Can you believe that?"

"Yes. I'll do anything you want."

"I'll marry you before I go if you still want that. I don't advise it, but I'll do it."

She said: "No," in so small a voice that it could hardly be heard in the tumult of the weather.

"What now?" Joe asked. "Do I stay the night?"

"I'd love it," she said. "But my charwoman's wedding celebrations won't stretch over to-morrow. She has her key, and she'll bring me a cup of tea in bed at half past eight. I'm afraid she wouldn't be as lenient as the Chancellor. She's a bawdy old thing in speech, but she draws the line in practice."

They got up and stood embraced, body to body, each aware of the other's heat. Joe whispered: "Just an hour."

She said: "Oh, my darling!" and led him by the hand into the bedroom.

It was half past ten when she opened the door upon Baker Street and said, kissing him: "Come early to-morrow, darling. I shan't be alive till you're here."

Joe whistled to a taxi-cab that was sloshing over the shining road in which the raindrops danced, and it stopped, and he dashed in, and she saw the red of his beard through the streaming glass, and then he was gone in a wild whoosh of Valkyrie wind.

She climbed her stairs on weak legs, feeling drained as she had done on those nights when Scroop would give her a look at a party, and they would unceremoniously leave and go back to Soho Square, palpitating side by side in a taxi, his arm around her, upon her breast. She fell rather than sat upon the easy-chair before the electric fire in her bedroom, hardly aware of the howling weather that had swallowed him up, hardly aware of anything but the slow ebb of feeling, till the telephone alongside her bed made her start as though a shot had been fired in the room.

She sat on the bed and took up the receiver. It was Septimus Pordage, scarcely intelligible in his agitation and distress. She understood at last that her mother was dead. Septimus was speaking from Throstle's Nest, where he had been invited to dinner, he said. Mrs. Halliwell had come rather late from a committee meeting in Smurthwaite, and had seemed tired and overdone. She had fallen on entering the house, and she was dead by the time a doctor arrived.

4

The news shocked her thoughts into order. She would have to travel through the night, and she rang up the garage where her car was housed and told them to have it at the door in half an hour. She must write to Joe. But where was he staying? He had not told her. She wrote to her charwoman. "Dear Mrs. Potter.—I have just received news of my mother's sudden death, and am motoring up to Yorkshire. I shall be away for some days. With this you will find a letter addressed to Mr. Joe Morrison, whom I am expecting to call upon me to-morrow. Please hand the letter to him."

She wrote to Joe: "Oh, darling! No sooner were you gone than I received the most dreadful news by telephone. My dear mother has died suddenly of some sort of stroke. I must get to Yorkshire at once and am motoring through the night. Darling, believe me, not to have you with me is insupportable. Especially at such a moment. Is it at all possible for you to drop everything and come after me by train? I don't know how I shall be able to go through this if you don't. Oh, please do, do. I can't bear this feeling of having been dropped from heaven into the darkest misery. Your loving, loving Joanna."

She put the two notes on the mantelpiece in the kitchen, threw

423

some things into a suitcase, dressed herself in travelling clothes, and was at the door as her car drew up. The chauffeur touched his cap. "Not the choicest night for travelling, my lady."

She hardly heard him. She got in and started off through the dreadful unabating storm. It was half past eleven.

5

The wind had dropped when Mrs. Potter got out of bed at six o'clock to make her old man's breakfast, but the sky was still turgid with cloud and Mrs. Potter's head with the fumes of festivity. When the old man was gone she sat down to her own rasher, and it nauseated her. What she wanted was a good day in bed, and that was what she'd be having if people had their rights. She was damned, she told herself, if she'd fag all the way to Baker Street this morning if it wasn't for Lady Scroop. Lady Scroop was all right, even if she was a lady. Look at the hat she had given her for the wedding. A proper fetching hat that was, and it caused a bit of a stir. All very well for Lady Scroop to make a joke about it and say that it was something a boy friend had given her and that she didn't want to wear any more. That was how Lady Scroop was. She was always pretending she wasn't helping you when she was. Mrs. Potter put the breakfast things on a tray and tottered towards the kitchen sink. The smell of congealed fat made her stomach heave, and she only just managed to get the tray down before discharging into a bucket.

Well, she told herself philosophically, a wedding wasn't much of a wedding if it didn't leave a few fat heads behind, and young Maryllin deserved the best. "I'll bet *she's* having a morning in bed, anyhow, and then some," Mrs. Potter thought with relish, looking out on the sagging clouds over the Limehouse roofs. "Well," she said, "I'll have an hour anyway, and then get cracking. Lady Scroop'll understand." She felt worse lying down than standing up. She was still lying down and beginning to groan while Joe Morrison was ringing and ringing at the door of the Baker Street flat, and getting no answer.

6

It was worse, Joe thought, than if the wind had continued to blow. That at least gave a vigour and urgency to any moment. But now, no wind, no rain, nothing but the dreary drifting dish-clouts overhead and the sodden earth beneath. A city of more than dreadful night, because he had come to it with what he thought a safe passport to paradise. He wandered along Baker Street and turned into Oxford Street, and listlessly looked at the books in Bumpus's, and circumnavigated Selfridge's, and was back at ten o'clock at the flat in Baker Street. And again he might have been knocking on the door of a tomb. He went into the tea-room beneath the flat and spent an hour there, looking at the foreign news in all the morning papers but seeing nothing of what he looked at. Then once more he climbed the stairs and knocked. Again there was no answer, but he could hear the shrilling of the telephone bell. It went on for a long time, and he knelt with the flap of the letter-box pushed in and his ear attentive as though that urgent noise could have some meaning for him. As indeed it had. It was Joanna ringing up to ask Mrs. Potter if Joe had been given her letter, and hoping desperately that Joe himself might be there to speak to her.

The ringing stopped, and Joe rose to his feet, dusted down his knees, and said: "Well, that's that."

He had used the beginning of his leave to make all his duty calls, hoping to have a few clear days with Joanna. Now he was at a loose end, and he thought of Hesba Lewison. Joe was not much interested in novels and had not read a word that Hesba had written. He called on her whenever he was in England because he knew her to be a reliable and generous helper of some who escaped from Hitler's hell. He had himself directed a few of them to her. She had never let him down. He rang her up from a call-box, and she said that she would be busy all day, but would like him to dine with her that night. "Could you be at *La Fine Bouche* at eight o'clock? I shall have two other guests whom you might like to meet." Joe thanked her and said he would be there.

It was twelve o'clock, and he did not again return to Baker Street. Had he done so, he would have heard the telephone bell ringing again. A belated Mrs. Potter, feeling none too bright, had arrived a quarter-of-an-hour before and read the note Joanna had left for her. She was sorry about poor Lady Scroop's mother, but unscrupulous in self-defense. What was easier, she thought, than to say that no one hadn't called for that letter addressed to Mr. Morrison? She left it standing by the tin clock on the kitchen mantelpiece, and she told her lie firmly when Lady Scroop asked if it had been called for.

"Are you sure, Mrs. Potter?"

"Quite sure, my lady. No one hasn't called since I been here, and you know what time I comes." Neat, she thought. Not even a lie, really.

Lady Scroop sounded proper upset. "I don't understand. It was most important. Is there any letter there for me?"

"Not a thing, my lady."

"Are you sure you've been in the flat all the time? I rang up an hour ago, and there was no answer."

Mrs. Potter was not caught by that one. "Well, my lady, I heard the ring, but I was in the— Well, actually, I don't like to say it, but you know how it is sometimes, quite sudden, my lady. And then the bell stopped ringing. I've been here all right."

There was a long silence, and she wondered if Lady Scroop had pushed off without saying good-bye. So she said: "Awfully sorry about your mother, my lady."

Lady Scroop was still there. She said: "Thank you, Mrs. Potter. If Mr. Morrison does call, ask him to ring me up here. You know the number, don't you?"

"Yes, my lady."

"Well, I think that's all. Good-bye."

Mrs. Potter didn't like telephones at the best of times, and this conversation made her feel quite bad. Seeing that it was gone twelve, which was her pushing-off time, she made a languid swipe here and there with a duster and set out for Limehouse.

7

Joe didn't want lunch. He wanted nothing but oblivion. He walked to his small back-street hotel, went to bed, and slept till seven o'clock. Then he bathed and dressed, had a drink in the bar, and strolled to *La Fine Bouche*. He didn't know what the drill was in Anthony's posh place, so he put on a dinner jacket to be on the safe side. Anyway, he welcomed the idea of a night out. A reaction had set in. He felt defrauded. He wanted to forget Joanna Scroop. And yet it couldn't be all her fault. Where had he gone wrong? He couldn't make it out. They had seemed all one, moving in harmony last night with every motion of mind and body. Why in hell had she run away? He felt as though he had possessed her in a dream—as he often had done—and awakened to find his mouth bitter and his arms empty.

While he slept the sky had cleared. As he strolled along Piccadilly with a raincoat over his arm, a tall red-bearded figure that took many a woman's eye, the stars were shining, the last rags of the late autumn leaves in the Green Park were caught by the city's lamps, and liberation from the ferocity of the weather lightened his sense of the darkness of human destiny, and of his own in particular. He was prepared to take this charming moment at its face value. Always, he was aware, a dangerous thing to do.

He found Hesba Lewison already arrived. She was in the foyer with a short dark middle-aged man and a girl—almost a child— whose sad beauty struck him at once. He had seen so much of it. Miss Lewison rose and went to meet him and led him towards her guests, saying: "Now, let's all have a drink before we go in. This is Joe Morrison, and this is Rudolph Schwann and his niece, Magda Schwann. Mr. Schwann is a naturalised Englishman. Miss Schwann is a German Jewess. I know these points interest you, Joe, and that you understand their significance. Now, what's it to be?"

The girl, Joe noticed, drank nothing. He offered her a cigarette and she declined it without speaking, with a mere shake of the head. She seemed frozen. He tried to draw her into conversation. "Have you been long in England, Miss Schwann?"

"A few months."

"What is it—a visit or are you hoping to stay?"

"I hoped at first to stay, but now I am going back."

She had nothing more to say, and Miss Lewison said: "We'll tell you about that presently, Joe."

They went into the restaurant, and Anthony Fieldhouse conducted them to their table. He was looking fat and prosperous, Joe thought, but his hair was going grey and there was a bald spot on the top of his head.

"How is Lottie?" Joe asked, and he knew he was asking it mechanically. He felt an enormous distance lying between himself and the man who had been the boy crying with him during their first day together at school.

"At home," Anthony said, "nursing our third."

"Give her my love, won't you?"

"She'll be delighted to hear of you. Have you been seeing anything of Joanna?"

"No," Joe said. "I've been up to the eyes."

"Well"—Anthony hovered, his eye on new arrivals.

"Off you go," Joe said. "Don't neglect the clients."

That was at half past eight, and Joanna, who had driven through the night, and been distracted by the conversation she had had with Mrs. Potter, and torn to pieces by the feeling of the house with the dead woman upstairs, was dropping with grief and tiredness. Septimus Pordage, who had hovered about the place all day, trying to persuade her to eat, trying to persuade her to sleep, followed her into Mrs. Halliwell's office. "If there is nothing more I can do, dear lady, I'll be off. I shall be here first thing in the morning to obey your lightest command. Are you sure you won't get off to bed now, or let me order you a little soup or a glass of wine?"

She got up from the swivel chair at her mother's desk and kissed him absent-mindedly. "You are a darling," she said. "I shall love to see you in the morning."

Septimus reluctantly took the dismissal and tiptoed out as though she were indeed asleep and he feared to wake her. She was displeased with herself because she knew the abounding kindness of his heart and was, nevertheless, glad to see him go. The double load of sorrow so tore at her nerves that she felt as though the mere buzzing of a fly would make her scream.

Now there was absolute quiet save for the companionable rustle of flames in the grate, a rustle as if the trees which, æons ago, this coal had been were visiting the earth again and shaking their leaves beneath the moon. In the blessed quiet, she began to think coherently for the first time since Septimus had rung up last night. There were many things she would have to do. For one, there would be letters to write and funeral invitations to send out. She hoped no one would come—that would have been her mother's wish—but some invitations there must be. She thought of Lottie and of her mother for whom Mrs. Halliwell had had a high regard. They, at all events, should be told at once. A day had already been lost. She would ring up Lottie at Pinner, ask her to pass the news on to Anthony and her mother, and then take Septimus's advice and try to sleep.

While Anthony was talking to Joe Morrison in *La Fine Bouche*, Lottie was asking herself whether she ought to ring him up and give him the news. "And Joanna says if we see anything of Joe Morrison we mustn't fail to let him know." But she didn't telephone. It was a rule that Anthony was not to be disturbed by private affairs during business hours. "He'll be here by midnight," Lottie told herself. "That'll be time enough."

There was no difficulty in recognising the double-crossing Nazi who could have been, as Joe told Joanna, a double double-crosser. In the first world war he lost an eye, and the empty socket was concealed behind a black monocle that gave a grim touch to his thin clean-shaven face. Joe often had occasion to call at the German Embassy when he was in London, and he recognised the young man sitting next to the monocled Kaspar Retz as a member of the Embassy staff. He told Hesba Lewison and Mr. Schwann what he knew of them, carefully saying nothing of his own associations with Retz. Miss Lewison, who had a great curiosity about human beings, said: "I wish you'd introduce me to them, Joe."

Schwann walked across the restaurant with them. Magda stayed where she was. Joe made the introductions, and Retz invited them all to sit down and have some coffee and a liqueur. But Joe went back to his table, not wishing to leave that sad child alone. Her uncle had persuaded her to take a Benedictine with her coffee, but she had not tasted it, and as Joe sat at her side she was still twirling the glass thoughtfully. Joe said with a smile: "Try it. It's good."

She smiled back at him: the first smile he had seen on her face that night. It improved her, he thought, and that was saying a good deal. "I think I will," she said, and sipped. "Will it give me courage?"

"Do you especially need courage at the moment?"

"Yes. I want to be very rude to you. I am puzzled."

"Tell me what's puzzling you."

"When you were talking to Mr. Fieldhouse, he asked you if you had been seeing anything of Joanna. Is that by any chance Lady Scroop?"

"Yes, it is. Do you know her?"

She didn't answer the question, but went on: "You said you hadn't seen her, and you said it in an off-hand way as if she didn't mean anything to you. But during dinner you and Miss Lewison talked about her, and I felt you were not—well, not indifferent to her."

He said rather curtly: "You are a very observant young woman, Miss Schwann."

"Now I have hurt you," she said, "and I did not wish to hurt you. I have listened to all three of you talking to-night, and I have admired you. You have been so willing to help anybody who has been like me in distress. So my wish is not to hurt you, but to help you. It is helpful, is it not, to know the truth?"

"That's a philosophical question," Joe said. "It can depend on the moment. I can think of a good many times when not to know the truth helped me over a bad patch. And don't mix up the truth with mere facts, which are another matter. Anyway, if there's anything you want to enlighten me about, fire away. I don't think you'll destroy me."

She said: "Lady Scroop is my uncle's mistress."

10

Magda was, as Joe had said, an observant young woman. It hadn't taken her long to realise that when Joanna took her to St. John's Wood it was not so that she might meet Chris's father but so that she might meet his step-mother, who clearly hated him. It was so that she might hear her beloved evilly spoken of. Why Joanna who had been so kind to her should want to do this she could not understand, but her revulsion of feeling was sharp. A stab in the back from a friend went doubly deep, and when that night Chris did not meet her, it was upon Joanna, not him, that her contempt was turned. For it was not clean anger that she felt: it was corroding contempt, eating into herself. Life had taught her no subtlety. Everything that had happened to her had been simple and above board: a loving family life, a happiness among companions at school, and then, swift and terrible, but still simple and obvious, the hatred and the persecution. She could understand all that; but that a friend should use the devious methods of Joanna: that was something she could not understand. It was contemptible.

These were the thoughts that were corroding her mind in those few hours when she felt herself utterly abandoned, wandering in a great darkness of the soul, and convinced that Joanna, who had used such dirty means to belittle Chris in her eyes, had also belittled her in his. How else account for his absence? And so it was that when she could no longer indulge and feed her sorrow by watching the lighters sliding like dark coffins over the dark river and was obliged to creep back to the only refuge she knew, she was prepared, with a child's simplicity, to believe anything monstrous about Joanna. When she silently opened the door and found her uncle and Joanna in one another's arms she was shocked and disgusted but not surprised. The moment merely told her how right she had been in all that she had been thinking of Lady Scroop. She never wanted to see her again, and only the chance finding of the brooch, with all the implications she gave to it, induced her to go to Baker Street to enjoy a small triumph.

Throughout the next few days she lived pathetically in hope of hearing from Chris; but no word came. His mind, she decided, had been permanently poisoned against her. What was worst of all was that this should be done by a woman who was her uncle's mistress. For she had no doubt that she was, and a mistress, in Magda's childish and puritan mind, was an abomination. From a mistress, what else could one expect save the contemptible conduct of which Joanna had been guilty?

On the night when Magda came back from Baker Street after handing the brooch to Joanna, with the satisfied feeling that a barrister might have on producing out of the hat the last clinching and damning piece of evidence, the almost mythical North family materialised for Schwann. He himself answered the telephone when Miss North rang up. She said she wished to remind Magda of a lecture that they had arranged to attend that night. He called Magda to the telephone and heard her say that No, she wouldn't be coming after all. There were other things she had to do.

What she had to do was be in the flat that night and every night, so that Lady Scroop should not come there to practice her abominations.

"I hope," Schwann said gently, "that you don't find this place too lonely at nights."

"I am all right so long as you are here."

"But I am going out to-night to dine with a friend."

So that was it. He would elude her after all! If his mistress didn't come here, he would go to her.

She spent a night of anguish. She knew the Baker Street flat well enough to indulge in an orgy of imagination about what was going on there. The sudden cutting off of her own passionate experience had left her mind neurotic and erotic, and it was while she was in this condition, which she felt at times would destroy her, that she made up her mind to return to Germany. There, whatever the perils, was a family with whom she would find affection and would not feel the contempt that was killing the love she had cherished for her uncle.

When Magda said: "Lady Scroop is my uncle's mistress" she expected at least to see Joe blench or tremble. She had liked this Joe Morrison, and because she liked him and because she had become aware of his feeling for Joanna, she felt it was right to leave him in no doubt as to the true nature of that enchantress. But she had become so bemused and obsessed by melodramatic fancy that she didn't know what to do or say next when Joe began to laugh. He had been solemn all through the meal, and her revelation seemed an odd thing to start his laughter.

Joe himself was surprised at the peace that spread through his mind when Magda had spoken. He looked at the girl and saw that she was serious. But he knew his Joanna. Almost without thought, everything within him repudiated what he had heard. It was not a matter even to be considered. And if you know your Joanna as well as that, he said, what's the matter with you? She's vanished. All right. Wait till you know why. Come to your senses. She didn't just go for the sake of giving you hell.

He said to Magda: "Lady Scroop and I are going to be married soon." He felt great joy in answering her in those words, brushing her aside like a fly from his nose.

"After what I have told you?"

"After everything you could possibly tell me."

"I have never dared to speak about this to my uncle. I think you should."

"I shall not. And if you are a wise girl you will not do so either."

He wondered what was behind it all, but he didn't wonder for long. There were other things for wonder, especially the sudden clarity of his mind and the confidence of his heart. He raised his brandy-glass to her. "Thank you, Miss Schwann," he said. "You are an angel, a messenger of light. Now here are your uncle and Miss Lewison. If you'll forgive me I'll go and have a few words with my German friends."

He said good-night to Rudolph and Hesba and walked over to sit at Retz's table.

12

The young man with Retz was named Lang. He was a cartoon German, stiff-haired and bull-necked, the sort of man who would know, one imagined, how to keep a *hausfrau* in order. Retz, with his eye black-shuttered, his scarred face and lean body, looked like a war-worn knight, dependable to death. But Joe was alert and watchful. As soon as he joined them, Lang got up and said to Retz: "I'll see you later, then, Kaspar?"

He clicked his heels to Joe and went.

Joe accepted a cigar from Retz but declined a drink. It had been an odd day, and this was an odd culmination. The restaurant had reached the peak of its evening activity. People were coming in from the theatres, beautiful women, well-dressed men. Trolleys rolled by, waiters hurried along with trays, cutlery clattered, glass and china clinked. Bottles in buckets of ice were reverently lifted in napkins, tilted over crystal. At a service-table the voices of a few waiters suddenly rose in sharp altercation. Joe saw Anthony Field-house appear there—in no hurry, with no obvious intention; it was as though he just happened to be on the spot—and the unseemly noise instantly stilled. It was a long way from Anthony's first dinner at the flat in Baker Street for the launching of *Vanguard*. Well, good luck to Anthony. This was his world, and he was in serene command of it. But Joe was glad it wasn't his world.

The thought of *Vanguard* and the flat inevitably took his mind back to Joanna. He found that he could still think of her with confidence and serenity.

A lovely blonde girl passed by their table with a famous actor whose third divorce had been reported in the papers that morning. Retz looked at her with slow insolent appraisal. "A type that appeals to me, Joe," he said. "To you, too, I imagine. She reminds me of Lady Scroop."

Joe controlled his tendency to show surprise at the words. "What on earth d'you know about Lady Scroop?" had been on the tip of his tongue. He smiled and said: "You know everything, Kaspar."

"Yes, Joe. That is where I have an advantage over you. You are a very good foreign correspondent, but you seem to take no interest in general news. It can be fascinating, and a small hint can take you a long way. I imagine that if you had read a few lines in the stop press of the *Yorkshire Post* this morning I should not now be having the pleasure of your company."

"And what do these wonderful lines tell us?"

"That Lady Scroop's mother died yesterday evening."

Even Retz could not fail to feel surprise at the light almost of joy that warmed Joe's face. "You are not glad surely that the old lady has kicked the bucket?"

"I am glad, almighty glad, that I know where Joanna is."

He got up. "You must excuse me, Kaspar, but I shall have to ring her up. Right now. I'll get Mr. Fieldhouse to put me through from here."

Retz said: "Sit down a moment, Joe. We can do better than that. I'm meeting Lang presently. It's a lovely moonlight night and he has proposed a run in his car. He will doubtless wish to show me attractive things like the country houses that the Embassy staff will occupy when the Fuehrer has conquered England. They are a pack of silly swine who little know the English, as I do and as you do. However, we can make use of Lang. Orders are orders, and I happen to be in a position to give them to him. We shall order him to drive us to Yorkshire. You shall surprise your Lady Scroop by appearing for breakfast."

It was an overwhelming temptation, but Joe hesitated. He looked at Retz's grim face and his mind weighed all his old confidence in the man against his new-come fears. Had anything but Joanna been in question he would have said No. He said: "Very well, Kaspar. Thank you."

"Good. And come now at once. Do not telephone. Say nothing to anyone. So the surprise and joy will be greater." He took Joe's arm and almost hustled him to the cloak-room where they put on their coats and then strolled together towards Hyde Park Corner.

13

They had stood there for only a few moments when Lang's car slid up, a shining powerful vehicle with Lang himself at the wheel. They were in and the car was moving away almost in one movement. There seemed something so odd, inevitable, preordained, that again Joe's brain questioned the wisdom of his impulse.

Retz leaned forward and said to Lang: "Get on to the Great North Road and keep going along it until I give you further orders."

He slid the glass panel across and pulled down the little blind that shut them into a small cosy world away from Lang. He unfolded a fur rug that lay on the seat and spread it over his knees and Joe's. They moved along as if on silk. Joe said: "You must regret at times, Kaspar, that you cannot for ever remain loyal to the Reich. It is so kind to its favoured servants."

Retz said: "Ribbentrop imagines himself to be an aristocrat. He is, in fact, the worst type of vulgarian. Everything about him must be like this car—fat and luxurious. I despise him. I am a soldier."

Joe looked sideways at the lean formidable countenance. "You must have been a pretty tough one at that, Kaspar. We are lucky to have you on our side. I shall be returning to Germany soon—perhaps in a week. How is the set-up? Do we go on as before?"

"No. Do nothing till you hear from me. Old Heuffer has been rumbled." Retz was proud of his English slang. Heuffer was the match-seller.

Joe was alarmed. "May that not be bad for you, Kaspar? The old rogue could tell a lot."

Retz said rather primly: "Heuffer was not a rogue. He was once a good musician, but he had the misfortune to be like you and me. He didn't like megalomaniacs and their ways. He was a good friend of freedom. He was afraid of only one thing—torture. He asked me long ago to give him the means of avoiding that. I did, and he was dead before he could be questioned. You have been wondering, I know, why the typescript of your book has not reached your publisher. That is why. I imagine Heuffer was too wise to have anything in his room that would involve me or you, but you never know. Anyway, it was common prudence at the moment to leave the thing behind."

"Thank you, Kaspar. I've been worrying about that."

"Don't worry, Joe. You know how things are. We must do what we can if and when the opportunity arises. But we can't afford to make mistakes. I can't anyway. If I seem slow off the mark, bear that in mind. I'm with you, and I do what I can. I hope I've given you proof enough of that. But one mistake is one too many in the Third Reich."

They were silent for a while. The car was clear of the town, and Lang had accelerated along the country roads. It was a wonderful night. The moon was high and bright, washing the fields in silver. The trees were still. Impossible to believe, Joe was thinking, that only twenty-four hours separated this moment from that in which he had run across the pavement in Baker Street through the drench of rain and the wild buffets of the wind. And he could hardly have been through the door when Joanna, alone, had to bear the shock of that sorrowful moment. The moon-milky filaments of the telegraph wires swooped and dipped, and the speed of the car would have seemed to him a bit on the alarming side but for the thought that it was taking him to her, and the faster the better.

He felt drowsy after his disturbing day and his over-heavy dinner.

He put his head back on the downy cushion of the car and was instantly more asleep than awake. And then he was wide awake again with a jerk, for through his bemused condition a thread of disbelief was creeping once more. Even if Retz were all that he had once imagined him to be, even if his new-come doubts were baseless, wasn't this a bit too much? Retz was not in London for fun. The long absence that this run to Yorkshire and back would entail—that would take some explaining; and if the true explanation were given—the sudden whim to deliver a lover to his distressed lady —wouldn't that sound frivolous and untenable?

He looked at Retz, and Retz was looking at him. In the light of a passing car the black monocle glittered.

Retz spoke in his old familiar voice. "You are lucky to be able to snatch forty winks in a car, Joe. I never can."

Joe asked the question that was in his mind. "When you get back to London to-morrow, won't you and Lang have trouble in explaining where you've been? I hope I'm not going to be responsible for putting you in a spot."

Retz laughed. "There are strange jobs to be done, you know, in the pass life has come to nowadays, and Lang has one of them. You know as well as I do that not all Englishmen regard the Reich with the contempt that you and I feel. What terrifies them is not Germany but Russia. They want to cherish Germany as a buffer between them and the Reds. They'd like to see those two at one another's throats, tearing one another to death. And there are some who go a good deal further than that and think the Fuehrer is setting a fine example of how the strong hand should run a country. Believe me, Joe, there are plenty of country houses where Ribbentrop is an honoured guest. Our dapper Lang is an unofficial liaison officer with some of these people. A social call here and there. What more natural than that he should occasionally be invited to stay the night, or that he should for once take me with him to see the natives in their natural setting? To your prejudiced eye he may look just a typical fat little German pig, but he has certain qualities. He has polished manners; he is adaptable; he is *persona grata* with ladies. Do not under-estimate that crafty little porker. It is like you, Joe, to be thinking of me. But you needn't. Use this chance to have a little sleep."

It was easy to follow that advice. Joe put his head down. The movement of the car lulled his senses. The little cubicle was heated by some electrical gadget. Soon he was soundly sleeping.

14

A change in the tempo of the car's progress brought him suddenly awake. He stretched and yawned, not aware for a moment where he was; then a sharp apprehension of danger alerted all his senses. He looked at his wrist watch. It was nearly two o'clock, and almost as bright as day. The car stopped.

"Where are we, Kaspar?" he asked.

Retz said: "Get out and see, Joe. I thought we might stretch our legs for a moment."

He got out, and Joe followed him, shivering in the sharp air, looking about him to see if any house or other sign of humanity were in sight. There was nothing. They had left the main road. What they were on now could hardly be called secondary. It was little more than a lane, shut closely in by high hazel hedges. Joe looked at this undistinguished English prospect, and something said in him: "Well, this is it."

From the lane a cart-track ran between fields, and this, too, was masked by hedges that had not been slashed for a long time. Lang was walking along this track, and Retz said: "You follow Lang, Joe."

There was nothing to do but obey. Lang was six yards or so ahead, his footsteps soundless, for the track was grassy, and, six yards behind Joe, Retz silently followed. The track twisted, so that, even had someone improbably passed by where the car was now standing, he would have seen nothing of that silent procession of three. The light of the moon was itself liquid silence, raining down.

When they had walked a few hundred yards the track widened into a bay, with a gate into a field on either side. Here, where the hedges fell away, the moonlight came strongly, as on to a stage.

Retz said: "This will do. Stand where you are, Joe, and turn towards me."

Joe did so, and saw the moonlight glint on the revolver in Retz's hand. Retz said: "You are a good chap in many ways, Joe, but I am going to shoot you."

He was speaking very quietly, and Joe found himself listening with a surprising calm that was beyond desperation or hope. This was not Jacopo. This was it.

"You see, Joe, to impound your manuscript is not enough. You are one of those rash fools who would write it all over again. However, your author's vanity will be pleased to know that your work has been read in the highest quarters—by the Fuehrer and by Dr. Goebbels. They are not pleased with you, Joe. You must admit that you were not complimentary to either. I have received no direct order to do what I am about to do, but I'm good at interpreting unspoken wishes. Of course, it's not only this book. You're too much of a nuisance in every sort of way, and you're the sort of man who'd go on being a nuisance. You don't learn. Well, we can't dally here all night. Farewell."

Joe saw him raise the revolver. He shut his eyes. The sound of the shot made him reel, but to his surprise he was able presently to open his eyes. Lang was leaning over Retz, and in his hand, too, was a revolver. Joe was unable to move, mystified by what had happened, his limbs shaking from shock. Lang put his revolver into his pocket and then, putting on a glove, removed the weapon from Retz's dead hand. Joe swayed forward and saw the hole in Retz's temple, a black stain near the black monocle. Lang walked to one of the field gates and fired Retz's revolver. He came back and looked at Joe. He was trembling and ghastly white. He put the revolver down by Retz's hand and said in a shaking voice: "There. That is a bullet missing from the chamber. They will find it in his brain. A clear case of suicide—eh?"

Joe said, in a voice that trembled like Lang's: "I don't know what this is all about."

Lang was walking along the track back towards the car, weaving from side to side as if drunk. Joe followed him hardly more steadily, and climbed into the seat next the driver's. Lang started the engine. Once at the wheel, he seemed to recover some control of himself. In a quarter of an hour they were off the secondary road, and Lang, away from the scene of his crime, became steady again.

They were driving back towards London. Presently Joe said: "Mr. Lang, you have saved my life and you have taken Retz's. I don't know why you did either. But, anyway, thank you."

Lang's colour was coming back. He stopped the car for a moment, took a flask from a pocket in the door, and swigged. He wiped the mouthpiece with a silk handkerchief and handed the flask to Joe. The brandy tingled through him and he felt better. "We both needed that," Lang said. "The night is cold and I am a coward. That is the first time I have killed a man."

They were buzzing along again, and Joe felt well enough to laugh. "Don't make a habit of it," he said.

Lang said: "What he told you about me—about visiting country houses and all that—that is true."

"I thought we were having a private conversation, and I'm sure Retz did."

"Yes, but Retz was a fool. He should have thought of the microphone."

"I see."

"He was quite right in telling you that I shall have no difficulty in explaining my movements. When I arranged in the restaurant to pick him up at Hyde Park Corner I did so because it is a busy place where no one was likely to notice such a commonplace thing as a car taking a passenger aboard. I didn't know how or where I should kill him, and your being with him made everything more difficult. Or so I thought. As it happened, he arranged his own execution perfectly. When I had shot him, I thought of shooting you, too."

"I'm surprised you didn't," Joe said sincerely. "I still don't understand why you let me off."

Lang said: "There were two reasons. The first one you will understand. The second perhaps not. As it turned out, it looked so perfectly like suicide. Well, so much the better, I thought. And then the second thing was this. He wanted to kill you, and even when he was dead it gave me satisfaction to prevent something that he wanted to do."

Yes, Joe said to himself, I can see that. And he marvelled at, was saddened by, the corrosion of mind and spirit behind Lang's words. He had seen so much of it, all over Europe, and here it was again in this small bull-necked fellow at his side, and he owed his life to it. A strange thought—that, in its own roundabout and odious way, hate had been his salvation. Was a man's word worth anything in such a world? Anyway, he decided to give it. "Mr. Lang," he said, "we are living in an odd world, a world that I don't like one little bit. Even those who govern great states have frankly laid it down that any lie or deception is permissible if it advances what they consider to be the state's interest. So perhaps to give you my word may seem meaningless. However, I give it. I shall not tell anybody what has happened to-night."

That must be so absolutely. Not even to Joanna would he say a word. And he began to think of Joanna again and of her present sorrow and of the future joys that they would share. He began to think of life, and the thought was exhilarating after the hate and death that had been his companions for what seemed now a long time. He stirred and stretched and felt his taut nerves relaxing, and he noticed that the moon was tumbling away towards the west. Not long, and it would be sunrise. He had been longing to ask Lang why he killed Retz, but now it didn't seem to matter. In a hateful environment he had killed him out of hate, as a lot of people would be killed before this thing was over, this strutting of murderous maniacs all over Europe. His own efforts to counter it by exposing it seemed small and ineffectual in face of an immense apathy, an immense sleepy ignorance that refused to be awakened. Told off by Dunkerley; told off by Whitehall. Watch your step, Joe Morrison. Not so many pot-shots at the grinning tigers and the slimy snakes. They don't like it, and we really mustn't annoy them.

What could one man do?

Absurdly, the words of a popular song went swinging through his mind. *I've got my love to keep me warm.* Well, he thought, that was a beginning, so long as there was a dormer in the roof with a lookout on the world. A pair of lovers was an improvement on a pair of haters. You could say that, anyway.

Lang was shut up again in whatever dark memories and speculations haunted his mind. He did not speak till they were on the fringes of the London suburbs, and then he said: "We had better not be seen arriving in London together, Mr. Morrison. We part here."

Joe got out and watched the car drive away. Not a soul was in sight, but, as he walked on, a light here and there appeared in a window, and here and there a man or a woman came out of a door, and presently the world was waking up and the day's traffic began to stir. The eastern sky was flushed when he came to a bus stop, and the light of day was shining when he rang the bell at his small hotel.

The night porter was just packing up. He looked at Joe, with his raincoat over his arm and his evening clothes a little rumpled, and gave him a knowing grin. "Hello, Mr. Morrison!" he said. "Did you get away safely before the old man came home from the night shift?"

Joe said with a conspiring wink: "What a night! But keep it under your hat, Frank."

He ran up the stairs to put a call through to Throstle's Nest.

EISE INCKLER
CIN'TI 5-62